BATMAN

A LOT OF LI'L GOTHAM

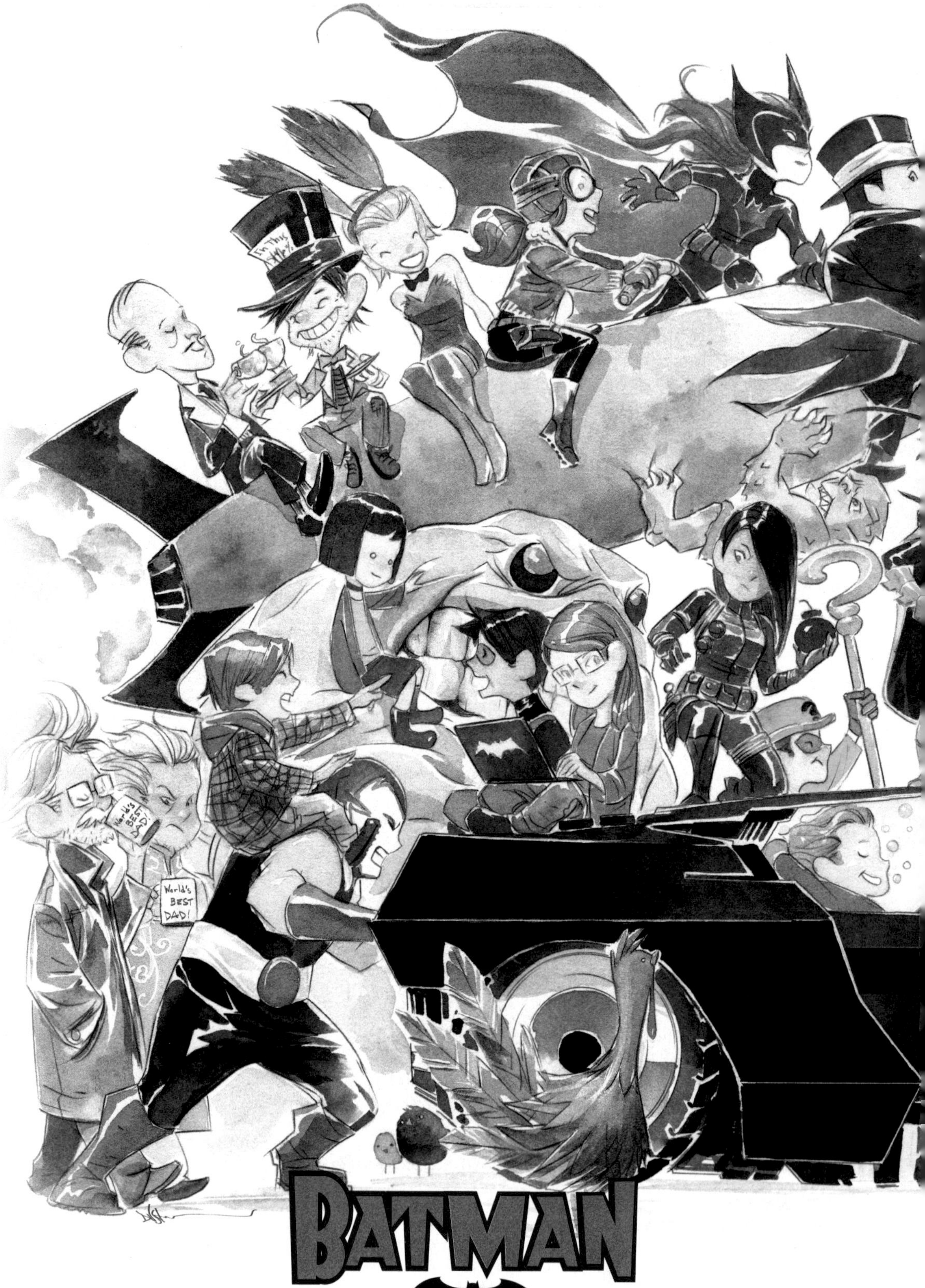
World's BEST DAD!

BATMAN

A LOT OF LI'L GOTHAM

DUSTIN NGUYEN & DEREK FRIDOLFS
writers

DUSTIN NGUYEN
artist & colorist

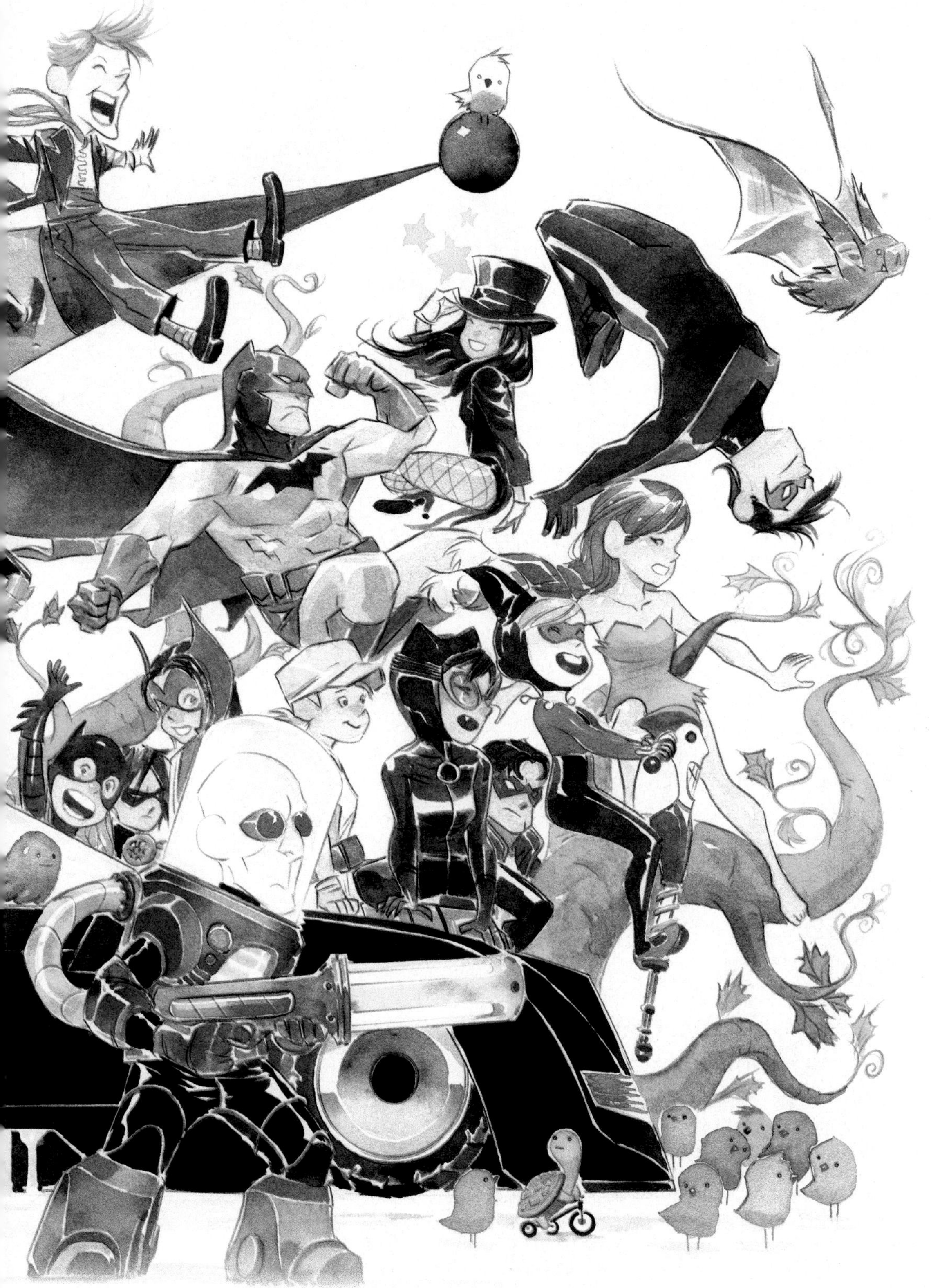

SAIDA TEMOFONTE
JOHN J. HILL
letterers

DUSTIN NGUYEN
collection & original series cover artist

BATMAN created by BOB KANE with BILL FINGER

KRISTY QUINN, SARAH GAYDOS, JANELLE SIEGEL Editors – Original Series
JESSICA CHEN Assistant Editor – Original Series
JEB WOODARD Group Editor – Collected Editions
ROBIN WILDMAN Editor – Collected Edition
STEVE COOK Design Director – Books
MEGEN BELLERSEN Publication Design

BOB HARRAS Senior VP – Editor-in-Chief, DC Comics
PAT McCALLUM Executive Editor, DC Comics

DIANE NELSON President
DAN DiDIO Publisher
JIM LEE Publisher
GEOFF JOHNS President & Chief Creative Officer
AMIT DESAI Executive VP – Business & Marketing Strategy,
Direct to Consumer & Global Franchise Management
SAM ADES Senior VP & General Manager, Digital Services
BOBBIE CHASE VP & Executive Editor, Young Reader & Talent Development
MARK CHIARELLO Senior VP – Art, Design & Collected Editions
JOHN CUNNINGHAM Senior VP – Sales & Trade Marketing
ANNE DePIES Senior VP – Business Strategy, Finance & Administration
DON FALLETTI VP – Manufacturing Operations
LAWRENCE GANEM VP – Editorial Administration & Talent Relations
ALISON GILL Senior VP – Manufacturing & Operations
HANK KANALZ Senior VP – Editorial Strategy & Administration
JAY KOGAN VP – Legal Affairs
JACK MAHAN VP – Business Affairs
NICK J. NAPOLITANO VP – Manufacturing Administration
EDDIE SCANNELL VP – Consumer Marketing
COURTNEY SIMMONS Senior VP – Publicity & Communications
JIM (SKI) SOKOLOWSKI VP – Comic Book Specialty Sales & Trade Marketing
NANCY SPEARS VP – Mass, Book, Digital Sales & Trade Marketing
MICHELE R. WELLS VP – Content Strategy

BATMAN: A LOT OF LI'L GOTHAM

DC Comics, 2900 West Alameda Ave., Burbank, CA 91505
Printed by LSC Communications, Owensville, MO, USA. 7/27/18. First Printing.
ISBN: 978-1-4012-7394-1

Library of Congress Cataloging-in-Publication Data is available.

PEFC Certified
Printed on paper from sustainably managed forests and controlled sources
PEFC
PEFC/29-31-337   www.pefc.org

CONTENTS

Unless otherwise listed, all stories written by Derek Fridolfs and Dustin Nguyen, with art by Dustin Nguyen and letters by Saida Temofonte.

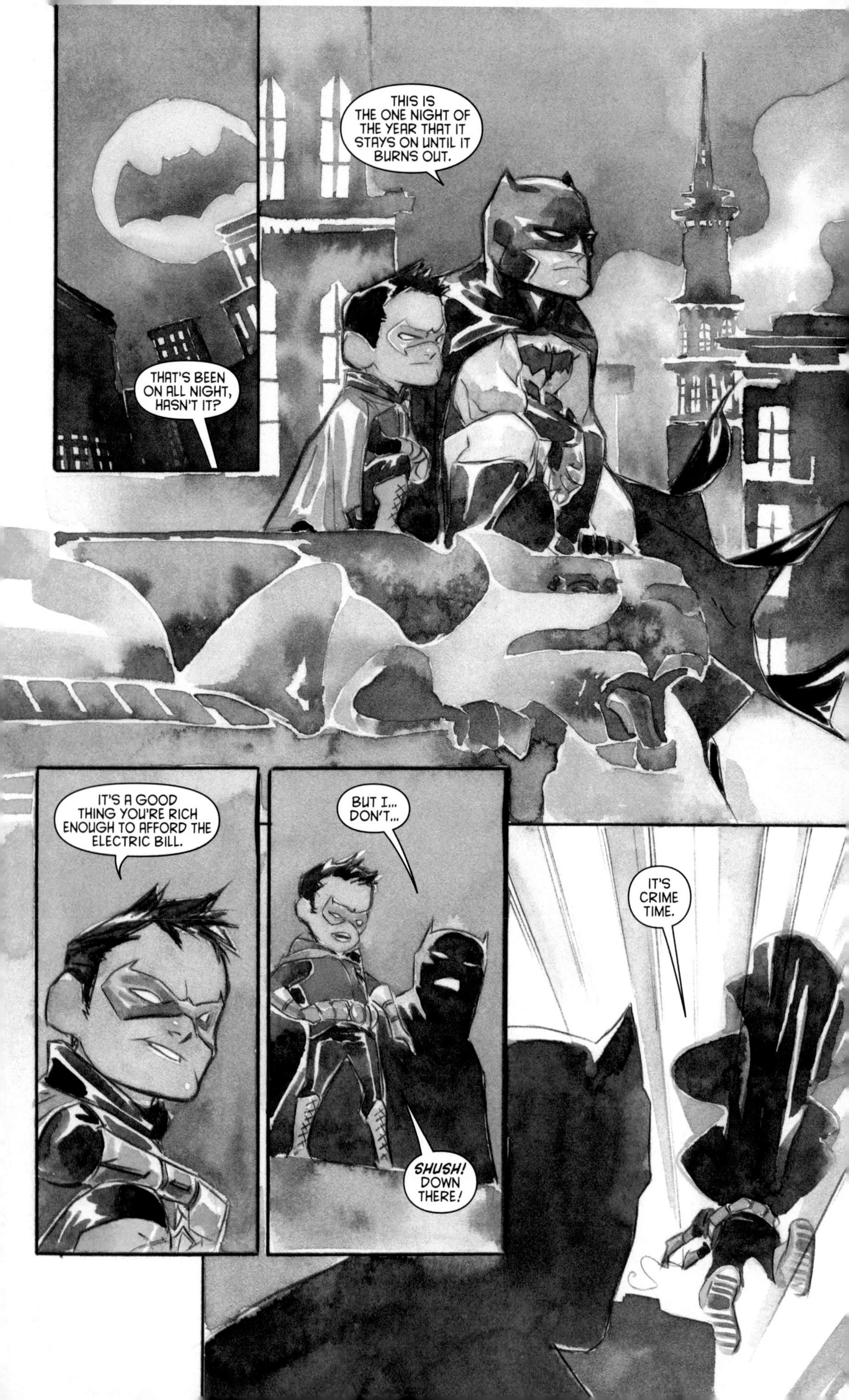
THAT'S BEEN ON ALL NIGHT, HASN'T IT?
THIS IS THE ONE NIGHT OF THE YEAR THAT IT STAYS ON UNTIL IT BURNS OUT.
IT'S A GOOD THING YOU'RE RICH ENOUGH TO AFFORD THE ELECTRIC BILL.
BUT I... DON'T...
SHUSH! DOWN THERE!
IT'S CRIME TIME.

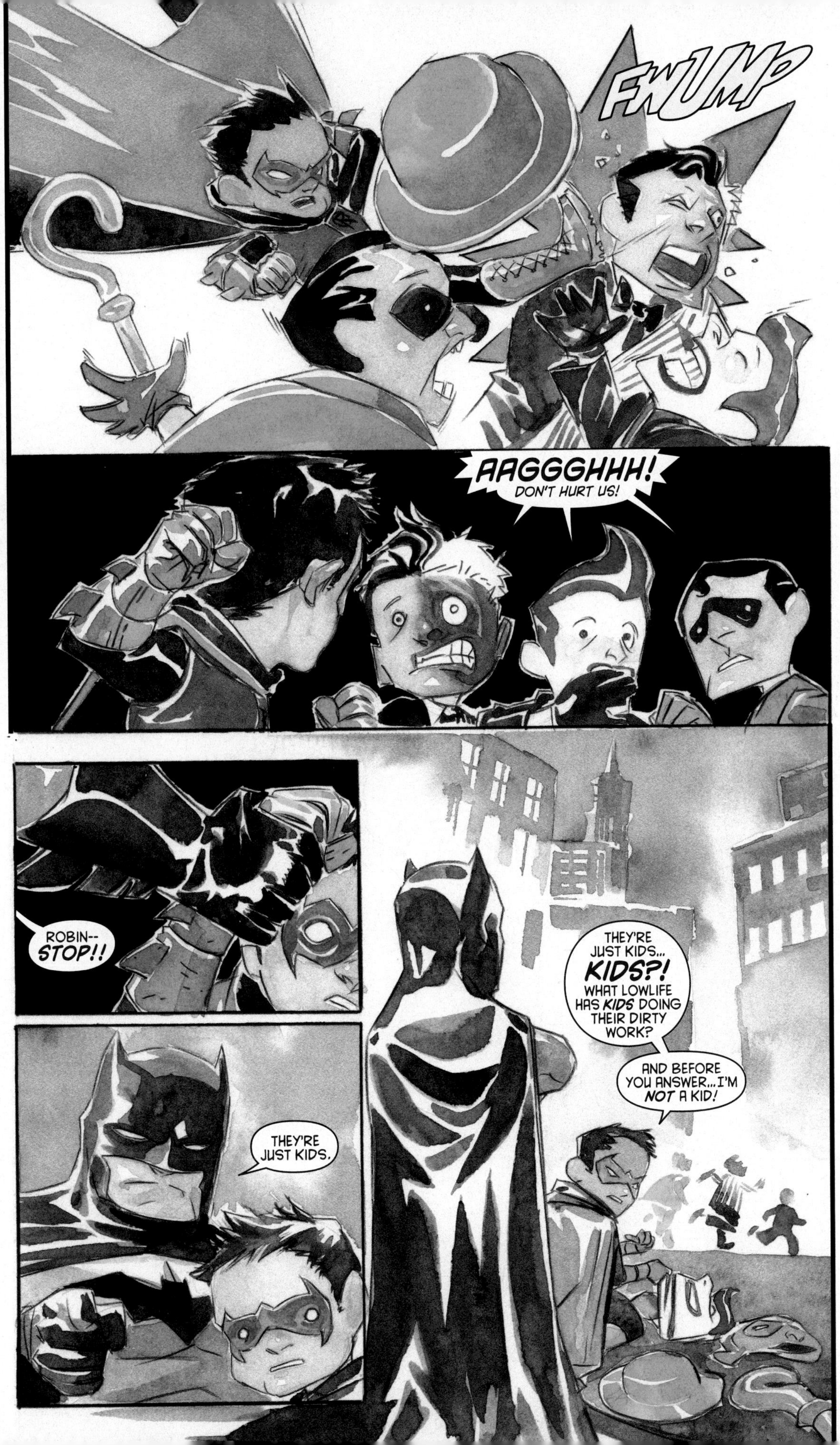
FWUMP
AAGGGHHH!
DON'T HURT US!
ROBIN--
STOP!!
THEY'RE
JUST KIDS.
THEY'RE
JUST KIDS...
KIDS?!
WHAT LOWLIFE
HAS KIDS DOING
THEIR DIRTY
WORK?
AND BEFORE
YOU ANSWER... I'M
NOT A KID!

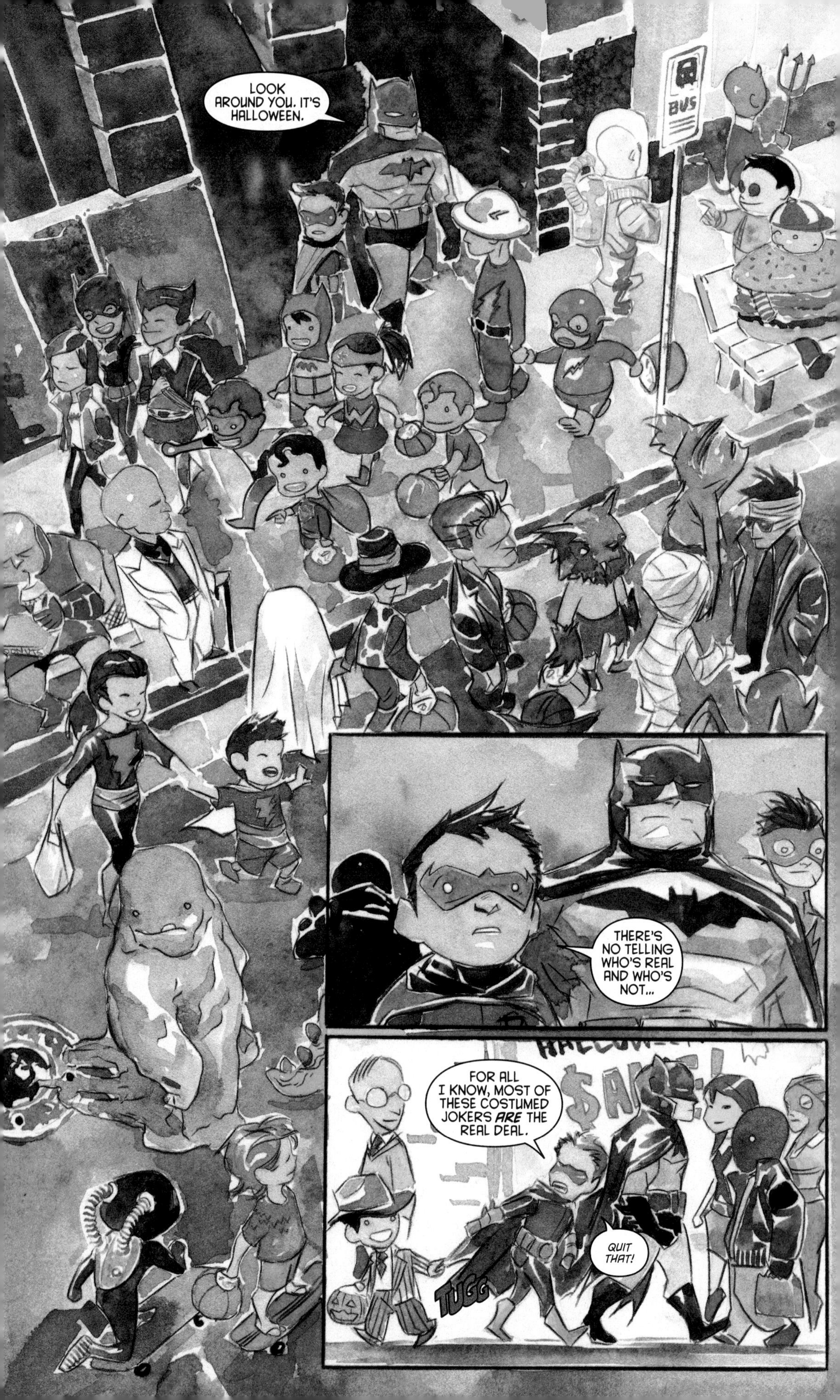
LOOK AROUND YOU. IT'S HALLOWEEN.
BUS
THERE'S NO TELLING WHO'S REAL AND WHO'S NOT...
FOR ALL I KNOW, MOST OF THESE COSTUMED JOKERS *ARE* THE REAL DEAL.
TUGG
QUIT THAT!

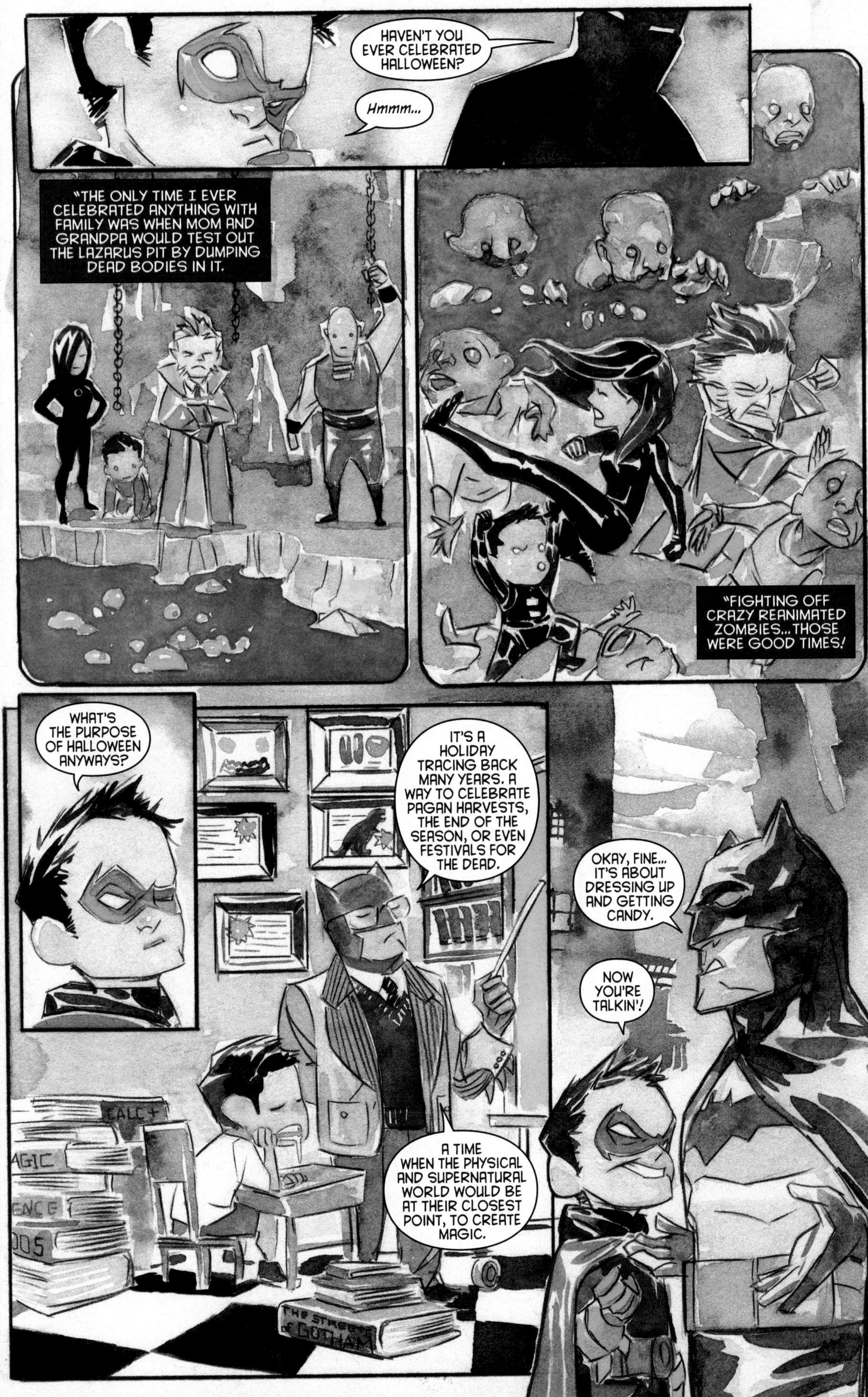

HAVEN'T YOU EVER CELEBRATED HALLOWEEN?
Hmmm...
"THE ONLY TIME I EVER CELEBRATED ANYTHING WITH FAMILY WAS WHEN MOM AND GRANDPA WOULD TEST OUT THE LAZARUS PIT BY DUMPING DEAD BODIES IN IT.
"FIGHTING OFF CRAZY REANIMATED ZOMBIES... THOSE WERE GOOD TIMES!
WHAT'S THE PURPOSE OF HALLOWEEN ANYWAYS?
IT'S A HOLIDAY TRACING BACK MANY YEARS. A WAY TO CELEBRATE PAGAN HARVESTS, THE END OF THE SEASON, OR EVEN FESTIVALS FOR THE DEAD.
A TIME WHEN THE PHYSICAL AND SUPERNATURAL WORLD WOULD BE AT THEIR CLOSEST POINT, TO CREATE MAGIC.
OKAY, FINE... IT'S ABOUT DRESSING UP AND GETTING CANDY.
NOW YOU'RE TALKIN'!

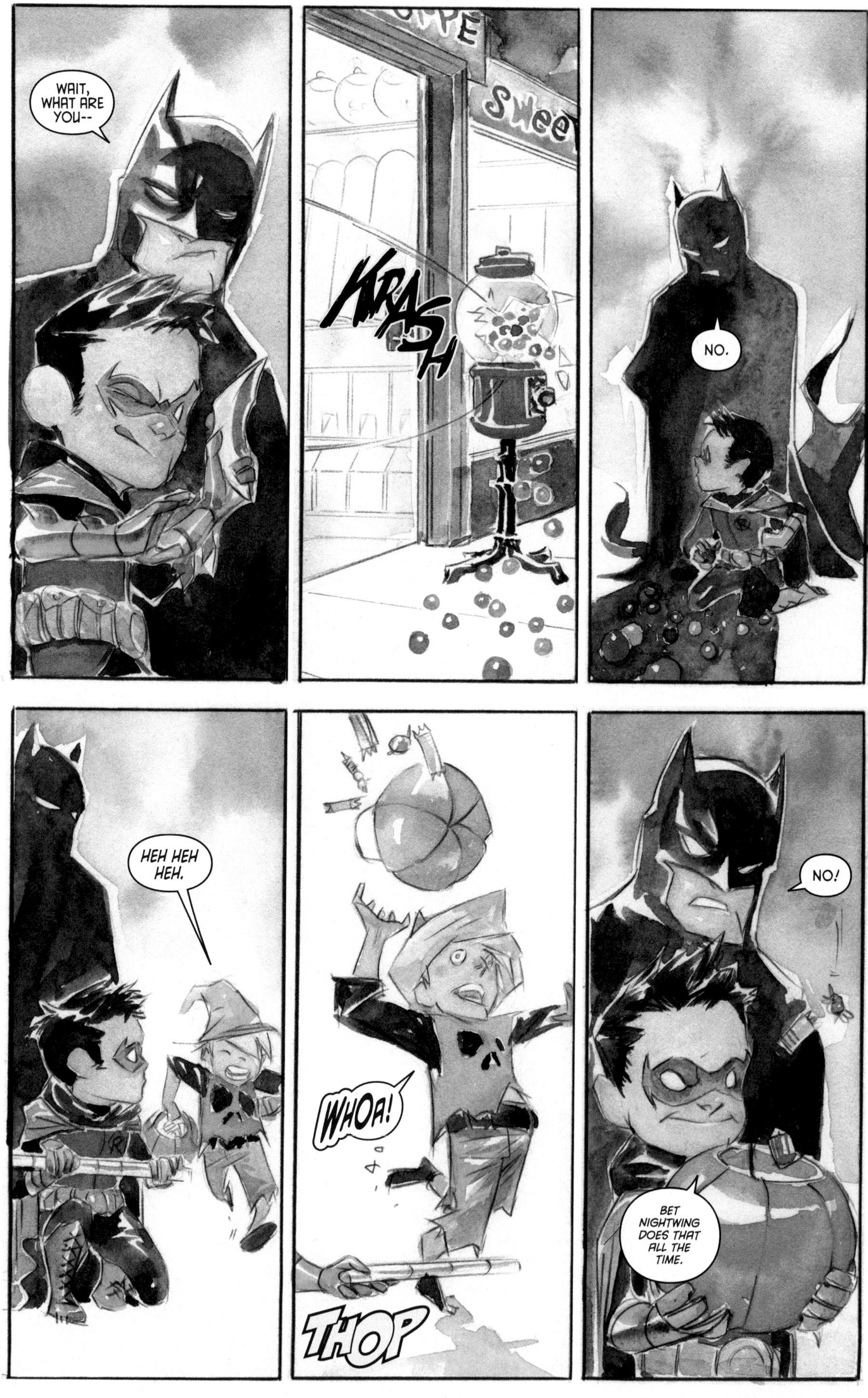
WAIT, WHAT ARE YOU--
SWEET
KRASH
NO.
HEH HEH HEH.
WHOA!
THOP
NO!
BET NIGHTWING DOES THAT ALL THE TIME.

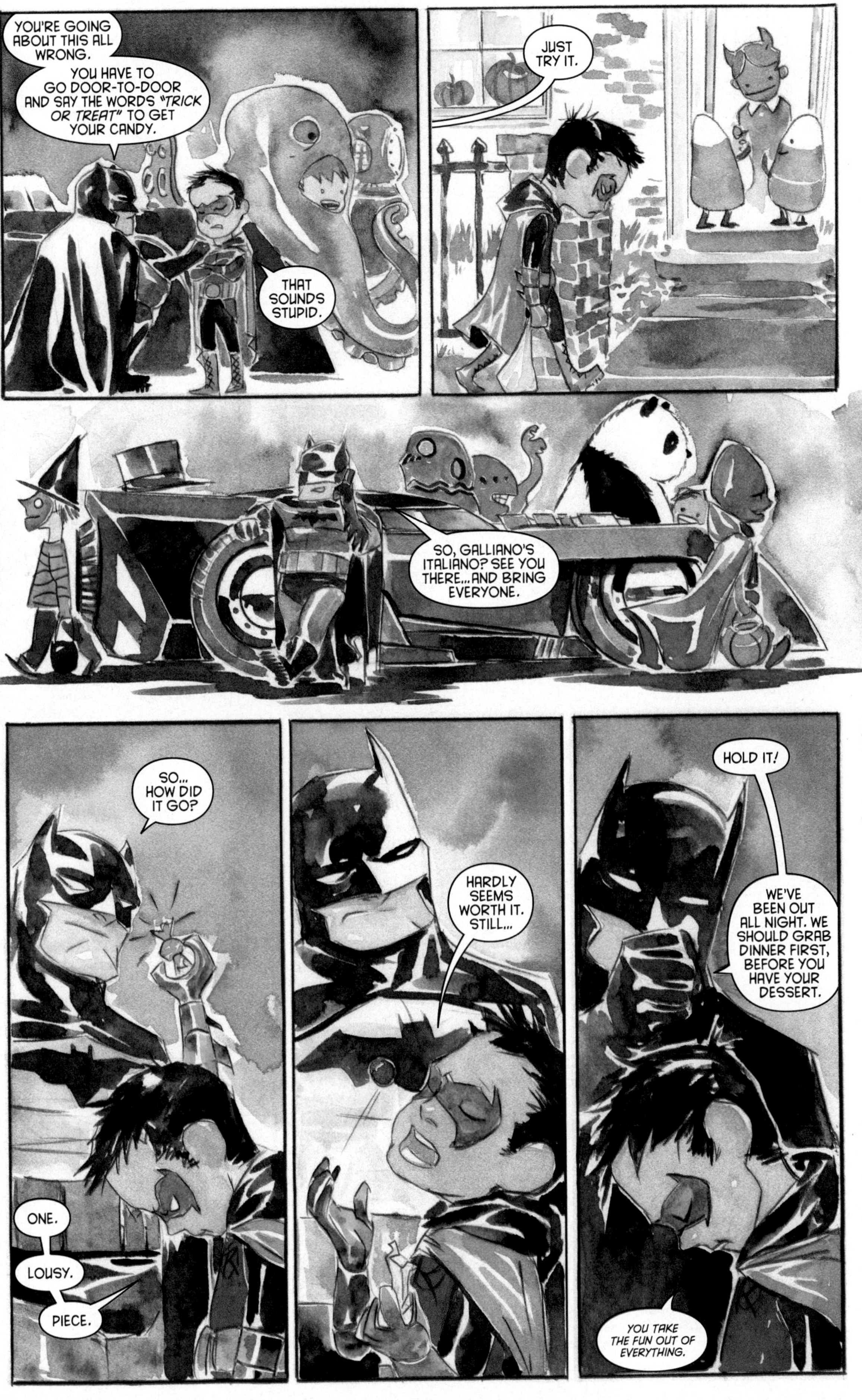
YOU'RE GOING ABOUT THIS ALL WRONG.
YOU HAVE TO GO DOOR-TO-DOOR AND SAY THE WORDS *"TRICK OR TREAT"* TO GET YOUR CANDY.
THAT SOUNDS STUPID.
JUST TRY IT.
SO, GALLIANO'S ITALIANO? SEE YOU THERE...AND BRING EVERYONE.
SO... HOW DID IT GO?
ONE.
LOUSY.
PIECE.
HARDLY SEEMS WORTH IT. STILL...
HOLD IT!
WE'VE BEEN OUT ALL NIGHT. WE SHOULD GRAB DINNER FIRST, BEFORE YOU HAVE YOUR DESSERT.
YOU TAKE THE FUN OUT OF EVERYTHING.

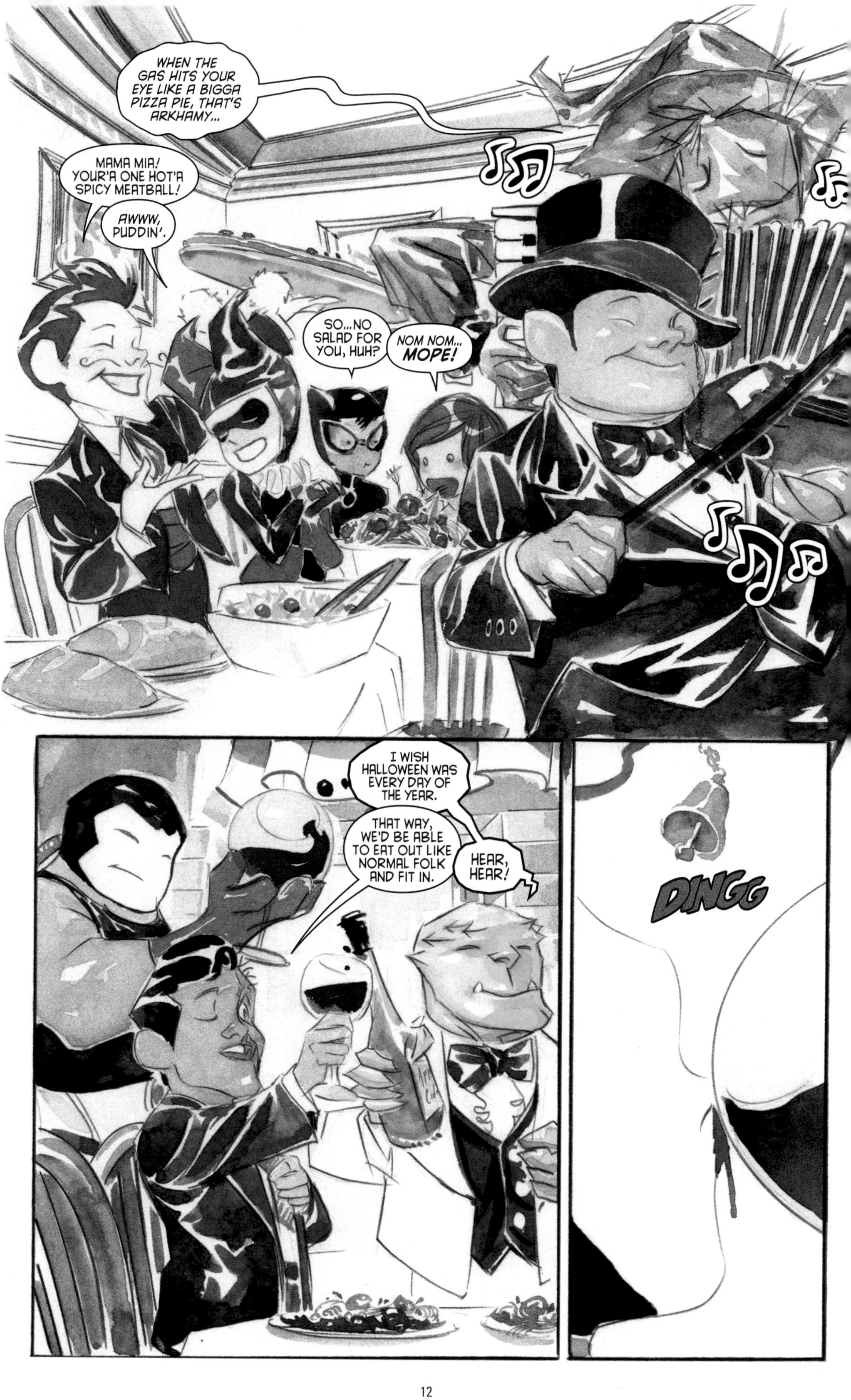
WHEN THE GAS HITS YOUR EYE LIKE A BIGGA PIZZA PIE, THAT'S ARKHAMY...
MAMA MIA! YOUR'A ONE HOT'A SPICY MEATBALL!
AWWW, PUDDIN'.
SO...NO SALAD FOR YOU, HUH?
NOM NOM... MOPE!
I WISH HALLOWEEN WAS EVERY DAY OF THE YEAR.
THAT WAY, WE'D BE ABLE TO EAT OUT LIKE NORMAL FOLK AND FIT IN.
HEAR, HEAR!
DINGG

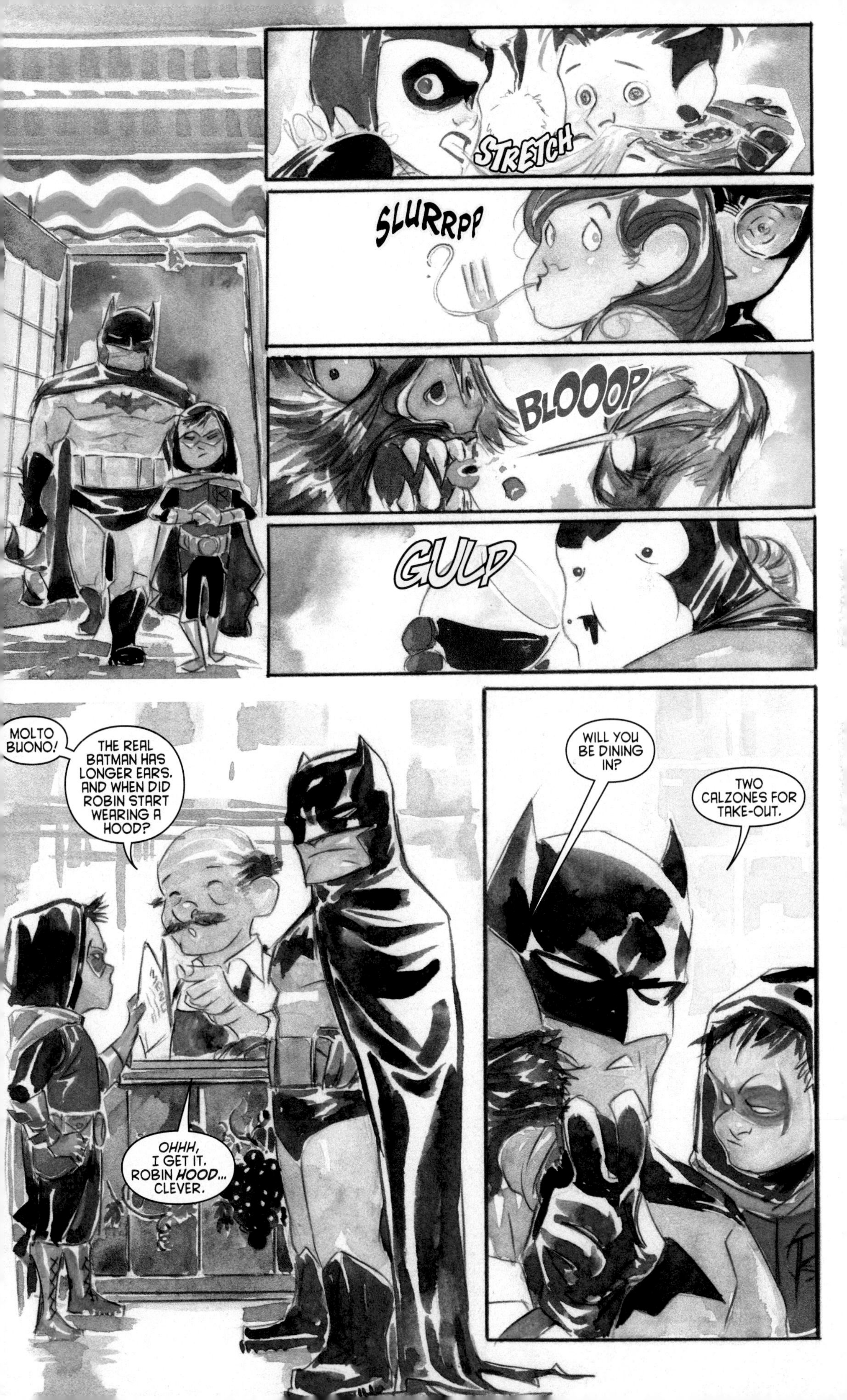
STRETCH
SLURRPP
BLOOOP
GULP
MOLTO BUONO!
THE REAL BATMAN HAS LONGER EARS. AND WHEN DID ROBIN START WEARING A HOOD?
OHHH, I GET IT. ROBIN HOOD... CLEVER.
WILL YOU BE DINING IN?
TWO CALZONES FOR TAKE-OUT.

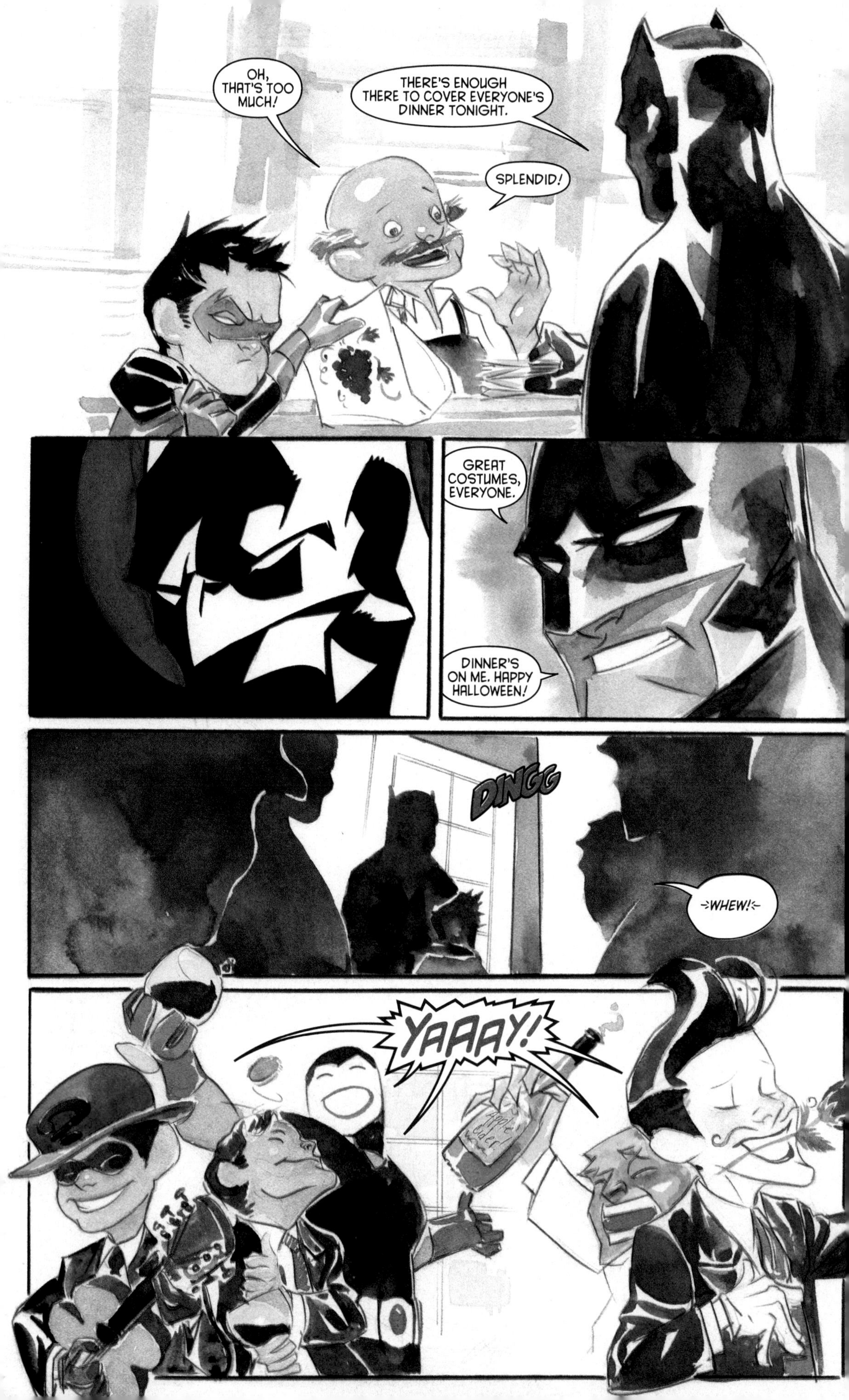
OH, THAT'S TOO MUCH!
THERE'S ENOUGH THERE TO COVER EVERYONE'S DINNER TONIGHT.
SPLENDID!
GREAT COSTUMES, EVERYONE.
DINNER'S ON ME. HAPPY HALLOWEEN!
DINGG
WHEW!
YAAAY!
Apple Cider!

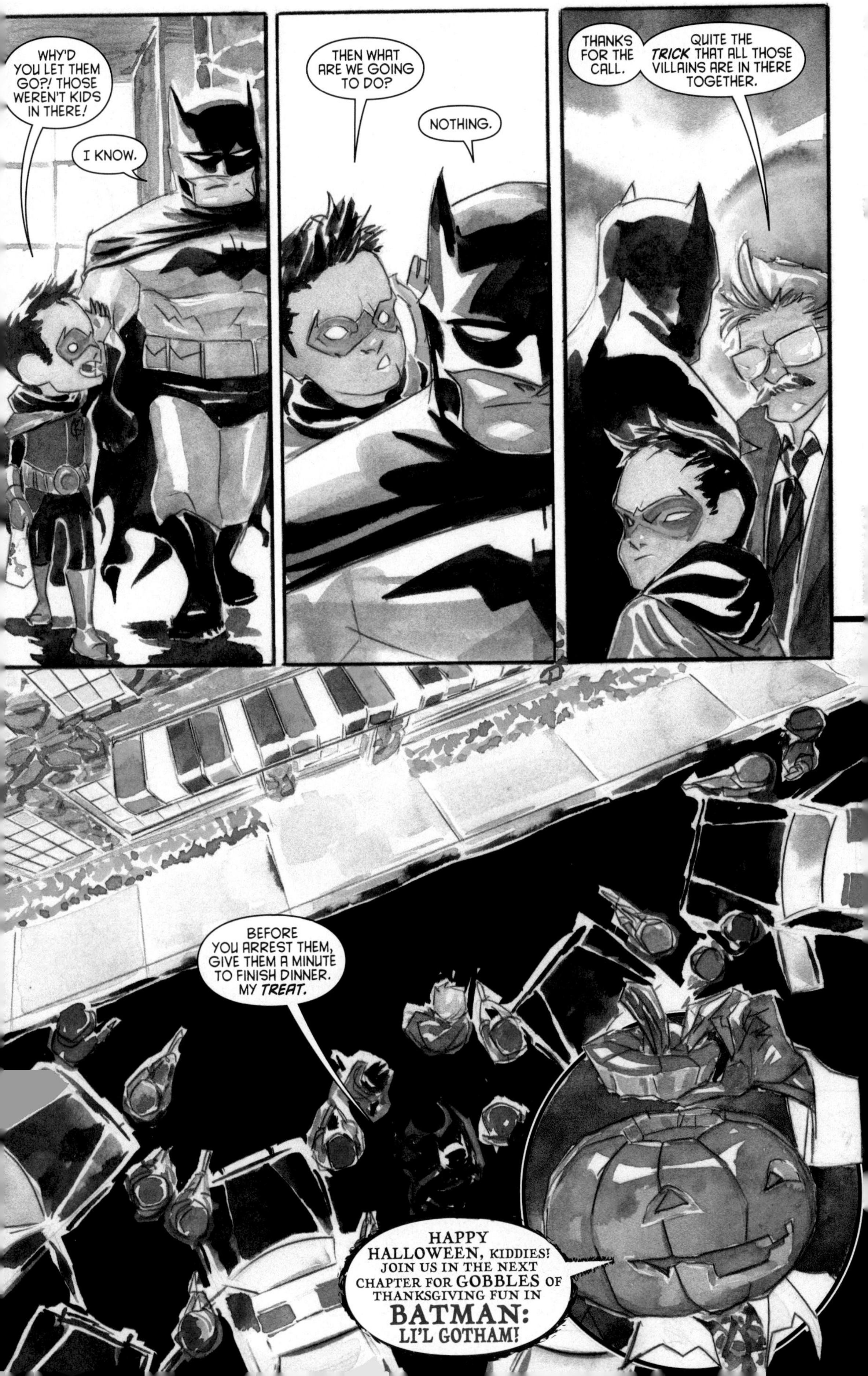
WHY'D YOU LET THEM GO?! THOSE WEREN'T KIDS IN THERE!
I KNOW.
THEN WHAT ARE WE GOING TO DO?
NOTHING.
THANKS FOR THE CALL.
QUITE THE TRICK THAT ALL THOSE VILLAINS ARE IN THERE TOGETHER.
BEFORE YOU ARREST THEM, GIVE THEM A MINUTE TO FINISH DINNER. MY TREAT.
HAPPY HALLOWEEN, KIDDIES! JOIN US IN THE NEXT CHAPTER FOR GOBBLES OF THANKSGIVING FUN IN BATMAN: LI'L GOTHAM!

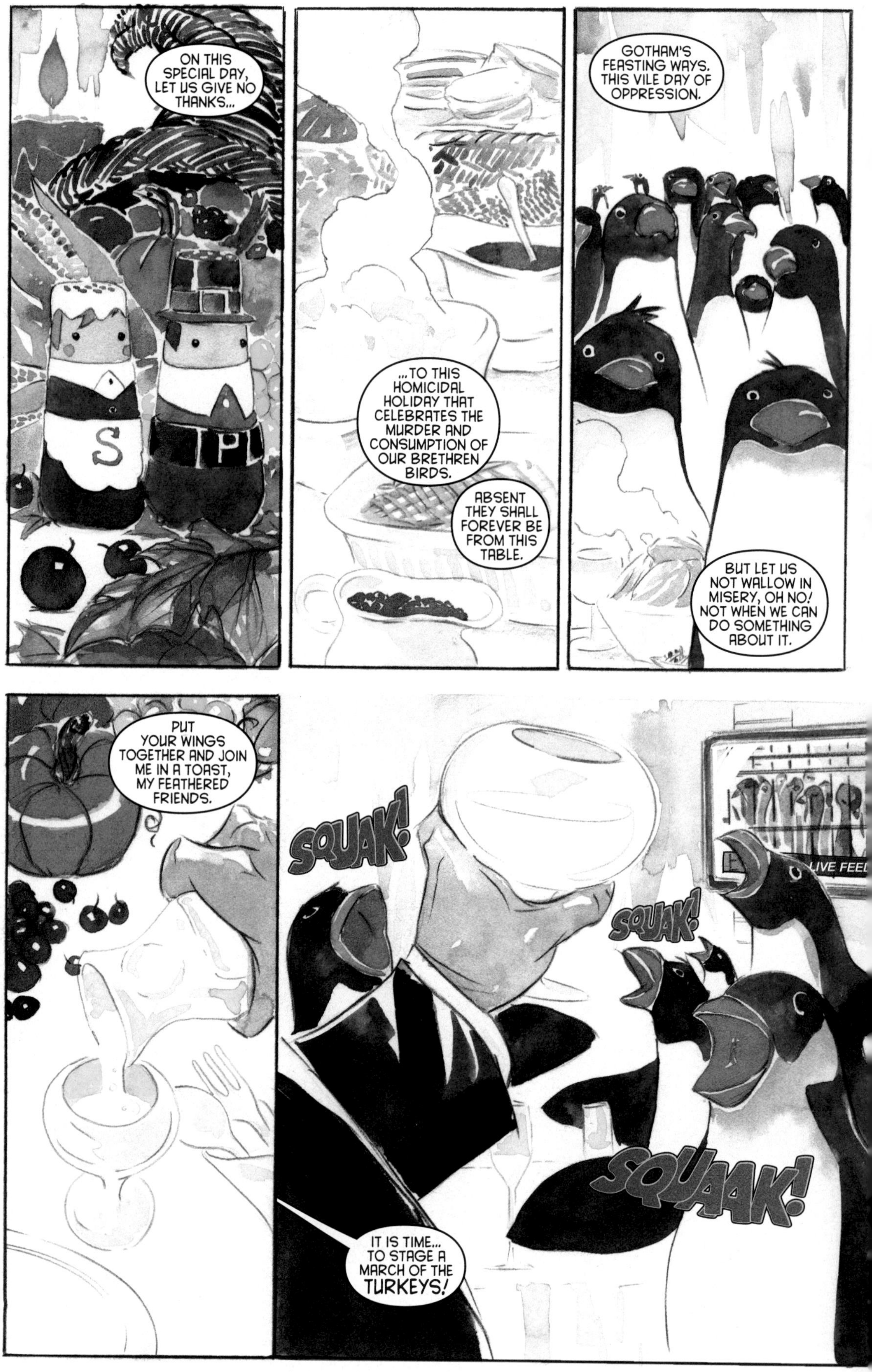

ON THIS SPECIAL DAY, LET US GIVE NO THANKS...
...TO THIS HOMICIDAL HOLIDAY THAT CELEBRATES THE MURDER AND CONSUMPTION OF OUR BRETHREN BIRDS.
ABSENT THEY SHALL FOREVER BE FROM THIS TABLE.
GOTHAM'S FEASTING WAYS. THIS VILE DAY OF OPPRESSION.
BUT LET US NOT WALLOW IN MISERY, OH NO! NOT WHEN WE CAN DO SOMETHING ABOUT IT.
PUT YOUR WINGS TOGETHER AND JOIN ME IN A TOAST, MY FEATHERED FRIENDS.
SQUAK!
LIVE FEED
SQUAK!
SQUAAK!
IT IS TIME... TO STAGE A MARCH OF THE TURKEYS!

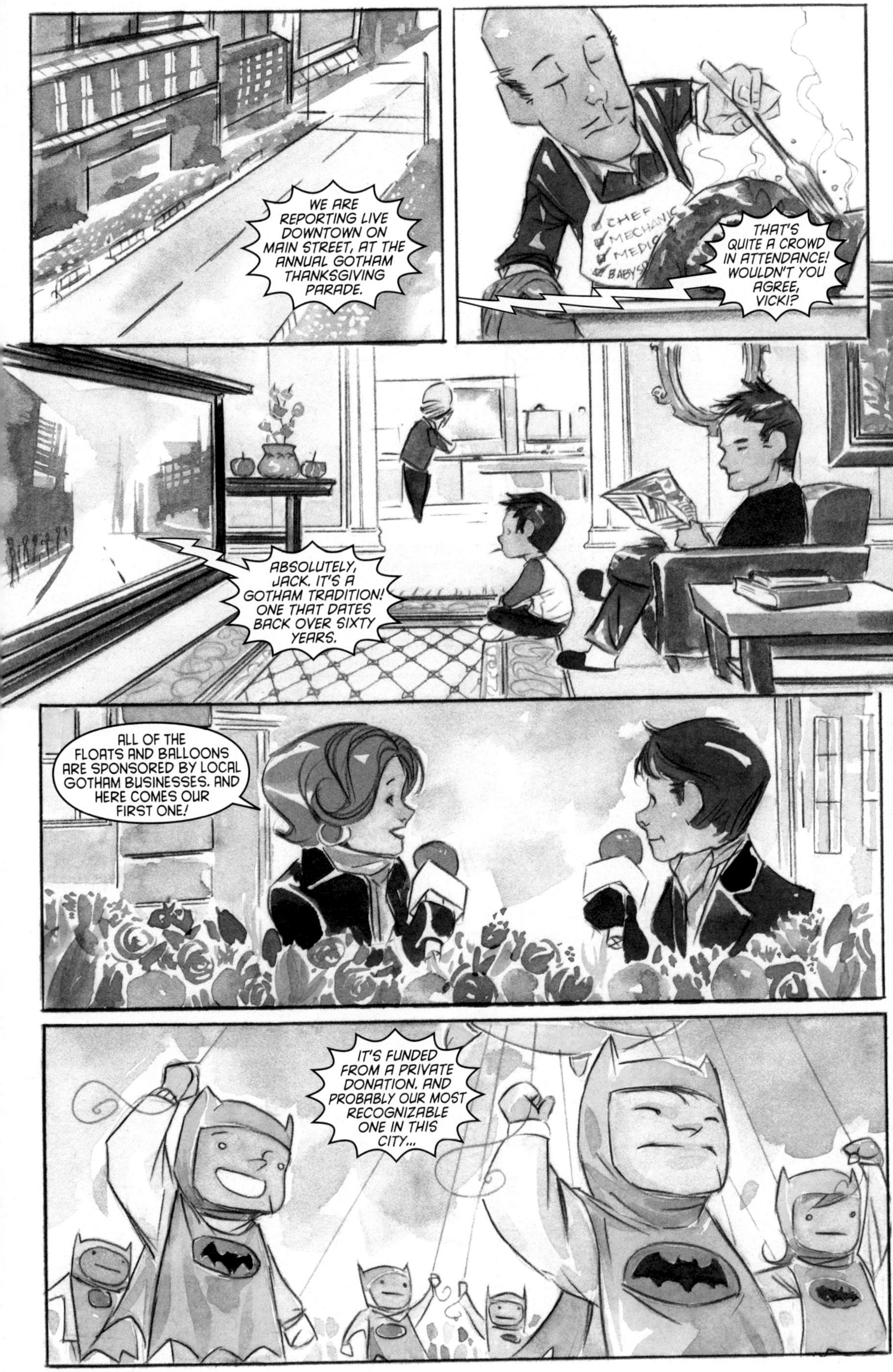
WE ARE REPORTING LIVE DOWNTOWN ON MAIN STREET, AT THE ANNUAL GOTHAM THANKSGIVING PARADE.
THAT'S QUITE A CROWD IN ATTENDANCE! WOULDN'T YOU AGREE, VICKI?
ABSOLUTELY, JACK. IT'S A GOTHAM TRADITION! ONE THAT DATES BACK OVER SIXTY YEARS.
ALL OF THE FLOATS AND BALLOONS ARE SPONSORED BY LOCAL GOTHAM BUSINESSES. AND HERE COMES OUR FIRST ONE!
IT'S FUNDED FROM A PRIVATE DONATION. AND PROBABLY OUR MOST RECOGNIZABLE ONE IN THIS CITY...

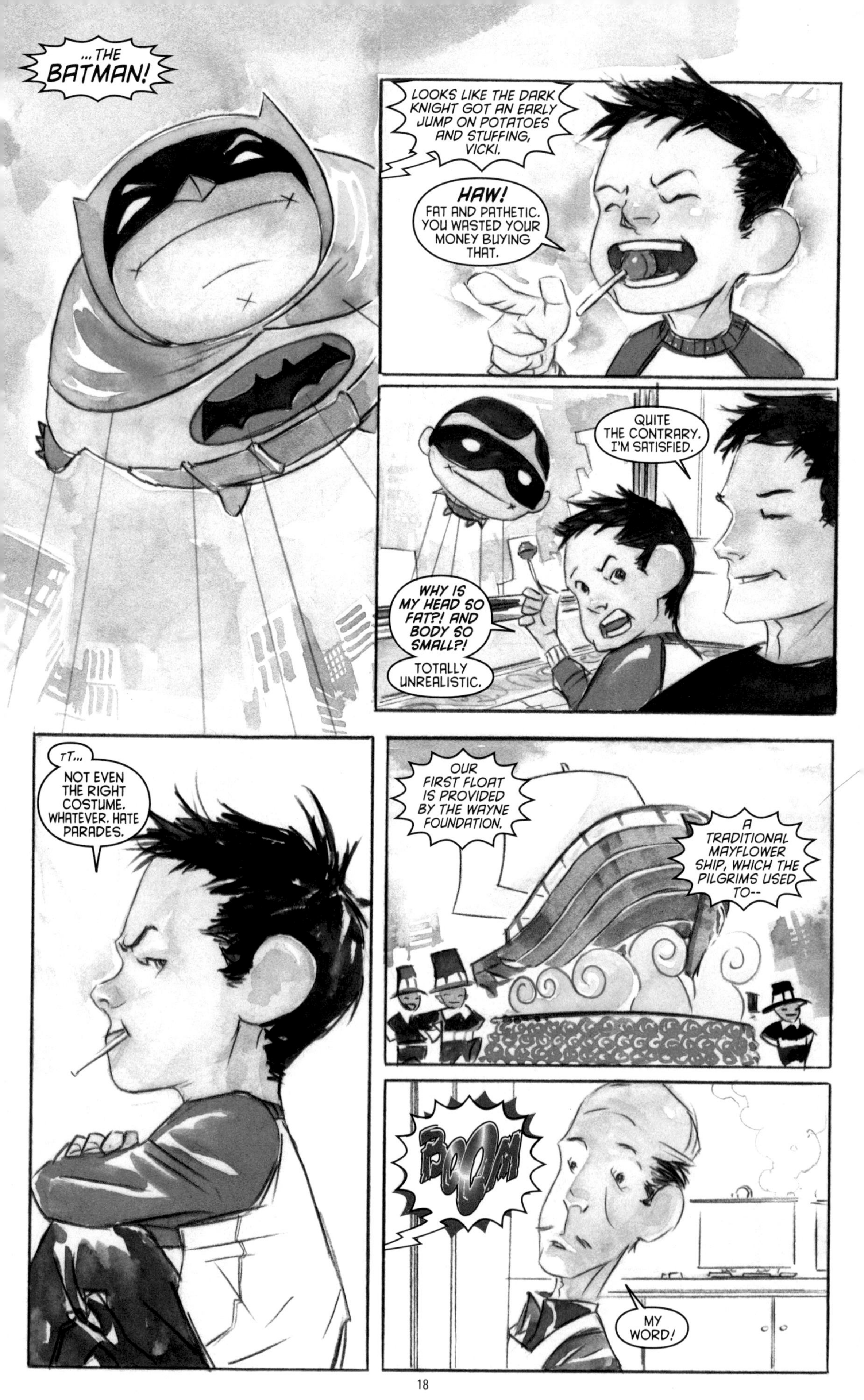
...THE BATMAN!
LOOKS LIKE THE DARK KNIGHT GOT AN EARLY JUMP ON POTATOES AND STUFFING, VICKI.
HAW! FAT AND PATHETIC. YOU WASTED YOUR MONEY BUYING THAT.
QUITE THE CONTRARY. I'M SATISFIED.
WHY IS MY HEAD SO FAT?! AND BODY SO SMALL?!
TOTALLY UNREALISTIC.
TT...
NOT EVEN THE RIGHT COSTUME. WHATEVER. HATE PARADES.
OUR FIRST FLOAT IS PROVIDED BY THE WAYNE FOUNDATION.
A TRADITIONAL MAYFLOWER SHIP, WHICH THE PILGRIMS USED TO--
BOOM
MY WORD!

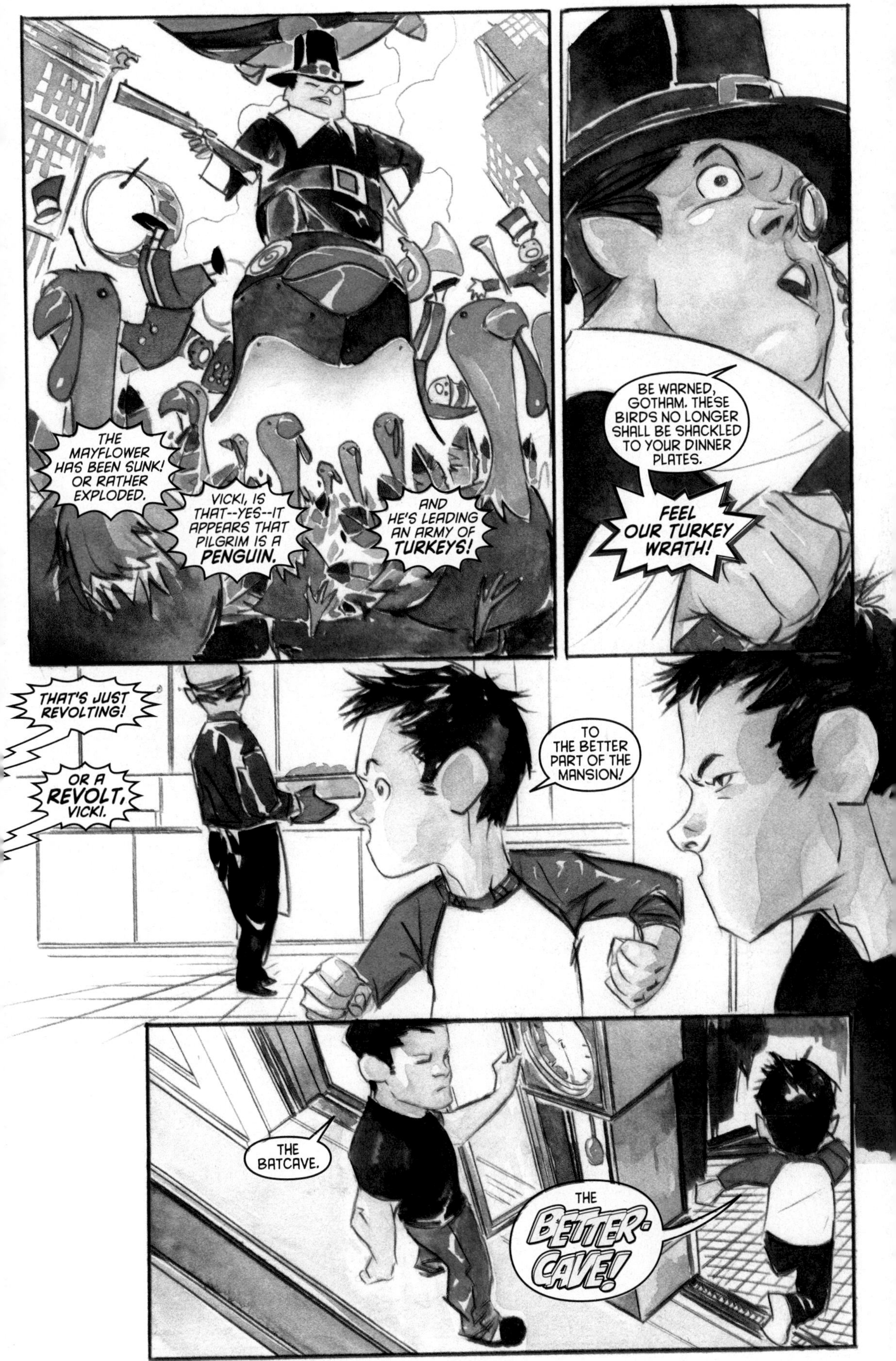
THE MAYFLOWER HAS BEEN SUNK! OR RATHER EXPLODED.
VICKI, IS THAT--YES--IT APPEARS THAT PILGRIM IS A PENGUIN.
AND HE'S LEADING AN ARMY OF TURKEYS!
BE WARNED, GOTHAM. THESE BIRDS NO LONGER SHALL BE SHACKLED TO YOUR DINNER PLATES.
FEEL OUR TURKEY WRATH!
THAT'S JUST REVOLTING!
OR A REVOLT, VICKI.
TO THE BETTER PART OF THE MANSION!
THE BATCAVE.
THE BETTER-CAVE!

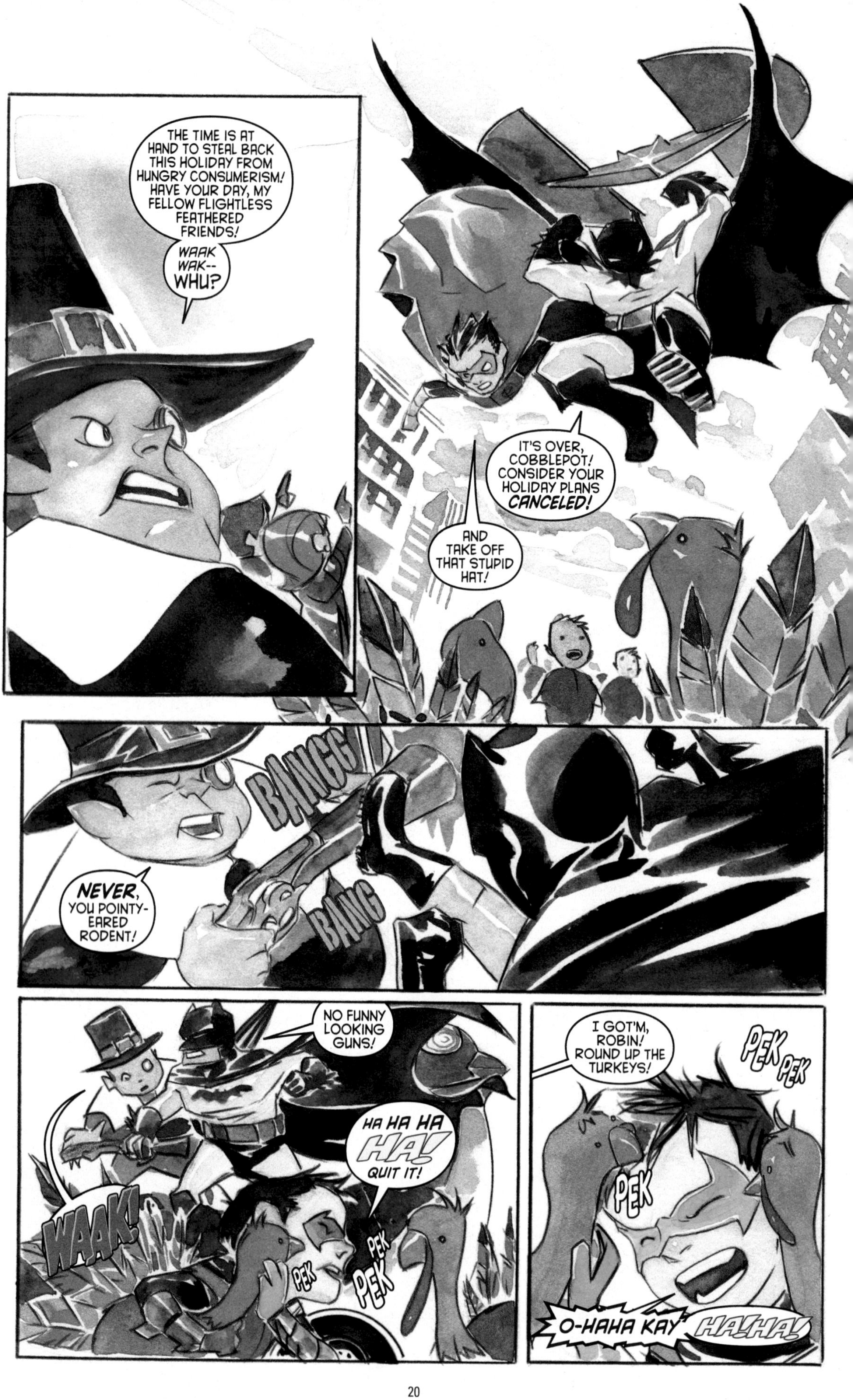
THE TIME IS AT HAND TO STEAL BACK THIS HOLIDAY FROM HUNGRY CONSUMERISM! HAVE YOUR DAY, MY FELLOW FLIGHTLESS FEATHERED FRIENDS!
WAAK WAK-- WHU?
IT'S OVER, COBBLEPOT! CONSIDER YOUR HOLIDAY PLANS CANCELED!
AND TAKE OFF THAT STUPID HAT!
BANGG
NEVER, YOU POINTY-EARED RODENT!
BANG
NO FUNNY LOOKING GUNS!
HA HA HA HA! QUIT IT!
WAAK!
PEK
PEK
PEK
I GOT'M, ROBIN! ROUND UP THE TURKEYS!
PEK PEK
PEK
O-HAHA KAY HA!HA!

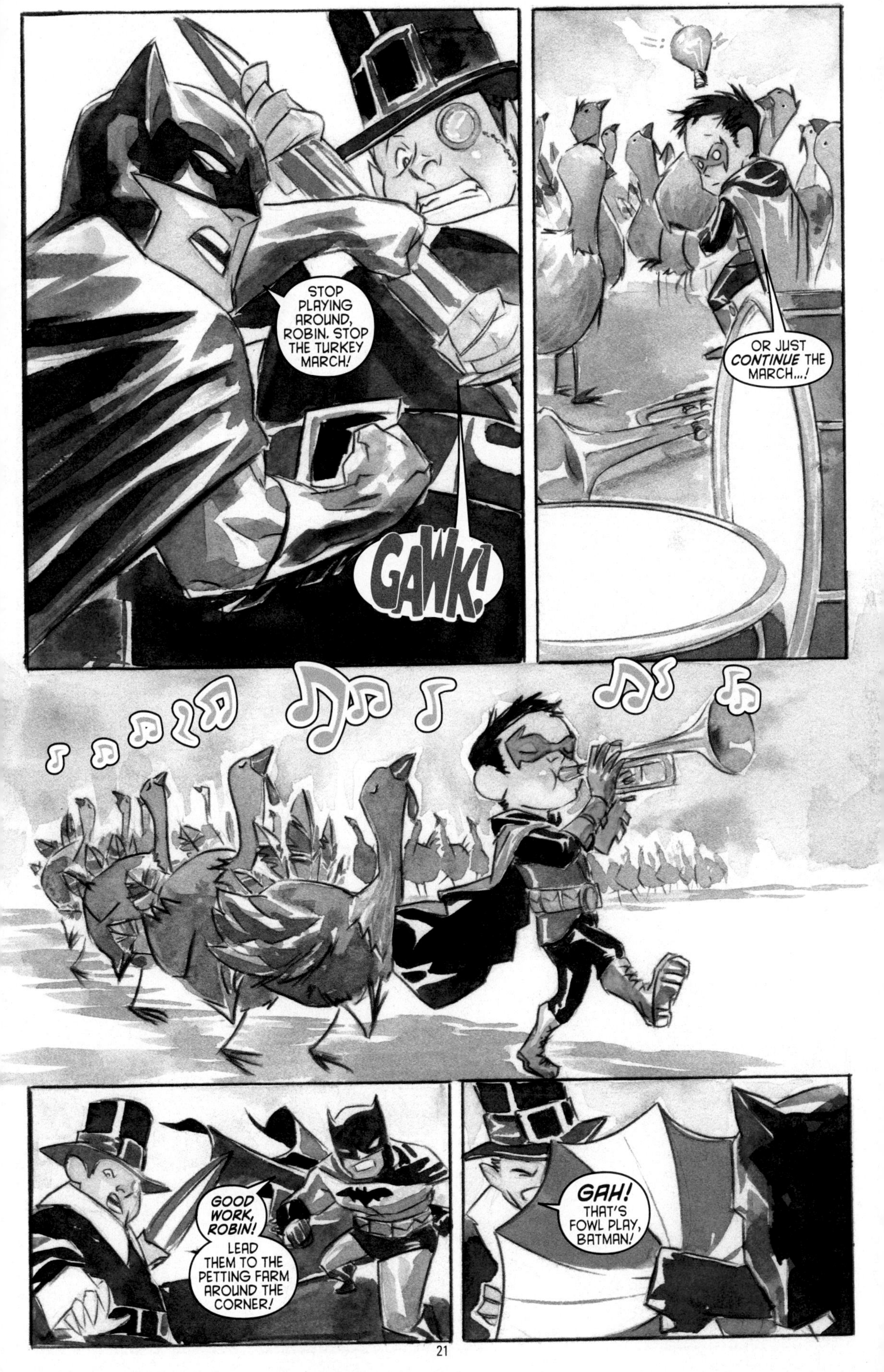
STOP PLAYING AROUND, ROBIN. STOP THE TURKEY MARCH!
GAWK!
OR JUST *CONTINUE* THE MARCH...!
GOOD WORK, ROBIN!
LEAD THEM TO THE PETTING FARM AROUND THE CORNER!
GAH! THAT'S FOWL PLAY, BATMAN!

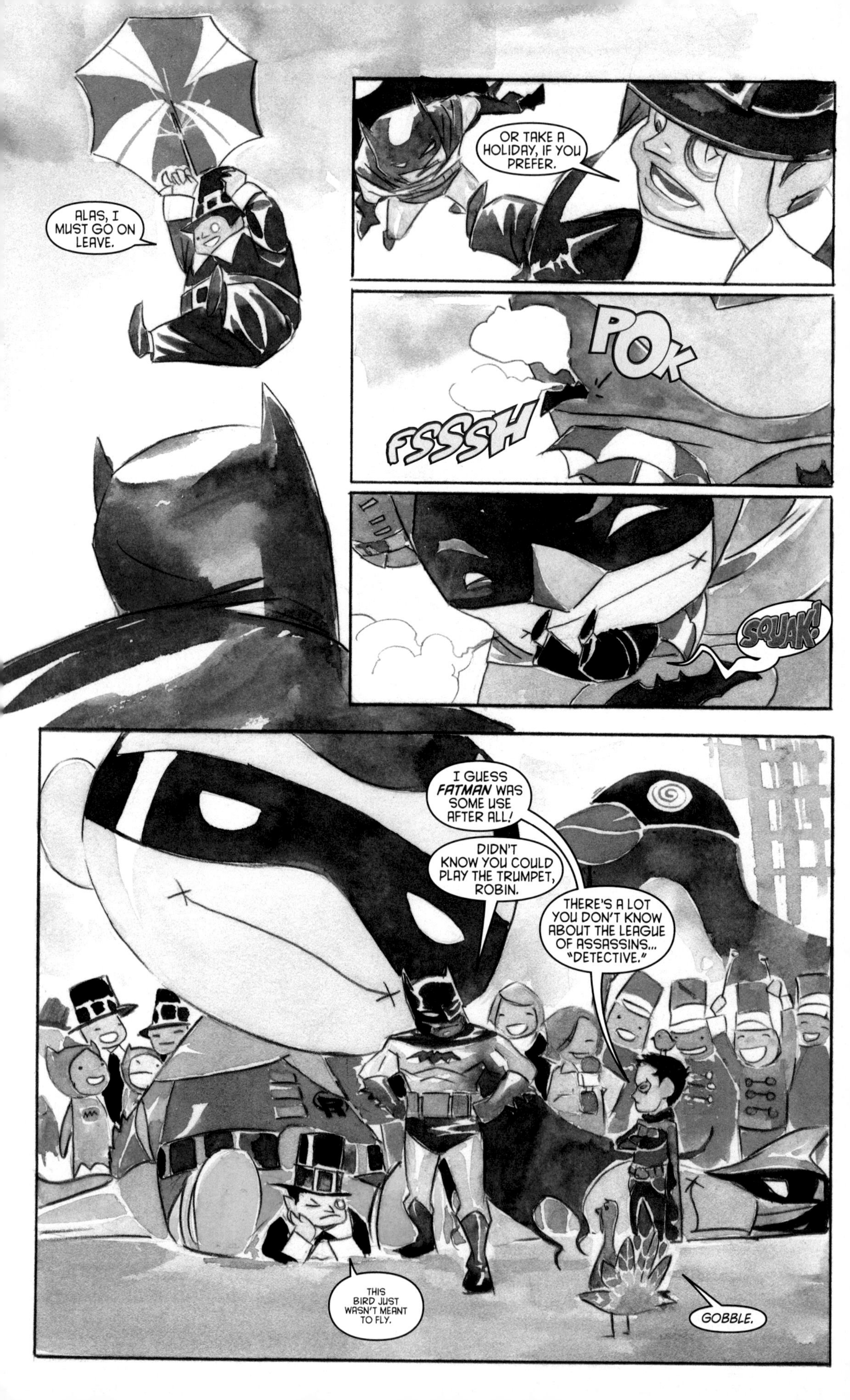
ALAS, I MUST GO ON LEAVE.
OR TAKE A HOLIDAY, IF YOU PREFER.
POK
FSSSH
SQUAK!
I GUESS FATMAN WAS SOME USE AFTER ALL!
DIDN'T KNOW YOU COULD PLAY THE TRUMPET, ROBIN.
THERE'S A LOT YOU DON'T KNOW ABOUT THE LEAGUE OF ASSASSINS... "DETECTIVE."
THIS BIRD JUST WASN'T MEANT TO FLY.
GOBBLE.

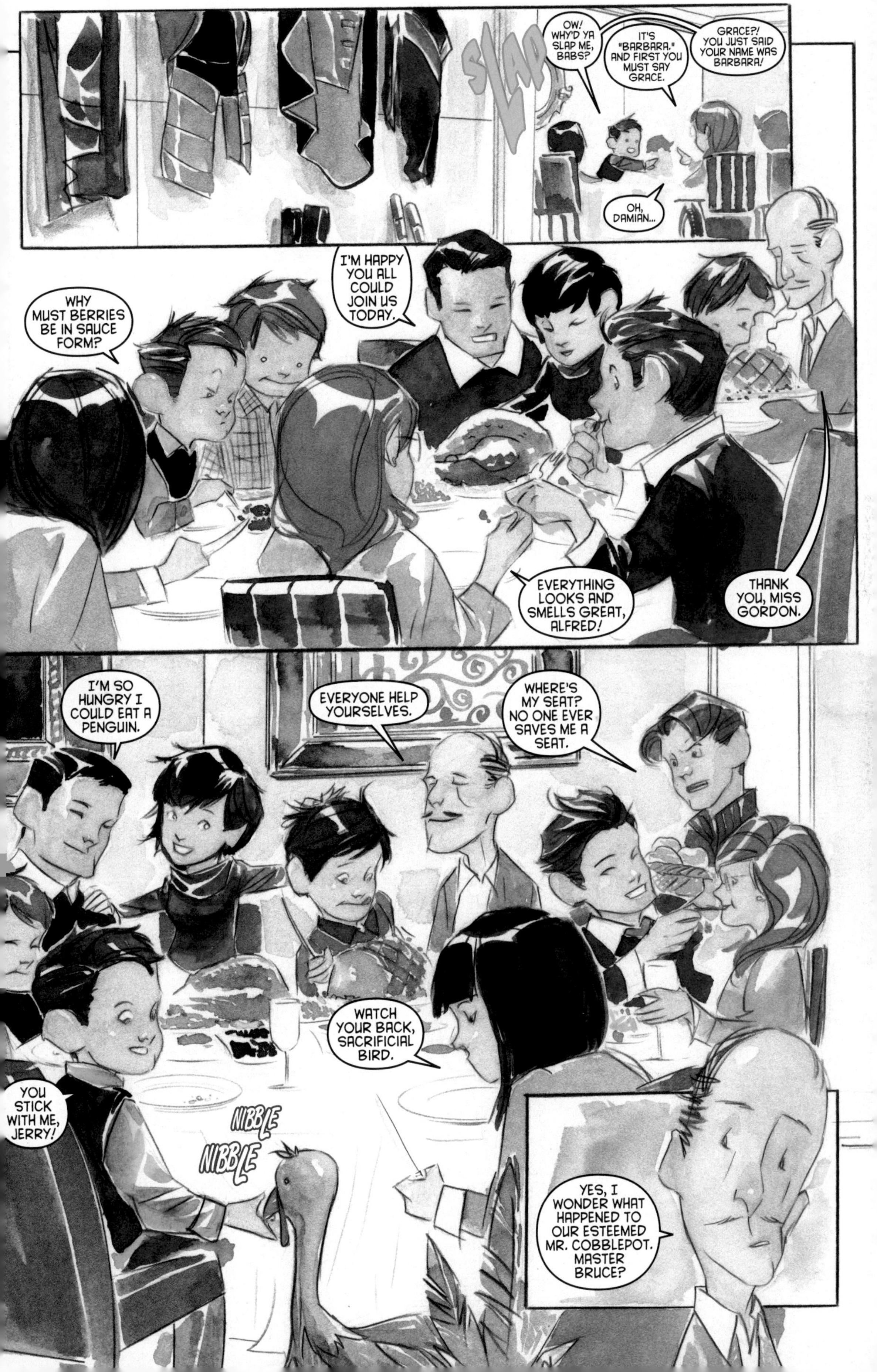
SLAP
OW! WHY'D YA SLAP ME, BABS?
IT'S "BARBARA." AND FIRST YOU MUST SAY GRACE.
GRACE?! YOU JUST SAID YOUR NAME WAS BARBARA!
OH, DAMIAN...
WHY MUST BERRIES BE IN SAUCE FORM?
I'M HAPPY YOU ALL COULD JOIN US TODAY.
EVERYTHING LOOKS AND SMELLS GREAT, ALFRED!
THANK YOU, MISS GORDON.
I'M SO HUNGRY I COULD EAT A PENGUIN.
EVERYONE HELP YOURSELVES.
WHERE'S MY SEAT? NO ONE EVER SAVES ME A SEAT.
WATCH YOUR BACK, SACRIFICIAL BIRD.
YOU STICK WITH ME, JERRY!
NIBBLE
NIBBLE
YES, I WONDER WHAT HAPPENED TO OUR ESTEEMED MR. COBBLEPOT. MASTER BRUCE?

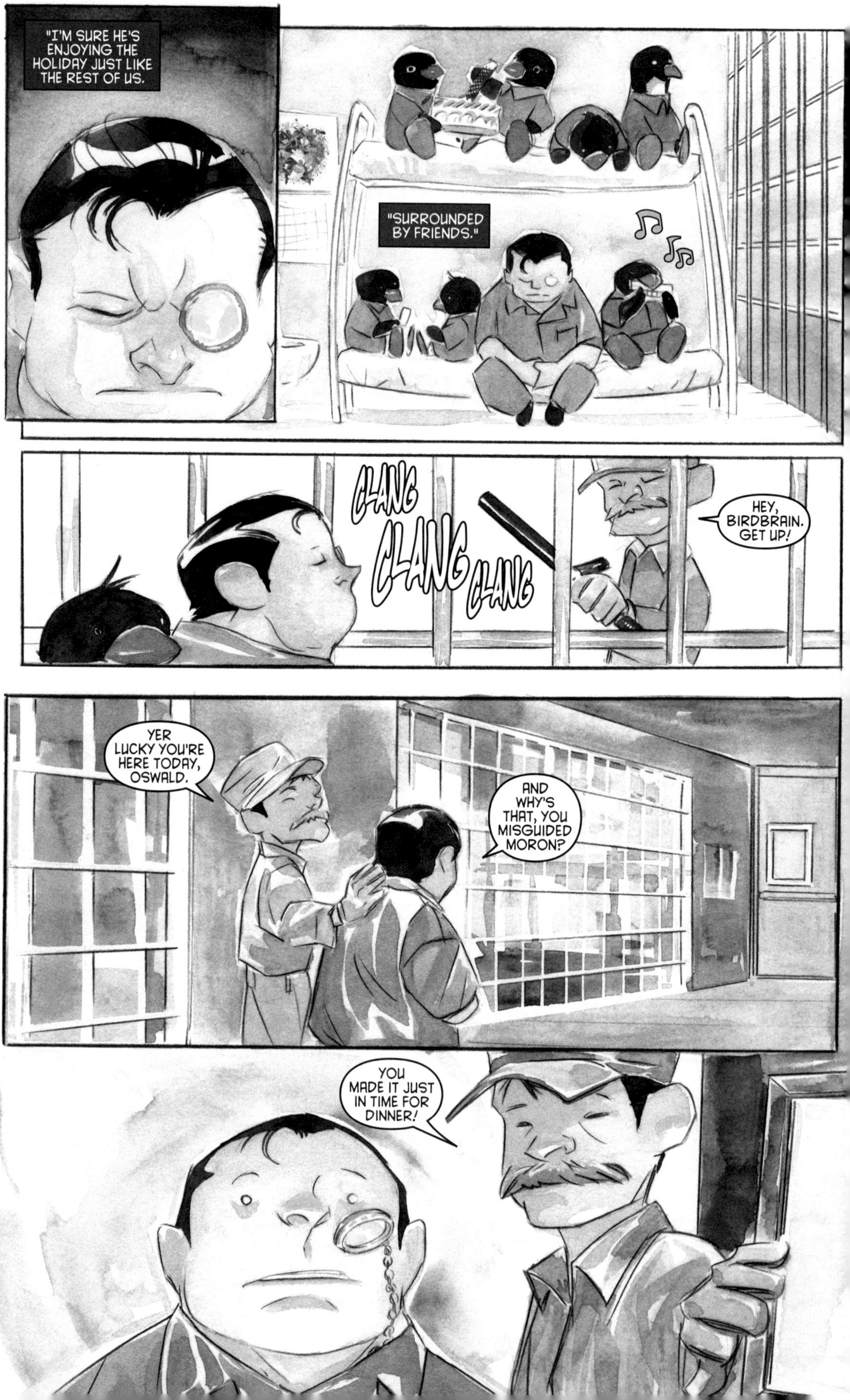
"I'M SURE HE'S ENJOYING THE HOLIDAY JUST LIKE THE REST OF US.
"SURROUNDED BY FRIENDS."
CLANG
CLANG
CLANG
CLANG
HEY, BIRDBRAIN. GET UP!
YER LUCKY YOU'RE HERE TODAY, OSWALD.
AND WHY'S THAT, YOU MISGUIDED MORON?
YOU MADE IT JUST IN TIME FOR DINNER!

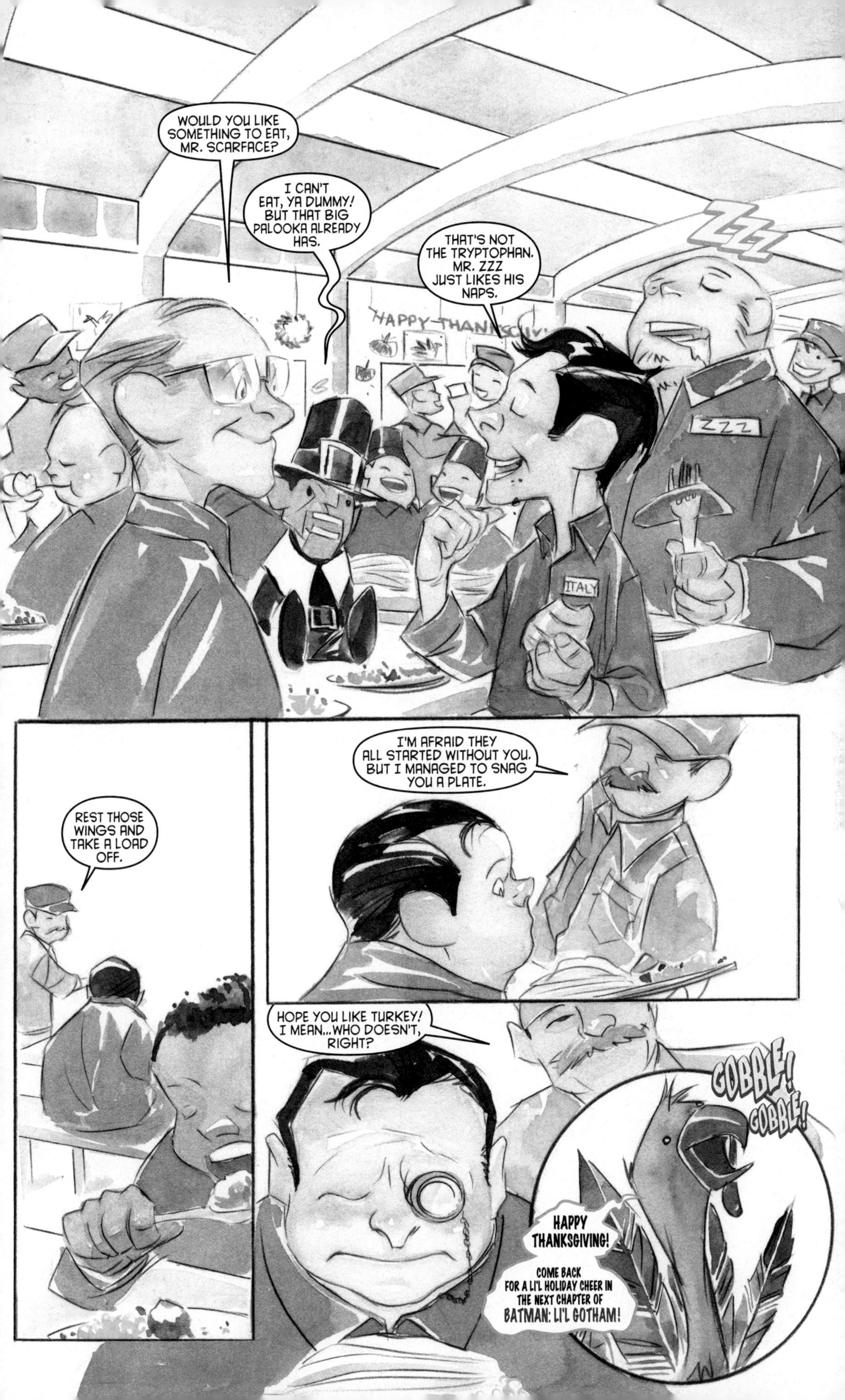
WOULD YOU LIKE SOMETHING TO EAT, MR. SCARFACE?
I CAN'T EAT, YA DUMMY! BUT THAT BIG PALOOKA ALREADY HAS.
THAT'S NOT THE TRYPTOPHAN. MR. ZZZ JUST LIKES HIS NAPS.
ZZZ
HAPPY THANKSGIV
ZZZ
ITALY
REST THOSE WINGS AND TAKE A LOAD OFF.
I'M AFRAID THEY ALL STARTED WITHOUT YOU. BUT I MANAGED TO SNAG YOU A PLATE.
HOPE YOU LIKE TURKEY! I MEAN...WHO DOESN'T, RIGHT?
GOBBLE! GOBBLE!
HAPPY THANKSGIVING!
COME BACK FOR A LI'L HOLIDAY CHEER IN THE NEXT CHAPTER OF BATMAN: LI'L GOTHAM!

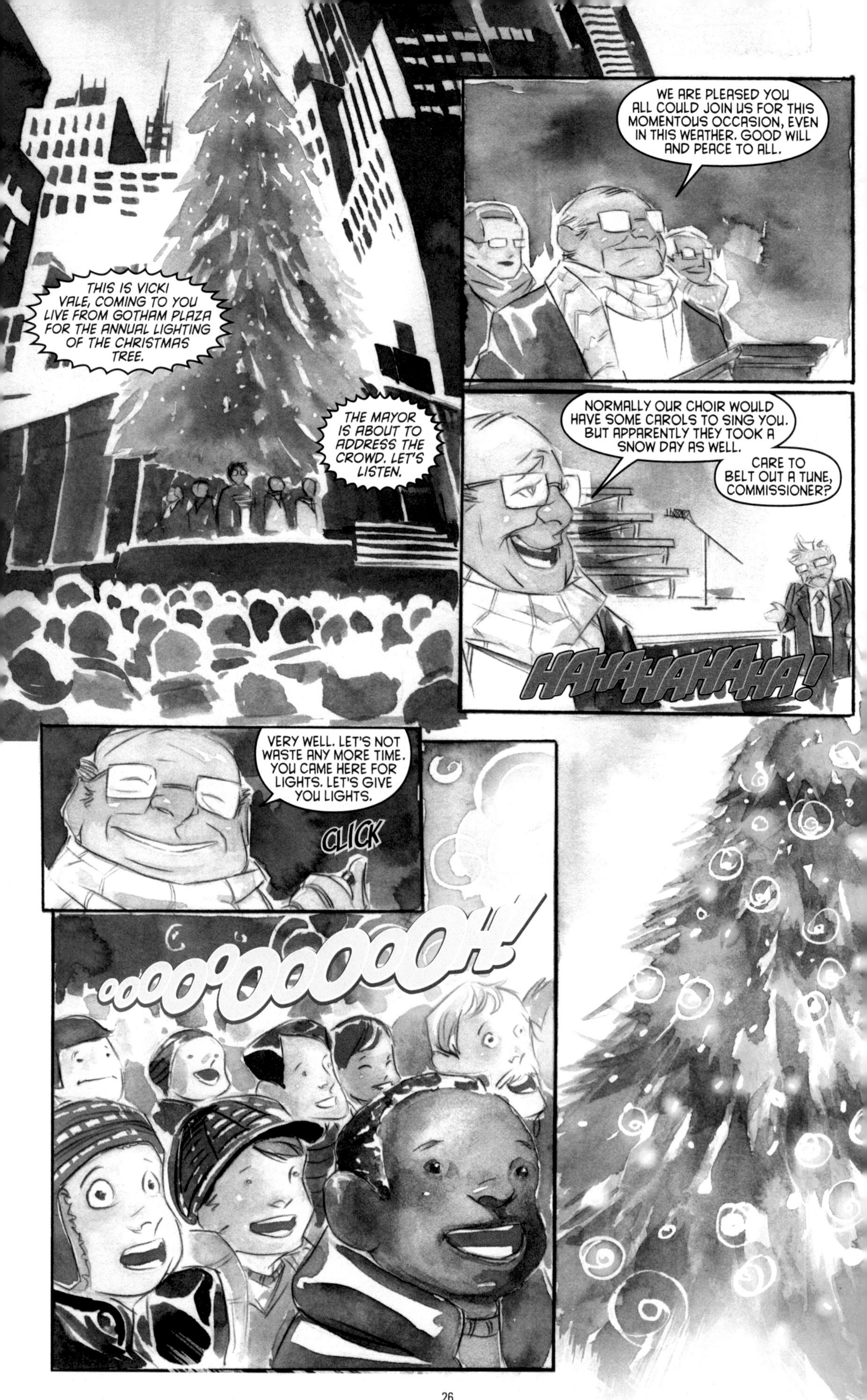
THIS IS VICKI VALE, COMING TO YOU LIVE FROM GOTHAM PLAZA FOR THE ANNUAL LIGHTING OF THE CHRISTMAS TREE.
THE MAYOR IS ABOUT TO ADDRESS THE CROWD. LET'S LISTEN.
WE ARE PLEASED YOU ALL COULD JOIN US FOR THIS MOMENTOUS OCCASION, EVEN IN THIS WEATHER. GOOD WILL AND PEACE TO ALL.
NORMALLY OUR CHOIR WOULD HAVE SOME CAROLS TO SING YOU. BUT APPARENTLY THEY TOOK A SNOW DAY AS WELL.
CARE TO BELT OUT A TUNE, COMMISSIONER?
HAHAHAHAHAHA!
VERY WELL. LET'S NOT WASTE ANY MORE TIME. YOU CAME HERE FOR LIGHTS. LET'S GIVE YOU LIGHTS.
CLICK
OOOOOOOOOOH!

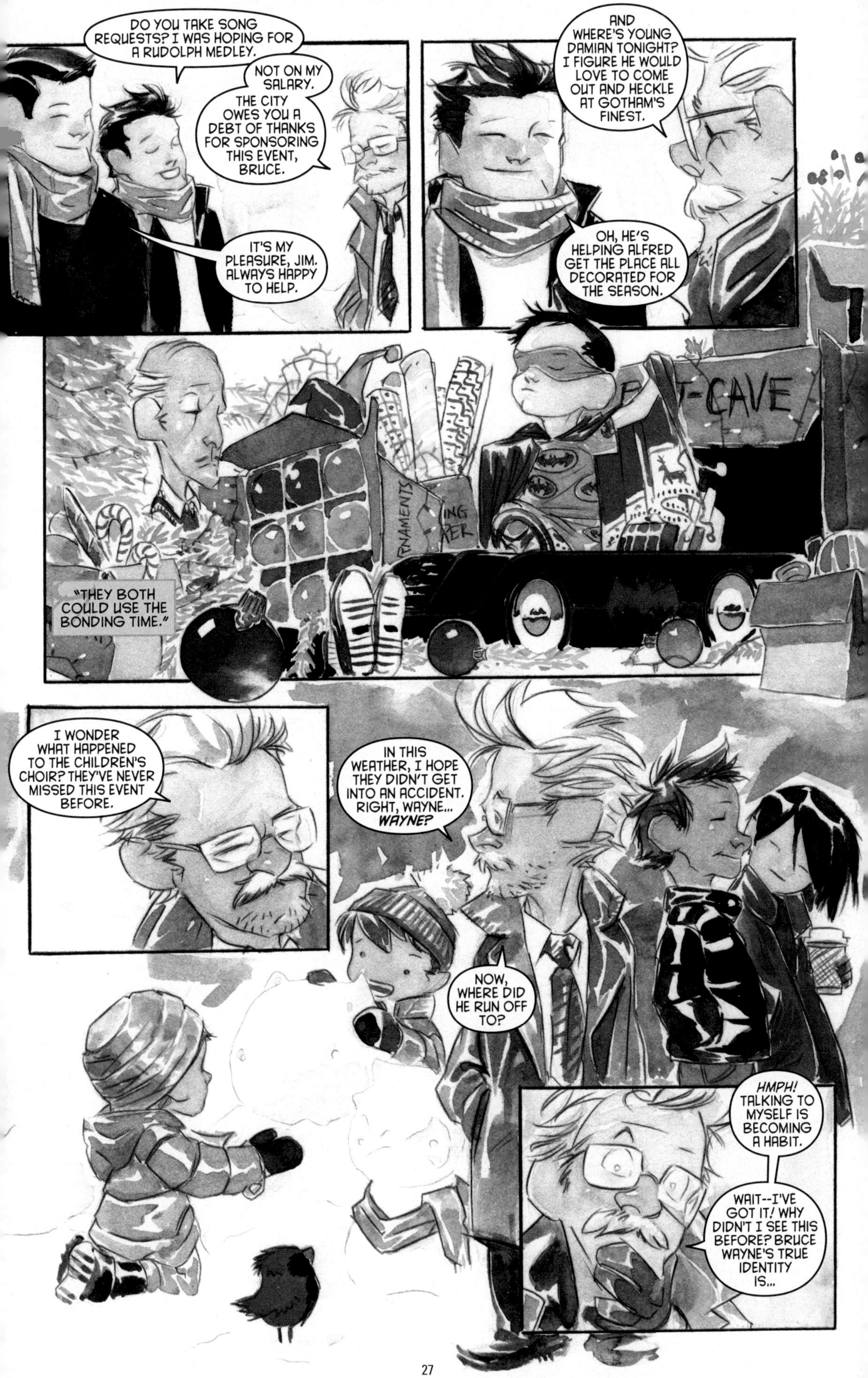
DO YOU TAKE SONG REQUESTS? I WAS HOPING FOR A RUDOLPH MEDLEY.
NOT ON MY SALARY.
THE CITY OWES YOU A DEBT OF THANKS FOR SPONSORING THIS EVENT, BRUCE.
IT'S MY PLEASURE, JIM. ALWAYS HAPPY TO HELP.
AND WHERE'S YOUNG DAMIAN TONIGHT? I FIGURE HE WOULD LOVE TO COME OUT AND HECKLE AT GOTHAM'S FINEST.
OH, HE'S HELPING ALFRED GET THE PLACE ALL DECORATED FOR THE SEASON.
"THEY BOTH COULD USE THE BONDING TIME."
I WONDER WHAT HAPPENED TO THE CHILDREN'S CHOIR? THEY'VE NEVER MISSED THIS EVENT BEFORE.
IN THIS WEATHER, I HOPE THEY DIDN'T GET INTO AN ACCIDENT. RIGHT, WAYNE... *WAYNE?*
NOW, WHERE DID HE RUN OFF TO?
HMPH! TALKING TO MYSELF IS BECOMING A HABIT.
WAIT--I'VE GOT IT! WHY DIDN'T I SEE THIS BEFORE? BRUCE WAYNE'S TRUE IDENTITY IS...

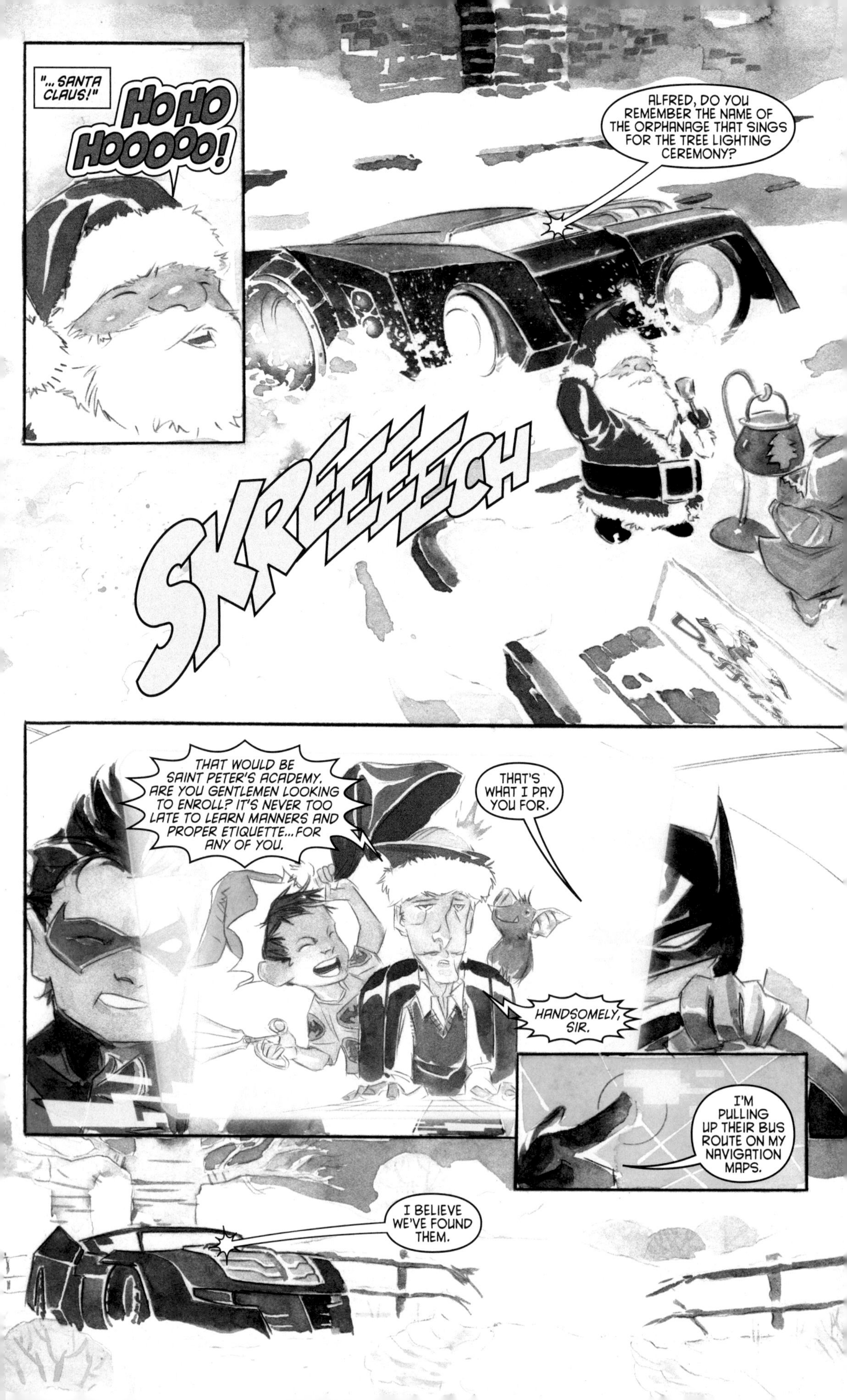

"...SANTA CLAUS!"
HO HO HOOOOO!
ALFRED, DO YOU REMEMBER THE NAME OF THE ORPHANAGE THAT SINGS FOR THE TREE LIGHTING CEREMONY?
SKREEEECH
THAT WOULD BE SAINT PETER'S ACADEMY. ARE YOU GENTLEMEN LOOKING TO ENROLL? IT'S NEVER TOO LATE TO LEARN MANNERS AND PROPER ETIQUETTE...FOR ANY OF YOU.
THAT'S WHAT I PAY YOU FOR.
HANDSOMELY, SIR.
I'M PULLING UP THEIR BUS ROUTE ON MY NAVIGATION MAPS.
I BELIEVE WE'VE FOUND THEM.

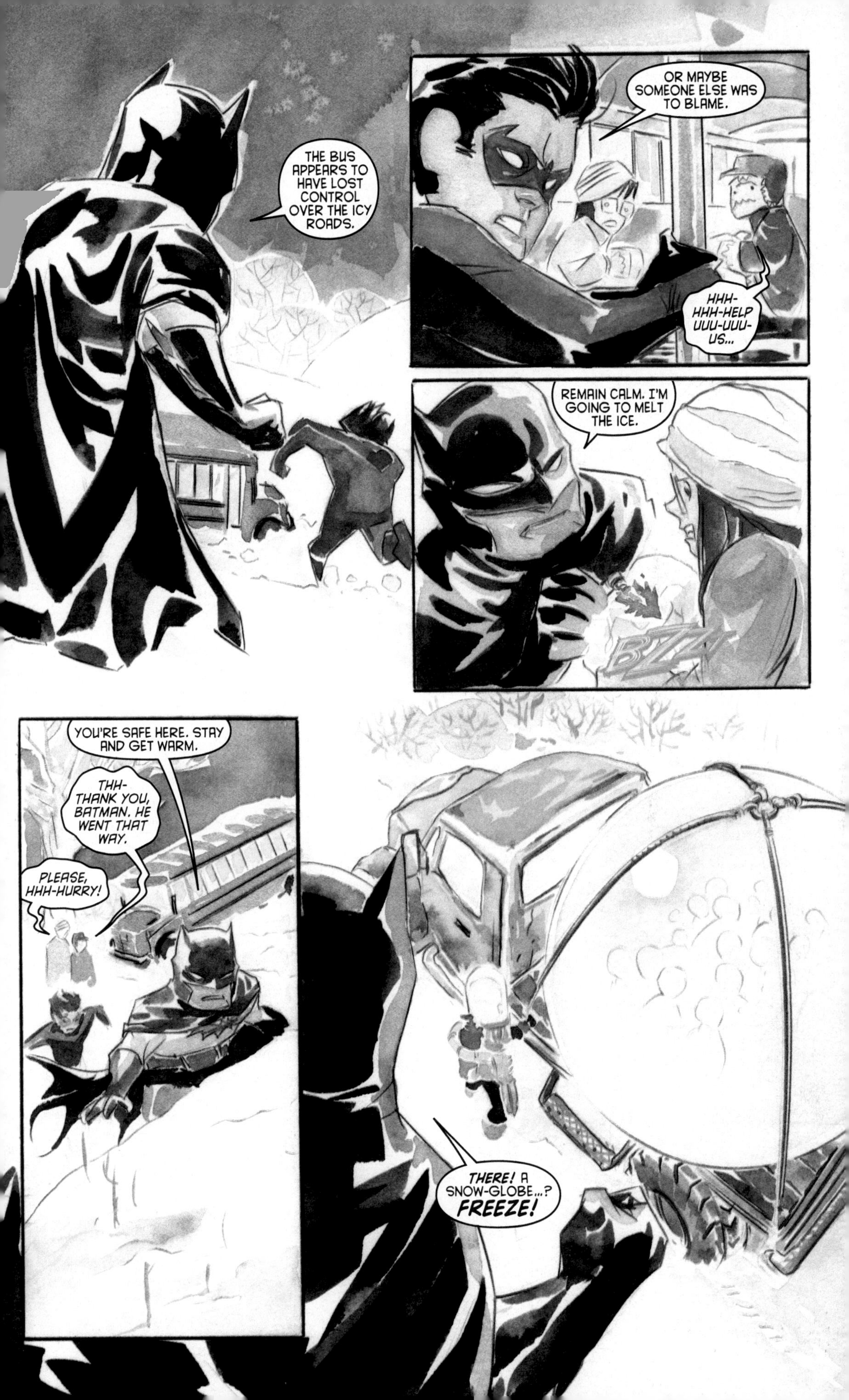

THE BUS APPEARS TO HAVE LOST CONTROL OVER THE ICY ROADS.
OR MAYBE SOMEONE ELSE WAS TO BLAME.
HHH-HHH-HELP UUU-UUU-US...
REMAIN CALM. I'M GOING TO MELT THE ICE.
BZZT
YOU'RE SAFE HERE. STAY AND GET WARM.
THH-THANK YOU, BATMAN. HE WENT THAT WAY.
PLEASE, HHH-HURRY!
THERE! A SNOW-GLOBE...? FREEZE!

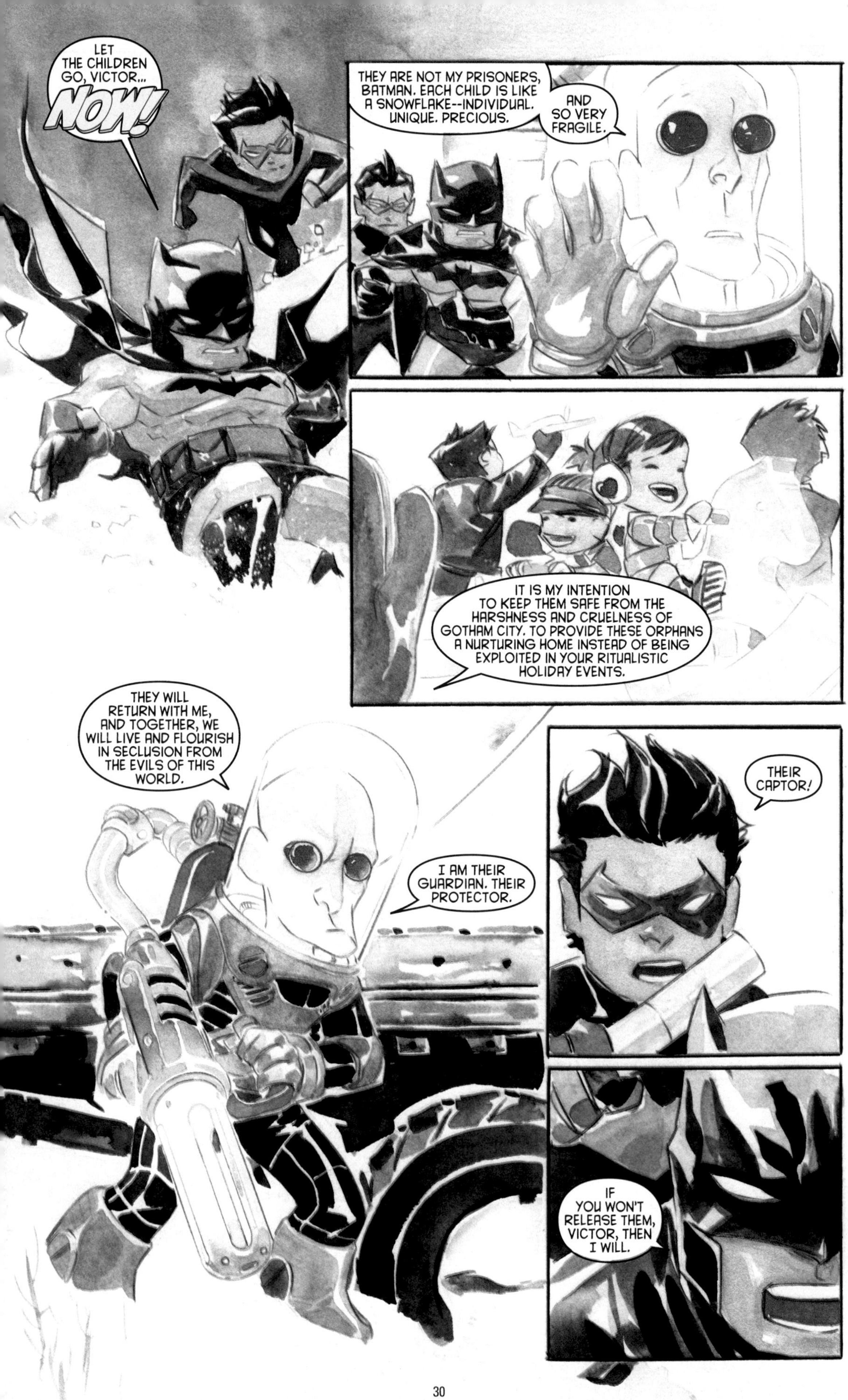
LET THE CHILDREN GO, VICTOR... NOW!
THEY ARE NOT MY PRISONERS, BATMAN. EACH CHILD IS LIKE A SNOWFLAKE--INDIVIDUAL. UNIQUE. PRECIOUS.
AND SO VERY FRAGILE.
IT IS MY INTENTION TO KEEP THEM SAFE FROM THE HARSHNESS AND CRUELNESS OF GOTHAM CITY. TO PROVIDE THESE ORPHANS A NURTURING HOME INSTEAD OF BEING EXPLOITED IN YOUR RITUALISTIC HOLIDAY EVENTS.
THEY WILL RETURN WITH ME, AND TOGETHER, WE WILL LIVE AND FLOURISH IN SECLUSION FROM THE EVILS OF THIS WORLD.
I AM THEIR GUARDIAN. THEIR PROTECTOR.
THEIR CAPTOR!
IF YOU WON'T RELEASE THEM, VICTOR, THEN I WILL.

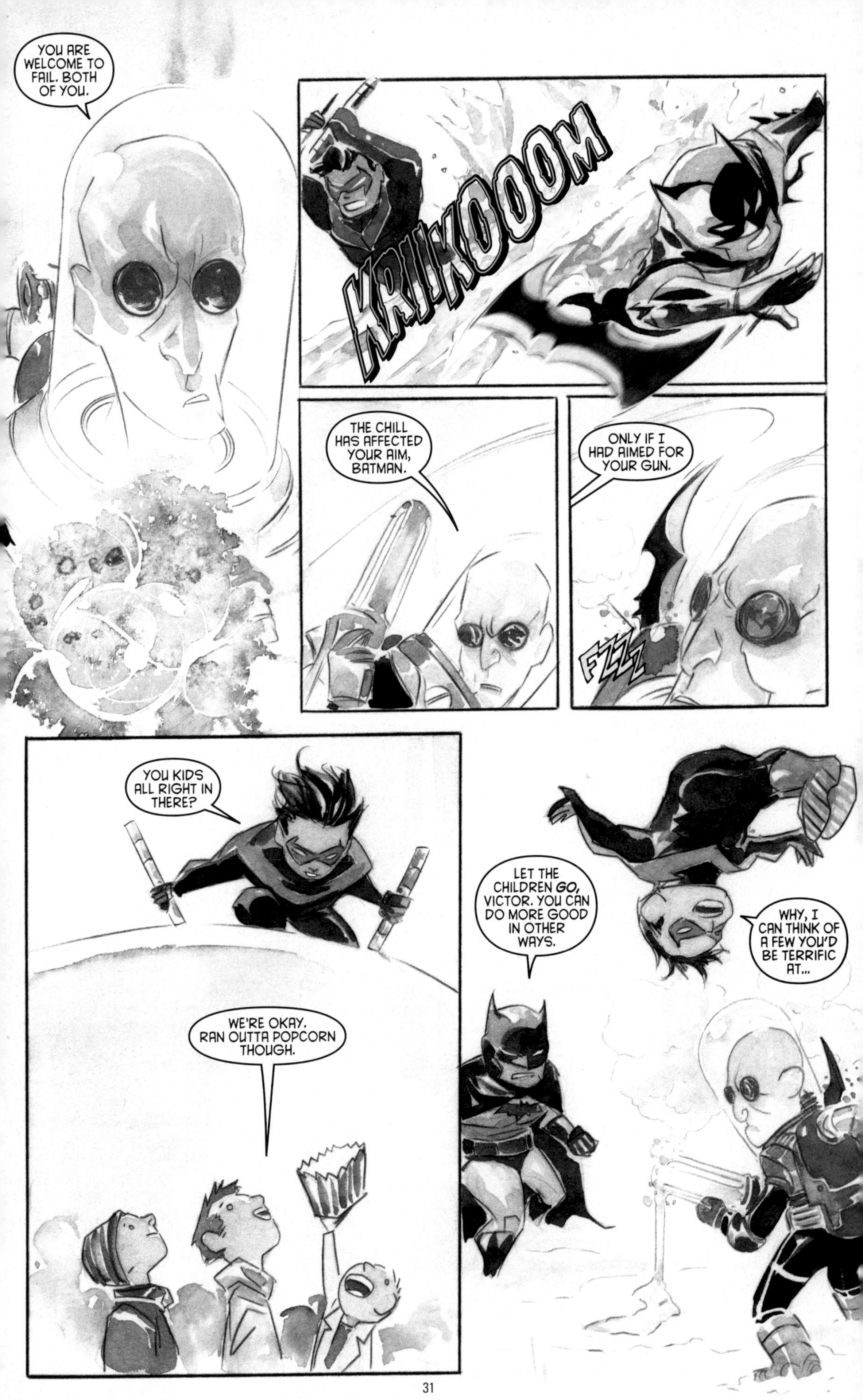
YOU ARE WELCOME TO FAIL. BOTH OF YOU.
KRIIKOOOM
THE CHILL HAS AFFECTED YOUR AIM, BATMAN.
ONLY IF I HAD AIMED FOR YOUR GUN.
FZZZ
YOU KIDS ALL RIGHT IN THERE?
WE'RE OKAY. RAN OUTTA POPCORN THOUGH.
LET THE CHILDREN GO, VICTOR. YOU CAN DO MORE GOOD IN OTHER WAYS.
WHY, I CAN THINK OF A FEW YOU'D BE TERRIFIC AT...

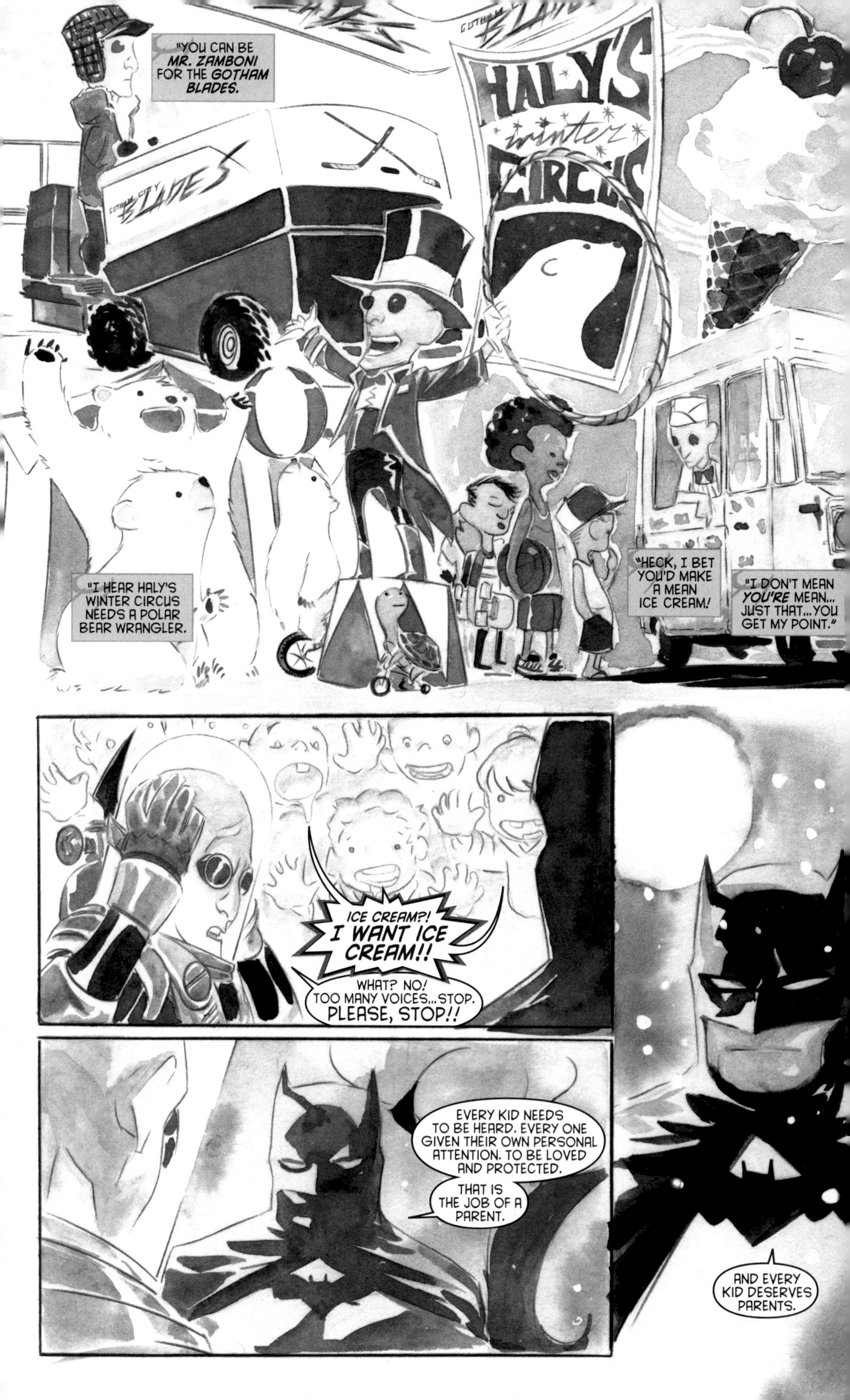
"YOU CAN BE MR. ZAMBONI FOR THE GOTHAM BLADES.
GOTHAM CITY BLADES
HALY'S winter CIRCUS
"I HEAR HALY'S WINTER CIRCUS NEEDS A POLAR BEAR WRANGLER.
"HECK, I BET YOU'D MAKE A MEAN ICE CREAM!
"I DON'T MEAN YOU'RE MEAN... JUST THAT... YOU GET MY POINT."
ICE CREAM?! I WANT ICE CREAM!!
WHAT? NO! TOO MANY VOICES... STOP. PLEASE, STOP!!
EVERY KID NEEDS TO BE HEARD. EVERY ONE GIVEN THEIR OWN PERSONAL ATTENTION. TO BE LOVED AND PROTECTED.
THAT IS THE JOB OF A PARENT.
AND EVERY KID DESERVES PARENTS.

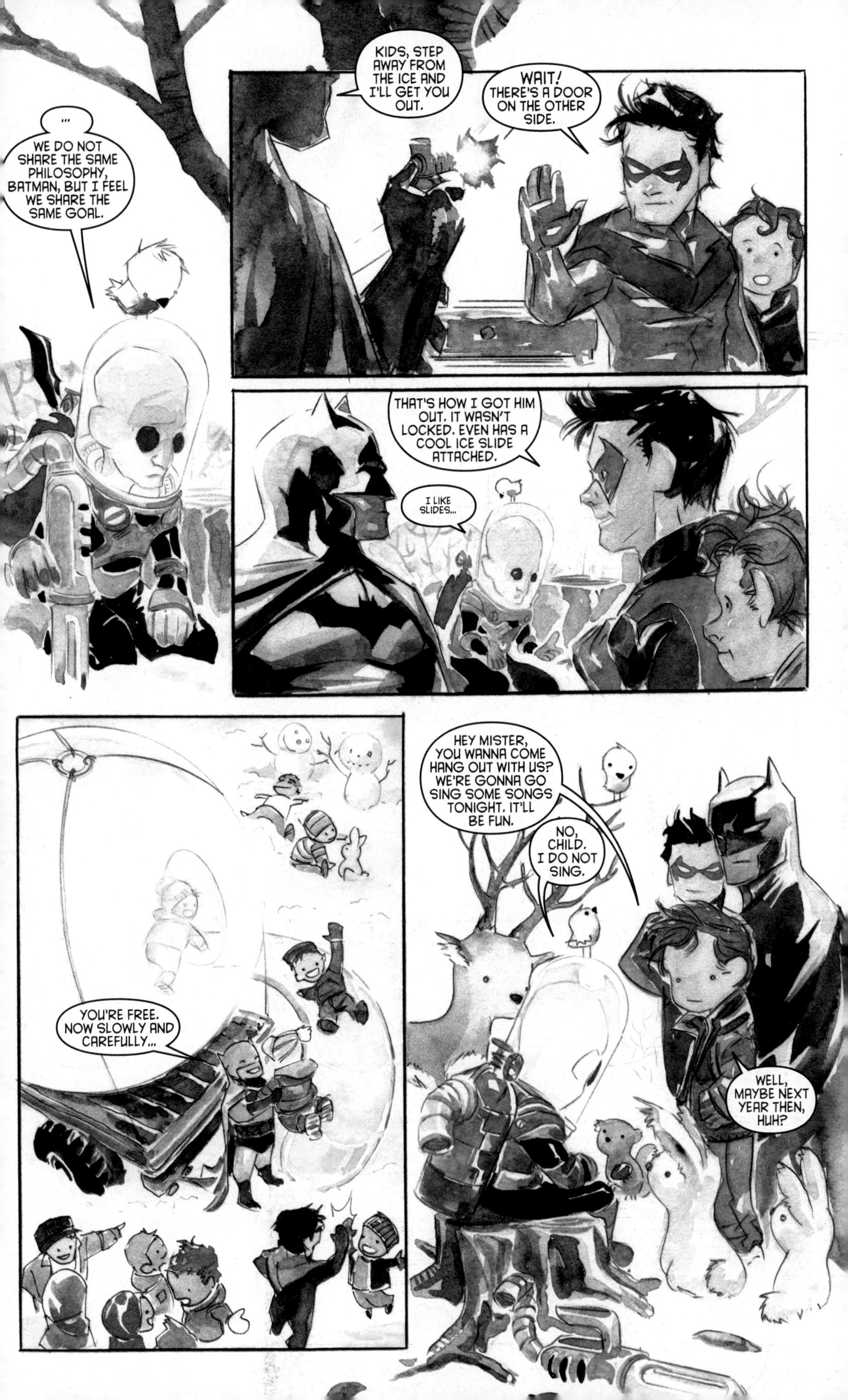

...
WE DO NOT SHARE THE SAME PHILOSOPHY, BATMAN, BUT I FEEL WE SHARE THE SAME GOAL.
KIDS, STEP AWAY FROM THE ICE AND I'LL GET YOU OUT.
WAIT! THERE'S A DOOR ON THE OTHER SIDE.
THAT'S HOW I GOT HIM OUT. IT WASN'T LOCKED. EVEN HAS A COOL ICE SLIDE ATTACHED.
I LIKE SLIDES...
YOU'RE FREE. NOW SLOWLY AND CAREFULLY...
HEY MISTER, YOU WANNA COME HANG OUT WITH US? WE'RE GONNA GO SING SOME SONGS TONIGHT. IT'LL BE FUN.
NO, CHILD. I DO NOT SING.
WELL, MAYBE NEXT YEAR THEN, HUH?

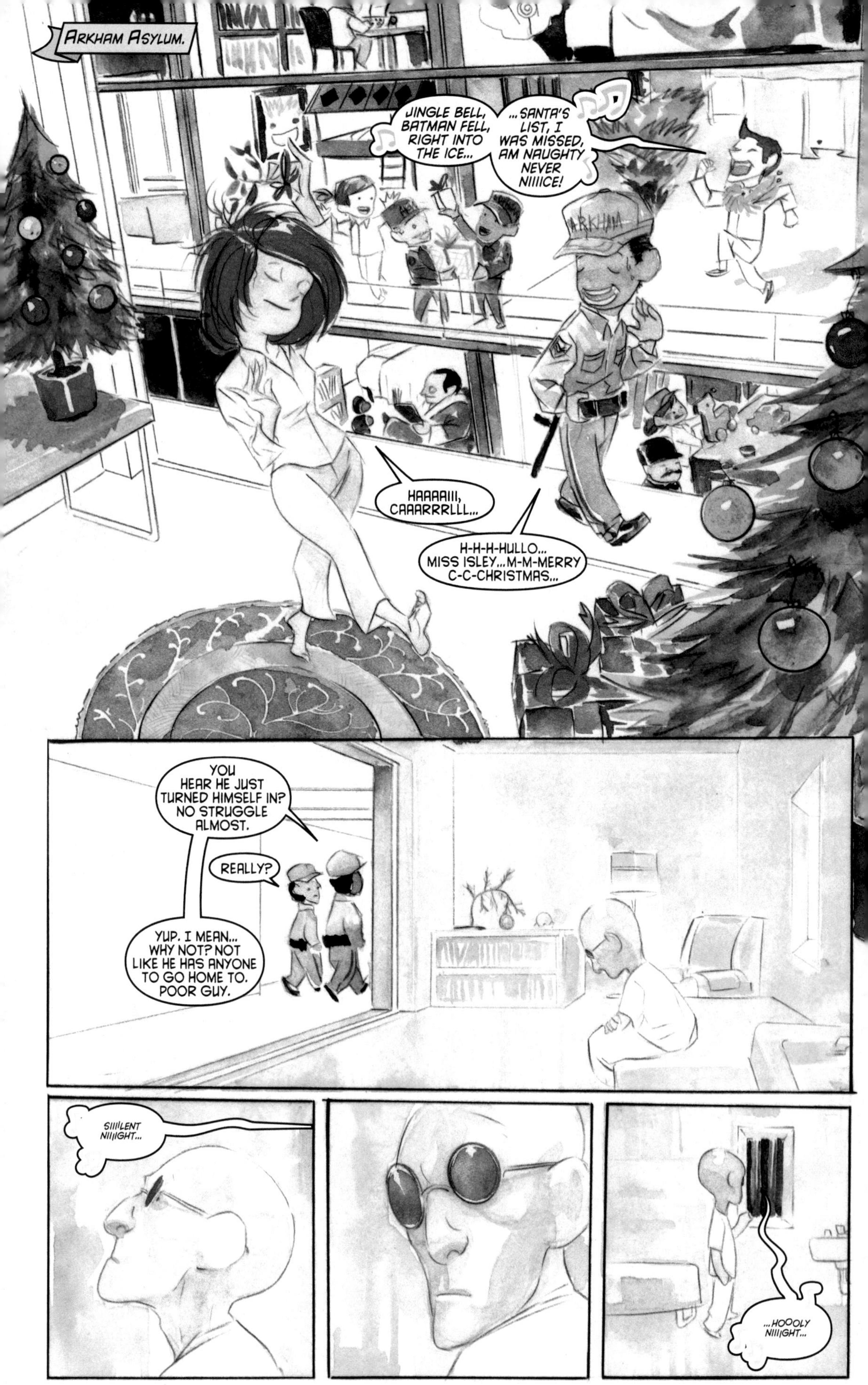

ARKHAM ASYLUM.
JINGLE BELL, BATMAN FELL, RIGHT INTO THE ICE...
...SANTA'S LIST, I WAS MISSED, AM NAUGHTY NEVER NIIIICE!
HAAAAIII, CAAARRRLLL...
H-H-H-HULLO... MISS ISLEY...M-M-MERRY C-C-CHRISTMAS...
YOU HEAR HE JUST TURNED HIMSELF IN? NO STRUGGLE ALMOST.
REALLY?
YUP. I MEAN... WHY NOT? NOT LIKE HE HAS ANYONE TO GO HOME TO. POOR GUY.
SIIIILENT NIIIIGHT...
...HOOOLY NIIIIGHT...

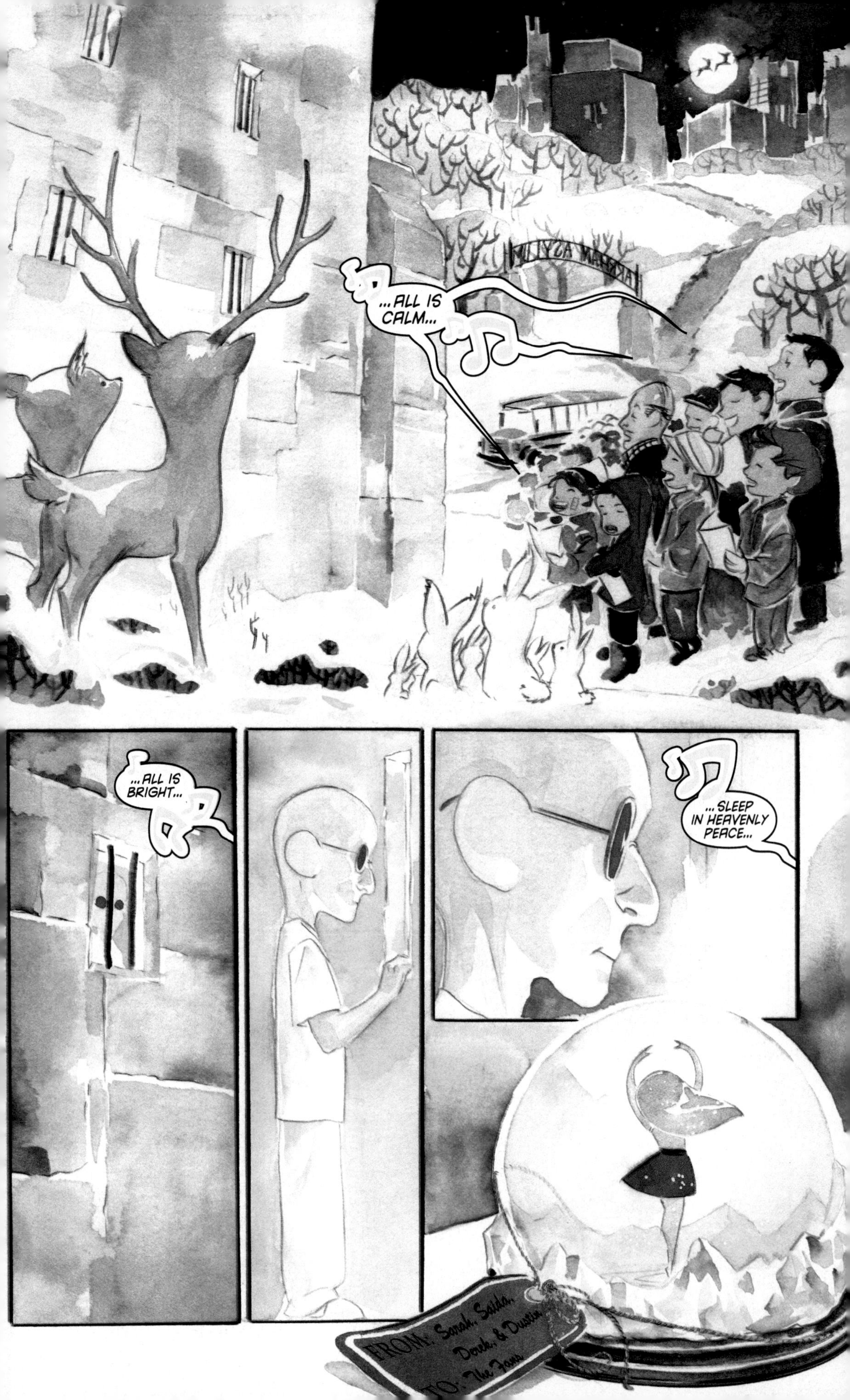
...ALL IS CALM...
...ALL IS BRIGHT...
...SLEEP IN HEAVENLY PEACE...
FROM: Sarah, Saida, Derek, & Dustin
TO: The Fans

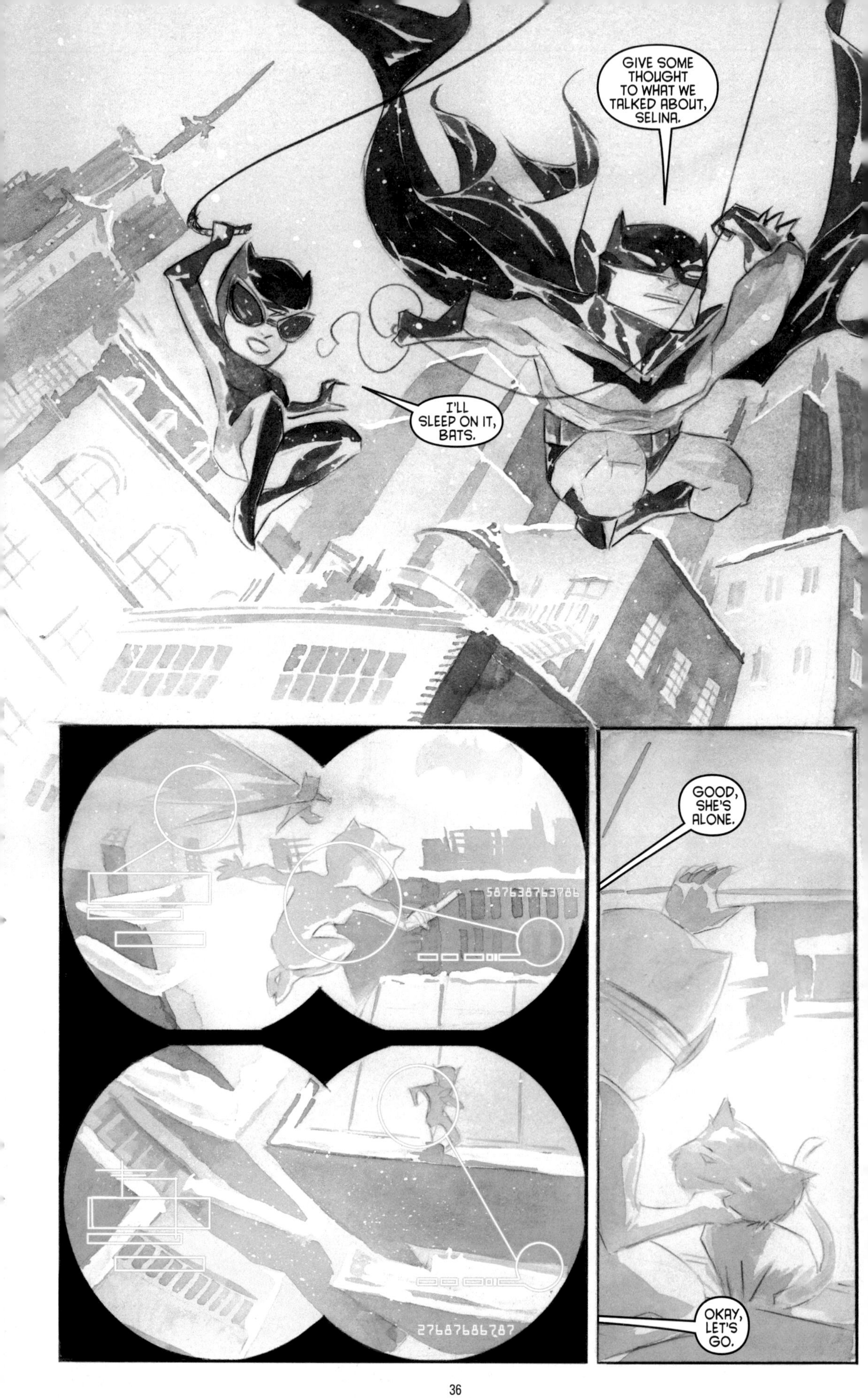
GIVE SOME THOUGHT TO WHAT WE TALKED ABOUT, SELINA.
I'LL SLEEP ON IT, BATS.
587638763786
27687686787
GOOD, SHE'S ALONE.
OKAY, LET'S GO.

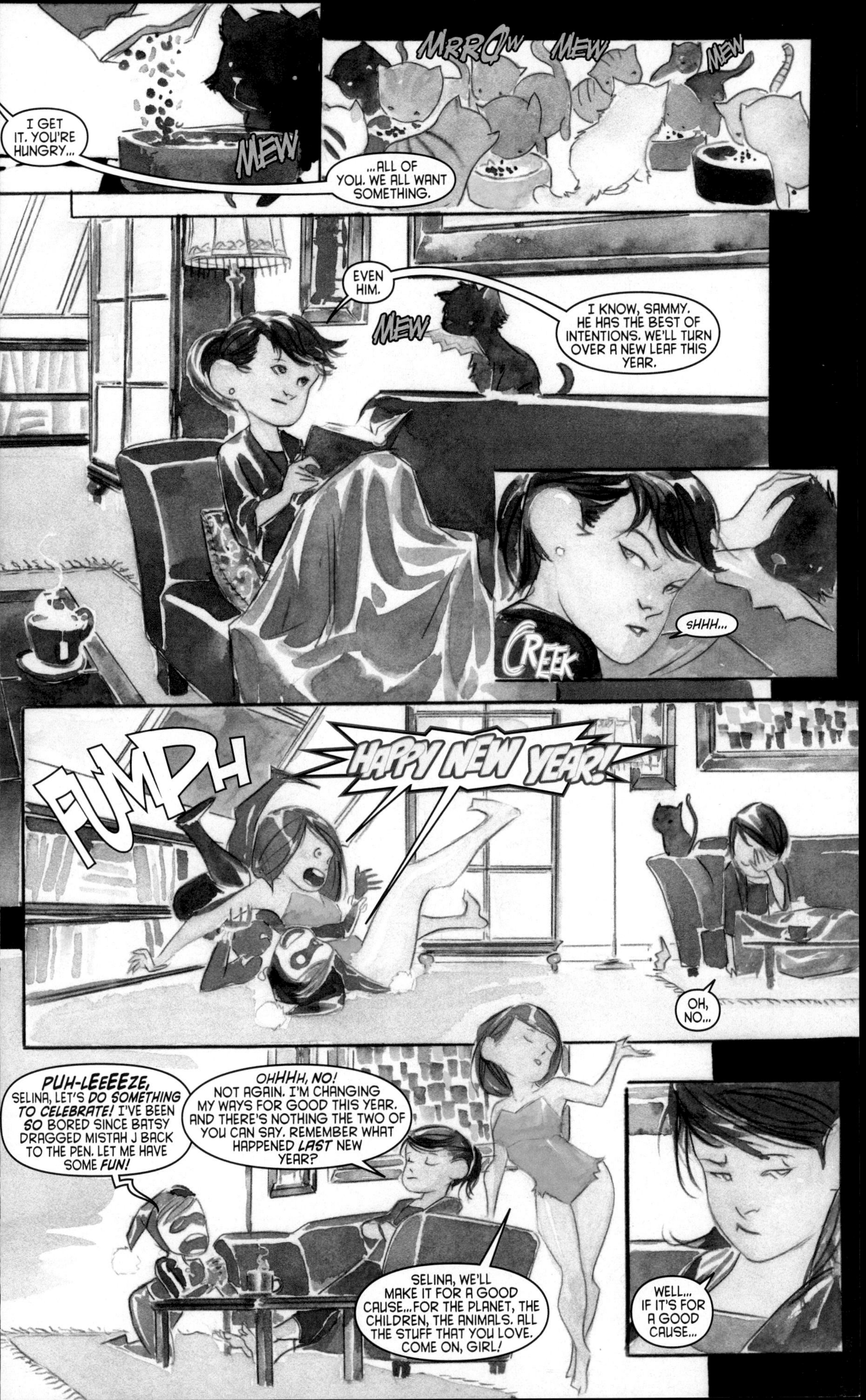
I GET IT. YOU'RE HUNGRY...
MEW
MRROW
MEW
MEW
...ALL OF YOU. WE ALL WANT SOMETHING.
EVEN HIM.
MEW
I KNOW, SAMMY. HE HAS THE BEST OF INTENTIONS. WE'LL TURN OVER A NEW LEAF THIS YEAR.
CREEK
SHHH...
FUMPH
HAPPY NEW YEAR!
OH, NO...
PUH-LEEEEZE, SELINA, LET'S DO SOMETHING TO CELEBRATE! I'VE BEEN SO BORED SINCE BATSY DRAGGED MISTAH J BACK TO THE PEN. LET ME HAVE SOME FUN!
OHHHH, NO! NOT AGAIN. I'M CHANGING MY WAYS FOR GOOD THIS YEAR. AND THERE'S NOTHING THE TWO OF YOU CAN SAY. REMEMBER WHAT HAPPENED LAST NEW YEAR?
SELINA, WE'LL MAKE IT FOR A GOOD CAUSE...FOR THE PLANET, THE CHILDREN, THE ANIMALS. ALL THE STUFF THAT YOU LOVE. COME ON, GIRL!
WELL... IF IT'S FOR A GOOD CAUSE...

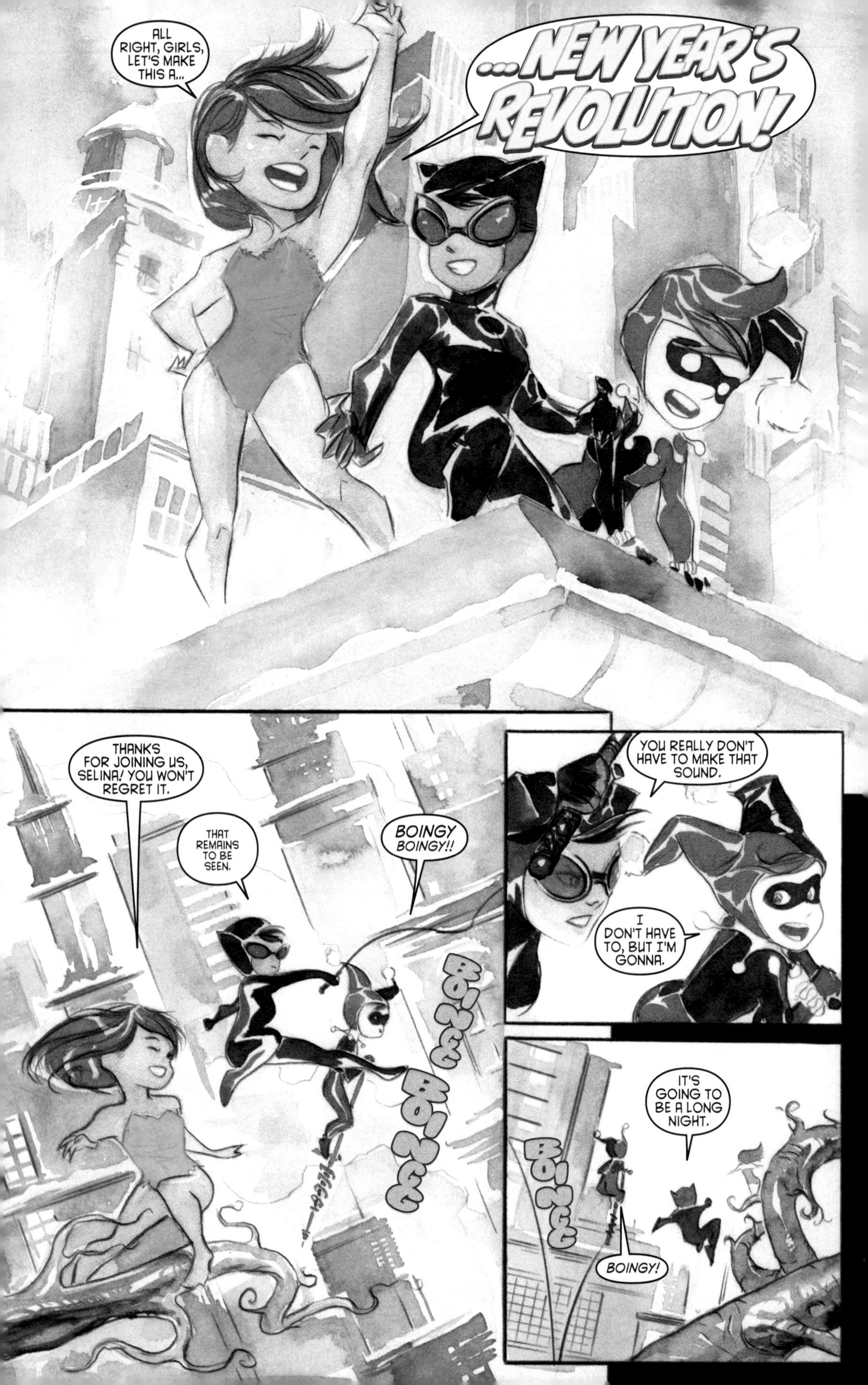
ALL RIGHT, GIRLS, LET'S MAKE THIS A...
...NEW YEAR'S REVOLUTION!
THANKS FOR JOINING US, SELINA! YOU WON'T REGRET IT.
THAT REMAINS TO BE SEEN.
BOINGY BOINGY!!
BOING
BOING
YOU REALLY DON'T HAVE TO MAKE THAT SOUND.
I DON'T HAVE TO, BUT I'M GONNA.
IT'S GOING TO BE A LONG NIGHT.
BOING
BOINGY!

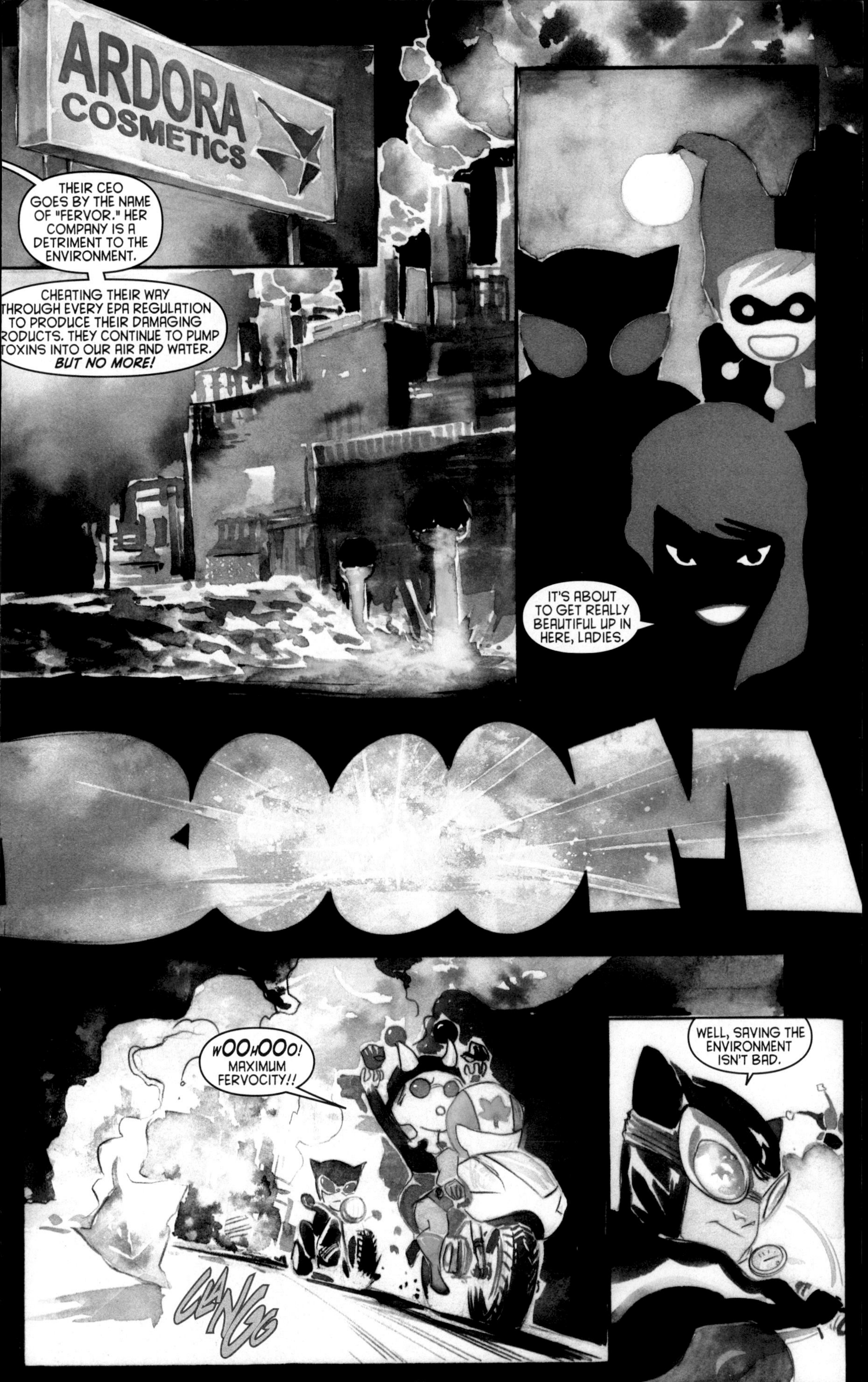
ARDORA COSMETICS
THEIR CEO GOES BY THE NAME OF "FERVOR." HER COMPANY IS A DETRIMENT TO THE ENVIRONMENT.
CHEATING THEIR WAY THROUGH EVERY EPA REGULATION TO PRODUCE THEIR DAMAGING PRODUCTS. THEY CONTINUE TO PUMP TOXINS INTO OUR AIR AND WATER. BUT NO MORE!
IT'S ABOUT TO GET REALLY BEAUTIFUL UP IN HERE, LADIES.
BOOOM
WOOHOOO! MAXIMUM FERVOCITY!!
CLANGG
WELL, SAVING THE ENVIRONMENT ISN'T BAD.

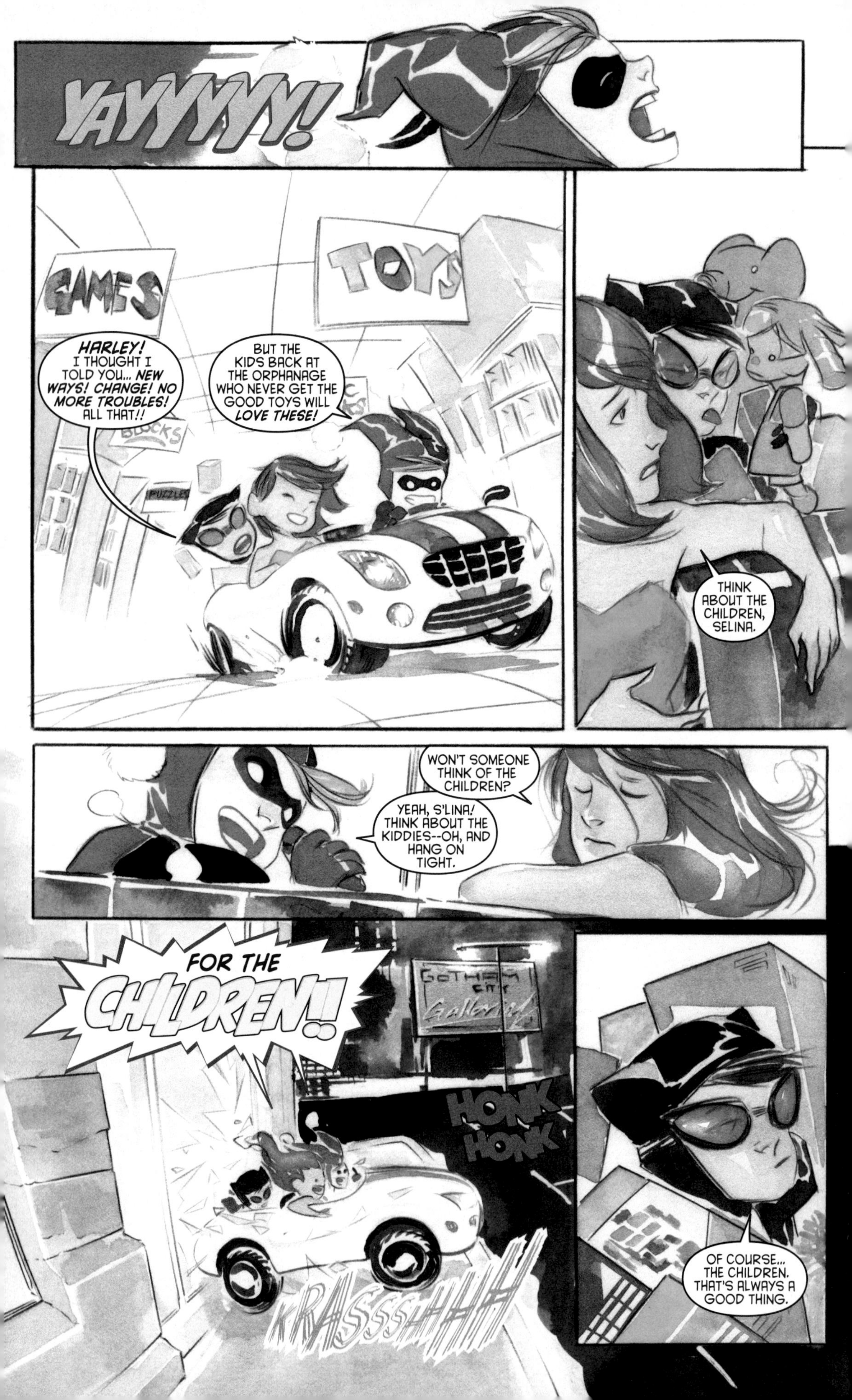
YAYYYYY!
GAMES
TOYS
HARLEY! I THOUGHT I TOLD YOU... NEW WAYS! CHANGE! NO MORE TROUBLES! ALL THAT!!
BUT THE KIDS BACK AT THE ORPHANAGE WHO NEVER GET THE GOOD TOYS WILL LOVE THESE!
BLOCKS
PUZZLES
THINK ABOUT THE CHILDREN, SELINA.
WON'T SOMEONE THINK OF THE CHILDREN?
YEAH, S'LINA! THINK ABOUT THE KIDDIES--OH, AND HANG ON TIGHT.
FOR THE CHILDREN!!
GOTHAM CITY Gallery
HONK HONK
KRASSSHHHH
OF COURSE... THE CHILDREN. THAT'S ALWAYS A GOOD THING.

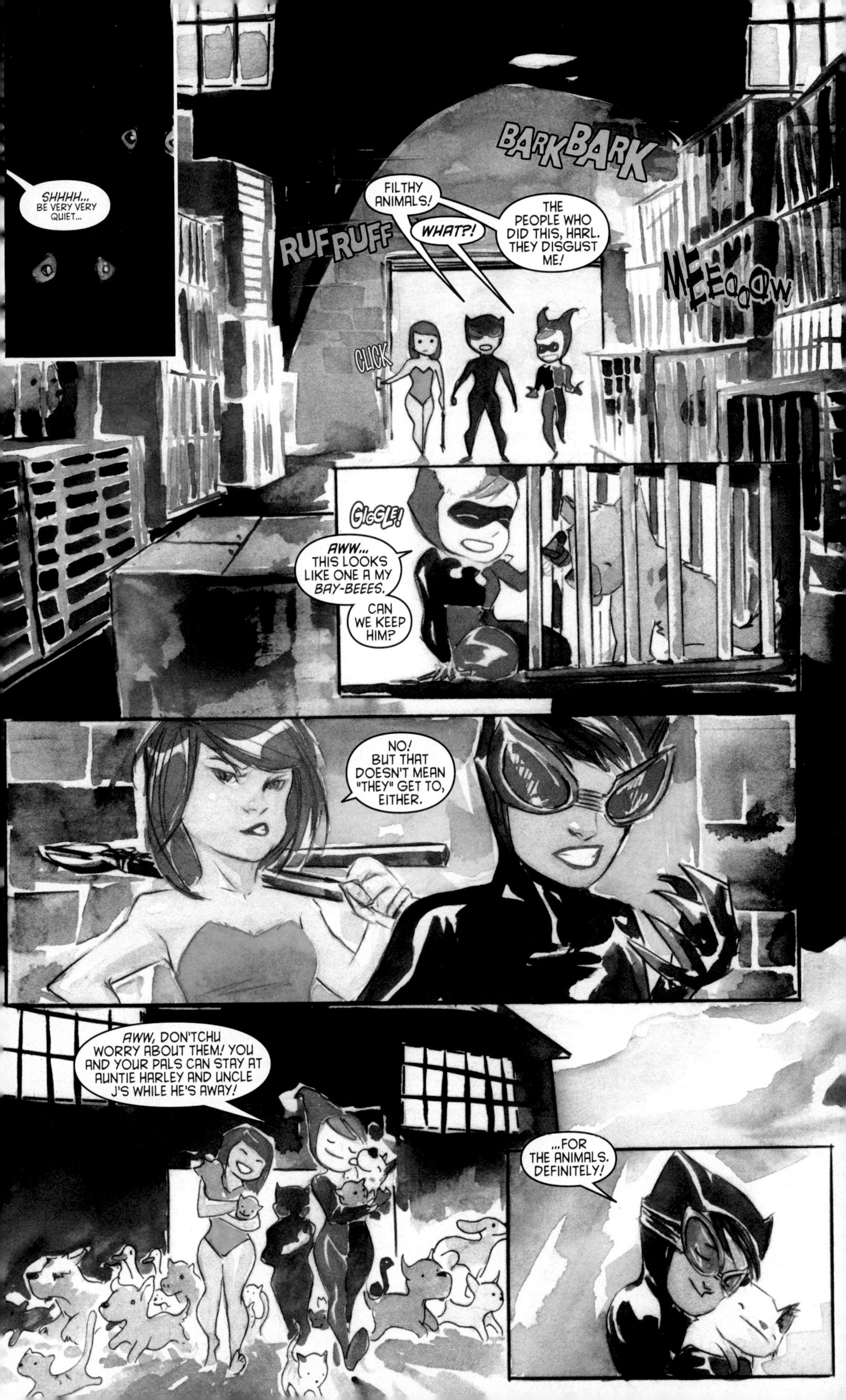

SHHHH...
BE VERY VERY QUIET...
BARK BARK
FILTHY ANIMALS!
RUF RUFF
WHAT?!
THE PEOPLE WHO DID THIS, HARL. THEY DISGUST ME!
MEEOOW
CLICK
GIGGLE!
AWW... THIS LOOKS LIKE ONE A MY BAY-BEEES.
CAN WE KEEP HIM?
NO! BUT THAT DOESN'T MEAN "THEY" GET TO, EITHER.
AWW, DON'TCHU WORRY ABOUT THEM! YOU AND YOUR PALS CAN STAY AT AUNTIE HARLEY AND UNCLE J'S WHILE HE'S AWAY!
...FOR THE ANIMALS. DEFINITELY!

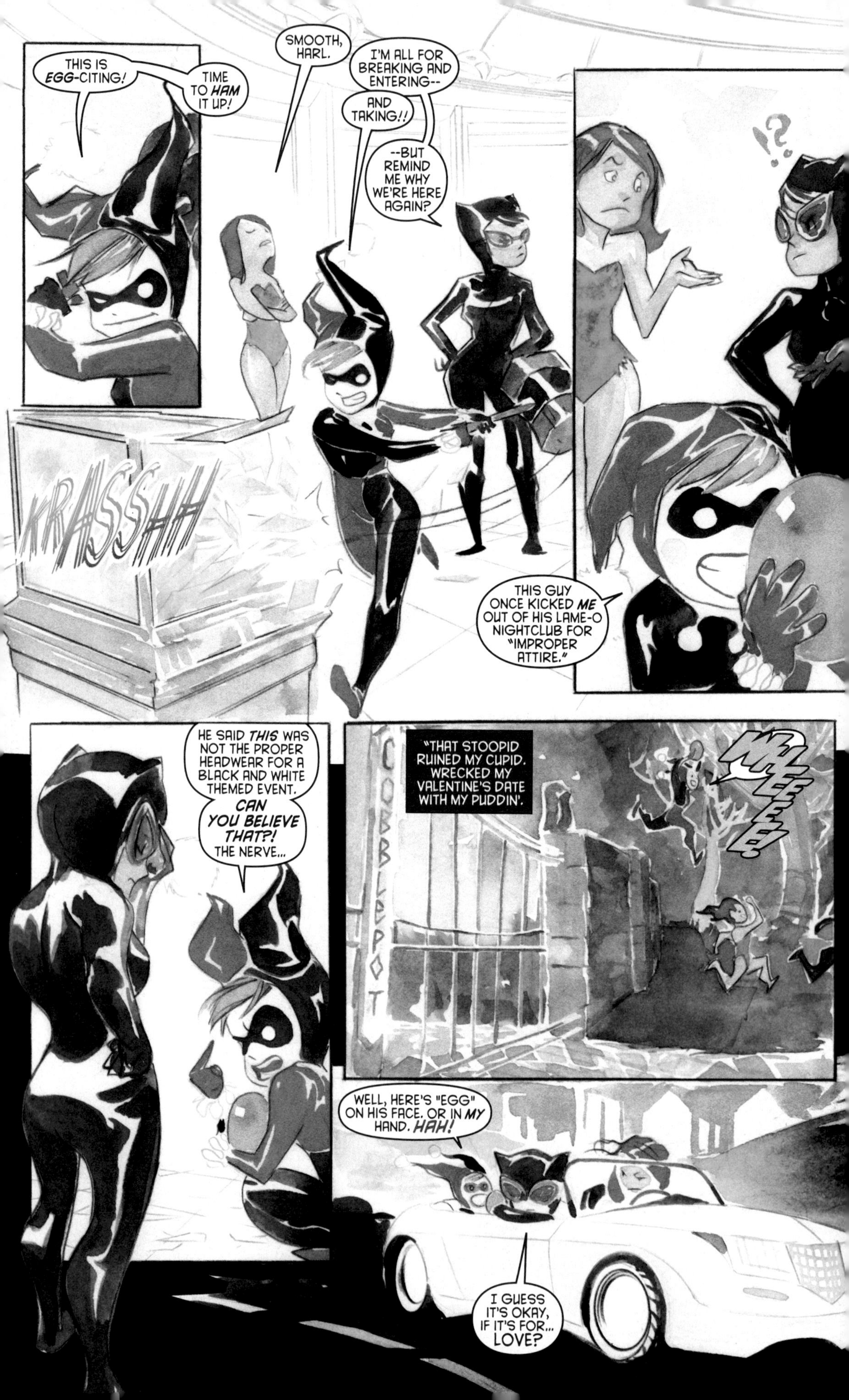
THIS IS EGG-CITING!
TIME TO HAM IT UP!
SMOOTH, HARL.
I'M ALL FOR BREAKING AND ENTERING--
AND TAKING!!
--BUT REMIND ME WHY WE'RE HERE AGAIN?
KRASSHH
!?
THIS GUY ONCE KICKED ME OUT OF HIS LAME-O NIGHTCLUB FOR "IMPROPER ATTIRE."
HE SAID THIS WAS NOT THE PROPER HEADWEAR FOR A BLACK AND WHITE THEMED EVENT. CAN YOU BELIEVE THAT?! THE NERVE...
COBBLEPOT
"THAT STOOPID RUINED MY CUPID. WRECKED MY VALENTINE'S DATE WITH MY PUDDIN'.
WHEEEEE!
WELL, HERE'S "EGG" ON HIS FACE. OR IN MY HAND. HAH!
I GUESS IT'S OKAY, IF IT'S FOR... LOVE?

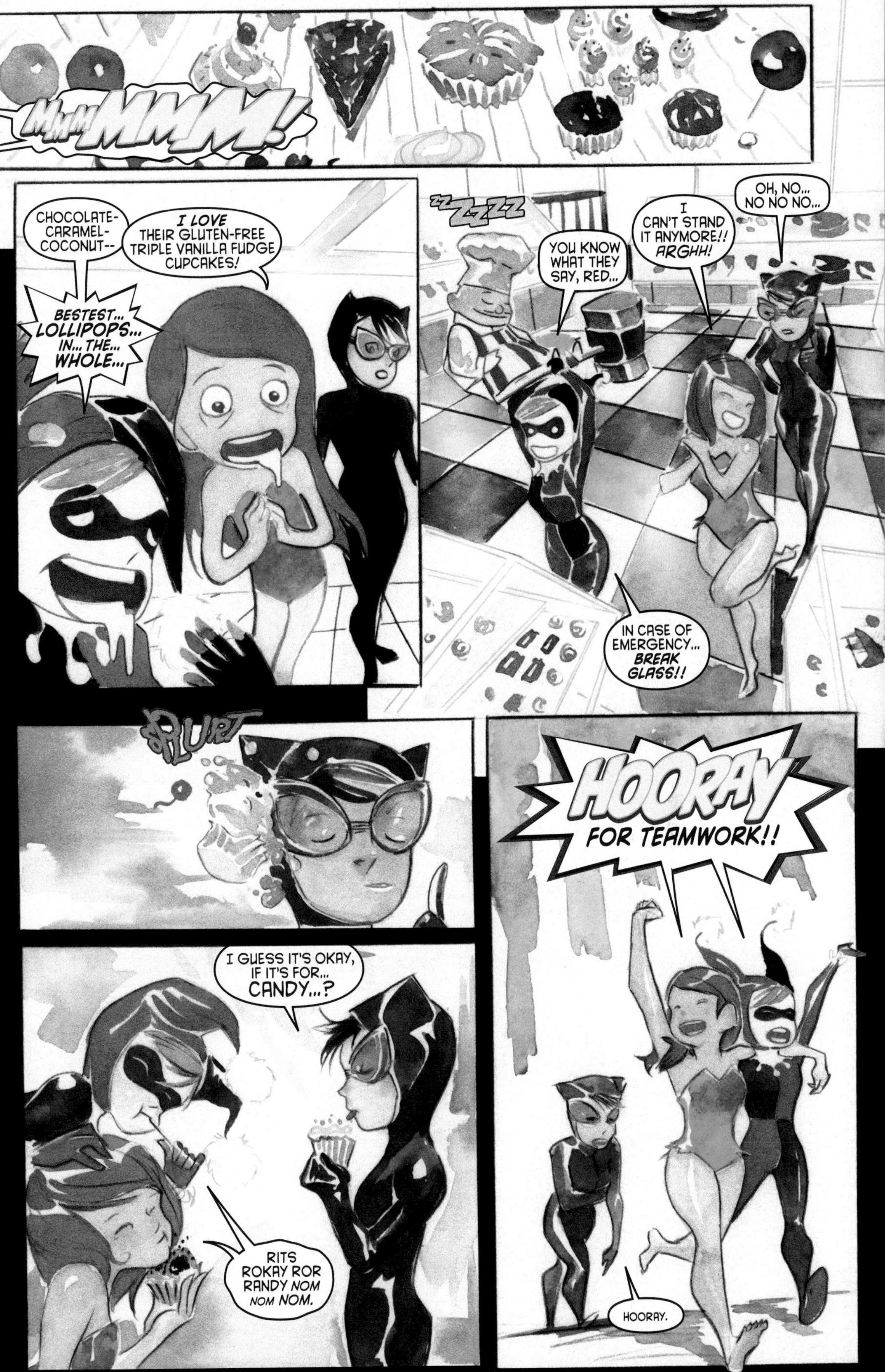
MMMMMMM!
CHOCOLATE-CARAMEL-COCONUT--
I LOVE THEIR GLUTEN-FREE TRIPLE VANILLA FUDGE CUPCAKES!
BESTEST... LOLLIPOPS... IN... THE... WHOLE...
ZZZZZZ
YOU KNOW WHAT THEY SAY, RED...
I CAN'T STAND IT ANYMORE!! ARGHH!
OH, NO... NO NO NO...
IN CASE OF EMERGENCY... BREAK GLASS!!
SPLURT
I GUESS IT'S OKAY, IF IT'S FOR... CANDY...?
RITS ROKAY ROR RANDY NOM NOM NOM.
HOORAY FOR TEAMWORK!!
HOORAY.

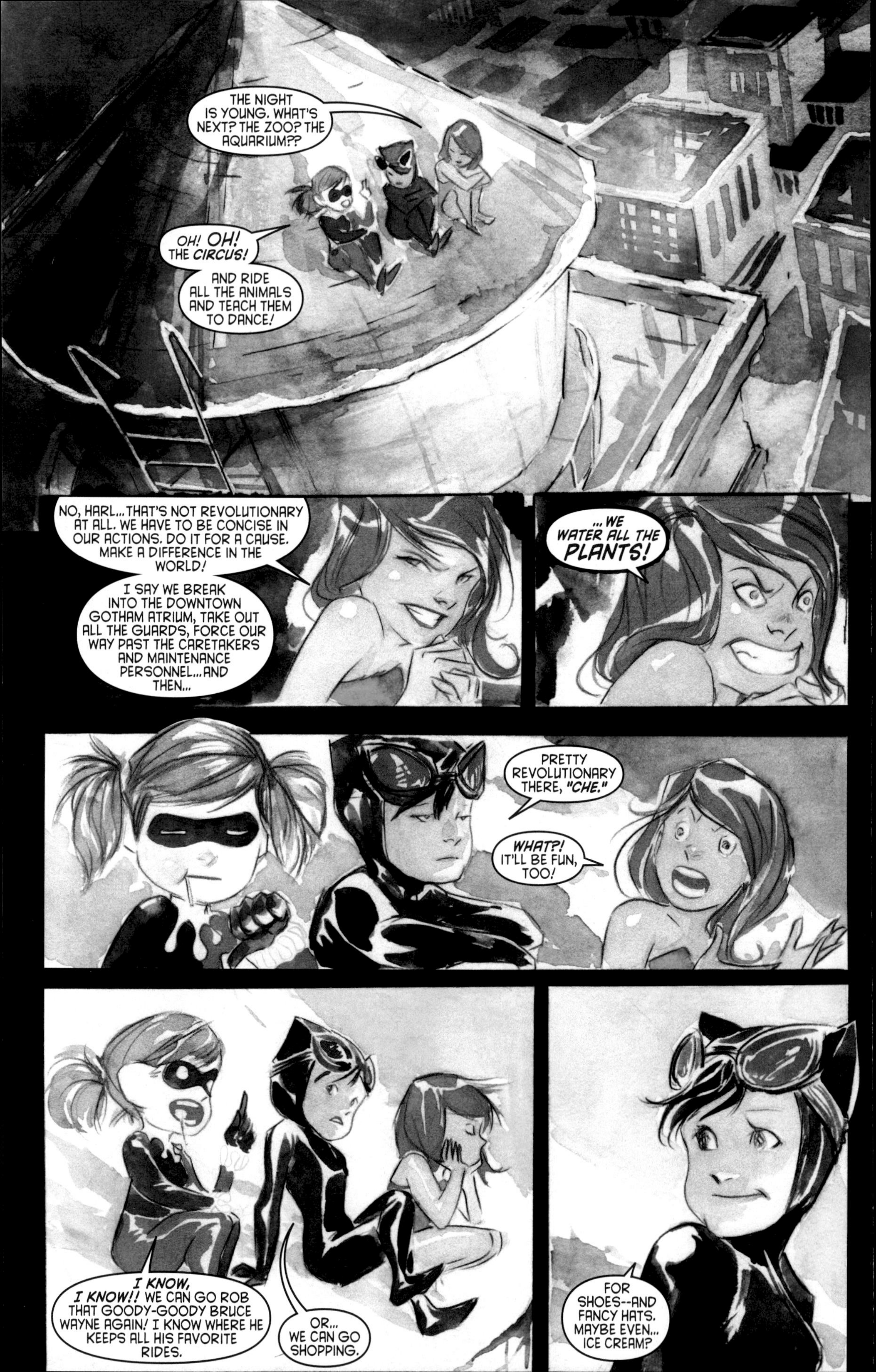
THE NIGHT IS YOUNG. WHAT'S NEXT? THE ZOO? THE AQUARIUM??
OH! **OH!** THE ***CIRCUS!***
AND RIDE ALL THE ANIMALS AND TEACH THEM TO DANCE!
NO, HARL... THAT'S NOT REVOLUTIONARY AT ALL. WE HAVE TO BE CONCISE IN OUR ACTIONS. DO IT FOR A CAUSE. MAKE A DIFFERENCE IN THE WORLD!
I SAY WE BREAK INTO THE DOWNTOWN GOTHAM ATRIUM, TAKE OUT ALL THE GUARDS, FORCE OUR WAY PAST THE CARETAKERS AND MAINTENANCE PERSONNEL... AND THEN...
...WE WATER ALL THE PLANTS!
PRETTY REVOLUTIONARY THERE, ***"CHE."***
WHAT?! IT'LL BE FUN, TOO!
I KNOW, I KNOW!! WE CAN GO ROB THAT GOODY-GOODY BRUCE WAYNE AGAIN! I KNOW WHERE HE KEEPS ALL HIS FAVORITE RIDES.
OR... WE CAN GO SHOPPING.
FOR SHOES--AND FANCY HATS. MAYBE EVEN... ICE CREAM?

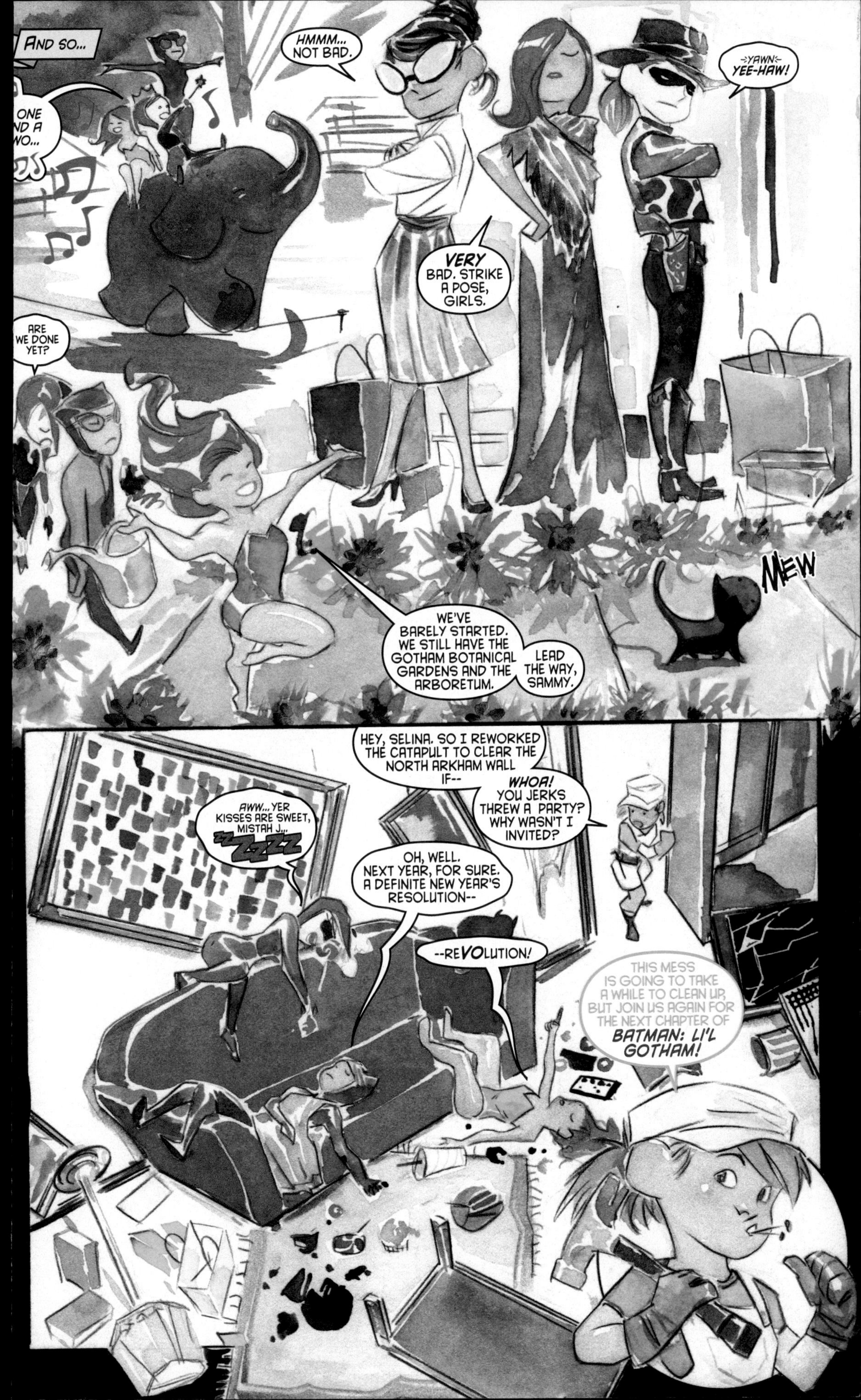
AND SO...
ONE
ND A
WO...
HMMM... NOT BAD.
>YAWN< YEE-HAW!
VERY BAD. STRIKE A POSE, GIRLS.
ARE WE DONE YET?
WE'VE BARELY STARTED. WE STILL HAVE THE GOTHAM BOTANICAL GARDENS AND THE ARBORETUM.
LEAD THE WAY, SAMMY.
MEW
HEY, SELINA. SO I REWORKED THE CATAPULT TO CLEAR THE NORTH ARKHAM WALL IF--
WHOA! YOU JERKS THREW A PARTY? WHY WASN'T I INVITED?
AWW... YER KISSES ARE SWEET, MISTAH J...
ZZZZZ
OH, WELL. NEXT YEAR, FOR SURE. A DEFINITE NEW YEAR'S RESOLUTION--
--REVOLUTION!
THIS MESS IS GOING TO TAKE A WHILE TO CLEAN UP, BUT JOIN US AGAIN FOR THE NEXT CHAPTER OF BATMAN: LI'L GOTHAM!

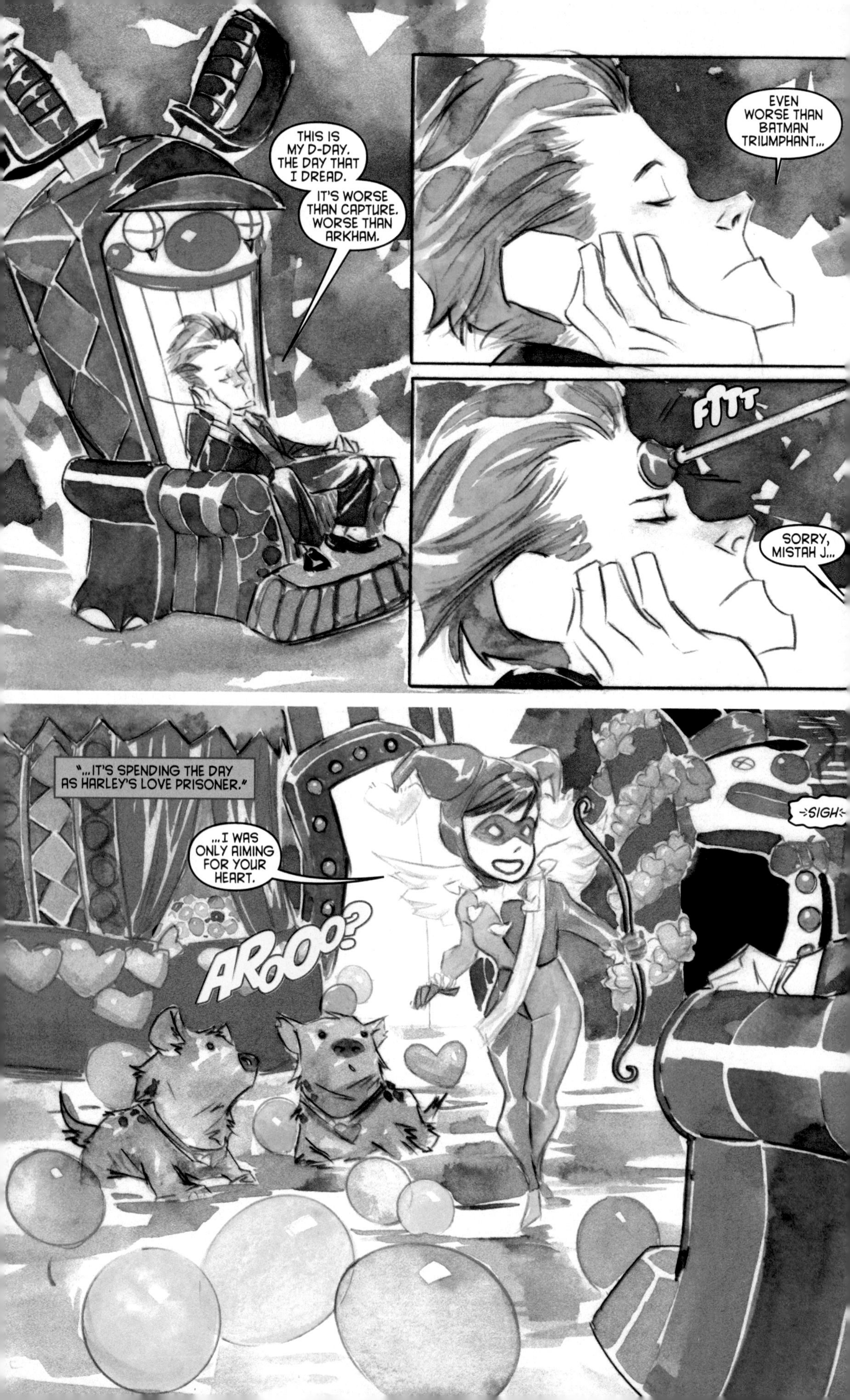
THIS IS MY D-DAY. THE DAY THAT I DREAD.
IT'S WORSE THAN CAPTURE. WORSE THAN ARKHAM.
EVEN WORSE THAN BATMAN TRIUMPHANT...
FTTT
SORRY, MISTAH J...
"...IT'S SPENDING THE DAY AS HARLEY'S LOVE PRISONER."
...I WAS ONLY AIMING FOR YOUR HEART.
SIGH
AROOO?

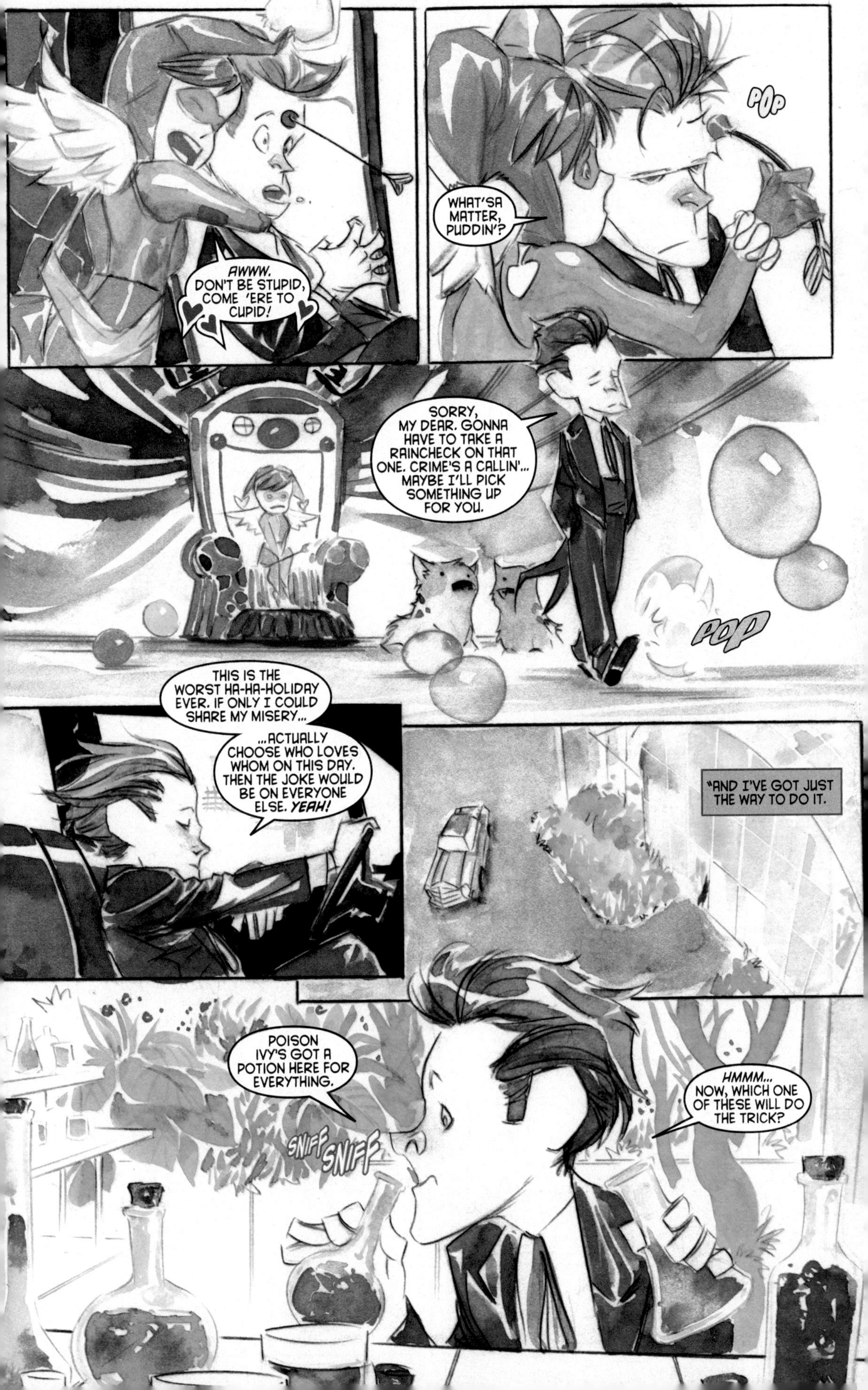
AWWW. DON'T BE STUPID, COME 'ERE TO CUPID!
POP
WHAT'SA MATTER, PUDDIN'?
SORRY, MY DEAR. GONNA HAVE TO TAKE A RAINCHECK ON THAT ONE. CRIME'S A CALLIN'... MAYBE I'LL PICK SOMETHING UP FOR YOU.
POP
THIS IS THE WORST HA-HA-HOLIDAY EVER. IF ONLY I COULD SHARE MY MISERY...
...ACTUALLY CHOOSE WHO LOVES WHOM ON THIS DAY. THEN THE JOKE WOULD BE ON EVERYONE ELSE. YEAH!
"AND I'VE GOT JUST THE WAY TO DO IT.
POISON IVY'S GOT A POTION HERE FOR EVERYTHING.
SNIFF SNIFF
HMMM... NOW, WHICH ONE OF THESE WILL DO THE TRICK?

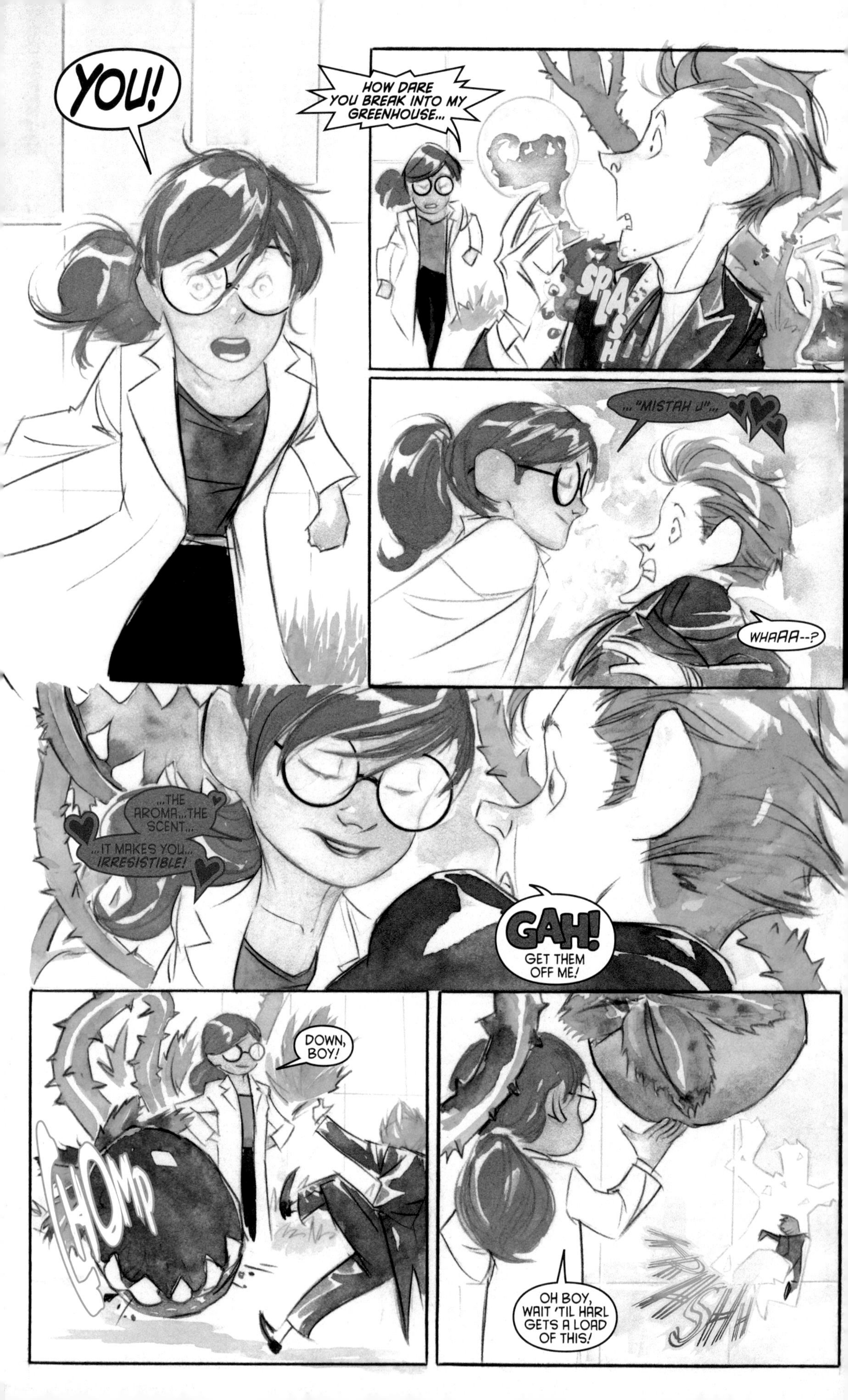
YOU!
HOW DARE YOU BREAK INTO MY GREENHOUSE...
SPLASH
..."MISTAH J"...
WHAAA--?
...THE AROMA...THE SCENT...
...IT MAKES YOU... IRRESISTIBLE!
GAH! GET THEM OFF ME!
DOWN, BOY!
CHOMP
OH BOY, WAIT 'TIL HARL GETS A LOAD OF THIS!
KRASHH

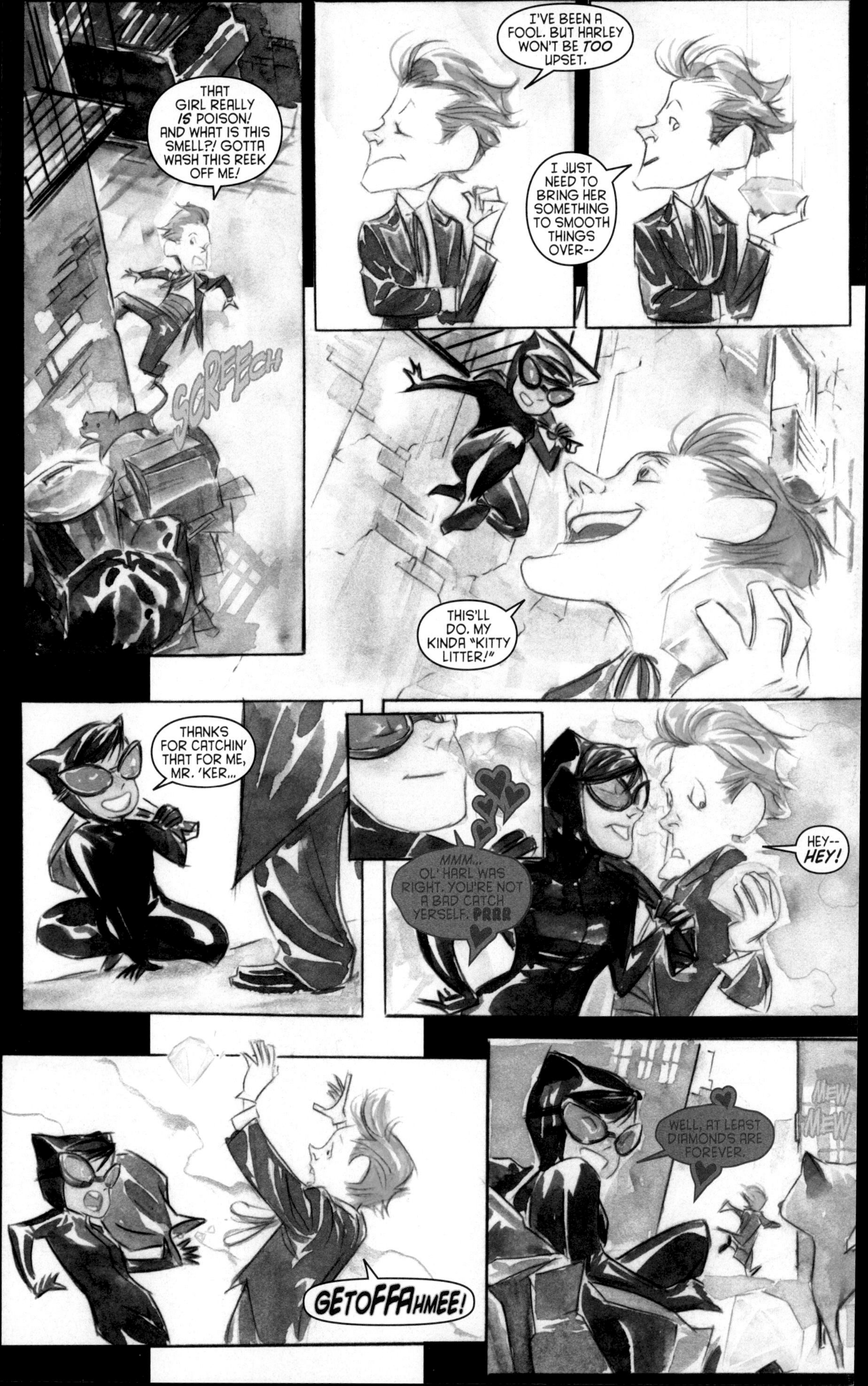
THAT GIRL REALLY *IS* POISON! AND WHAT IS THIS SMELL?! GOTTA WASH THIS REEK OFF ME!
SCREECH
I'VE BEEN A FOOL. BUT HARLEY WON'T BE *TOO* UPSET.
I JUST NEED TO BRING HER SOMETHING TO SMOOTH THINGS OVER--
THIS'LL DO. MY KINDA "KITTY LITTER!"
THANKS FOR CATCHIN' THAT FOR ME, MR. 'KER...
MMM... OL' HARL WAS RIGHT. YOU'RE NOT A BAD CATCH YERSELF. PRRR
HEY-- *HEY!*
GETOFFAHMEE!
WELL, AT LEAST DIAMONDS ARE FOREVER.
MEW MEW

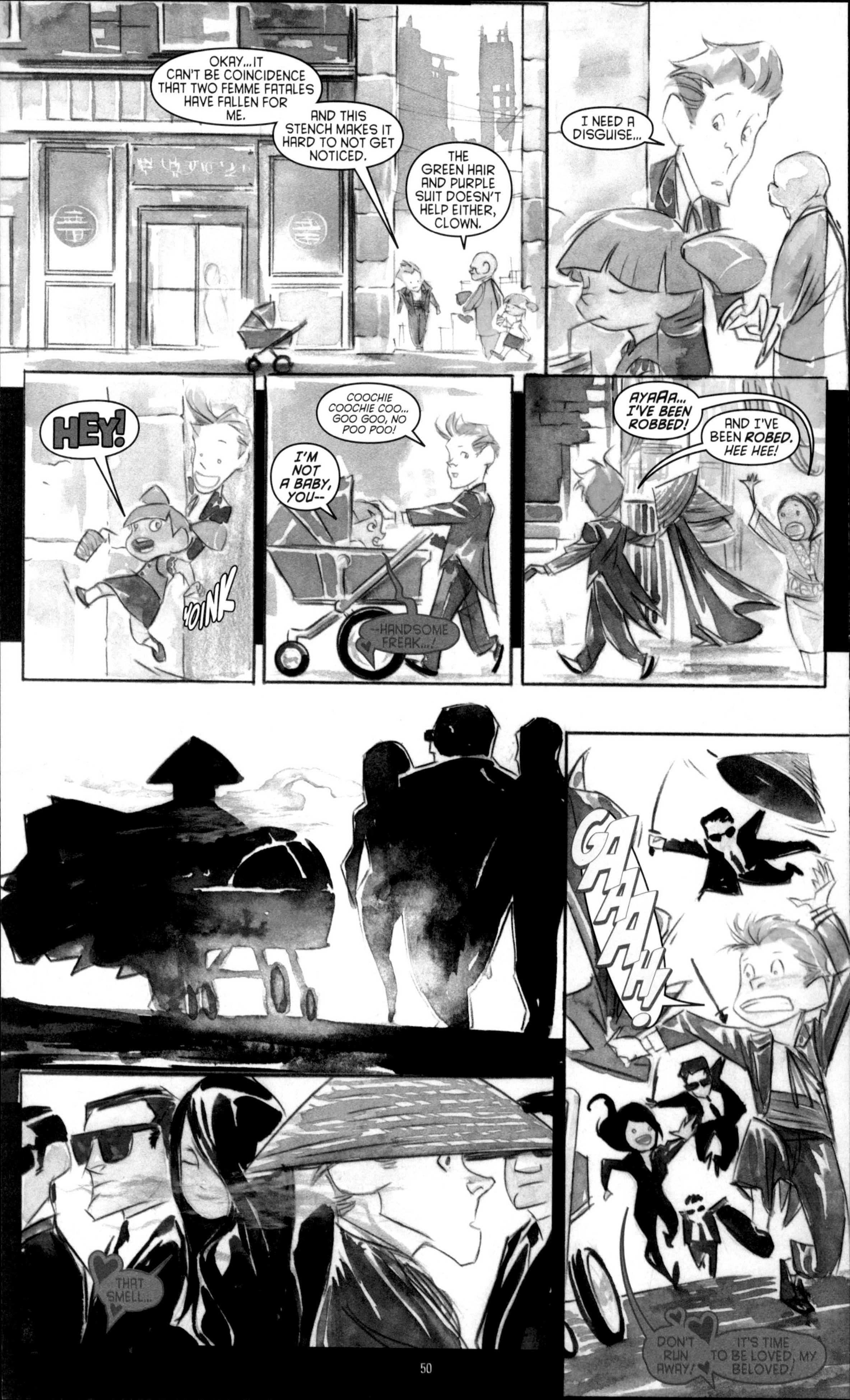
OKAY...IT CAN'T BE COINCIDENCE THAT TWO FEMME FATALES HAVE FALLEN FOR ME.
AND THIS STENCH MAKES IT HARD TO NOT GET NOTICED.
THE GREEN HAIR AND PURPLE SUIT DOESN'T HELP EITHER, CLOWN.
I NEED A DISGUISE...
HEY!
YOINK
COOCHIE COOCHIE COO... GOO GOO, NO POO POO!
I'M NOT A BABY, YOU--
--HANDSOME FREAK...!
AYAAA... I'VE BEEN ROBBED!
AND I'VE BEEN ROBED. HEE HEE!
THAT SMELL...
GAAAAH!
DON'T RUN AWAY!
IT'S TIME TO BE LOVED, MY BELOVED!

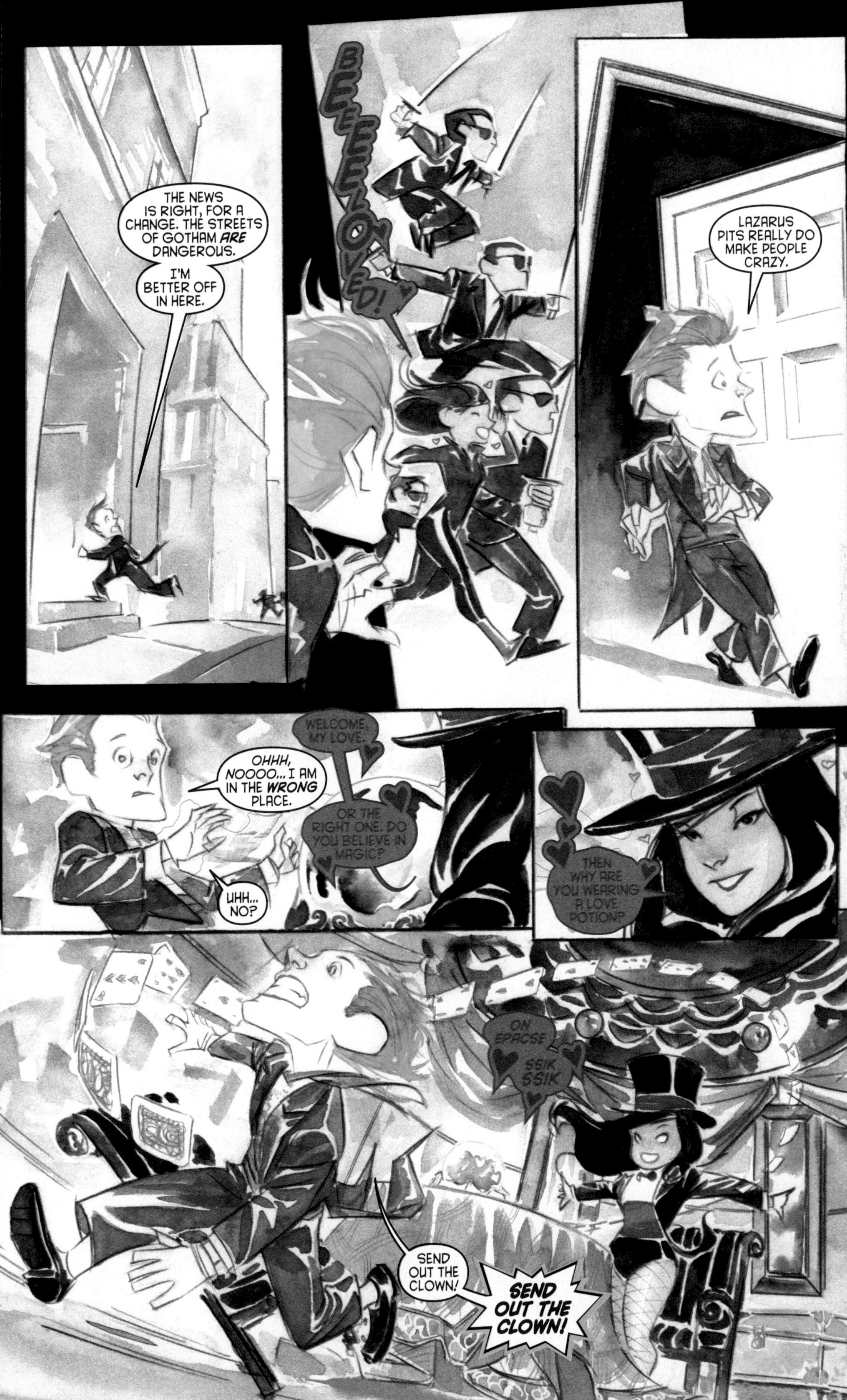
THE NEWS IS RIGHT, FOR A CHANGE. THE STREETS OF GOTHAM ARE DANGEROUS.
I'M BETTER OFF IN HERE.
BEEEEELOVED!
LAZARUS PITS REALLY DO MAKE PEOPLE CRAZY.
OHHH, NOOOO... I AM IN THE WRONG PLACE.
WELCOME, MY LOVE.
OR THE RIGHT ONE. DO YOU BELIEVE IN MAGIC?
UHH... NO?
THEN WHY ARE YOU WEARING A LOVE POTION?
ON EPACSE
SSIK SSIK
SEND OUT THE CLOWN!
SEND OUT THE CLOWN!

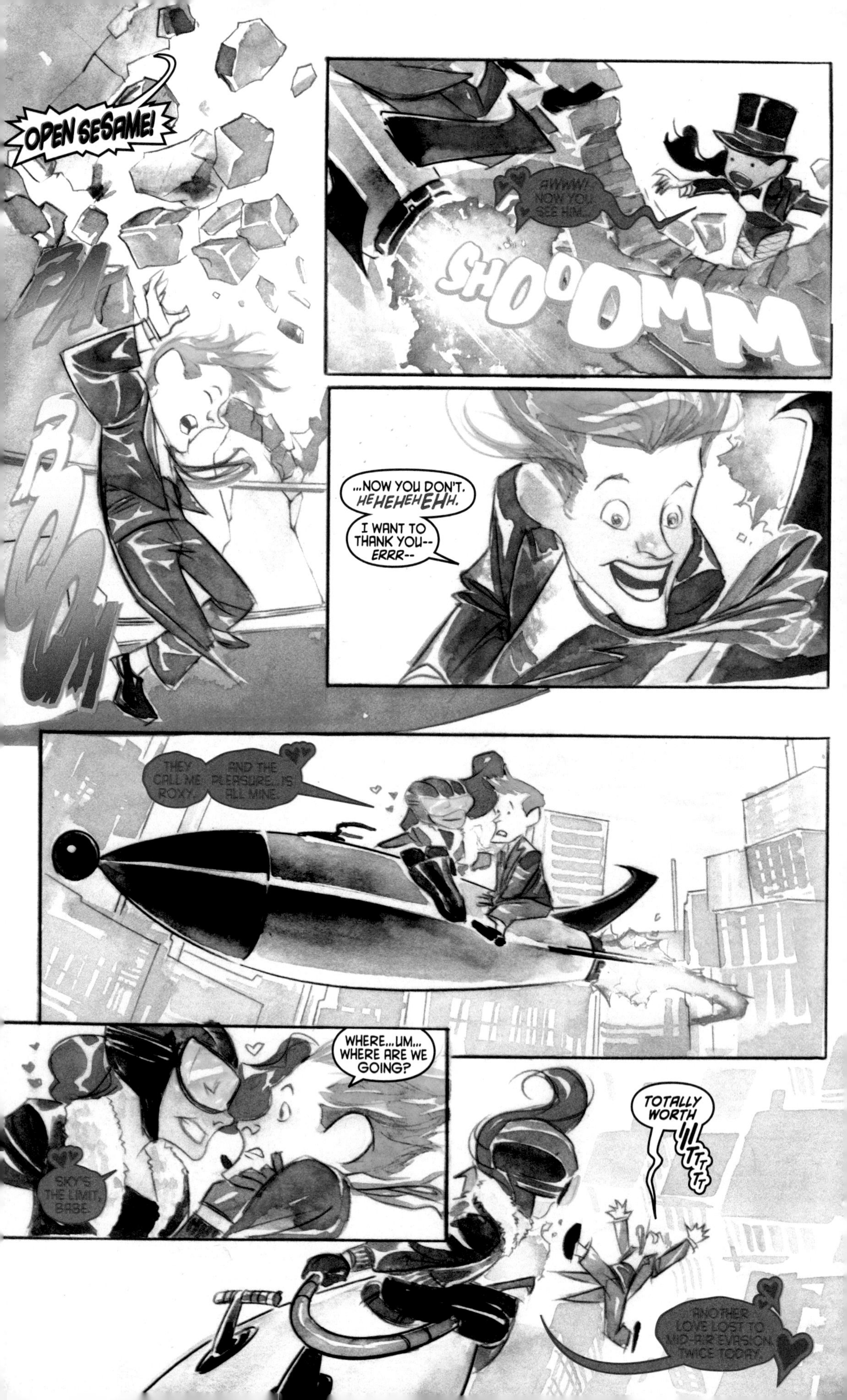
OPEN SESAME!
AWWW! NOW YOU SEE HIM...
SHOOOOMMM
...NOW YOU DON'T. HEHEHEHEHH.
I WANT TO THANK YOU-- ERRR--
THEY CALL ME ROXY.
AND THE PLEASURE... IS ALL MINE.
WHERE... UM... WHERE ARE WE GOING?
SKY'S THE LIMIT, BABE.
TOTALLY WORTH IIIITTTT
ANOTHER LOVE LOST TO MID-AIR EVASION. TWICE TODAY.

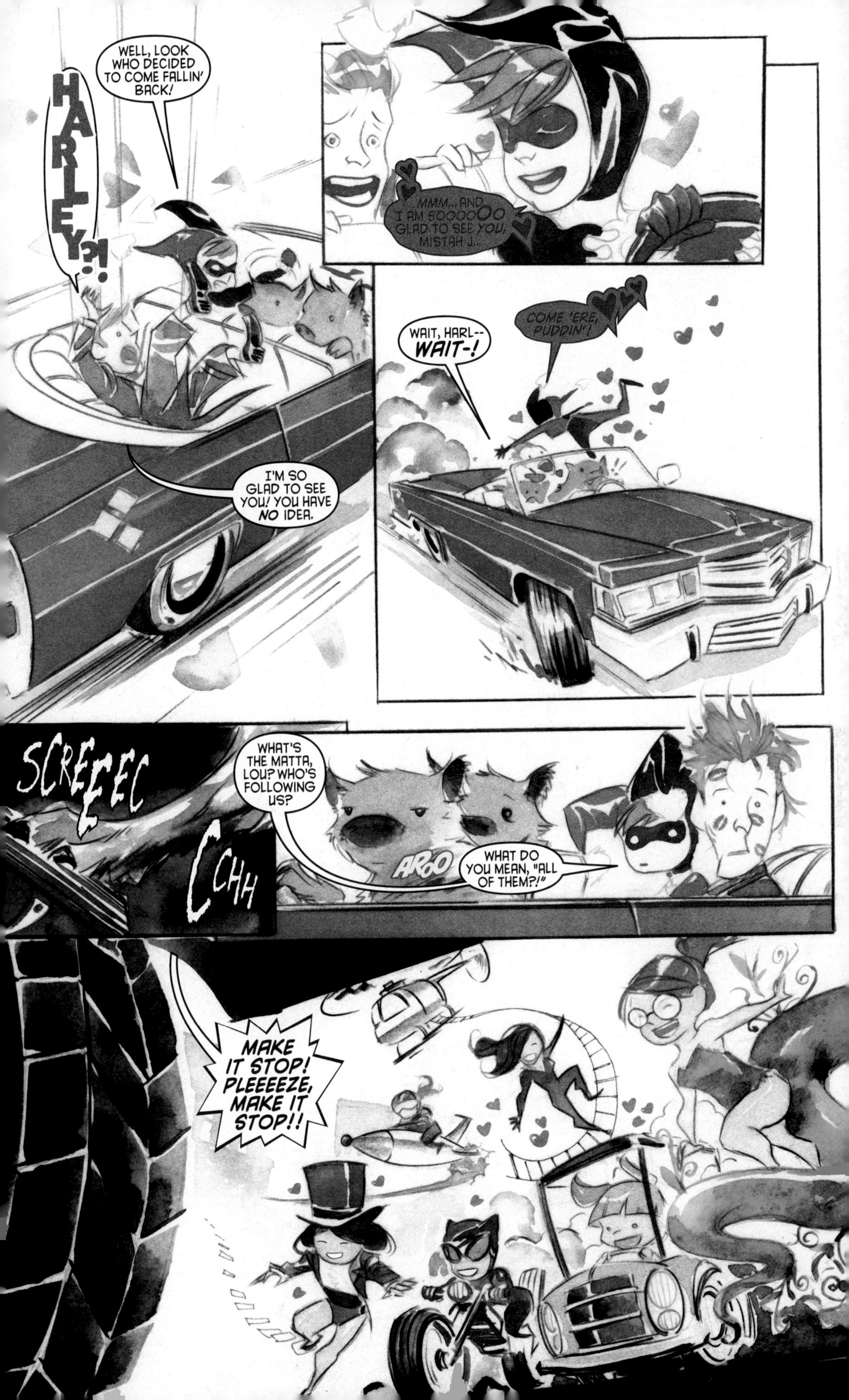
WELL, LOOK WHO DECIDED TO COME FALLIN' BACK!
HARLEY?!
MMM... AND I AM SOOOOOOO GLAD TO SEE YOU, MISTAH J...
I'M SO GLAD TO SEE YOU! YOU HAVE NO IDEA.
WAIT, HARL-- WAIT-!
COME 'ERE, PUDDIN'!
SCREEEC
CCHH
WHAT'S THE MATTA, LOU? WHO'S FOLLOWING US?
AROO
WHAT DO YOU MEAN, "ALL OF THEM?!"
MAKE IT STOP! PLEEEEZE, MAKE IT STOP!!

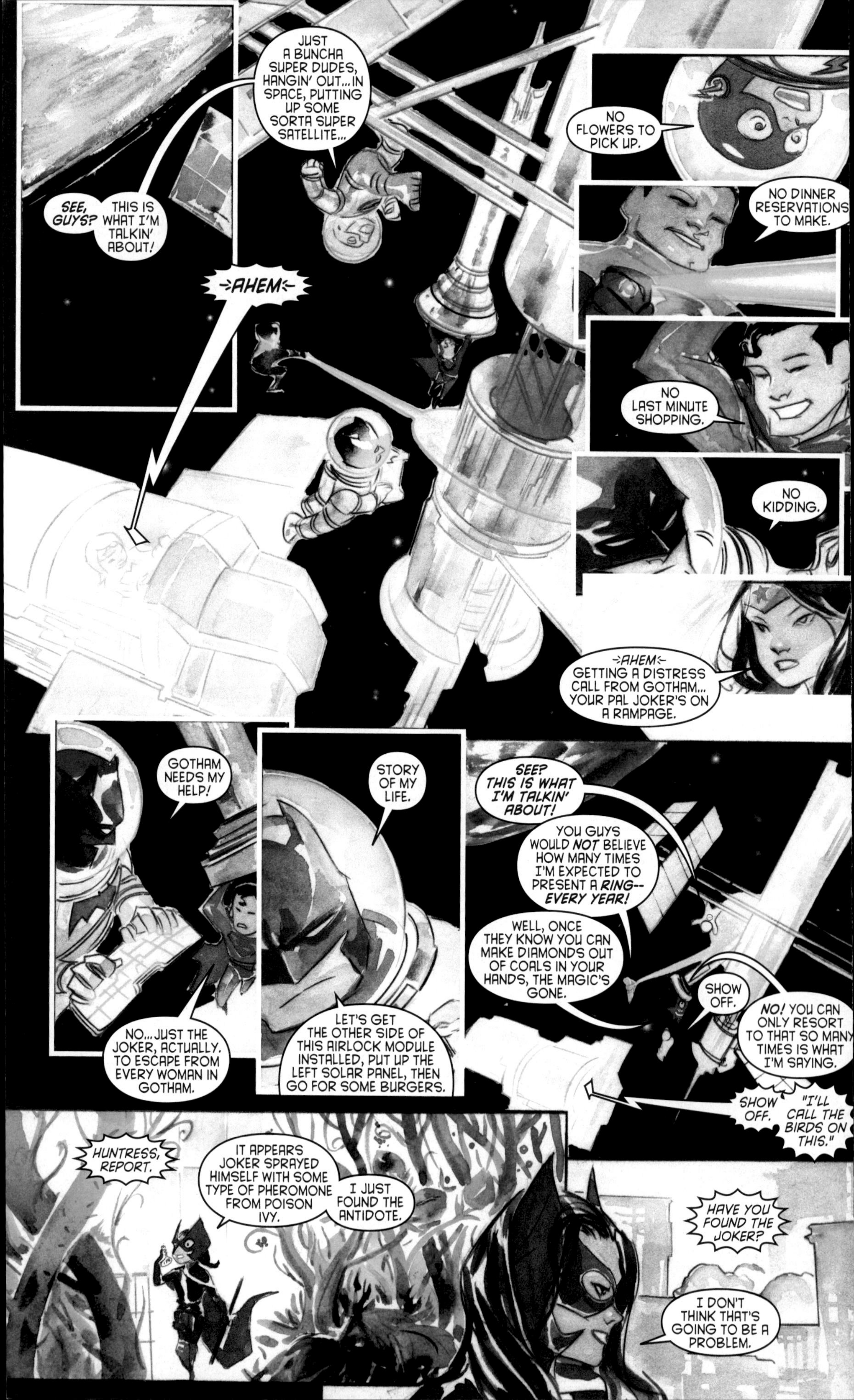
JUST A BUNCHA SUPER DUDES, HANGIN' OUT...IN SPACE, PUTTING UP SOME SORTA SUPER SATELLITE...
SEE, GUYS?
THIS IS WHAT I'M TALKIN' ABOUT!
NO FLOWERS TO PICK UP.
NO DINNER RESERVATIONS TO MAKE.
NO LAST MINUTE SHOPPING.
NO KIDDING.
AHEM
AHEM GETTING A DISTRESS CALL FROM GOTHAM... YOUR PAL JOKER'S ON A RAMPAGE.
GOTHAM NEEDS MY HELP!
NO... JUST THE JOKER, ACTUALLY. TO ESCAPE FROM EVERY WOMAN IN GOTHAM.
STORY OF MY LIFE.
LET'S GET THE OTHER SIDE OF THIS AIRLOCK MODULE INSTALLED, PUT UP THE LEFT SOLAR PANEL, THEN GO FOR SOME BURGERS.
SEE? THIS IS WHAT I'M TALKIN' ABOUT!
YOU GUYS WOULD NOT BELIEVE HOW MANY TIMES I'M EXPECTED TO PRESENT A RING-- EVERY YEAR!
WELL, ONCE THEY KNOW YOU CAN MAKE DIAMONDS OUT OF COALS IN YOUR HANDS, THE MAGIC'S GONE.
SHOW OFF.
NO! YOU CAN ONLY RESORT TO THAT SO MANY TIMES IS WHAT I'M SAYING.
SHOW OFF.
"I'LL CALL THE BIRDS ON THIS."
HUNTRESS, REPORT.
IT APPEARS JOKER SPRAYED HIMSELF WITH SOME TYPE OF PHEROMONE FROM POISON IVY.
I JUST FOUND THE ANTIDOTE.
HAVE YOU FOUND THE JOKER?
I DON'T THINK THAT'S GOING TO BE A PROBLEM.

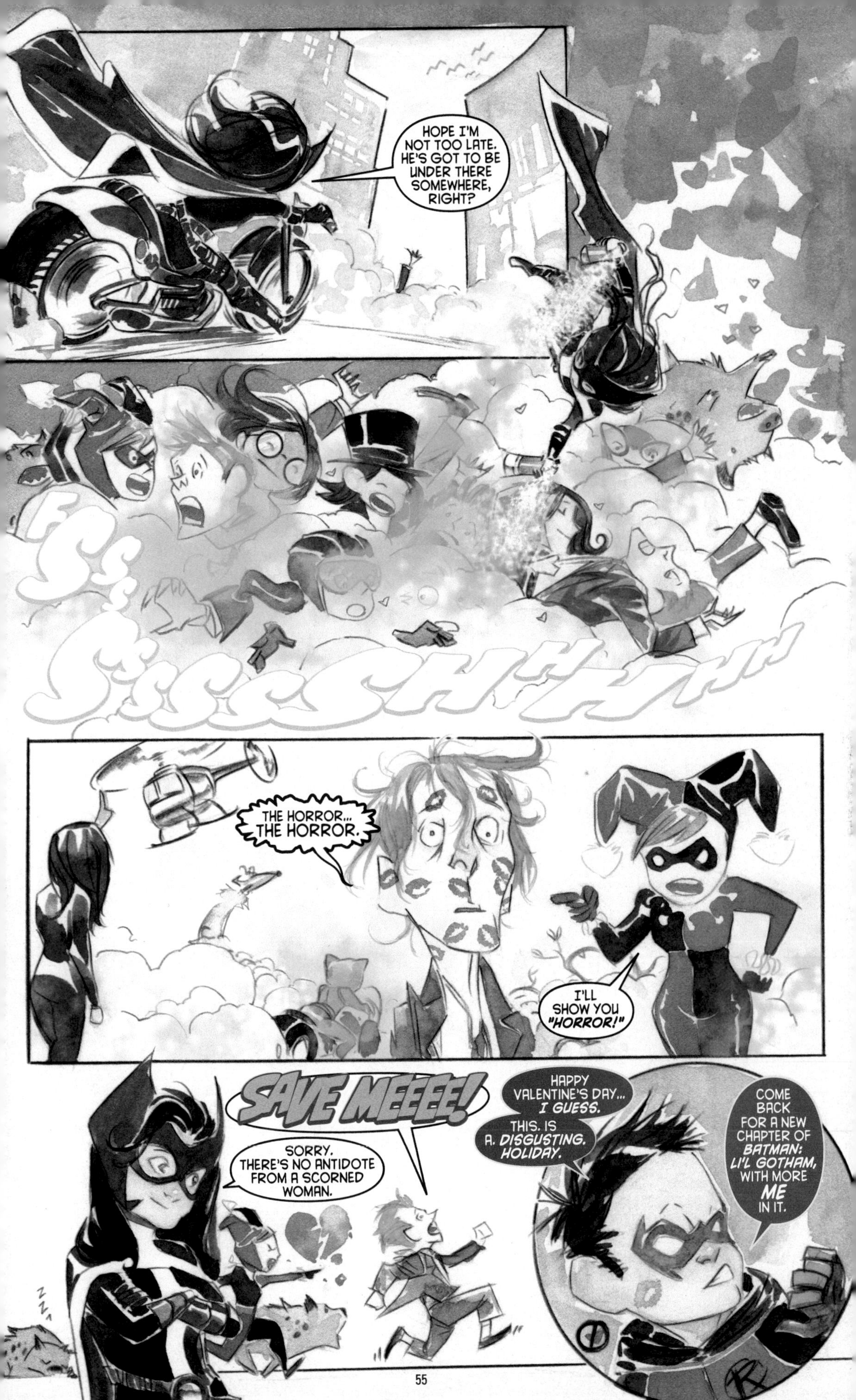
HOPE I'M NOT TOO LATE. HE'S GOT TO BE UNDER THERE SOMEWHERE, RIGHT?
FSSSSSSSHHHHH
THE HORROR... THE HORROR.
I'LL SHOW YOU "HORROR!"
SAVE MEEEE!
SORRY. THERE'S NO ANTIDOTE FROM A SCORNED WOMAN.
HAPPY VALENTINE'S DAY... I GUESS.
THIS. IS A. DISGUSTING. HOLIDAY.
COME BACK FOR A NEW CHAPTER OF BATMAN: LI'L GOTHAM, WITH MORE ME IN IT.
ZZZ

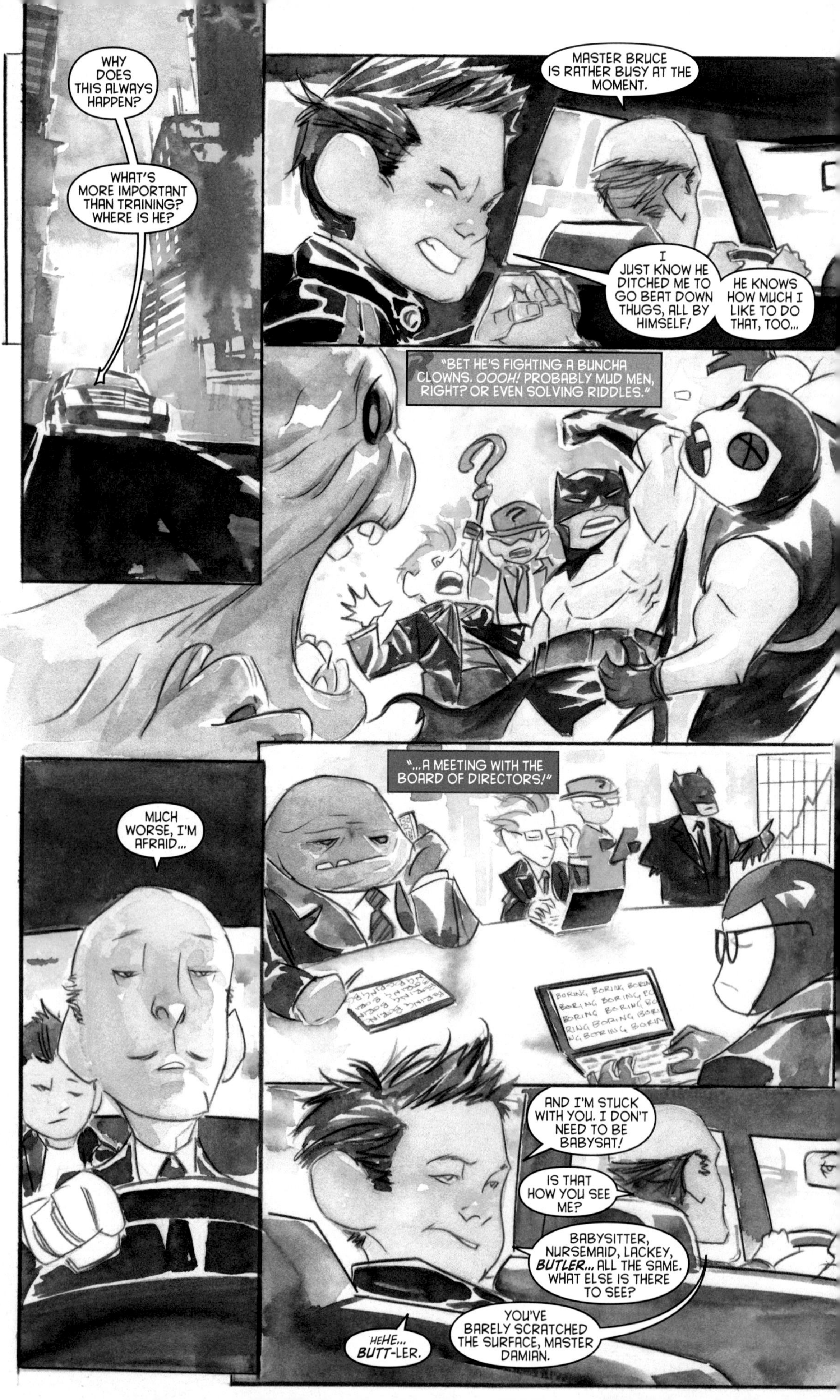
WHY DOES THIS ALWAYS HAPPEN?
WHAT'S MORE IMPORTANT THAN TRAINING? WHERE IS HE?
MASTER BRUCE IS RATHER BUSY AT THE MOMENT.
I JUST KNOW HE DITCHED ME TO GO BEAT DOWN THUGS, ALL BY HIMSELF!
HE KNOWS HOW MUCH I LIKE TO DO THAT, TOO...
"BET HE'S FIGHTING A BUNCHA CLOWNS. OOOH! PROBABLY MUD MEN, RIGHT? OR EVEN SOLVING RIDDLES."
MUCH WORSE, I'M AFRAID...
"...A MEETING WITH THE BOARD OF DIRECTORS!"
BORING BORING BORING BORING BORING BORING
BORING BORING BORING BORING BORING BORING BORING BORING
AND I'M STUCK WITH YOU. I DON'T NEED TO BE BABYSAT!
IS THAT HOW YOU SEE ME?
BABYSITTER, NURSEMAID, LACKEY, BUTLER... ALL THE SAME. WHAT ELSE IS THERE TO SEE?
YOU'VE BARELY SCRATCHED THE SURFACE, MASTER DAMIAN.
HEHE... BUTT-LER.

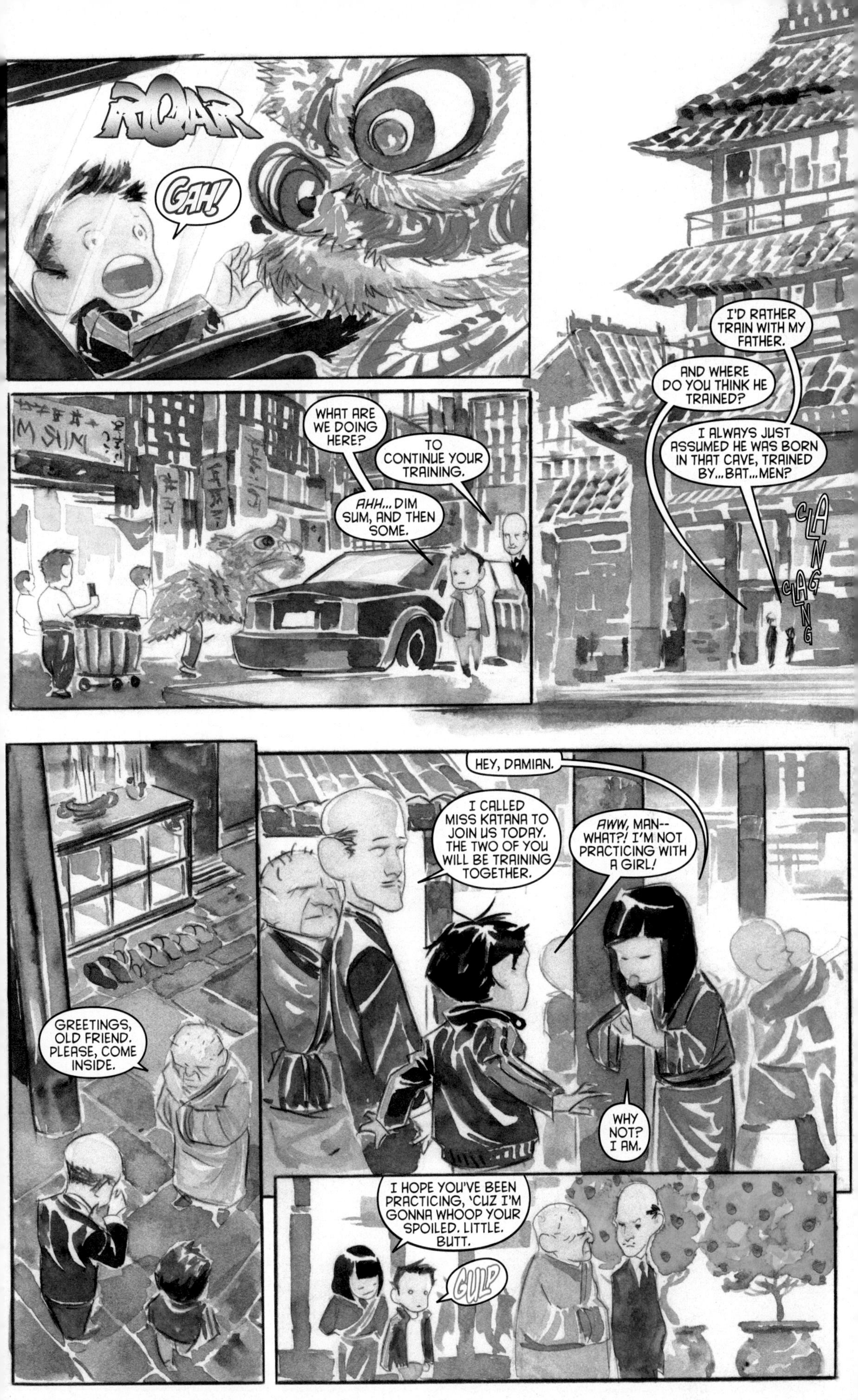
ROAR
GAH!
WHAT ARE WE DOING HERE?
TO CONTINUE YOUR TRAINING.
AHH... DIM SUM, AND THEN SOME.
I'D RATHER TRAIN WITH MY FATHER.
AND WHERE DO YOU THINK HE TRAINED?
I ALWAYS JUST ASSUMED HE WAS BORN IN THAT CAVE, TRAINED BY... BAT... MEN?
CLANG
CLANG
GREETINGS, OLD FRIEND. PLEASE, COME INSIDE.
HEY, DAMIAN.
I CALLED MISS KATANA TO JOIN US TODAY. THE TWO OF YOU WILL BE TRAINING TOGETHER.
AWW, MAN-- WHAT?! I'M NOT PRACTICING WITH A GIRL!
WHY NOT? I AM.
I HOPE YOU'VE BEEN PRACTICING, 'CUZ I'M GONNA WHOOP YOUR SPOILED. LITTLE. BUTT.
GULP

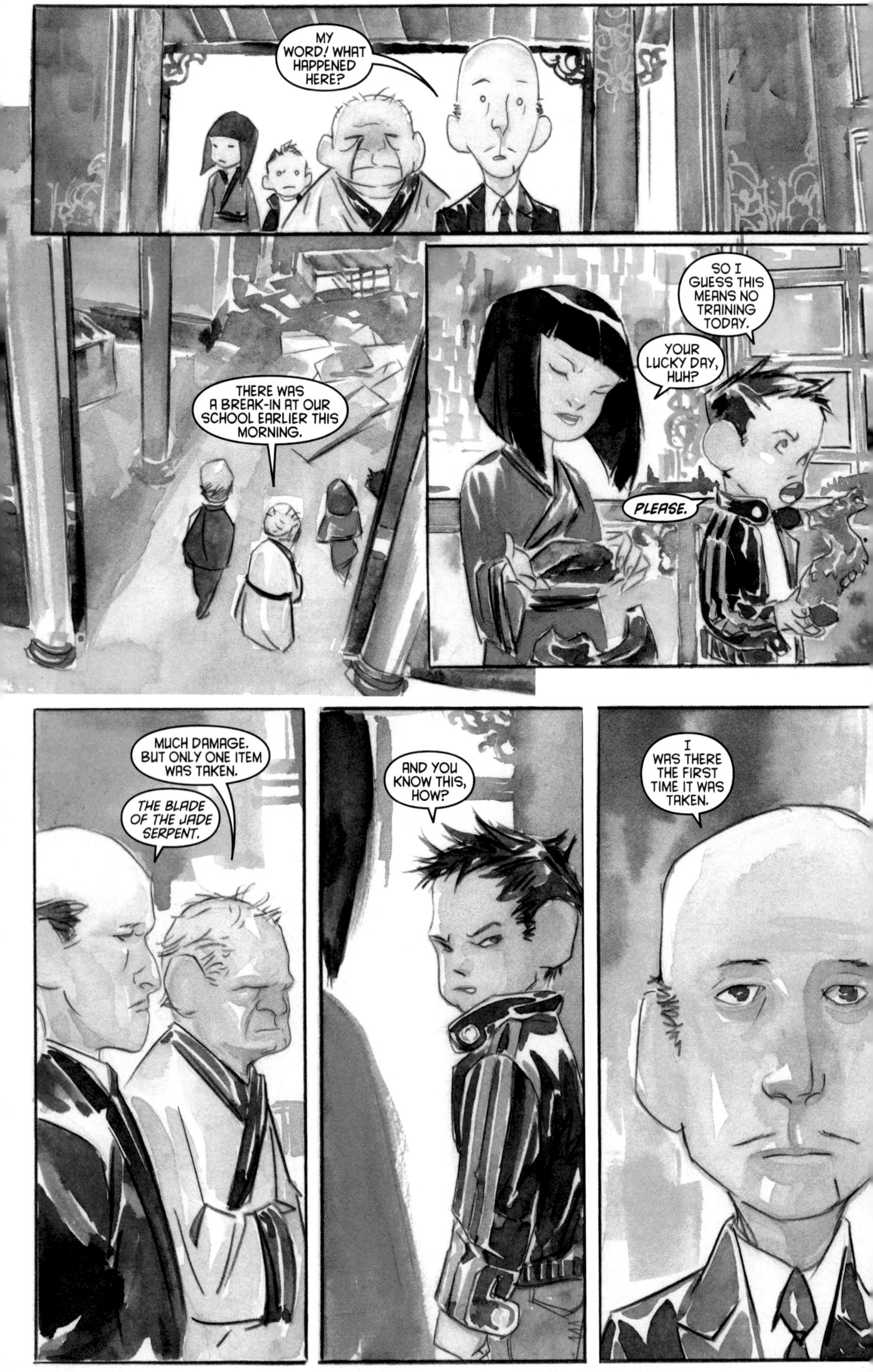
MY WORD! WHAT HAPPENED HERE?
THERE WAS A BREAK-IN AT OUR SCHOOL EARLIER THIS MORNING.
SO I GUESS THIS MEANS NO TRAINING TODAY.
YOUR LUCKY DAY, HUH?
PLEASE.
MUCH DAMAGE. BUT ONLY ONE ITEM WAS TAKEN.
THE BLADE OF THE JADE SERPENT.
AND YOU KNOW THIS, HOW?
I WAS THERE THE FIRST TIME IT WAS TAKEN.

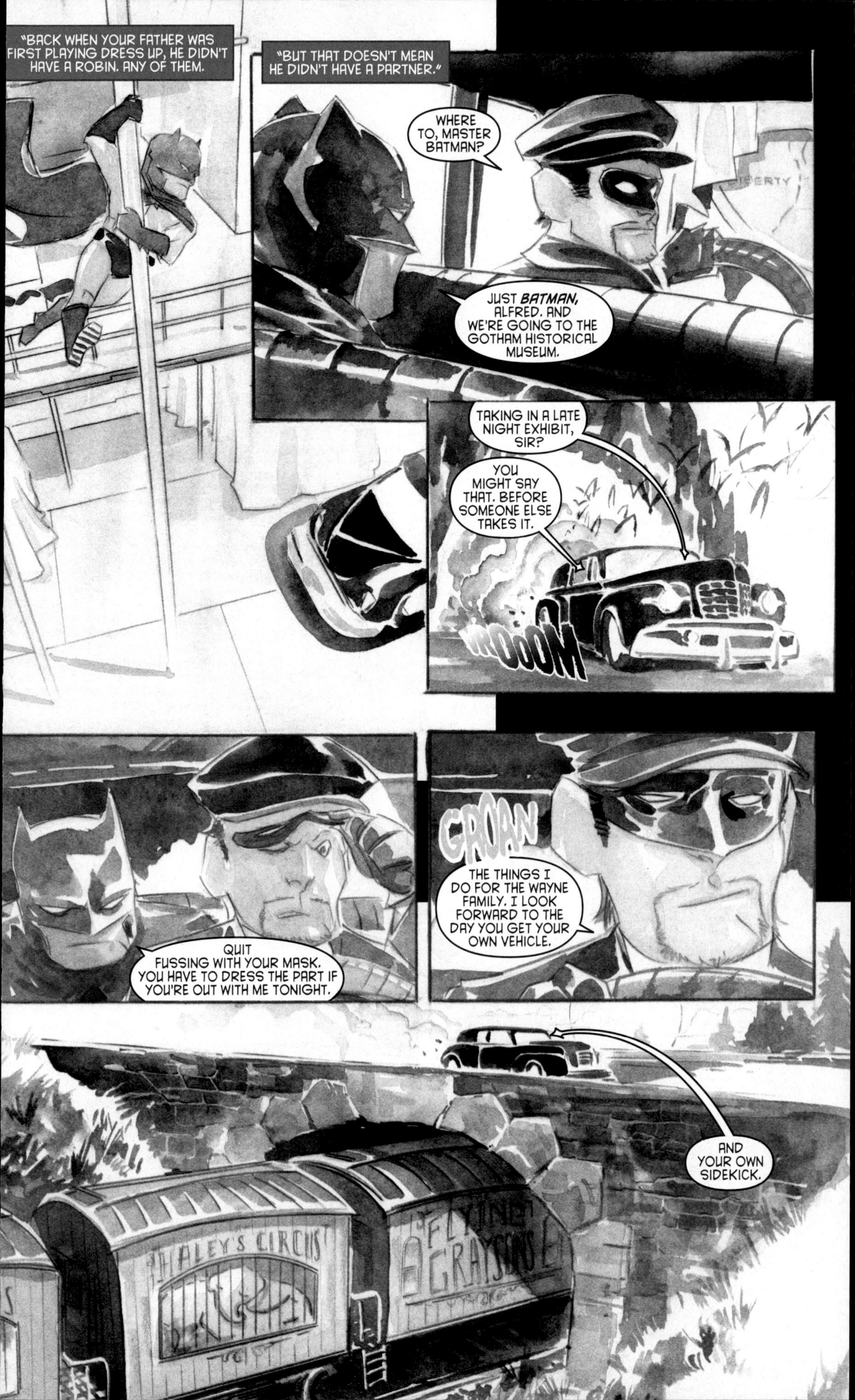
"BACK WHEN YOUR FATHER WAS FIRST PLAYING DRESS UP, HE DIDN'T HAVE A ROBIN. ANY OF THEM.
"BUT THAT DOESN'T MEAN HE DIDN'T HAVE A PARTNER."
WHERE TO, MASTER BATMAN?
JUST BATMAN, ALFRED. AND WE'RE GOING TO THE GOTHAM HISTORICAL MUSEUM.
TAKING IN A LATE NIGHT EXHIBIT, SIR?
YOU MIGHT SAY THAT. BEFORE SOMEONE ELSE TAKES IT.
VROOOOM
QUIT FUSSING WITH YOUR MASK. YOU HAVE TO DRESS THE PART IF YOU'RE OUT WITH ME TONIGHT.
GROAN
THE THINGS I DO FOR THE WAYNE FAMILY. I LOOK FORWARD TO THE DAY YOU GET YOUR OWN VEHICLE.
AND YOUR OWN SIDEKICK.
HALEY'S CIRCUS
FLYING GRAYSONS

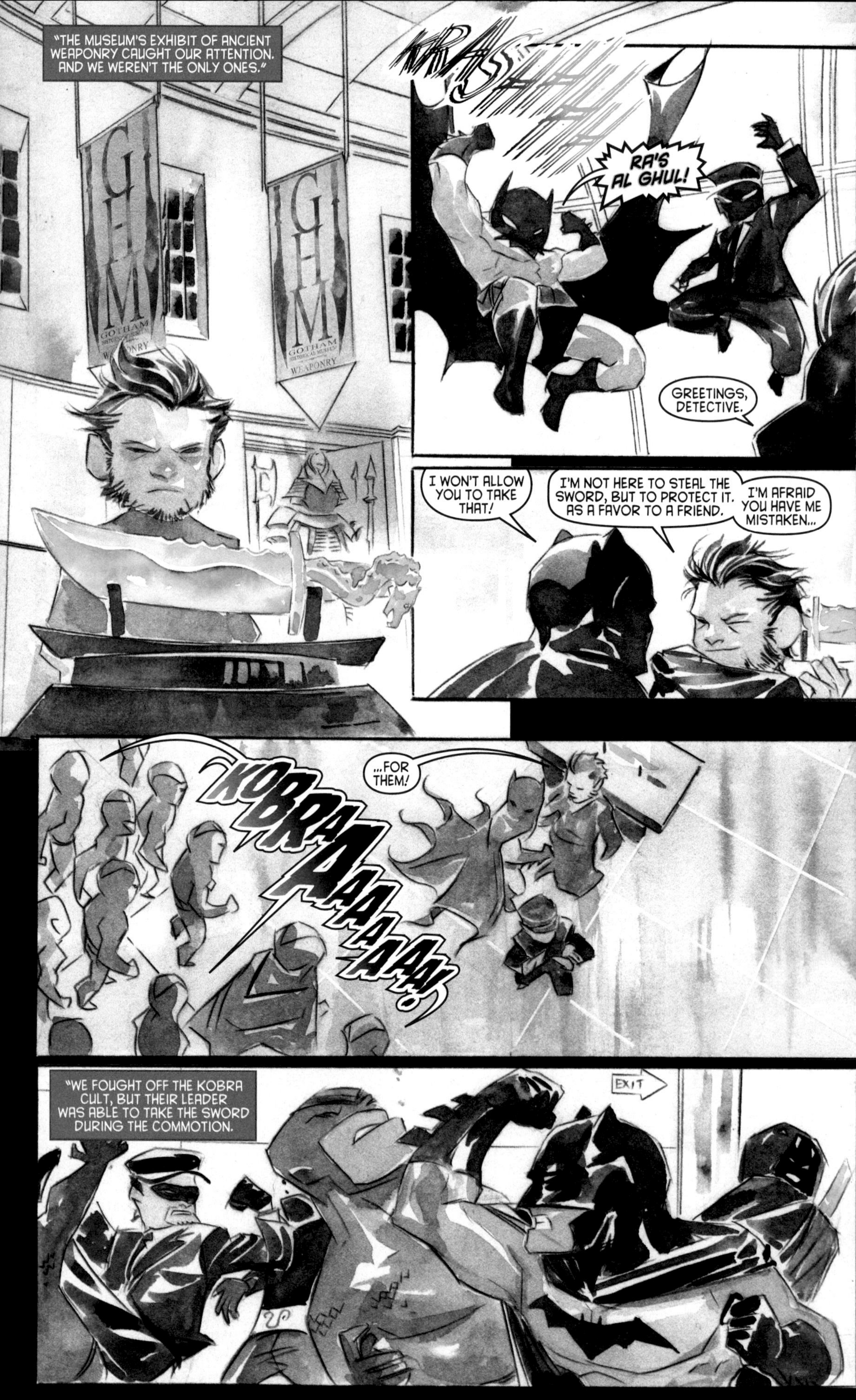
"THE MUSEUM'S EXHIBIT OF ANCIENT WEAPONRY CAUGHT OUR ATTENTION. AND WE WEREN'T THE ONLY ONES."
GHM
GOTHAM HISTORICAL MUSEUM
WEAPONRY
KRASSHHH
RA'S AL GHUL!
GREETINGS, DETECTIVE.
I WON'T ALLOW YOU TO TAKE THAT!
I'M NOT HERE TO STEAL THE SWORD, BUT TO PROTECT IT. AS A FAVOR TO A FRIEND.
I'M AFRAID YOU HAVE ME MISTAKEN...
...FOR THEM!
KOBRAAAAAAA!
"WE FOUGHT OFF THE KOBRA CULT, BUT THEIR LEADER WAS ABLE TO TAKE THE SWORD DURING THE COMMOTION.
EXIT

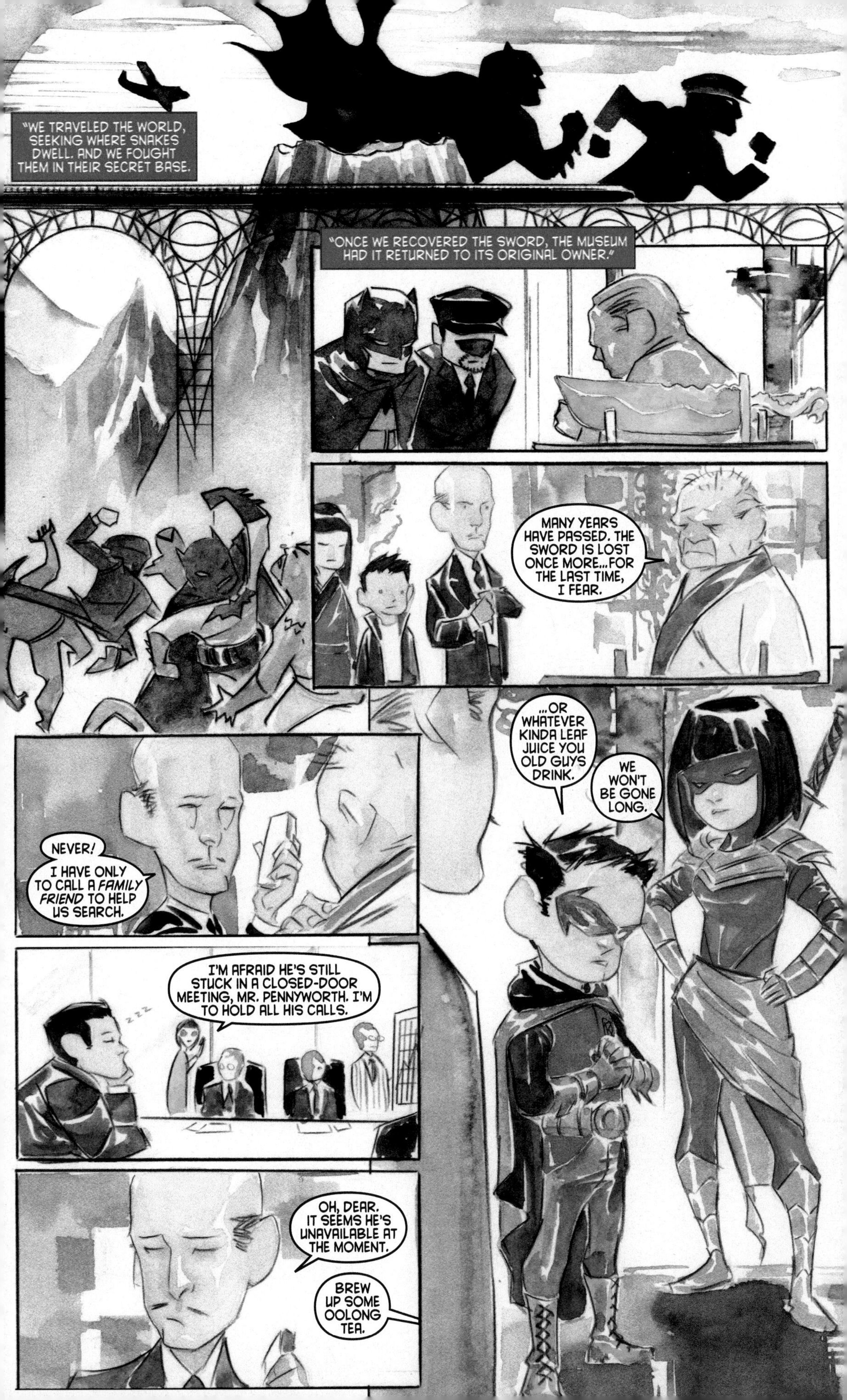

"WE TRAVELED THE WORLD, SEEKING WHERE SNAKES DWELL. AND WE FOUGHT THEM IN THEIR SECRET BASE.
"ONCE WE RECOVERED THE SWORD, THE MUSEUM HAD IT RETURNED TO ITS ORIGINAL OWNER."
MANY YEARS HAVE PASSED. THE SWORD IS LOST ONCE MORE...FOR THE LAST TIME, I FEAR.
NEVER!
I HAVE ONLY TO CALL A *FAMILY FRIEND* TO HELP US SEARCH.
I'M AFRAID HE'S STILL STUCK IN A CLOSED-DOOR MEETING, MR. PENNYWORTH. I'M TO HOLD ALL HIS CALLS.
ZZZ
OH, DEAR. IT SEEMS HE'S UNAVAILABLE AT THE MOMENT.
BREW UP SOME OOLONG TEA.
...OR WHATEVER KINDA LEAF JUICE YOU OLD GUYS DRINK.
WE WON'T BE GONE LONG.

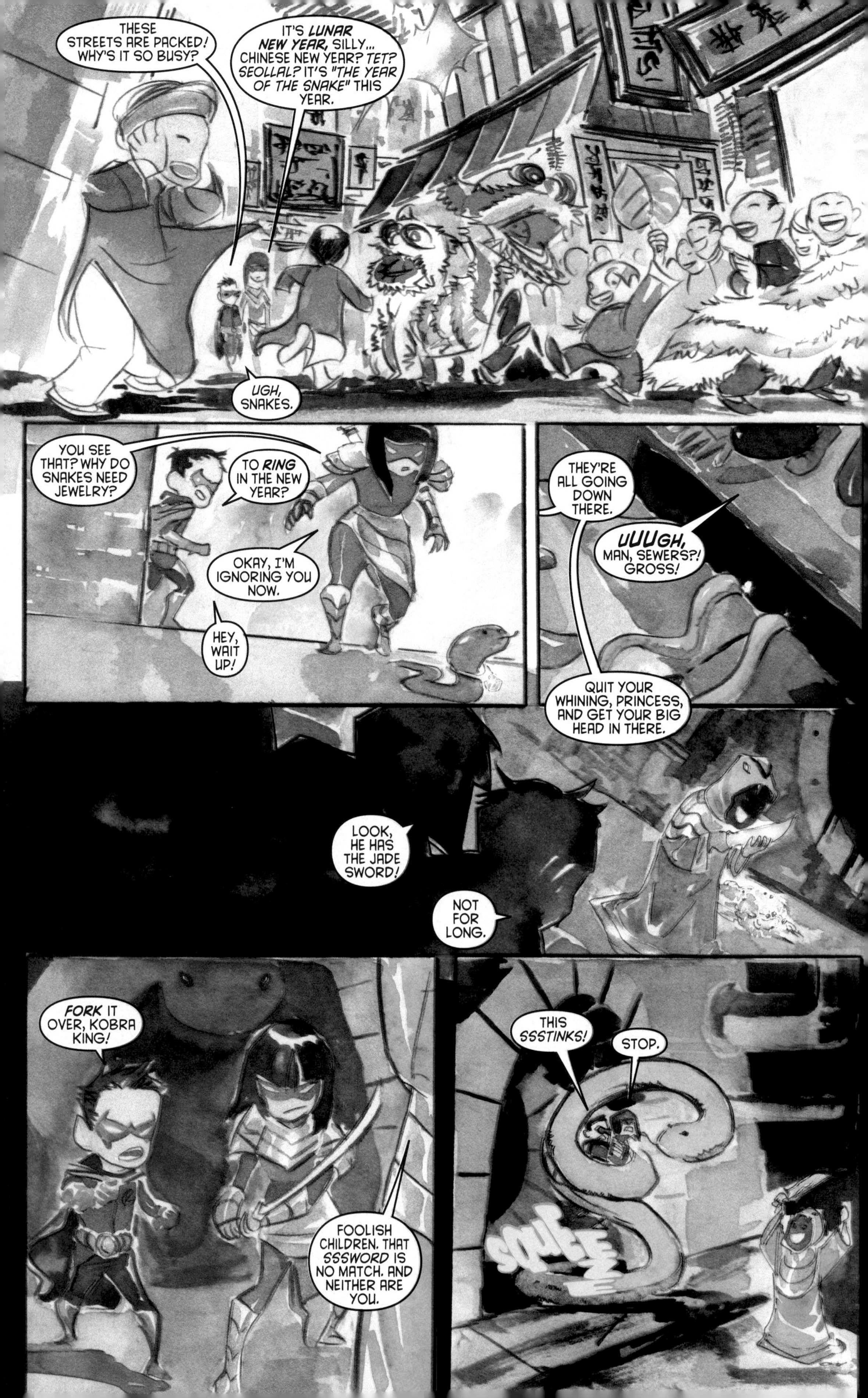
THESE STREETS ARE PACKED! WHY'S IT SO BUSY?
IT'S LUNAR NEW YEAR, SILLY... CHINESE NEW YEAR? TET? SEOLLAL? IT'S "THE YEAR OF THE SNAKE" THIS YEAR.
UGH, SNAKES.
YOU SEE THAT? WHY DO SNAKES NEED JEWELRY?
TO RING IN THE NEW YEAR?
OKAY, I'M IGNORING YOU NOW.
HEY, WAIT UP!
THEY'RE ALL GOING DOWN THERE.
UUUGH, MAN, SEWERS?! GROSS!
QUIT YOUR WHINING, PRINCESS, AND GET YOUR BIG HEAD IN THERE.
LOOK, HE HAS THE JADE SWORD!
NOT FOR LONG.
FORK IT OVER, KOBRA KING!
FOOLISH CHILDREN. THAT SSSWORD IS NO MATCH. AND NEITHER ARE YOU.
THIS SSSTINKS!
STOP.
SQUEEEEE

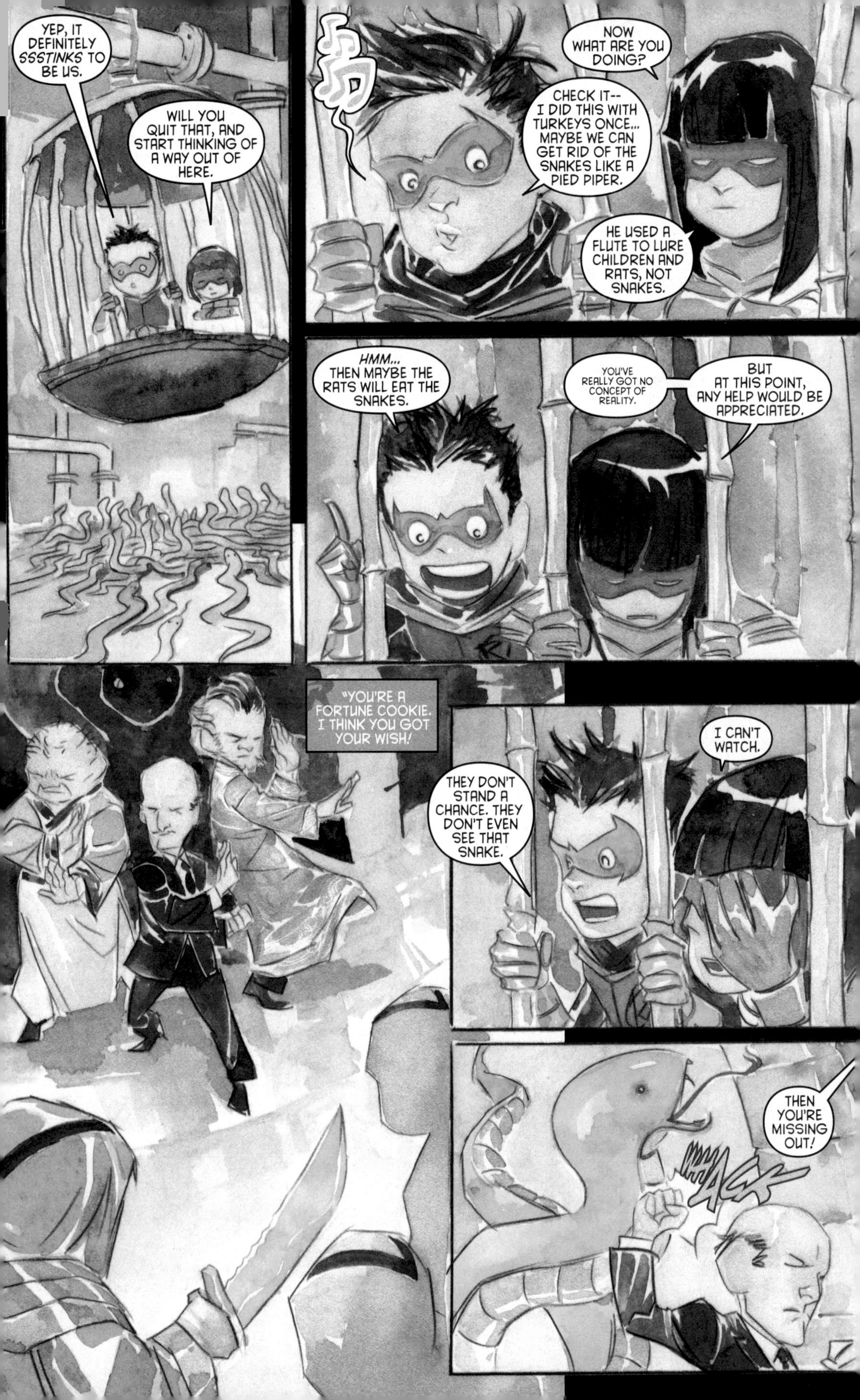
YEP, IT DEFINITELY SSSTINKS TO BE US.
WILL YOU QUIT THAT, AND START THINKING OF A WAY OUT OF HERE.
NOW WHAT ARE YOU DOING?
CHECK IT-- I DID THIS WITH TURKEYS ONCE... MAYBE WE CAN GET RID OF THE SNAKES LIKE A PIED PIPER.
HE USED A FLUTE TO LURE CHILDREN AND RATS, NOT SNAKES.
HMM... THEN MAYBE THE RATS WILL EAT THE SNAKES.
YOU'VE REALLY GOT NO CONCEPT OF REALITY.
BUT AT THIS POINT, ANY HELP WOULD BE APPRECIATED.
"YOU'RE A FORTUNE COOKIE. I THINK YOU GOT YOUR WISH!
I CAN'T WATCH.
THEY DON'T STAND A CHANCE. THEY DON'T EVEN SEE THAT SNAKE.
THEN YOU'RE MISSING OUT!
WHACK

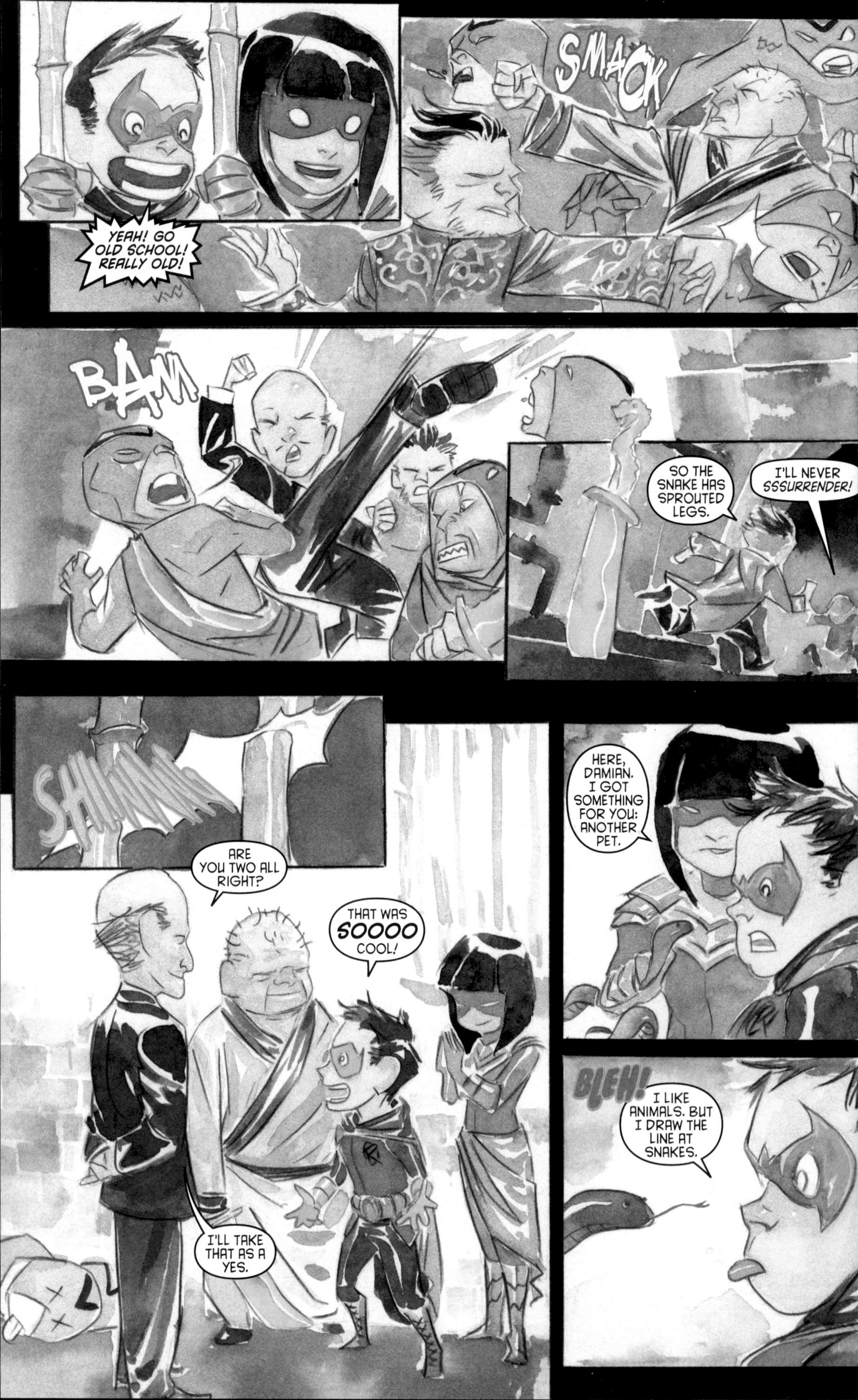

YEAH! GO OLD SCHOOL! REALLY OLD!
SMACK
BAM
SO THE SNAKE HAS SPROUTED LEGS.
I'LL NEVER SSSURRENDER!
SHING
ARE YOU TWO ALL RIGHT?
THAT WAS SOOOO COOL!
I'LL TAKE THAT AS A YES.
HERE, DAMIAN. I GOT SOMETHING FOR YOU: ANOTHER PET.
BLEH!
I LIKE ANIMALS. BUT I DRAW THE LINE AT SNAKES.

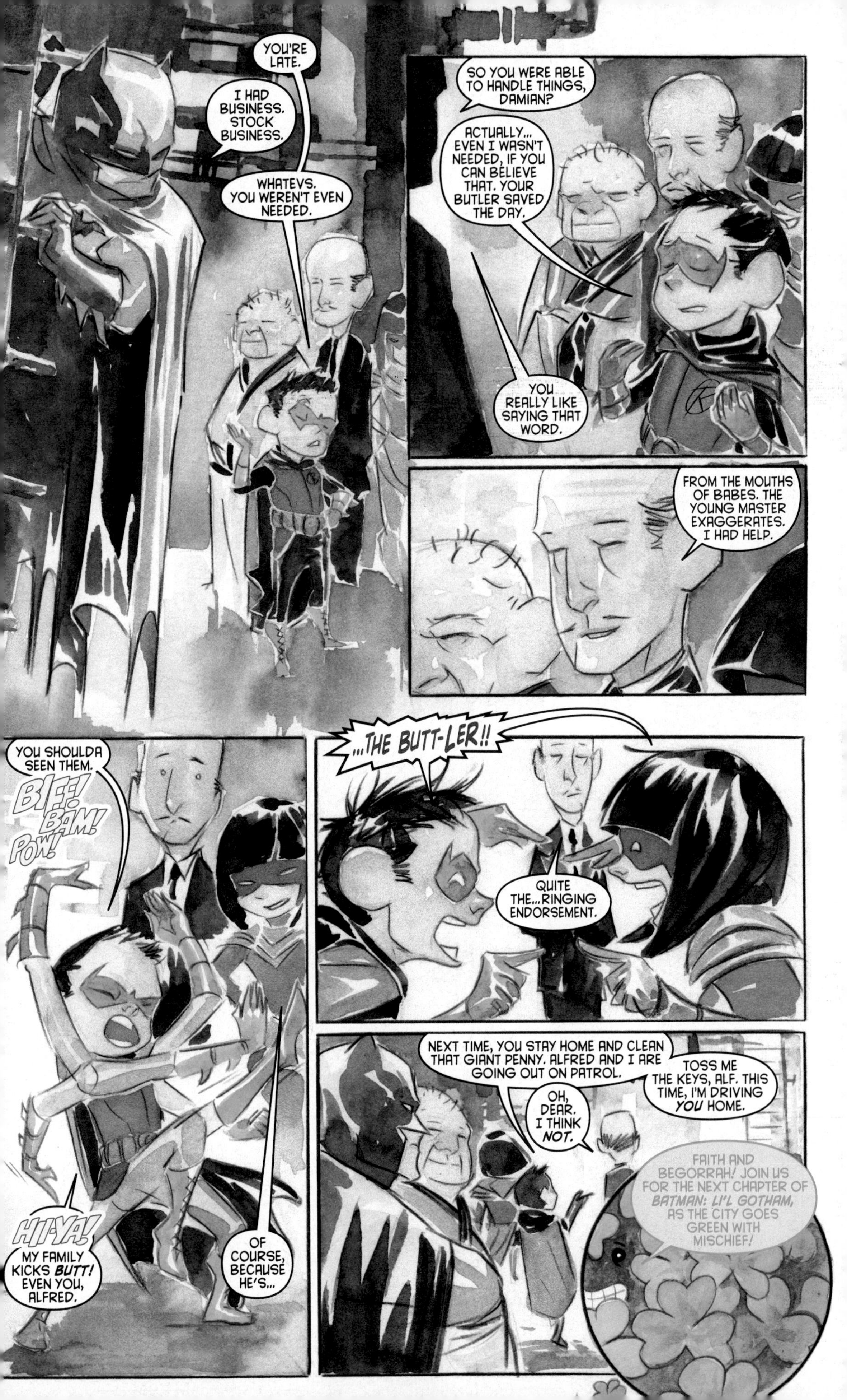
YOU'RE LATE.
I HAD BUSINESS. STOCK BUSINESS.
WHATEVS. YOU WEREN'T EVEN NEEDED.
SO YOU WERE ABLE TO HANDLE THINGS, DAMIAN?
ACTUALLY... EVEN I WASN'T NEEDED, IF YOU CAN BELIEVE THAT. YOUR BUTLER SAVED THE DAY.
YOU REALLY LIKE SAYING THAT WORD.
FROM THE MOUTHS OF BABES. THE YOUNG MASTER EXAGGERATES. I HAD HELP.
YOU SHOULDA SEEN THEM.
BIFF! BAM! POW!
HI-YA!
MY FAMILY KICKS *BUTT*! EVEN YOU, ALFRED.
OF COURSE, BECAUSE HE'S...
...THE BUTT-LER!!
QUITE THE...RINGING ENDORSEMENT.
NEXT TIME, YOU STAY HOME AND CLEAN THAT GIANT PENNY. ALFRED AND I ARE GOING OUT ON PATROL.
OH, DEAR. I THINK *NOT*.
TOSS ME THE KEYS, ALF. THIS TIME, I'M DRIVING *YOU* HOME.
FAITH AND BEGORRAH! JOIN US FOR THE NEXT CHAPTER OF *BATMAN: LI'L GOTHAM*, AS THE CITY GOES GREEN WITH MISCHIEF!

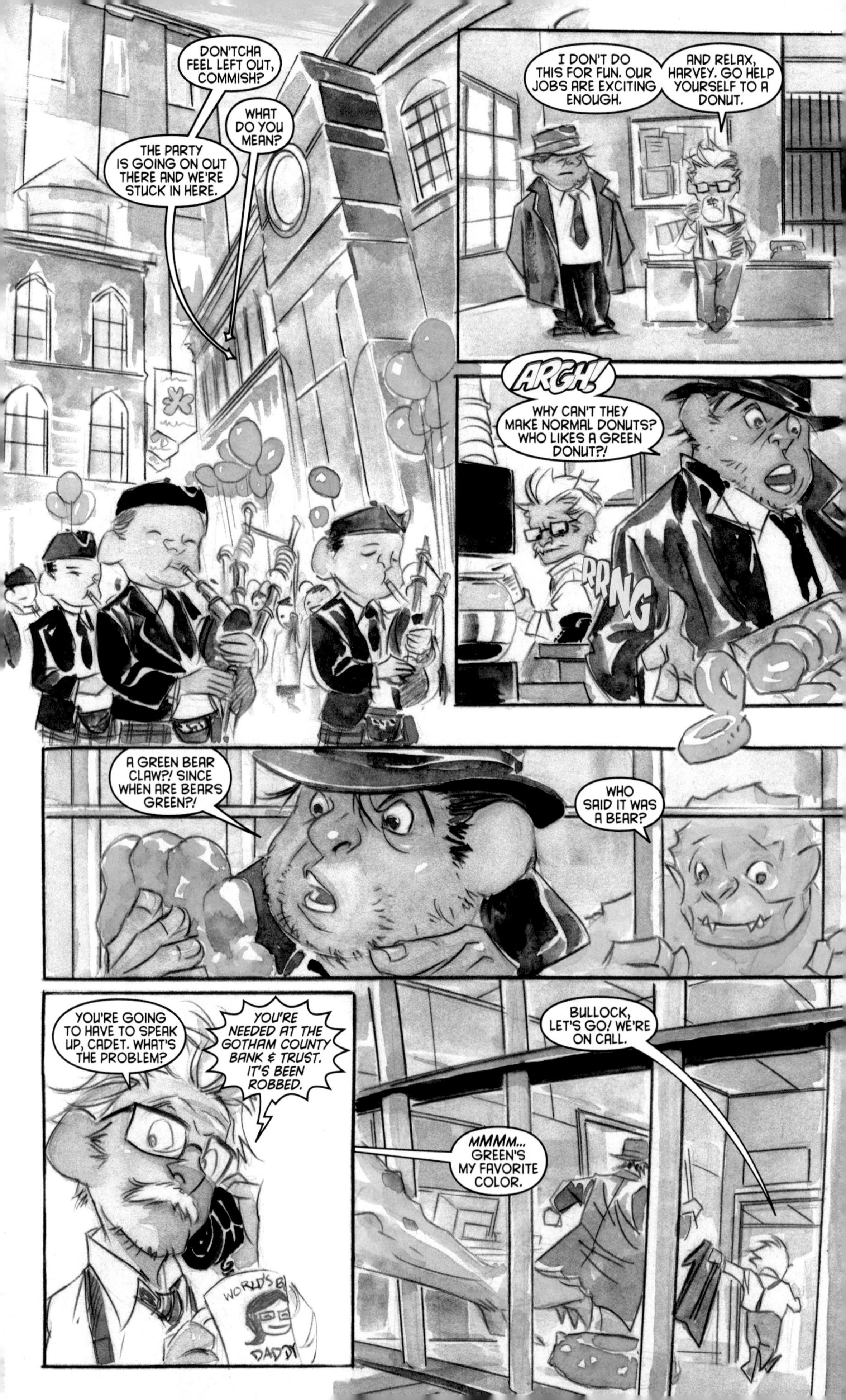

DON'TCHA FEEL LEFT OUT, COMMISH?
WHAT DO YOU MEAN?
THE PARTY IS GOING ON OUT THERE AND WE'RE STUCK IN HERE.
I DON'T DO THIS FOR FUN. OUR JOBS ARE EXCITING ENOUGH.
AND RELAX, HARVEY. GO HELP YOURSELF TO A DONUT.
ARGH!
WHY CAN'T THEY MAKE NORMAL DONUTS? WHO LIKES A GREEN DONUT?!
RRNG
A GREEN BEAR CLAW?! SINCE WHEN ARE BEARS GREEN?!
WHO SAID IT WAS A BEAR?
YOU'RE GOING TO HAVE TO SPEAK UP, CADET. WHAT'S THE PROBLEM?
YOU'RE NEEDED AT THE GOTHAM COUNTY BANK & TRUST. IT'S BEEN ROBBED.
BULLOCK, LET'S GO! WE'RE ON CALL.
MMMM... GREEN'S MY FAVORITE COLOR.

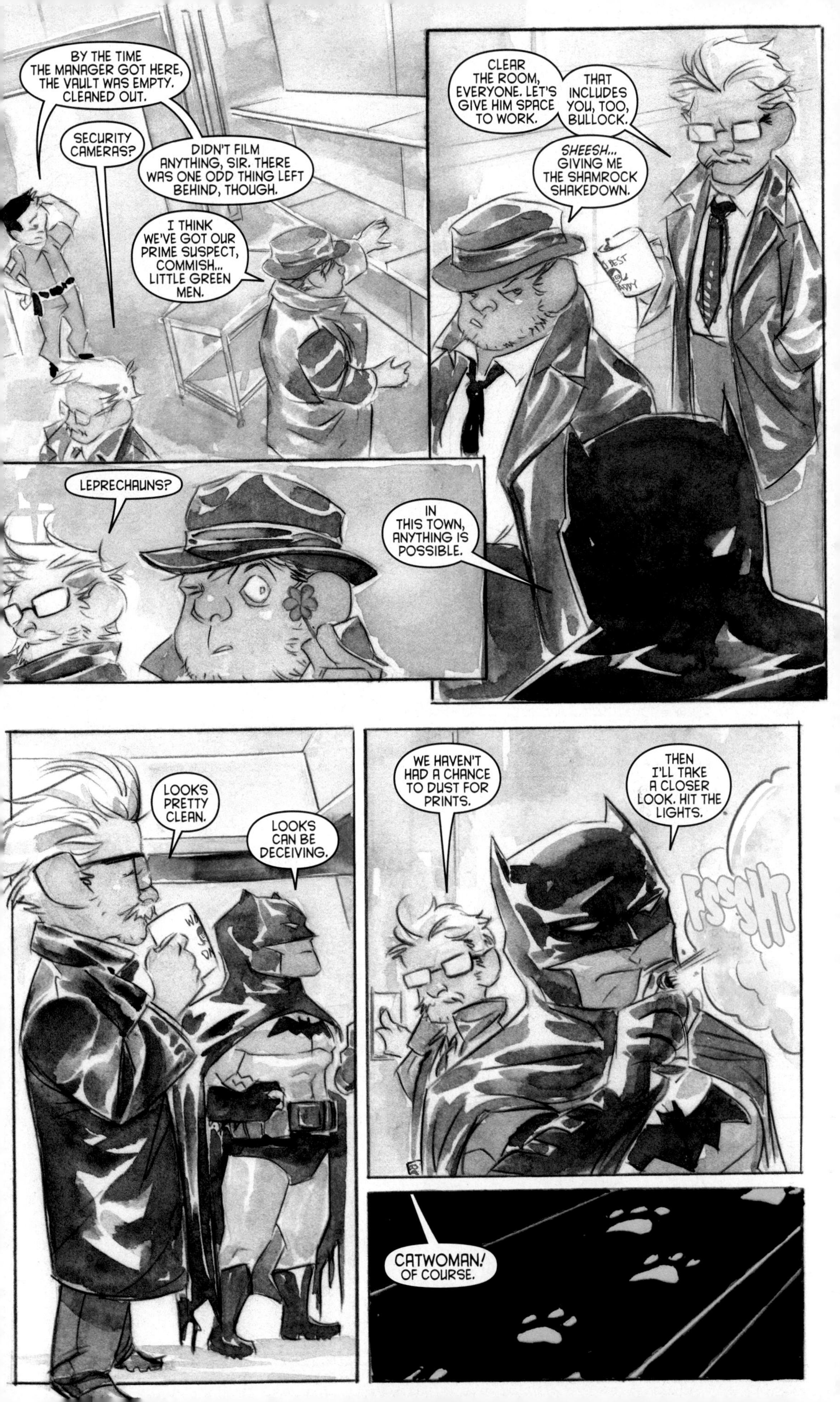

BY THE TIME THE MANAGER GOT HERE, THE VAULT WAS EMPTY. CLEANED OUT.
SECURITY CAMERAS?
DIDN'T FILM ANYTHING, SIR. THERE WAS ONE ODD THING LEFT BEHIND, THOUGH.
I THINK WE'VE GOT OUR PRIME SUSPECT, COMMISH... LITTLE GREEN MEN.
CLEAR THE ROOM, EVERYONE. LET'S GIVE HIM SPACE TO WORK.
THAT INCLUDES YOU, TOO, BULLOCK.
SHEESH... GIVING ME THE SHAMROCK SHAKEDOWN.
BEST DADDY
LEPRECHAUNS?
IN THIS TOWN, ANYTHING IS POSSIBLE.
LOOKS PRETTY CLEAN.
LOOKS CAN BE DECEIVING.
WE HAVEN'T HAD A CHANCE TO DUST FOR PRINTS.
THEN I'LL TAKE A CLOSER LOOK. HIT THE LIGHTS.
FSSSHT
CATWOMAN! OF COURSE.

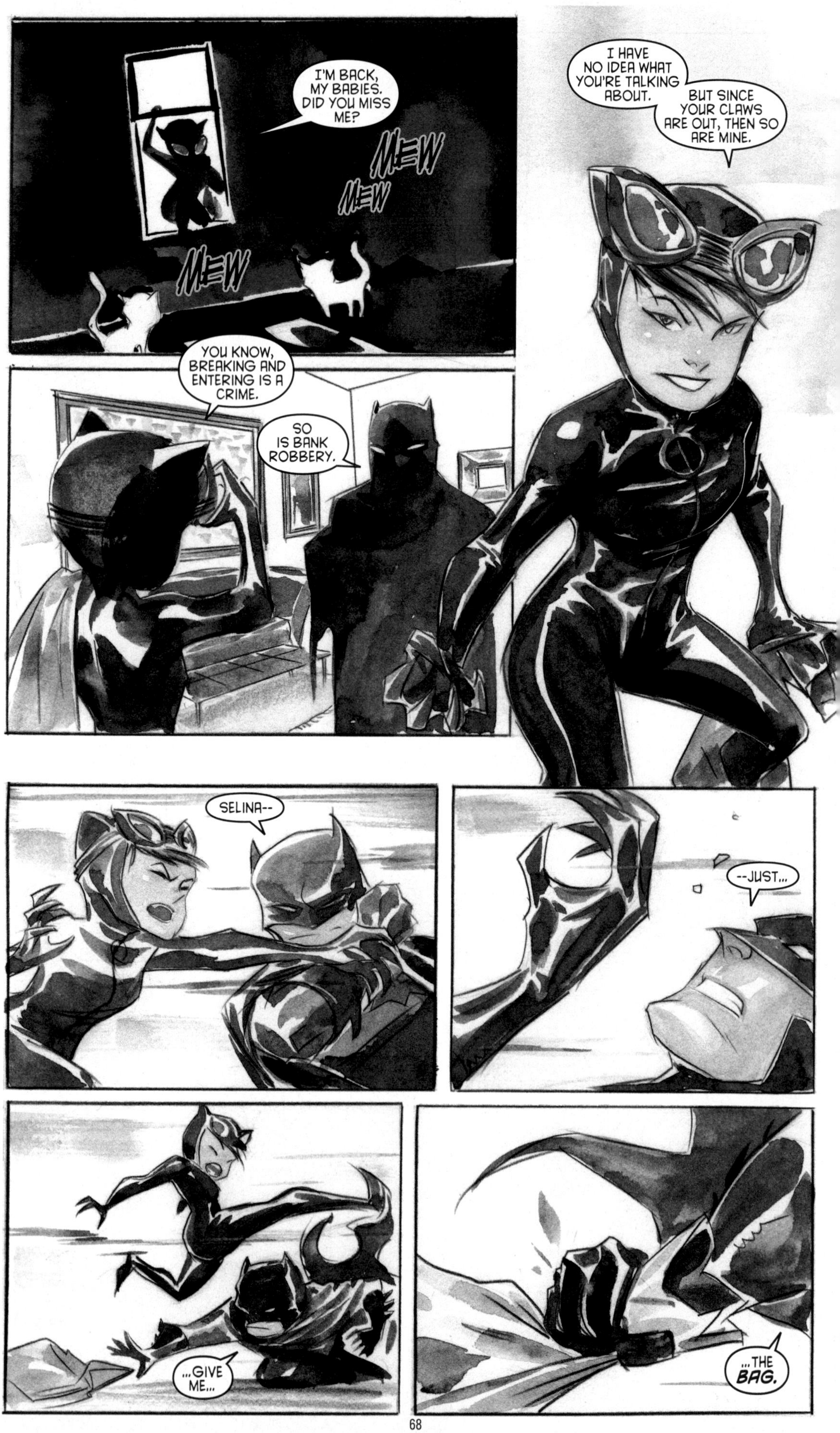
I'M BACK, MY BABIES. DID YOU MISS ME?
MEW
MEW
MEW
I HAVE NO IDEA WHAT YOU'RE TALKING ABOUT.
BUT SINCE YOUR CLAWS ARE OUT, THEN SO ARE MINE.
YOU KNOW, BREAKING AND ENTERING IS A CRIME.
SO IS BANK ROBBERY.
SELINA--
--JUST...
...GIVE ME...
...THE *BAG.*

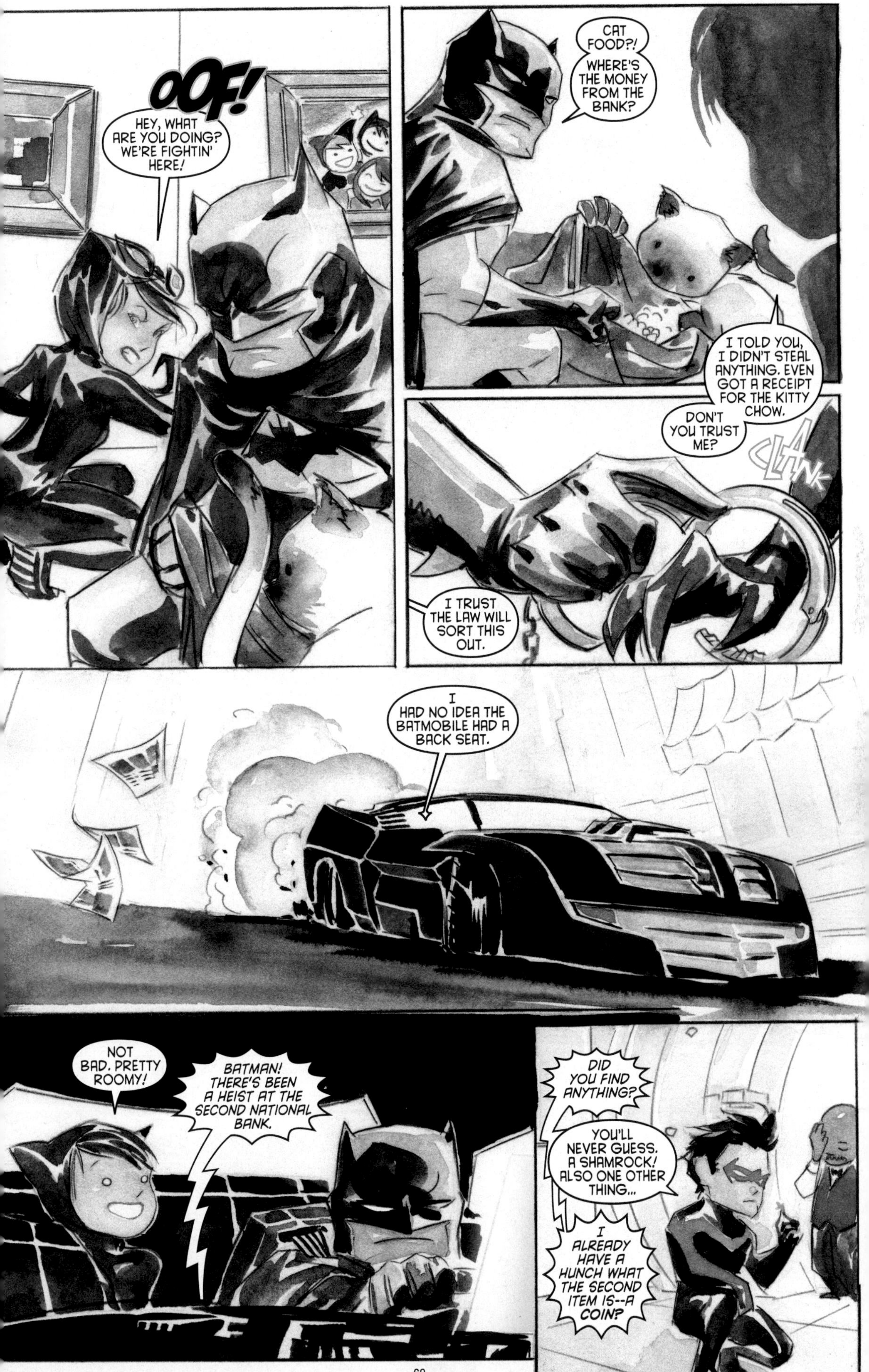
OOF!
HEY, WHAT ARE YOU DOING? WE'RE FIGHTIN' HERE!
CAT FOOD?! WHERE'S THE MONEY FROM THE BANK?
I TOLD YOU, I DIDN'T STEAL ANYTHING. EVEN GOT A RECEIPT FOR THE KITTY CHOW.
DON'T YOU TRUST ME?
CLANK
I TRUST THE LAW WILL SORT THIS OUT.
I HAD NO IDEA THE BATMOBILE HAD A BACK SEAT.
NOT BAD. PRETTY ROOMY!
BATMAN! THERE'S BEEN A HEIST AT THE SECOND NATIONAL BANK.
DID YOU FIND ANYTHING?
YOU'LL NEVER GUESS. A SHAMROCK! ALSO ONE OTHER THING...
I ALREADY HAVE A HUNCH WHAT THE SECOND ITEM IS--A COIN?

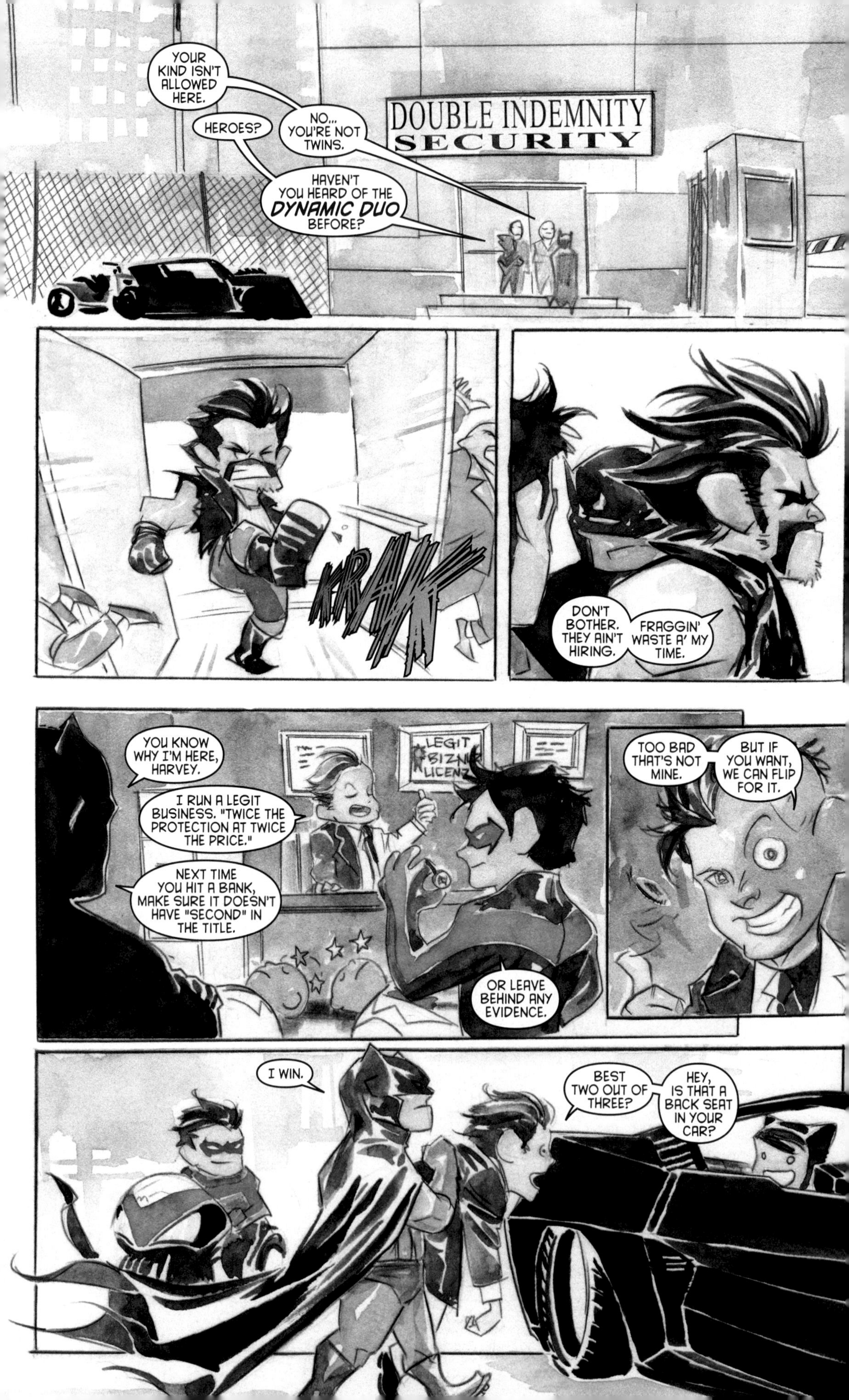
YOUR KIND ISN'T ALLOWED HERE.
HEROES?
NO... YOU'RE NOT TWINS.
HAVEN'T YOU HEARD OF THE DYNAMIC DUO BEFORE?
DOUBLE INDEMNITY SECURITY
KRAK
DON'T BOTHER. THEY AIN'T HIRING.
FRAGGIN' WASTE A' MY TIME.
YOU KNOW WHY I'M HERE, HARVEY.
I RUN A LEGIT BUSINESS. "TWICE THE PROTECTION AT TWICE THE PRICE."
NEXT TIME YOU HIT A BANK, MAKE SURE IT DOESN'T HAVE "SECOND" IN THE TITLE.
OR LEAVE BEHIND ANY EVIDENCE.
TOO BAD THAT'S NOT MINE.
BUT IF YOU WANT, WE CAN FLIP FOR IT.
I WIN.
BEST TWO OUT OF THREE?
HEY, IS THAT A BACK SEAT IN YOUR CAR?

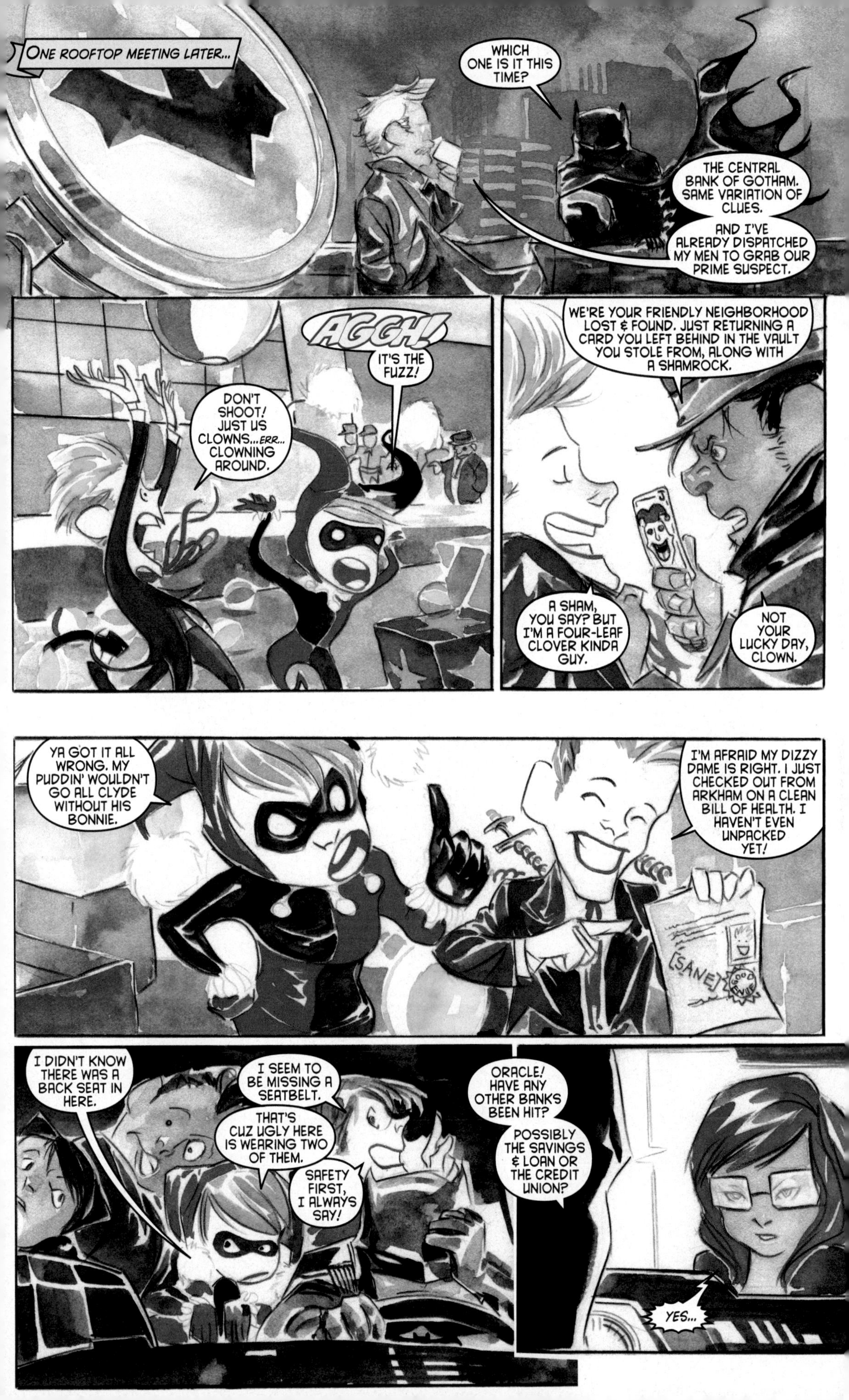
ONE ROOFTOP MEETING LATER...
WHICH ONE IS IT THIS TIME?
THE CENTRAL BANK OF GOTHAM. SAME VARIATION OF CLUES.
AND I'VE ALREADY DISPATCHED MY MEN TO GRAB OUR PRIME SUSPECT.
AGGH!
IT'S THE FUZZ!
DON'T SHOOT! JUST US CLOWNS...ERR... CLOWNING AROUND.
WE'RE YOUR FRIENDLY NEIGHBORHOOD LOST & FOUND. JUST RETURNING A CARD YOU LEFT BEHIND IN THE VAULT YOU STOLE FROM, ALONG WITH A SHAMROCK.
A SHAM, YOU SAY? BUT I'M A FOUR-LEAF CLOVER KINDA GUY.
NOT YOUR LUCKY DAY, CLOWN.
YA GOT IT ALL WRONG. MY PUDDIN' WOULDN'T GO ALL CLYDE WITHOUT HIS BONNIE.
I'M AFRAID MY DIZZY DAME IS RIGHT. I JUST CHECKED OUT FROM ARKHAM ON A CLEAN BILL OF HEALTH. I HAVEN'T EVEN UNPACKED YET!
SANE
I DIDN'T KNOW THERE WAS A BACK SEAT IN HERE.
I SEEM TO BE MISSING A SEATBELT.
THAT'S CUZ UGLY HERE IS WEARING TWO OF THEM.
SAFETY FIRST, I ALWAYS SAY!
ORACLE! HAVE ANY OTHER BANKS BEEN HIT?
POSSIBLY THE SAVINGS & LOAN OR THE CREDIT UNION?
YES...

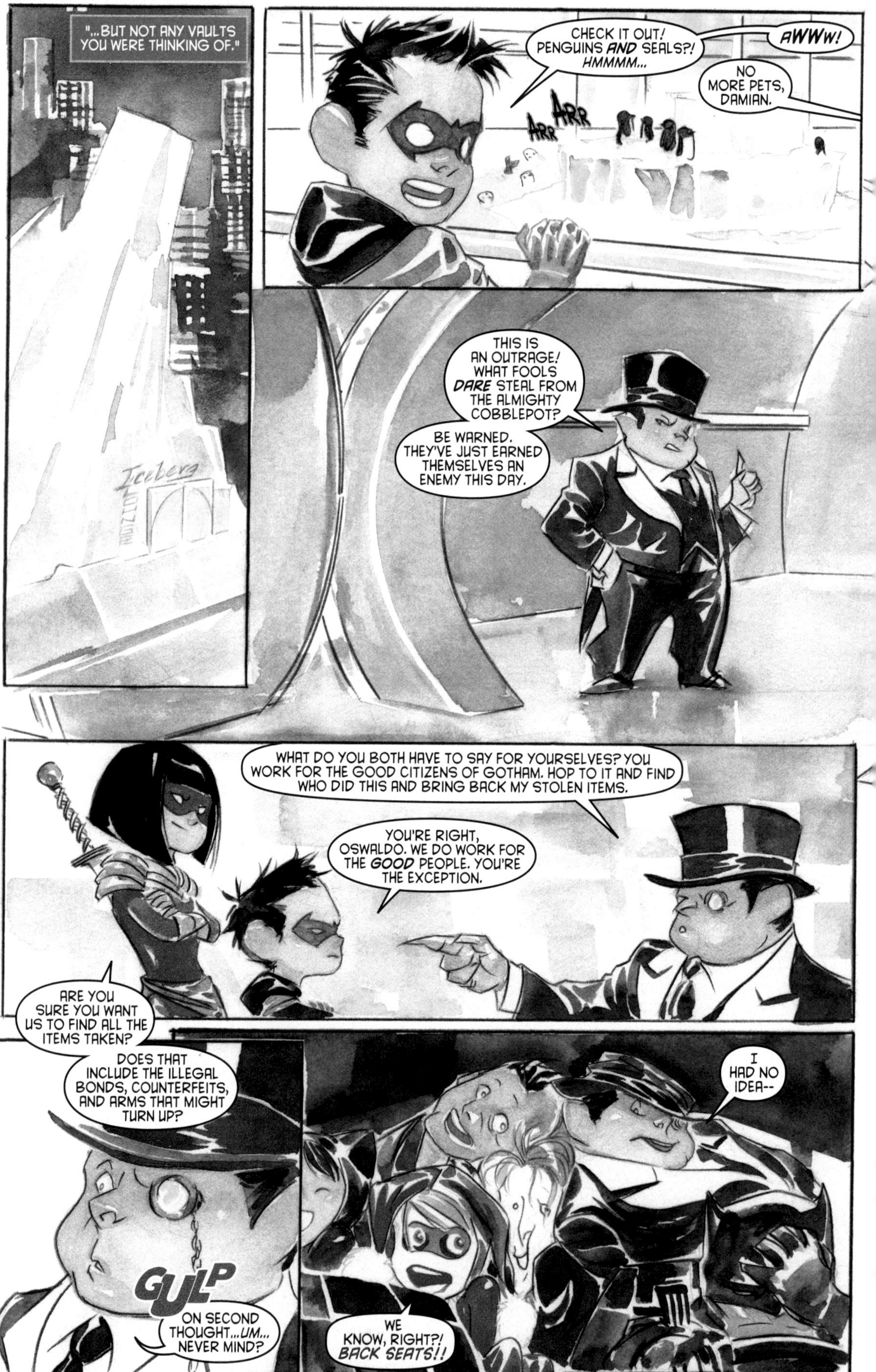
"...BUT NOT ANY VAULTS YOU WERE THINKING OF."
Iceberg
CHECK IT OUT! PENGUINS AND SEALS?! HMMMM...
AWWW!
NO MORE PETS, DAMIAN.
ARR ARR
THIS IS AN OUTRAGE! WHAT FOOLS DARE STEAL FROM THE ALMIGHTY COBBLEPOT?
BE WARNED. THEY'VE JUST EARNED THEMSELVES AN ENEMY THIS DAY.
WHAT DO YOU BOTH HAVE TO SAY FOR YOURSELVES? YOU WORK FOR THE GOOD CITIZENS OF GOTHAM. HOP TO IT AND FIND WHO DID THIS AND BRING BACK MY STOLEN ITEMS.
YOU'RE RIGHT, OSWALDO. WE DO WORK FOR THE GOOD PEOPLE. YOU'RE THE EXCEPTION.
ARE YOU SURE YOU WANT US TO FIND ALL THE ITEMS TAKEN?
DOES THAT INCLUDE THE ILLEGAL BONDS, COUNTERFEITS, AND ARMS THAT MIGHT TURN UP?
GULP
ON SECOND THOUGHT...UM... NEVER MIND?
I HAD NO IDEA--
WE KNOW, RIGHT?! BACK SEATS!!

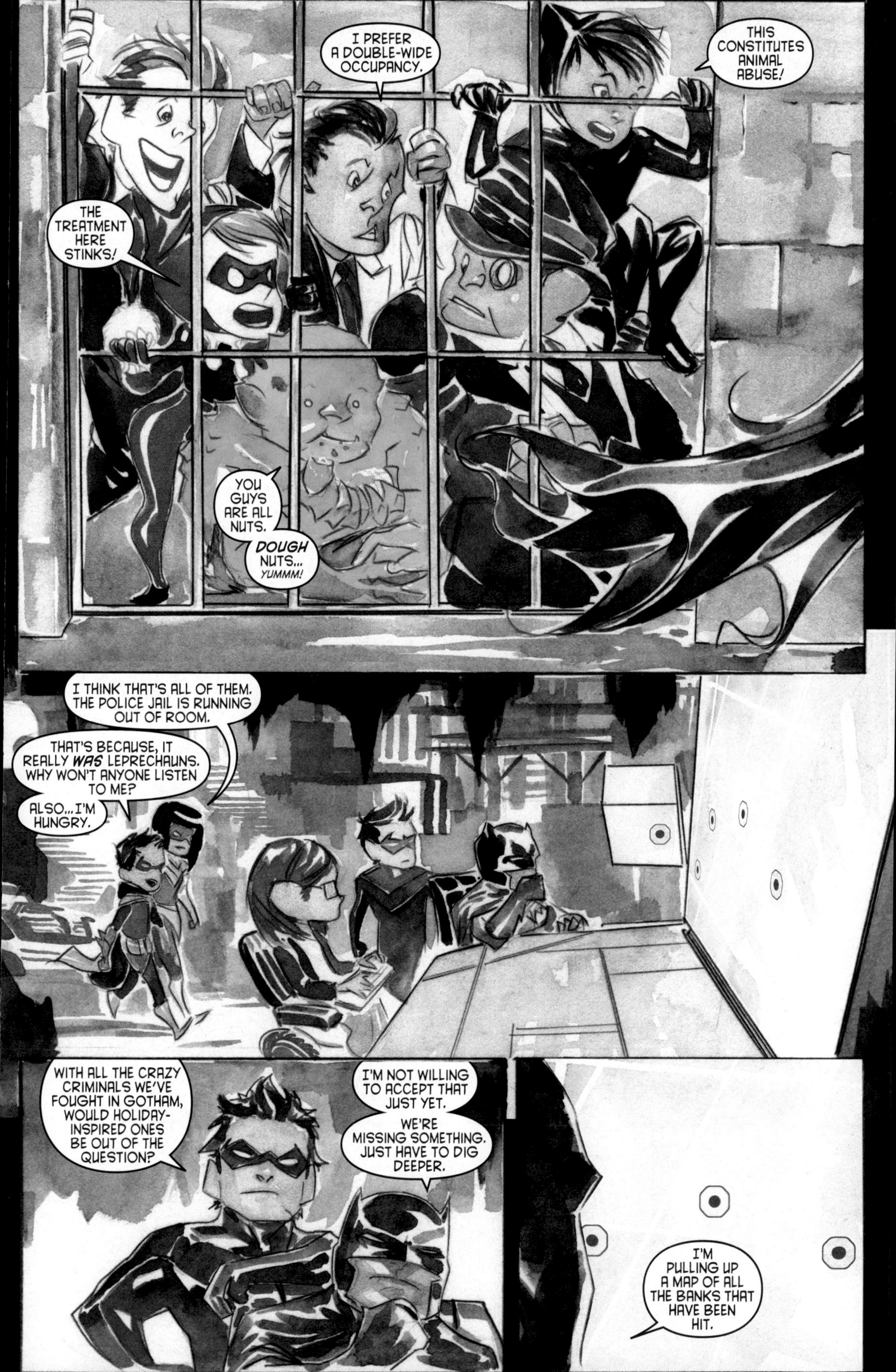
THE TREATMENT HERE STINKS!
I PREFER A DOUBLE-WIDE OCCUPANCY.
THIS CONSTITUTES ANIMAL ABUSE!
YOU GUYS ARE ALL NUTS.
DOUGH NUTS... YUMMM!
I THINK THAT'S ALL OF THEM. THE POLICE JAIL IS RUNNING OUT OF ROOM.
THAT'S BECAUSE, IT REALLY WAS LEPRECHAUNS. WHY WON'T ANYONE LISTEN TO ME?
ALSO...I'M HUNGRY.
WITH ALL THE CRAZY CRIMINALS WE'VE FOUGHT IN GOTHAM, WOULD HOLIDAY-INSPIRED ONES BE OUT OF THE QUESTION?
I'M NOT WILLING TO ACCEPT THAT JUST YET.
WE'RE MISSING SOMETHING. JUST HAVE TO DIG DEEPER.
I'M PULLING UP A MAP OF ALL THE BANKS THAT HAVE BEEN HIT.

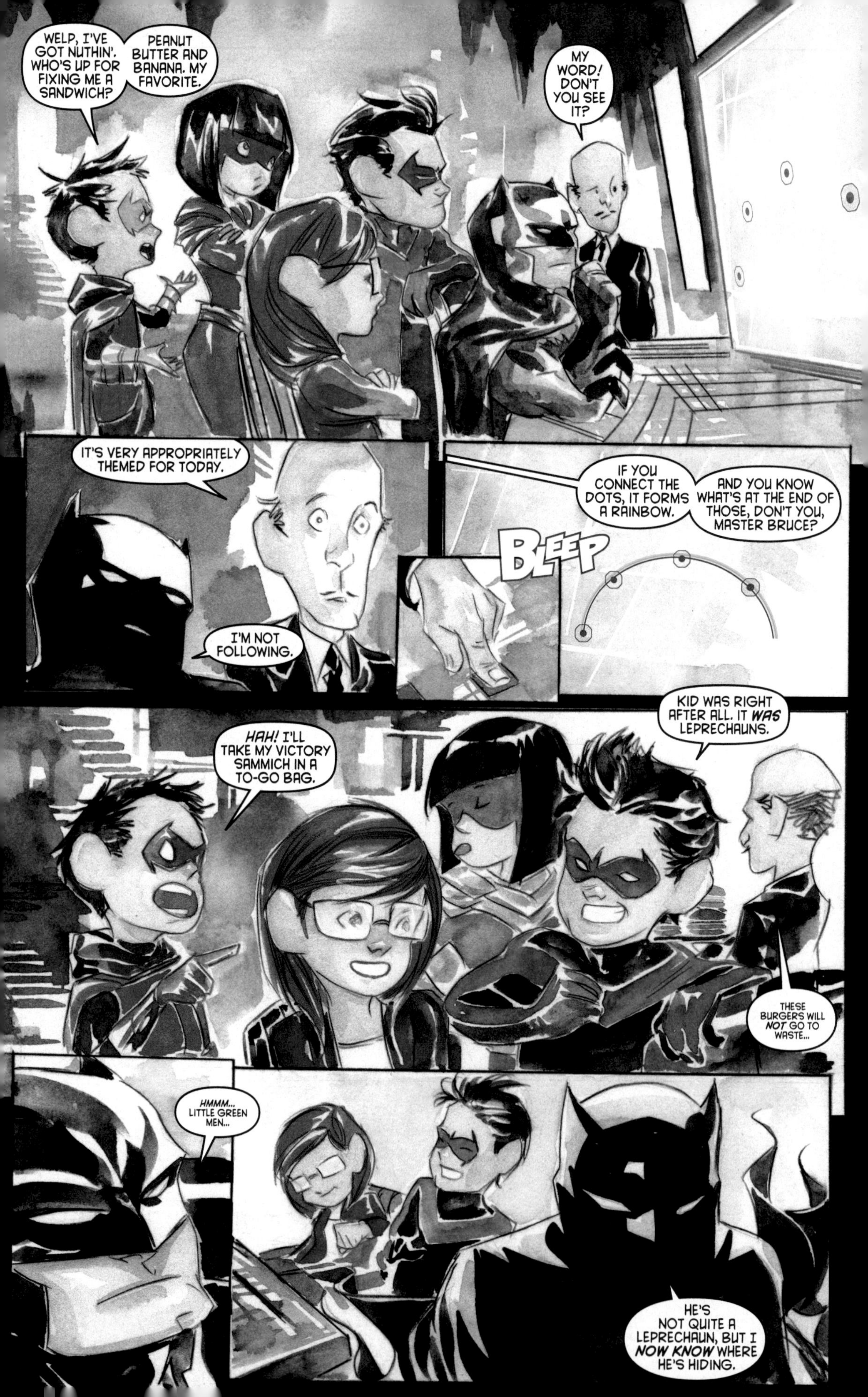
WELP, I'VE GOT NUTHIN'. WHO'S UP FOR FIXING ME A SANDWICH?
PEANUT BUTTER AND BANANA. MY FAVORITE.
MY WORD! DON'T YOU SEE IT?
IT'S VERY APPROPRIATELY THEMED FOR TODAY.
I'M NOT FOLLOWING.
BLEEP
IF YOU CONNECT THE DOTS, IT FORMS A RAINBOW.
AND YOU KNOW WHAT'S AT THE END OF THOSE, DON'T YOU, MASTER BRUCE?
HAH! I'LL TAKE MY VICTORY SAMMICH IN A TO-GO BAG.
KID WAS RIGHT AFTER ALL. IT WAS LEPRECHAUNS.
THESE BURGERS WILL NOT GO TO WASTE...
HMMM... LITTLE GREEN MEN...
HE'S NOT QUITE A LEPRECHAUN, BUT I NOW KNOW WHERE HE'S HIDING.

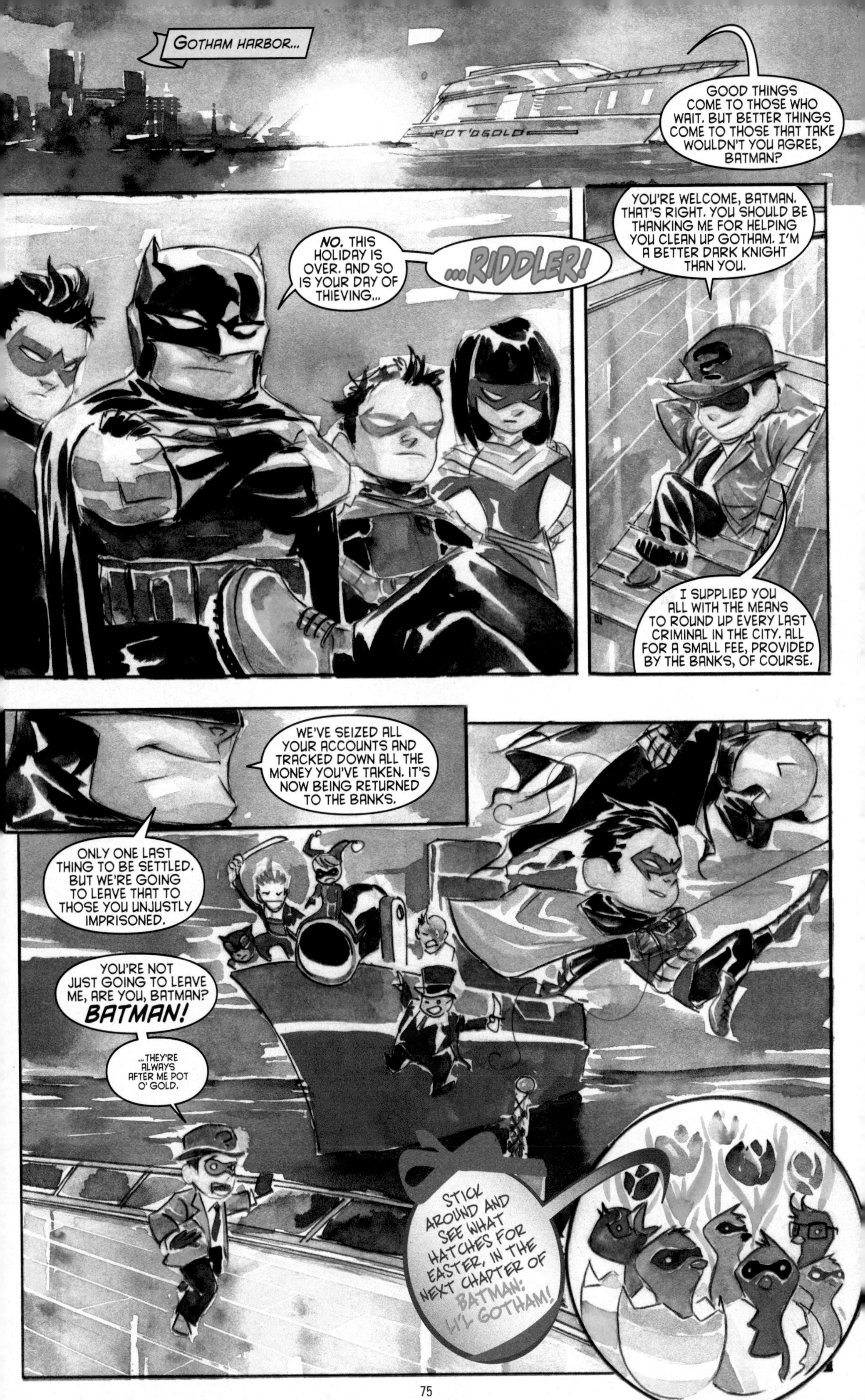
GOTHAM HARBOR...
POT 'O GOLD
GOOD THINGS COME TO THOSE WHO WAIT. BUT BETTER THINGS COME TO THOSE THAT TAKE WOULDN'T YOU AGREE, BATMAN?
NO. THIS HOLIDAY IS OVER. AND SO IS YOUR DAY OF THIEVING...
...RIDDLER!
YOU'RE WELCOME, BATMAN. THAT'S RIGHT. YOU SHOULD BE THANKING ME FOR HELPING YOU CLEAN UP GOTHAM. I'M A BETTER DARK KNIGHT THAN YOU.
I SUPPLIED YOU ALL WITH THE MEANS TO ROUND UP EVERY LAST CRIMINAL IN THE CITY. ALL FOR A SMALL FEE, PROVIDED BY THE BANKS, OF COURSE.
WE'VE SEIZED ALL YOUR ACCOUNTS AND TRACKED DOWN ALL THE MONEY YOU'VE TAKEN. IT'S NOW BEING RETURNED TO THE BANKS.
ONLY ONE LAST THING TO BE SETTLED. BUT WE'RE GOING TO LEAVE THAT TO THOSE YOU UNJUSTLY IMPRISONED.
YOU'RE NOT JUST GOING TO LEAVE ME, ARE YOU, BATMAN? BATMAN!
...THEY'RE ALWAYS AFTER ME POT O' GOLD.
STICK AROUND AND SEE WHAT HATCHES FOR EASTER, IN THE NEXT CHAPTER OF BATMAN: LI'L GOTHAM!

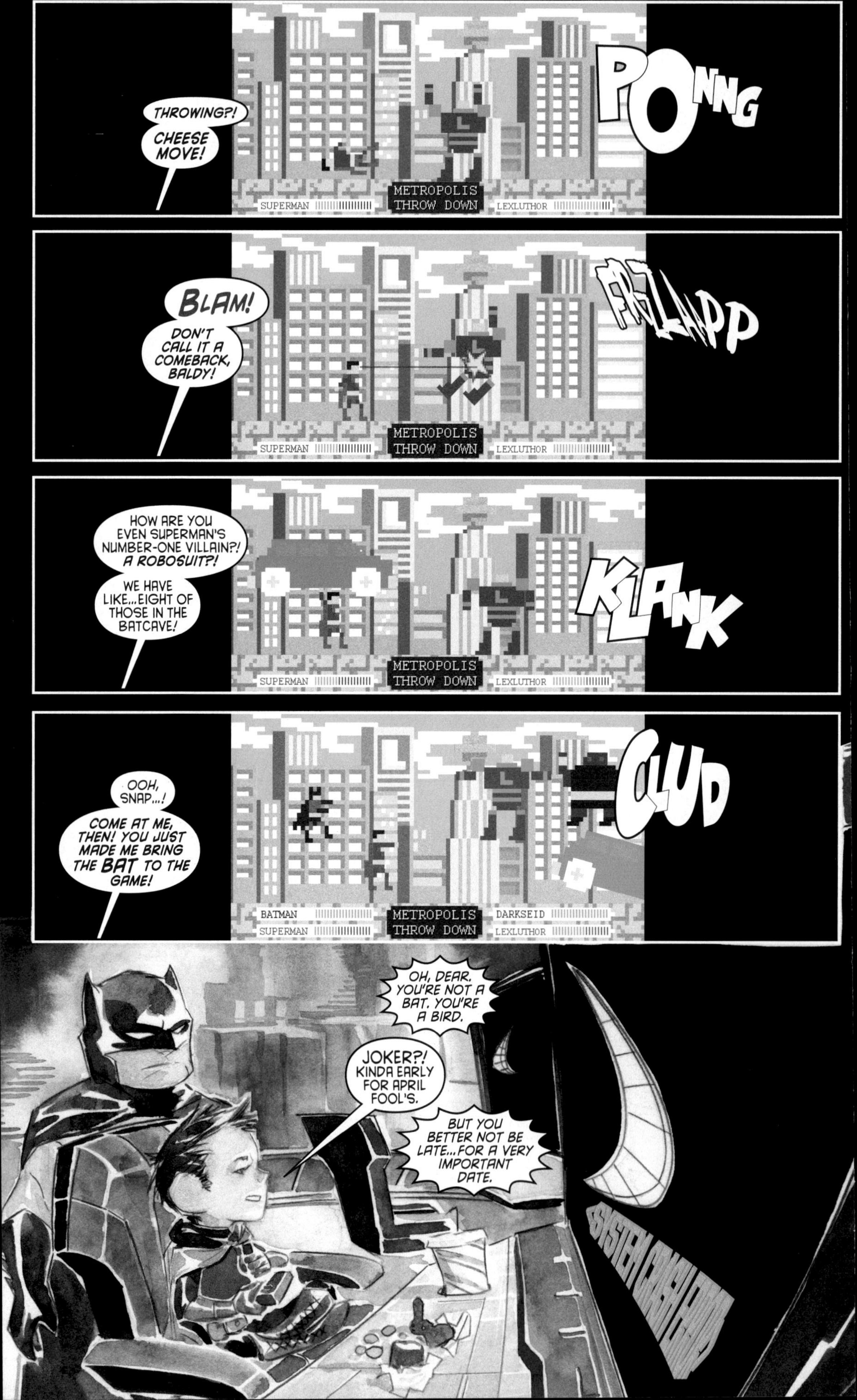
THROWING?!
CHEESE MOVE!
PONNG
METROPOLIS THROW DOWN
SUPERMAN
LEXLUTHOR
BLAM!
DON'T CALL IT A COMEBACK, BALDY!
FRZLAAPP
METROPOLIS THROW DOWN
SUPERMAN
LEXLUTHOR
HOW ARE YOU EVEN SUPERMAN'S NUMBER-ONE VILLAIN?! A ROBOSUIT?!
WE HAVE LIKE...EIGHT OF THOSE IN THE BATCAVE!
KLANK
METROPOLIS THROW DOWN
SUPERMAN
LEXLUTHOR
OOH, SNAP...!
COME AT ME, THEN! YOU JUST MADE ME BRING THE BAT TO THE GAME!
CLUD
BATMAN
SUPERMAN
METROPOLIS THROW DOWN
DARKSEID
LEXLUTHOR
OH, DEAR. YOU'RE NOT A BAT. YOU'RE A BIRD.
JOKER?! KINDA EARLY FOR APRIL FOOL'S.
BUT YOU BETTER NOT BE LATE...FOR A VERY IMPORTANT DATE.
SYSTEM CRASH ERROR

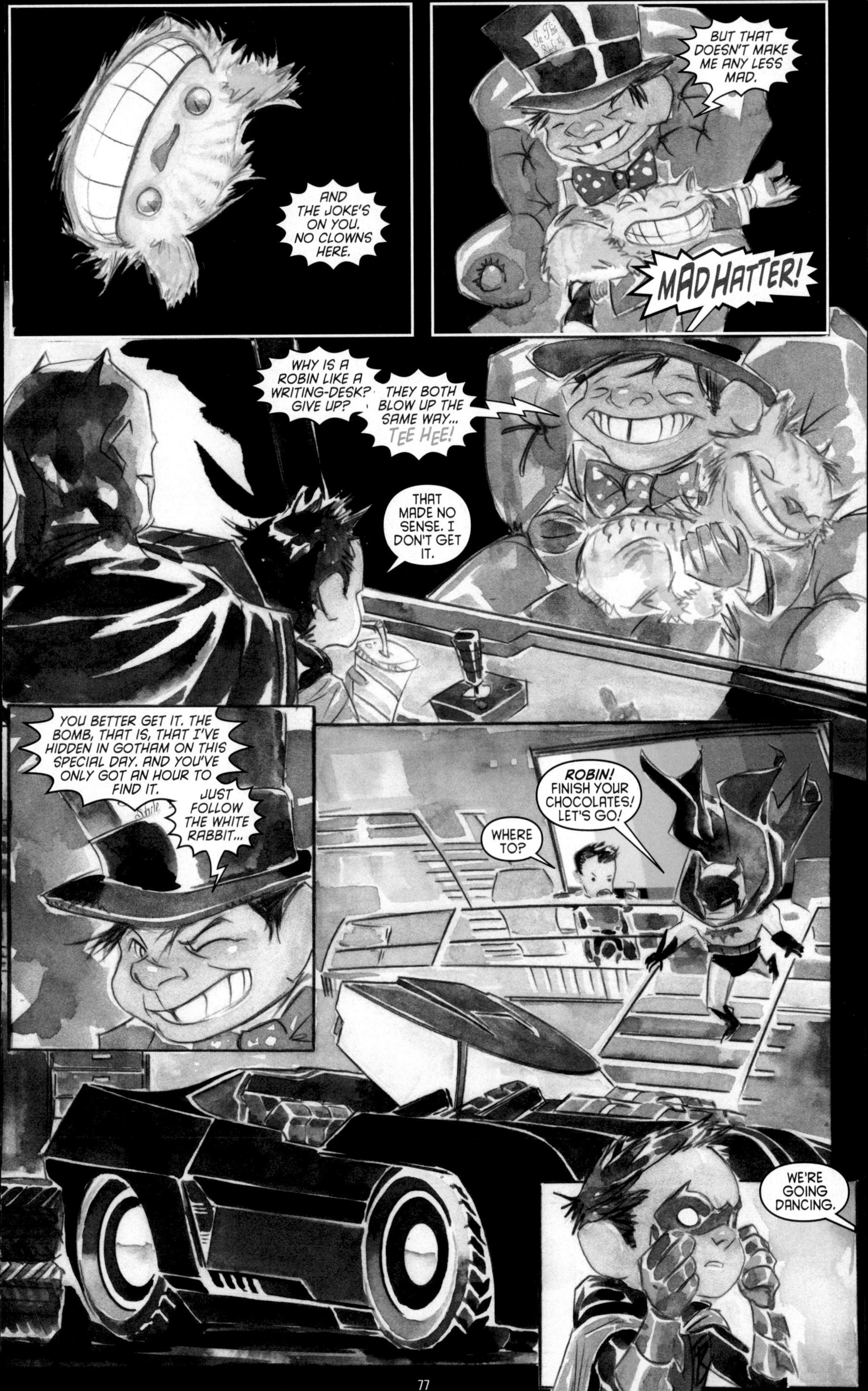
AND THE JOKE'S ON YOU. NO CLOWNS HERE.
BUT THAT DOESN'T MAKE ME ANY LESS MAD.
MAD HATTER!
WHY IS A ROBIN LIKE A WRITING-DESK? GIVE UP?
THEY BOTH BLOW UP THE SAME WAY... TEE HEE!
THAT MADE NO SENSE. I DON'T GET IT.
YOU BETTER GET IT. THE BOMB, THAT IS, THAT I'VE HIDDEN IN GOTHAM ON THIS SPECIAL DAY. AND YOU'VE ONLY GOT AN HOUR TO FIND IT.
JUST FOLLOW THE WHITE RABBIT...
ROBIN! FINISH YOUR CHOCOLATES! LET'S GO!
WHERE TO?
WE'RE GOING DANCING.

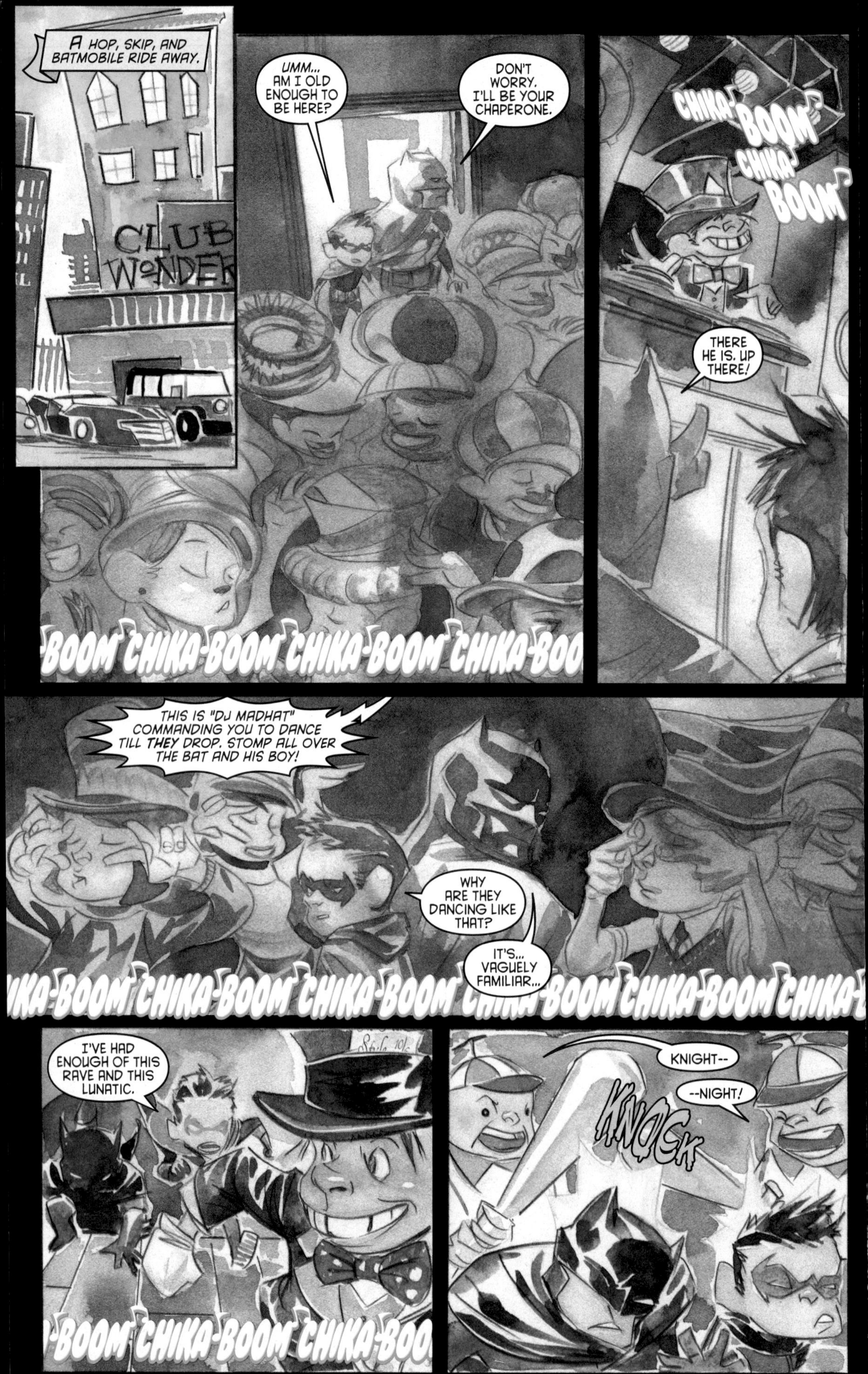
A HOP, SKIP, AND BATMOBILE RIDE AWAY.
CLUB WONDER
UMM... AM I OLD ENOUGH TO BE HERE?
DON'T WORRY. I'LL BE YOUR CHAPERONE.
-BOOM CHIKA-BOOM CHIKA-BOOM CHIKA-BOO
CHIKA-BOOM CHIKA-BOOM
THERE HE IS. UP THERE!
THIS IS "DJ MADHAT" COMMANDING YOU TO DANCE TILL **THEY** DROP. STOMP ALL OVER THE BAT AND HIS BOY!
WHY ARE THEY DANCING LIKE THAT?
IT'S... VAGUELY FAMILIAR...
IKA-BOOM CHIKA-BOOM CHIKA-BOOM CHIKA-BOOM CHIKA-
I'VE HAD ENOUGH OF THIS RAVE AND THIS LUNATIC.
-BOOM CHIKA-BOOM CHIKA-BOO
KNIGHT--
--NIGHT!
KNOCK

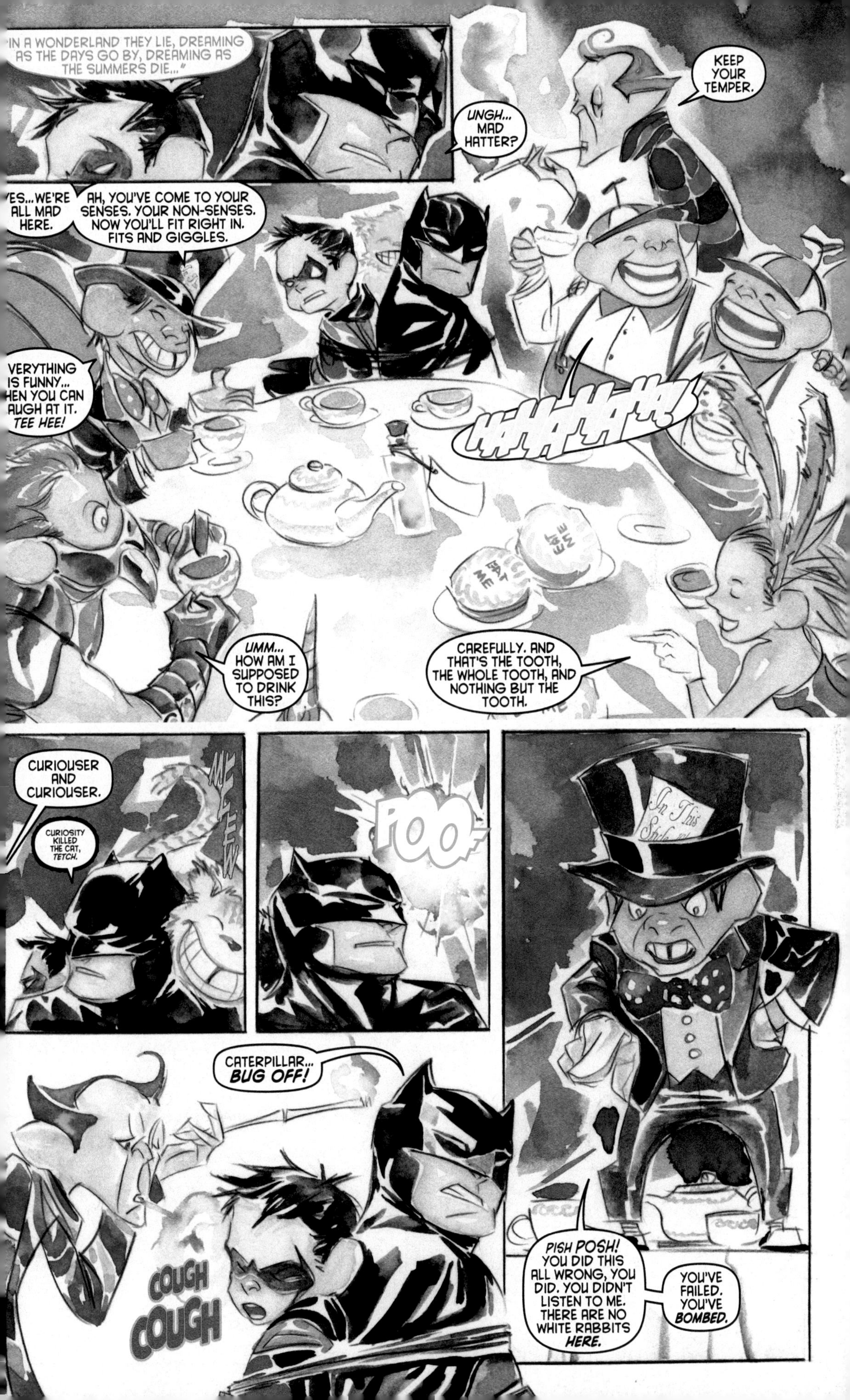

"IN A WONDERLAND THEY LIE, DREAMING AS THE DAYS GO BY, DREAMING AS THE SUMMER'S DIE..."
UNGH... MAD HATTER?
KEEP YOUR TEMPER.
YES... WE'RE ALL MAD HERE.
AH, YOU'VE COME TO YOUR SENSES. YOUR NON-SENSES. NOW YOU'LL FIT RIGHT IN. FITS AND GIGGLES.
VERYTHING IS FUNNY... HEN YOU CAN AUGH AT IT. TEE HEE!
HAHAHAHA!
EAT ME
EAT ME
UMM... HOW AM I SUPPOSED TO DRINK THIS?
CAREFULLY. AND THAT'S THE TOOTH, THE WHOLE TOOTH, AND NOTHING BUT THE TOOTH.
CURIOUSER AND CURIOUSER.
CURIOSITY KILLED THE CAT, TETCH.
MEEEW
POOF
In This Style
CATERPILLAR... BUG OFF!
COUGH COUGH
PISH POSH! YOU DID THIS ALL WRONG, YOU DID. YOU DIDN'T LISTEN TO ME. THERE ARE NO WHITE RABBITS HERE.
YOU'VE FAILED. YOU'VE BOMBED.

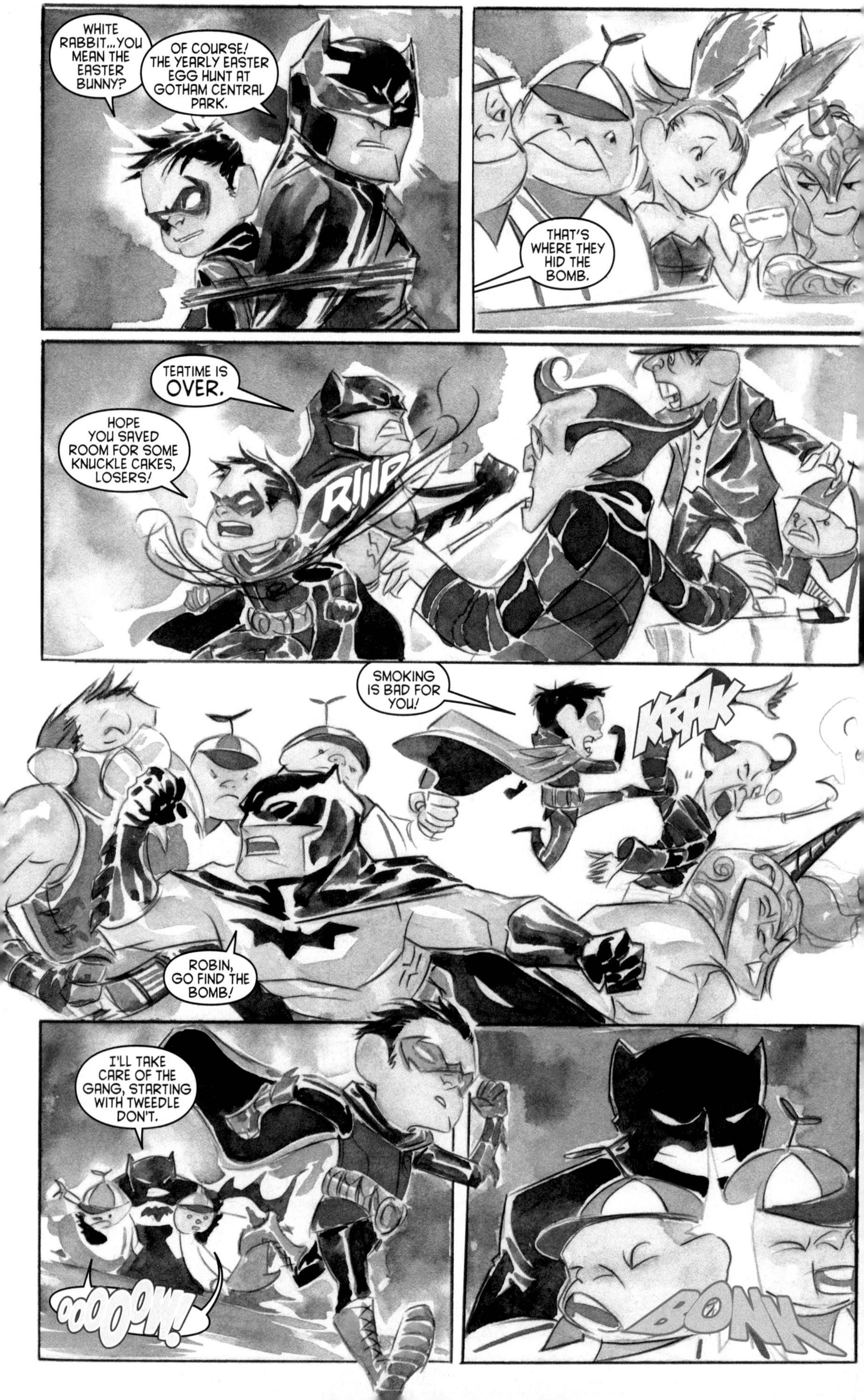
WHITE RABBIT...YOU MEAN THE EASTER BUNNY?
OF COURSE! THE YEARLY EASTER EGG HUNT AT GOTHAM CENTRAL PARK.
THAT'S WHERE THEY HID THE BOMB.
TEATIME IS OVER.
HOPE YOU SAVED ROOM FOR SOME KNUCKLE CAKES, LOSERS!
RIIIP
SMOKING IS BAD FOR YOU!
KRAK
ROBIN, GO FIND THE BOMB!
I'LL TAKE CARE OF THE GANG, STARTING WITH TWEEDLE DON'T.
OOOOOW!
BONK

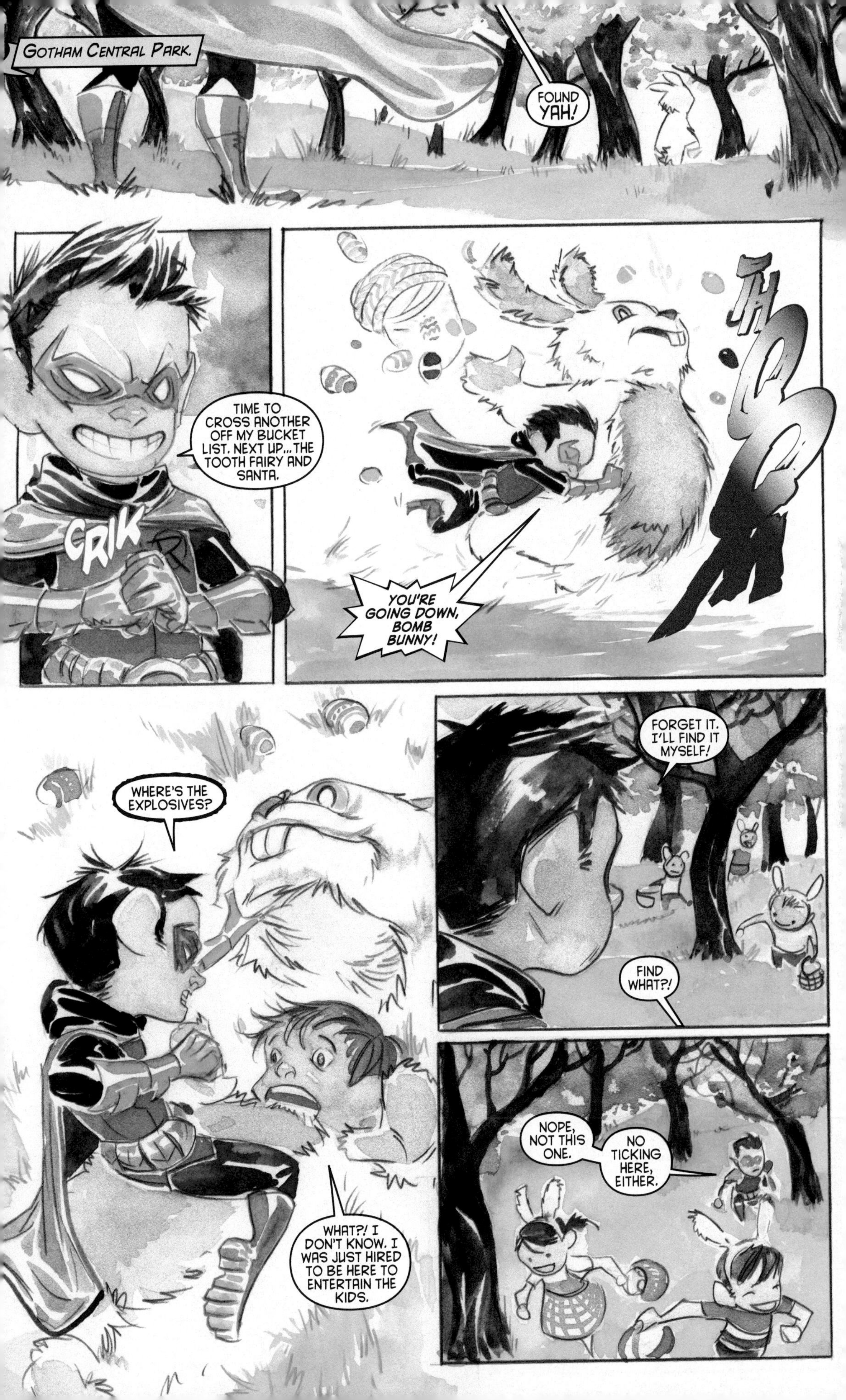

GOTHAM CENTRAL PARK.
FOUND YAH!
TIME TO CROSS ANOTHER OFF MY BUCKET LIST. NEXT UP...THE TOOTH FAIRY AND SANTA.
CRIK
THOOM
YOU'RE GOING DOWN, BOMB BUNNY!
WHERE'S THE EXPLOSIVES?
WHAT?! I DON'T KNOW. I WAS JUST HIRED TO BE HERE TO ENTERTAIN THE KIDS.
FORGET IT. I'LL FIND IT MYSELF!
FIND WHAT?!
NOPE, NOT THIS ONE.
NO TICKING HERE, EITHER.

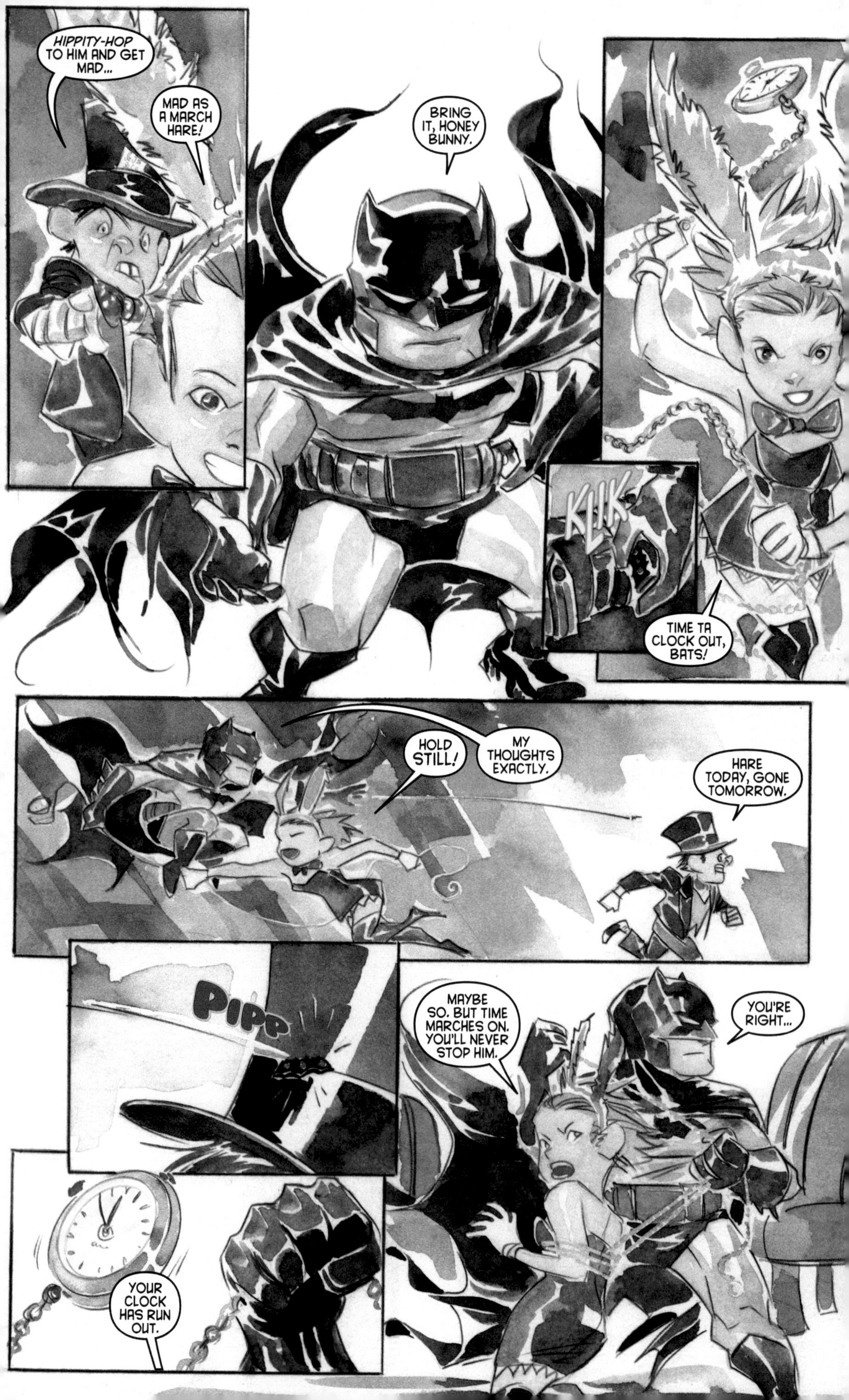
HIPPITY-HOP TO HIM AND GET MAD...
MAD AS A MARCH HARE!
BRING IT, HONEY BUNNY.
KLIK
TIME TA CLOCK OUT, BATS!
HOLD STILL!
MY THOUGHTS EXACTLY.
HARE TODAY, GONE TOMORROW.
PIPP
MAYBE SO. BUT TIME MARCHES ON. YOU'LL NEVER STOP HIM.
YOU'RE RIGHT...
YOUR CLOCK HAS RUN OUT.

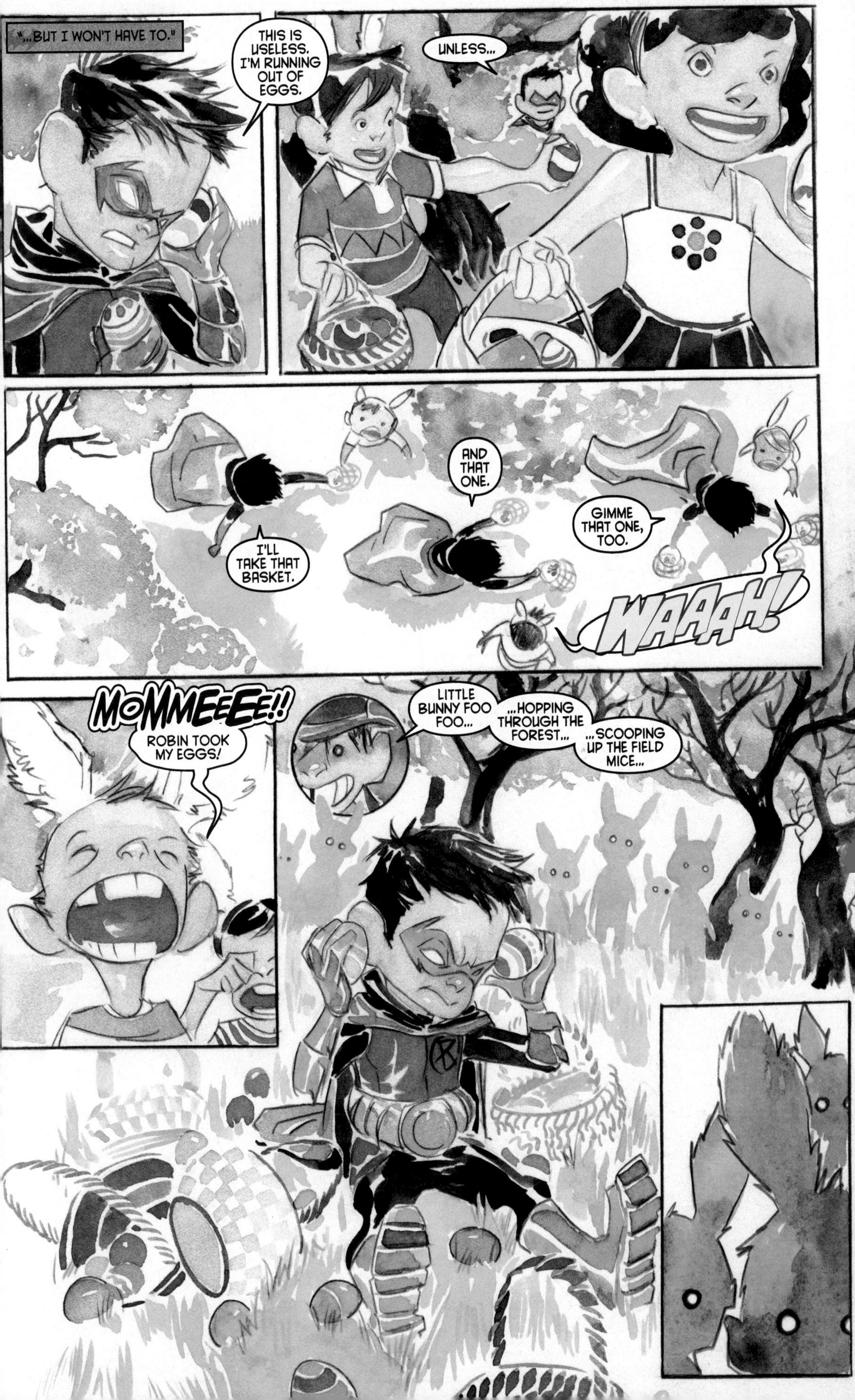
"...BUT I WON'T HAVE TO."
THIS IS USELESS. I'M RUNNING OUT OF EGGS.
UNLESS...
I'LL TAKE THAT BASKET.
AND THAT ONE.
GIMME THAT ONE, TOO.
WAAAH!
MOMMEEEEE!!
ROBIN TOOK MY EGGS!
LITTLE BUNNY FOO FOO...
...HOPPING THROUGH THE FOREST...
...SCOOPING UP THE FIELD MICE...

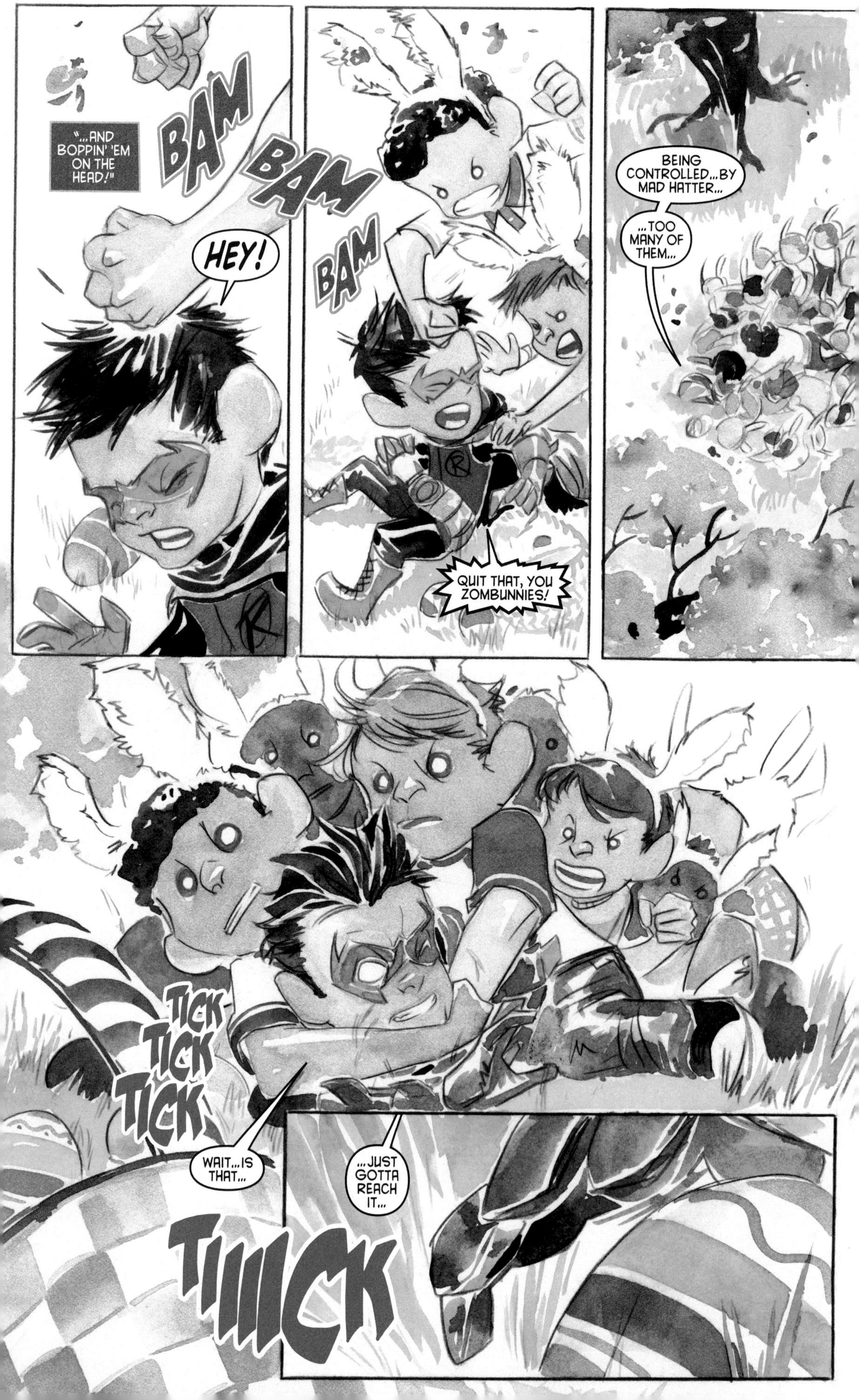
"...AND BOPPIN' 'EM ON THE HEAD!"
BAM
HEY!
BAM
BAM
BAM
QUIT THAT, YOU ZOMBUNNIES!
BEING CONTROLLED...BY MAD HATTER...
...TOO MANY OF THEM...
TICK
TICK
TICK
WAIT...IS THAT...
...JUST GOTTA REACH IT...
TIIIICK

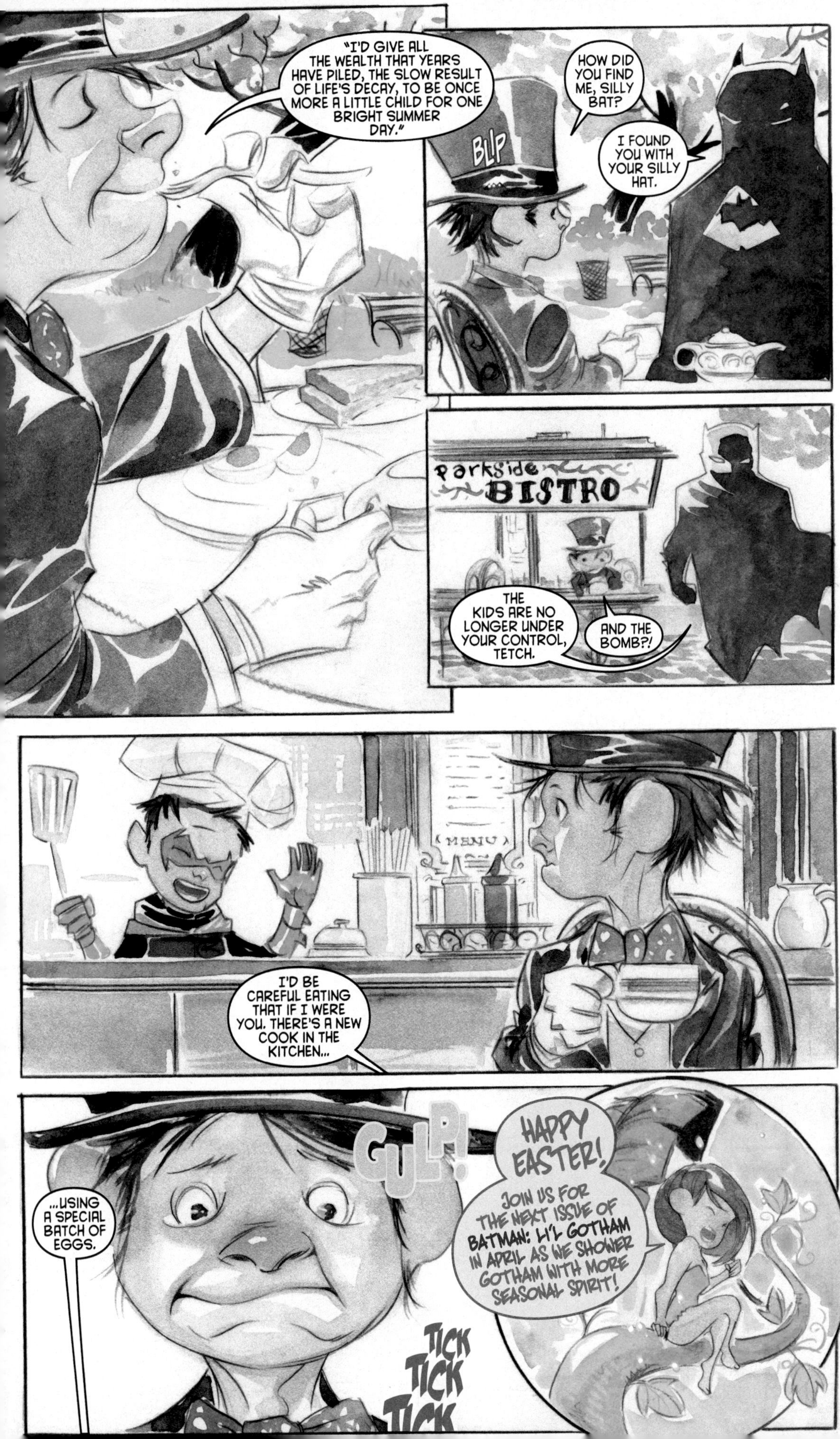
"I'D GIVE ALL THE WEALTH THAT YEARS HAVE PILED, THE SLOW RESULT OF LIFE'S DECAY, TO BE ONCE MORE A LITTLE CHILD FOR ONE BRIGHT SUMMER DAY."
BLIP
HOW DID YOU FIND ME, SILLY BAT?
I FOUND YOU WITH YOUR SILLY HAT.
Parkside BISTRO
THE KIDS ARE NO LONGER UNDER YOUR CONTROL, TETCH.
AND THE BOMB?!
MENU
I'D BE CAREFUL EATING THAT IF I WERE YOU. THERE'S A NEW COOK IN THE KITCHEN...
GULP!
...USING A SPECIAL BATCH OF EGGS.
HAPPY EASTER!
JOIN US FOR THE NEXT ISSUE OF BATMAN: LI'L GOTHAM IN APRIL AS WE SHOWER GOTHAM WITH MORE SEASONAL SPIRIT!
TICK
TICK
TICK

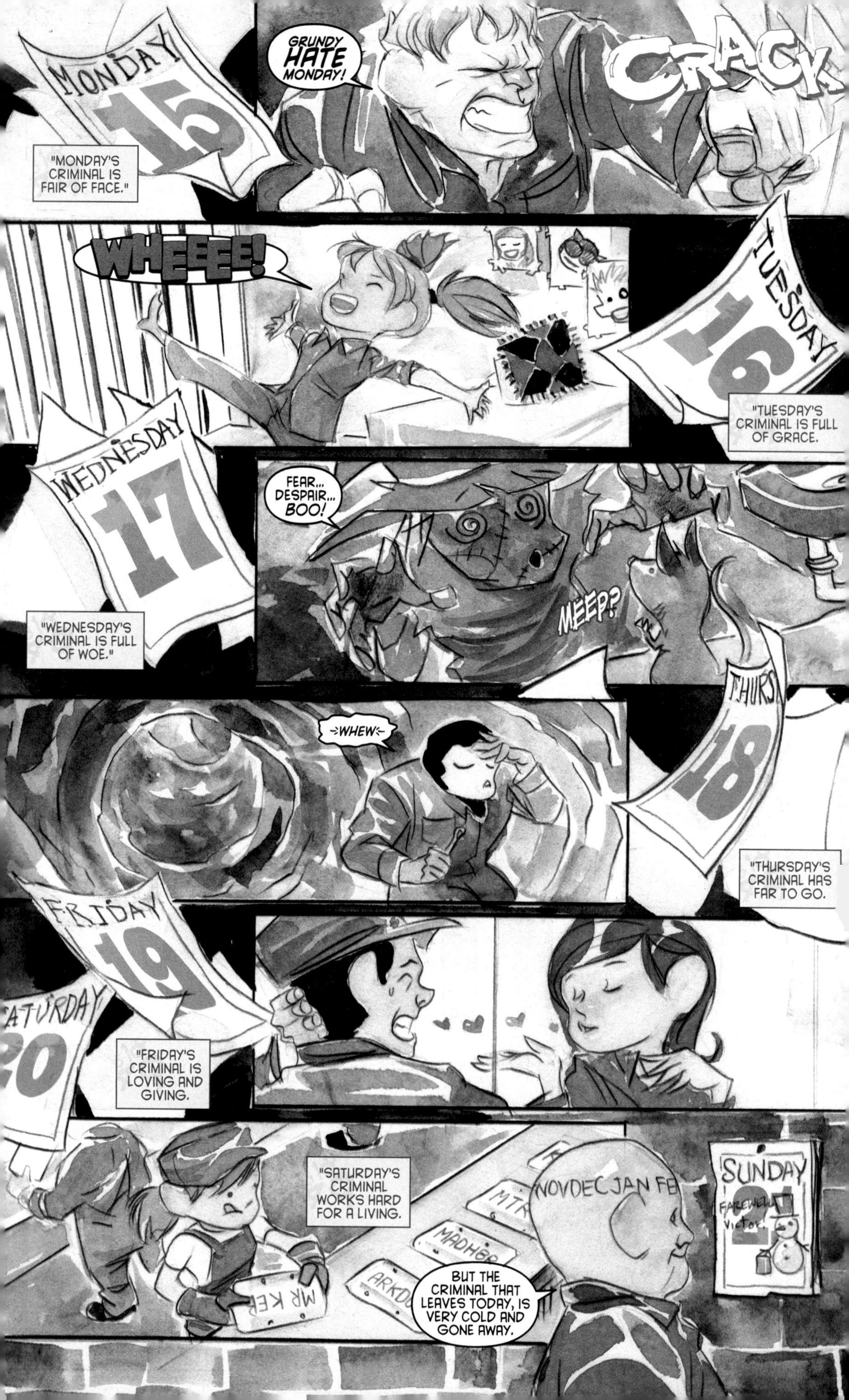
MONDAY
15
GRUNDY HATE MONDAY!
CRACK
"MONDAY'S CRIMINAL IS FAIR OF FACE."
WHEEEEE!
TUESDAY
16
"TUESDAY'S CRIMINAL IS FULL OF GRACE.
WEDNESDAY
17
FEAR... DESPAIR... BOO!
MEEP?
"WEDNESDAY'S CRIMINAL IS FULL OF WOE."
THURS
18
-WHEW-
"THURSDAY'S CRIMINAL HAS FAR TO GO.
FRIDAY
19
SATURDAY
20
"FRIDAY'S CRIMINAL IS LOVING AND GIVING.
"SATURDAY'S CRIMINAL WORKS HARD FOR A LIVING.
NOVDECJAN FE
SUNDAY
FAREWELL Victor
MTR
MADHO
ARKO
MR KE
BUT THE CRIMINAL THAT LEAVES TODAY, IS VERY COLD AND GONE AWAY.

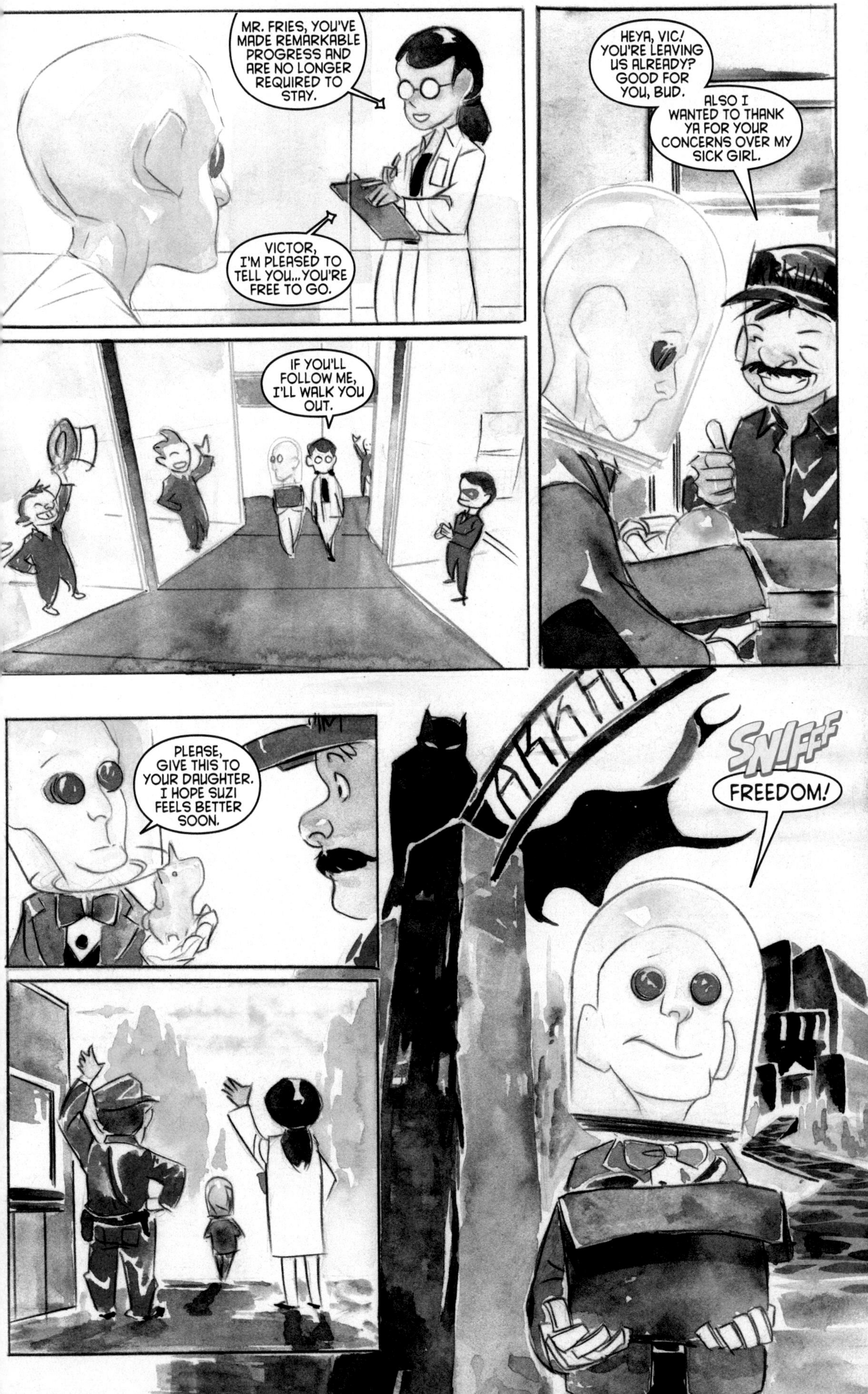
MR. FRIES, YOU'VE MADE REMARKABLE PROGRESS AND ARE NO LONGER REQUIRED TO STAY.
VICTOR, I'M PLEASED TO TELL YOU...YOU'RE FREE TO GO.
HEYA, VIC! YOU'RE LEAVING US ALREADY? GOOD FOR YOU, BUD.
ALSO I WANTED TO THANK YA FOR YOUR CONCERNS OVER MY SICK GIRL.
IF YOU'LL FOLLOW ME, I'LL WALK YOU OUT.
PLEASE, GIVE THIS TO YOUR DAUGHTER. I HOPE SUZI FEELS BETTER SOON.
SNIFFF
FREEDOM!

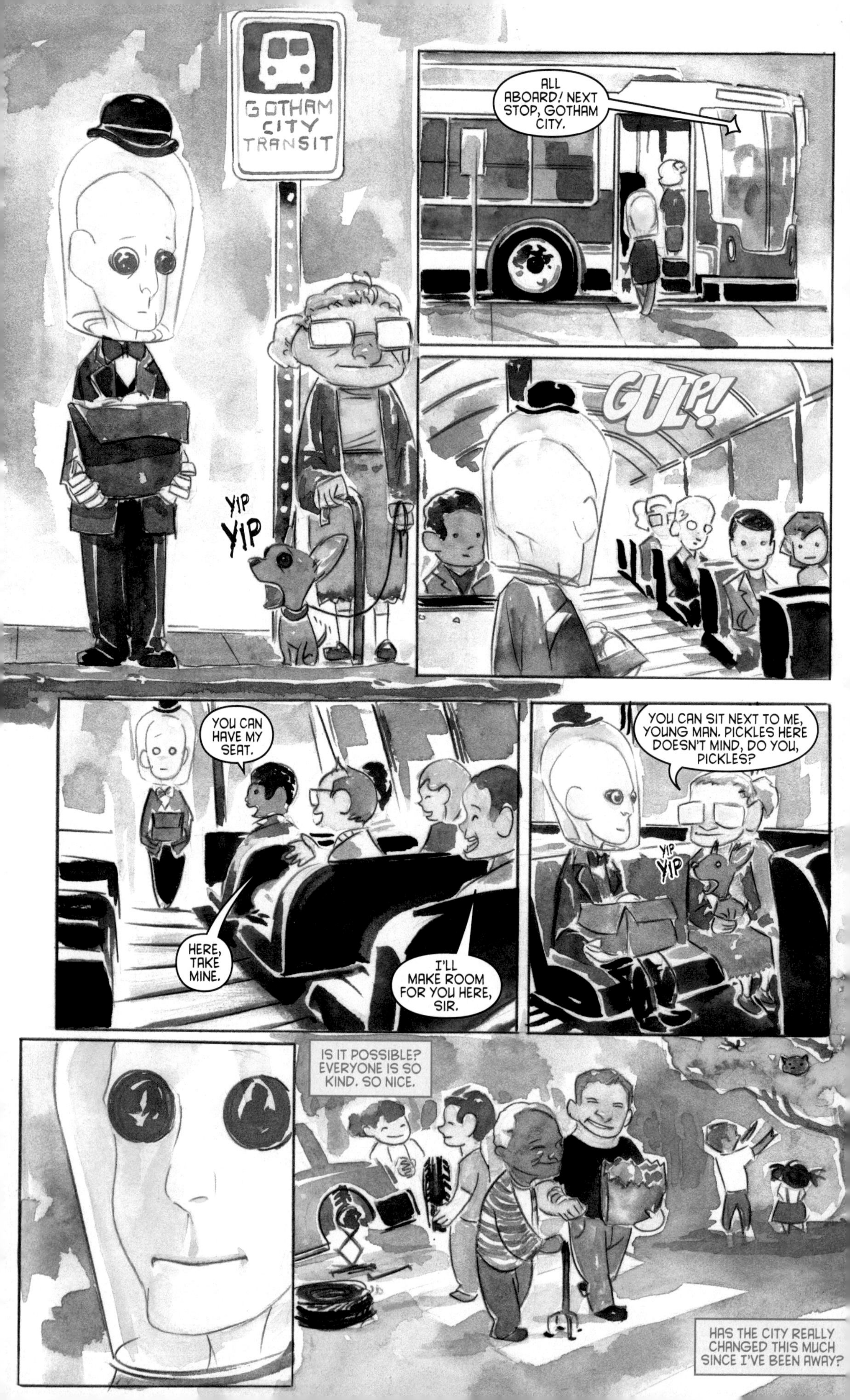
GOTHAM CITY TRANSIT
YIP YIP
ALL ABOARD! NEXT STOP, GOTHAM CITY.
GULP!
YOU CAN HAVE MY SEAT.
HERE, TAKE MINE.
I'LL MAKE ROOM FOR YOU HERE, SIR.
YOU CAN SIT NEXT TO ME, YOUNG MAN. PICKLES HERE DOESN'T MIND, DO YOU, PICKLES?
YIP YIP
IS IT POSSIBLE? EVERYONE IS SO KIND. SO NICE.
HAS THE CITY REALLY CHANGED THIS MUCH SINCE I'VE BEEN AWAY?

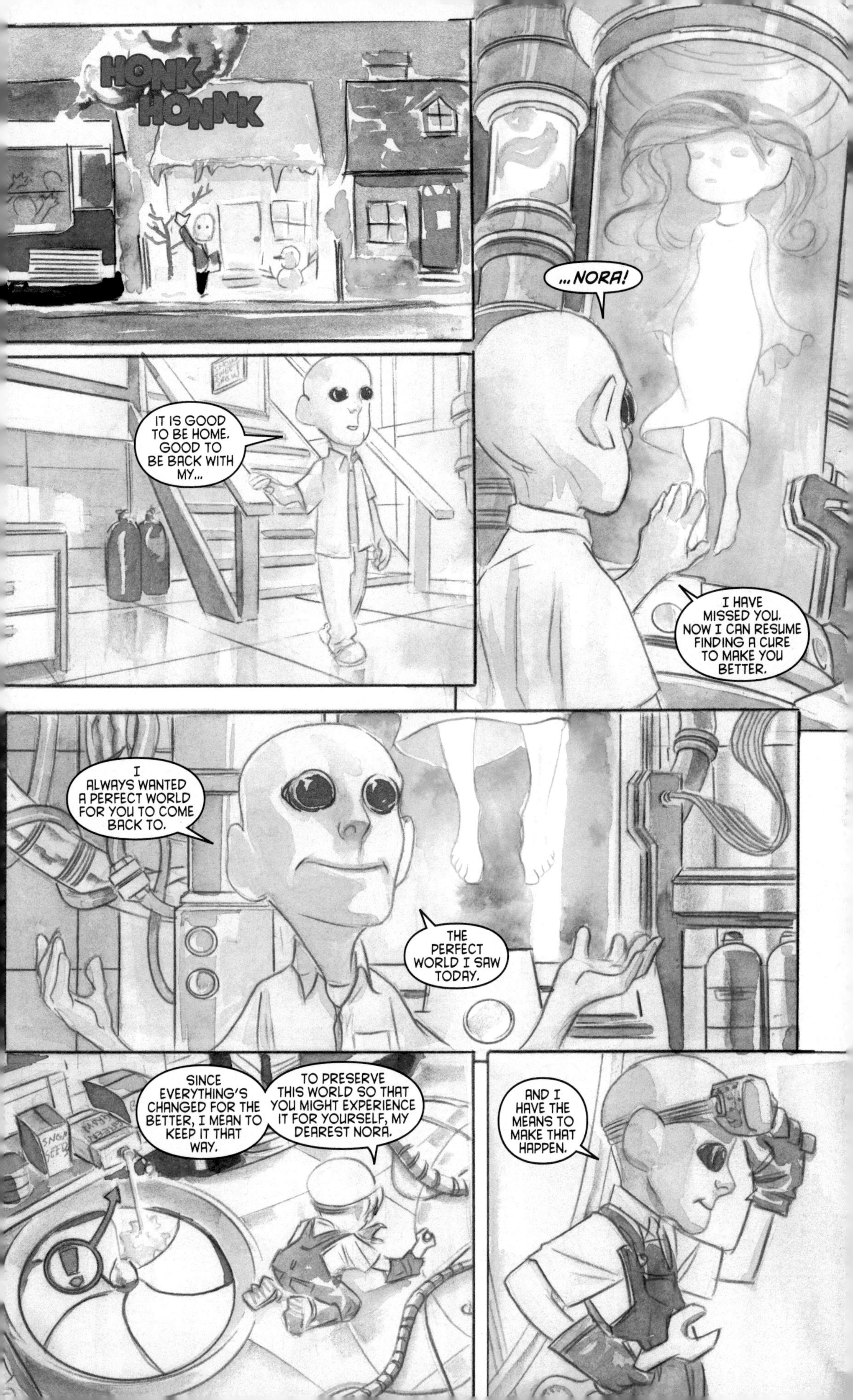
HONK
HONNK
IT IS GOOD TO BE HOME. GOOD TO BE BACK WITH MY...
...NORA!
I HAVE MISSED YOU. NOW I CAN RESUME FINDING A CURE TO MAKE YOU BETTER.
I ALWAYS WANTED A PERFECT WORLD FOR YOU TO COME BACK TO.
THE PERFECT WORLD I SAW TODAY.
SINCE EVERYTHING'S CHANGED FOR THE BETTER, I MEAN TO KEEP IT THAT WAY.
TO PRESERVE THIS WORLD SO THAT YOU MIGHT EXPERIENCE IT FOR YOURSELF, MY DEAREST NORA.
AND I HAVE THE MEANS TO MAKE THAT HAPPEN.

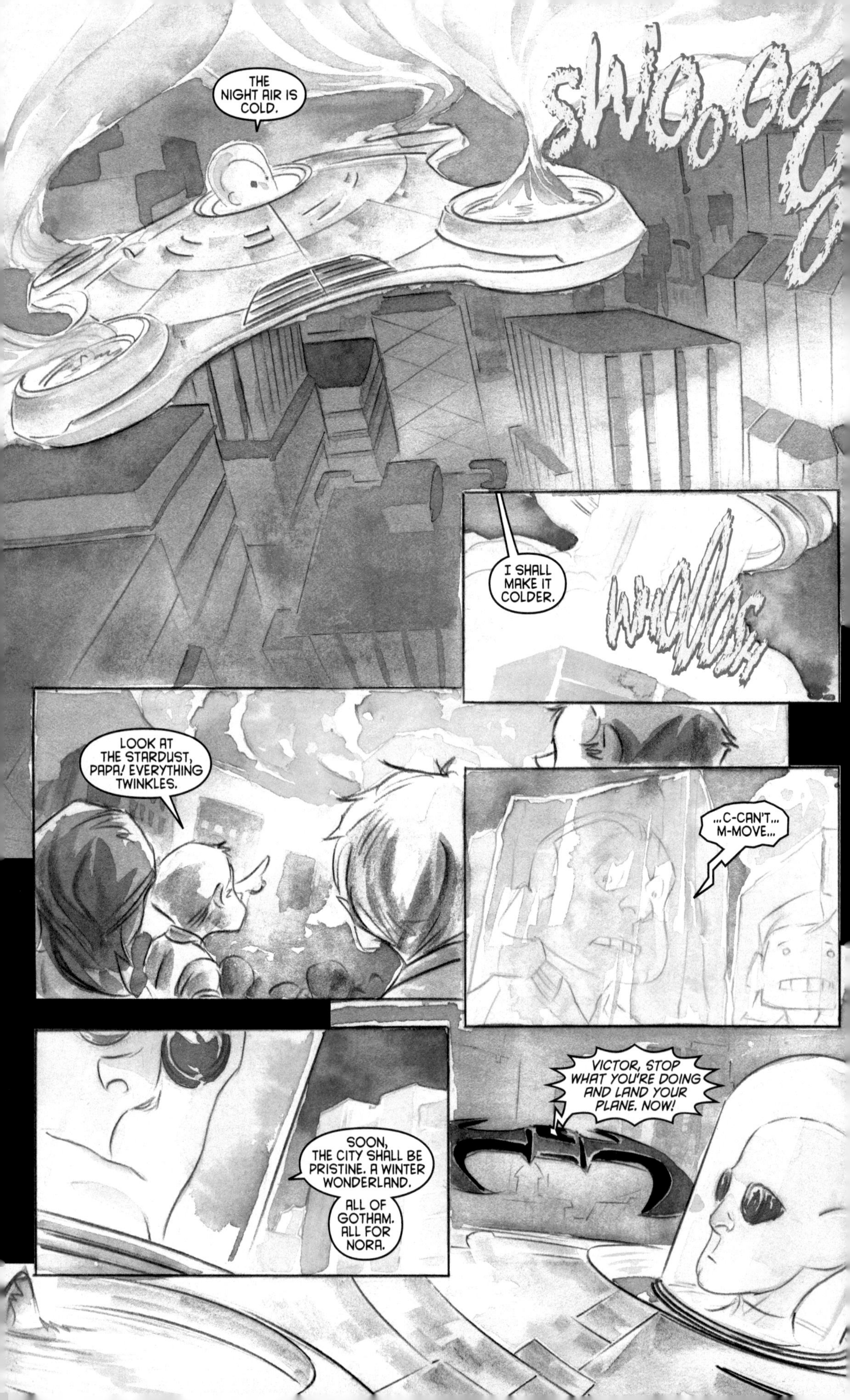
THE NIGHT AIR IS COLD.
SHWOOOOG
I SHALL MAKE IT COLDER.
WHOOSH
LOOK AT THE STARDUST, PAPA! EVERYTHING TWINKLES.
...C-CAN'T... M-MOVE...
SOON, THE CITY SHALL BE PRISTINE. A WINTER WONDERLAND.
ALL OF GOTHAM. ALL FOR NORA.
VICTOR, STOP WHAT YOU'RE DOING AND LAND YOUR PLANE. NOW!

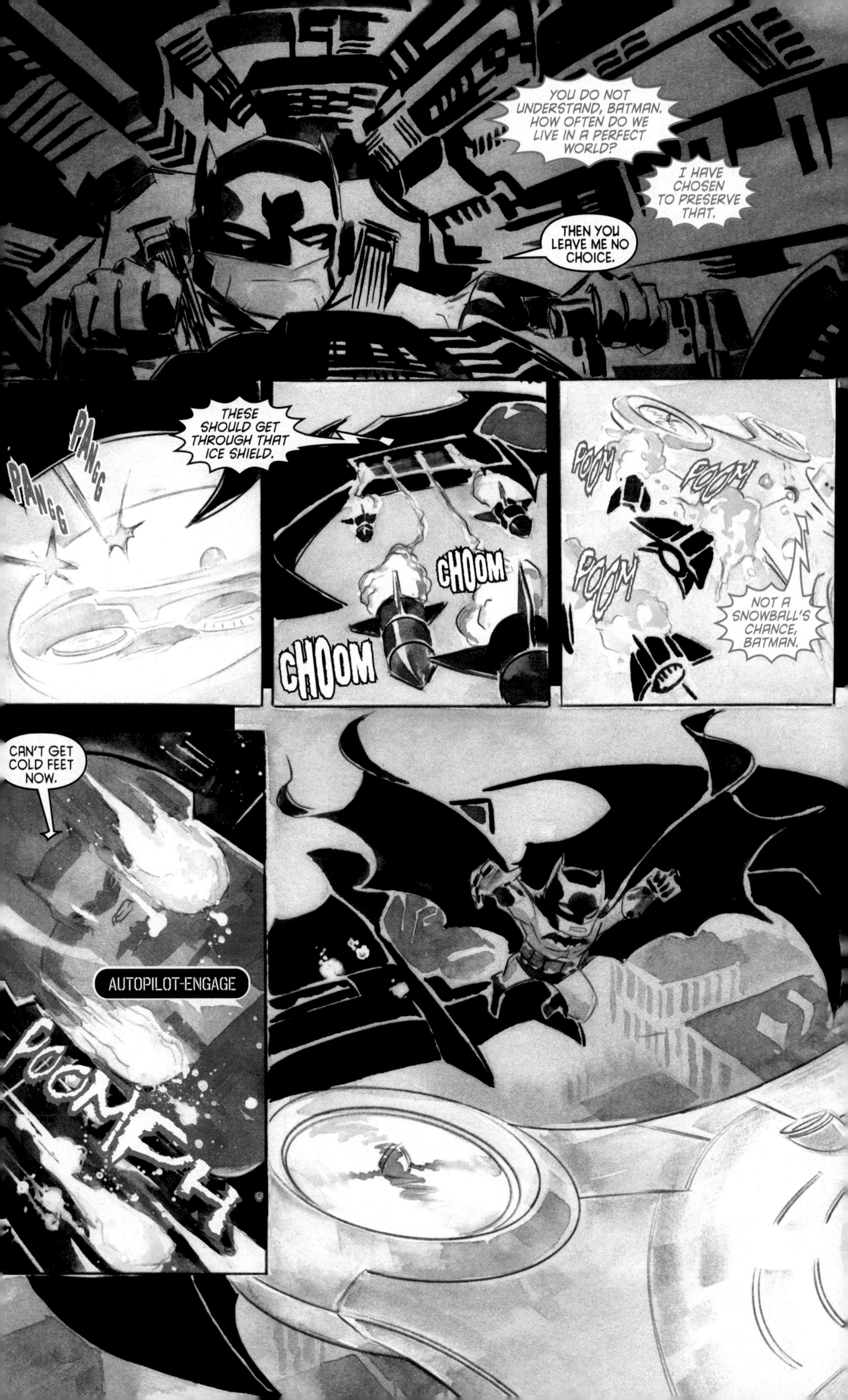
YOU DO NOT UNDERSTAND, BATMAN. HOW OFTEN DO WE LIVE IN A PERFECT WORLD?
I HAVE CHOSEN TO PRESERVE THAT.
THEN YOU LEAVE ME NO CHOICE.
PANGG
PANGG
THESE SHOULD GET THROUGH THAT ICE SHIELD.
CHOOM
CHOOM
POOM
POOM
POOM
NOT A SNOWBALL'S CHANCE, BATMAN.
CAN'T GET COLD FEET NOW.
AUTOPILOT-ENGAGE
POOMFF

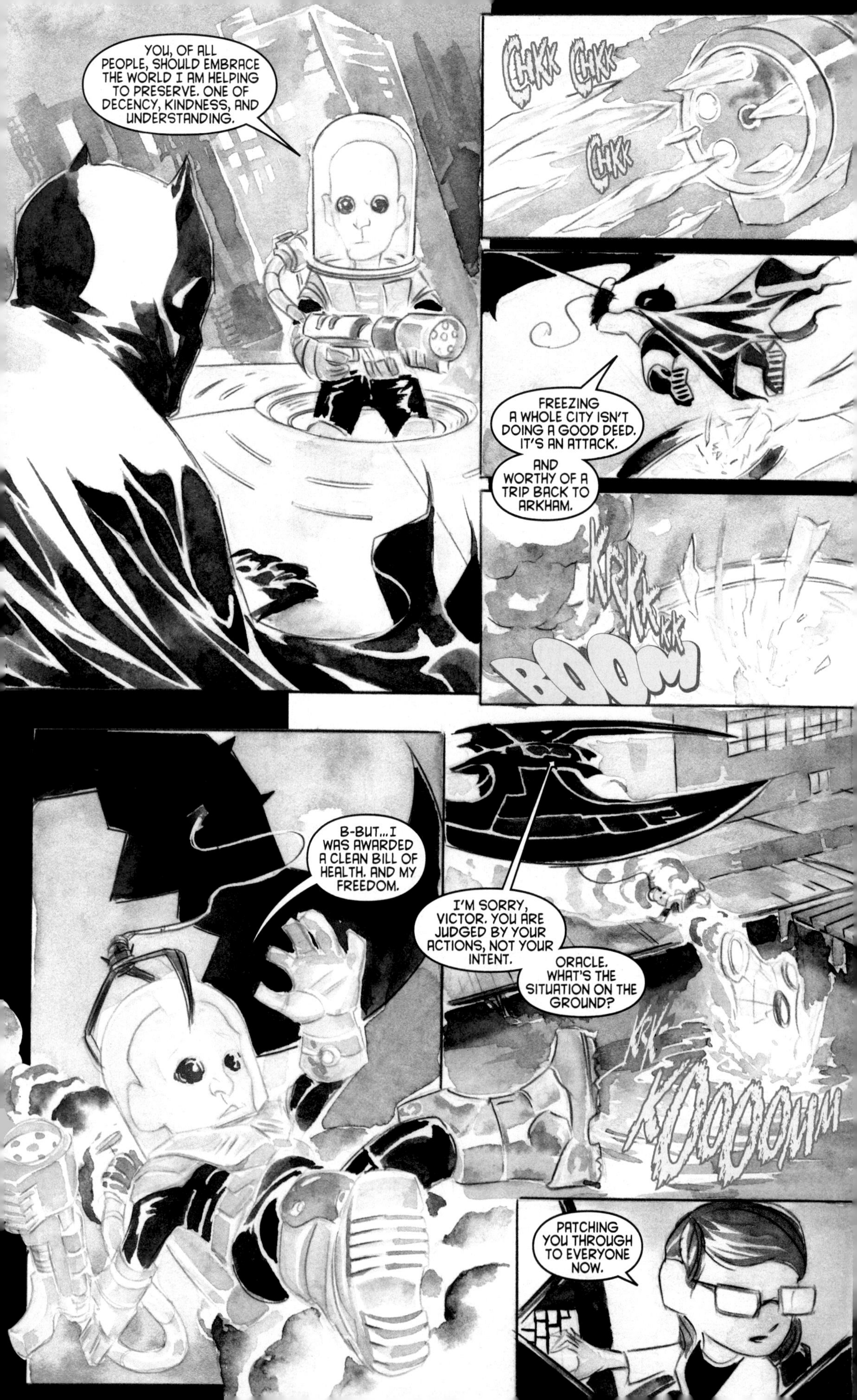
YOU, OF ALL PEOPLE, SHOULD EMBRACE THE WORLD I AM HELPING TO PRESERVE. ONE OF DECENCY, KINDNESS, AND UNDERSTANDING.
CHKK CHKK
CHKK
FREEZING A WHOLE CITY ISN'T DOING A GOOD DEED. IT'S AN ATTACK.
AND WORTHY OF A TRIP BACK TO ARKHAM.
KRKKKK
BOOM
B-BUT...I WAS AWARDED A CLEAN BILL OF HEALTH. AND MY FREEDOM.
I'M SORRY, VICTOR. YOU ARE JUDGED BY YOUR ACTIONS, NOT YOUR INTENT.
ORACLE. WHAT'S THE SITUATION ON THE GROUND?
KOOOOMM
PATCHING YOU THROUGH TO EVERYONE NOW.

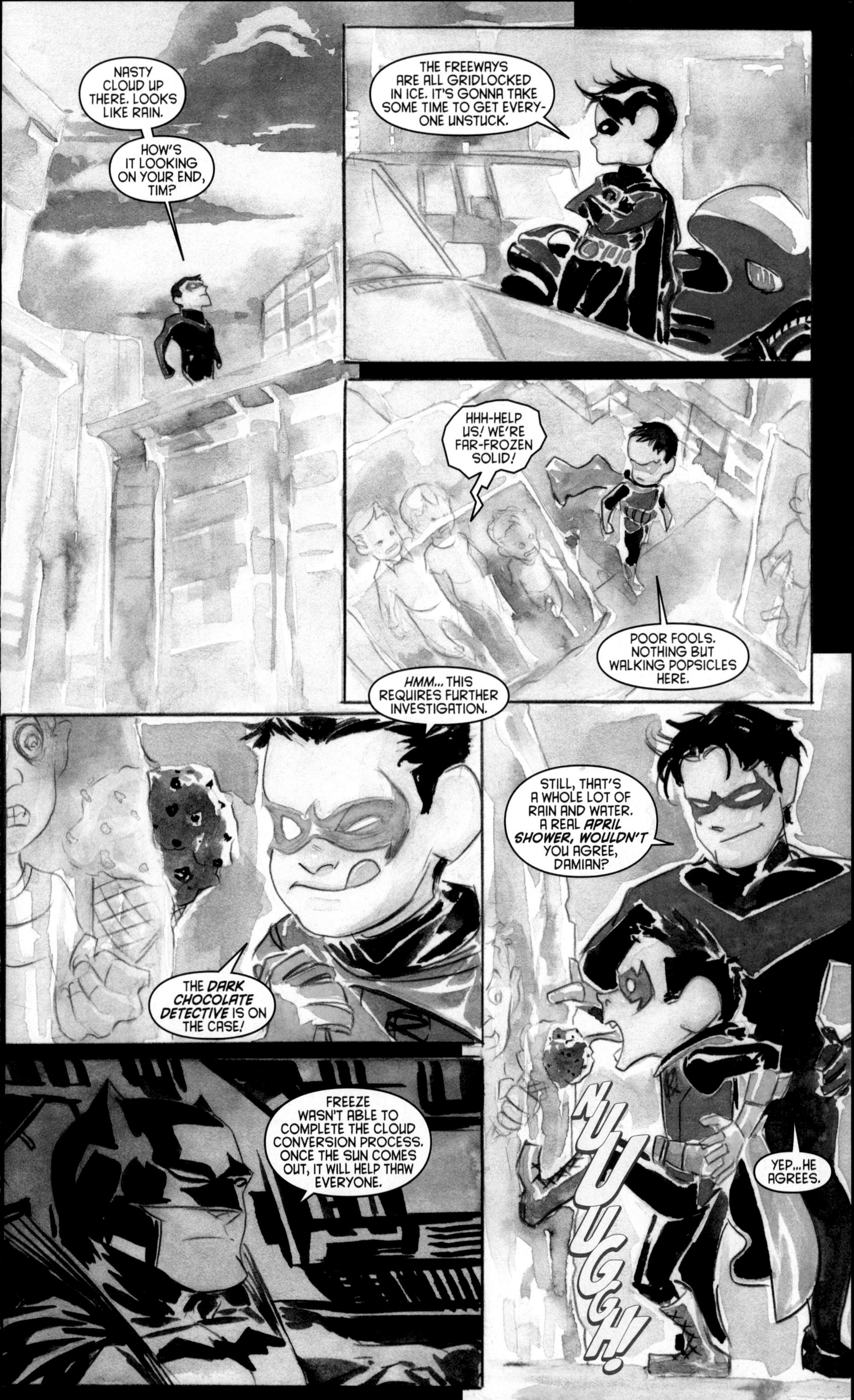
NASTY CLOUD UP THERE. LOOKS LIKE RAIN.
HOW'S IT LOOKING ON YOUR END, TIM?
THE FREEWAYS ARE ALL GRIDLOCKED IN ICE. IT'S GONNA TAKE SOME TIME TO GET EVERY-ONE UNSTUCK.
HHH-HELP US! WE'RE FAR-FROZEN SOLID!
POOR FOOLS. NOTHING BUT WALKING POPSICLES HERE.
HMM... THIS REQUIRES FURTHER INVESTIGATION.
THE DARK CHOCOLATE DETECTIVE IS ON THE CASE!
FREEZE WASN'T ABLE TO COMPLETE THE CLOUD CONVERSION PROCESS. ONCE THE SUN COMES OUT, IT WILL HELP THAW EVERYONE.
STILL, THAT'S A WHOLE LOT OF RAIN AND WATER. A REAL APRIL SHOWER, WOULDN'T YOU AGREE, DAMIAN?
NUUUUGGH!
YEP... HE AGREES.

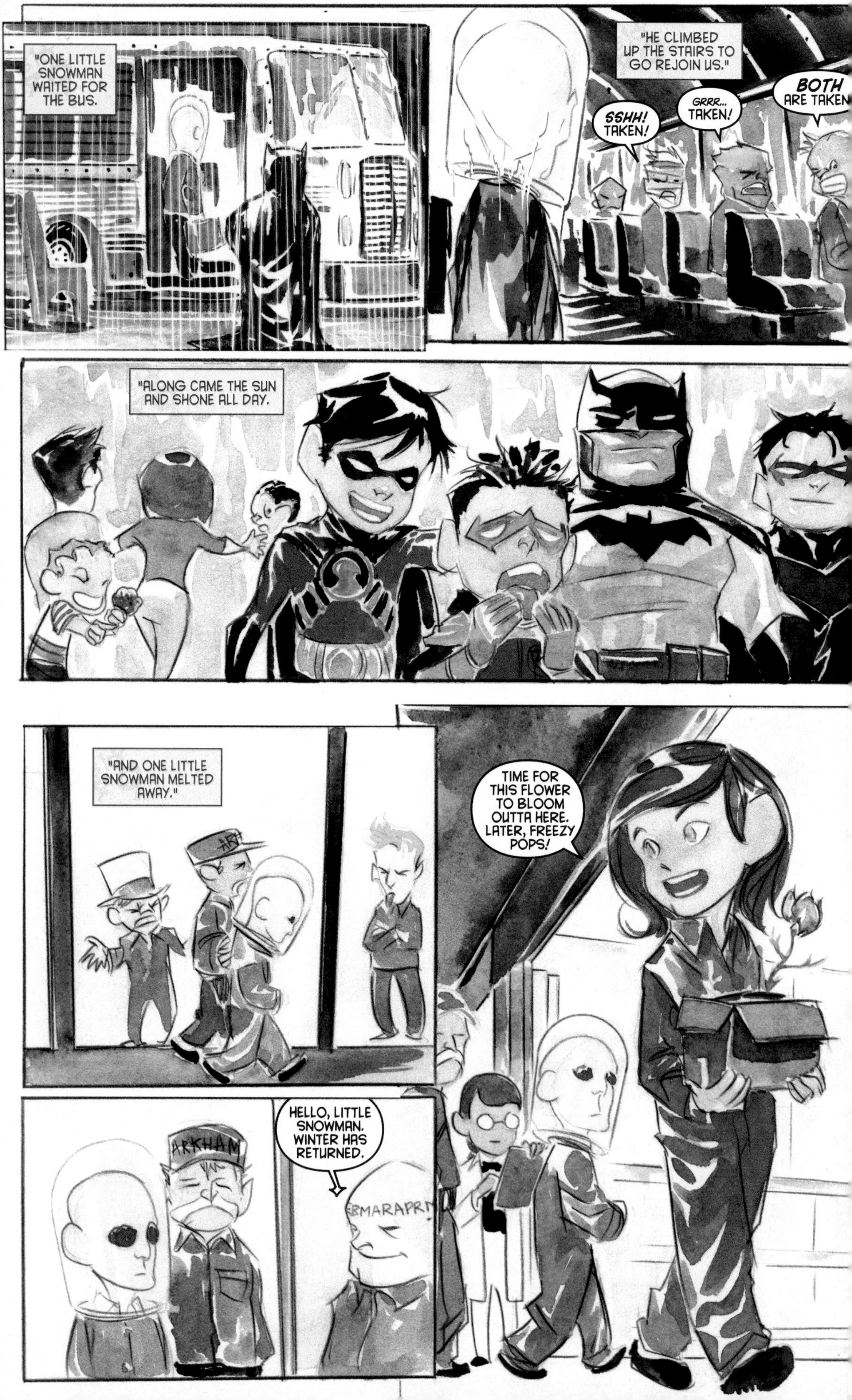
"ONE LITTLE SNOWMAN WAITED FOR THE BUS.
"HE CLIMBED UP THE STAIRS TO GO REJOIN US."
SSHH! TAKEN!
GRRR... TAKEN!
BOTH ARE TAKEN
"ALONG CAME THE SUN AND SHONE ALL DAY.
"AND ONE LITTLE SNOWMAN MELTED AWAY."
TIME FOR THIS FLOWER TO BLOOM OUTTA HERE. LATER, FREEZY POPS!
ARKHAM
HELLO, LITTLE SNOWMAN. WINTER HAS RETURNED.

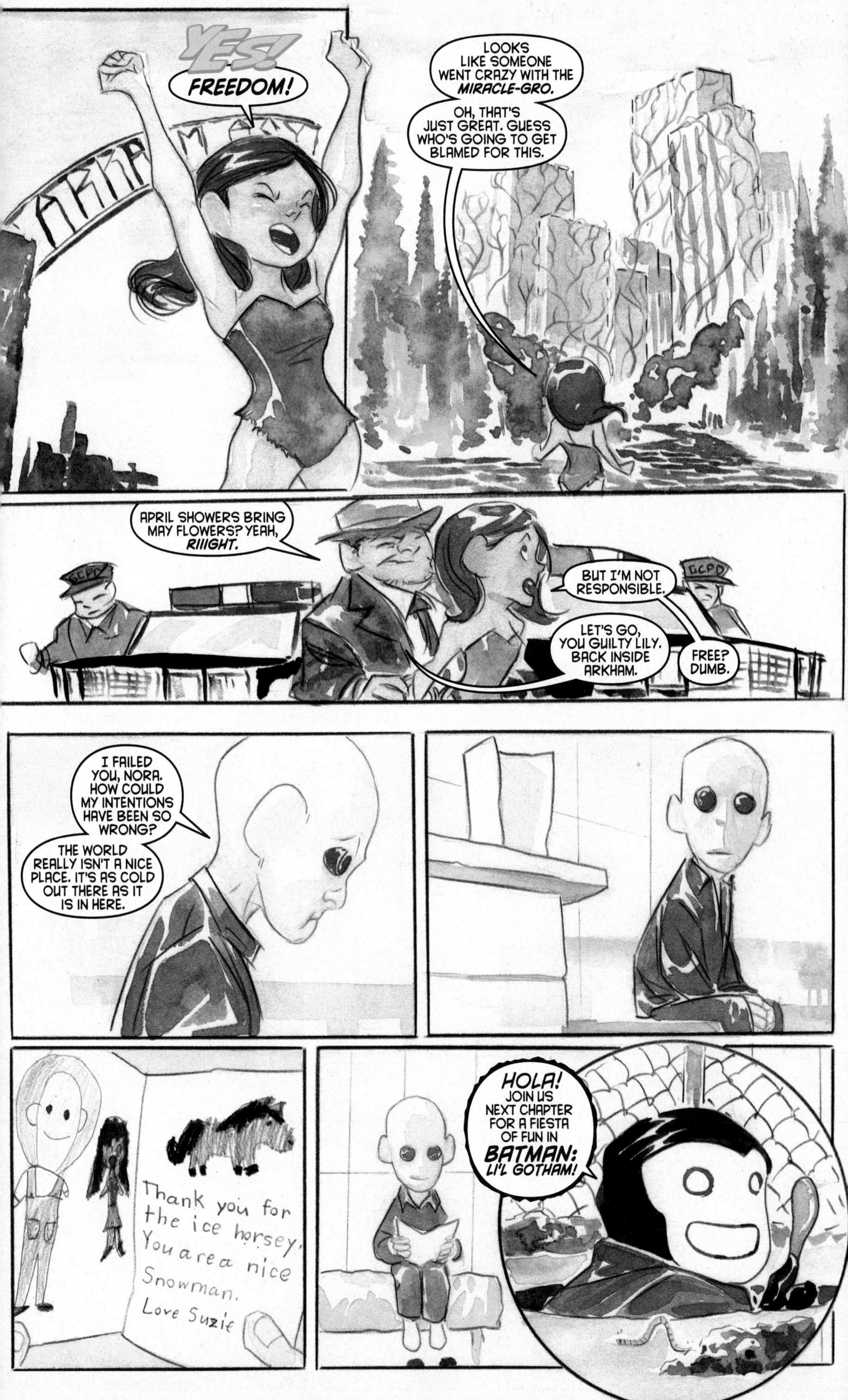
YES!
FREEDOM!
ARKHAM ASYLUM
LOOKS LIKE SOMEONE WENT CRAZY WITH THE MIRACLE-GRO.
OH, THAT'S JUST GREAT. GUESS WHO'S GOING TO GET BLAMED FOR THIS.
APRIL SHOWERS BRING MAY FLOWERS? YEAH, RIIIGHT.
BUT I'M NOT RESPONSIBLE.
LET'S GO, YOU GUILTY LILY. BACK INSIDE ARKHAM.
FREE? DUMB.
GCPD
I FAILED YOU, NORA. HOW COULD MY INTENTIONS HAVE BEEN SO WRONG?
THE WORLD REALLY ISN'T A NICE PLACE. IT'S AS COLD OUT THERE AS IT IS IN HERE.
Thank you for the ice horsey. You are a nice Snowman. Love Suzie
HOLA! JOIN US NEXT CHAPTER FOR A FIESTA OF FUN IN BATMAN: LI'L GOTHAM!

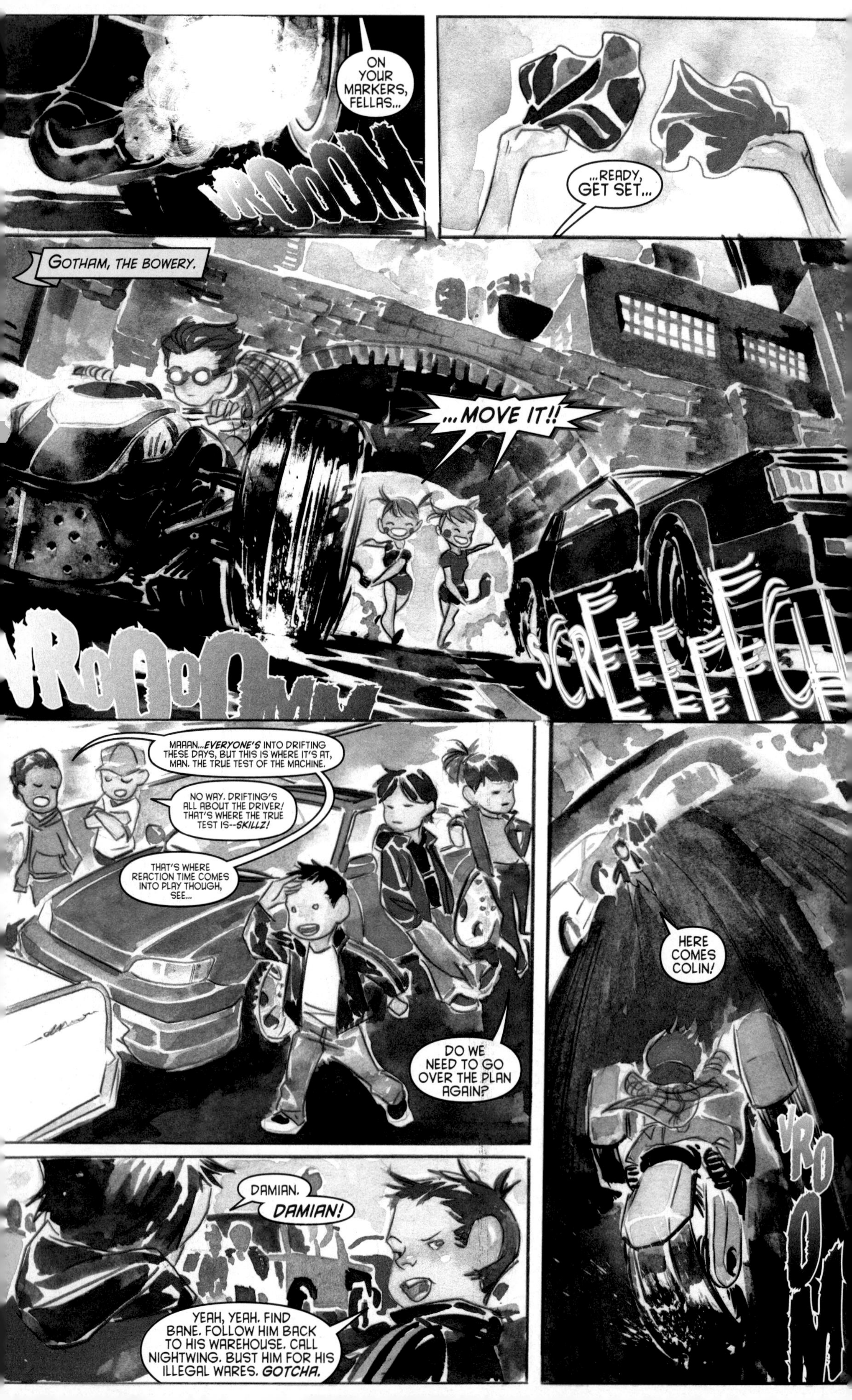
ON YOUR MARKERS, FELLAS...
VROOOM
...READY, GET SET...
GOTHAM, THE BOWERY.
...MOVE IT!!
VROOOOMM
SCREEEEECH
MAAAN...EVERYONE'S INTO DRIFTING THESE DAYS, BUT THIS IS WHERE IT'S AT, MAN. THE TRUE TEST OF THE MACHINE.
NO WAY. DRIFTING'S ALL ABOUT THE DRIVER! THAT'S WHERE THE TRUE TEST IS--SKILLZ!
THAT'S WHERE REACTION TIME COMES INTO PLAY THOUGH, SEE...
DO WE NEED TO GO OVER THE PLAN AGAIN?
HERE COMES COLIN!
DAMIAN.
DAMIAN!
YEAH, YEAH. FIND BANE. FOLLOW HIM BACK TO HIS WAREHOUSE. CALL NIGHTWING. BUST HIM FOR HIS ILLEGAL WARES. GOTCHA.

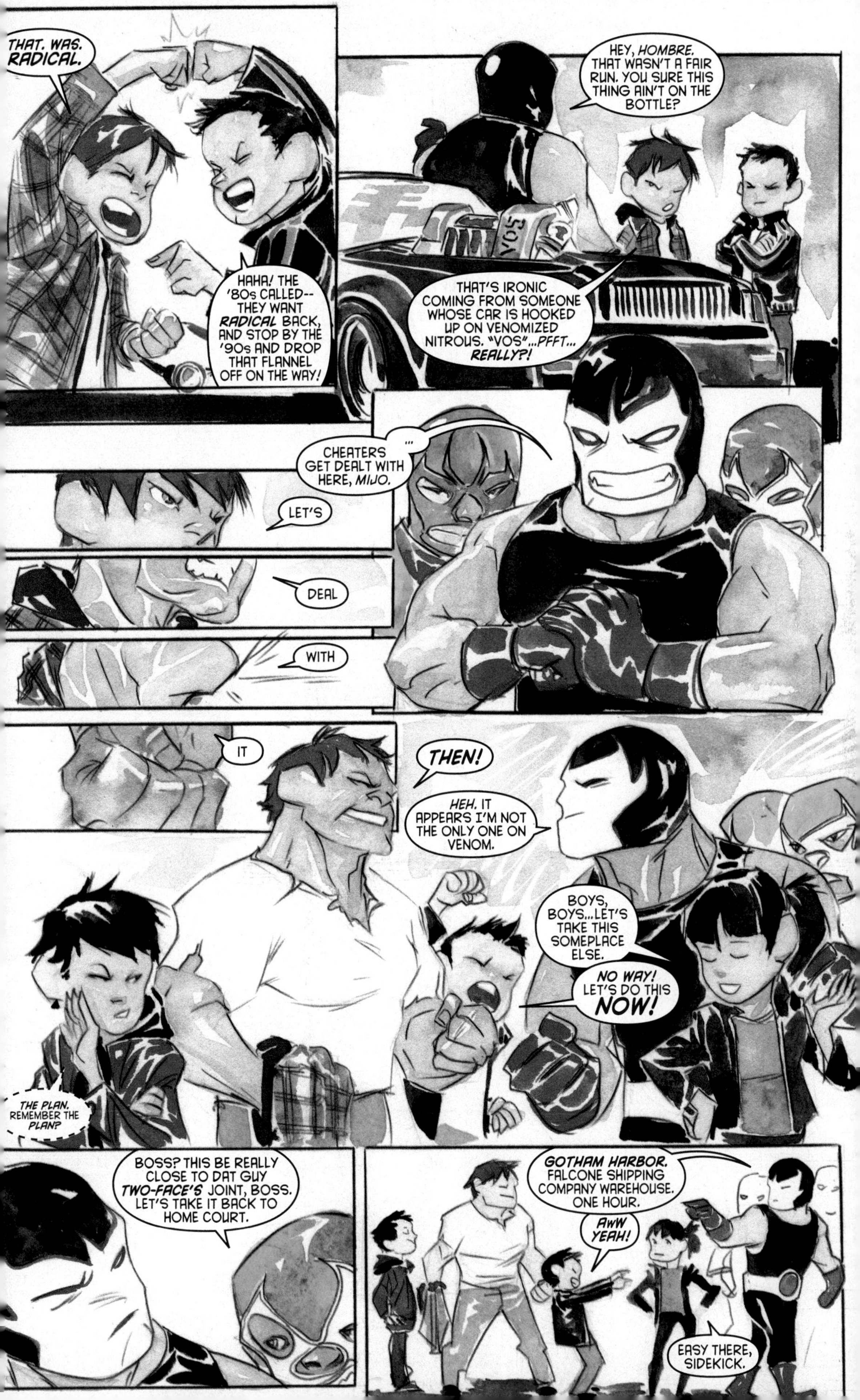
THAT. WAS. RADICAL.
HAHA! THE '80s CALLED-- THEY WANT RADICAL BACK, AND STOP BY THE '90s AND DROP THAT FLANNEL OFF ON THE WAY!
HEY, HOMBRE. THAT WASN'T A FAIR RUN. YOU SURE THIS THING AIN'T ON THE BOTTLE?
THAT'S IRONIC COMING FROM SOMEONE WHOSE CAR IS HOOKED UP ON VENOMIZED NITROUS. "VOS"...PFFT... REALLY?!
VOS
CHEATERS GET DEALT WITH HERE, MIJO.
LET'S
DEAL
WITH
IT
THEN!
HEH. IT APPEARS I'M NOT THE ONLY ONE ON VENOM.
BOYS, BOYS...LET'S TAKE THIS SOMEPLACE ELSE.
NO WAY! LET'S DO THIS NOW!
THE PLAN. REMEMBER THE PLAN?
BOSS? THIS BE REALLY CLOSE TO DAT GUY TWO-FACE'S JOINT, BOSS. LET'S TAKE IT BACK TO HOME COURT.
GOTHAM HARBOR. FALCONE SHIPPING COMPANY WAREHOUSE. ONE HOUR.
AWW YEAH!
EASY THERE, SIDEKICK.

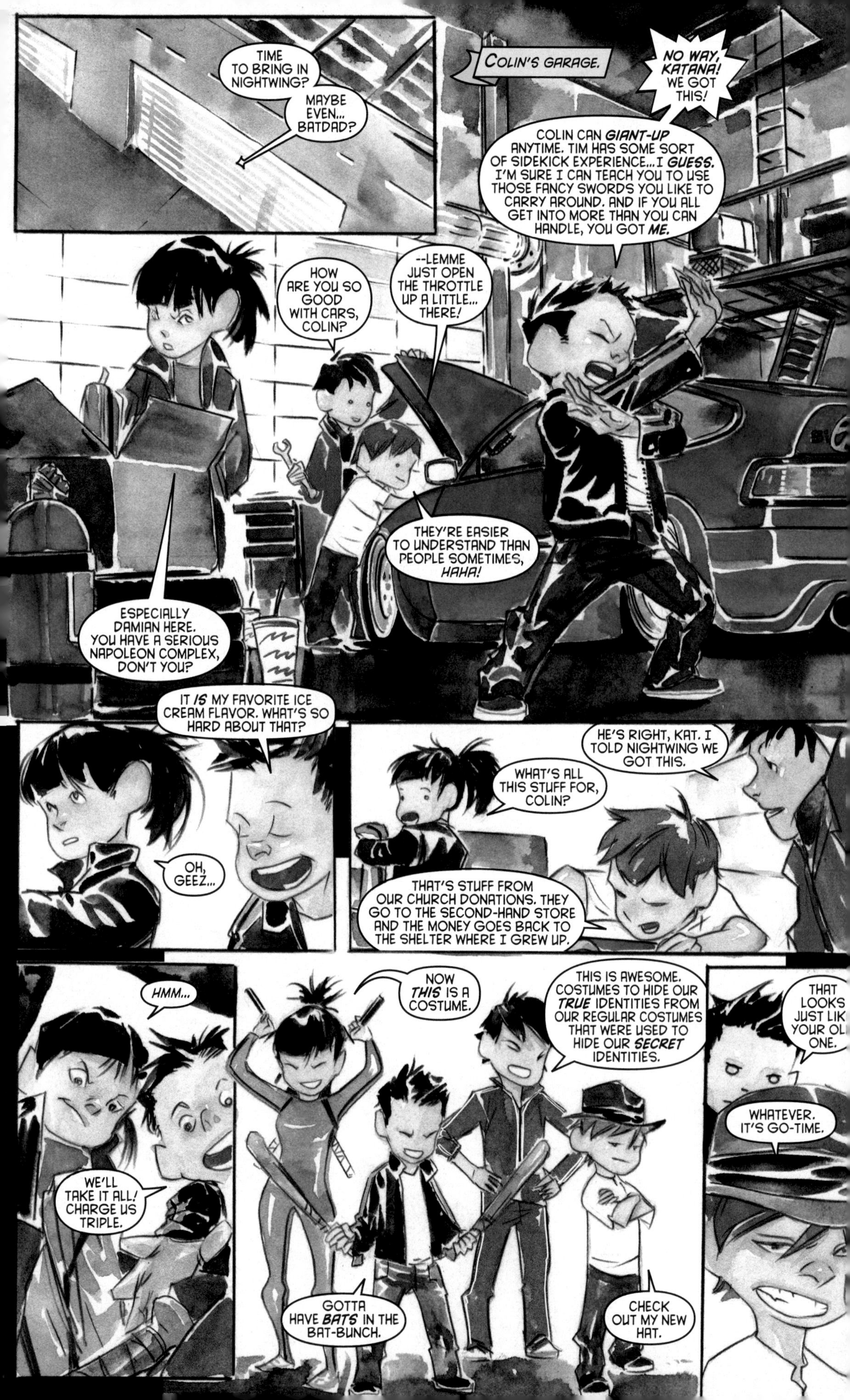

TIME TO BRING IN NIGHTWING?
MAYBE EVEN... BATDAD?
COLIN'S GARAGE.
NO WAY, KATANA! WE GOT THIS!
COLIN CAN GIANT-UP ANYTIME. TIM HAS SOME SORT OF SIDEKICK EXPERIENCE... I GUESS. I'M SURE I CAN TEACH YOU TO USE THOSE FANCY SWORDS YOU LIKE TO CARRY AROUND. AND IF YOU ALL GET INTO MORE THAN YOU CAN HANDLE, YOU GOT ME.
HOW ARE YOU SO GOOD WITH CARS, COLIN?
--LEMME JUST OPEN THE THROTTLE UP A LITTLE... THERE!
THEY'RE EASIER TO UNDERSTAND THAN PEOPLE SOMETIMES, HAHA!
ESPECIALLY DAMIAN HERE. YOU HAVE A SERIOUS NAPOLEON COMPLEX, DON'T YOU?
IT IS MY FAVORITE ICE CREAM FLAVOR. WHAT'S SO HARD ABOUT THAT?
OH, GEEZ...
WHAT'S ALL THIS STUFF FOR, COLIN?
HE'S RIGHT, KAT. I TOLD NIGHTWING WE GOT THIS.
THAT'S STUFF FROM OUR CHURCH DONATIONS. THEY GO TO THE SECOND-HAND STORE AND THE MONEY GOES BACK TO THE SHELTER WHERE I GREW UP.
HMM...
WE'LL TAKE IT ALL! CHARGE US TRIPLE.
NOW THIS IS A COSTUME.
THIS IS AWESOME. COSTUMES TO HIDE OUR TRUE IDENTITIES FROM OUR REGULAR COSTUMES THAT WERE USED TO HIDE OUR SECRET IDENTITIES.
GOTTA HAVE BATS IN THE BAT-BUNCH.
CHECK OUT MY NEW HAT.
THAT LOOKS JUST LIK YOUR OL ONE.
WHATEVER. IT'S GO-TIME.

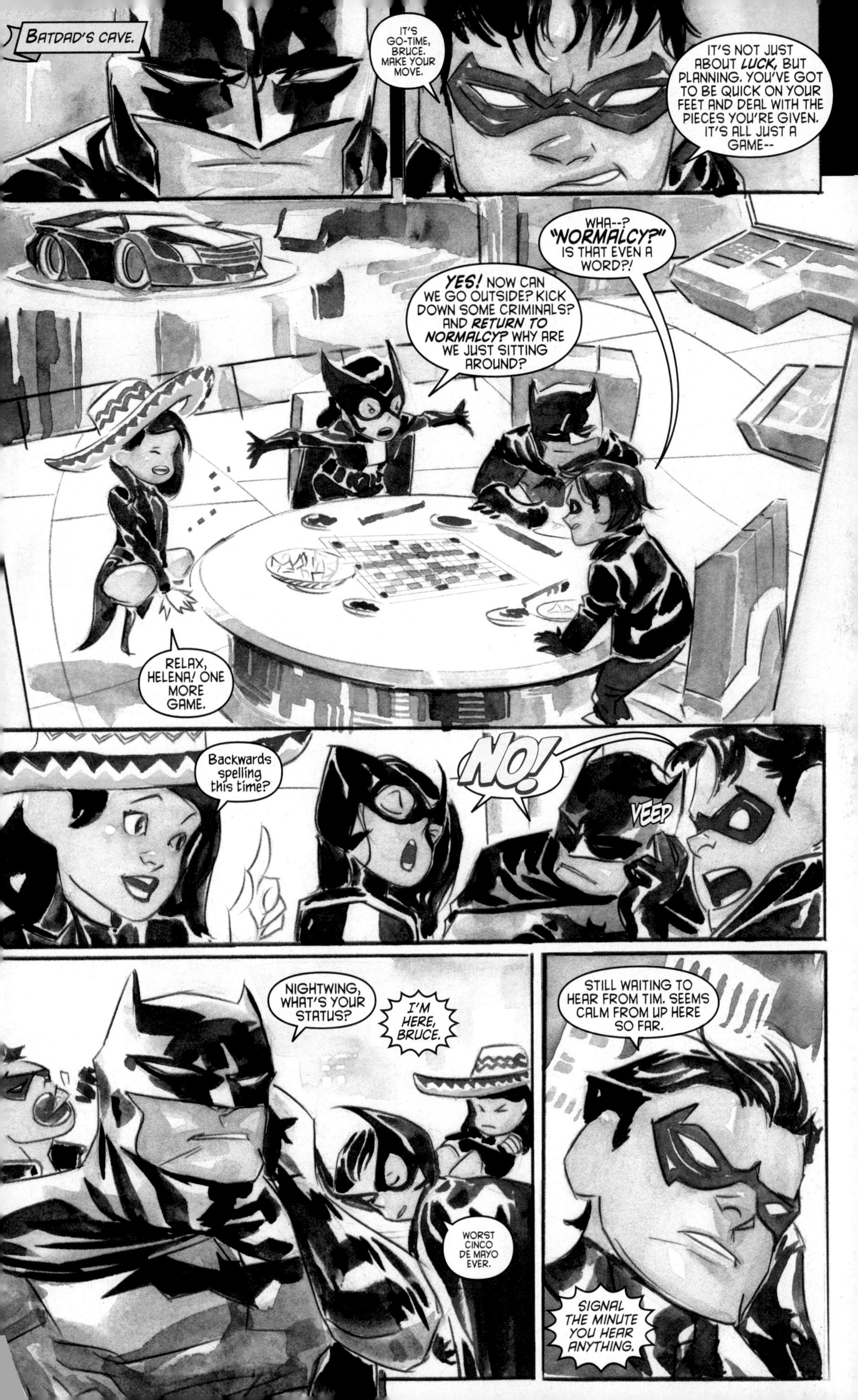
BATDAD'S CAVE.
IT'S GO-TIME, BRUCE. MAKE YOUR MOVE.
IT'S NOT JUST ABOUT LUCK, BUT PLANNING. YOU'VE GOT TO BE QUICK ON YOUR FEET AND DEAL WITH THE PIECES YOU'RE GIVEN. IT'S ALL JUST A GAME--
YES! NOW CAN WE GO OUTSIDE? KICK DOWN SOME CRIMINALS? AND RETURN TO NORMALCY? WHY ARE WE JUST SITTING AROUND?
WHA--? "NORMALCY?" IS THAT EVEN A WORD?!
RELAX, HELENA! ONE MORE GAME.
Backwards spelling this time?
NO!
VEEP
NIGHTWING, WHAT'S YOUR STATUS?
I'M HERE, BRUCE.
WORST CINCO DE MAYO EVER.
STILL WAITING TO HEAR FROM TIM. SEEMS CALM FROM UP HERE SO FAR.
SIGNAL THE MINUTE YOU HEAR ANYTHING.

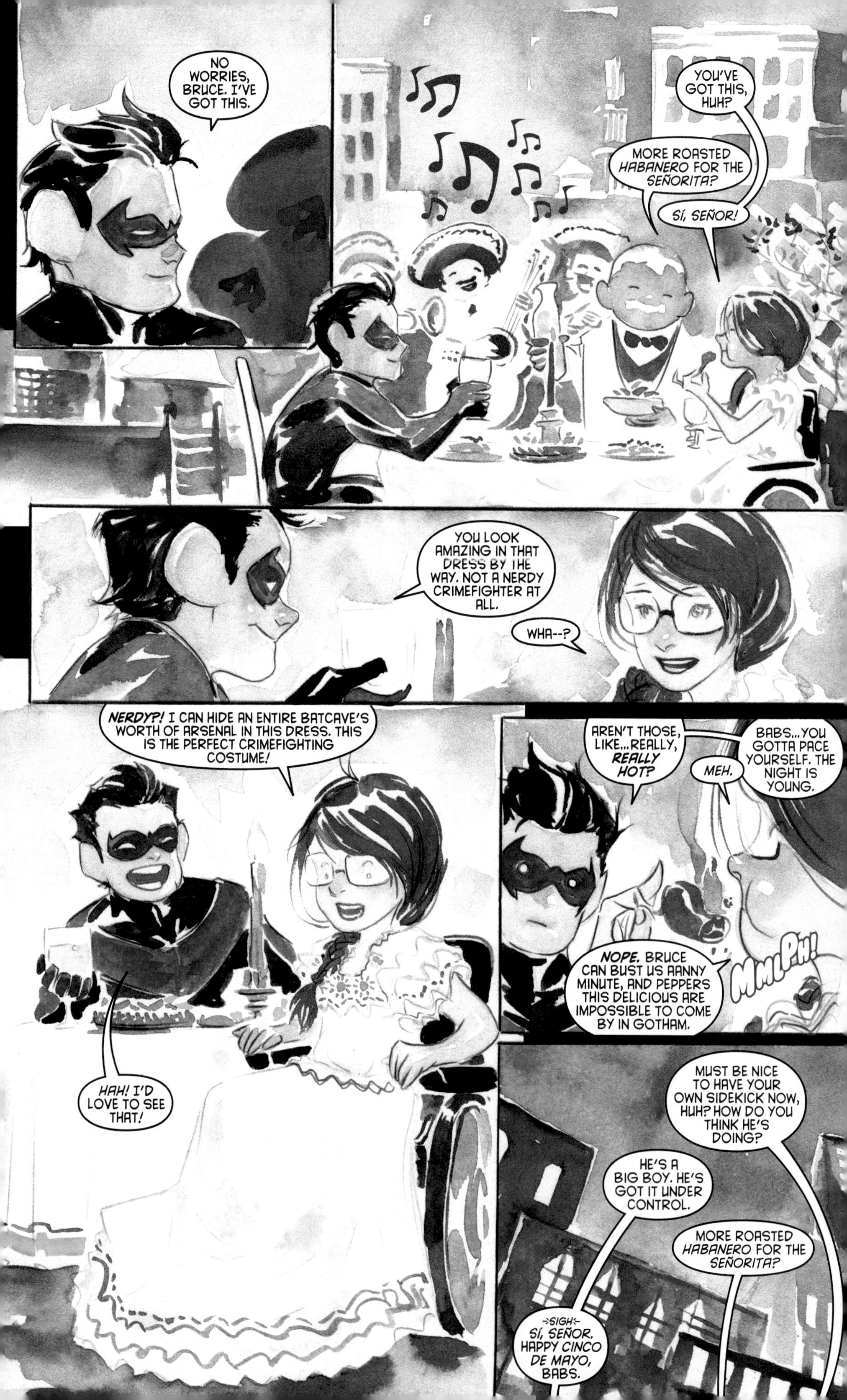
NO WORRIES, BRUCE. I'VE GOT THIS.
YOU'VE GOT THIS, HUH?
MORE ROASTED HABANERO FOR THE SEÑORITA?
SÍ, SEÑOR!
YOU LOOK AMAZING IN THAT DRESS BY THE WAY. NOT A NERDY CRIMEFIGHTER AT ALL.
WHA--?
NERDY?! I CAN HIDE AN ENTIRE BATCAVE'S WORTH OF ARSENAL IN THIS DRESS. THIS IS THE PERFECT CRIMEFIGHTING COSTUME!
HAH! I'D LOVE TO SEE THAT!
AREN'T THOSE, LIKE...REALLY, REALLY HOT?
BABS...YOU GOTTA PACE YOURSELF. THE NIGHT IS YOUNG.
MEH.
NOPE. BRUCE CAN BUST US AANNY MINUTE, AND PEPPERS THIS DELICIOUS ARE IMPOSSIBLE TO COME BY IN GOTHAM.
MMLPH!
MUST BE NICE TO HAVE YOUR OWN SIDEKICK NOW, HUH? HOW DO YOU THINK HE'S DOING?
HE'S A BIG BOY. HE'S GOT IT UNDER CONTROL.
MORE ROASTED HABANERO FOR THE SEÑORITA?
SIGH
SÍ, SEÑOR. HAPPY CINCO DE MAYO, BABS.

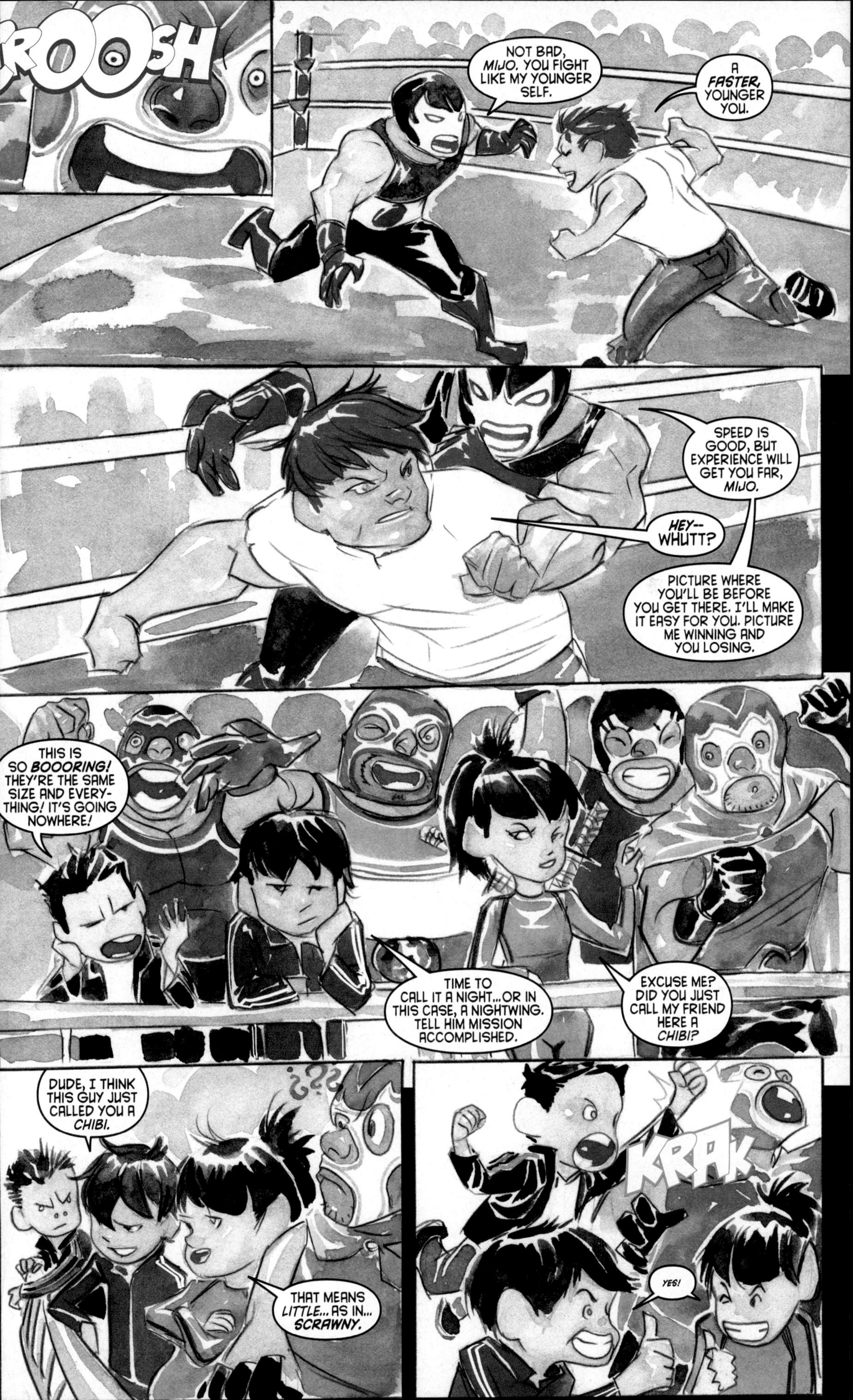
KROOSH
NOT BAD, MIJO. YOU FIGHT LIKE MY YOUNGER SELF.
A FASTER, YOUNGER YOU.
SPEED IS GOOD, BUT EXPERIENCE WILL GET YOU FAR, MIJO.
HEY-- WHUTT?
PICTURE WHERE YOU'LL BE BEFORE YOU GET THERE. I'LL MAKE IT EASY FOR YOU. PICTURE ME WINNING AND YOU LOSING.
THIS IS SO BOOORING! THEY'RE THE SAME SIZE AND EVERY-THING! IT'S GOING NOWHERE!
TIME TO CALL IT A NIGHT...OR IN THIS CASE, A NIGHTWING. TELL HIM MISSION ACCOMPLISHED.
EXCUSE ME? DID YOU JUST CALL MY FRIEND HERE A CHIBI?
DUDE, I THINK THIS GUY JUST CALLED YOU A CHIBI.
???
THAT MEANS LITTLE... AS IN... SCRAWNY.
KRAK
YES!

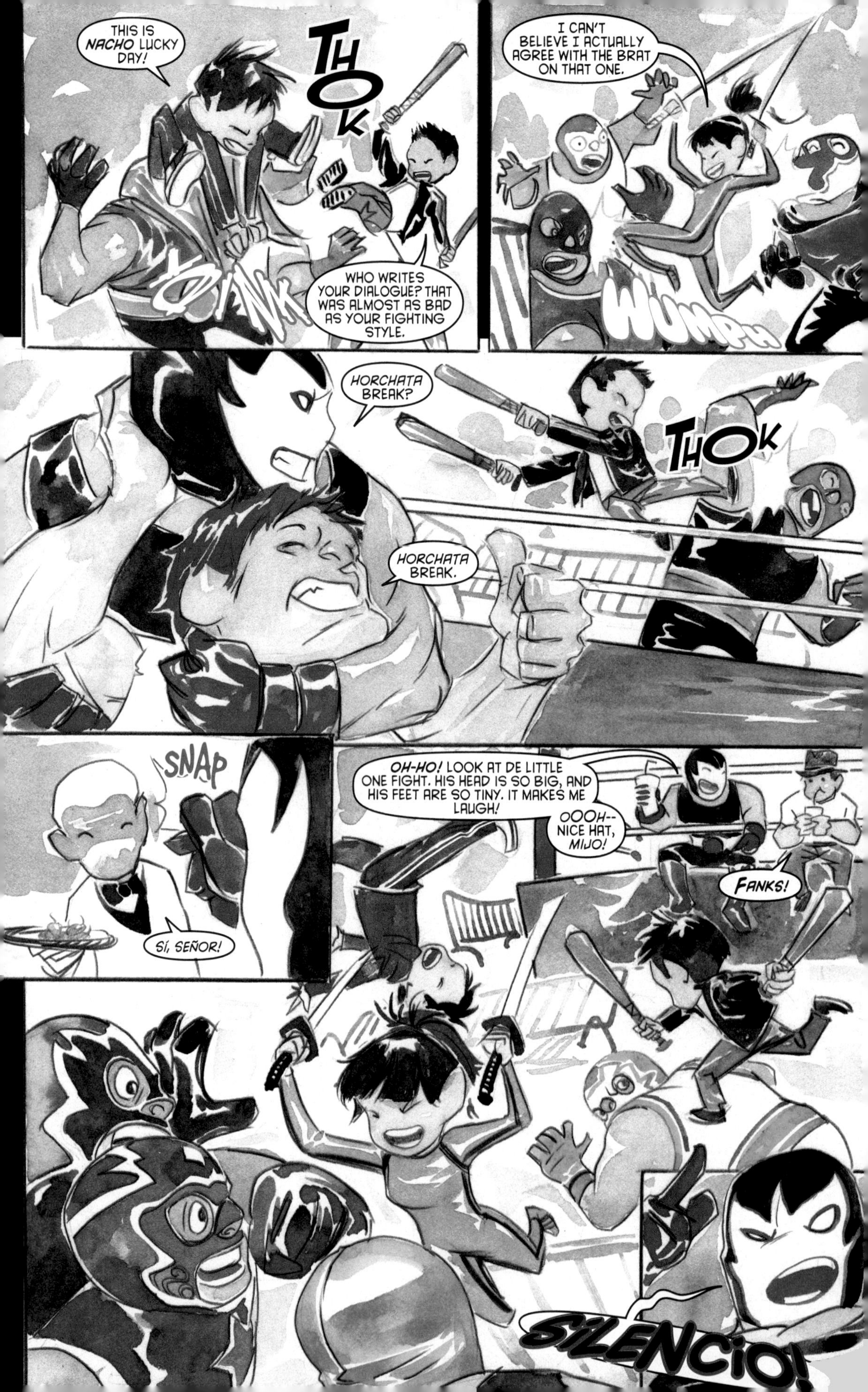
THIS IS NACHO LUCKY DAY!
THOK
YOINK
WHO WRITES YOUR DIALOGUE? THAT WAS ALMOST AS BAD AS YOUR FIGHTING STYLE.
I CAN'T BELIEVE I ACTUALLY AGREE WITH THE BRAT ON THAT ONE.
WUMPH
HORCHATA BREAK?
THOK
HORCHATA BREAK.
SNAP
SÍ, SEÑOR!
OH-HO! LOOK AT DE LITTLE ONE FIGHT. HIS HEAD IS SO BIG, AND HIS FEET ARE SO TINY. IT MAKES ME LAUGH!
OOOH-- NICE HAT, MIJO!
FANKS!
SILENCIO!

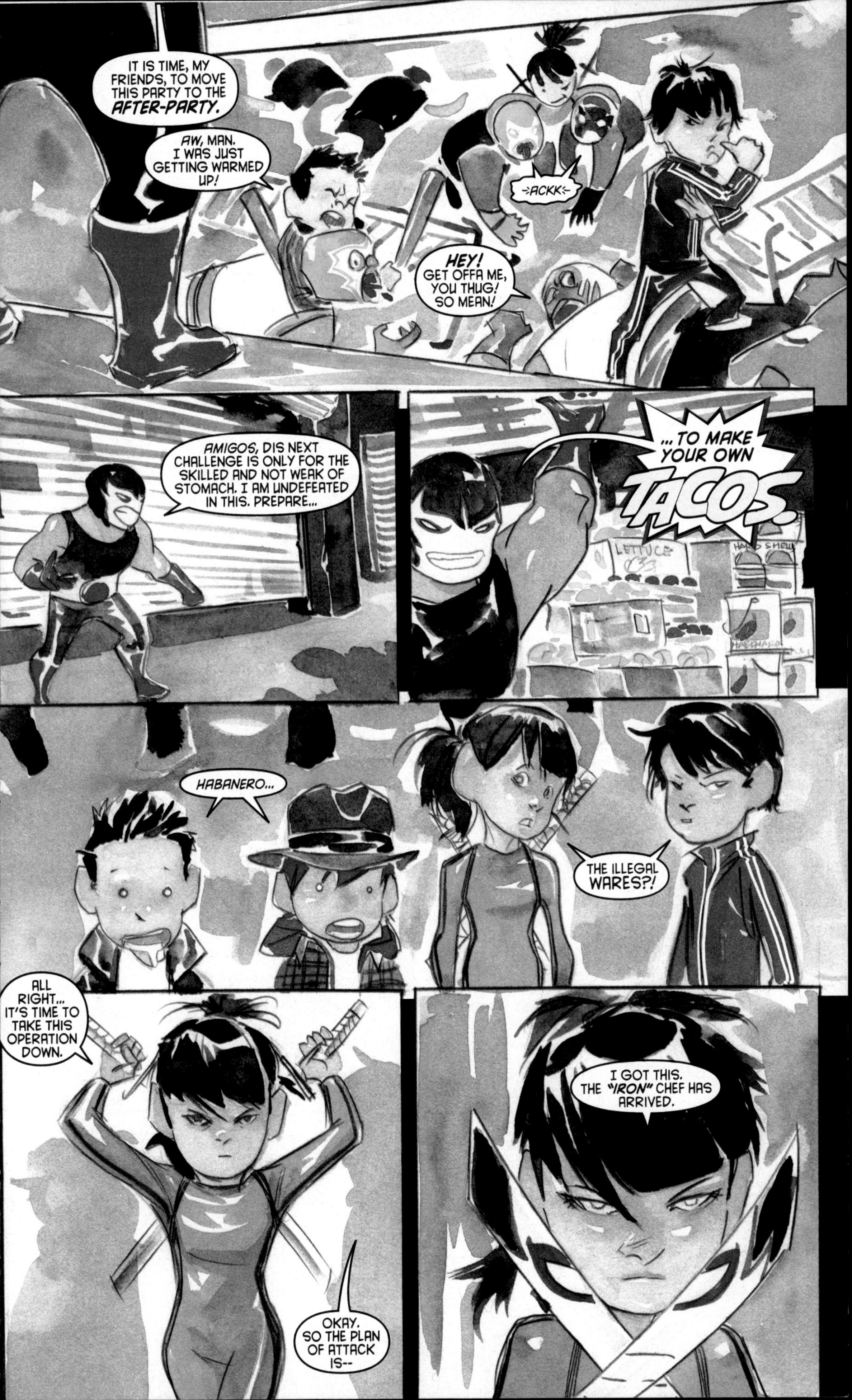
IT IS TIME, MY FRIENDS, TO MOVE THIS PARTY TO THE AFTER-PARTY.
AW, MAN. I WAS JUST GETTING WARMED UP!
ACKK
HEY! GET OFFA ME, YOU THUG! SO MEAN!
AMIGOS, DIS NEXT CHALLENGE IS ONLY FOR THE SKILLED AND NOT WEAK OF STOMACH. I AM UNDEFEATED IN THIS. PREPARE...
...TO MAKE YOUR OWN TACOS.
LETTUCE
HABANERO...
THE ILLEGAL WARES?!
ALL RIGHT... IT'S TIME TO TAKE THIS OPERATION DOWN.
OKAY. SO THE PLAN OF ATTACK IS--
I GOT THIS. THE "IRON" CHEF HAS ARRIVED.

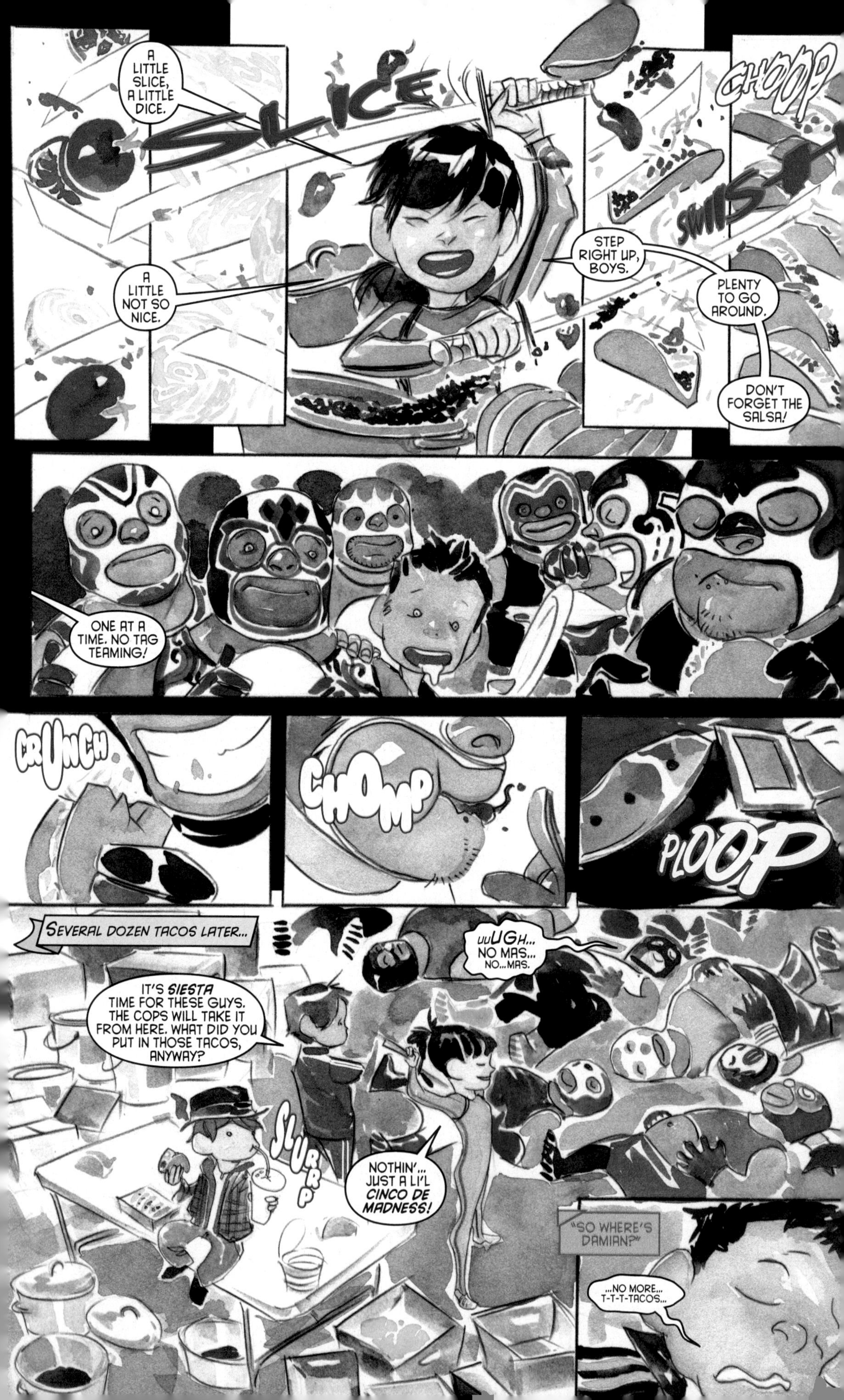
A LITTLE SLICE, A LITTLE DICE.
SLICE
A LITTLE NOT SO NICE.
STEP RIGHT UP, BOYS.
CHOOP
SWISH
PLENTY TO GO AROUND.
DON'T FORGET THE SALSA!
ONE AT A TIME. NO TAG TEAMING!
CRUNCH
CHOMP
PLOOP
SEVERAL DOZEN TACOS LATER...
UUUGH... NO MAS... NO...MAS.
IT'S SIESTA TIME FOR THESE GUYS. THE COPS WILL TAKE IT FROM HERE. WHAT DID YOU PUT IN THOSE TACOS, ANYWAY?
SLURRP
NOTHIN'... JUST A LI'L CINCO DE MADNESS!
"SO WHERE'S DAMIAN?"
...NO MORE... T-T-T-TACOS...

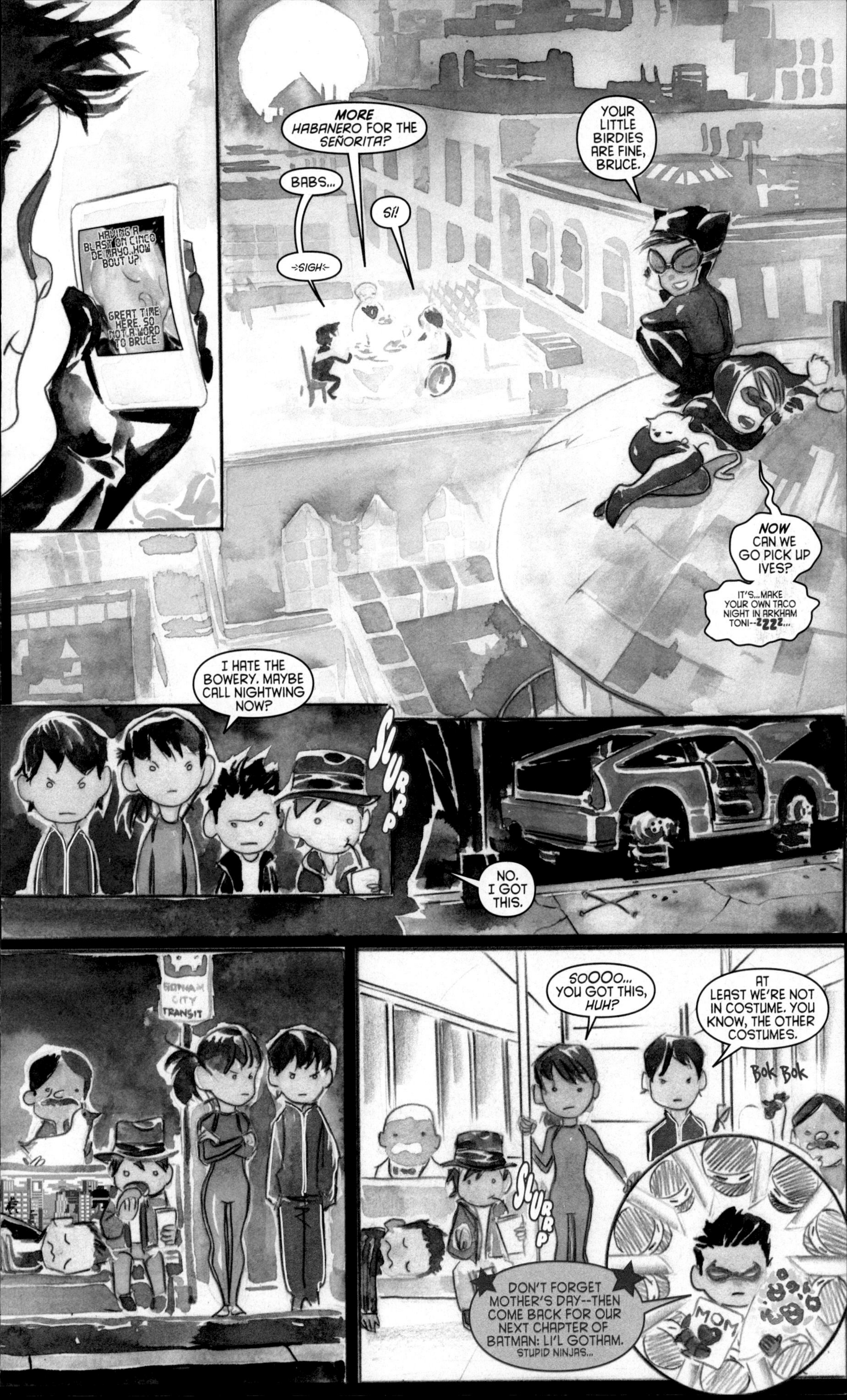
HAVING A BLAST ON CINCO DE MAYO..HOW BOUT U?
GREAT TIME HERE. SO NOT A WORD TO BRUCE.
MORE HABANERO FOR THE SEÑORITA?
BABS...
SÍ!
-SIGH-
YOUR LITTLE BIRDIES ARE FINE, BRUCE.
NOW CAN WE GO PICK UP IVES?
IT'S...MAKE YOUR OWN TACO NIGHT IN ARKHAM TONI--ZZZZ...
I HATE THE BOWERY. MAYBE CALL NIGHTWING NOW?
SLURRP
NO. I GOT THIS.
GOTHAM CITY TRANSIT
SOOOO... YOU GOT THIS, HUH?
AT LEAST WE'RE NOT IN COSTUME. YOU KNOW, THE OTHER COSTUMES.
BOK BOK
SLURRP
DON'T FORGET MOTHER'S DAY--THEN COME BACK FOR OUR NEXT CHAPTER OF BATMAN: LI'L GOTHAM.
STUPID NINJAS...
MOM

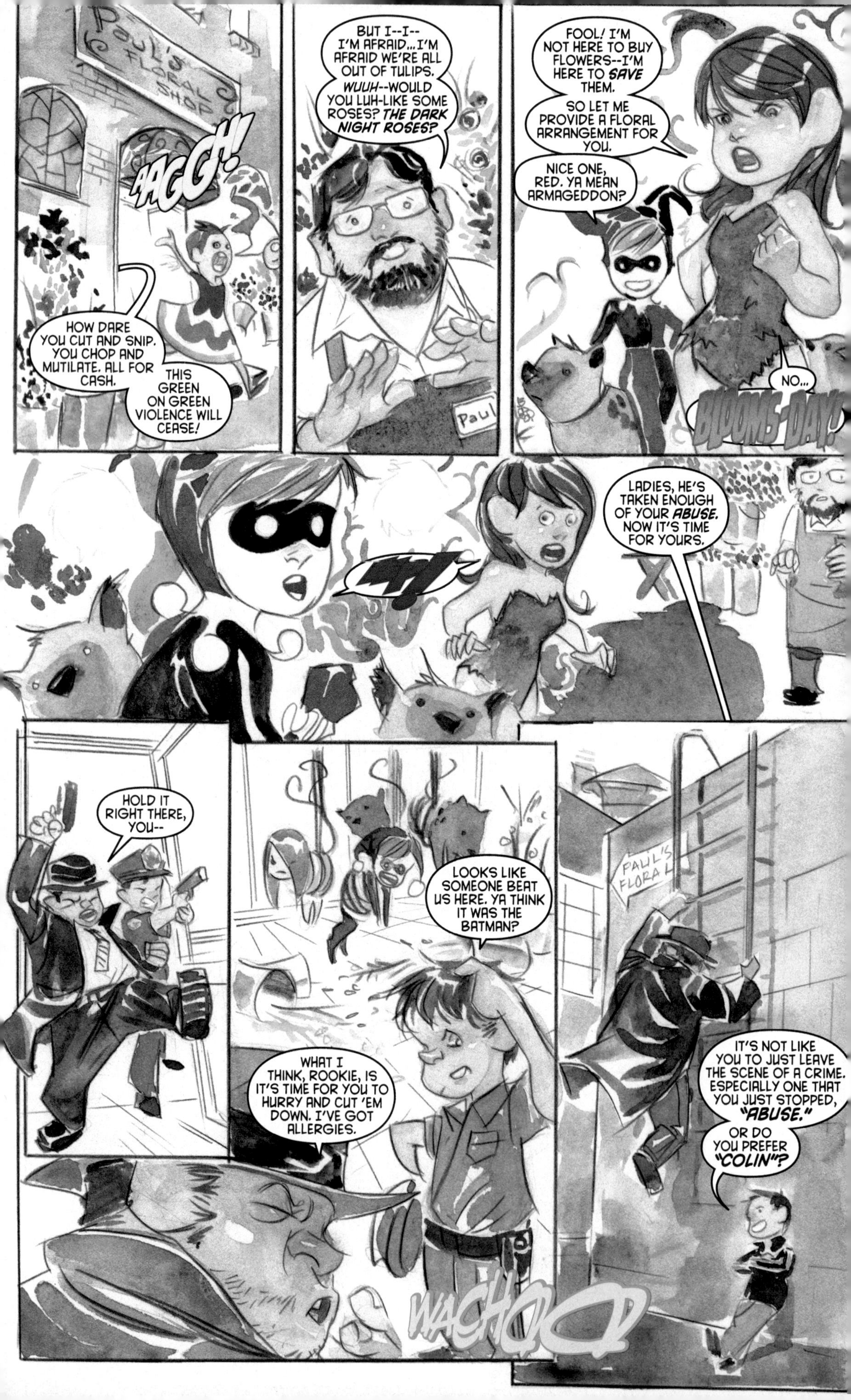
PAUL'S FLORAL SHOP
AAGGH!
HOW DARE YOU CUT AND SNIP. YOU CHOP AND MUTILATE. ALL FOR CASH.
THIS GREEN ON GREEN VIOLENCE WILL CEASE!
BUT I--I-- I'M AFRAID... I'M AFRAID WE'RE ALL OUT OF TULIPS. WUUH--WOULD YOU LUH-LIKE SOME ROSES? THE DARK NIGHT ROSES?
Paul
FOOL! I'M NOT HERE TO BUY FLOWERS--I'M HERE TO SAVE THEM.
SO LET ME PROVIDE A FLORAL ARRANGEMENT FOR YOU.
NICE ONE, RED. YA MEAN ARMAGEDDON?
NO...
BLOOMS-DAY!
LADIES, HE'S TAKEN ENOUGH OF YOUR ABUSE. NOW IT'S TIME FOR YOURS.
HOLD IT RIGHT THERE, YOU--
LOOKS LIKE SOMEONE BEAT US HERE. YA THINK IT WAS THE BATMAN?
WHAT I THINK, ROOKIE, IS IT'S TIME FOR YOU TO HURRY AND CUT 'EM DOWN. I'VE GOT ALLERGIES.
WACHOO
PAUL'S FLORAL
IT'S NOT LIKE YOU TO JUST LEAVE THE SCENE OF A CRIME. ESPECIALLY ONE THAT YOU JUST STOPPED, "ABUSE."
OR DO YOU PREFER "COLIN"?

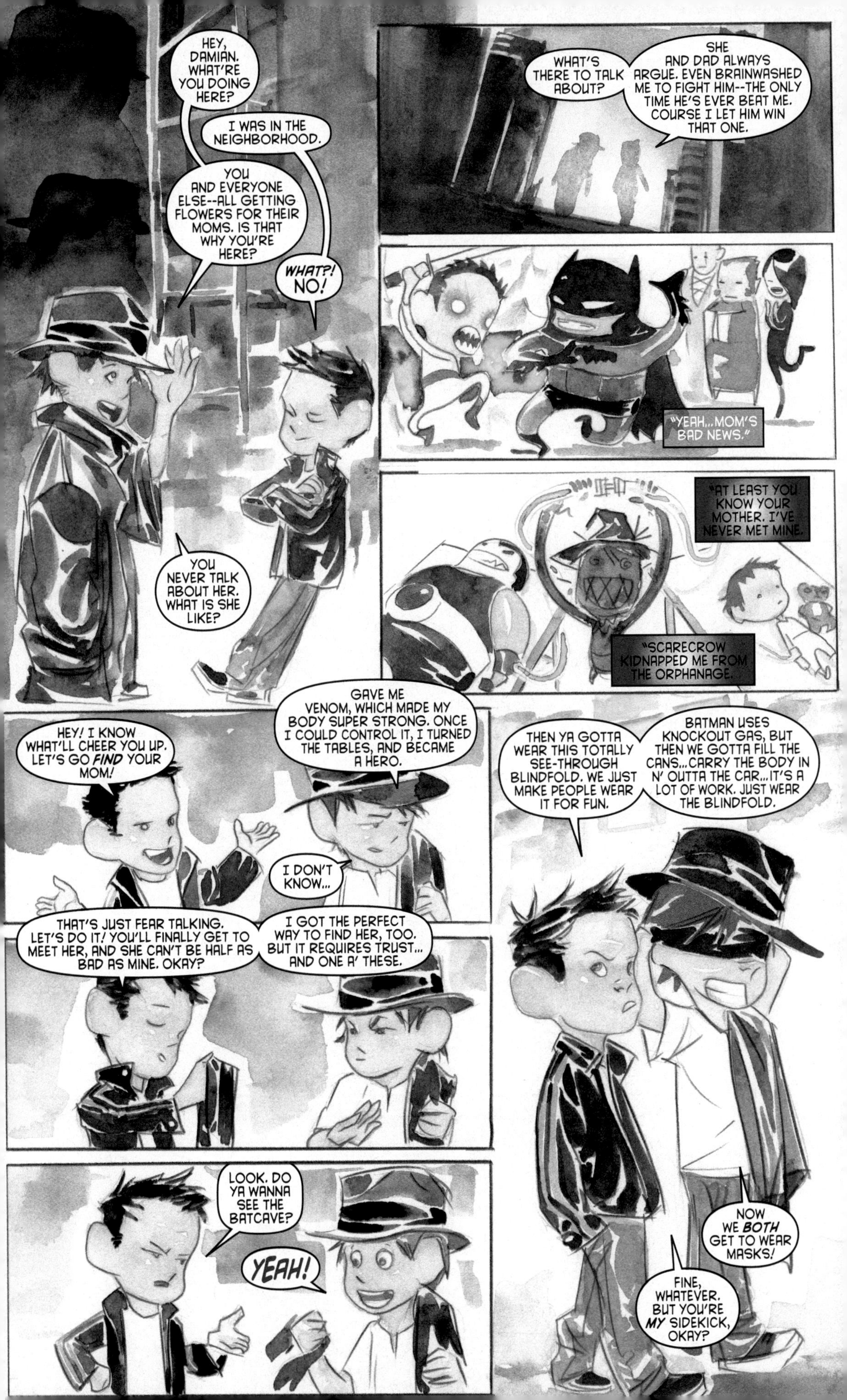
HEY, DAMIAN. WHAT'RE YOU DOING HERE?
I WAS IN THE NEIGHBORHOOD.
YOU AND EVERYONE ELSE--ALL GETTING FLOWERS FOR THEIR MOMS. IS THAT WHY YOU'RE HERE?
WHAT?! NO!
YOU NEVER TALK ABOUT HER. WHAT IS SHE LIKE?
WHAT'S THERE TO TALK ABOUT?
SHE AND DAD ALWAYS ARGUE. EVEN BRAINWASHED ME TO FIGHT HIM--THE ONLY TIME HE'S EVER BEAT ME. COURSE I LET HIM WIN THAT ONE.
"YEAH... MOM'S BAD NEWS."
"AT LEAST YOU KNOW YOUR MOTHER. I'VE NEVER MET MINE.
"SCARECROW KIDNAPPED ME FROM THE ORPHANAGE.
GAVE ME VENOM, WHICH MADE MY BODY SUPER STRONG. ONCE I COULD CONTROL IT, I TURNED THE TABLES, AND BECAME A HERO.
HEY! I KNOW WHAT'LL CHEER YOU UP. LET'S GO FIND YOUR MOM!
I DON'T KNOW...
THAT'S JUST FEAR TALKING. LET'S DO IT! YOU'LL FINALLY GET TO MEET HER, AND SHE CAN'T BE HALF AS BAD AS MINE. OKAY?
I GOT THE PERFECT WAY TO FIND HER, TOO. BUT IT REQUIRES TRUST... AND ONE A' THESE.
LOOK. DO YA WANNA SEE THE BATCAVE?
YEAH!
BATMAN USES KNOCKOUT GAS, BUT THEN WE GOTTA FILL THE CANS... CARRY THE BODY IN N' OUTTA THE CAR... IT'S A LOT OF WORK. JUST WEAR THE BLINDFOLD.
THEN YA GOTTA WEAR THIS TOTALLY SEE-THROUGH BLINDFOLD. WE JUST MAKE PEOPLE WEAR IT FOR FUN.
NOW WE BOTH GET TO WEAR MASKS!
FINE, WHATEVER. BUT YOU'RE MY SIDEKICK, OKAY?

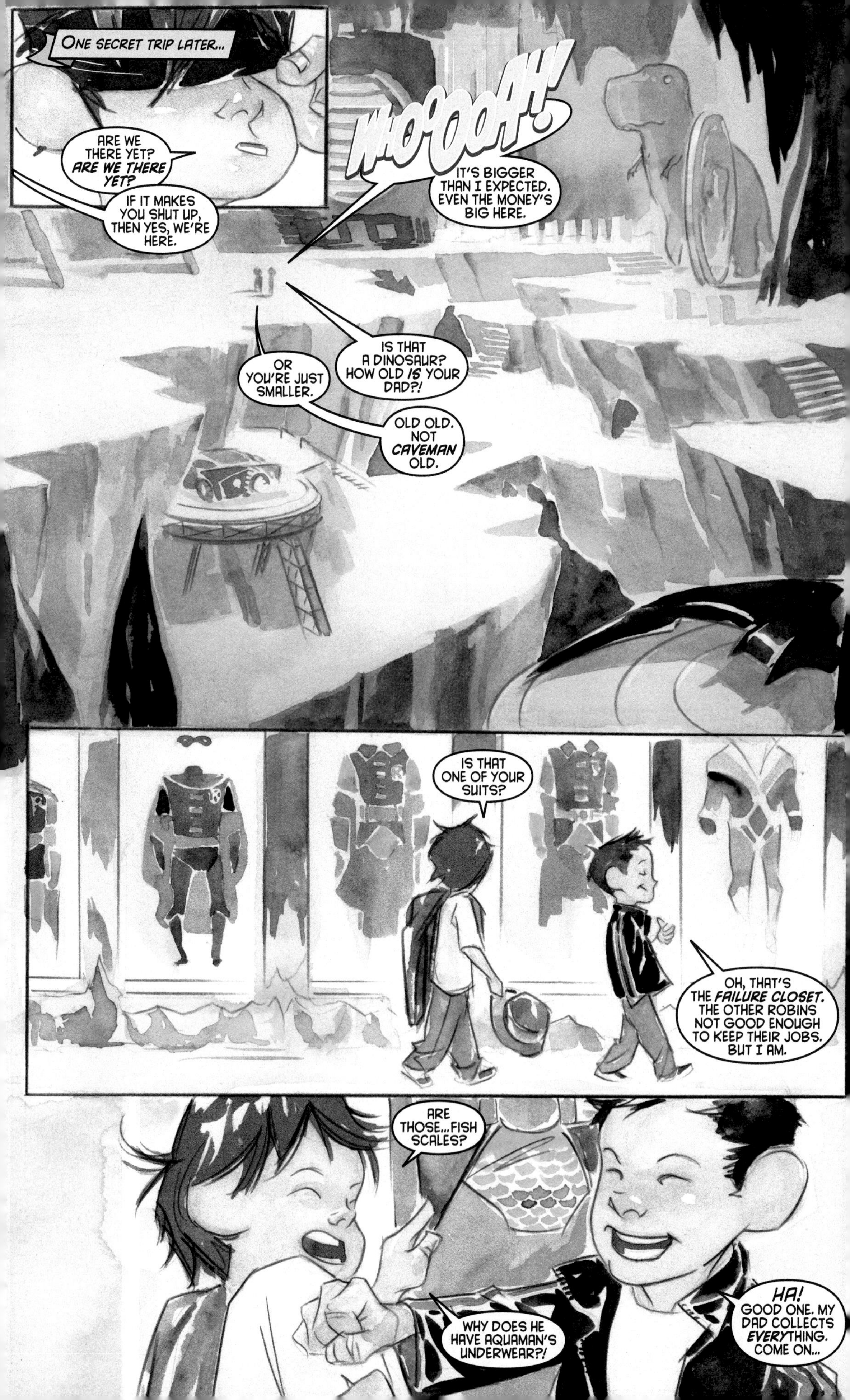

ONE SECRET TRIP LATER...
ARE WE THERE YET? ARE WE THERE YET?
IF IT MAKES YOU SHUT UP, THEN YES, WE'RE HERE.
WHOOOOAH!
IT'S BIGGER THAN I EXPECTED. EVEN THE MONEY'S BIG HERE.
OR YOU'RE JUST SMALLER.
IS THAT A DINOSAUR? HOW OLD IS YOUR DAD?!
OLD OLD. NOT CAVEMAN OLD.
IS THAT ONE OF YOUR SUITS?
OH, THAT'S THE FAILURE CLOSET. THE OTHER ROBINS NOT GOOD ENOUGH TO KEEP THEIR JOBS. BUT I AM.
ARE THOSE...FISH SCALES?
WHY DOES HE HAVE AQUAMAN'S UNDERWEAR?!
HA! GOOD ONE. MY DAD COLLECTS EVERYTHING. COME ON...

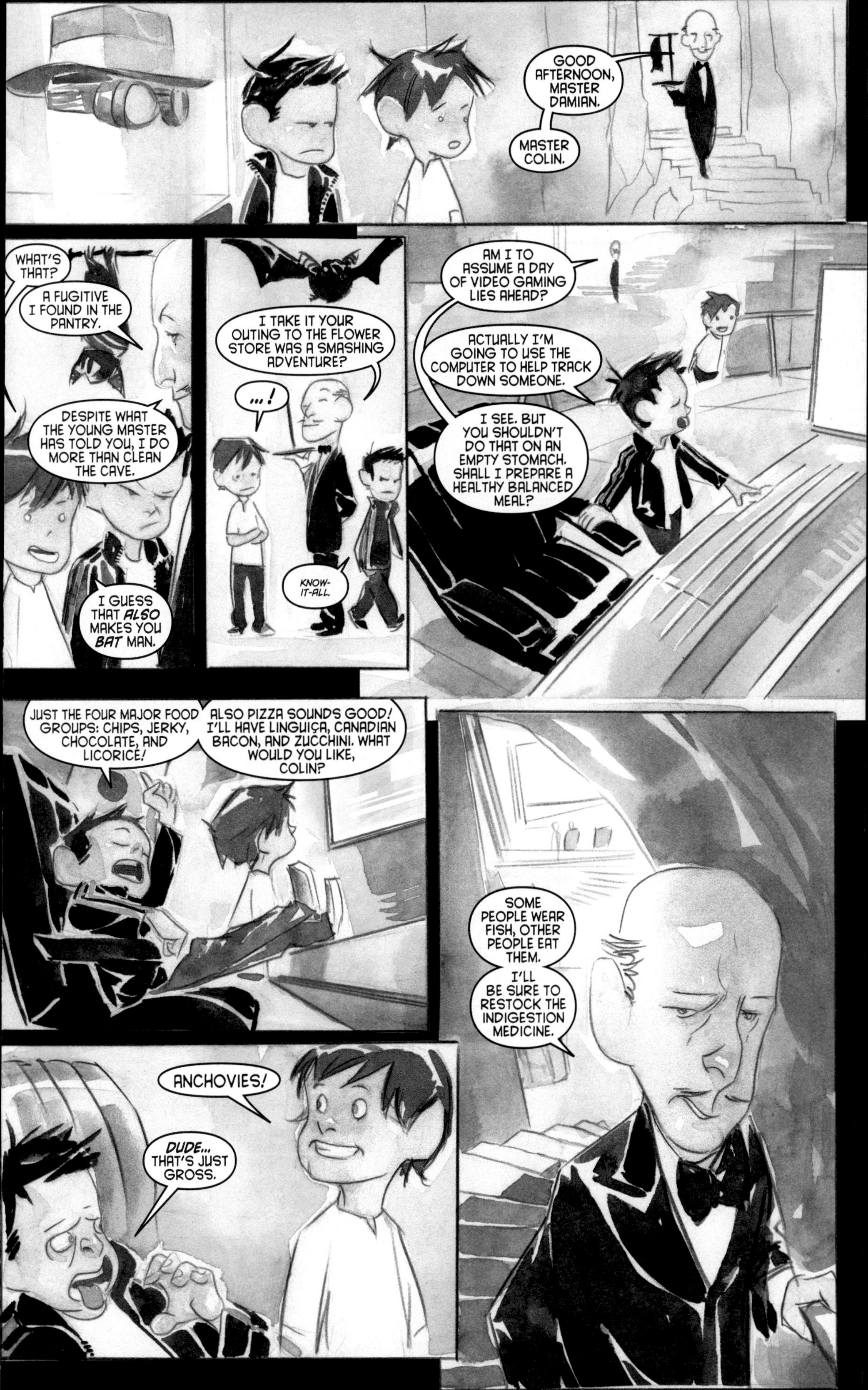
GOOD AFTERNOON, MASTER DAMIAN.
MASTER COLIN.
WHAT'S THAT?
A FUGITIVE I FOUND IN THE PANTRY.
DESPITE WHAT THE YOUNG MASTER HAS TOLD YOU, I DO MORE THAN CLEAN THE CAVE.
I GUESS THAT *ALSO* MAKES YOU *BAT* MAN.
I TAKE IT YOUR OUTING TO THE FLOWER STORE WAS A SMASHING ADVENTURE?
...!
KNOW-IT-ALL.
AM I TO ASSUME A DAY OF VIDEO GAMING LIES AHEAD?
ACTUALLY I'M GOING TO USE THE COMPUTER TO HELP TRACK DOWN SOMEONE.
I SEE. BUT YOU SHOULDN'T DO THAT ON AN EMPTY STOMACH. SHALL I PREPARE A HEALTHY BALANCED MEAL?
JUST THE FOUR MAJOR FOOD GROUPS: CHIPS, JERKY, CHOCOLATE, AND LICORICE!
ALSO PIZZA SOUNDS GOOD! I'LL HAVE LINGUIÇA, CANADIAN BACON, AND ZUCCHINI. WHAT WOULD YOU LIKE, COLIN?
ANCHOVIES!
DUDE... THAT'S JUST GROSS.
SOME PEOPLE WEAR FISH, OTHER PEOPLE EAT THEM.
I'LL BE SURE TO RESTOCK THE INDIGESTION MEDICINE.

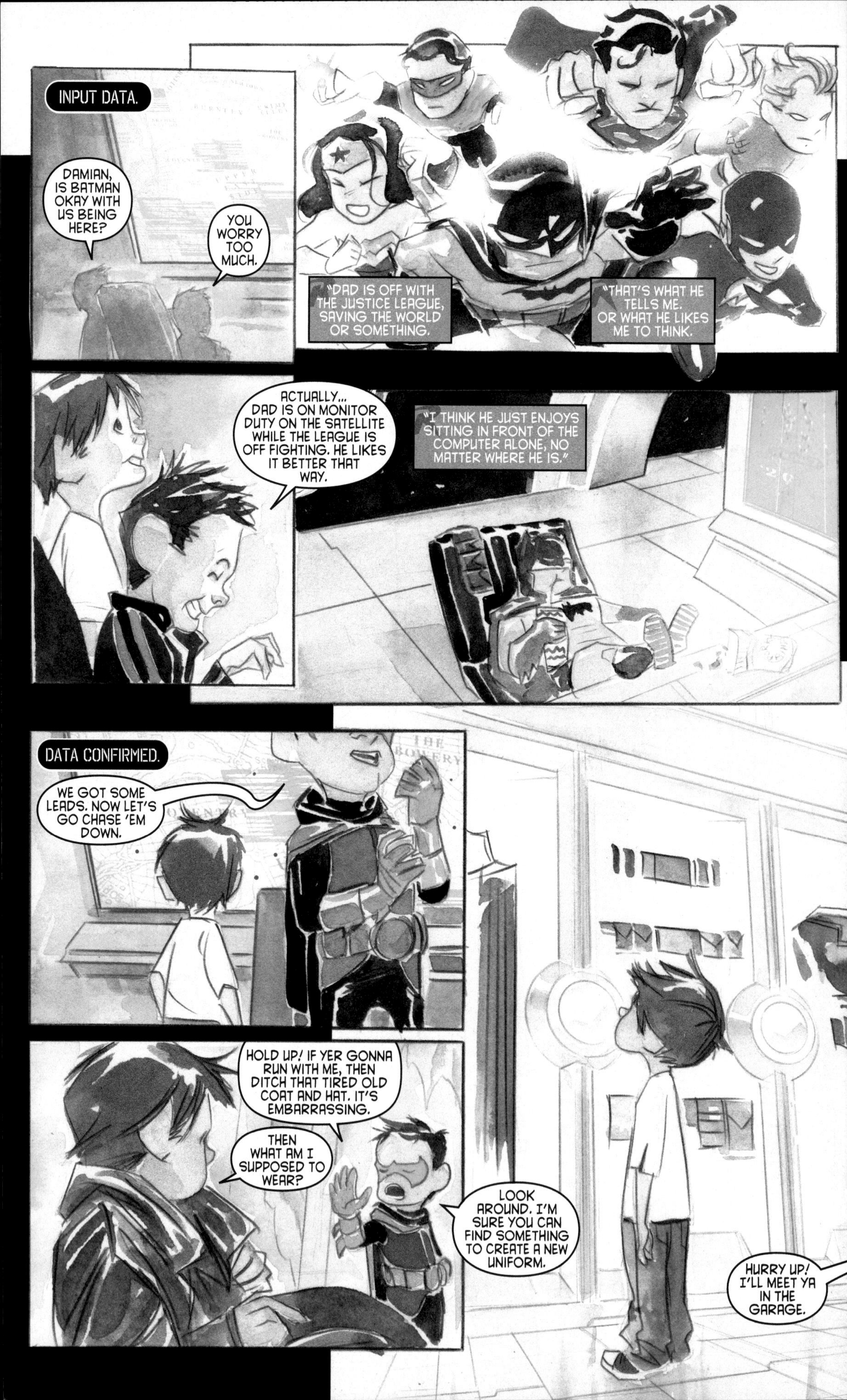
INPUT DATA.
DAMIAN, IS BATMAN OKAY WITH US BEING HERE?
YOU WORRY TOO MUCH.
"DAD IS OFF WITH THE JUSTICE LEAGUE, SAVING THE WORLD OR SOMETHING.
"THAT'S WHAT HE TELLS ME. OR WHAT HE LIKES ME TO THINK.
ACTUALLY... DAD IS ON MONITOR DUTY ON THE SATELLITE WHILE THE LEAGUE IS OFF FIGHTING. HE LIKES IT BETTER THAT WAY.
"I THINK HE JUST ENJOYS SITTING IN FRONT OF THE COMPUTER ALONE, NO MATTER WHERE HE IS."
DATA CONFIRMED.
WE GOT SOME LEADS. NOW LET'S GO CHASE 'EM DOWN.
HOLD UP! IF YER GONNA RUN WITH ME, THEN DITCH THAT TIRED OLD COAT AND HAT. IT'S EMBARRASSING.
THEN WHAT AM I SUPPOSED TO WEAR?
LOOK AROUND. I'M SURE YOU CAN FIND SOMETHING TO CREATE A NEW UNIFORM.
HURRY UP! I'LL MEET YA IN THE GARAGE.

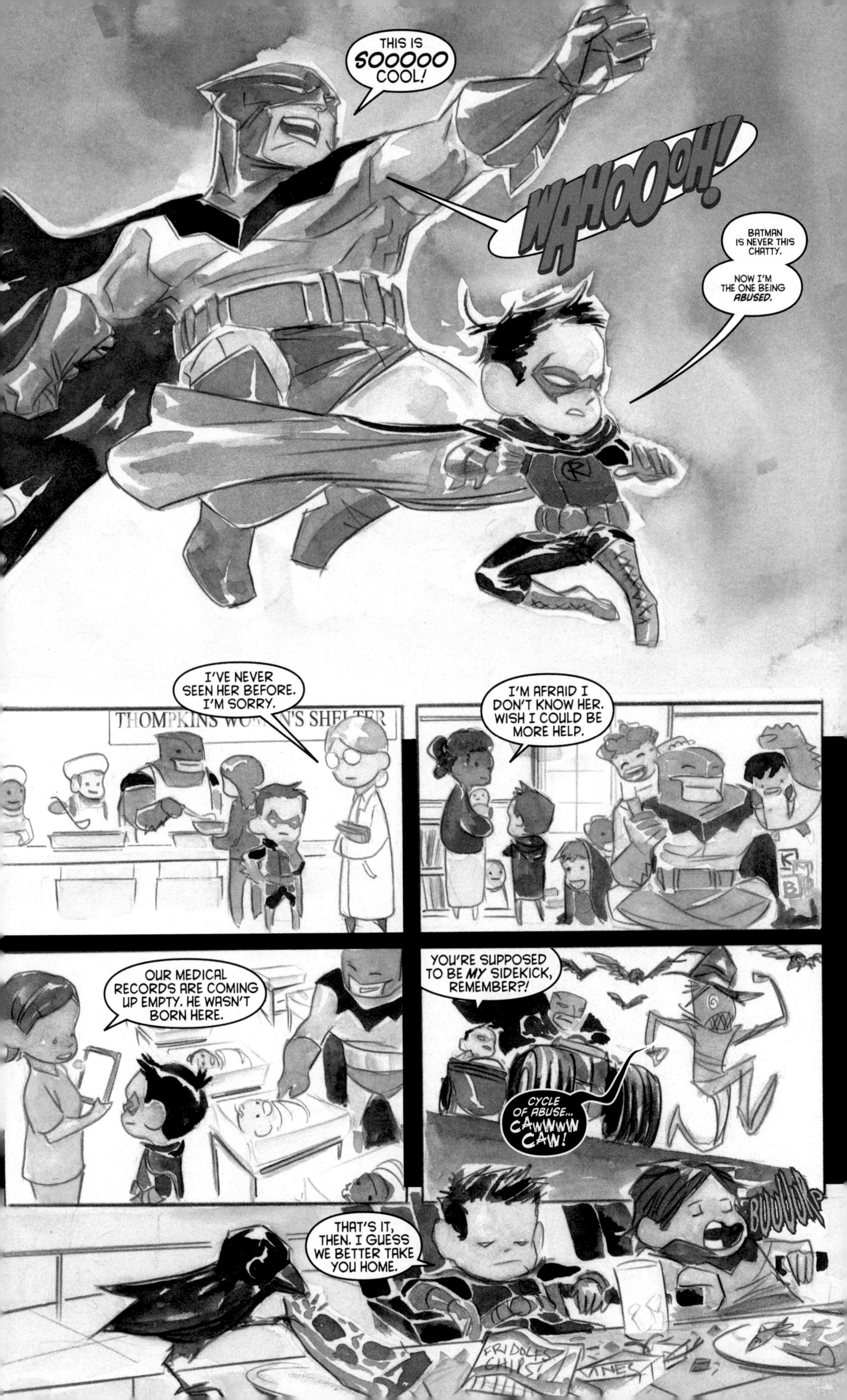
THIS IS *SOOOOO* COOL!
WAHOOOOH!
BATMAN IS NEVER THIS CHATTY.
NOW I'M THE ONE BEING *ABUSED.*
I'VE NEVER SEEN HER BEFORE. I'M SORRY.
I'M AFRAID I DON'T KNOW HER. WISH I COULD BE MORE HELP.
OUR MEDICAL RECORDS ARE COMING UP EMPTY. HE WASN'T BORN HERE.
YOU'RE SUPPOSED TO BE *MY* SIDEKICK, REMEMBER?!
CYCLE OF ABUSE... CAWWWW CAW!
THAT'S IT, THEN. I GUESS WE BETTER TAKE YOU HOME.

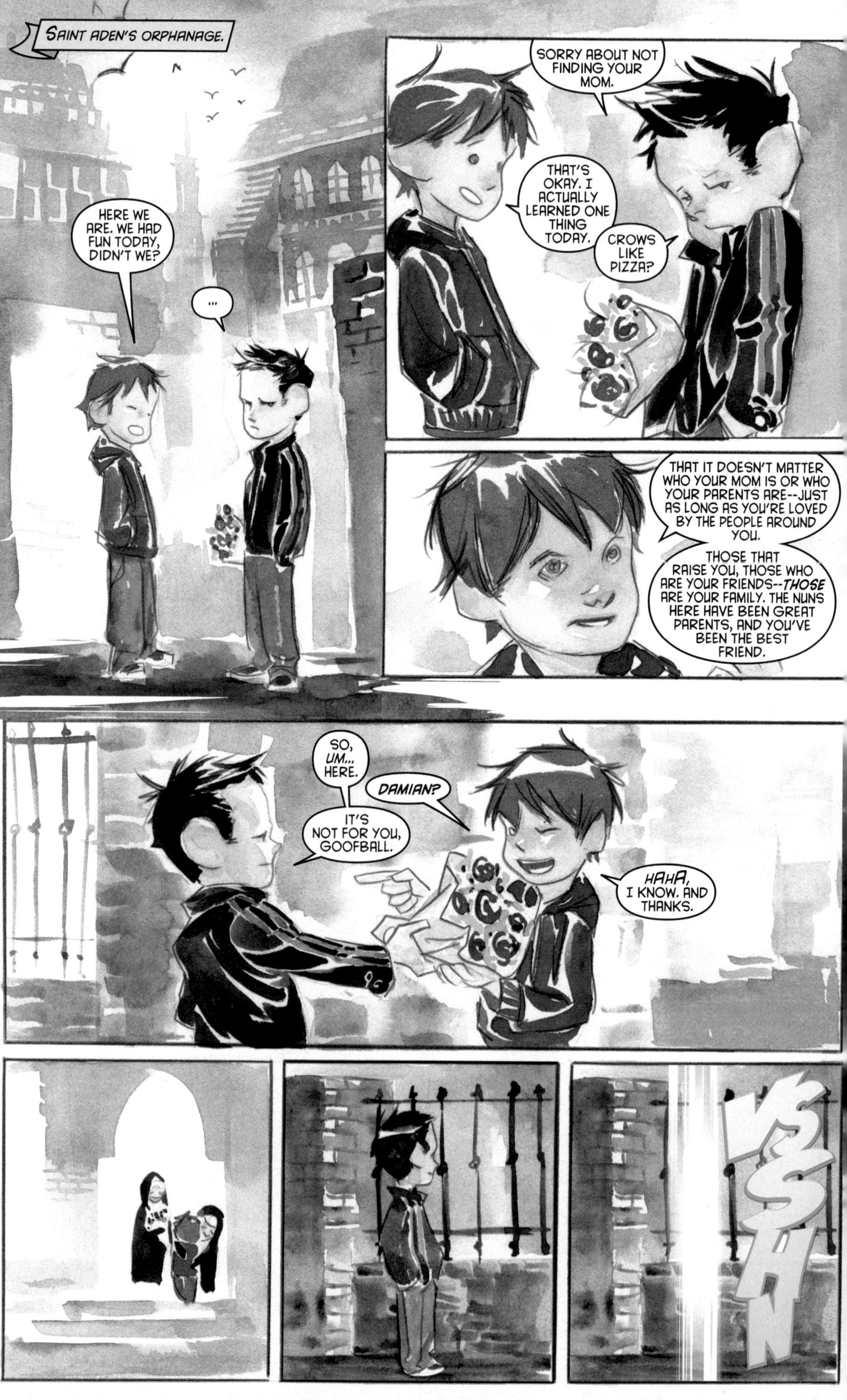
SAINT ADEN'S ORPHANAGE.
HERE WE ARE. WE HAD FUN TODAY, DIDN'T WE?
...
SORRY ABOUT NOT FINDING YOUR MOM.
THAT'S OKAY. I ACTUALLY LEARNED ONE THING TODAY.
CROWS LIKE PIZZA?
THAT IT DOESN'T MATTER WHO YOUR MOM IS OR WHO YOUR PARENTS ARE--JUST AS LONG AS YOU'RE LOVED BY THE PEOPLE AROUND YOU.
THOSE THAT RAISE YOU, THOSE WHO ARE YOUR FRIENDS--THOSE ARE YOUR FAMILY. THE NUNS HERE HAVE BEEN GREAT PARENTS, AND YOU'VE BEEN THE BEST FRIEND.
SO, UM... HERE.
DAMIAN?
IT'S NOT FOR YOU, GOOFBALL.
HAHA, I KNOW. AND THANKS.
VSSHH

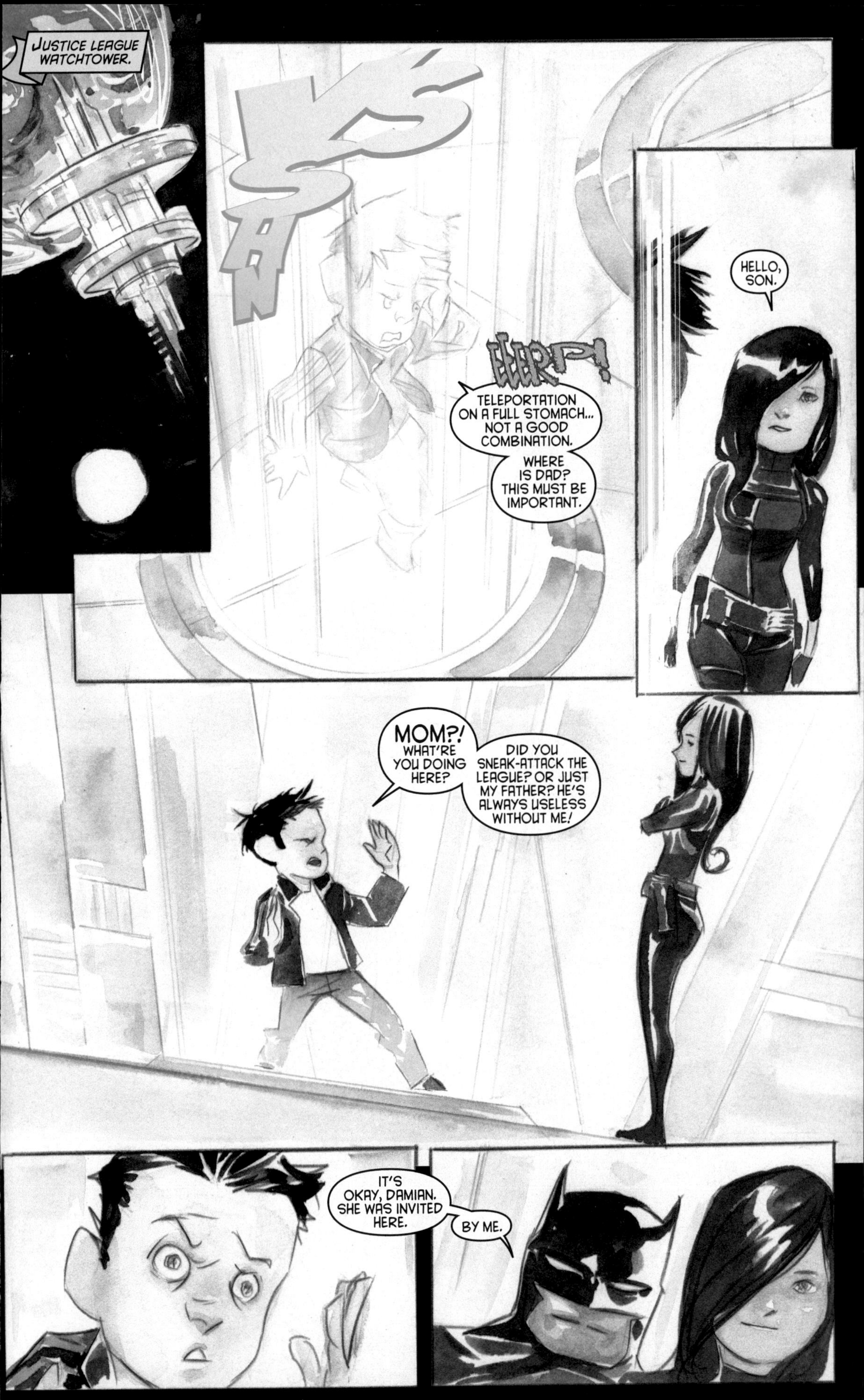

JUSTICE LEAGUE WATCHTOWER.
VSSH
TELEPORTATION ON A FULL STOMACH... NOT A GOOD COMBINATION.
WHERE IS DAD? THIS MUST BE IMPORTANT.
EEERP!
HELLO, SON.
MOM?! WHAT'RE YOU DOING HERE?
DID YOU SNEAK-ATTACK THE LEAGUE? OR JUST MY FATHER? HE'S ALWAYS USELESS WITHOUT ME!
IT'S OKAY, DAMIAN. SHE WAS INVITED HERE.
BY ME.

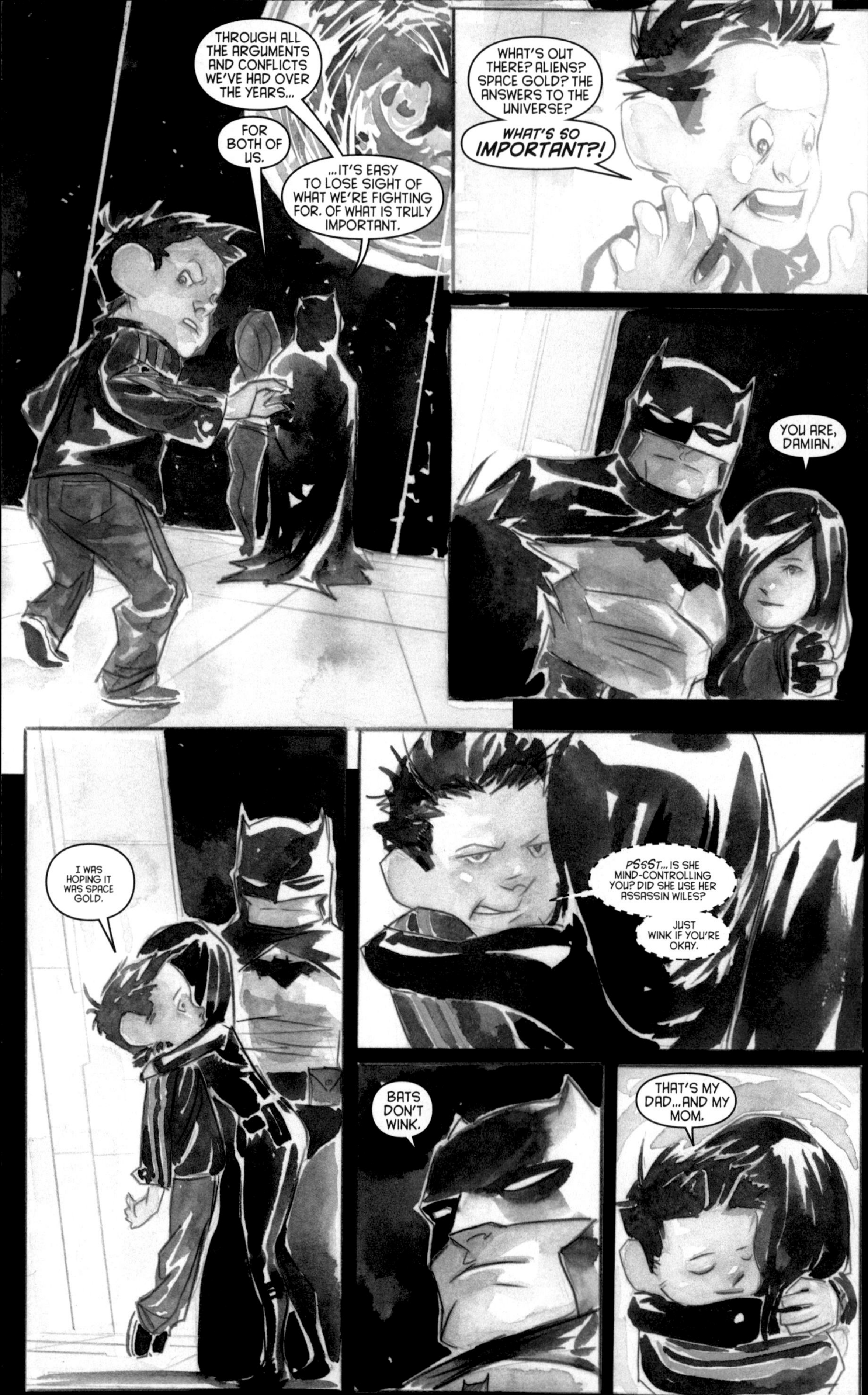
THROUGH ALL THE ARGUMENTS AND CONFLICTS WE'VE HAD OVER THE YEARS...
FOR BOTH OF US.
...IT'S EASY TO LOSE SIGHT OF WHAT WE'RE FIGHTING FOR. OF WHAT IS TRULY IMPORTANT.
WHAT'S OUT THERE? ALIENS? SPACE GOLD? THE ANSWERS TO THE UNIVERSE?
WHAT'S SO IMPORTANT?!
YOU ARE, DAMIAN.
I WAS HOPING IT WAS SPACE GOLD.
PSSST... IS SHE MIND-CONTROLLING YOU? DID SHE USE HER ASSASSIN WILES?
JUST WINK IF YOU'RE OKAY.
BATS DON'T WINK.
THAT'S MY DAD...AND MY MOM.

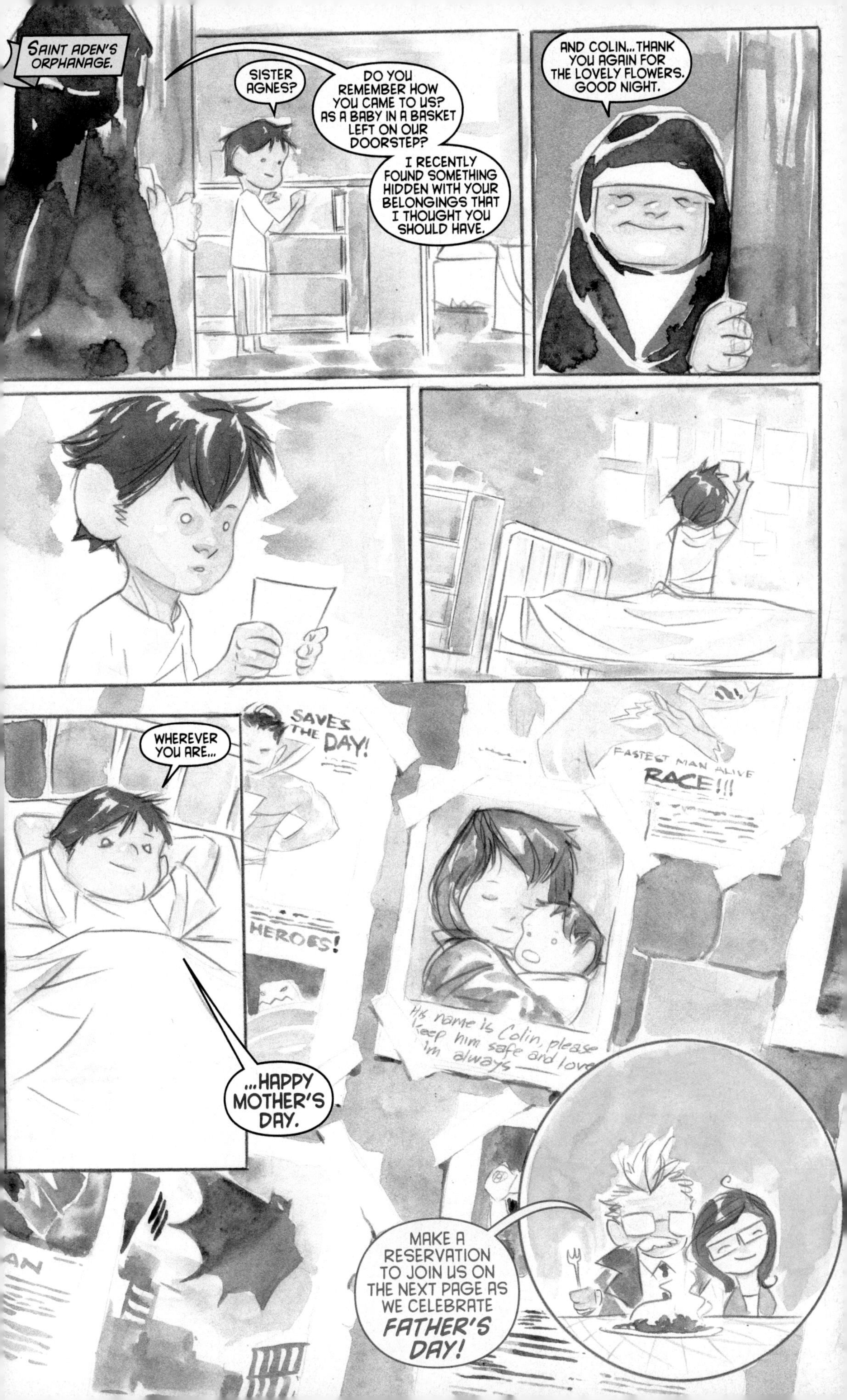

SAINT ADEN'S ORPHANAGE.
SISTER AGNES?
DO YOU REMEMBER HOW YOU CAME TO US? AS A BABY IN A BASKET LEFT ON OUR DOORSTEP?
I RECENTLY FOUND SOMETHING HIDDEN WITH YOUR BELONGINGS THAT I THOUGHT YOU SHOULD HAVE.
AND COLIN... THANK YOU AGAIN FOR THE LOVELY FLOWERS. GOOD NIGHT.
WHEREVER YOU ARE...
SAVES THE DAY!
FASTEST MAN ALIVE
RACE!!!
HEROES!
His name is Colin, please keep him safe and love
I'm always
...HAPPY MOTHER'S DAY.
MAKE A RESERVATION TO JOIN US ON THE NEXT PAGE AS WE CELEBRATE FATHER'S DAY!

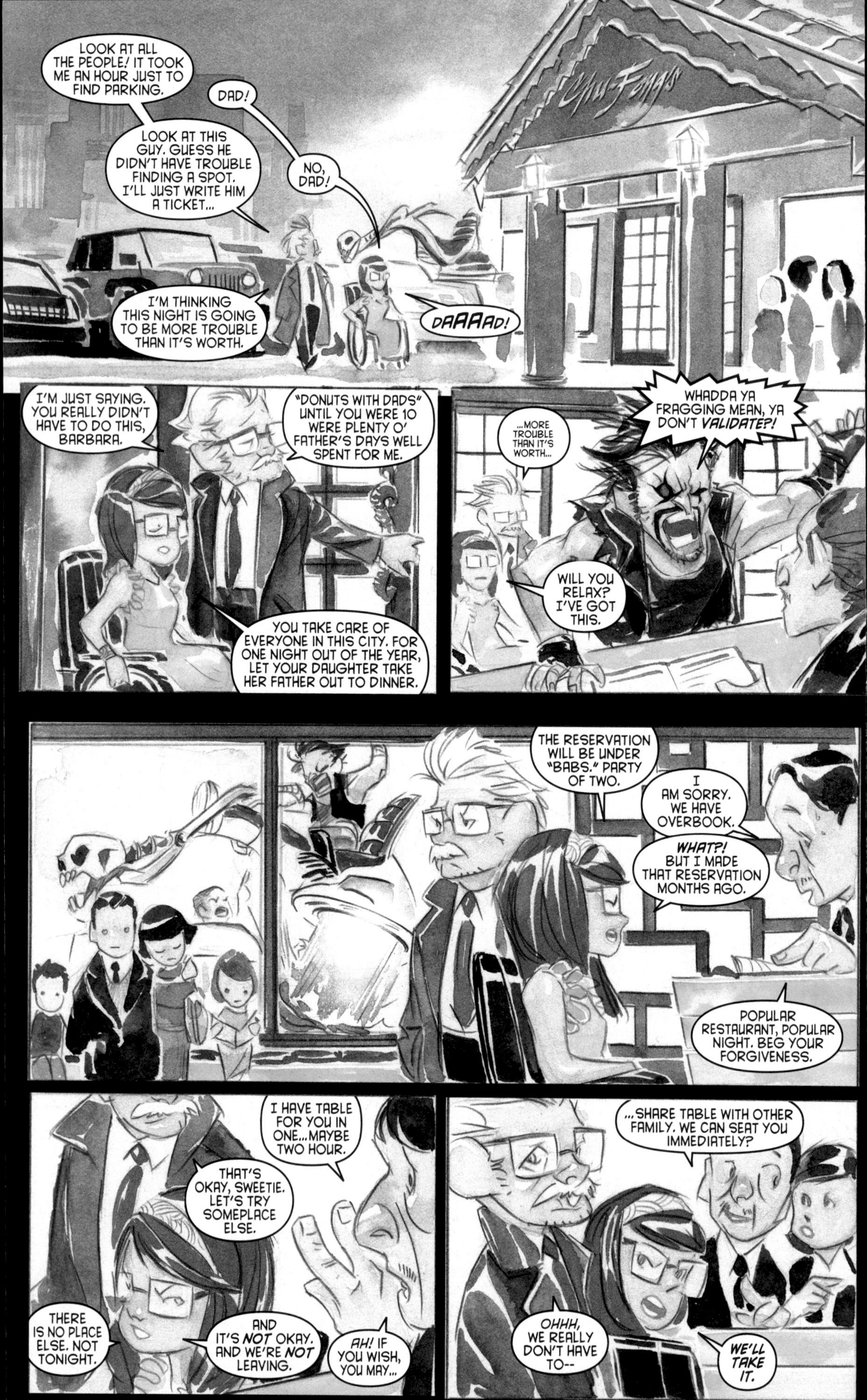
LOOK AT ALL THE PEOPLE! IT TOOK ME AN HOUR JUST TO FIND PARKING.
DAD!
LOOK AT THIS GUY. GUESS HE DIDN'T HAVE TROUBLE FINDING A SPOT. I'LL JUST WRITE HIM A TICKET...
NO, DAD!
I'M THINKING THIS NIGHT IS GOING TO BE MORE TROUBLE THAN IT'S WORTH.
DAAAAD!
I'M JUST SAYING. YOU REALLY DIDN'T HAVE TO DO THIS, BARBARA.
"DONUTS WITH DADS" UNTIL YOU WERE 10 WERE PLENTY O' FATHER'S DAYS WELL SPENT FOR ME.
YOU TAKE CARE OF EVERYONE IN THIS CITY. FOR ONE NIGHT OUT OF THE YEAR, LET YOUR DAUGHTER TAKE HER FATHER OUT TO DINNER.
WHADDA YA FRAGGING MEAN, YA DON'T *VALIDATE?!*
...MORE TROUBLE THAN IT'S WORTH...
WILL YOU RELAX? I'VE GOT THIS.
THE RESERVATION WILL BE UNDER "BABS." PARTY OF TWO.
I AM SORRY. WE HAVE OVERBOOK.
WHAT?! BUT I MADE THAT RESERVATION MONTHS AGO.
POPULAR RESTAURANT, POPULAR NIGHT. BEG YOUR FORGIVENESS.
I HAVE TABLE FOR YOU IN ONE...MAYBE TWO HOUR.
THAT'S OKAY, SWEETIE. LET'S TRY SOMEPLACE ELSE.
THERE IS NO PLACE ELSE. NOT TONIGHT.
AND IT'S *NOT* OKAY. AND WE'RE *NOT* LEAVING.
AH! IF YOU WISH, YOU MAY...
...SHARE TABLE WITH OTHER FAMILY. WE CAN SEAT YOU IMMEDIATELY?
OHHH, WE REALLY DON'T HAVE TO--
WE'LL TAKE IT.

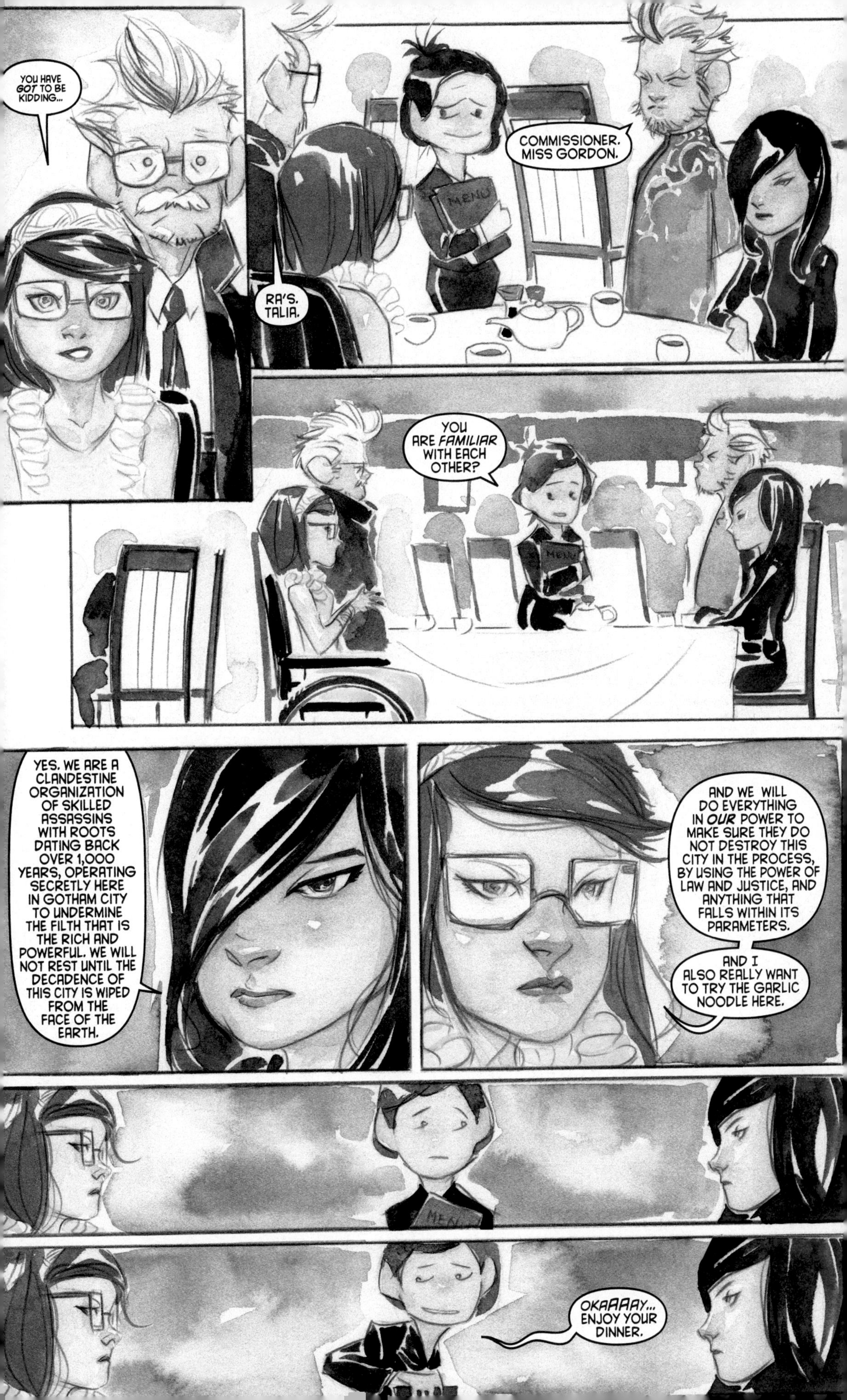

YOU HAVE GOT TO BE KIDDING...
COMMISSIONER. MISS GORDON.
RA'S. TALIA.
YOU ARE FAMILIAR WITH EACH OTHER?
YES. WE ARE A CLANDESTINE ORGANIZATION OF SKILLED ASSASSINS WITH ROOTS DATING BACK OVER 1,000 YEARS, OPERATING SECRETLY HERE IN GOTHAM CITY TO UNDERMINE THE FILTH THAT IS THE RICH AND POWERFUL. WE WILL NOT REST UNTIL THE DECADENCE OF THIS CITY IS WIPED FROM THE FACE OF THE EARTH.
AND WE WILL DO EVERYTHING IN OUR POWER TO MAKE SURE THEY DO NOT DESTROY THIS CITY IN THE PROCESS, BY USING THE POWER OF LAW AND JUSTICE, AND ANYTHING THAT FALLS WITHIN ITS PARAMETERS.
AND I ALSO REALLY WANT TO TRY THE GARLIC NOODLE HERE.
OKAAAAY... ENJOY YOUR DINNER.

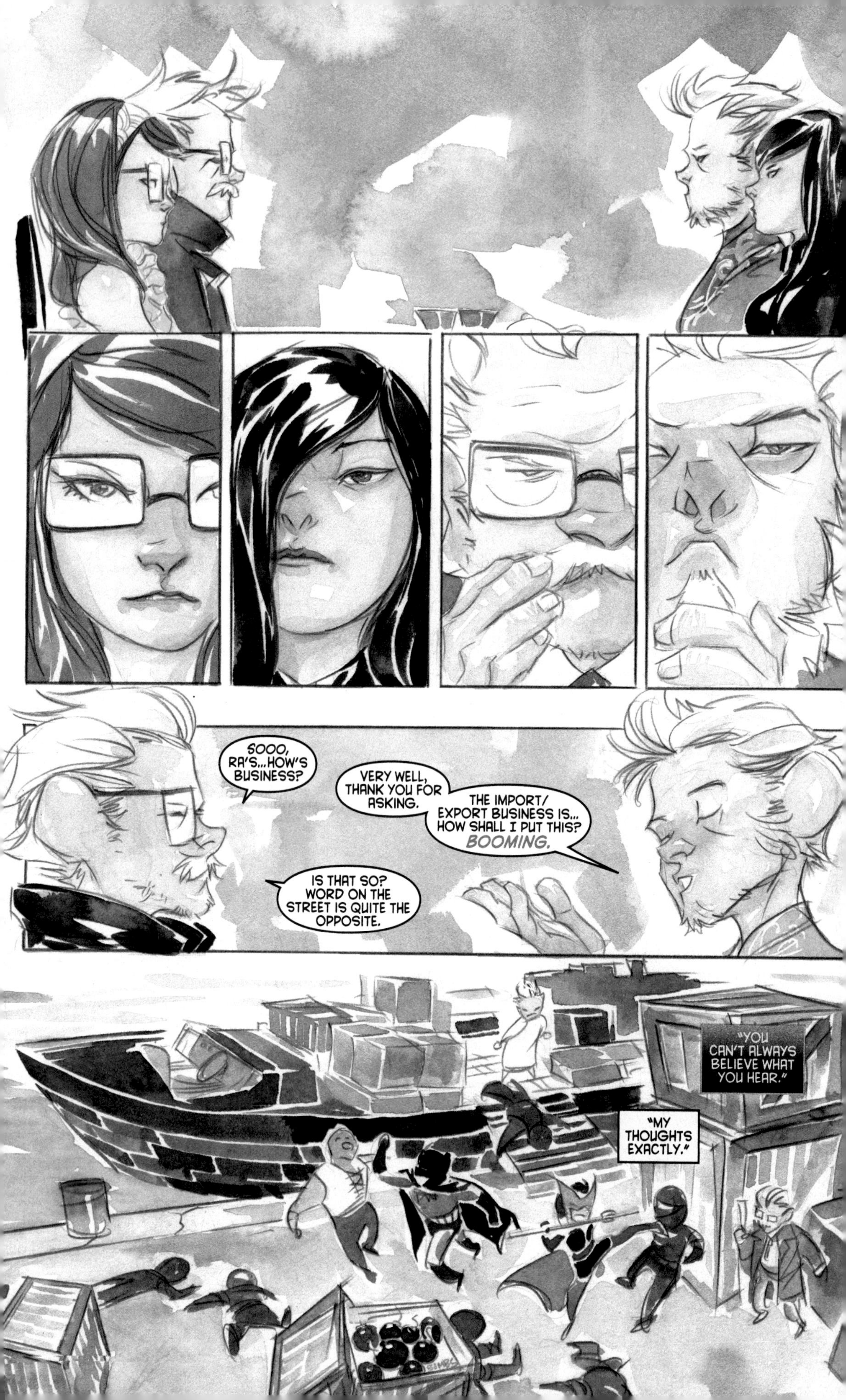
SOOO, RA'S...HOW'S BUSINESS?
VERY WELL, THANK YOU FOR ASKING.
THE IMPORT/ EXPORT BUSINESS IS... HOW SHALL I PUT THIS? BOOMING.
IS THAT SO? WORD ON THE STREET IS QUITE THE OPPOSITE.
"YOU CAN'T ALWAYS BELIEVE WHAT YOU HEAR."
"MY THOUGHTS EXACTLY."

IS THAT MY SON? OR BRUCE? I MUST TALK TO THEM. I INSIST.

AND I *RESIST.* FORGET IT.

I HOPE I'M NOT DISTURBING YOU, MISS GORDON.

NOT AT ALL, ALFRED. BESIDES, THERE'S ALREADY *PLENTY* HERE TO BE *DISTURBED* ABOUT.

WHY? WHAT'S UP?

I'M CALLING TO INFORM YOU SINCE YOU'RE MY EMERGENCY CONTACT NUMBER. JUST IN CASE, SAY...THE MANSION WERE TO BURN DOWN.

WHAT ARE THE BOYS UP TO *THIS* TIME?

THE YOUNG MASTERS HAVE DECIDED TO COOK ME A SPECIAL DINNER.

YOU'VE BEEN LIKE A FATHER TO THEM. IT'S THE LEAST THEY CAN DO. HOW DOES IT FEEL TO BE THE ONE WAITED ON?

A NEW EXPERIENCE. FOR ME AND FOR THEM. IF YOU'RE LOOKING FOR A WORD, YOU MAY USE "FRIGHTENED."

I IMAGINE BEING LOCKED UP IN ARKHAM IS MORE PLEASANT THAN BEING CONFINED TO THE KITCHEN.

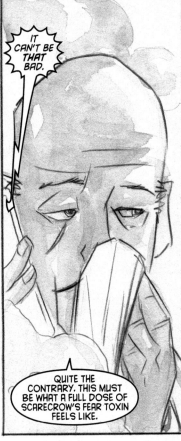

IT CAN'T BE THAT BAD.

QUITE THE CONTRARY. THIS MUST BE WHAT A FULL DOSE OF SCARECROW'S FEAR TOXIN FEELS LIKE.

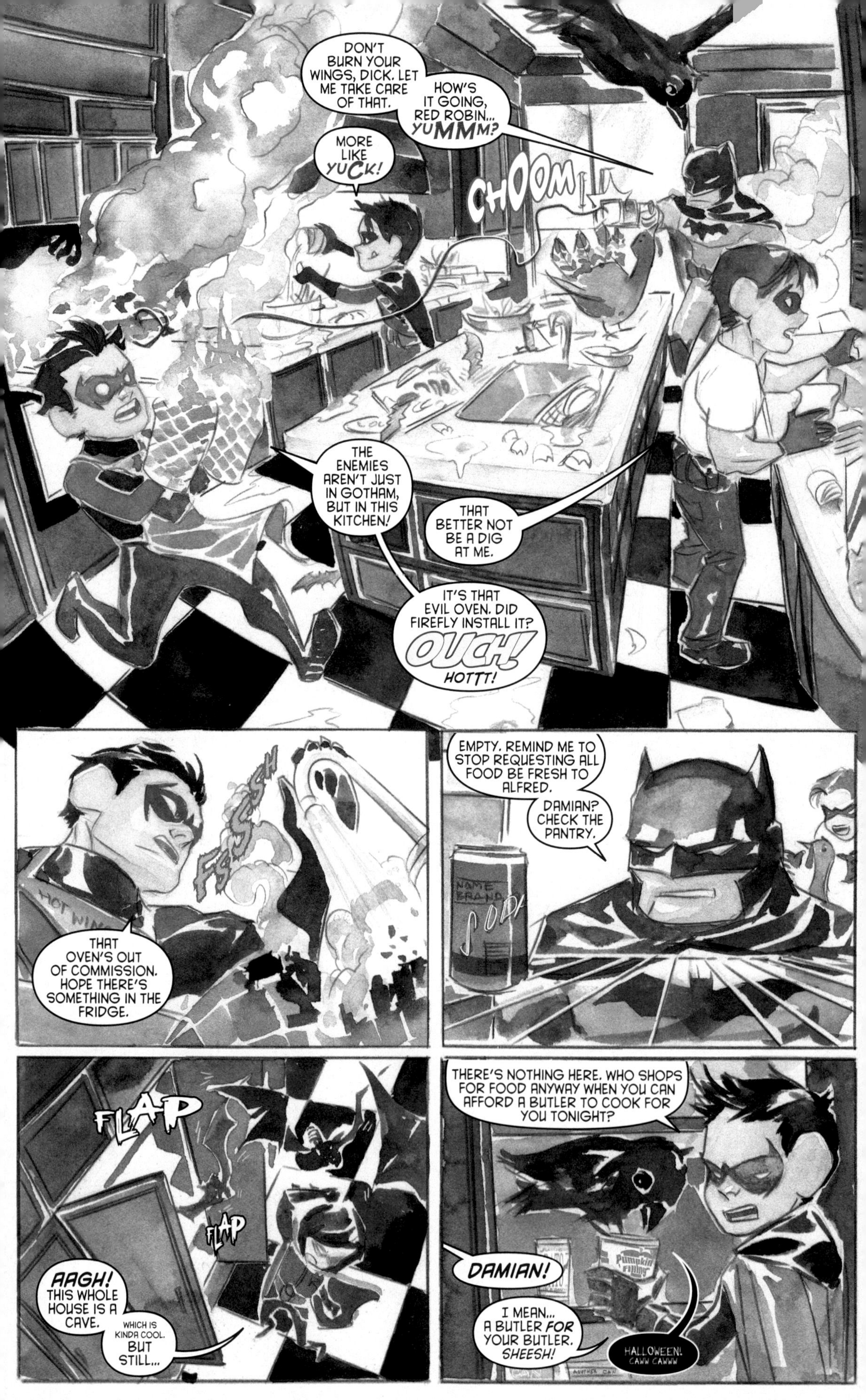
DON'T BURN YOUR WINGS, DICK. LET ME TAKE CARE OF THAT.
HOW'S IT GOING, RED ROBIN... YUMMM?
MORE LIKE YUCK!
CHOOM
THE ENEMIES AREN'T JUST IN GOTHAM, BUT IN THIS KITCHEN!
THAT BETTER NOT BE A DIG AT ME.
IT'S THAT EVIL OVEN. DID FIREFLY INSTALL IT?
OUCH!
HOTTT!
FSSSH
THAT OVEN'S OUT OF COMMISSION. HOPE THERE'S SOMETHING IN THE FRIDGE.
EMPTY. REMIND ME TO STOP REQUESTING ALL FOOD BE FRESH TO ALFRED.
DAMIAN? CHECK THE PANTRY.
NAME BRAND SODA
FLAP
FLAP
AAGH! THIS WHOLE HOUSE IS A CAVE.
WHICH IS KINDA COOL. BUT STILL...
THERE'S NOTHING HERE. WHO SHOPS FOR FOOD ANYWAY WHEN YOU CAN AFFORD A BUTLER TO COOK FOR YOU TONIGHT?
DAMIAN!
I MEAN... A BUTLER FOR YOUR BUTLER. SHEESH!
HALLOWEEN! CAWW CAWWW

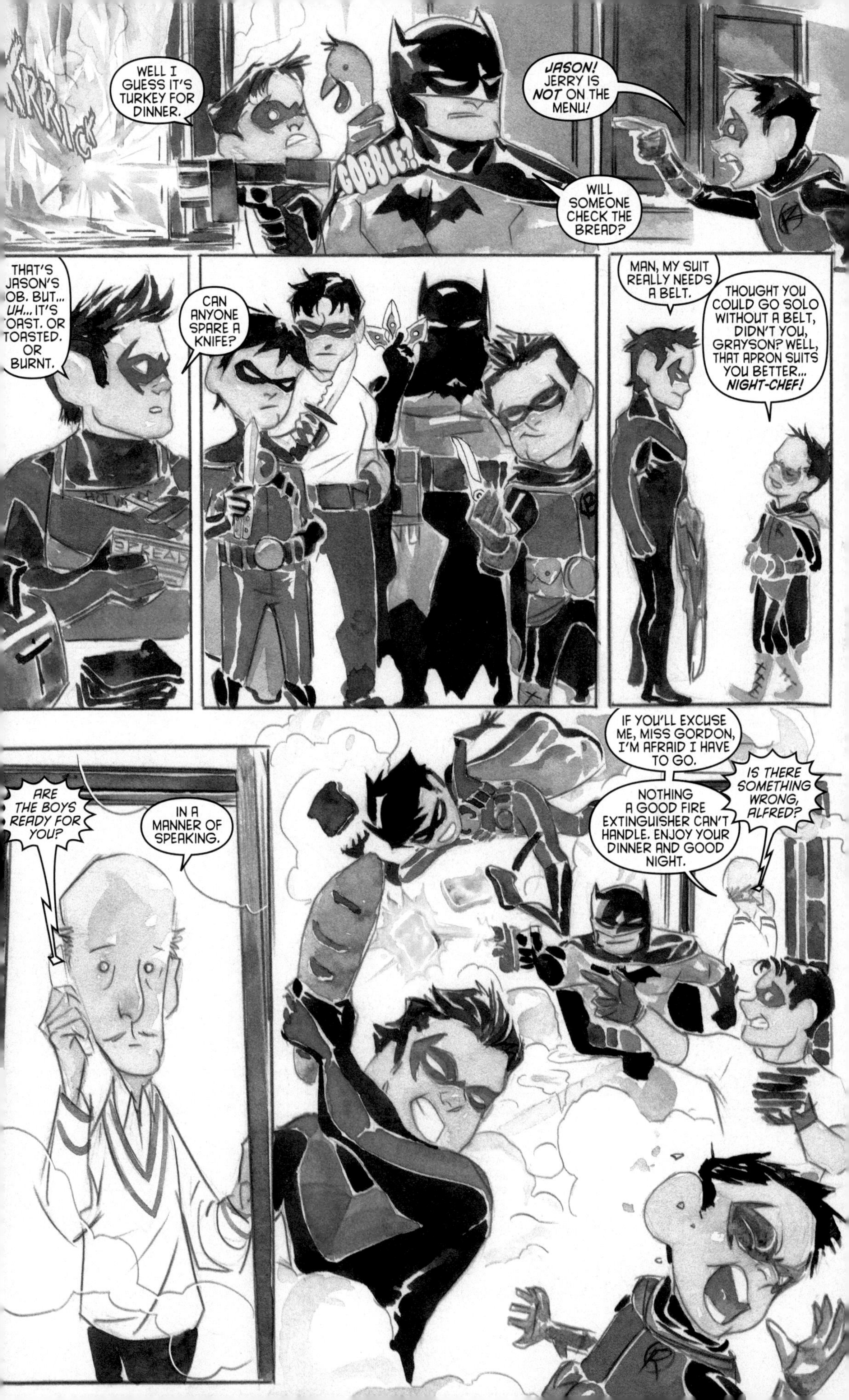
WELL I GUESS IT'S TURKEY FOR DINNER.
GOBBLE?!
JASON! JERRY IS NOT ON THE MENU!
WILL SOMEONE CHECK THE BREAD?
THAT'S JASON'S OB. BUT... UH... IT'S OAST. OR TOASTED. OR BURNT.
CAN ANYONE SPARE A KNIFE?
MAN, MY SUIT REALLY NEEDS A BELT.
THOUGHT YOU COULD GO SOLO WITHOUT A BELT, DIDN'T YOU, GRAYSON? WELL, THAT APRON SUITS YOU BETTER... NIGHT-CHEF!
ARE THE BOYS READY FOR YOU?
IN A MANNER OF SPEAKING.
IF YOU'LL EXCUSE ME, MISS GORDON, I'M AFRAID I HAVE TO GO.
IS THERE SOMETHING WRONG, ALFRED?
NOTHING A GOOD FIRE EXTINGUISHER CAN'T HANDLE. ENJOY YOUR DINNER AND GOOD NIGHT.

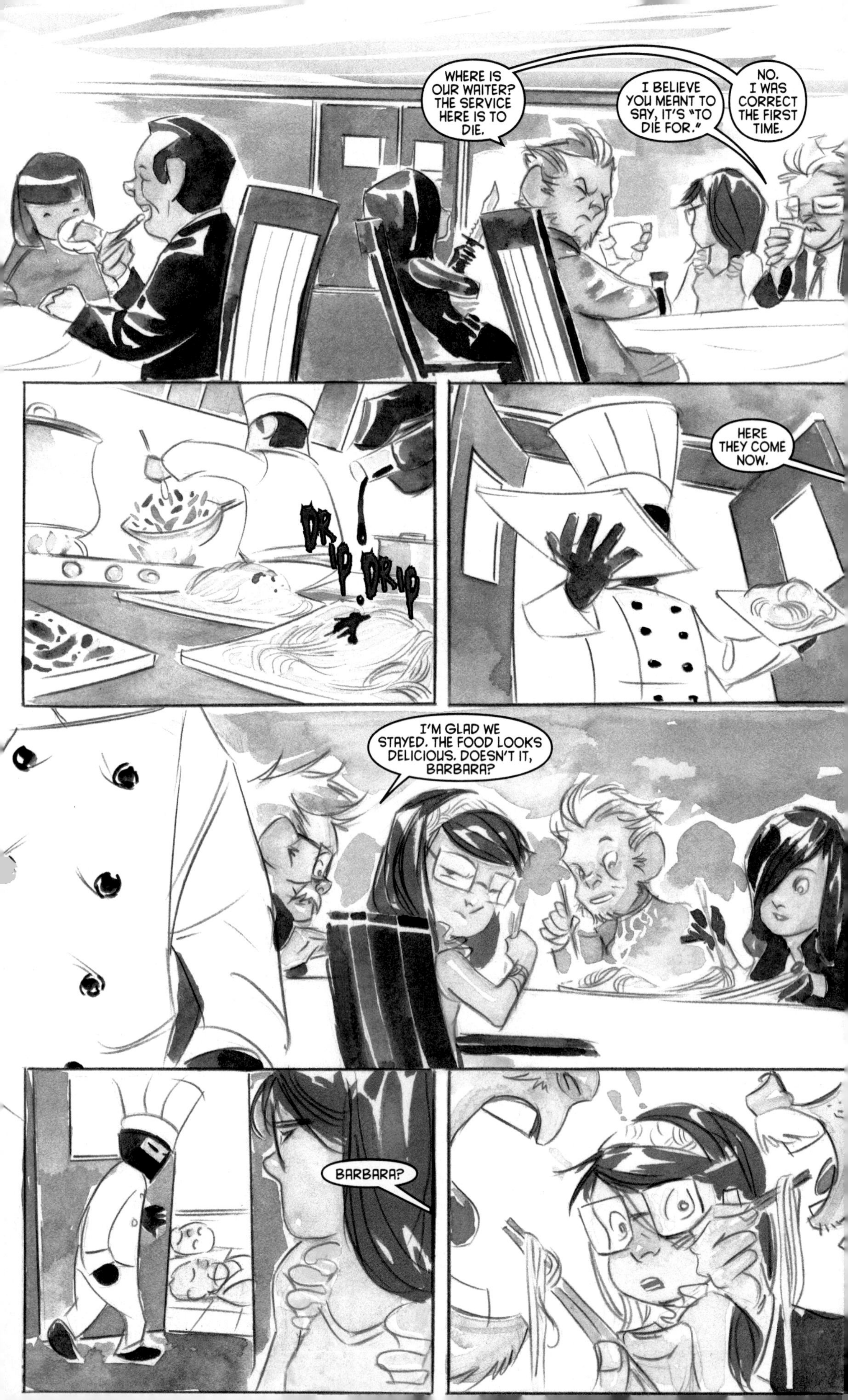
WHERE IS OUR WAITER? THE SERVICE HERE IS TO DIE.
I BELIEVE YOU MEANT TO SAY, IT'S "TO DIE FOR."
NO. I WAS CORRECT THE FIRST TIME.
DRIP DRIP
HERE THEY COME NOW.
I'M GLAD WE STAYED. THE FOOD LOOKS DELICIOUS. DOESN'T IT, BARBARA?
BARBARA?

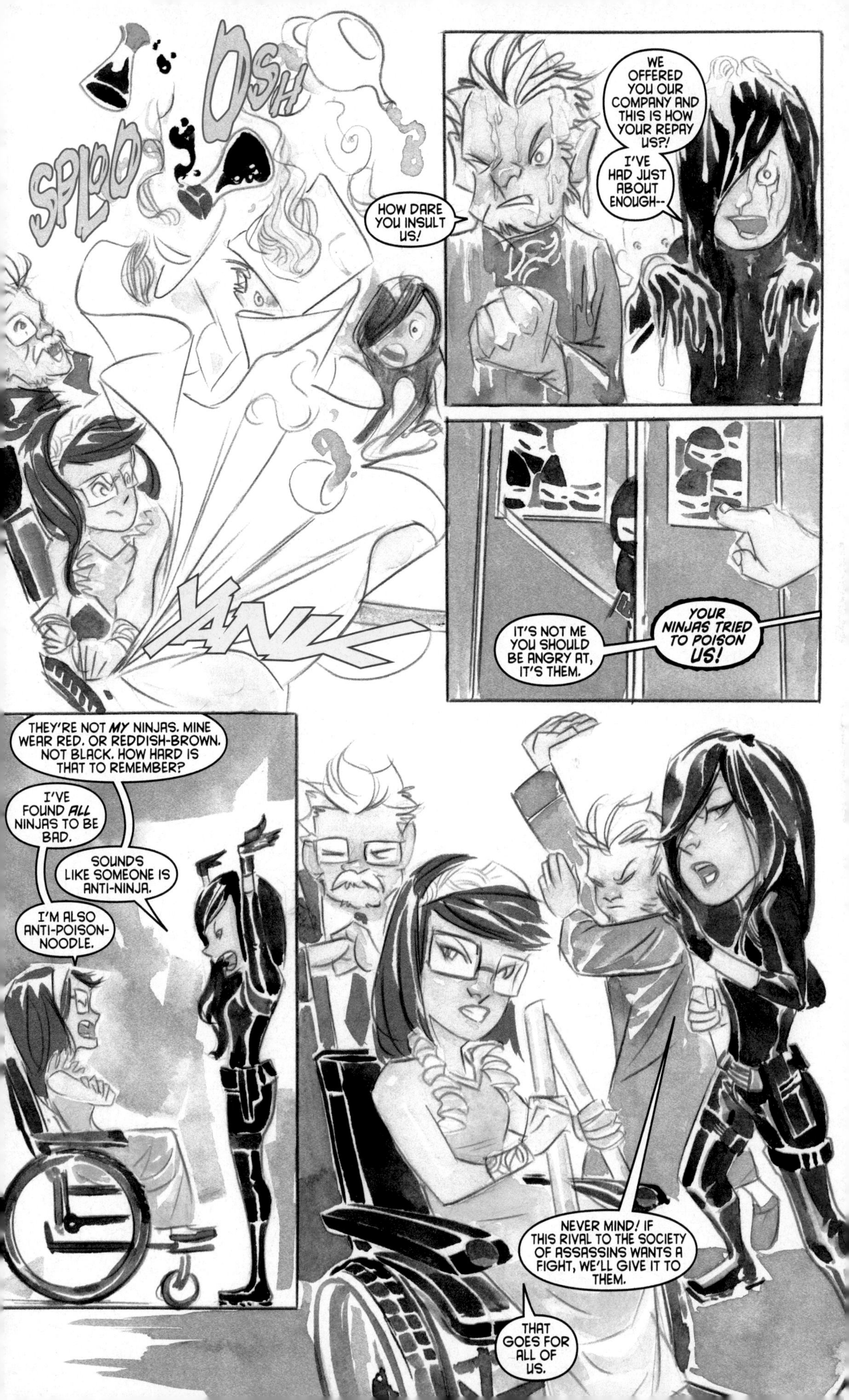
SPLOOSH
YANK
HOW DARE YOU INSULT US!
WE OFFERED YOU OUR COMPANY AND THIS IS HOW YOUR REPAY US?!
I'VE HAD JUST ABOUT ENOUGH--
IT'S NOT ME YOU SHOULD BE ANGRY AT, IT'S THEM.
YOUR NINJAS TRIED TO POISON US!
THEY'RE NOT MY NINJAS. MINE WEAR RED. OR REDDISH-BROWN. NOT BLACK. HOW HARD IS THAT TO REMEMBER?
I'VE FOUND ALL NINJAS TO BE BAD.
SOUNDS LIKE SOMEONE IS ANTI-NINJA.
I'M ALSO ANTI-POISON-NOODLE.
NEVER MIND! IF THIS RIVAL TO THE SOCIETY OF ASSASSINS WANTS A FIGHT, WE'LL GIVE IT TO THEM.
THAT GOES FOR ALL OF US.

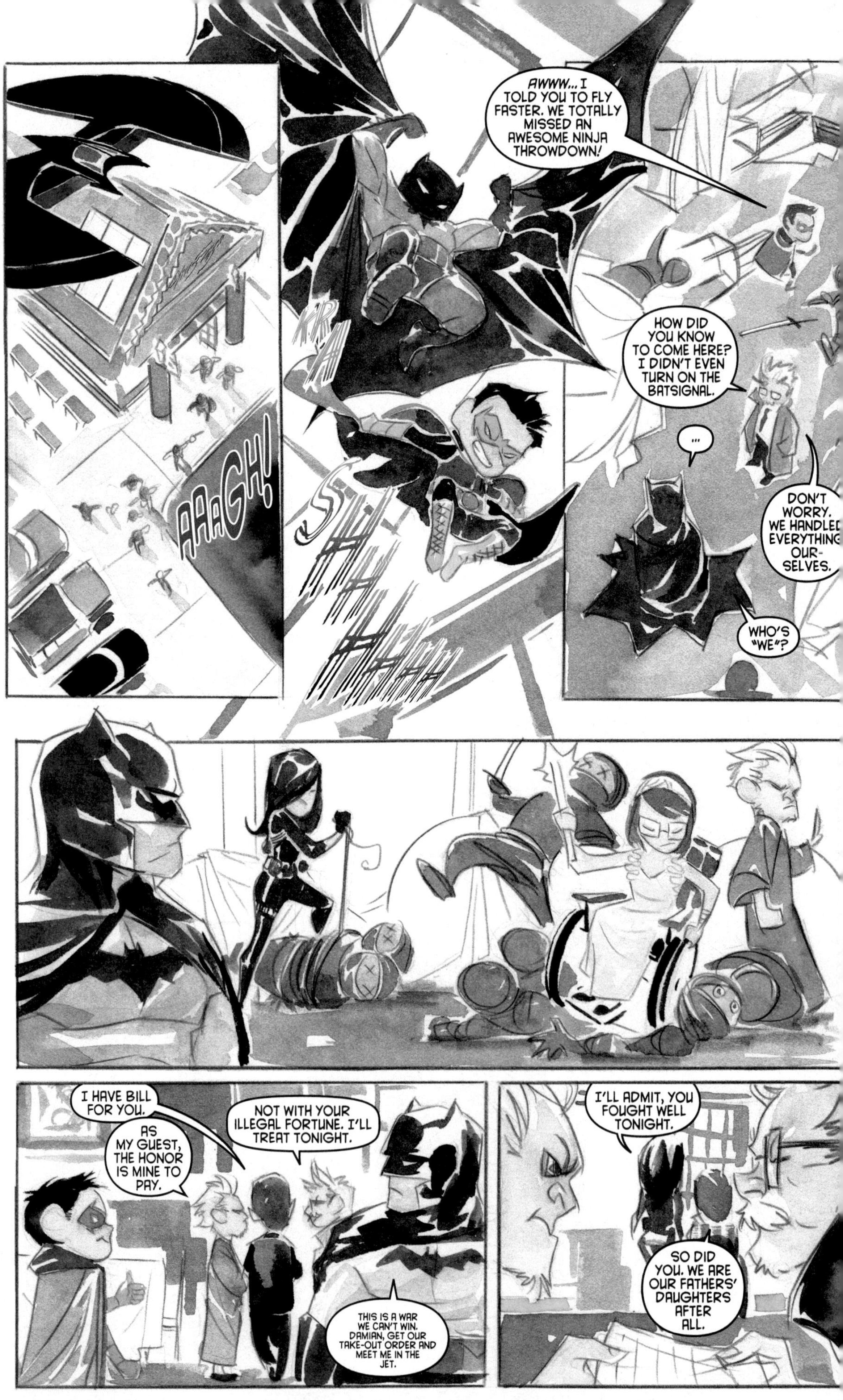

AAAGH!
KRA
AWWW... I TOLD YOU TO FLY FASTER. WE TOTALLY MISSED AN AWESOME NINJA THROWDOWN!
SSHHHHH
HOW DID YOU KNOW TO COME HERE? I DIDN'T EVEN TURN ON THE BATSIGNAL.
...
DON'T WORRY. WE HANDLED EVERYTHING OUR-SELVES.
WHO'S "WE"?
I HAVE BILL FOR YOU.
AS MY GUEST, THE HONOR IS MINE TO PAY.
NOT WITH YOUR ILLEGAL FORTUNE. I'LL TREAT TONIGHT.
THIS IS A WAR WE CAN'T WIN. DAMIAN, GET OUR TAKE-OUT ORDER AND MEET ME IN THE JET.
I'LL ADMIT, YOU FOUGHT WELL TONIGHT.
SO DID YOU. WE ARE OUR FATHERS' DAUGHTERS AFTER ALL.

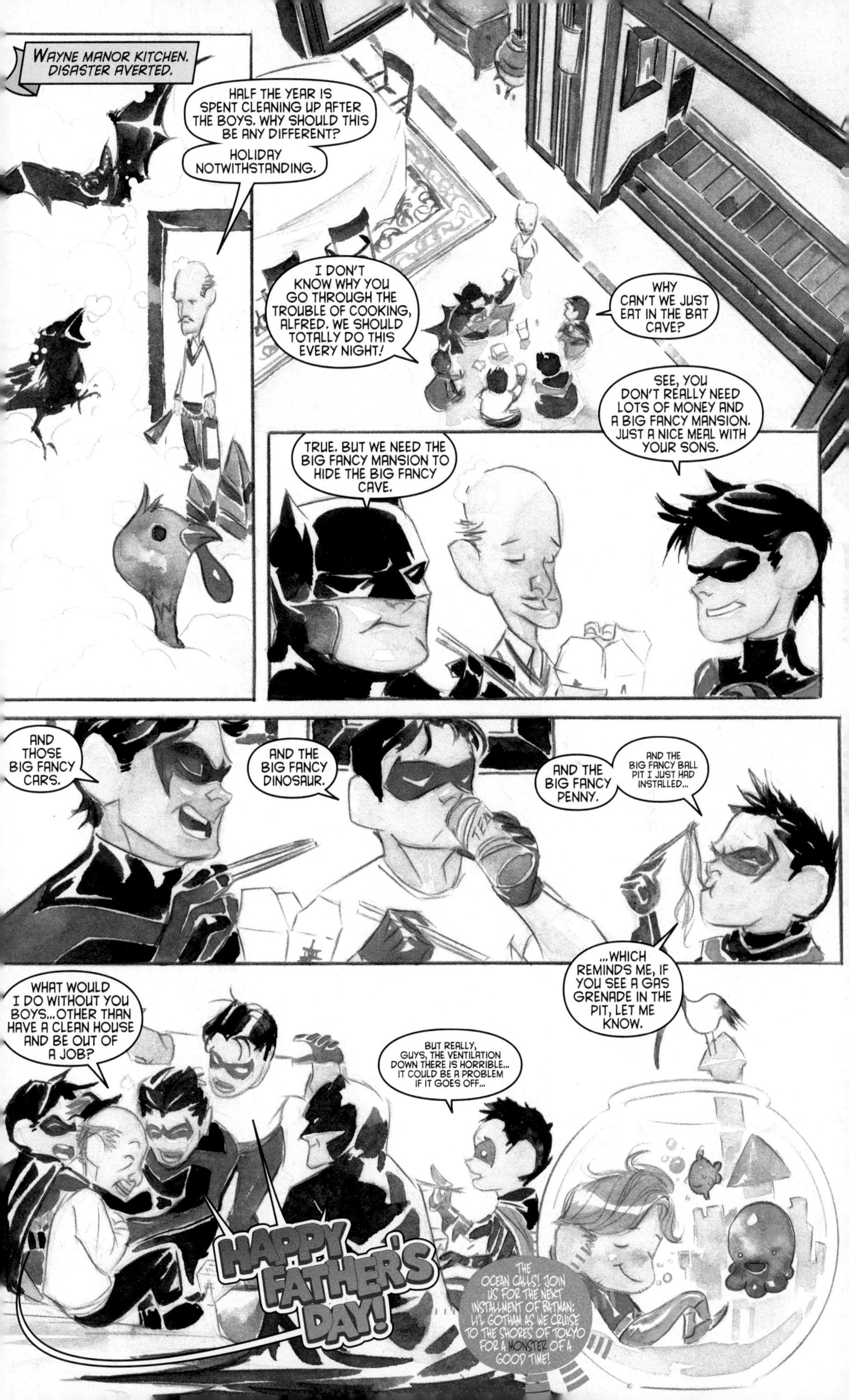
WAYNE MANOR KITCHEN. DISASTER AVERTED.
HALF THE YEAR IS SPENT CLEANING UP AFTER THE BOYS. WHY SHOULD THIS BE ANY DIFFERENT?
HOLIDAY NOTWITHSTANDING.
I DON'T KNOW WHY YOU GO THROUGH THE TROUBLE OF COOKING, ALFRED. WE SHOULD TOTALLY DO THIS EVERY NIGHT!
WHY CAN'T WE JUST EAT IN THE BAT CAVE?
SEE, YOU DON'T REALLY NEED LOTS OF MONEY AND A BIG FANCY MANSION. JUST A NICE MEAL WITH YOUR SONS.
TRUE. BUT WE NEED THE BIG FANCY MANSION TO HIDE THE BIG FANCY CAVE.
AND THOSE BIG FANCY CARS.
AND THE BIG FANCY DINOSAUR.
AND THE BIG FANCY PENNY.
AND THE BIG FANCY BALL PIT I JUST HAD INSTALLED...
...WHICH REMINDS ME, IF YOU SEE A GAS GRENADE IN THE PIT, LET ME KNOW.
WHAT WOULD I DO WITHOUT YOU BOYS...OTHER THAN HAVE A CLEAN HOUSE AND BE OUT OF A JOB?
BUT REALLY, GUYS, THE VENTILATION DOWN THERE IS HORRIBLE... IT COULD BE A PROBLEM IF IT GOES OFF...
HAPPY FATHER'S DAY!
THE OCEAN CALLS! JOIN US FOR THE NEXT INSTALLMENT OF BATMAN: LI'L GOTHAM AS WE CRUISE TO THE SHORES OF TOKYO FOR A MONSTER OF A GOOD TIME!

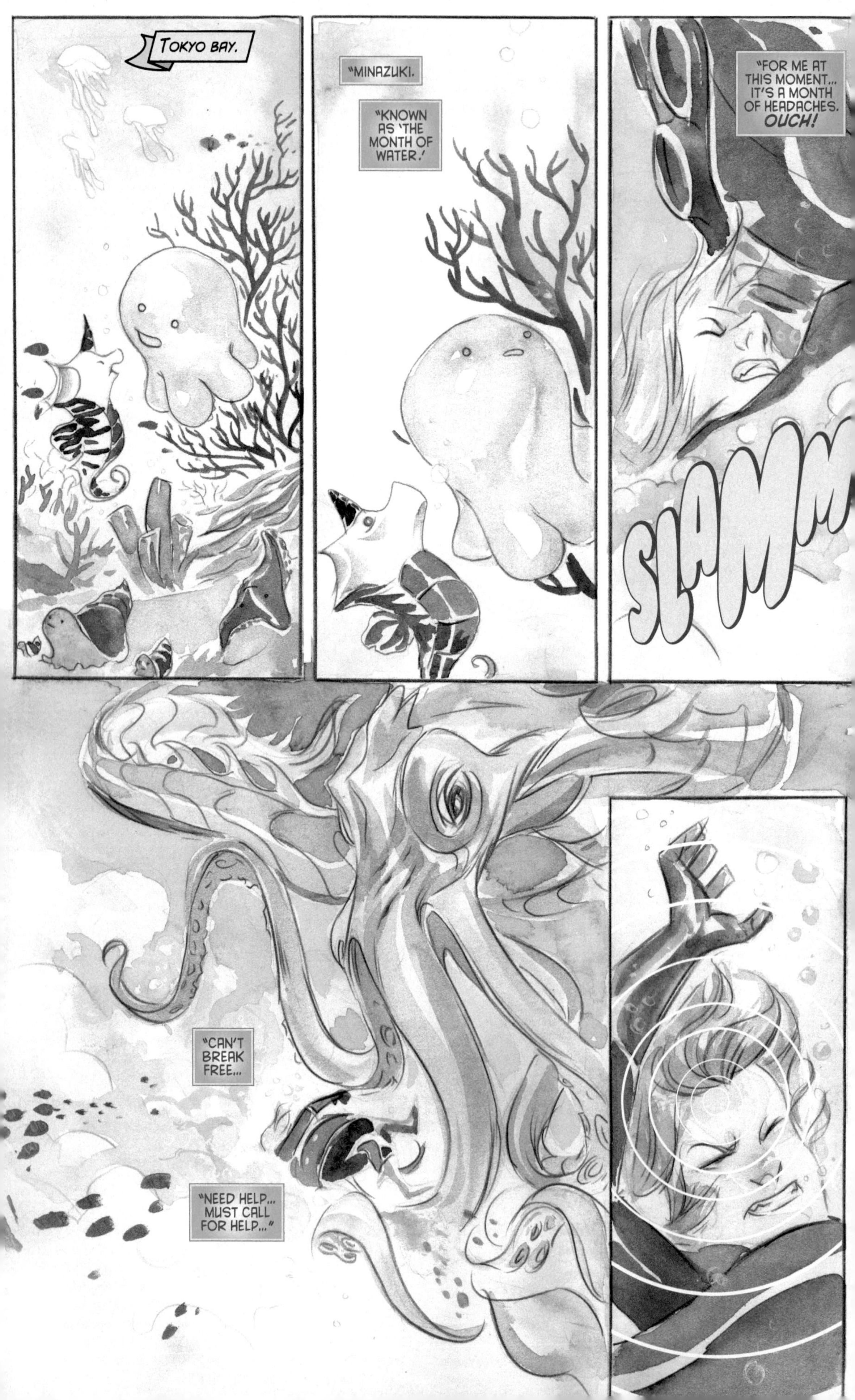
TOKYO BAY.
"MINAZUKI.
"KNOWN AS 'THE MONTH OF WATER.'
"FOR ME AT THIS MOMENT... IT'S A MONTH OF HEADACHES. OUCH!
SLAMM
"CAN'T BREAK FREE...
"NEED HELP... MUST CALL FOR HELP..."

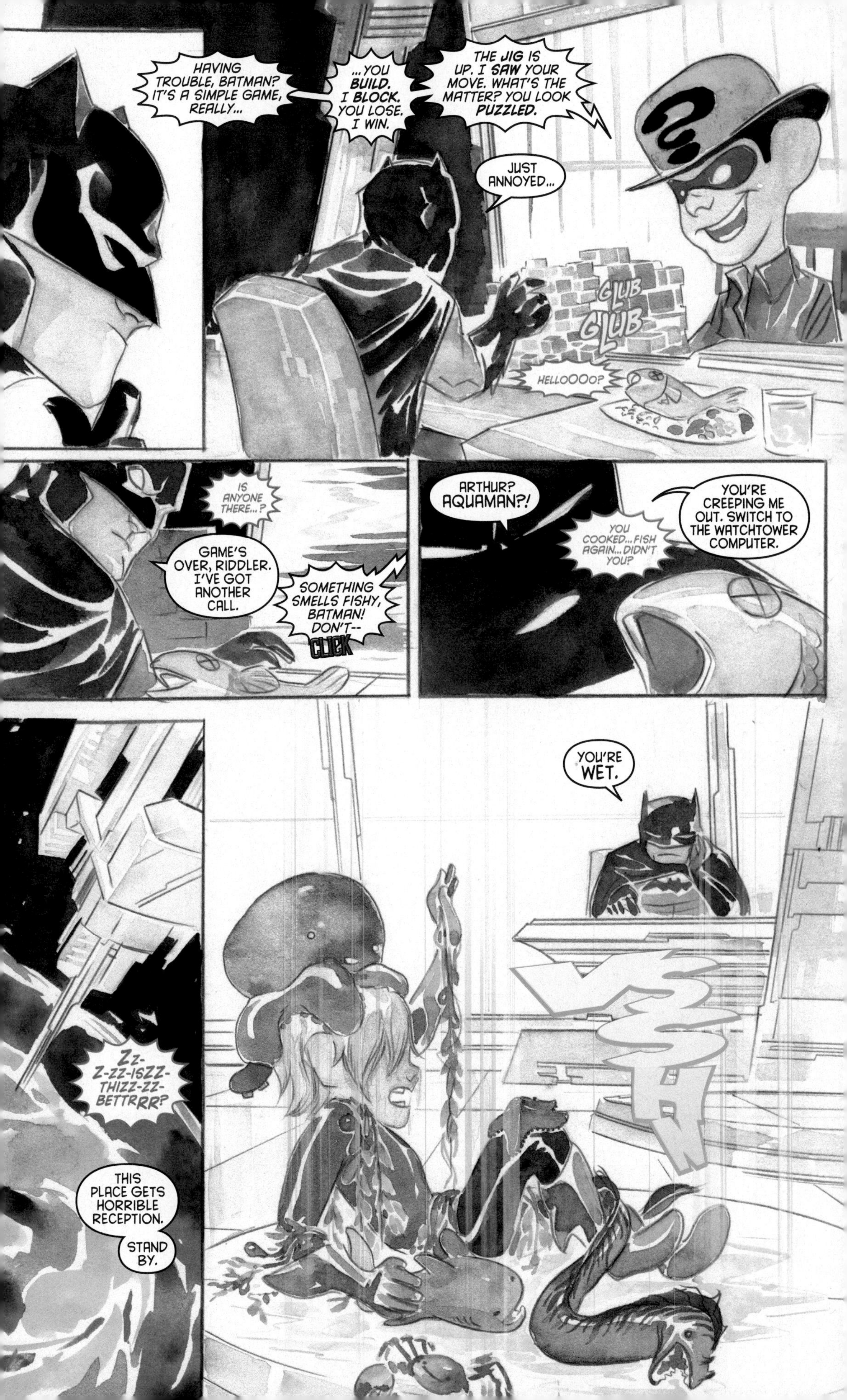
HAVING TROUBLE, BATMAN? IT'S A SIMPLE GAME, REALLY...
...YOU BUILD. I BLOCK. YOU LOSE. I WIN.
THE JIG IS UP. I SAW YOUR MOVE. WHAT'S THE MATTER? YOU LOOK PUZZLED.
JUST ANNOYED...
GLUB GLUB
HELLOOOO?
IS ANYONE THERE...?
GAME'S OVER, RIDDLER. I'VE GOT ANOTHER CALL.
SOMETHING SMELLS FISHY, BATMAN! DON'T--
CLICK
ARTHUR? AQUAMAN?!
YOU COOKED...FISH AGAIN...DIDN'T YOU?
YOU'RE CREEPING ME OUT. SWITCH TO THE WATCHTOWER COMPUTER.
ZZ-Z-ZZ-ISZZ-THIZZ-ZZ-BETTRRR?
THIS PLACE GETS HORRIBLE RECEPTION.
STAND BY.
YOU'RE WET.

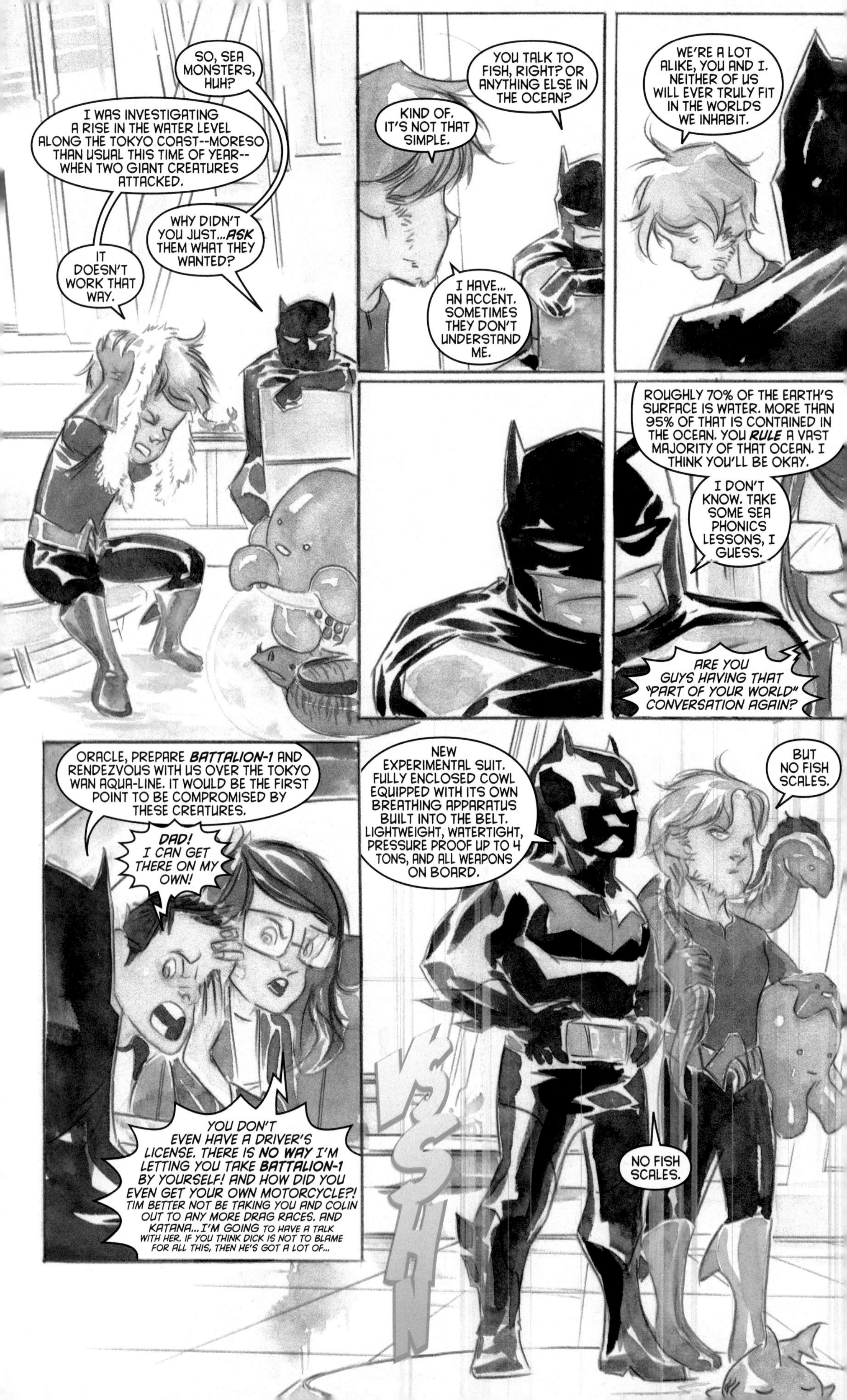

I WAS INVESTIGATING A RISE IN THE WATER LEVEL ALONG THE TOKYO COAST--MORESO THAN USUAL THIS TIME OF YEAR--WHEN TWO GIANT CREATURES ATTACKED.
SO, SEA MONSTERS, HUH?
WHY DIDN'T YOU JUST...ASK THEM WHAT THEY WANTED?
IT DOESN'T WORK THAT WAY.
YOU TALK TO FISH, RIGHT? OR ANYTHING ELSE IN THE OCEAN?
KIND OF. IT'S NOT THAT SIMPLE.
I HAVE... AN ACCENT. SOMETIMES THEY DON'T UNDERSTAND ME.
WE'RE A LOT ALIKE, YOU AND I. NEITHER OF US WILL EVER TRULY FIT IN THE WORLDS WE INHABIT.
ROUGHLY 70% OF THE EARTH'S SURFACE IS WATER. MORE THAN 95% OF THAT IS CONTAINED IN THE OCEAN. YOU RULE A VAST MAJORITY OF THAT OCEAN. I THINK YOU'LL BE OKAY.
I DON'T KNOW. TAKE SOME SEA PHONICS LESSONS, I GUESS.
ARE YOU GUYS HAVING THAT "PART OF YOUR WORLD" CONVERSATION AGAIN?
ORACLE, PREPARE BATTALION-1 AND RENDEZVOUS WITH US OVER THE TOKYO WAN AQUA-LINE. IT WOULD BE THE FIRST POINT TO BE COMPROMISED BY THESE CREATURES.
DAD! I CAN GET THERE ON MY OWN!
YOU DON'T EVEN HAVE A DRIVER'S LICENSE. THERE IS NO WAY I'M LETTING YOU TAKE BATTALION-1 BY YOURSELF! AND HOW DID YOU EVEN GET YOUR OWN MOTORCYCLE?! TIM BETTER NOT BE TAKING YOU AND COLIN OUT TO ANY MORE DRAG RACES. AND KATANA...I'M GOING TO HAVE A TALK WITH HER. IF YOU THINK DICK IS NOT TO BLAME FOR ALL THIS, THEN HE'S GOT A LOT OF...
NEW EXPERIMENTAL SUIT. FULLY ENCLOSED COWL EQUIPPED WITH ITS OWN BREATHING APPARATUS BUILT INTO THE BELT. LIGHTWEIGHT, WATERTIGHT, PRESSURE PROOF UP TO 4 TONS, AND ALL WEAPONS ON BOARD.
BUT NO FISH SCALES.
NO FISH SCALES.
VSHH

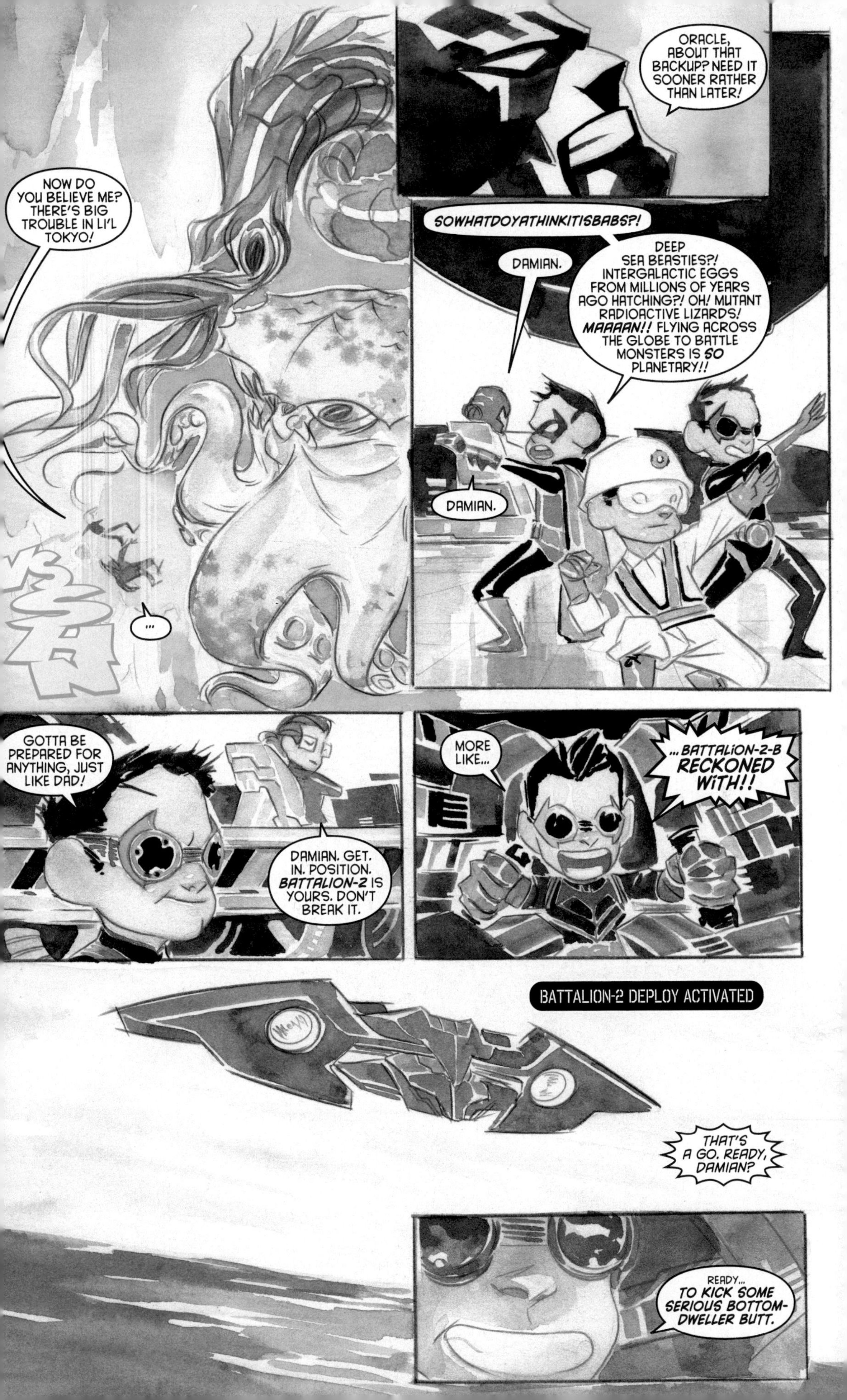
ORACLE, ABOUT THAT BACKUP? NEED IT SOONER RATHER THAN LATER!
NOW DO YOU BELIEVE ME? THERE'S BIG TROUBLE IN LI'L TOKYO!
...
SOWHATDOYATHINKITISBABS?!
DAMIAN.
DEEP SEA BEASTIES?! INTERGALACTIC EGGS FROM MILLIONS OF YEARS AGO HATCHING?! OH! MUTANT RADIOACTIVE LIZARDS! MAAAAN!! FLYING ACROSS THE GLOBE TO BATTLE MONSTERS IS SO PLANETARY!!
DAMIAN.
GOTTA BE PREPARED FOR ANYTHING, JUST LIKE DAD!
DAMIAN. GET. IN. POSITION. BATTALION-2 IS YOURS. DON'T BREAK IT.
MORE LIKE...
...BATTALION-2-B RECKONED WITH!!
BATTALION-2 DEPLOY ACTIVATED
THAT'S A GO. READY, DAMIAN?
READY... TO KICK SOME SERIOUS BOTTOM-DWELLER BUTT.

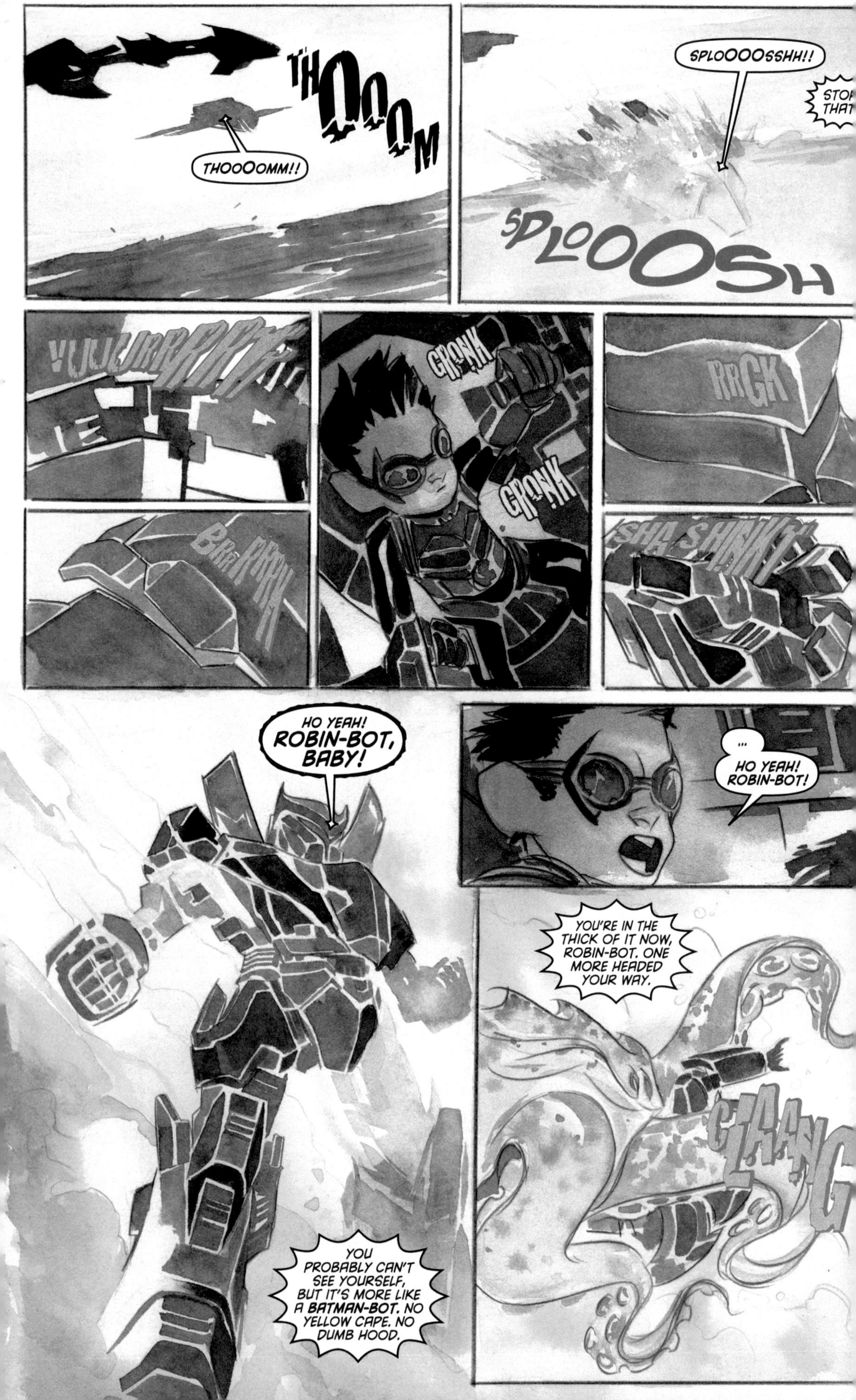
THOOOM
THOOOOMM!!
SPLOOOOSSHH!!
SPLOOOSH
VJJJJRRRRRK
GRONK
GRONK
RRGK
BRRRRRK
SHASHNK
HO YEAH! ROBIN-BOT, BABY!
... HO YEAH! ROBIN-BOT!
YOU'RE IN THE THICK OF IT NOW, ROBIN-BOT. ONE MORE HEADED YOUR WAY.
CLAANG
YOU PROBABLY CAN'T SEE YOURSELF, BUT IT'S MORE LIKE A BATMAN-BOT. NO YELLOW CAPE. NO DUMB HOOD.

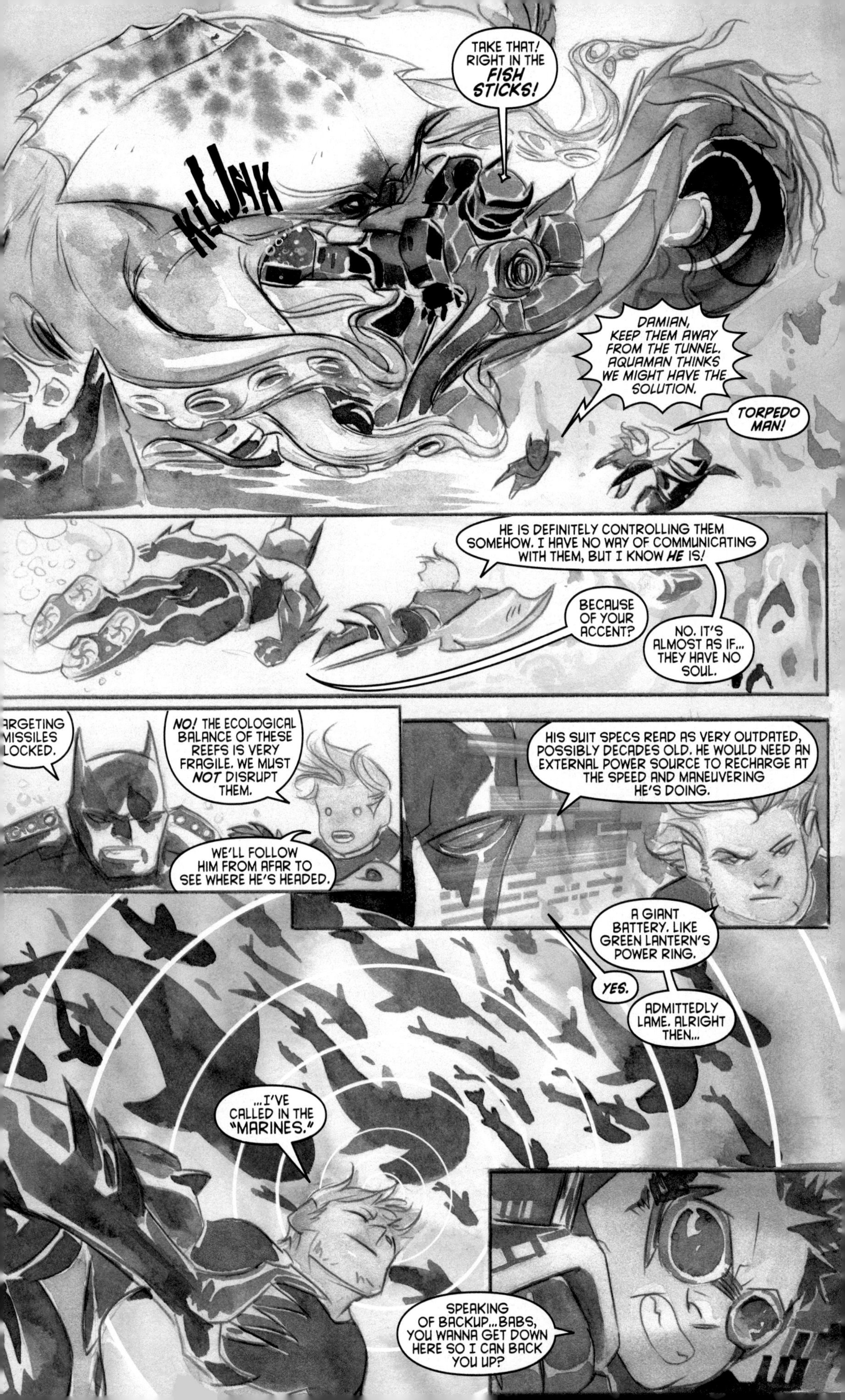
TAKE THAT! RIGHT IN THE FISH STICKS!
KLUNK
DAMIAN, KEEP THEM AWAY FROM THE TUNNEL. AQUAMAN THINKS WE MIGHT HAVE THE SOLUTION.
TORPEDO MAN!
HE IS DEFINITELY CONTROLLING THEM SOMEHOW. I HAVE NO WAY OF COMMUNICATING WITH THEM, BUT I KNOW HE IS!
BECAUSE OF YOUR ACCENT?
NO. IT'S ALMOST AS IF... THEY HAVE NO SOUL.
ARGETING MISSILES LOCKED.
NO! THE ECOLOGICAL BALANCE OF THESE REEFS IS VERY FRAGILE. WE MUST NOT DISRUPT THEM.
WE'LL FOLLOW HIM FROM AFAR TO SEE WHERE HE'S HEADED.
HIS SUIT SPECS READ AS VERY OUTDATED, POSSIBLY DECADES OLD. HE WOULD NEED AN EXTERNAL POWER SOURCE TO RECHARGE AT THE SPEED AND MANEUVERING HE'S DOING.
A GIANT BATTERY. LIKE GREEN LANTERN'S POWER RING.
YES.
ADMITTEDLY LAME. ALRIGHT THEN...
...I'VE CALLED IN THE "MARINES."
SPEAKING OF BACKUP... BABS, YOU WANNA GET DOWN HERE SO I CAN BACK YOU UP?

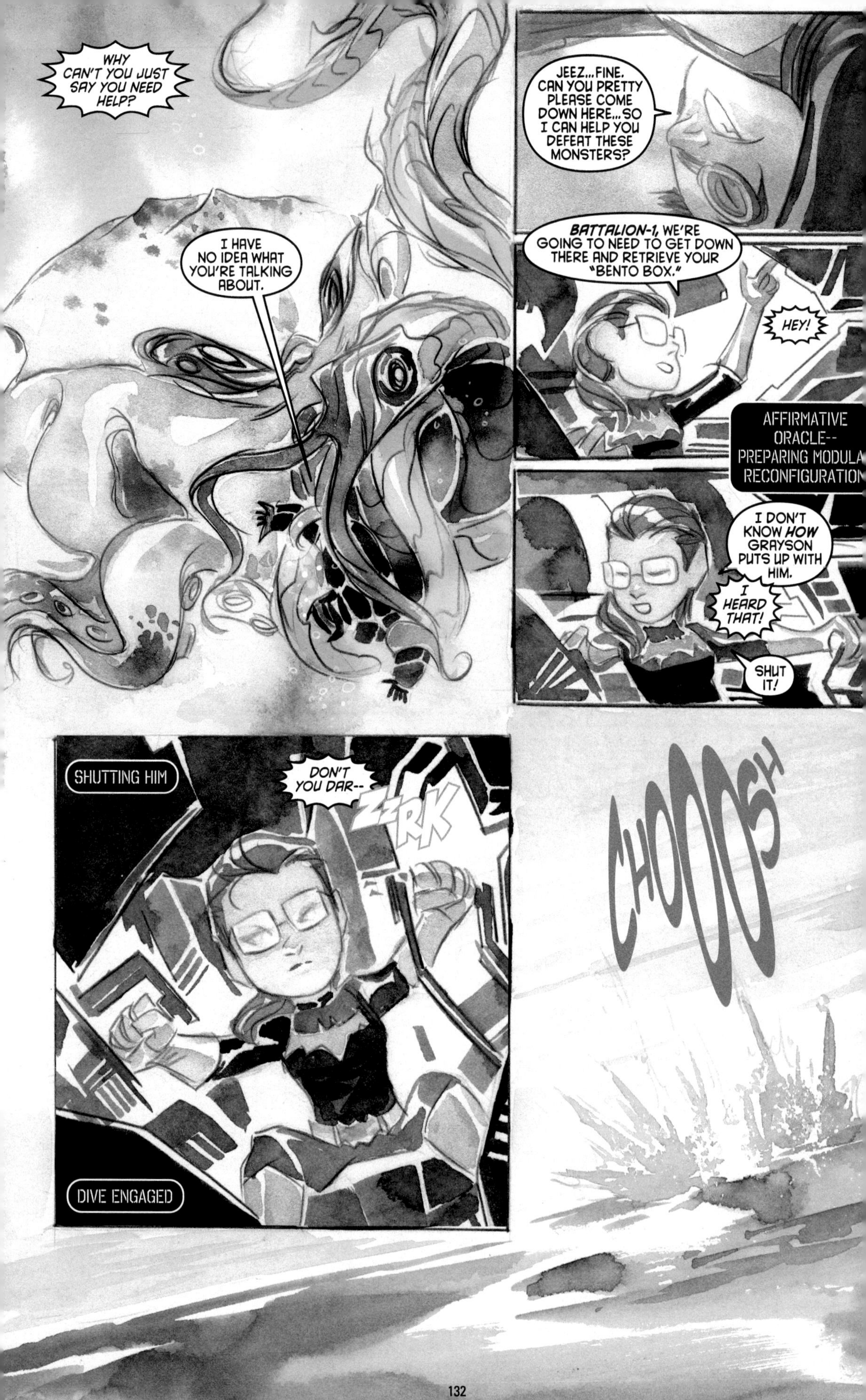

WHY CAN'T YOU JUST SAY YOU NEED HELP?
I HAVE NO IDEA WHAT YOU'RE TALKING ABOUT.
JEEZ...FINE. CAN YOU PRETTY PLEASE COME DOWN HERE...SO I CAN HELP YOU DEFEAT THESE MONSTERS?
BATTALION-1, WE'RE GOING TO NEED TO GET DOWN THERE AND RETRIEVE YOUR "BENTO BOX."
HEY!
AFFIRMATIVE ORACLE-- PREPARING MODULA RECONFIGURATION
I DON'T KNOW HOW GRAYSON PUTS UP WITH HIM.
I HEARD THAT!
SHUT IT!
SHUTTING HIM
DON'T YOU DAR--
ZZRK
DIVE ENGAGED
CHOOOSH

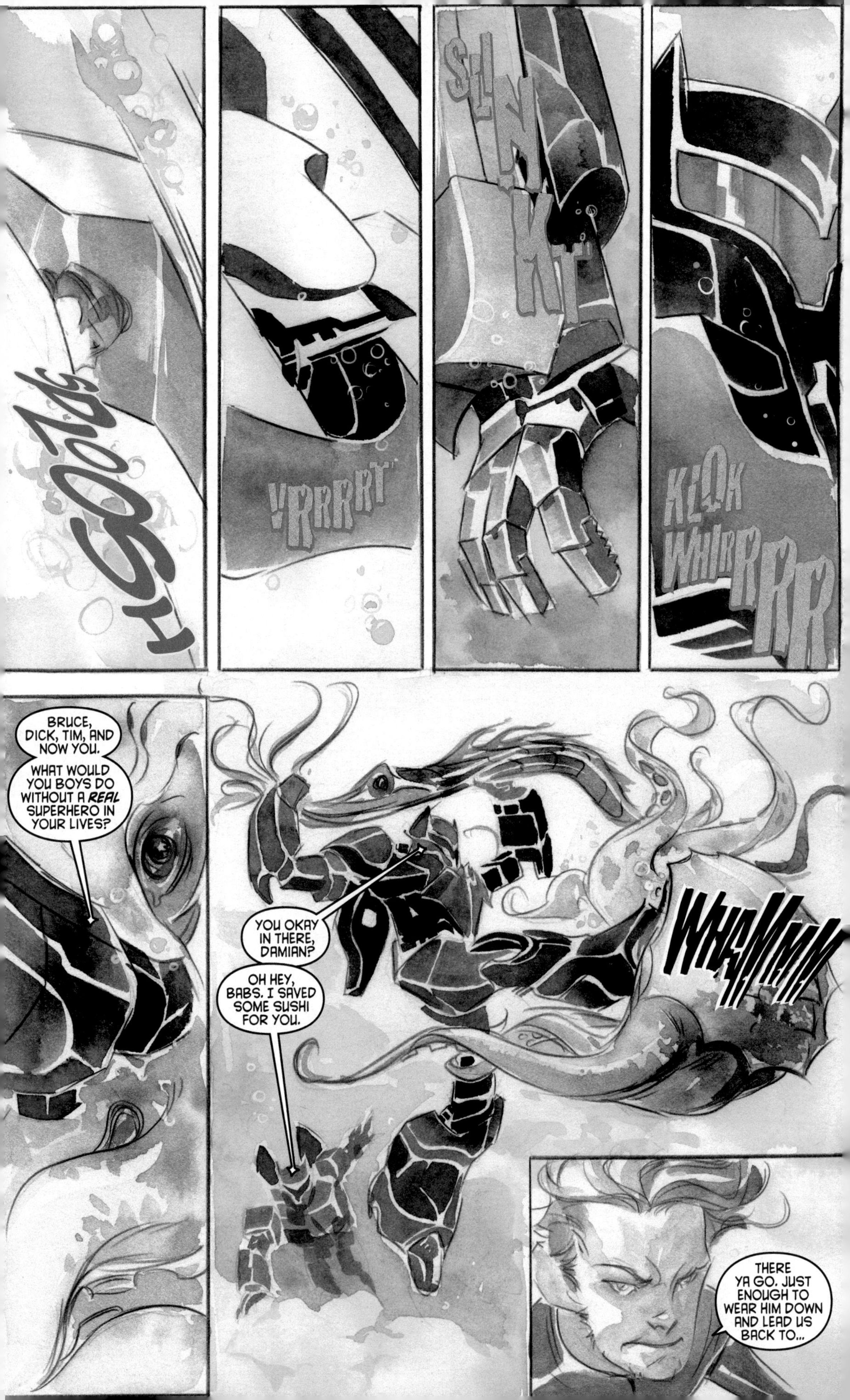

BRUCE, DICK, TIM, AND NOW YOU.
WHAT WOULD YOU BOYS DO WITHOUT A *REAL* SUPERHERO IN YOUR LIVES?
YOU OKAY IN THERE, DAMIAN?
OH HEY, BABS. I SAVED SOME SUSHI FOR YOU.
THERE YA GO. JUST ENOUGH TO WEAR HIM DOWN AND LEAD US BACK TO...

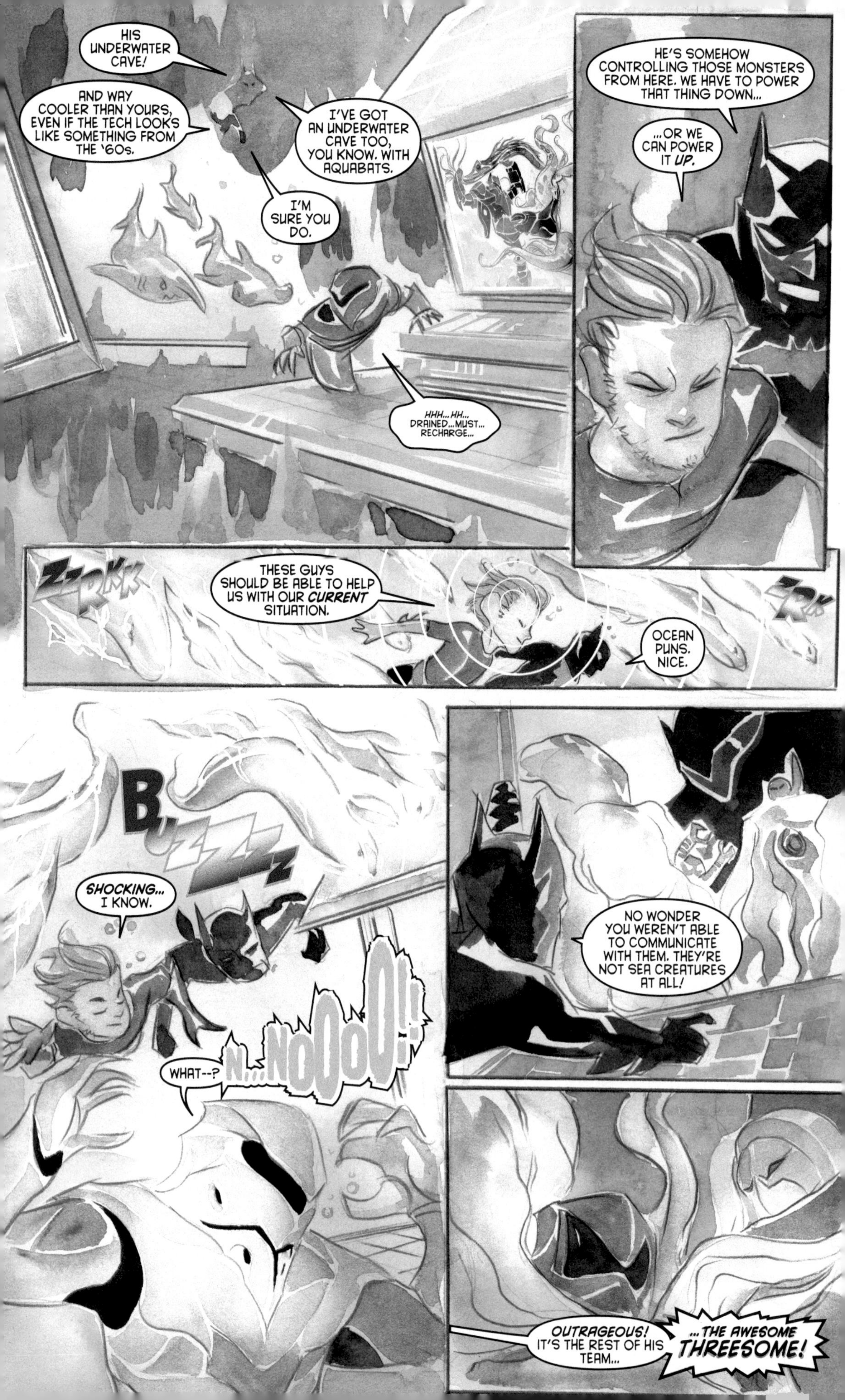
HIS UNDERWATER CAVE!
AND WAY COOLER THAN YOURS, EVEN IF THE TECH LOOKS LIKE SOMETHING FROM THE '60s.
I'VE GOT AN UNDERWATER CAVE TOO, YOU KNOW. WITH AQUABATS.
I'M SURE YOU DO.
HHH... HH... DRAINED... MUST... RECHARGE...
HE'S SOMEHOW CONTROLLING THOSE MONSTERS FROM HERE. WE HAVE TO POWER THAT THING DOWN...
...OR WE CAN POWER IT UP.
ZZRKK
THESE GUYS SHOULD BE ABLE TO HELP US WITH OUR CURRENT SITUATION.
OCEAN PUNS. NICE.
ZRK
BUZZZZ
SHOCKING... I KNOW.
WHAT--?
N...NOOOO!!
NO WONDER YOU WEREN'T ABLE TO COMMUNICATE WITH THEM. THEY'RE NOT SEA CREATURES AT ALL!
OUTRAGEOUS! IT'S THE REST OF HIS TEAM...
...THE AWESOME THREESOME!

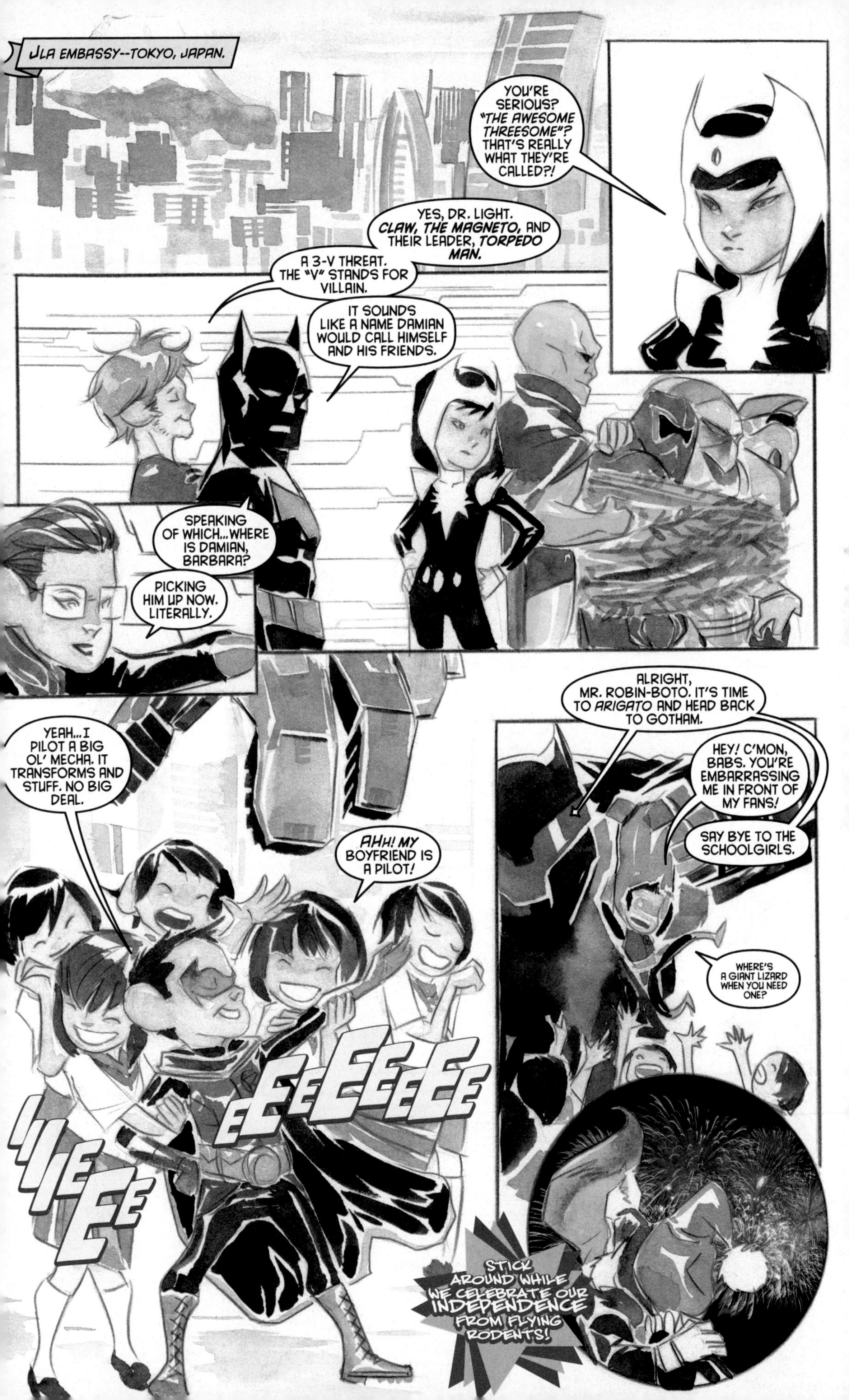
JLA EMBASSY--TOKYO, JAPAN.
YOU'RE SERIOUS? "THE AWESOME THREESOME"? THAT'S REALLY WHAT THEY'RE CALLED?!
YES, DR. LIGHT. CLAW, THE MAGNETO, AND THEIR LEADER, TORPEDO MAN.
A 3-V THREAT. THE "V" STANDS FOR VILLAIN.
IT SOUNDS LIKE A NAME DAMIAN WOULD CALL HIMSELF AND HIS FRIENDS.
SPEAKING OF WHICH...WHERE IS DAMIAN, BARBARA?
PICKING HIM UP NOW. LITERALLY.
YEAH...I PILOT A BIG OL' MECHA. IT TRANSFORMS AND STUFF. NO BIG DEAL.
AHH! MY BOYFRIEND IS A PILOT!
IIIIEEE
EEEEEEEEEE
ALRIGHT, MR. ROBIN-BOTO. IT'S TIME TO ARIGATO AND HEAD BACK TO GOTHAM.
HEY! C'MON, BABS. YOU'RE EMBARRASSING ME IN FRONT OF MY FANS!
SAY BYE TO THE SCHOOLGIRLS.
WHERE'S A GIANT LIZARD WHEN YOU NEED ONE?
STICK AROUND WHILE WE CELEBRATE OUR INDEPENDENCE FROM FLYING RODENTS!

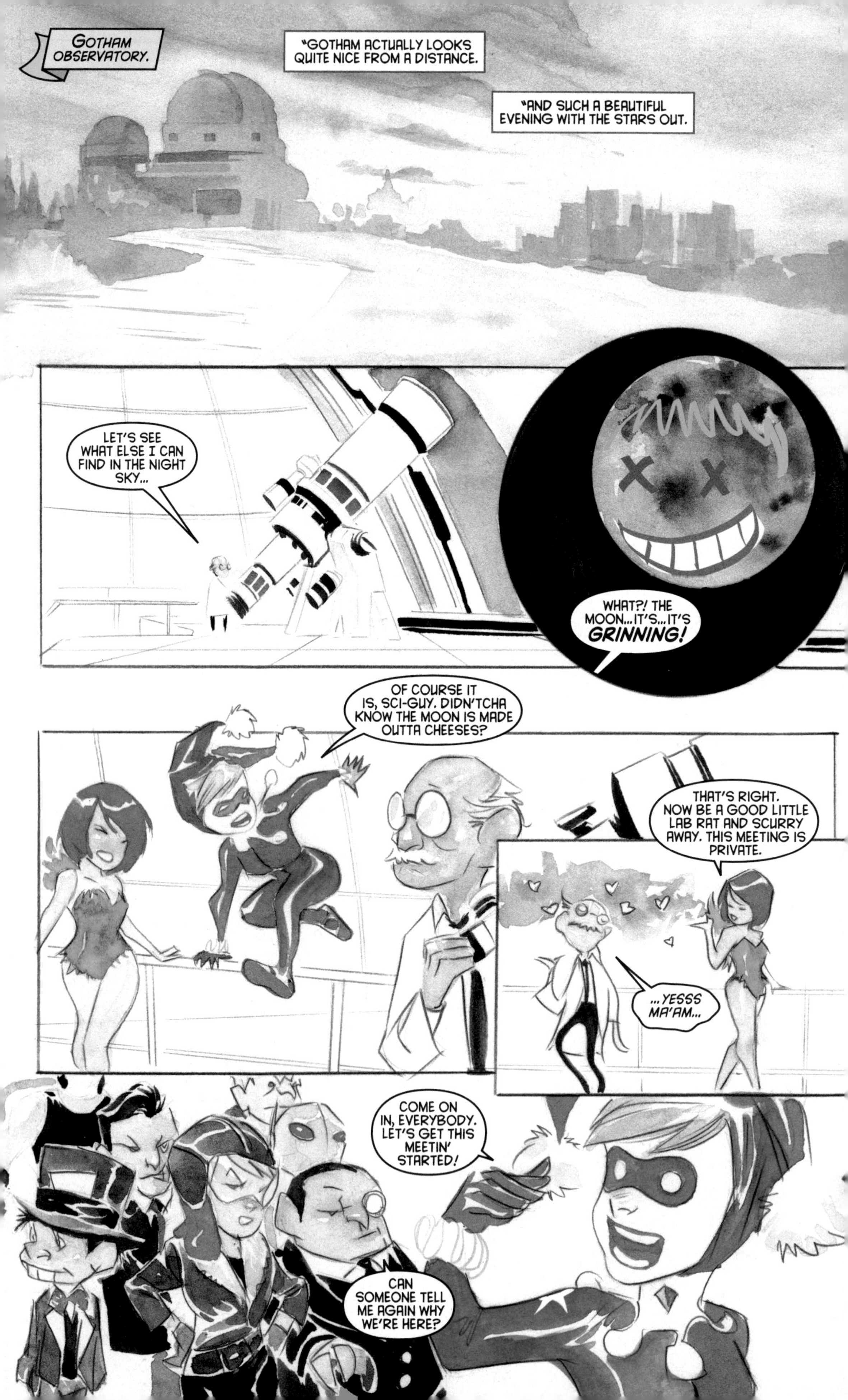
GOTHAM OBSERVATORY.
"GOTHAM ACTUALLY LOOKS QUITE NICE FROM A DISTANCE.
"AND SUCH A BEAUTIFUL EVENING WITH THE STARS OUT.
LET'S SEE WHAT ELSE I CAN FIND IN THE NIGHT SKY...
WHAT?! THE MOON...IT'S...IT'S GRINNING!
OF COURSE IT IS, SCI-GUY. DIDN'TCHA KNOW THE MOON IS MADE OUTTA CHEESES?
THAT'S RIGHT. NOW BE A GOOD LITTLE LAB RAT AND SCURRY AWAY. THIS MEETING IS PRIVATE.
...YESSS MA'AM...
COME ON IN, EVERYBODY. LET'S GET THIS MEETIN' STARTED!
CAN SOMEONE TELL ME AGAIN WHY WE'RE HERE?

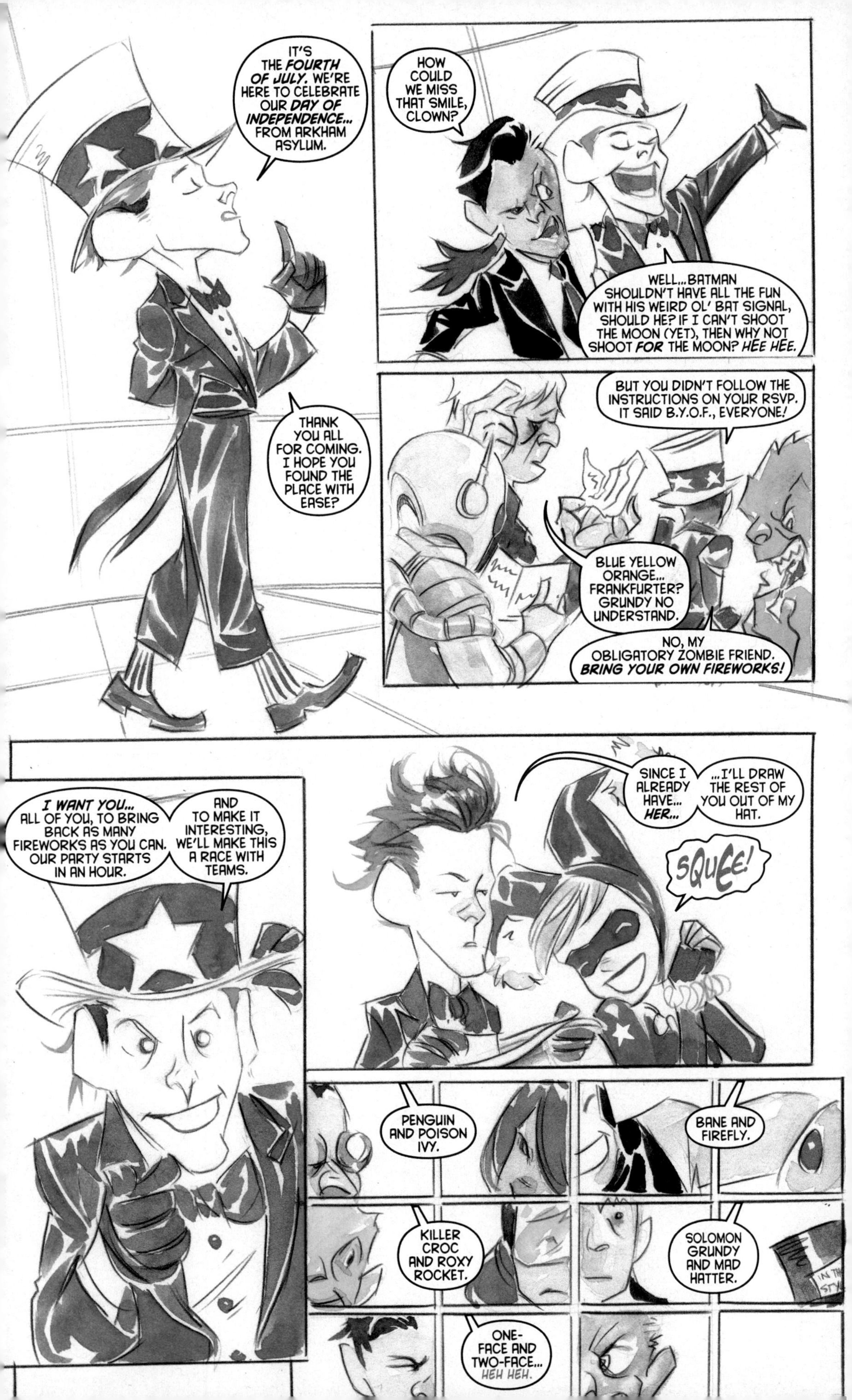
IT'S THE *FOURTH OF JULY.* WE'RE HERE TO CELEBRATE OUR *DAY OF INDEPENDENCE...* FROM ARKHAM ASYLUM.
THANK YOU ALL FOR COMING. I HOPE YOU FOUND THE PLACE WITH EASE?
HOW COULD WE MISS THAT SMILE, CLOWN?
WELL...BATMAN SHOULDN'T HAVE ALL THE FUN WITH HIS WEIRD OL' BAT SIGNAL, SHOULD HE? IF I CAN'T SHOOT THE MOON (YET), THEN WHY NOT SHOOT *FOR* THE MOON? *HEE HEE.*
BUT YOU DIDN'T FOLLOW THE INSTRUCTIONS ON YOUR RSVP. IT SAID B.Y.O.F., EVERYONE!
BLUE YELLOW ORANGE... FRANKFURTER? GRUNDY NO UNDERSTAND.
NO, MY OBLIGATORY ZOMBIE FRIEND. ***BRING YOUR OWN FIREWORKS!***
I WANT YOU... ALL OF YOU, TO BRING BACK AS MANY FIREWORKS AS YOU CAN. OUR PARTY STARTS IN AN HOUR.
AND TO MAKE IT INTERESTING, WE'LL MAKE THIS A RACE WITH TEAMS.
SINCE I ALREADY HAVE... *HER...*
...I'LL DRAW THE REST OF YOU OUT OF MY HAT.
SQUEE!
PENGUIN AND POISON IVY.
BANE AND FIREFLY.
KILLER CROC AND ROXY ROCKET.
SOLOMON GRUNDY AND MAD HATTER.
ONE-FACE AND TWO-FACE... HEH HEH.

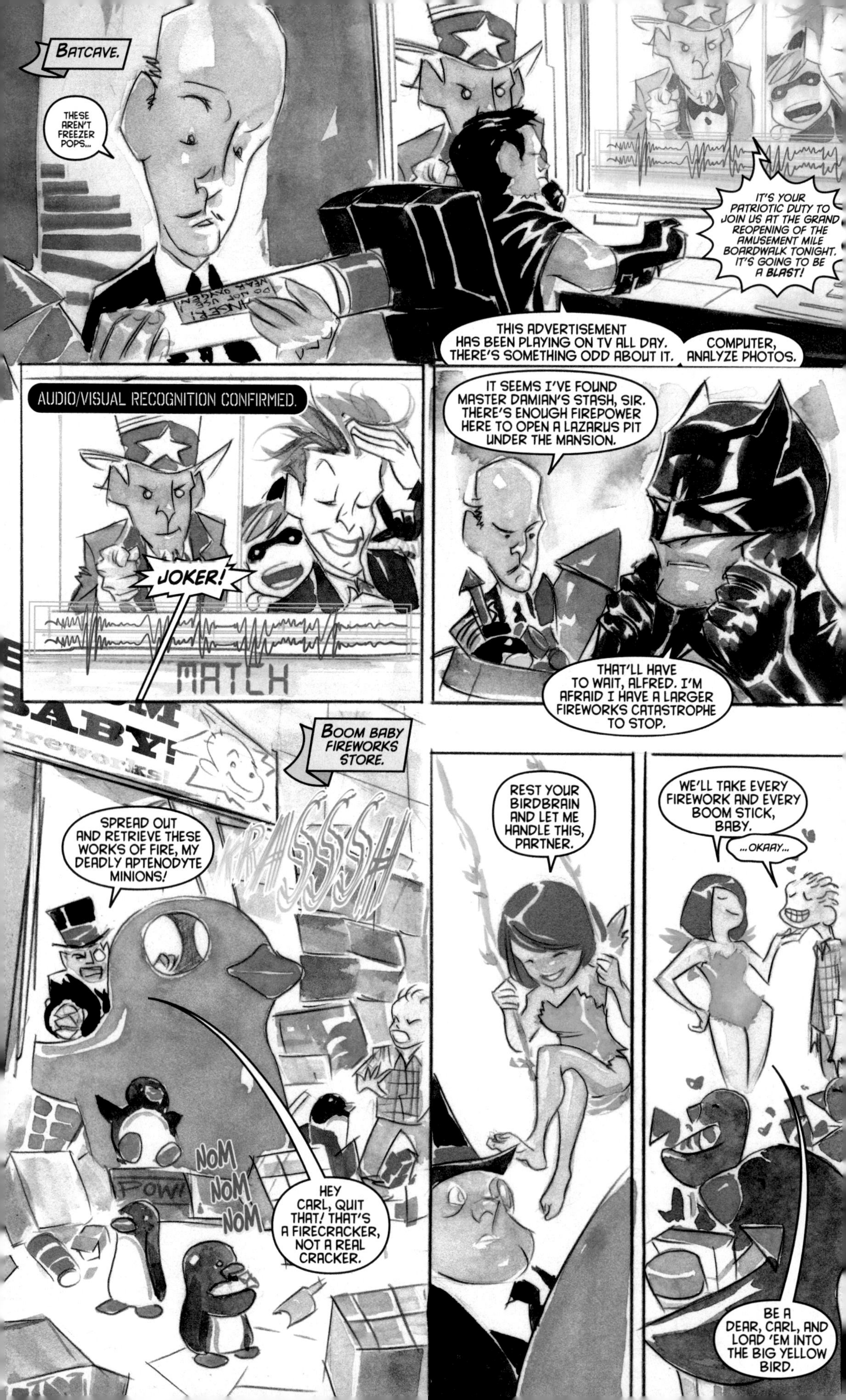
BATCAVE.
THESE AREN'T FREEZER POPS...
IT'S YOUR PATRIOTIC DUTY TO JOIN US AT THE GRAND REOPENING OF THE AMUSEMENT MILE BOARDWALK TONIGHT. IT'S GOING TO BE A BLAST!
THIS ADVERTISEMENT HAS BEEN PLAYING ON TV ALL DAY. THERE'S SOMETHING ODD ABOUT IT.
COMPUTER, ANALYZE PHOTOS.
AUDIO/VISUAL RECOGNITION CONFIRMED.
JOKER!
MATCH
IT SEEMS I'VE FOUND MASTER DAMIAN'S STASH, SIR. THERE'S ENOUGH FIREPOWER HERE TO OPEN A LAZARUS PIT UNDER THE MANSION.
THAT'LL HAVE TO WAIT, ALFRED. I'M AFRAID I HAVE A LARGER FIREWORKS CATASTROPHE TO STOP.
BOOM BABY FIREWORKS STORE.
SPREAD OUT AND RETRIEVE THESE WORKS OF FIRE, MY DEADLY APTENODYTE MINIONS!
KRASSSSH
NOM NOM NOM
POW!
HEY CARL, QUIT THAT! THAT'S A FIRECRACKER, NOT A REAL CRACKER.
REST YOUR BIRDBRAIN AND LET ME HANDLE THIS, PARTNER.
WE'LL TAKE EVERY FIREWORK AND EVERY BOOM STICK, BABY.
...OKAAY...
BE A DEAR, CARL, AND LOAD 'EM INTO THE BIG YELLOW BIRD.

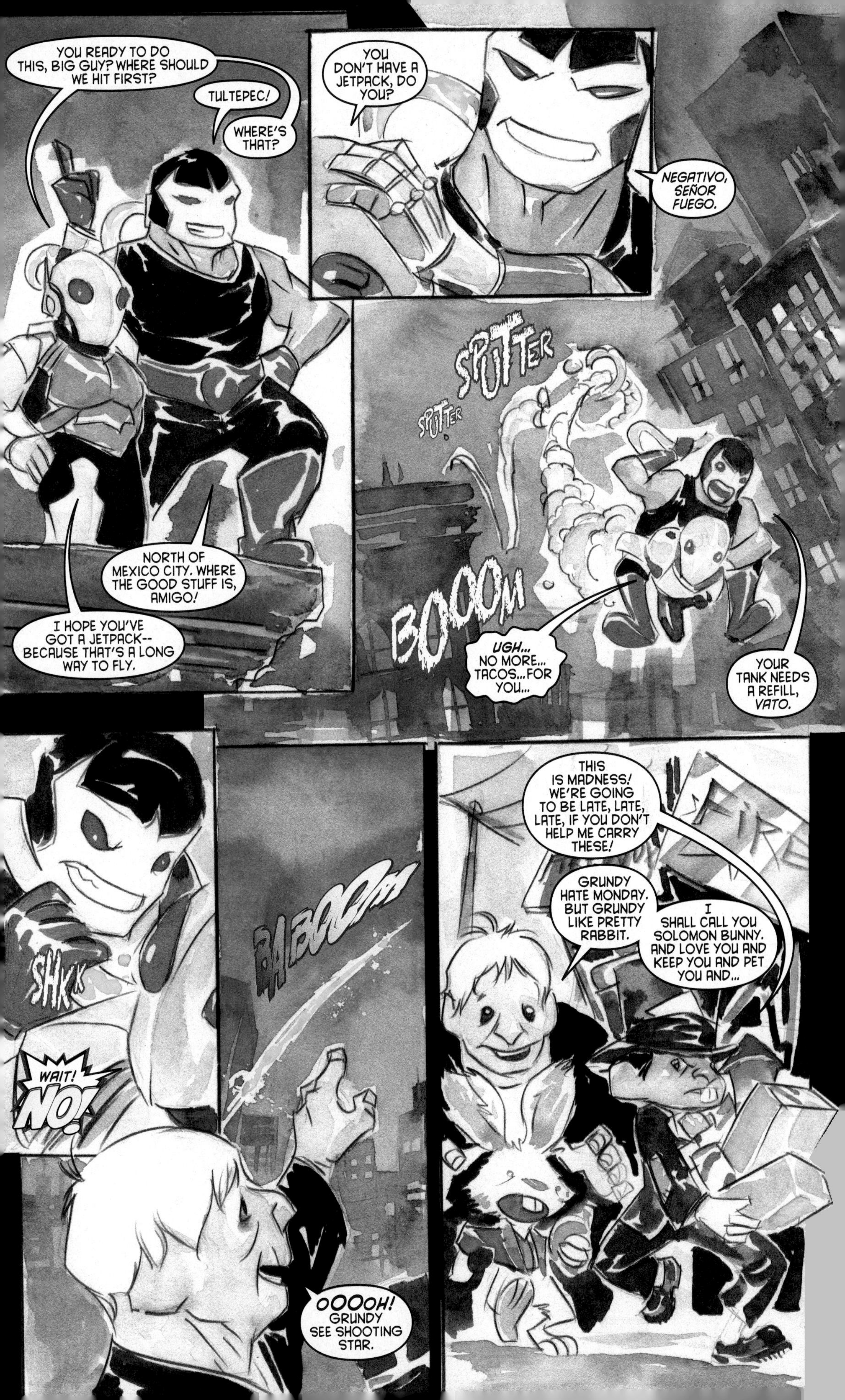
YOU READY TO DO THIS, BIG GUY? WHERE SHOULD WE HIT FIRST?
TULTEPEC!
WHERE'S THAT?
NORTH OF MEXICO CITY. WHERE THE GOOD STUFF IS, AMIGO!
I HOPE YOU'VE GOT A JETPACK-- BECAUSE THAT'S A LONG WAY TO FLY.
YOU DON'T HAVE A JETPACK, DO YOU?
NEGATIVO, SEÑOR FUEGO.
SPUTTER
SPUTTER
BOOOM
UGH... NO MORE... TACOS...FOR YOU...
YOUR TANK NEEDS A REFILL, VATO.
SHKK
WAIT! NO!
BABOOM
OOOOH! GRUNDY SEE SHOOTING STAR.
THIS IS MADNESS! WE'RE GOING TO BE LATE, LATE, LATE, IF YOU DON'T HELP ME CARRY THESE!
GRUNDY HATE MONDAY. BUT GRUNDY LIKE PRETTY RABBIT.
I SHALL CALL YOU SOLOMON BUNNY. AND LOVE YOU AND KEEP YOU AND PET YOU AND...

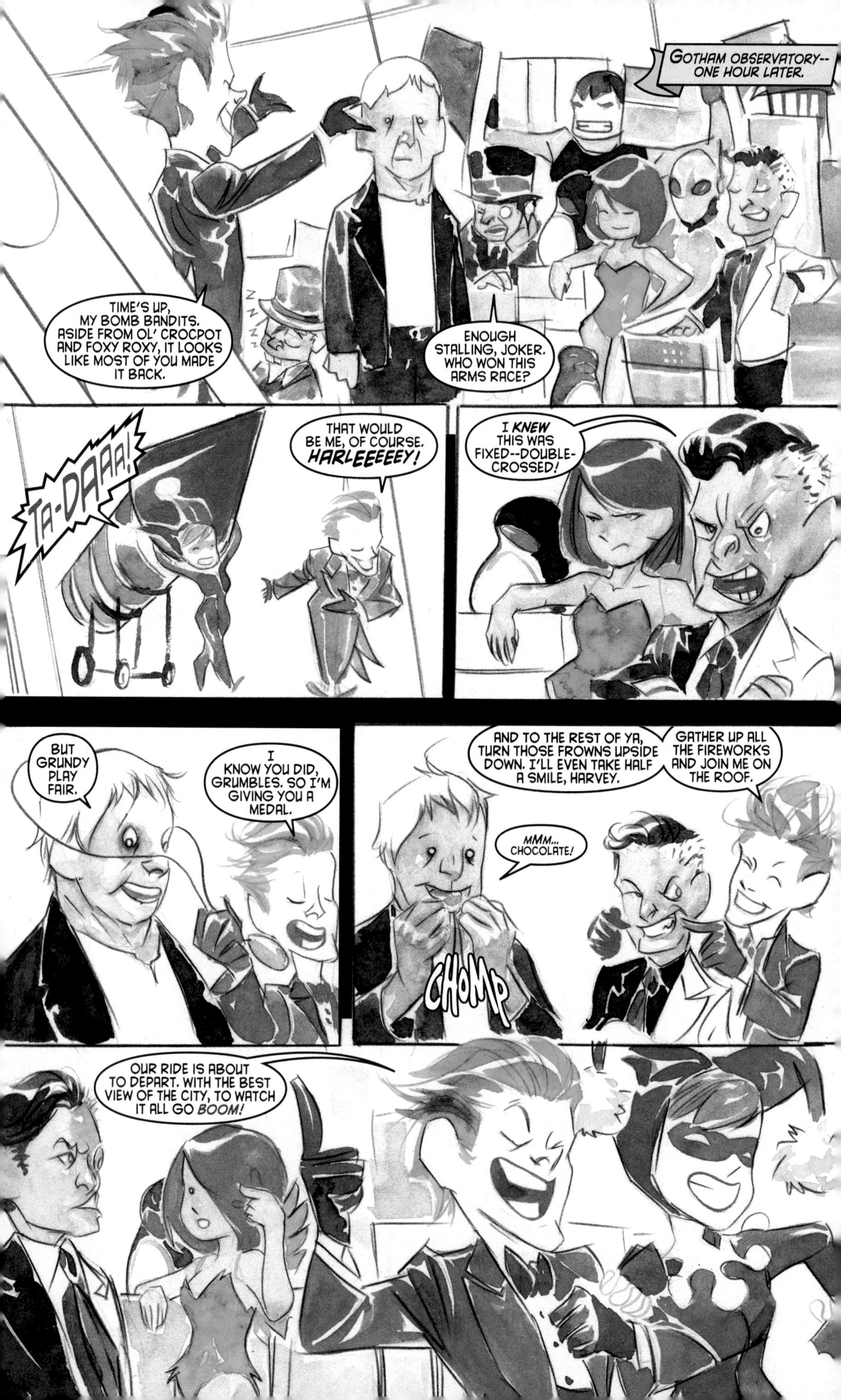
GOTHAM OBSERVATORY--
ONE HOUR LATER.
TIME'S UP, MY BOMB BANDITS. ASIDE FROM OL' CROCPOT AND FOXY ROXY, IT LOOKS LIKE MOST OF YOU MADE IT BACK.
ENOUGH STALLING, JOKER. WHO WON THIS ARMS RACE?
TA-DAAAA!
THAT WOULD BE ME, OF COURSE. HARLEEEEEY!
I KNEW THIS WAS FIXED--DOUBLE-CROSSED!
BUT GRUNDY PLAY FAIR.
I KNOW YOU DID, GRUMBLES. SO I'M GIVING YOU A MEDAL.
AND TO THE REST OF YA, TURN THOSE FROWNS UPSIDE DOWN. I'LL EVEN TAKE HALF A SMILE, HARVEY.
GATHER UP ALL THE FIREWORKS AND JOIN ME ON THE ROOF.
MMM... CHOCOLATE!
CHOMP
OUR RIDE IS ABOUT TO DEPART. WITH THE BEST VIEW OF THE CITY, TO WATCH IT ALL GO BOOM!

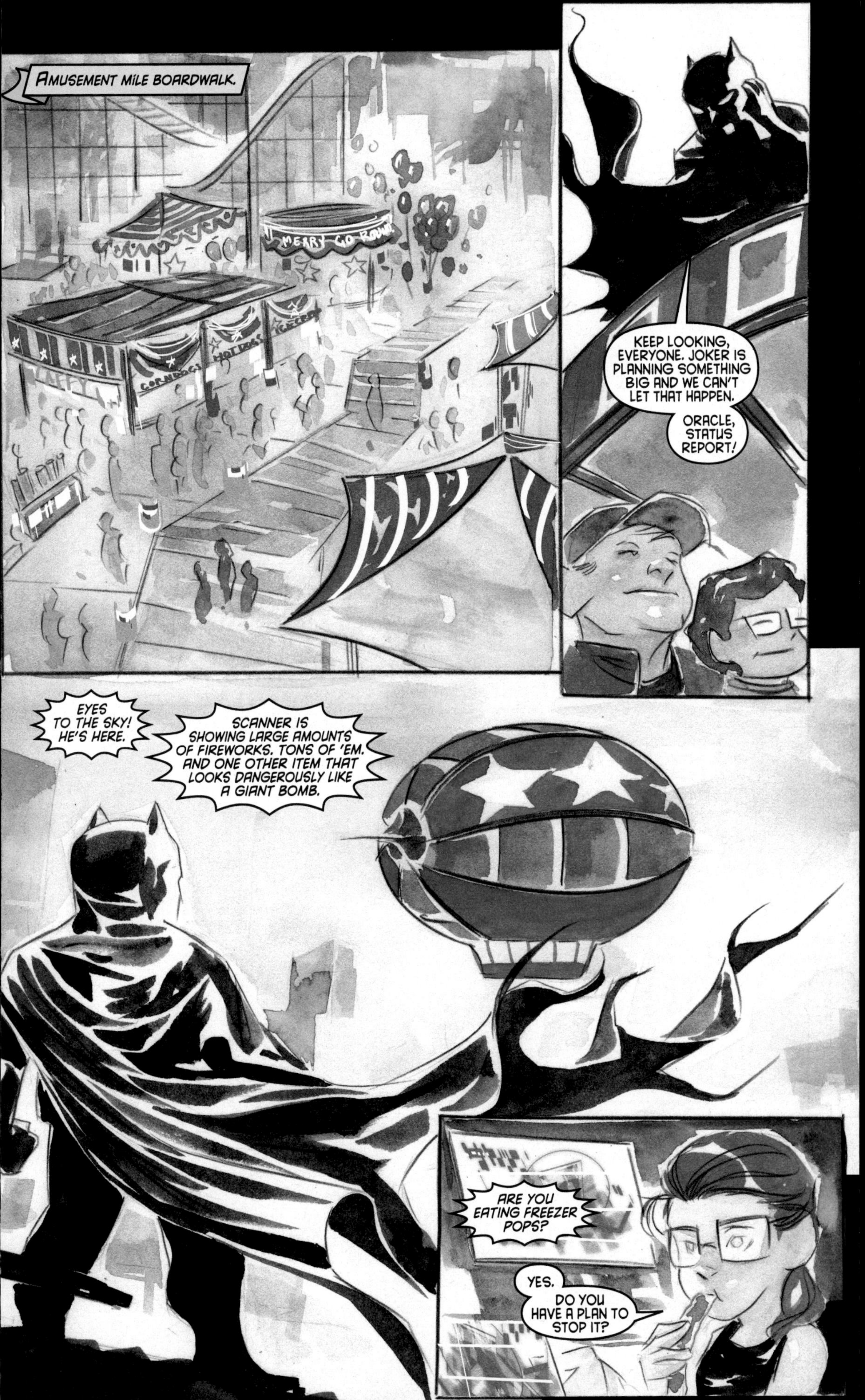
AMUSEMENT MILE BOARDWALK.
MERRY GO ROUND
CORNDOGS
HOT DOGS
KEEP LOOKING, EVERYONE. JOKER IS PLANNING SOMETHING BIG AND WE CAN'T LET THAT HAPPEN.
ORACLE, STATUS REPORT!
EYES TO THE SKY! HE'S HERE.
SCANNER IS SHOWING LARGE AMOUNTS OF FIREWORKS. TONS OF 'EM. AND ONE OTHER ITEM THAT LOOKS DANGEROUSLY LIKE A GIANT BOMB.
ARE YOU EATING FREEZER POPS?
YES.
DO YOU HAVE A PLAN TO STOP IT?

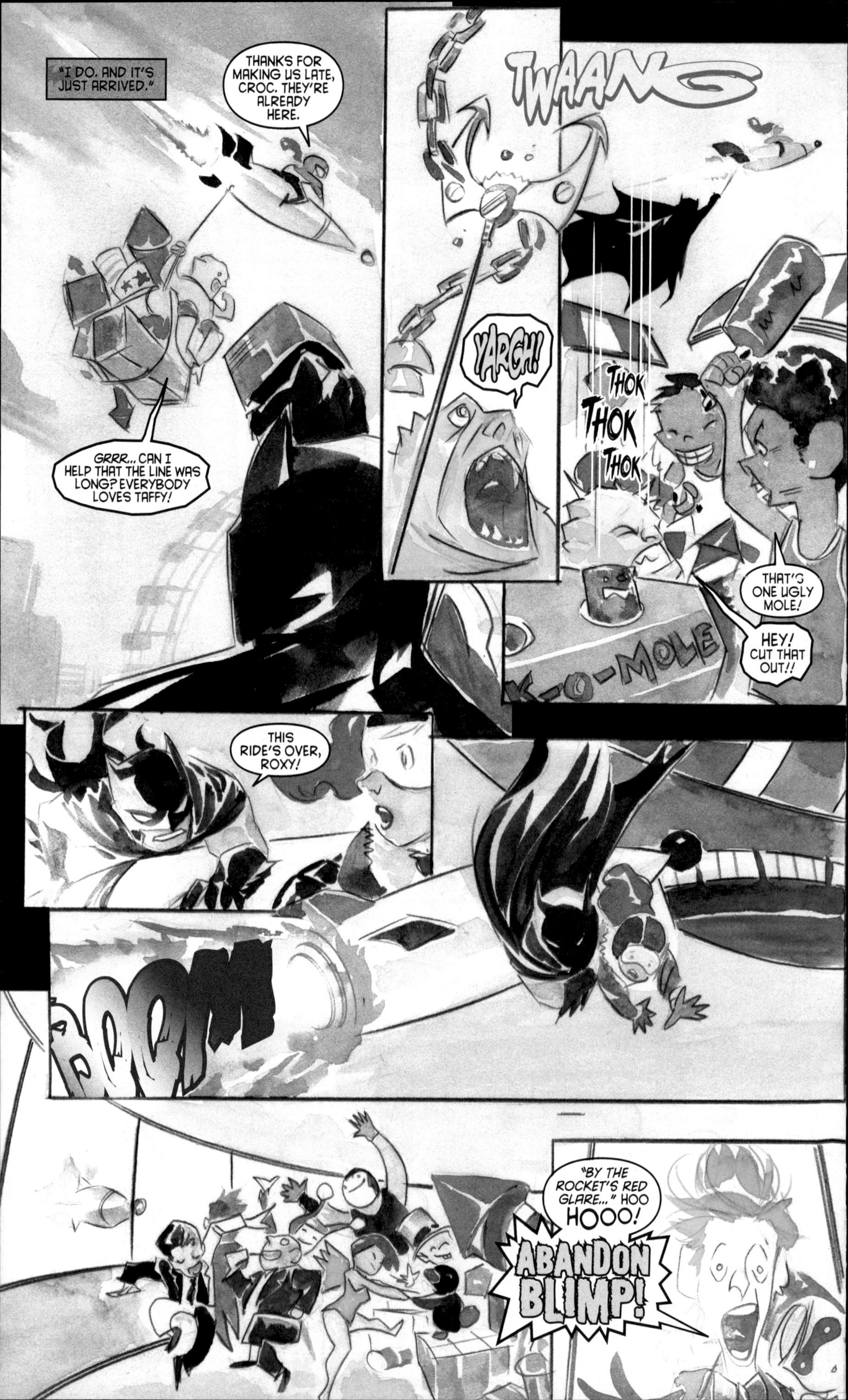
"I DO. AND IT'S JUST ARRIVED."
THANKS FOR MAKING US LATE, CROC. THEY'RE ALREADY HERE.
GRRR... CAN I HELP THAT THE LINE WAS LONG? EVERYBODY LOVES TAFFY!
YARGH!
TWAANG
THOK THOK THOK
THAT'S ONE UGLY MOLE!
HEY! CUT THAT OUT!!
-O-MOLE
THIS RIDE'S OVER, ROXY!
BOOM
"BY THE ROCKET'S RED GLARE..." HOO HOOO!
ABANDON BLIMP!

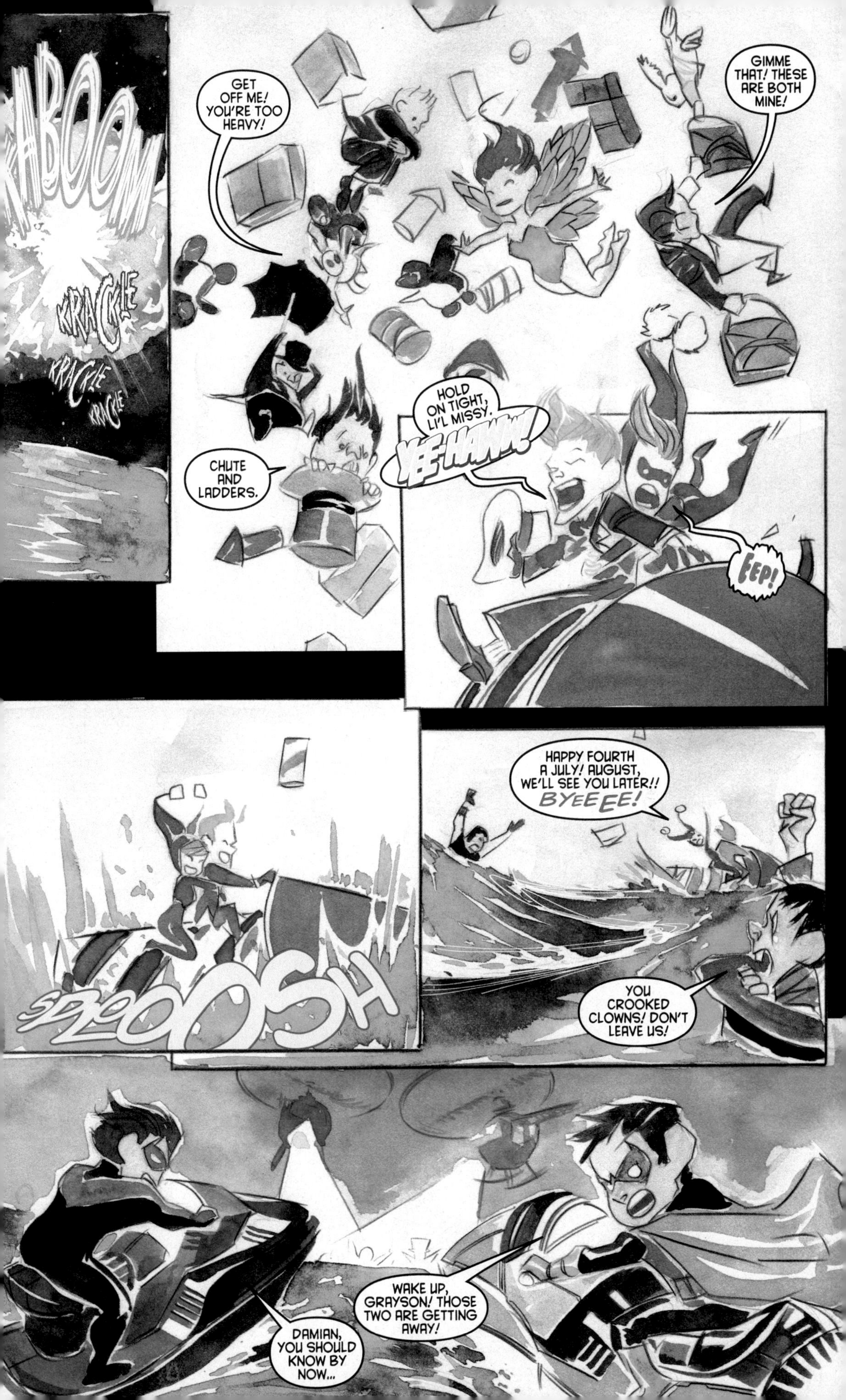
KABOOM
KRACKLE
KRACKLE
KRACKLE
GET OFF ME! YOU'RE TOO HEAVY!
GIMME THAT! THESE ARE BOTH MINE!
CHUTE AND LADDERS.
HOLD ON TIGHT, LI'L MISSY.
YEE-HAWW!
EEP!
SPLOOOSH
HAPPY FOURTH A JULY! AUGUST, WE'LL SEE YOU LATER!! BYEEEE!
YOU CROOKED CLOWNS! DON'T LEAVE US!
WAKE UP, GRAYSON! THOSE TWO ARE GETTING AWAY!
DAMIAN, YOU SHOULD KNOW BY NOW...

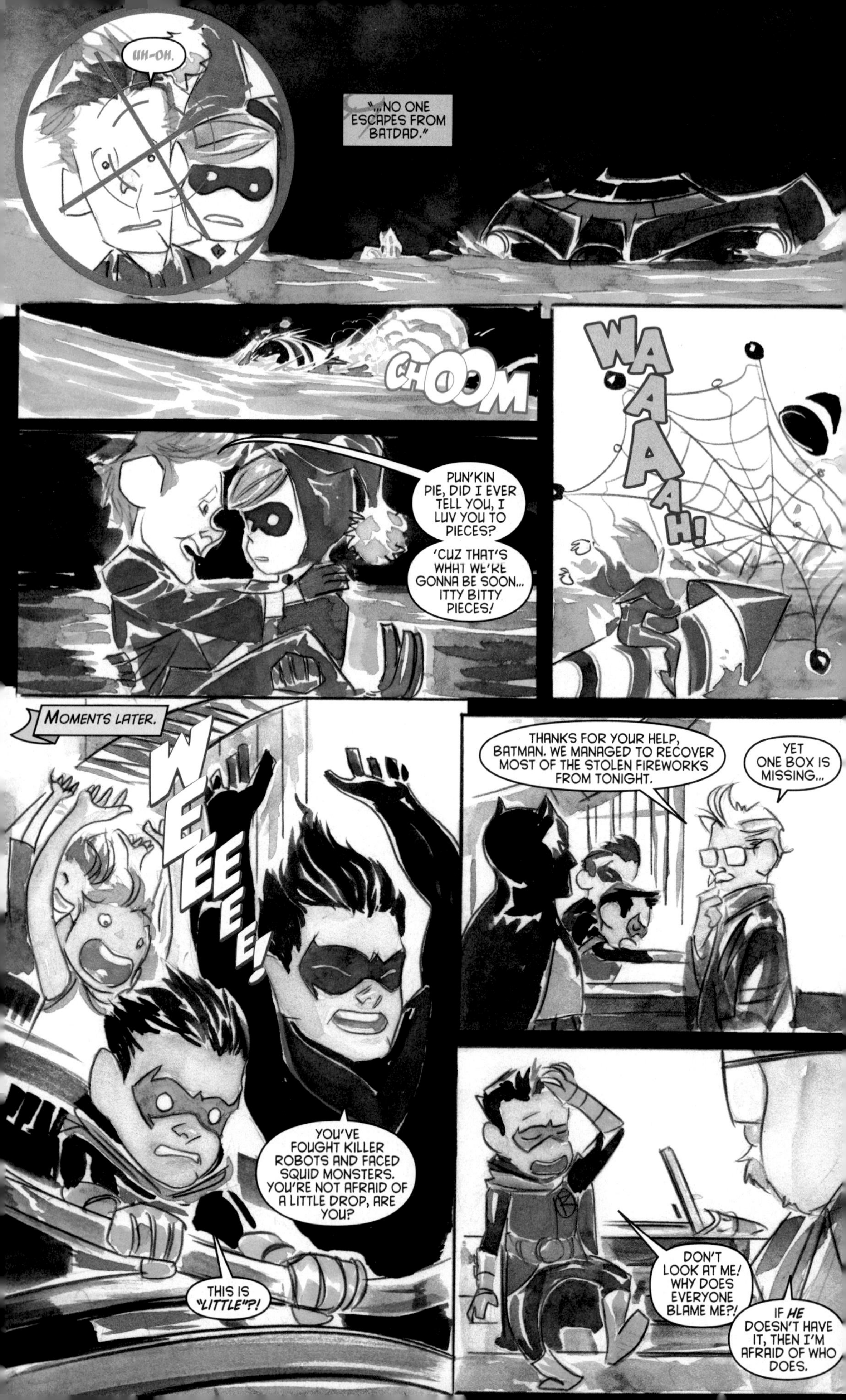

UH-OH.
"...NO ONE ESCAPES FROM BATDAD."
CHOOM
PUN'KIN PIE, DID I EVER TELL YOU, I LUV YOU TO PIECES?
'CUZ THAT'S WHAT WE'RE GONNA BE SOON... ITTY BITTY PIECES!
WAAAAAH!
MOMENTS LATER.
WEEEEEE!
YOU'VE FOUGHT KILLER ROBOTS AND FACED SQUID MONSTERS. YOU'RE NOT AFRAID OF A LITTLE DROP, ARE YOU?
THIS IS "LITTLE"?!
THANKS FOR YOUR HELP, BATMAN. WE MANAGED TO RECOVER MOST OF THE STOLEN FIREWORKS FROM TONIGHT.
YET ONE BOX IS MISSING...
DON'T LOOK AT ME! WHY DOES EVERYONE BLAME ME?!
IF HE DOESN'T HAVE IT, THEN I'M AFRAID OF WHO DOES.

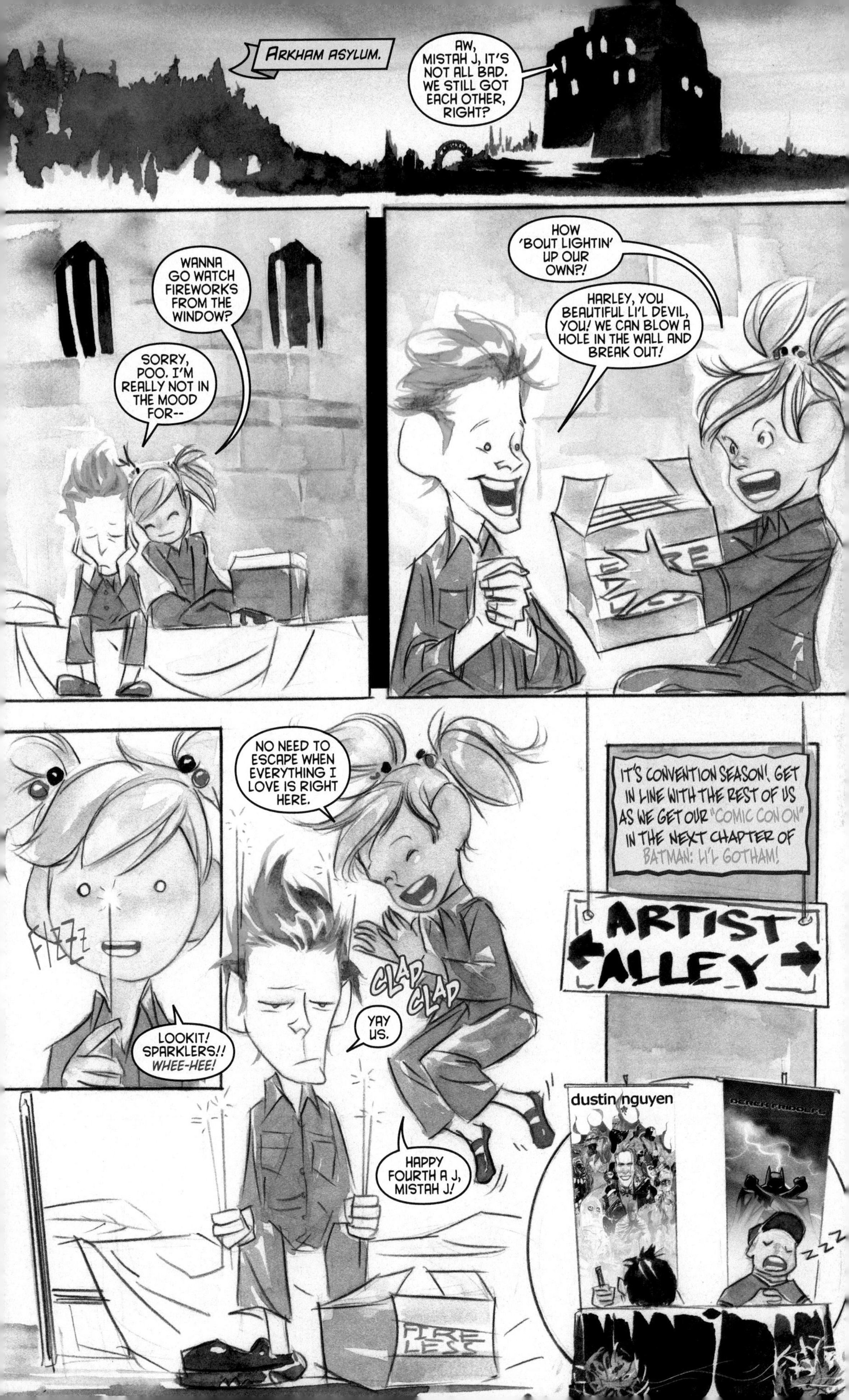
ARKHAM ASYLUM.
AW, MISTAH J, IT'S NOT ALL BAD. WE STILL GOT EACH OTHER, RIGHT?
WANNA GO WATCH FIREWORKS FROM THE WINDOW?
SORRY, POO. I'M REALLY NOT IN THE MOOD FOR--
HOW 'BOUT LIGHTIN' UP OUR OWN?!
HARLEY, YOU BEAUTIFUL LI'L DEVIL, YOU! WE CAN BLOW A HOLE IN THE WALL AND BREAK OUT!
FIZZZ
LOOKIT! SPARKLERS!! WHEE-HEE!
NO NEED TO ESCAPE WHEN EVERYTHING I LOVE IS RIGHT HERE.
CLAP CLAP
YAY US.
HAPPY FOURTH A J, MISTAH J!
FIRE LESS
IT'S CONVENTION SEASON! GET IN LINE WITH THE REST OF US AS WE GET OUR "COMIC CON ON" IN THE NEXT CHAPTER OF BATMAN: LI'L GOTHAM!
ARTIST ALLEY
dustin nguyen
ZZZ

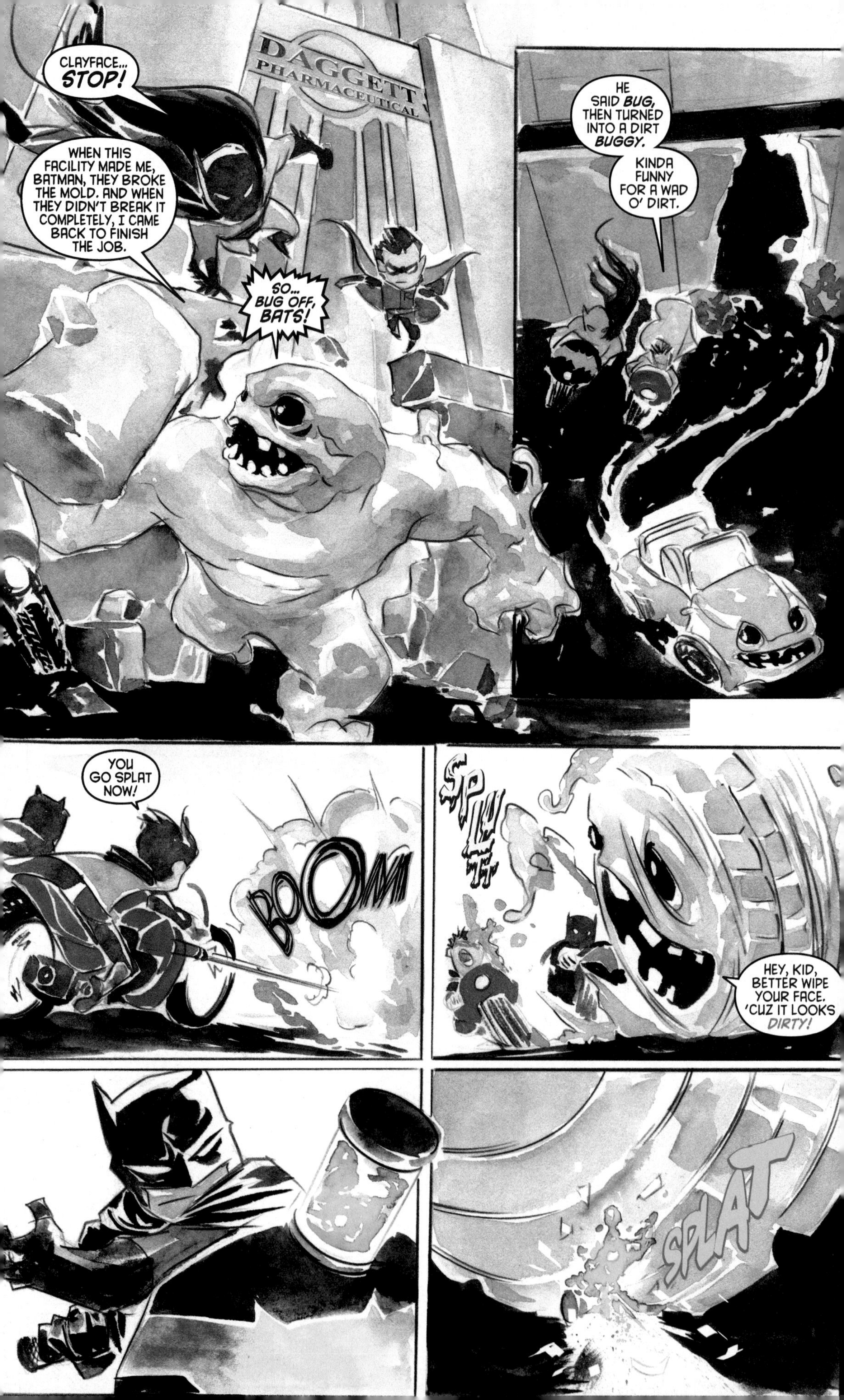
DAGGETT PHARMACEUTICAL
CLAYFACE... STOP!
WHEN THIS FACILITY MADE ME, BATMAN, THEY BROKE THE MOLD. AND WHEN THEY DIDN'T BREAK IT COMPLETELY, I CAME BACK TO FINISH THE JOB.
SO... BUG OFF, BATS!
HE SAID BUG, THEN TURNED INTO A DIRT BUGGY.
KINDA FUNNY FOR A WAD O' DIRT.
YOU GO SPLAT NOW!
BOOM
HEY, KID, BETTER WIPE YOUR FACE. 'CUZ IT LOOKS DIRTY!
SPLAT

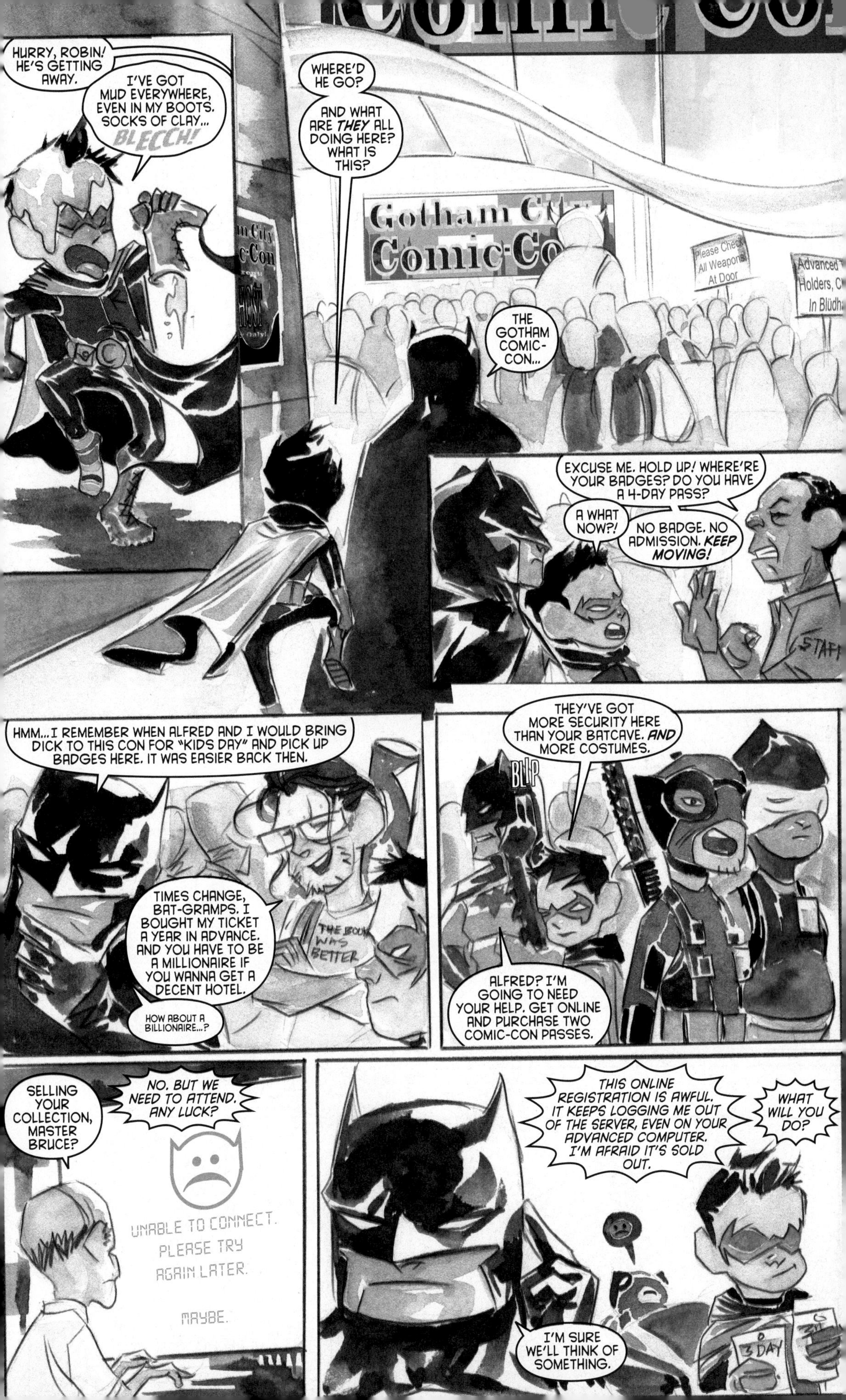
HURRY, ROBIN! HE'S GETTING AWAY.
I'VE GOT MUD EVERYWHERE, EVEN IN MY BOOTS. SOCKS OF CLAY... BLECCH!
WHERE'D HE GO?
AND WHAT ARE THEY ALL DOING HERE? WHAT IS THIS?
Gotham City Comic-Con
Please Check All Weapons At Door
THE GOTHAM COMIC-CON...
EXCUSE ME. HOLD UP! WHERE'RE YOUR BADGES? DO YOU HAVE A 4-DAY PASS?
A WHAT NOW?!
NO BADGE. NO ADMISSION. KEEP MOVING!
STAFF
HMM...I REMEMBER WHEN ALFRED AND I WOULD BRING DICK TO THIS CON FOR "KIDS DAY" AND PICK UP BADGES HERE. IT WAS EASIER BACK THEN.
TIMES CHANGE, BAT-GRAMPS. I BOUGHT MY TICKET A YEAR IN ADVANCE. AND YOU HAVE TO BE A MILLIONAIRE IF YOU WANNA GET A DECENT HOTEL.
HOW ABOUT A BILLIONAIRE...?
THE BOOK WAS BETTER
THEY'VE GOT MORE SECURITY HERE THAN YOUR BATCAVE. AND MORE COSTUMES.
BLIP
ALFRED? I'M GOING TO NEED YOUR HELP. GET ONLINE AND PURCHASE TWO COMIC-CON PASSES.
SELLING YOUR COLLECTION, MASTER BRUCE?
NO. BUT WE NEED TO ATTEND. ANY LUCK?
UNABLE TO CONNECT. PLEASE TRY AGAIN LATER.
MAYBE.
THIS ONLINE REGISTRATION IS AWFUL. IT KEEPS LOGGING ME OUT OF THE SERVER, EVEN ON YOUR ADVANCED COMPUTER. I'M AFRAID IT'S SOLD OUT.
WHAT WILL YOU DO?
I'M SURE WE'LL THINK OF SOMETHING.
3 DAY

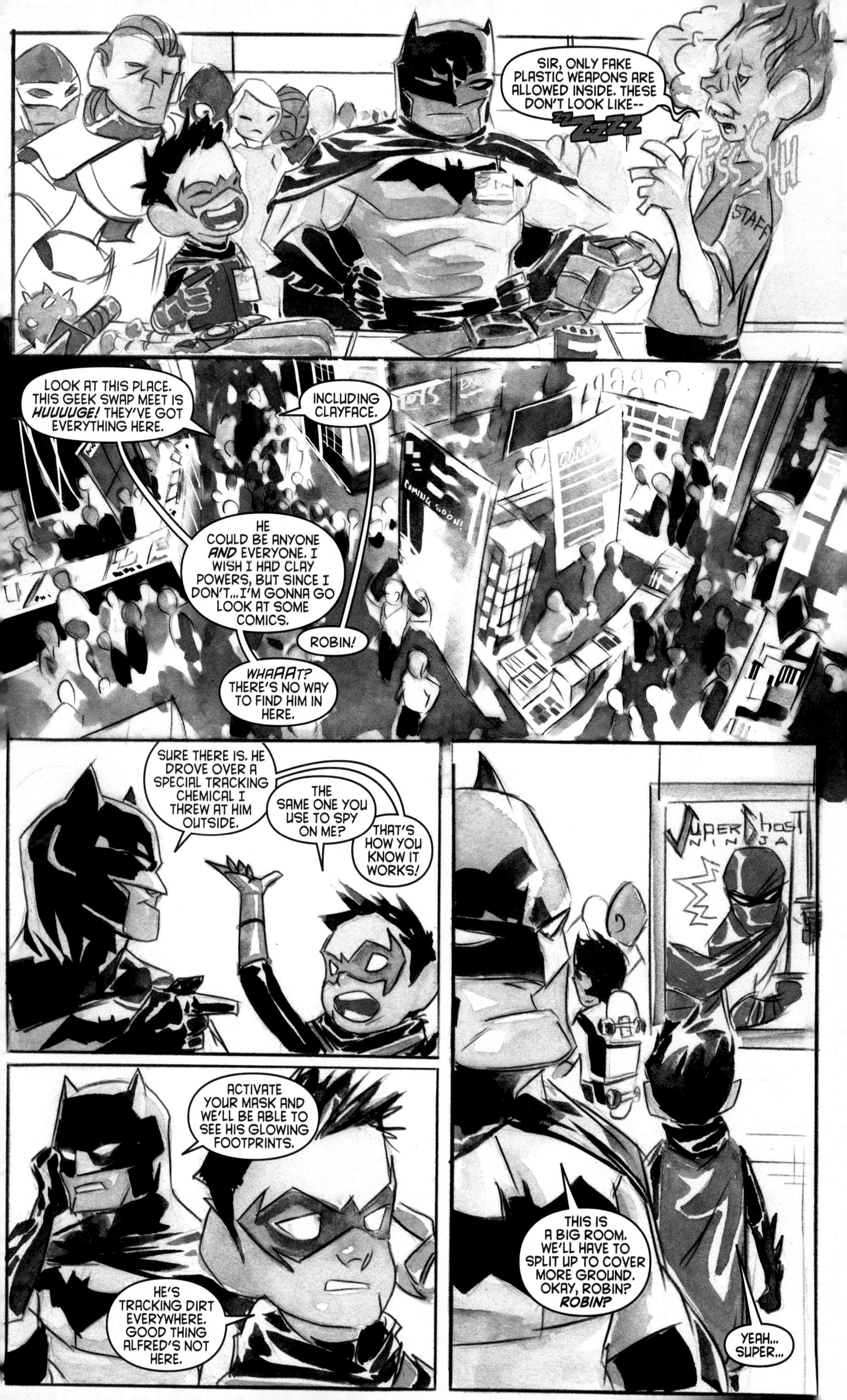

SIR, ONLY FAKE PLASTIC WEAPONS ARE ALLOWED INSIDE. THESE DON'T LOOK LIKE--
ZZZZZ
FSSSHH
STAFF
LOOK AT THIS PLACE. THIS GEEK SWAP MEET IS HUUUUGE! THEY'VE GOT EVERYTHING HERE.
INCLUDING CLAYFACE.
COMING SOON!
HE COULD BE ANYONE AND EVERYONE. I WISH I HAD CLAY POWERS, BUT SINCE I DON'T...I'M GONNA GO LOOK AT SOME COMICS.
ROBIN!
WHAAAT? THERE'S NO WAY TO FIND HIM IN HERE.
SURE THERE IS. HE DROVE OVER A SPECIAL TRACKING CHEMICAL I THREW AT HIM OUTSIDE.
THE SAME ONE YOU USE TO SPY ON ME?
THAT'S HOW YOU KNOW IT WORKS!
ACTIVATE YOUR MASK AND WE'LL BE ABLE TO SEE HIS GLOWING FOOTPRINTS.
HE'S TRACKING DIRT EVERYWHERE. GOOD THING ALFRED'S NOT HERE.
SUPER GHOST NINJA
THIS IS A BIG ROOM. WE'LL HAVE TO SPLIT UP TO COVER MORE GROUND. OKAY, ROBIN? ROBIN?
YEAH... SUPER...

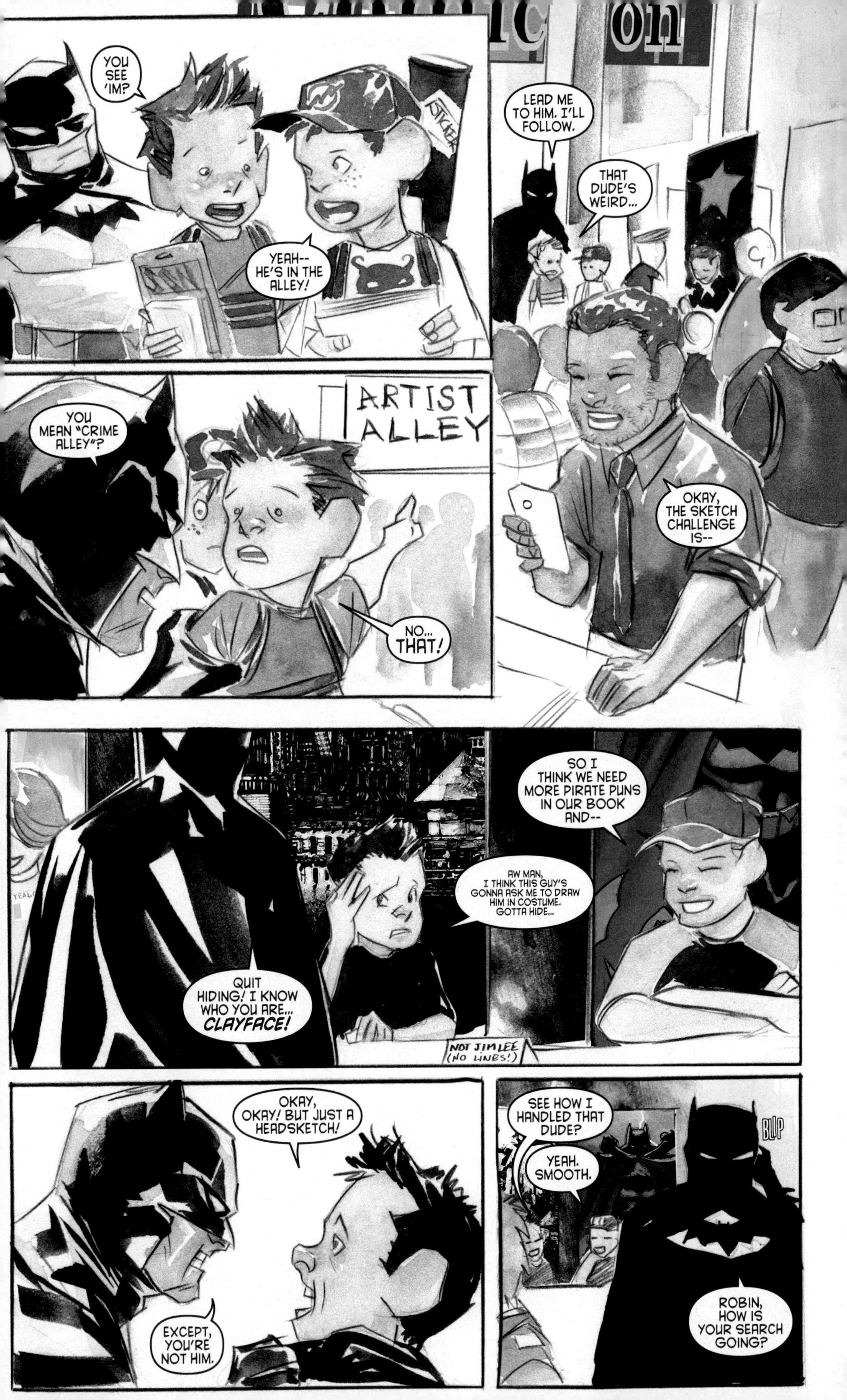
YOU SEE 'IM?
YEAH-- HE'S IN THE ALLEY!
YOU MEAN "CRIME ALLEY"?
ARTIST ALLEY
NO... THAT!
LEAD ME TO HIM. I'LL FOLLOW.
THAT DUDE'S WEIRD...
OKAY, THE SKETCH CHALLENGE IS--
AW MAN, I THINK THIS GUY'S GONNA ASK ME TO DRAW HIM IN COSTUME. GOTTA HIDE...
QUIT HIDING! I KNOW WHO YOU ARE... *CLAYFACE!*
NOT JIM LEE (NO LINES!)
SO I THINK WE NEED MORE PIRATE PUNS IN OUR BOOK AND--
OKAY, OKAY! BUT JUST A HEADSKETCH!
EXCEPT, YOU'RE NOT HIM.
SEE HOW I HANDLED THAT DUDE?
YEAH. SMOOTH.
BLIP
ROBIN, HOW IS YOUR SEARCH GOING?

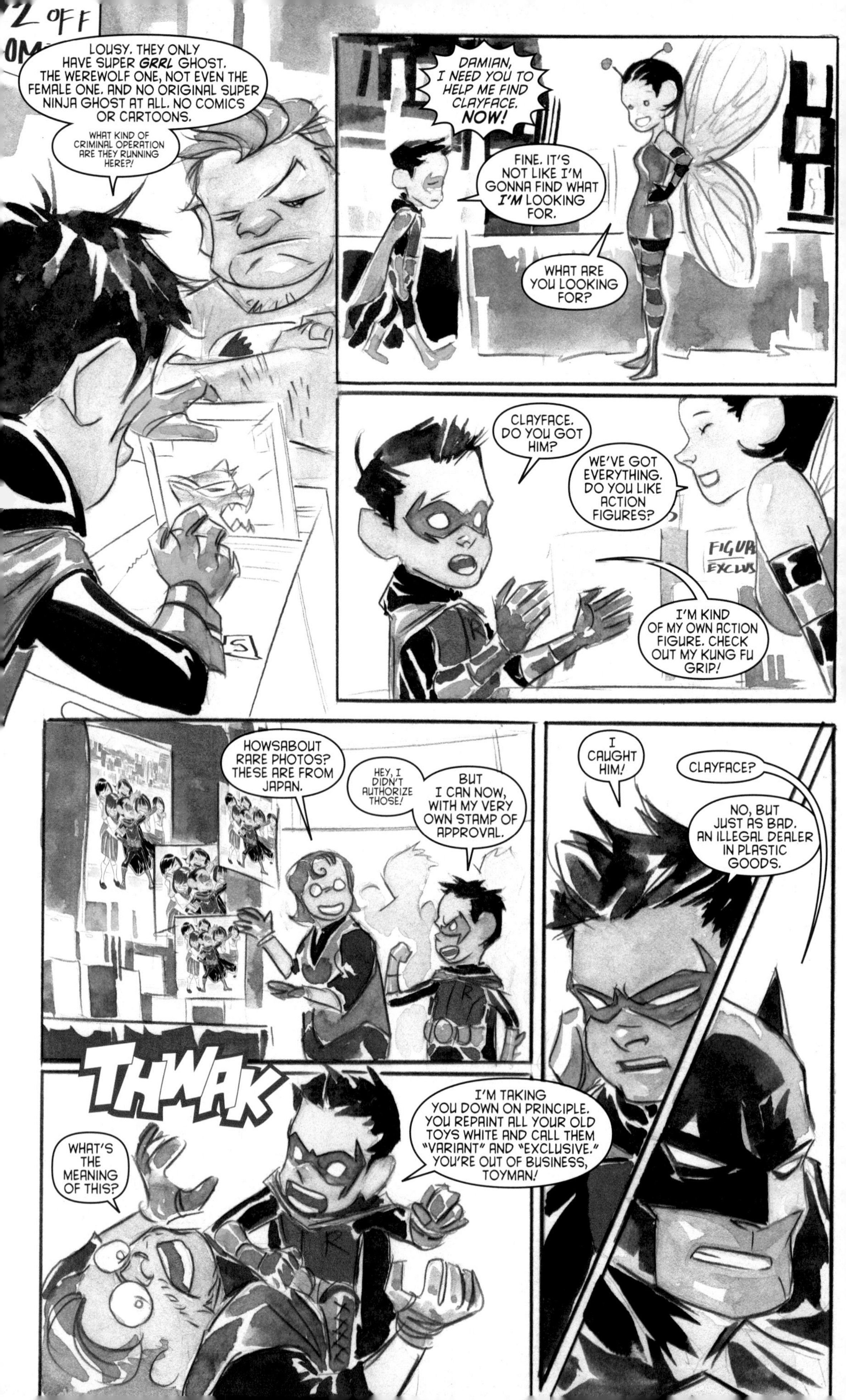
LOUSY. THEY ONLY HAVE SUPER GRRL GHOST. THE WEREWOLF ONE, NOT EVEN THE FEMALE ONE. AND NO ORIGINAL SUPER NINJA GHOST AT ALL. NO COMICS OR CARTOONS.
WHAT KIND OF CRIMINAL OPERATION ARE THEY RUNNING HERE?!
DAMIAN, I NEED YOU TO HELP ME FIND CLAYFACE. NOW!
FINE. IT'S NOT LIKE I'M GONNA FIND WHAT I'M LOOKING FOR.
WHAT ARE YOU LOOKING FOR?
CLAYFACE. DO YOU GOT HIM?
WE'VE GOT EVERYTHING. DO YOU LIKE ACTION FIGURES?
I'M KIND OF MY OWN ACTION FIGURE. CHECK OUT MY KUNG FU GRIP!
HOWSABOUT RARE PHOTOS? THESE ARE FROM JAPAN.
HEY, I DIDN'T AUTHORIZE THOSE!
BUT I CAN NOW, WITH MY VERY OWN STAMP OF APPROVAL.
THWAK
WHAT'S THE MEANING OF THIS?
I'M TAKING YOU DOWN ON PRINCIPLE. YOU REPAINT ALL YOUR OLD TOYS WHITE AND CALL THEM "VARIANT" AND "EXCLUSIVE." YOU'RE OUT OF BUSINESS, TOYMAN!
I CAUGHT HIM!
CLAYFACE?
NO, BUT JUST AS BAD. AN ILLEGAL DEALER IN PLASTIC GOODS.

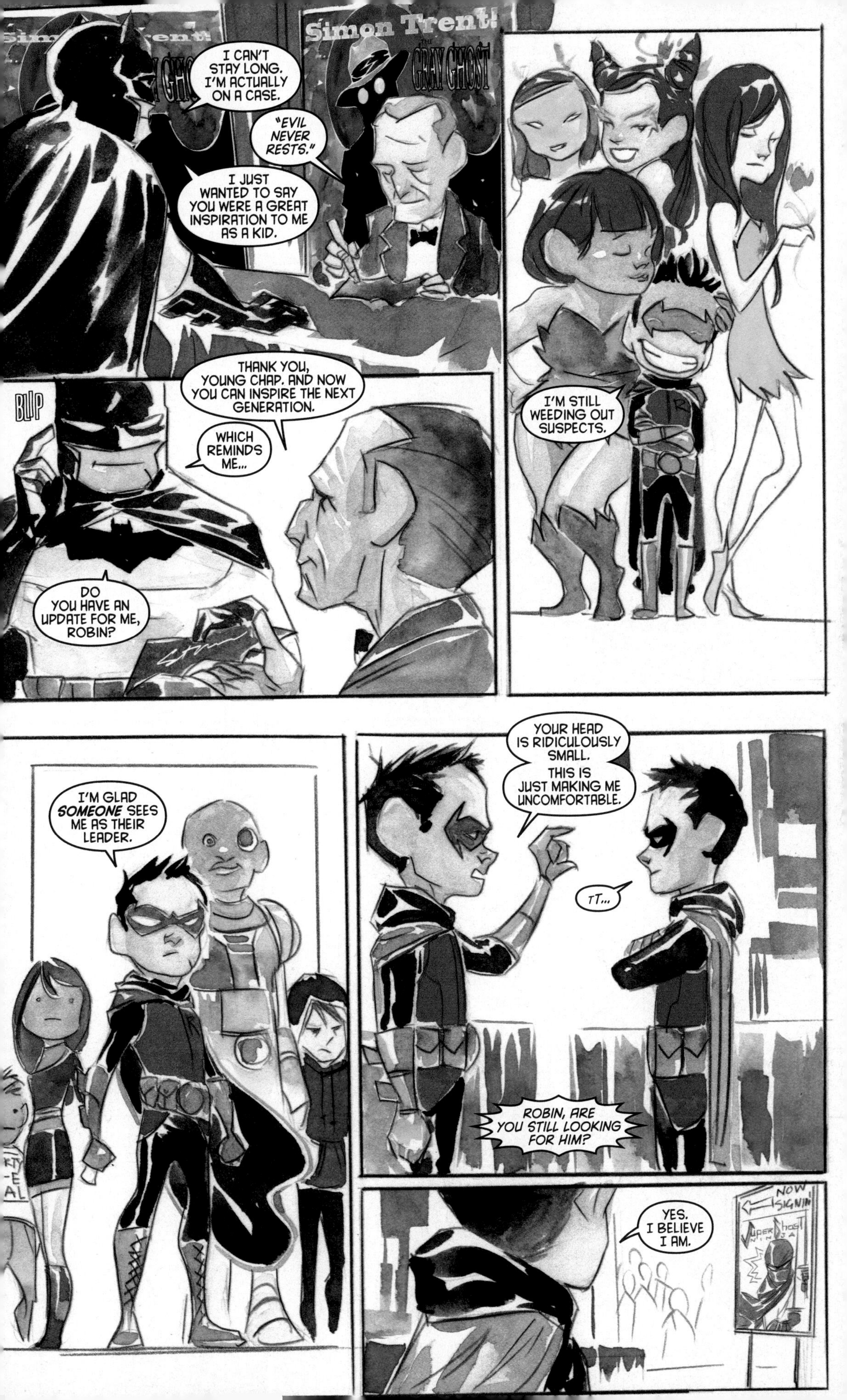

Simon Trent!
THE GRAY GHOST
I CAN'T STAY LONG. I'M ACTUALLY ON A CASE.
"EVIL NEVER RESTS."
I JUST WANTED TO SAY YOU WERE A GREAT INSPIRATION TO ME AS A KID.
THANK YOU, YOUNG CHAP. AND NOW YOU CAN INSPIRE THE NEXT GENERATION.
WHICH REMINDS ME...
BLIP
DO YOU HAVE AN UPDATE FOR ME, ROBIN?
I'M STILL WEEDING OUT SUSPECTS.
I'M GLAD SOMEONE SEES ME AS THEIR LEADER.
YOUR HEAD IS RIDICULOUSLY SMALL.
THIS IS JUST MAKING ME UNCOMFORTABLE.
TT...
ROBIN, ARE YOU STILL LOOKING FOR HIM?
YES. I BELIEVE I AM.
NOW SIGNIN

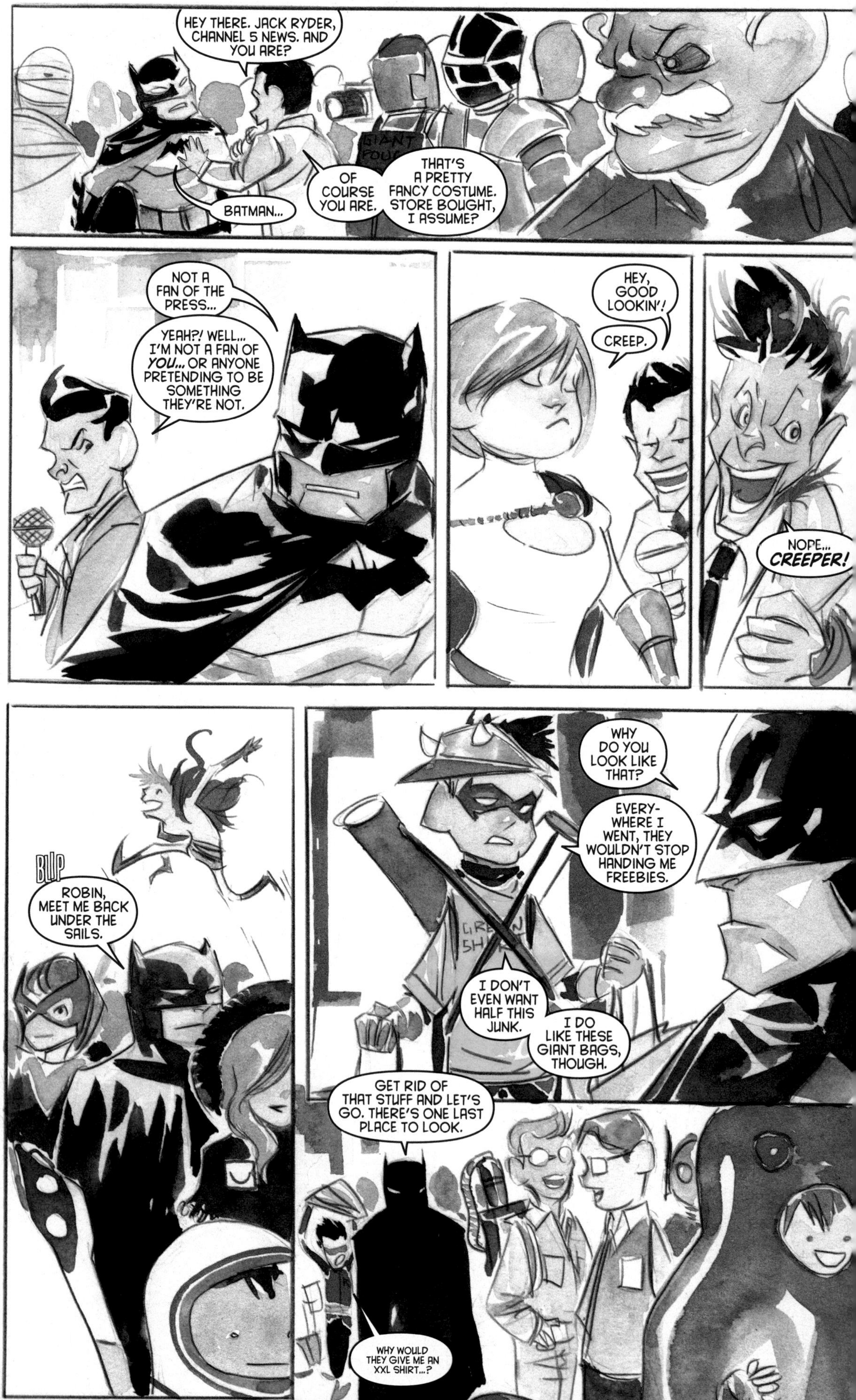
HEY THERE. JACK RYDER, CHANNEL 5 NEWS. AND YOU ARE?
BATMAN...
OF COURSE YOU ARE.
THAT'S A PRETTY FANCY COSTUME. STORE BOUGHT, I ASSUME?
NOT A FAN OF THE PRESS...
YEAH?! WELL... I'M NOT A FAN OF YOU... OR ANYONE PRETENDING TO BE SOMETHING THEY'RE NOT.
HEY, GOOD LOOKIN'!
CREEP.
NOPE... CREEPER!
BLIP
ROBIN, MEET ME BACK UNDER THE SAILS.
WHY DO YOU LOOK LIKE THAT?
EVERY-WHERE I WENT, THEY WOULDN'T STOP HANDING ME FREEBIES.
I DON'T EVEN WANT HALF THIS JUNK.
I DO LIKE THESE GIANT BAGS, THOUGH.
GET RID OF THAT STUFF AND LET'S GO. THERE'S ONE LAST PLACE TO LOOK.
WHY WOULD THEY GIVE ME AN XXL SHIRT...?

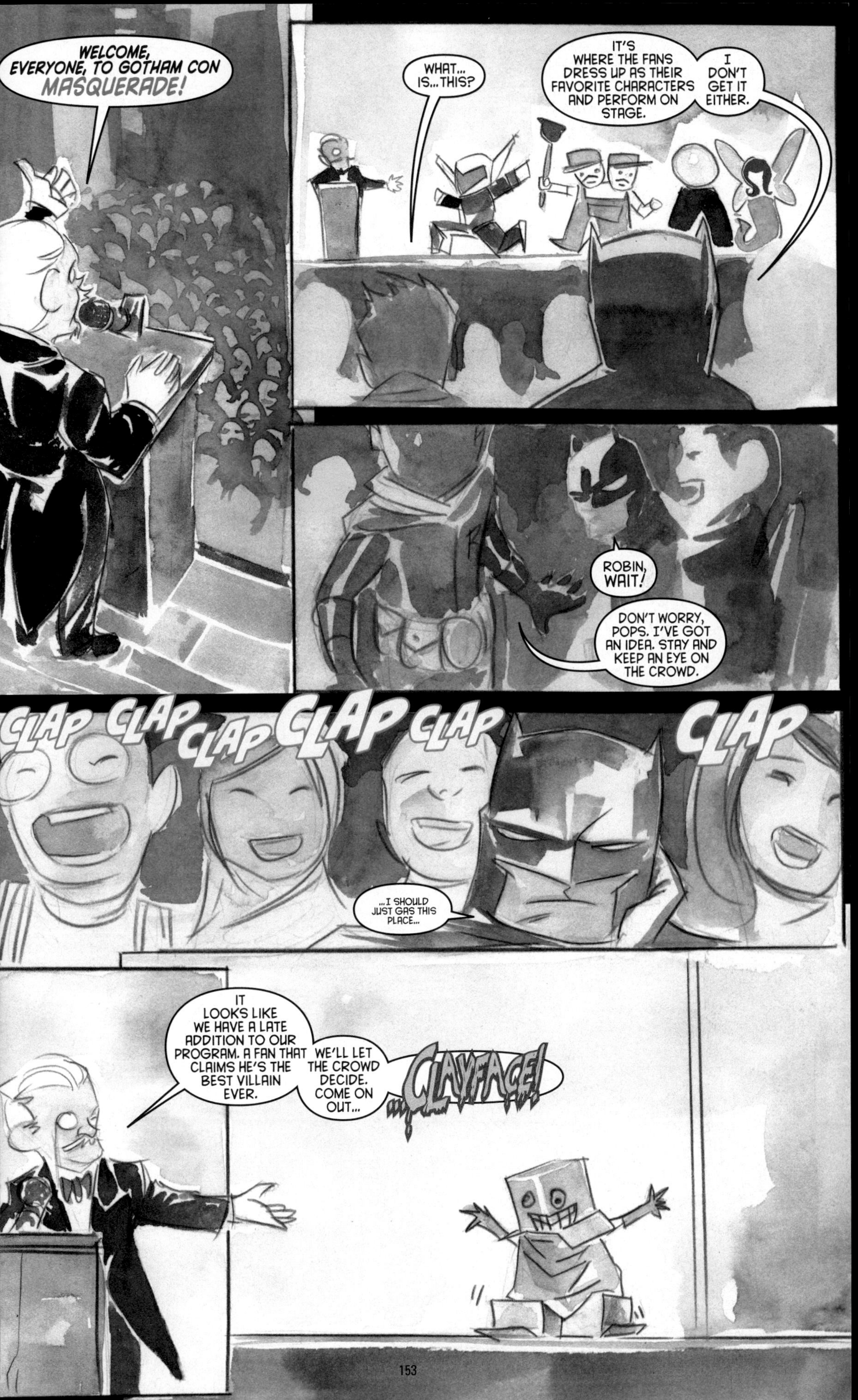
WELCOME, EVERYONE, TO GOTHAM CON MASQUERADE!
WHAT... IS... THIS?
IT'S WHERE THE FANS DRESS UP AS THEIR FAVORITE CHARACTERS AND PERFORM ON STAGE.
I DON'T GET IT EITHER.
ROBIN, WAIT!
DON'T WORRY, POPS. I'VE GOT AN IDEA. STAY AND KEEP AN EYE ON THE CROWD.
CLAP CLAP CLAP CLAP CLAP CLAP
...I SHOULD JUST GAS THIS PLACE...
IT LOOKS LIKE WE HAVE A LATE ADDITION TO OUR PROGRAM. A FAN THAT CLAIMS HE'S THE BEST VILLAIN EVER.
WE'LL LET THE CROWD DECIDE. COME ON OUT...
...CLAYFACE!

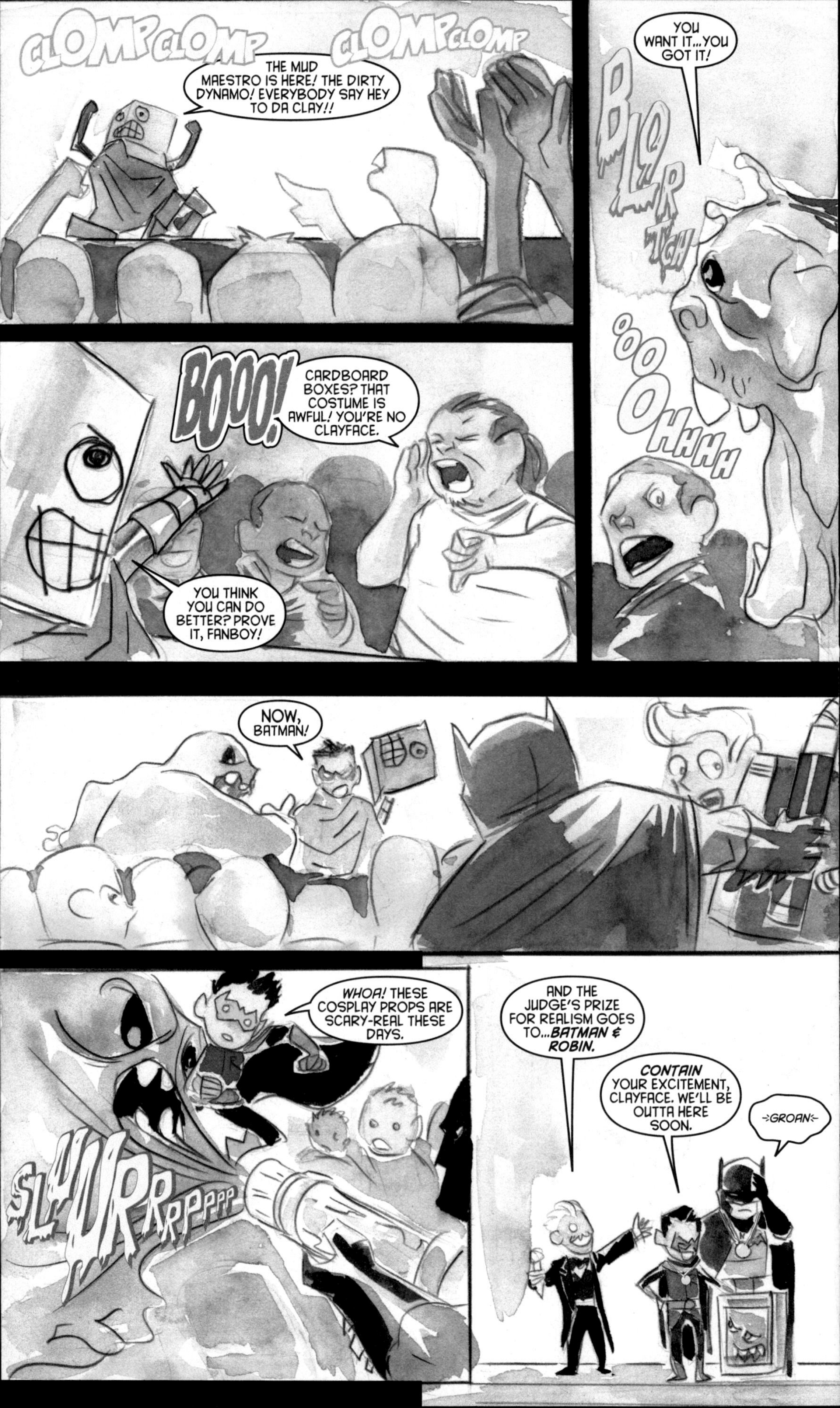
CLOMP CLOMP CLOMP CLOMP
THE MUD MAESTRO IS HERE! THE DIRTY DYNAMO! EVERYBODY SAY HEY TO DA CLAY!!
YOU WANT IT...YOU GOT IT!
BLORTCH
BOOO!
CARDBOARD BOXES? THAT COSTUME IS AWFUL! YOU'RE NO CLAYFACE.
YOU THINK YOU CAN DO BETTER? PROVE IT, FANBOY!
OOOOHHHHH
NOW, BATMAN!
WHOA! THESE COSPLAY PROPS ARE SCARY-REAL THESE DAYS.
SLURRRPPPP
AND THE JUDGE'S PRIZE FOR REALISM GOES TO...BATMAN & ROBIN.
CONTAIN YOUR EXCITEMENT, CLAYFACE. WE'LL BE OUTTA HERE SOON.
GROAN

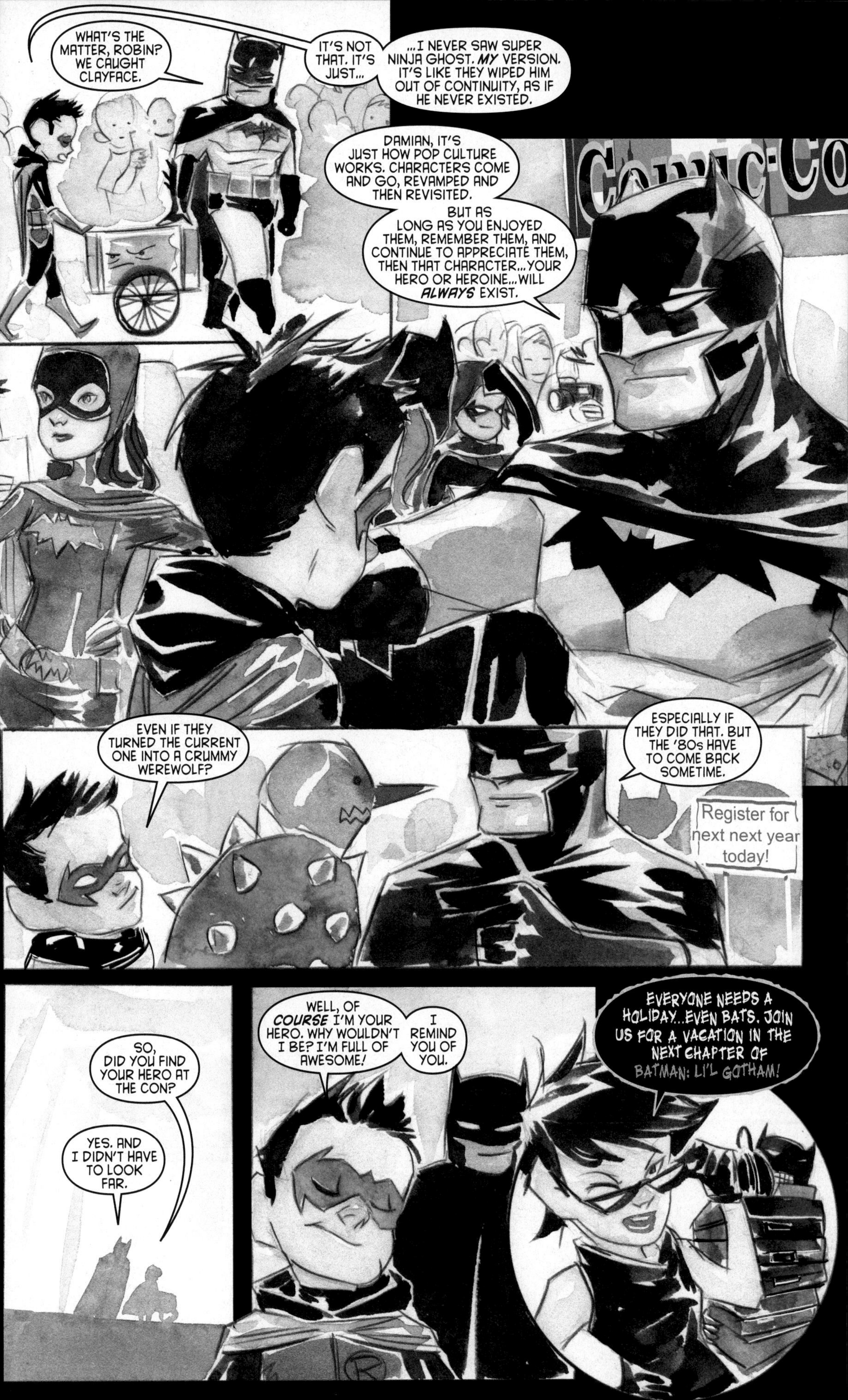
WHAT'S THE MATTER, ROBIN? WE CAUGHT CLAYFACE.
IT'S NOT THAT. IT'S JUST...
...I NEVER SAW SUPER NINJA GHOST. MY VERSION. IT'S LIKE THEY WIPED HIM OUT OF CONTINUITY, AS IF HE NEVER EXISTED.
DAMIAN, IT'S JUST HOW POP CULTURE WORKS. CHARACTERS COME AND GO, REVAMPED AND THEN REVISITED.
BUT AS LONG AS YOU ENJOYED THEM, REMEMBER THEM, AND CONTINUE TO APPRECIATE THEM, THEN THAT CHARACTER...YOUR HERO OR HEROINE...WILL ALWAYS EXIST.
EVEN IF THEY TURNED THE CURRENT ONE INTO A CRUMMY WEREWOLF?
ESPECIALLY IF THEY DID THAT. BUT THE '80s HAVE TO COME BACK SOMETIME.
Register for next next year today!
SO, DID YOU FIND YOUR HERO AT THE CON?
YES. AND I DIDN'T HAVE TO LOOK FAR.
WELL, OF COURSE I'M YOUR HERO. WHY WOULDN'T I BE? I'M FULL OF AWESOME!
I REMIND YOU OF YOU.
EVERYONE NEEDS A HOLIDAY...EVEN BATS. JOIN US FOR A VACATION IN THE NEXT CHAPTER OF BATMAN: LI'L GOTHAM!

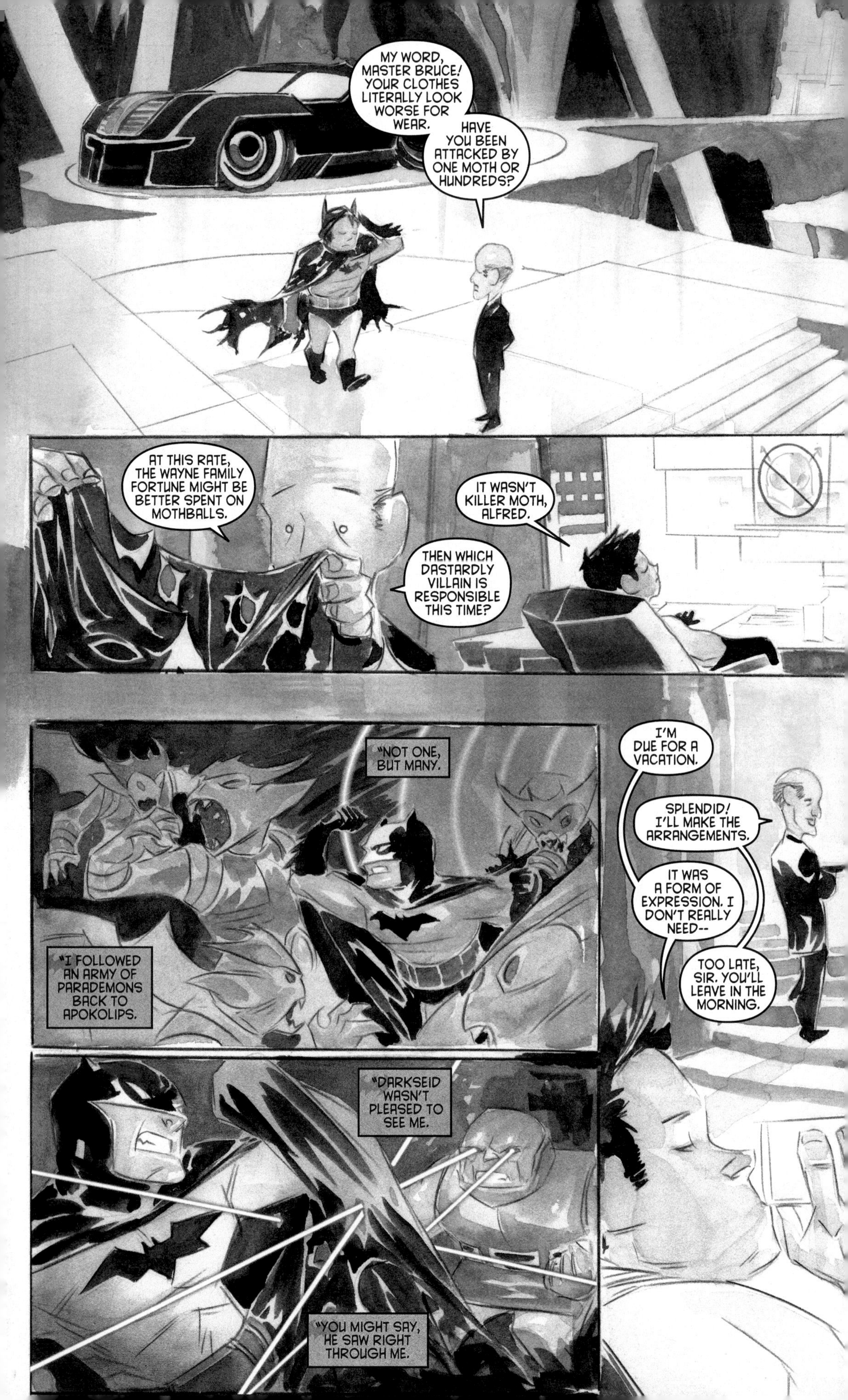
MY WORD, MASTER BRUCE! YOUR CLOTHES LITERALLY LOOK WORSE FOR WEAR.
HAVE YOU BEEN ATTACKED BY ONE MOTH OR HUNDREDS?
AT THIS RATE, THE WAYNE FAMILY FORTUNE MIGHT BE BETTER SPENT ON MOTHBALLS.
IT WASN'T KILLER MOTH, ALFRED.
THEN WHICH DASTARDLY VILLAIN IS RESPONSIBLE THIS TIME?
"NOT ONE, BUT MANY.
"I FOLLOWED AN ARMY OF PARADEMONS BACK TO APOKOLIPS.
"DARKSEID WASN'T PLEASED TO SEE ME.
"YOU MIGHT SAY, HE SAW RIGHT THROUGH ME.
I'M DUE FOR A VACATION.
SPLENDID! I'LL MAKE THE ARRANGEMENTS.
IT WAS A FORM OF EXPRESSION. I DON'T REALLY NEED--
TOO LATE, SIR. YOU'LL LEAVE IN THE MORNING.

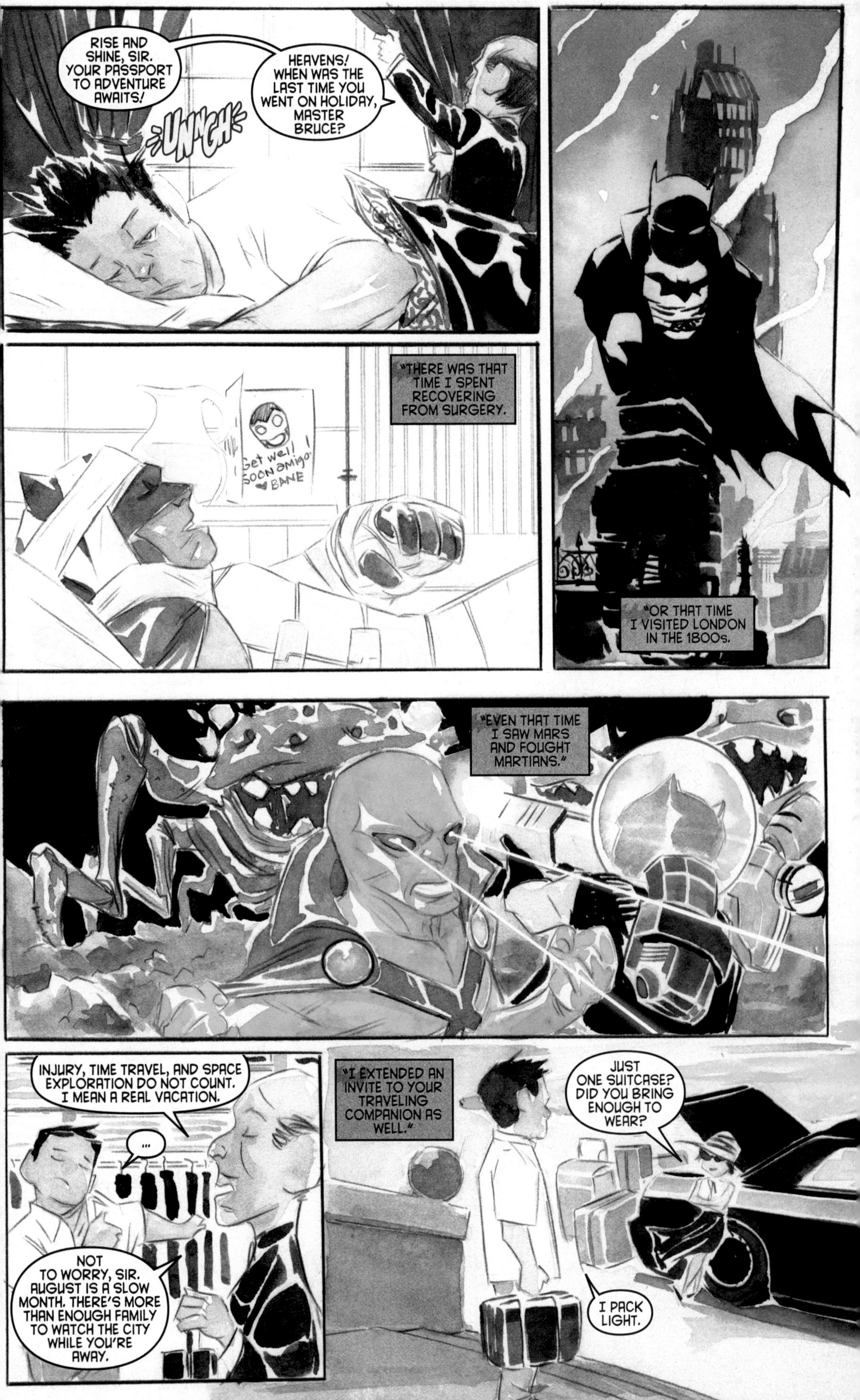
RISE AND SHINE, SIR. YOUR PASSPORT TO ADVENTURE AWAITS!
UNNGH
HEAVENS! WHEN WAS THE LAST TIME YOU WENT ON HOLIDAY, MASTER BRUCE?
"THERE WAS THAT TIME I SPENT RECOVERING FROM SURGERY.
Get well soon amigo! ♥ BANE
"OR THAT TIME I VISITED LONDON IN THE 1800s.
"EVEN THAT TIME I SAW MARS AND FOUGHT MARTIANS."
INJURY, TIME TRAVEL, AND SPACE EXPLORATION DO NOT COUNT. I MEAN A REAL VACATION.
...
NOT TO WORRY, SIR. AUGUST IS A SLOW MONTH. THERE'S MORE THAN ENOUGH FAMILY TO WATCH THE CITY WHILE YOU'RE AWAY.
"I EXTENDED AN INVITE TO YOUR TRAVELING COMPANION AS WELL."
JUST ONE SUITCASE? DID YOU BRING ENOUGH TO WEAR?
I PACK LIGHT.

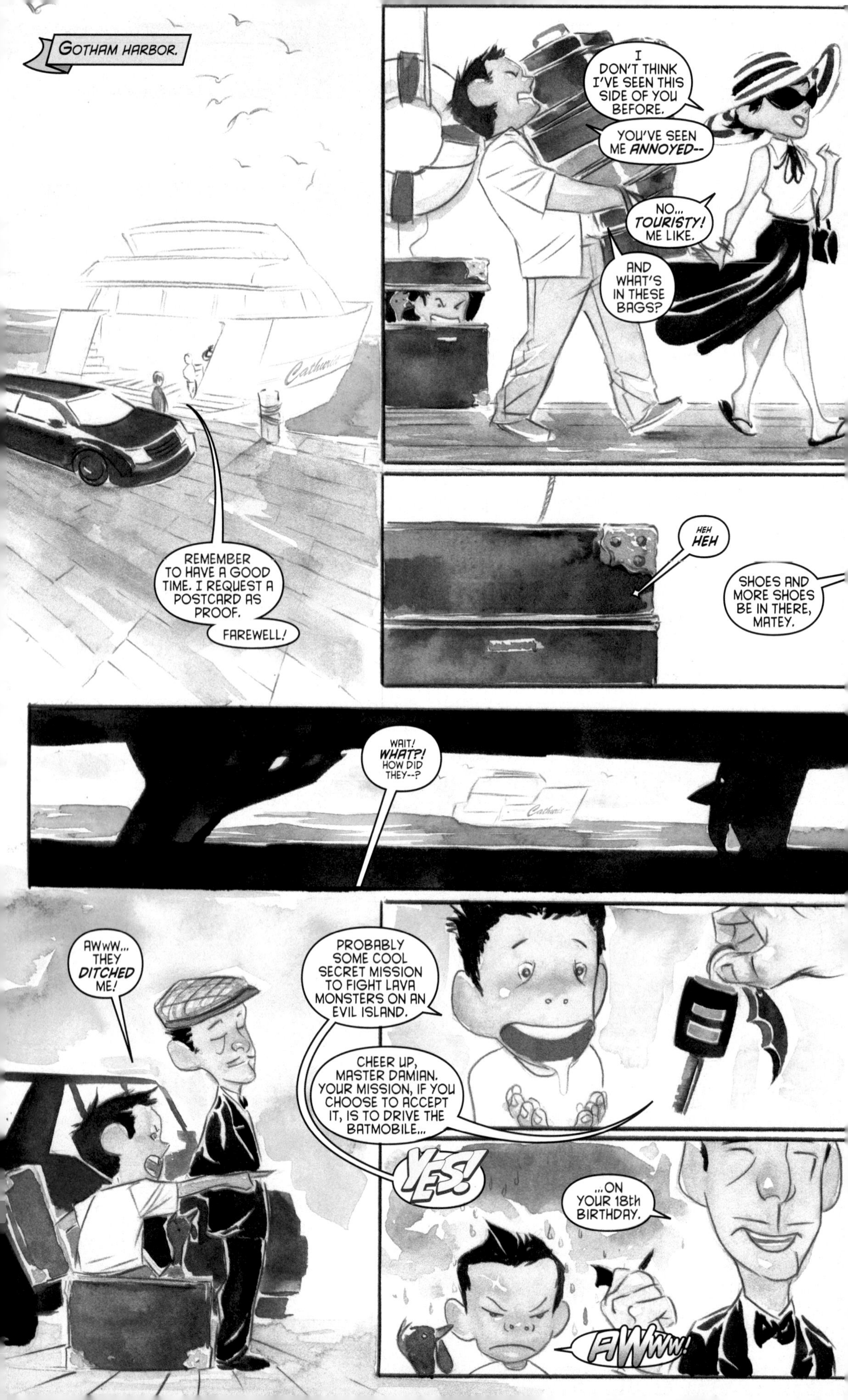
GOTHAM HARBOR.
I DON'T THINK I'VE SEEN THIS SIDE OF YOU BEFORE.
YOU'VE SEEN ME ANNOYED--
NO... TOURISTY! ME LIKE.
AND WHAT'S IN THESE BAGS?
REMEMBER TO HAVE A GOOD TIME. I REQUEST A POSTCARD AS PROOF.
FAREWELL!
HEH HEH
SHOES AND MORE SHOES BE IN THERE, MATEY.
WAIT! WHAT?! HOW DID THEY--?
AWWW... THEY DITCHED ME!
PROBABLY SOME COOL SECRET MISSION TO FIGHT LAVA MONSTERS ON AN EVIL ISLAND.
CHEER UP, MASTER DAMIAN. YOUR MISSION, IF YOU CHOOSE TO ACCEPT IT, IS TO DRIVE THE BATMOBILE...
YES!
...ON YOUR 18th BIRTHDAY.
AWWW!

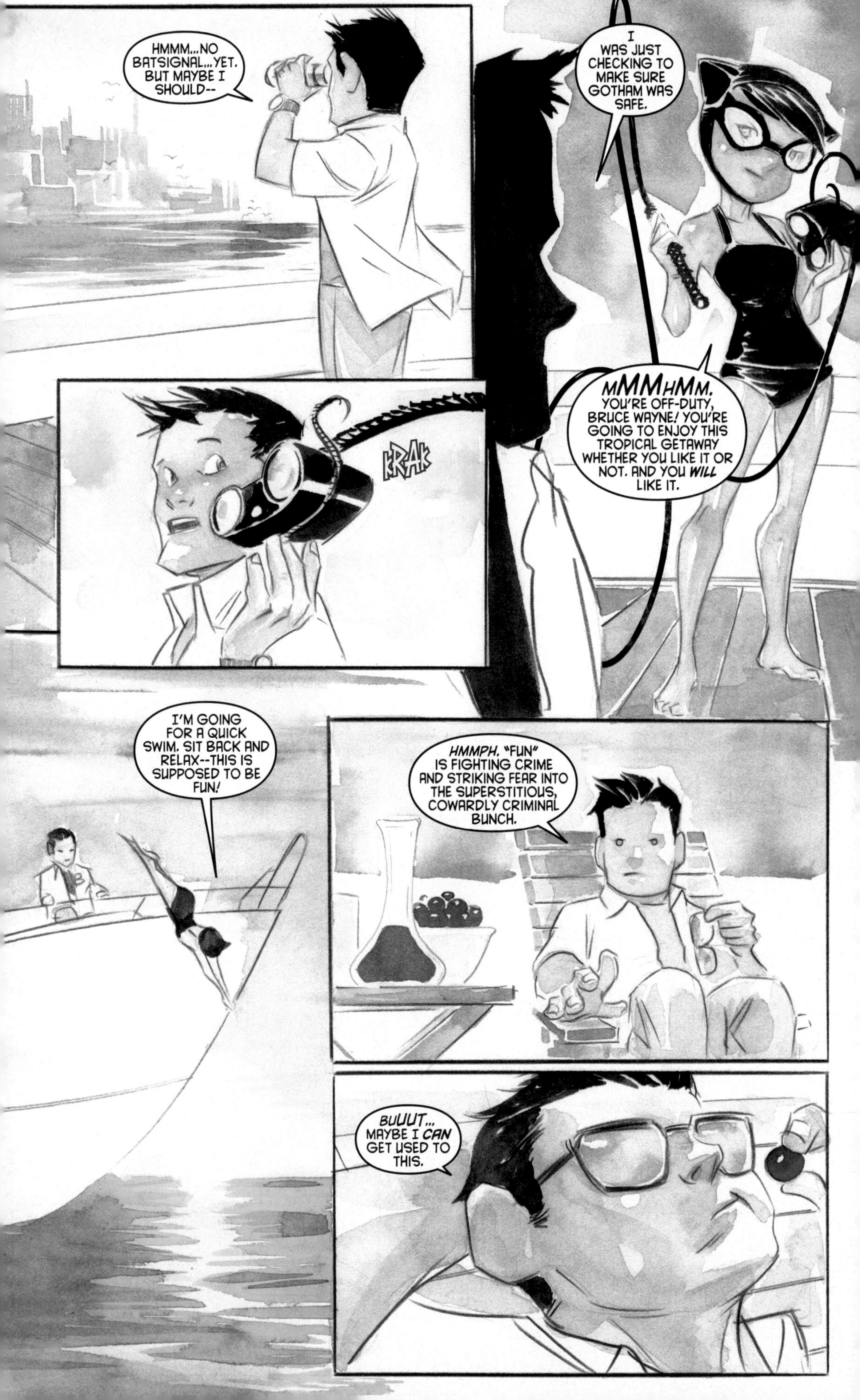
HMMM...NO BATSIGNAL...YET. BUT MAYBE I SHOULD--
I WAS JUST CHECKING TO MAKE SURE GOTHAM WAS SAFE.
kRAk
MMMHMM. YOU'RE OFF-DUTY, BRUCE WAYNE! YOU'RE GOING TO ENJOY THIS TROPICAL GETAWAY WHETHER YOU LIKE IT OR NOT. AND YOU *WILL* LIKE IT.
I'M GOING FOR A QUICK SWIM. SIT BACK AND RELAX--THIS IS SUPPOSED TO BE FUN!
HMMPH. "FUN" IS FIGHTING CRIME AND STRIKING FEAR INTO THE SUPERSTITIOUS, COWARDLY CRIMINAL BUNCH.
BUUUT... MAYBE I *CAN* GET USED TO THIS.

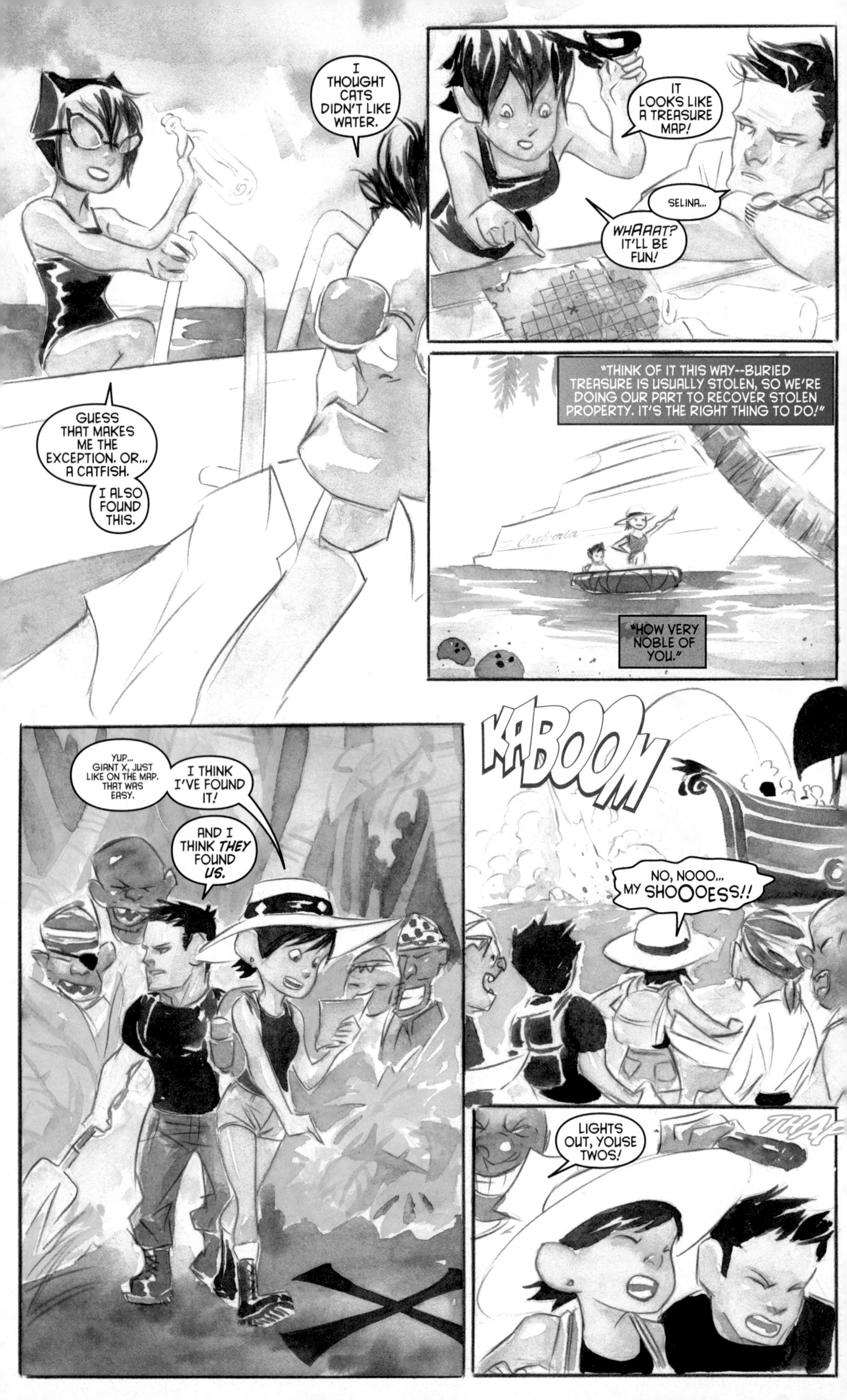
I THOUGHT CATS DIDN'T LIKE WATER.
GUESS THAT MAKES ME THE EXCEPTION. OR... A CATFISH.
I ALSO FOUND THIS.
IT LOOKS LIKE A TREASURE MAP!
SELINA...
WHAAAT? IT'LL BE FUN!
"THINK OF IT THIS WAY--BURIED TREASURE IS USUALLY STOLEN, SO WE'RE DOING OUR PART TO RECOVER STOLEN PROPERTY. IT'S THE RIGHT THING TO DO!"
"HOW VERY NOBLE OF YOU."
I THINK I'VE FOUND IT!
YUP... GIANT X, JUST LIKE ON THE MAP. THAT WAS EASY.
AND I THINK THEY FOUND US.
KABOOM
NO, NOOO... MY SHOOOESS!!
LIGHTS OUT, YOUSE TWOS!

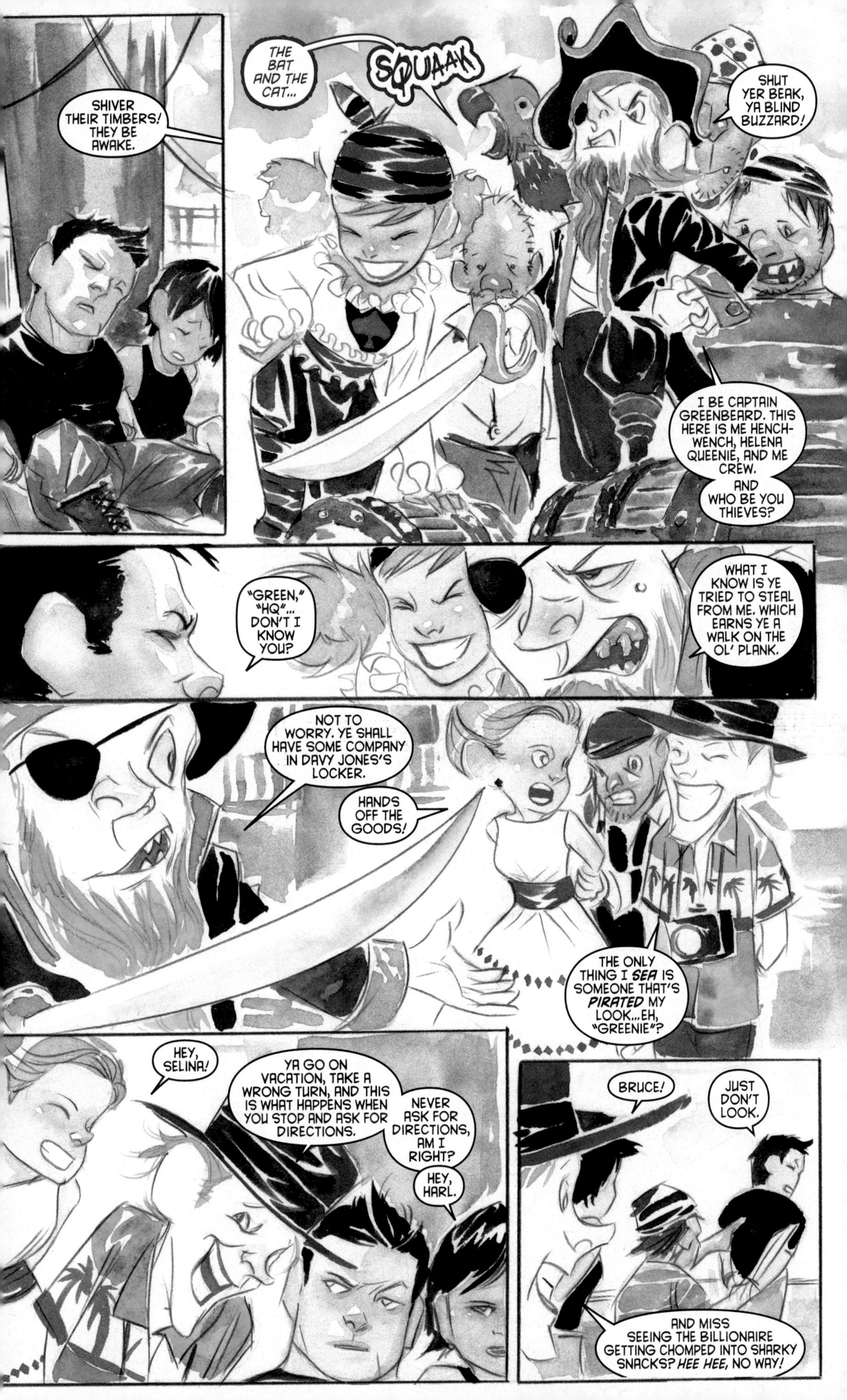
SHIVER THEIR TIMBERS! THEY BE AWAKE.
THE BAT AND THE CAT...
SQUAAK
SHUT YER BEAK, YA BLIND BUZZARD!
I BE CAPTAIN GREENBEARD. THIS HERE IS ME HENCH-WENCH, HELENA QUEENIE, AND ME CREW.
AND WHO BE YOU THIEVES?
"GREEN," "HQ"... DON'T I KNOW YOU?
WHAT I KNOW IS YE TRIED TO STEAL FROM ME. WHICH EARNS YE A WALK ON THE OL' PLANK.
NOT TO WORRY. YE SHALL HAVE SOME COMPANY IN DAVY JONES'S LOCKER.
HANDS OFF THE GOODS!
THE ONLY THING I SEA IS SOMEONE THAT'S PIRATED MY LOOK...EH, "GREENIE"?
HEY, SELINA!
YA GO ON VACATION, TAKE A WRONG TURN, AND THIS IS WHAT HAPPENS WHEN YOU STOP AND ASK FOR DIRECTIONS.
NEVER ASK FOR DIRECTIONS, AM I RIGHT?
HEY, HARL.
BRUCE!
JUST DON'T LOOK.
AND MISS SEEING THE BILLIONAIRE GETTING CHOMPED INTO SHARKY SNACKS? HEE HEE, NO WAY!

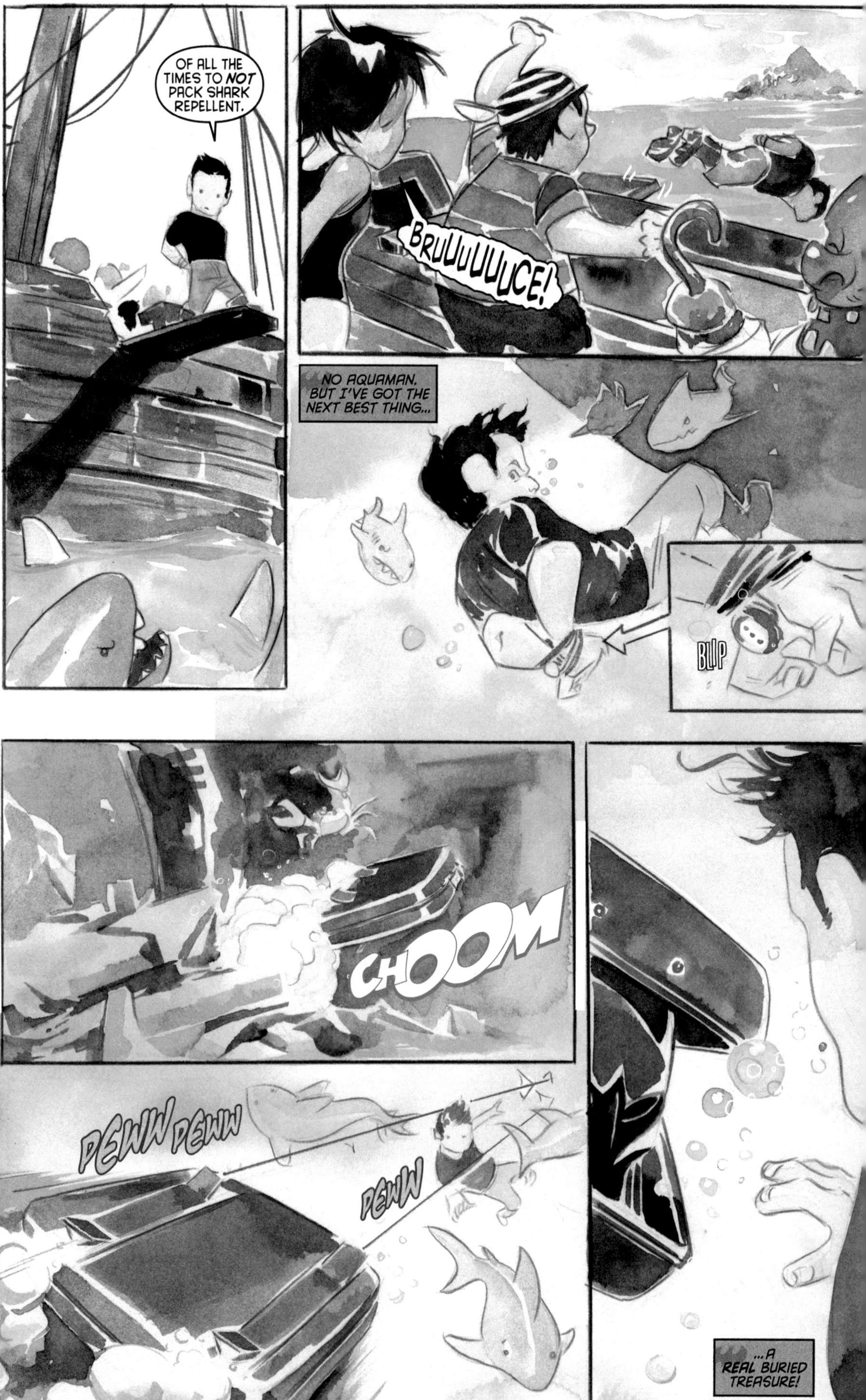
OF ALL THE TIMES TO NOT PACK SHARK REPELLENT.
BRUUUUUUCE!
NO AQUAMAN. BUT I'VE GOT THE NEXT BEST THING...
BLIP
CHOOM
PEWW PEWW
PEWW
...A REAL BURIED TREASURE!

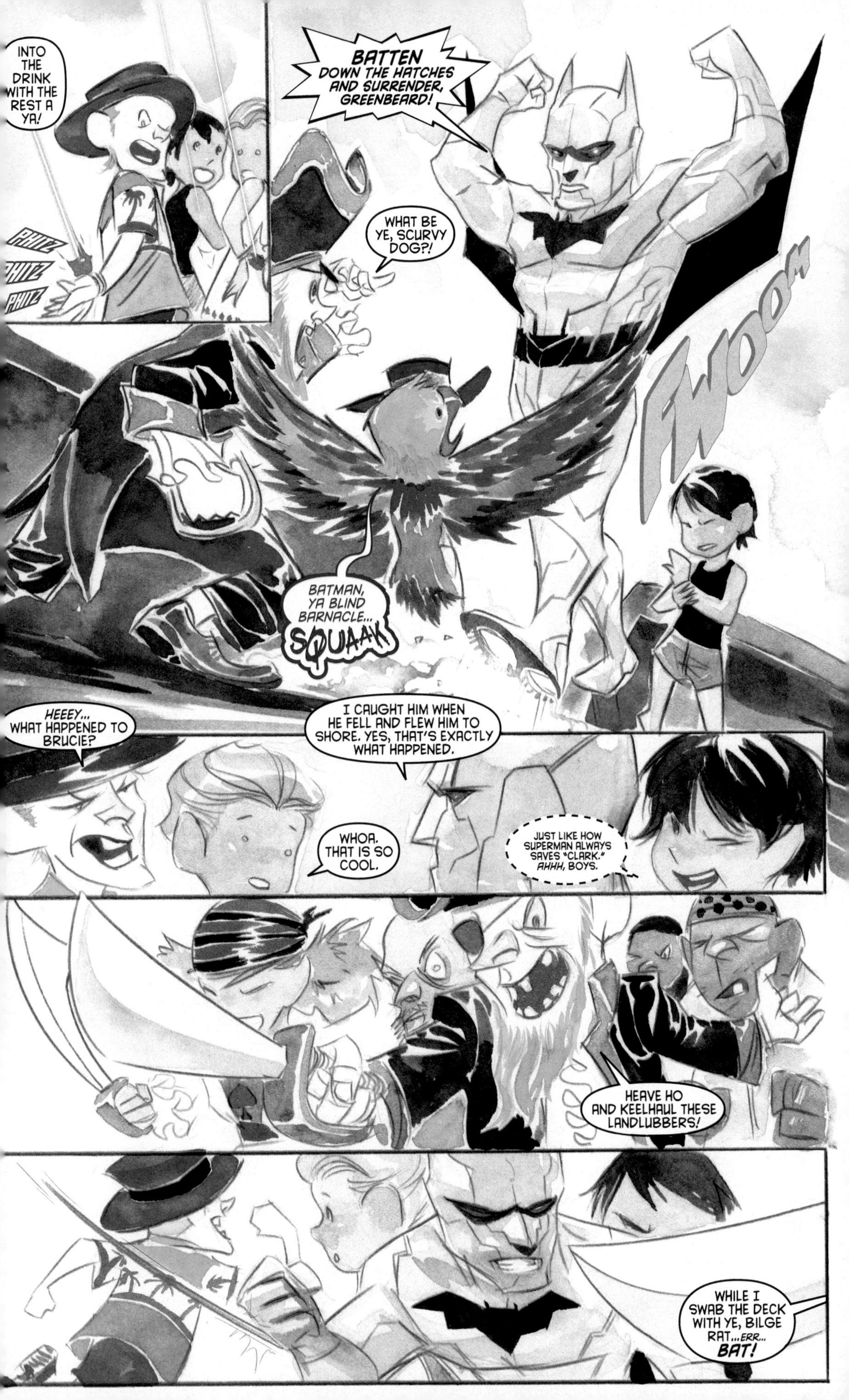
INTO THE DRINK WITH THE REST A YA!
PHITZ
PHITZ
PHITZ
BATTEN DOWN THE HATCHES AND SURRENDER, GREENBEARD!
WHAT BE YE, SCURVY DOG?!
FWOOM
BATMAN, YA BLIND BARNACLE...
SQUAAK
HEEEY... WHAT HAPPENED TO BRUCIE?
I CAUGHT HIM WHEN HE FELL AND FLEW HIM TO SHORE. YES, THAT'S EXACTLY WHAT HAPPENED.
WHOA. THAT IS SO COOL.
JUST LIKE HOW SUPERMAN ALWAYS SAVES "CLARK." AHHH, BOYS.
HEAVE HO AND KEELHAUL THESE LANDLUBBERS!
WHILE I SWAB THE DECK WITH YE, BILGE RAT...ERR... BAT!

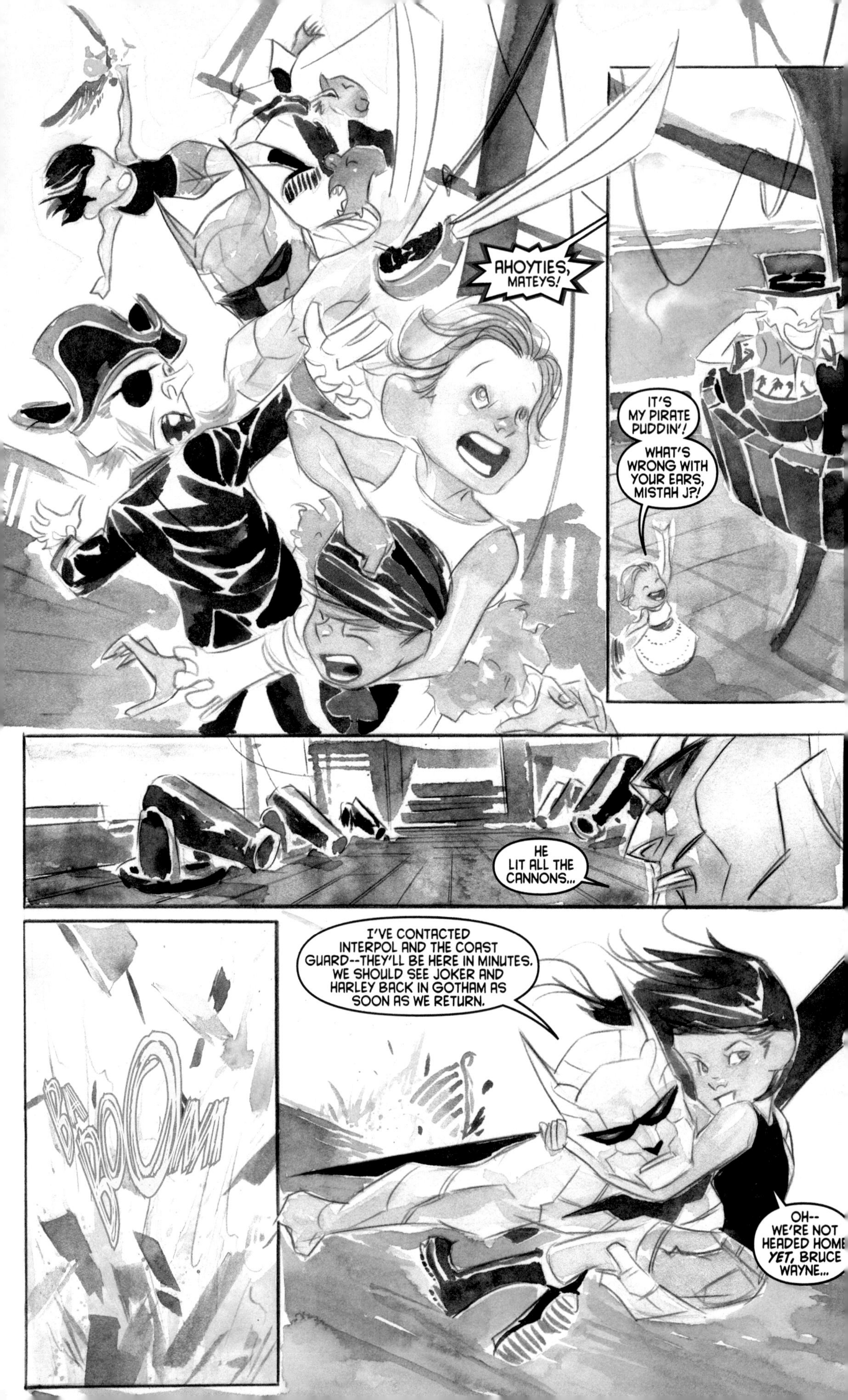
AHOYTIES, MATEYS!
IT'S MY PIRATE PUDDIN'!
WHAT'S WRONG WITH YOUR EARS, MISTAH J?!
HE LIT ALL THE CANNONS...
I'VE CONTACTED INTERPOL AND THE COAST GUARD--THEY'LL BE HERE IN MINUTES. WE SHOULD SEE JOKER AND HARLEY BACK IN GOTHAM AS SOON AS WE RETURN.
BABOOM
OH-- WE'RE NOT HEADED HOME *YET*, BRUCE WAYNE...

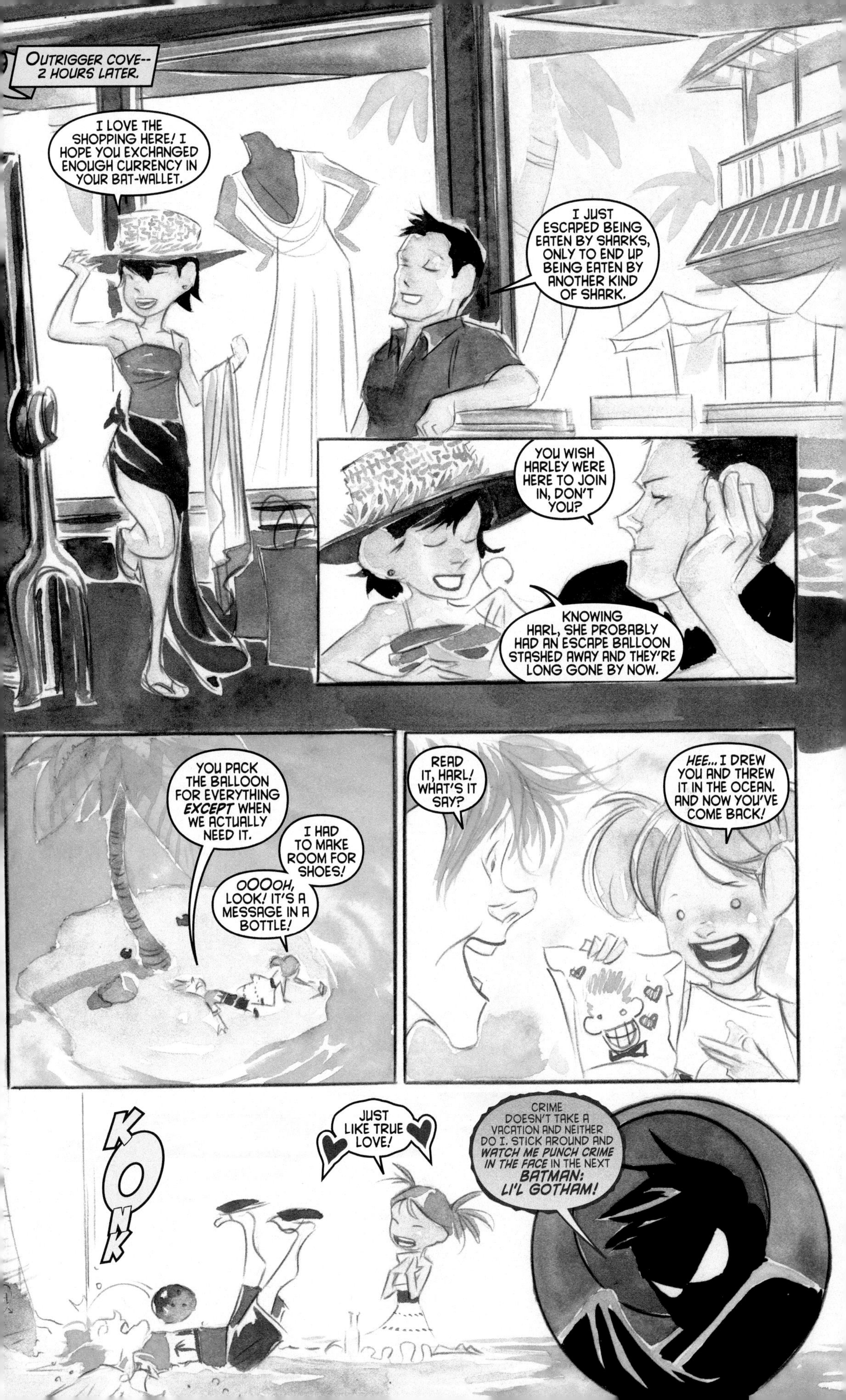
OUTRIGGER COVE-- 2 HOURS LATER.
I LOVE THE SHOPPING HERE! I HOPE YOU EXCHANGED ENOUGH CURRENCY IN YOUR BAT-WALLET.
I JUST ESCAPED BEING EATEN BY SHARKS, ONLY TO END UP BEING EATEN BY ANOTHER KIND OF SHARK.
YOU WISH HARLEY WERE HERE TO JOIN IN, DON'T YOU?
KNOWING HARL, SHE PROBABLY HAD AN ESCAPE BALLOON STASHED AWAY AND THEY'RE LONG GONE BY NOW.
YOU PACK THE BALLOON FOR EVERYTHING *EXCEPT* WHEN WE ACTUALLY NEED IT.
I HAD TO MAKE ROOM FOR SHOES!
OOOOH, LOOK! IT'S A MESSAGE IN A BOTTLE!
READ IT, HARL! WHAT'S IT SAY?
HEE... I DREW YOU AND THREW IT IN THE OCEAN. AND NOW YOU'VE COME BACK!
KONK
JUST LIKE TRUE LOVE!
CRIME DOESN'T TAKE A VACATION AND NEITHER DO I. STICK AROUND AND *WATCH ME PUNCH CRIME IN THE FACE* IN THE NEXT *BATMAN: LI'L GOTHAM!*

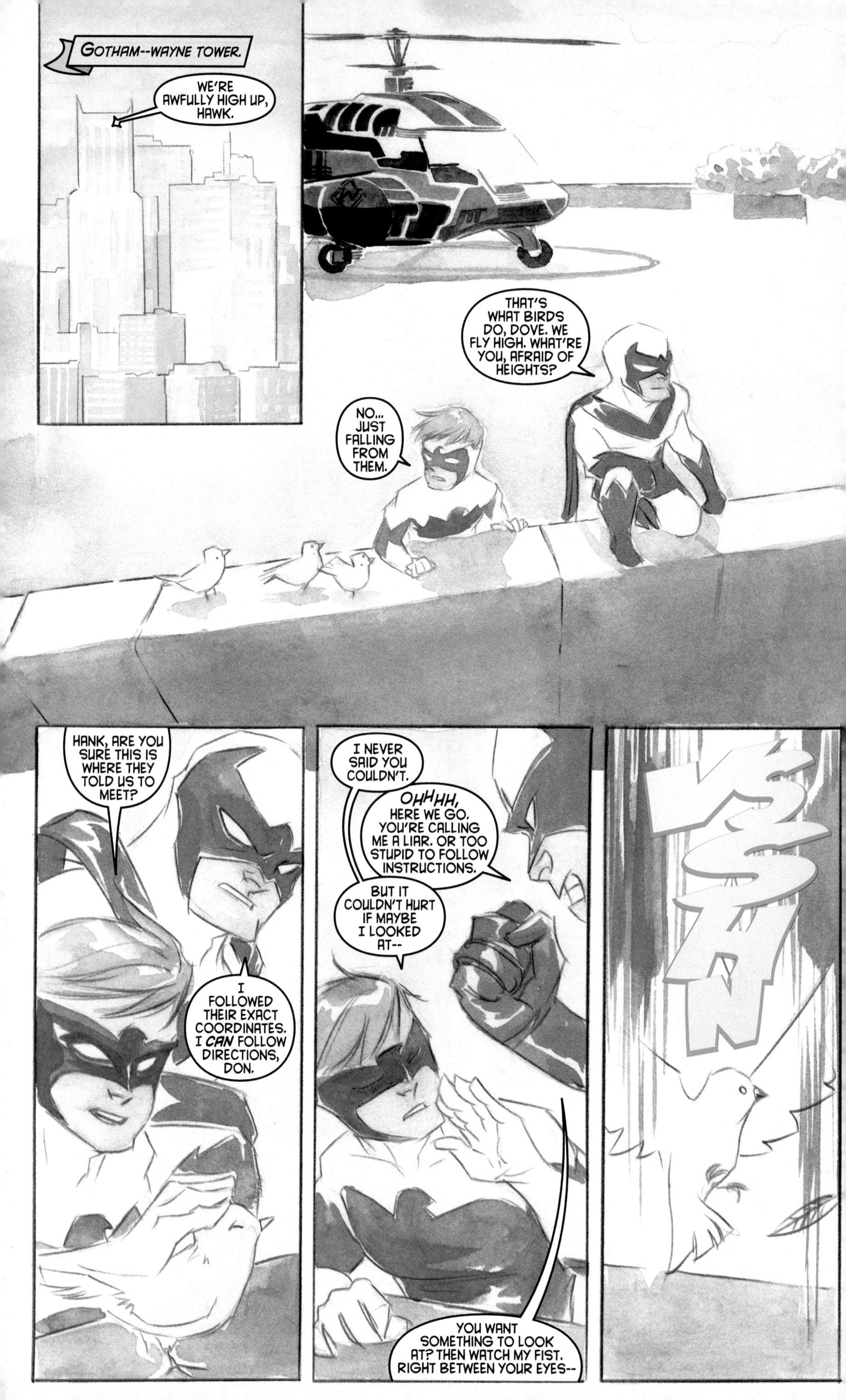
GOTHAM--WAYNE TOWER.
WE'RE AWFULLY HIGH UP, HAWK.
THAT'S WHAT BIRDS DO, DOVE. WE FLY HIGH. WHAT'RE YOU, AFRAID OF HEIGHTS?
NO... JUST FALLING FROM THEM.
HANK, ARE YOU SURE THIS IS WHERE THEY TOLD US TO MEET?
I FOLLOWED THEIR EXACT COORDINATES. I CAN FOLLOW DIRECTIONS, DON.
I NEVER SAID YOU COULDN'T.
OHHHH, HERE WE GO. YOU'RE CALLING ME A LIAR. OR TOO STUPID TO FOLLOW INSTRUCTIONS.
BUT IT COULDN'T HURT IF MAYBE I LOOKED AT--
YOU WANT SOMETHING TO LOOK AT? THEN WATCH MY FIST. RIGHT BETWEEN YOUR EYES--
VSHH

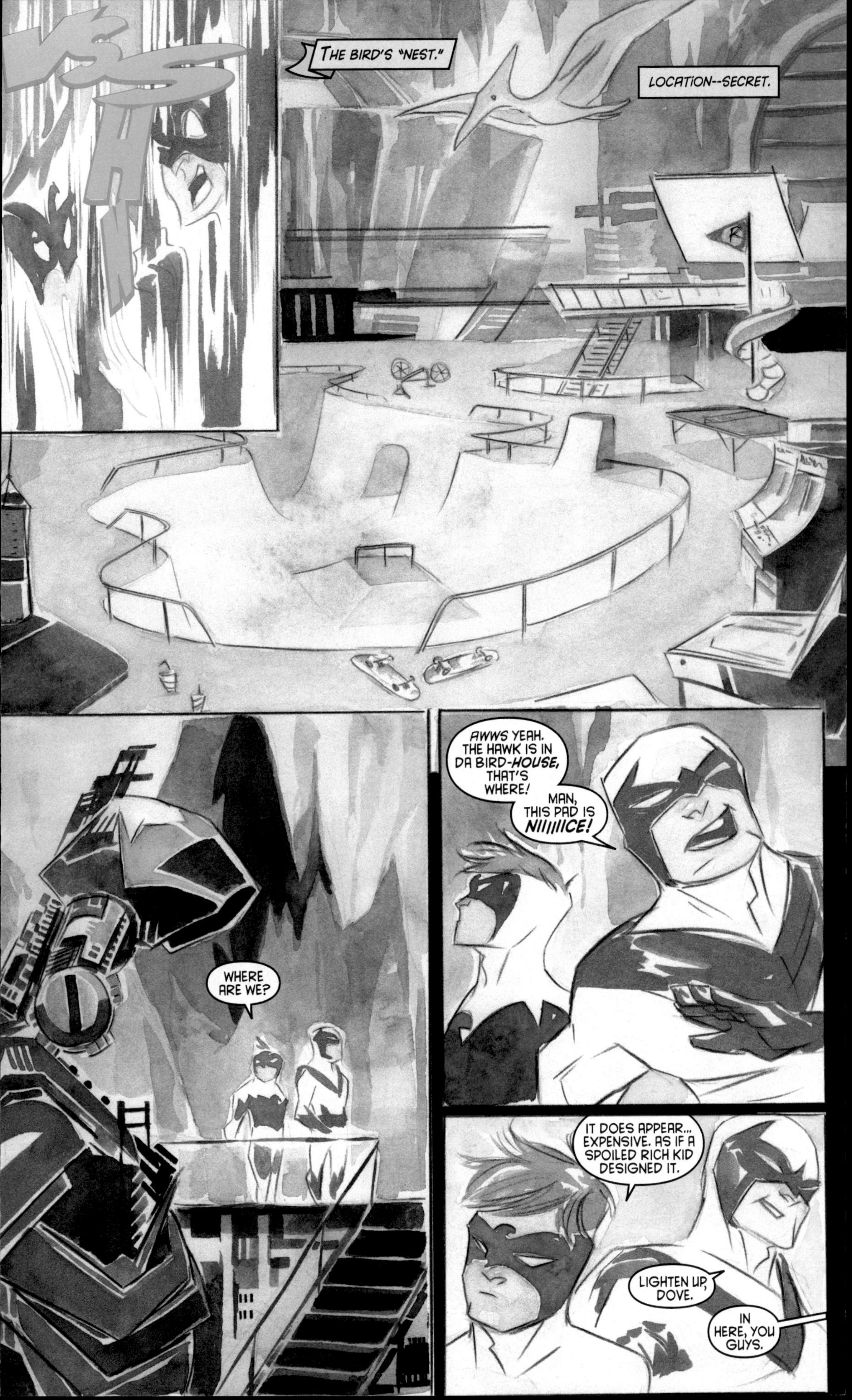

THE BIRD'S "NEST."
LOCATION--SECRET.
WHERE ARE WE?
AWWS YEAH. THE HAWK IS IN DA BIRD-HOUSE, THAT'S WHERE!
MAN, THIS PAD IS NIIIIIICE!
IT DOES APPEAR... EXPENSIVE. AS IF A SPOILED RICH KID DESIGNED IT.
LIGHTEN UP, DOVE.
IN HERE, YOU GUYS.

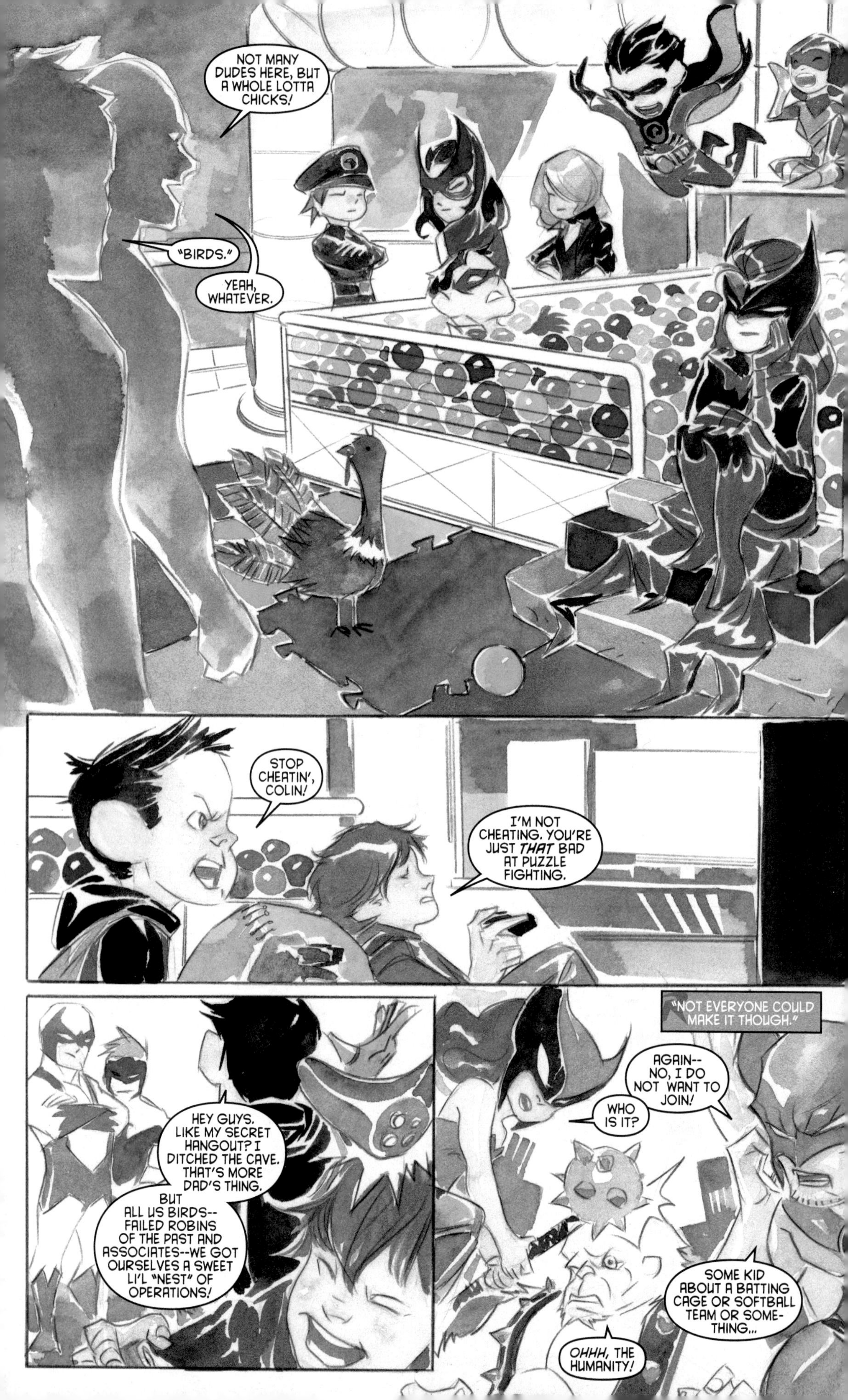
NOT MANY DUDES HERE, BUT A WHOLE LOTTA CHICKS!
"BIRDS."
YEAH, WHATEVER.
STOP CHEATIN', COLIN!
I'M NOT CHEATING. YOU'RE JUST *THAT* BAD AT PUZZLE FIGHTING.
HEY GUYS. LIKE MY SECRET HANGOUT? I DITCHED THE CAVE. THAT'S MORE DAD'S THING.
BUT ALL US BIRDS--FAILED ROBINS OF THE PAST AND ASSOCIATES--WE GOT OURSELVES A SWEET LI'L "NEST" OF OPERATIONS!
"NOT EVERYONE COULD MAKE IT THOUGH."
AGAIN--NO, I DO NOT WANT TO JOIN!
WHO IS IT?
SOME KID ABOUT A BATTING CAGE OR SOFTBALL TEAM OR SOME-THING...
OHHH, THE HUMANITY!

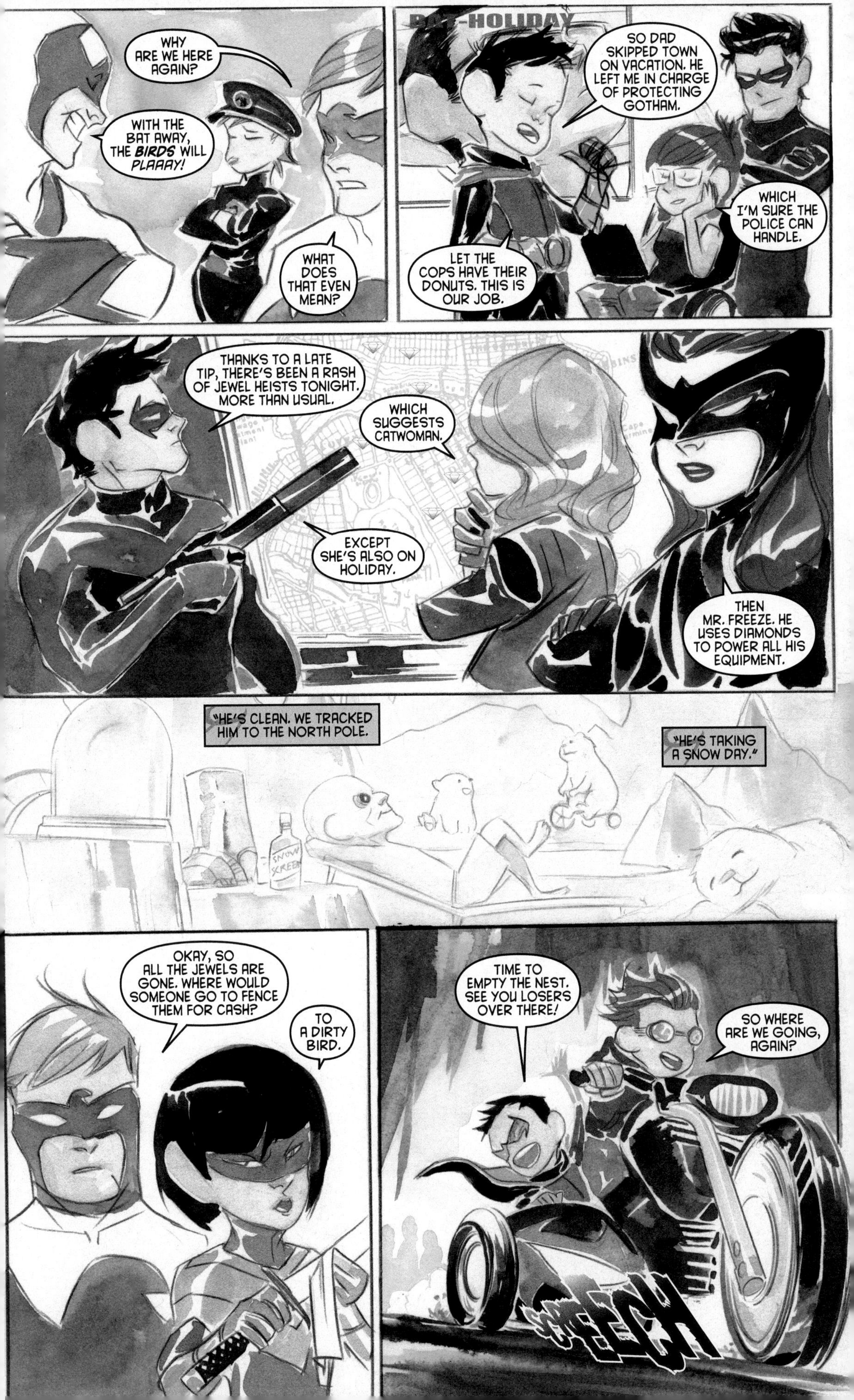
BAT-HOLIDAY
WHY ARE WE HERE AGAIN?
WITH THE BAT AWAY, THE *BIRDS* WILL *PLAAAY!*
WHAT DOES THAT EVEN MEAN?
SO DAD SKIPPED TOWN ON VACATION. HE LEFT ME IN CHARGE OF PROTECTING GOTHAM.
WHICH I'M SURE THE POLICE CAN HANDLE.
LET THE COPS HAVE THEIR DONUTS. THIS IS OUR JOB.
THANKS TO A LATE TIP, THERE'S BEEN A RASH OF JEWEL HEISTS TONIGHT. MORE THAN USUAL.
WHICH SUGGESTS CATWOMAN.
EXCEPT SHE'S ALSO ON HOLIDAY.
THEN MR. FREEZE. HE USES DIAMONDS TO POWER ALL HIS EQUIPMENT.
"HE'S CLEAN. WE TRACKED HIM TO THE NORTH POLE.
"HE'S TAKING A SNOW DAY."
OKAY, SO ALL THE JEWELS ARE GONE. WHERE WOULD SOMEONE GO TO FENCE THEM FOR CASH?
TO A DIRTY BIRD.
TIME TO EMPTY THE NEST. SEE YOU LOSERS OVER THERE!
SO WHERE ARE WE GOING, AGAIN?

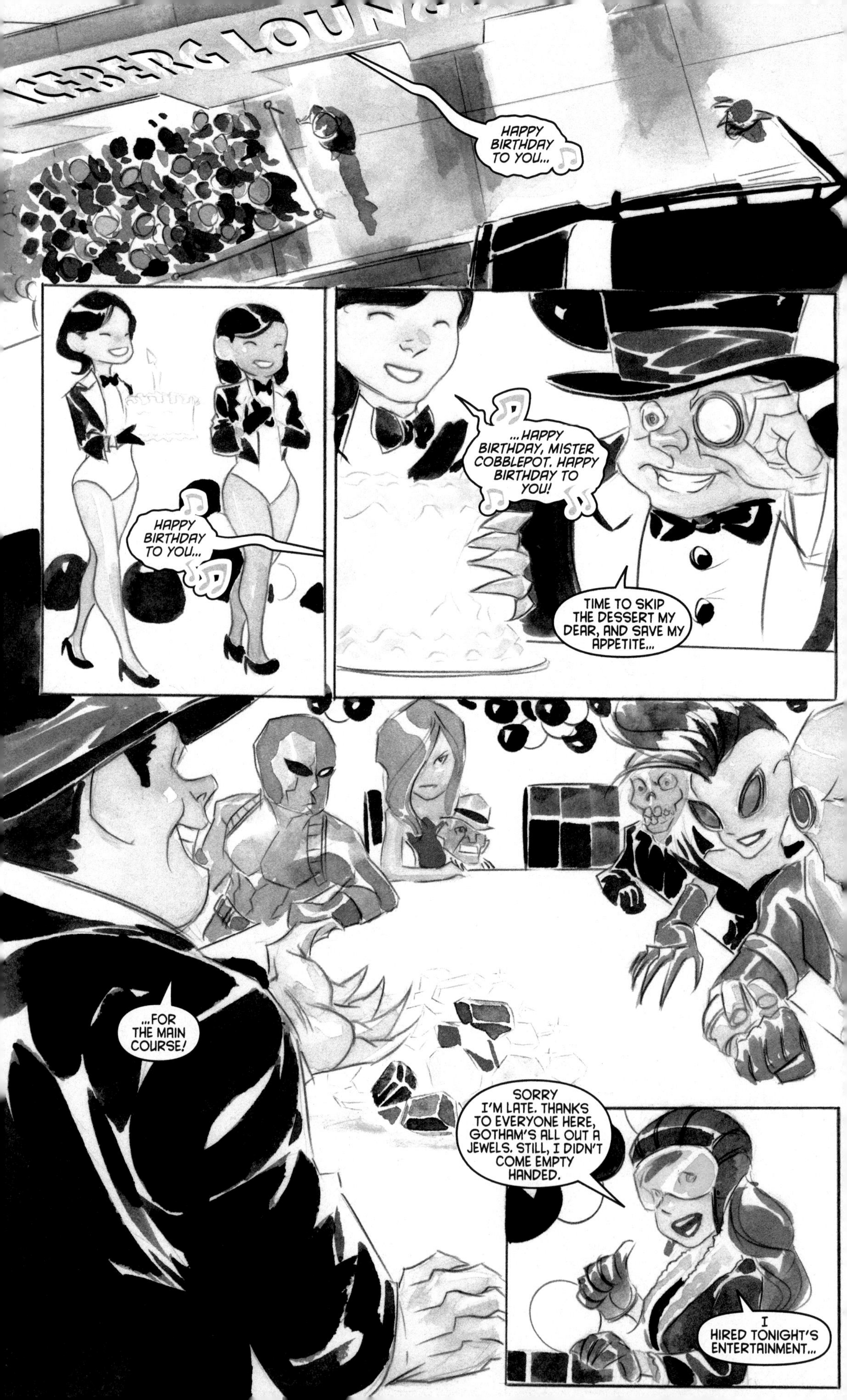

ICEBERG LOUNGE
HAPPY BIRTHDAY TO YOU...
HAPPY BIRTHDAY TO YOU...
...HAPPY BIRTHDAY, MISTER COBBLEPOT. HAPPY BIRTHDAY TO YOU!
TIME TO SKIP THE DESSERT MY DEAR, AND SAVE MY APPETITE...
...FOR THE MAIN COURSE!
SORRY I'M LATE. THANKS TO EVERYONE HERE, GOTHAM'S ALL OUT A JEWELS. STILL, I DIDN'T COME EMPTY HANDED.
I HIRED TONIGHT'S ENTERTAINMENT...

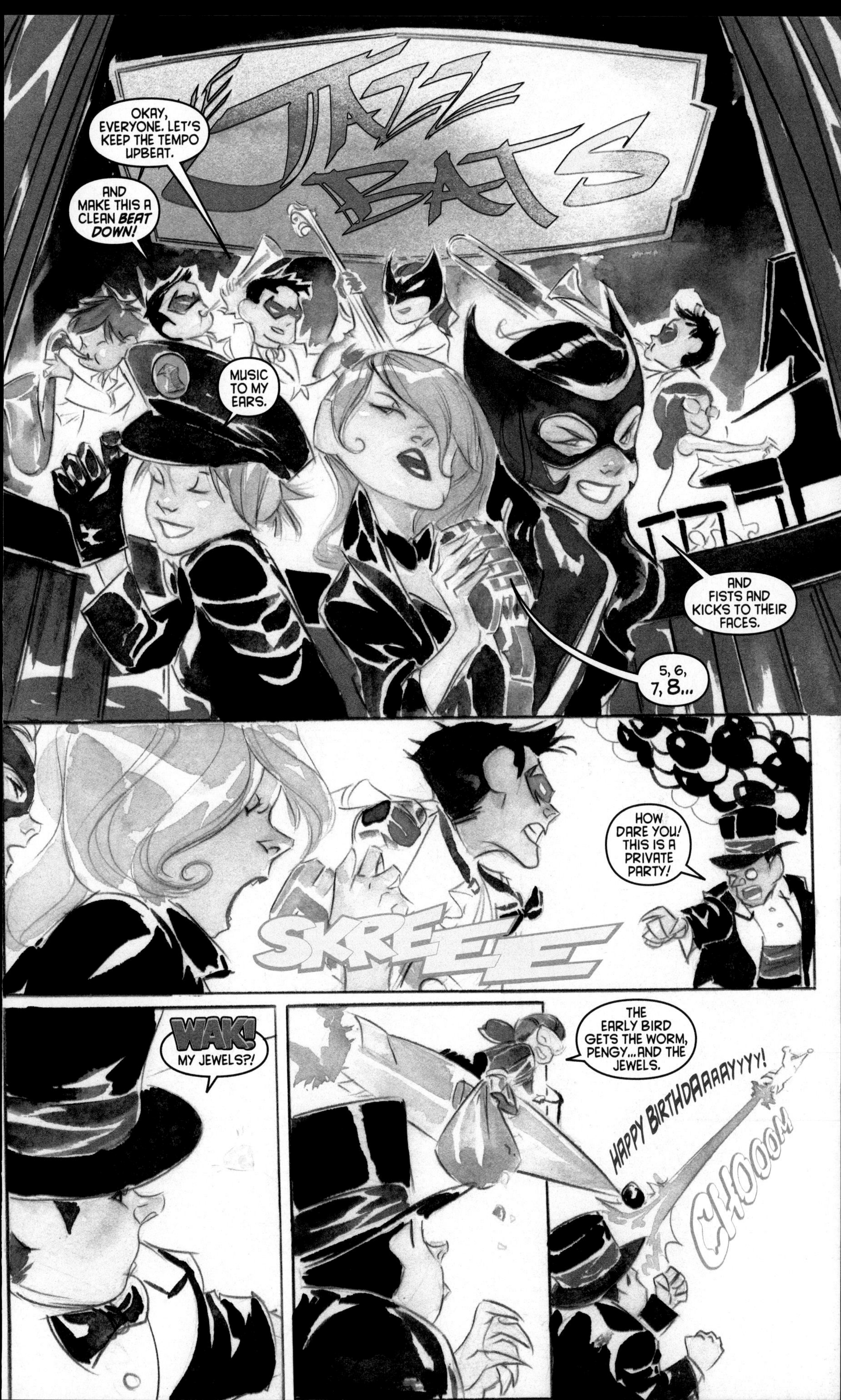

JAZZ BATS
OKAY, EVERYONE. LET'S KEEP THE TEMPO UPBEAT.
AND MAKE THIS A CLEAN *BEAT DOWN!*
MUSIC TO MY EARS.
AND FISTS AND KICKS TO THEIR FACES.
5, 6, 7, 8,...
HOW DARE YOU! THIS IS A PRIVATE PARTY!
SKREEE
WAK!
MY JEWELS?!
THE EARLY BIRD GETS THE WORM, PENGY...AND THE JEWELS.
HAPPY BIRTHDAAAAYYYY!
CHOOOM

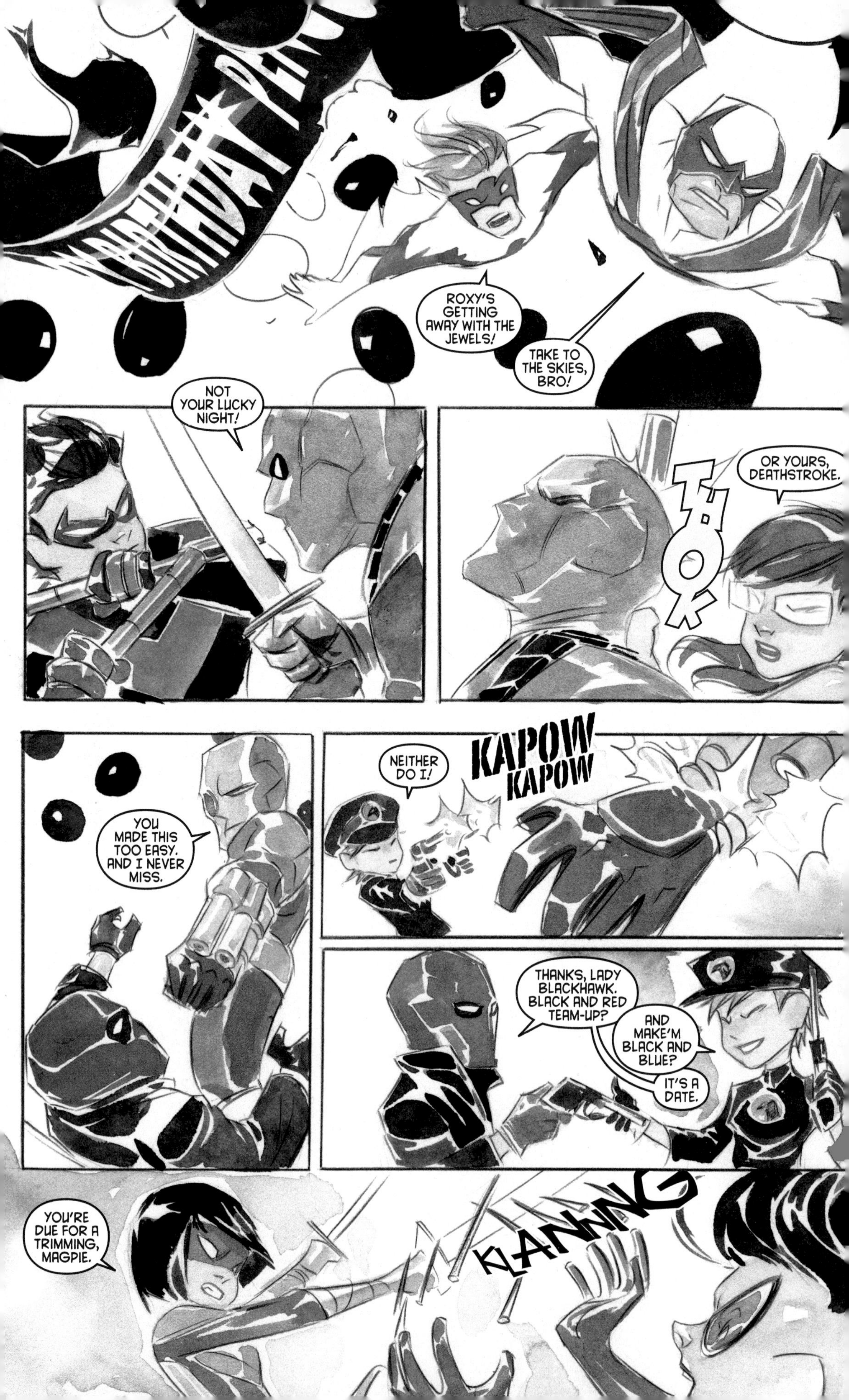
ROXY'S GETTING AWAY WITH THE JEWELS!
TAKE TO THE SKIES, BRO!
NOT YOUR LUCKY NIGHT!
THOK
OR YOURS, DEATHSTROKE.
YOU MADE THIS TOO EASY. AND I NEVER MISS.
NEITHER DO I!
KAPOW
KAPOW
THANKS, LADY BLACKHAWK. BLACK AND RED TEAM-UP?
AND MAKE'M BLACK AND BLUE?
IT'S A DATE.
YOU'RE DUE FOR A TRIMMING, MAGPIE.
KLANNNG

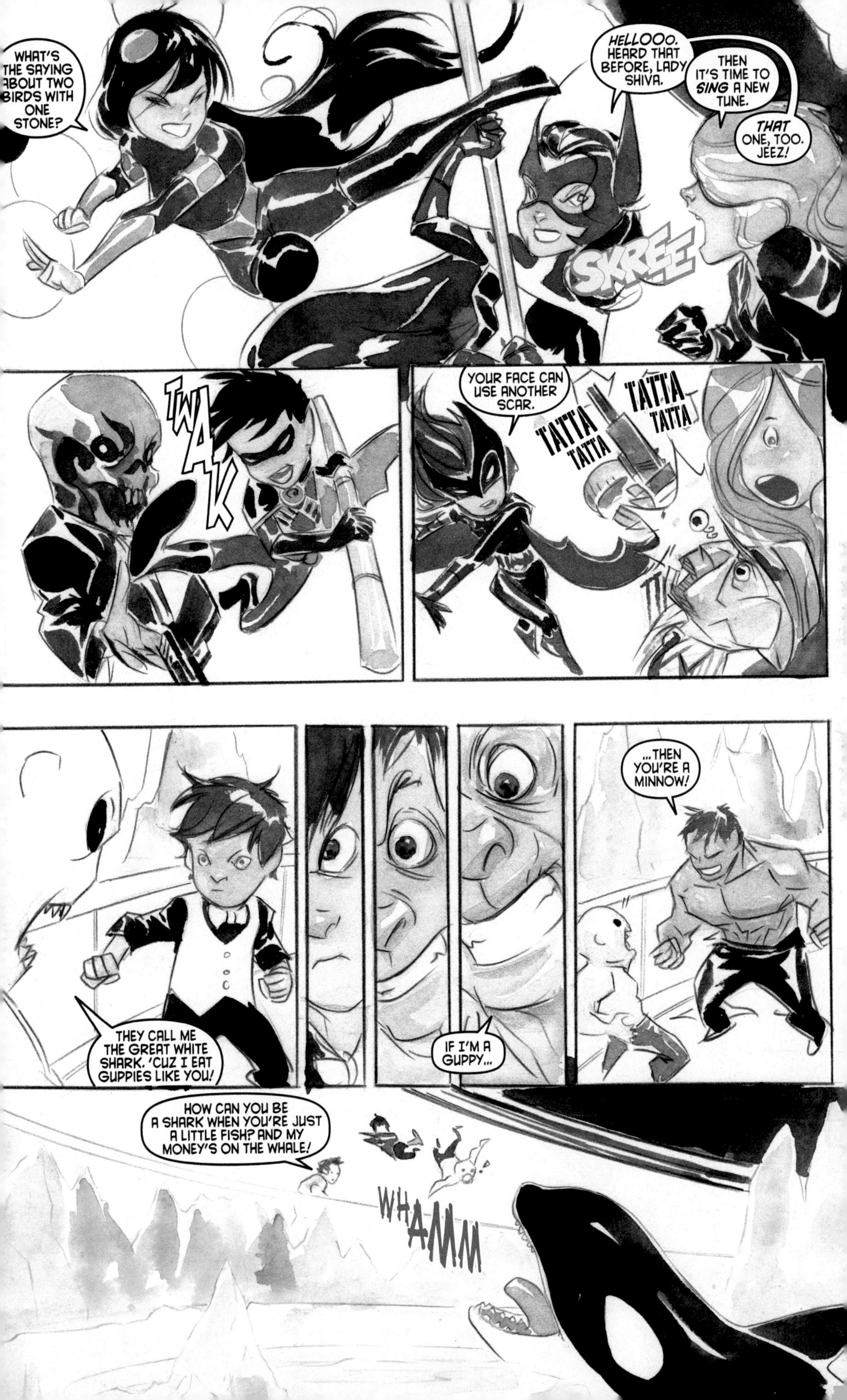

WHAT'S THE SAYING ABOUT TWO BIRDS WITH ONE STONE?
HELLOOO. HEARD THAT BEFORE, LADY SHIVA.
THEN IT'S TIME TO SING A NEW TUNE.
THAT ONE, TOO. JEEZ!
SKREE
TWAK
YOUR FACE CAN USE ANOTHER SCAR.
TATTA TATTA
TATTA TATTA
THEY CALL ME THE GREAT WHITE SHARK. 'CUZ I EAT GUPPIES LIKE YOU!
IF I'M A GUPPY...
...THEN YOU'RE A MINNOW!
HOW CAN YOU BE A SHARK WHEN YOU'RE JUST A LITTLE FISH? AND MY MONEY'S ON THE WHALE!
WHAMM

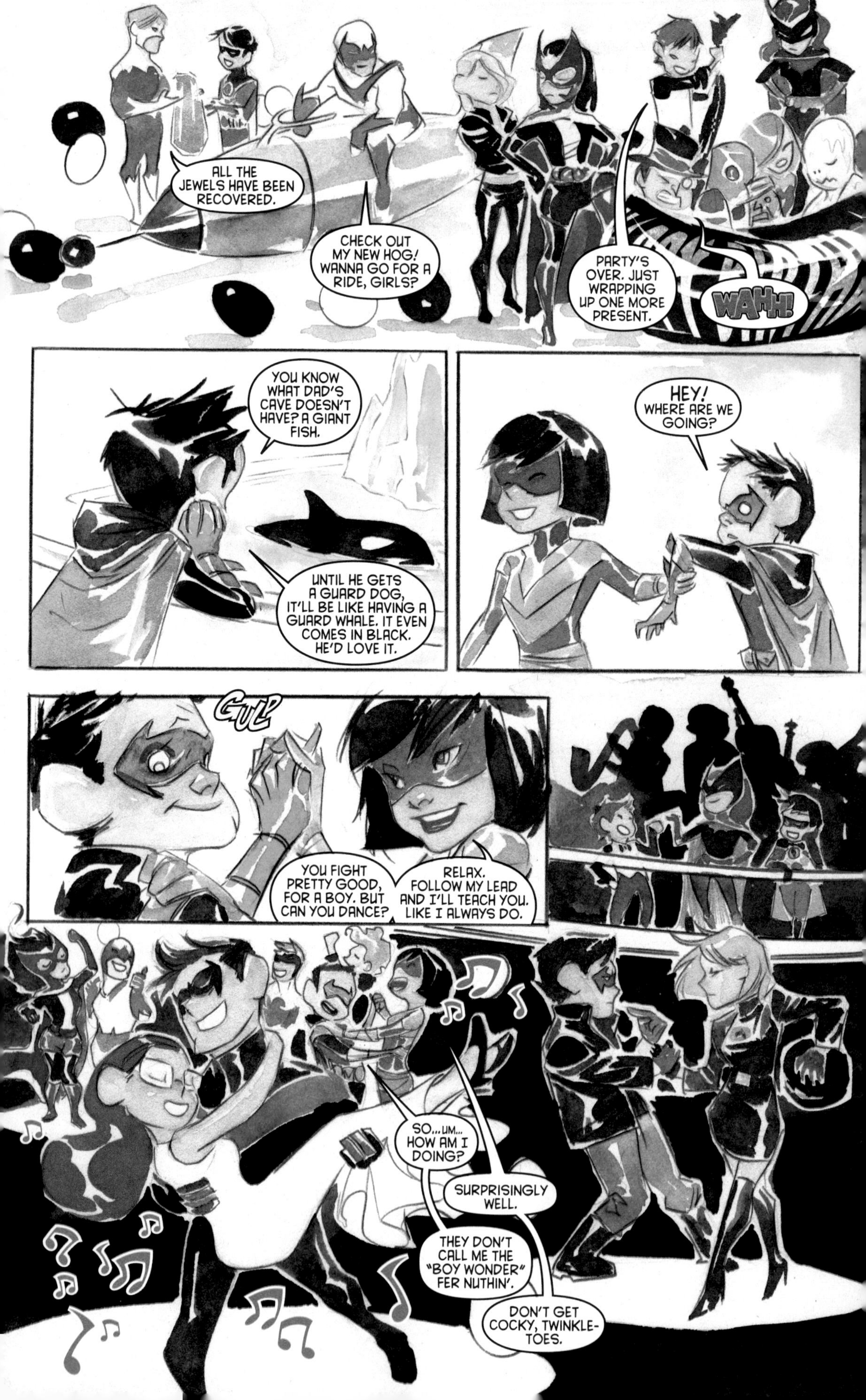
ALL THE JEWELS HAVE BEEN RECOVERED.
CHECK OUT MY NEW HOG! WANNA GO FOR A RIDE, GIRLS?
PARTY'S OVER. JUST WRAPPING UP ONE MORE PRESENT.
WAHH!
YOU KNOW WHAT DAD'S CAVE DOESN'T HAVE? A GIANT FISH.
UNTIL HE GETS A GUARD DOG, IT'LL BE LIKE HAVING A GUARD WHALE. IT EVEN COMES IN BLACK. HE'D LOVE IT.
HEY! WHERE ARE WE GOING?
GULP
YOU FIGHT PRETTY GOOD, FOR A BOY. BUT CAN YOU DANCE?
RELAX. FOLLOW MY LEAD AND I'LL TEACH YOU. LIKE I ALWAYS DO.
SO...UM... HOW AM I DOING?
SURPRISINGLY WELL.
THEY DON'T CALL ME THE "BOY WONDER" FER NUTHIN'.
DON'T GET COCKY, TWINKLE-TOES.

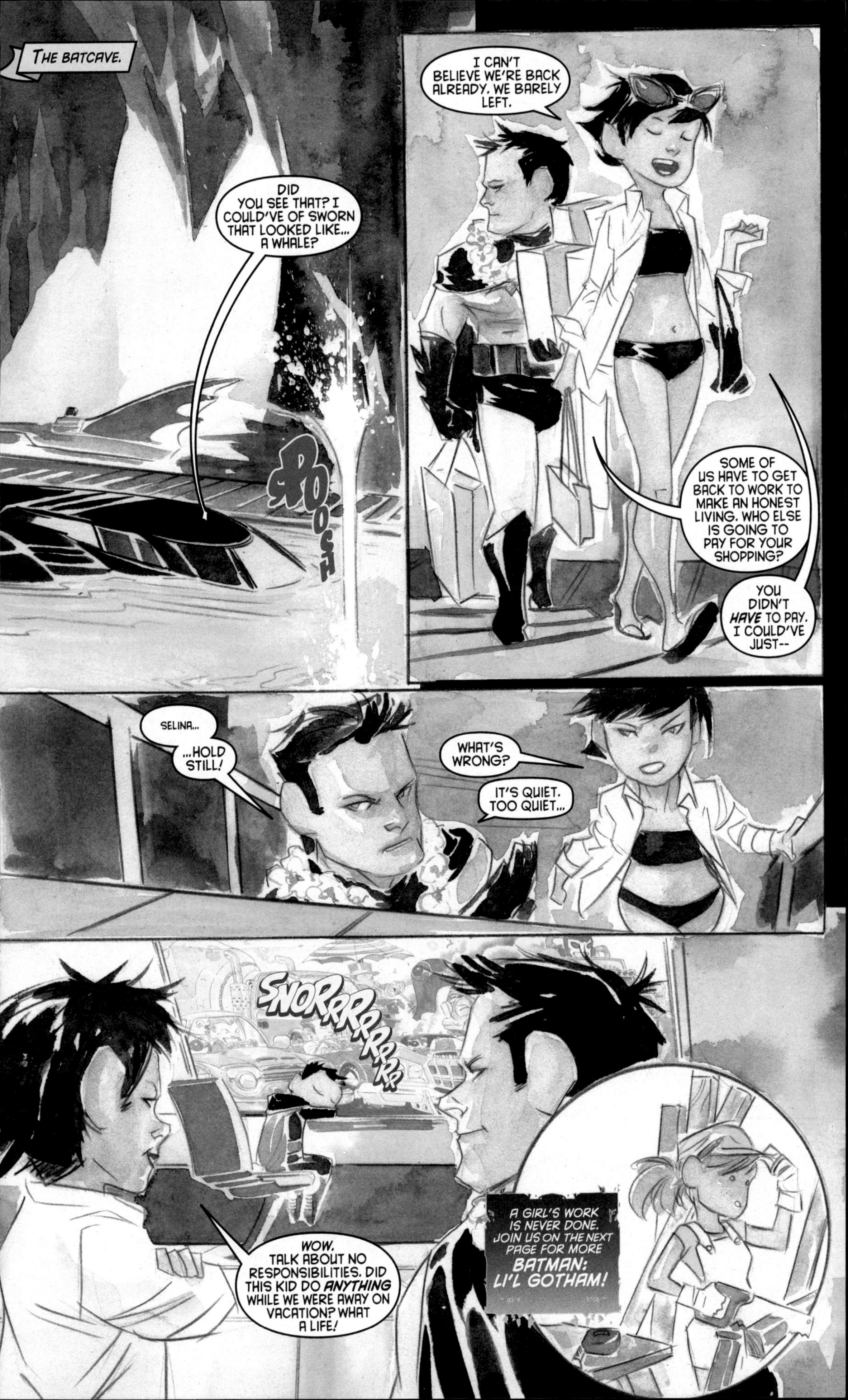
THE BATCAVE.
I CAN'T BELIEVE WE'RE BACK ALREADY. WE BARELY LEFT.
DID YOU SEE THAT? I COULD'VE OF SWORN THAT LOOKED LIKE... A WHALE?
SPROOOSH
SOME OF US HAVE TO GET BACK TO WORK TO MAKE AN HONEST LIVING. WHO ELSE IS GOING TO PAY FOR YOUR SHOPPING?
YOU DIDN'T HAVE TO PAY. I COULD'VE JUST--
SELINA...
...HOLD STILL!
WHAT'S WRONG?
IT'S QUIET. TOO QUIET...
SNORRRRRRRRR
WOW. TALK ABOUT NO RESPONSIBILITIES. DID THIS KID DO ANYTHING WHILE WE WERE AWAY ON VACATION? WHAT A LIFE!
A GIRL'S WORK IS NEVER DONE. JOIN US ON THE NEXT PAGE FOR MORE BATMAN: LI'L GOTHAM!

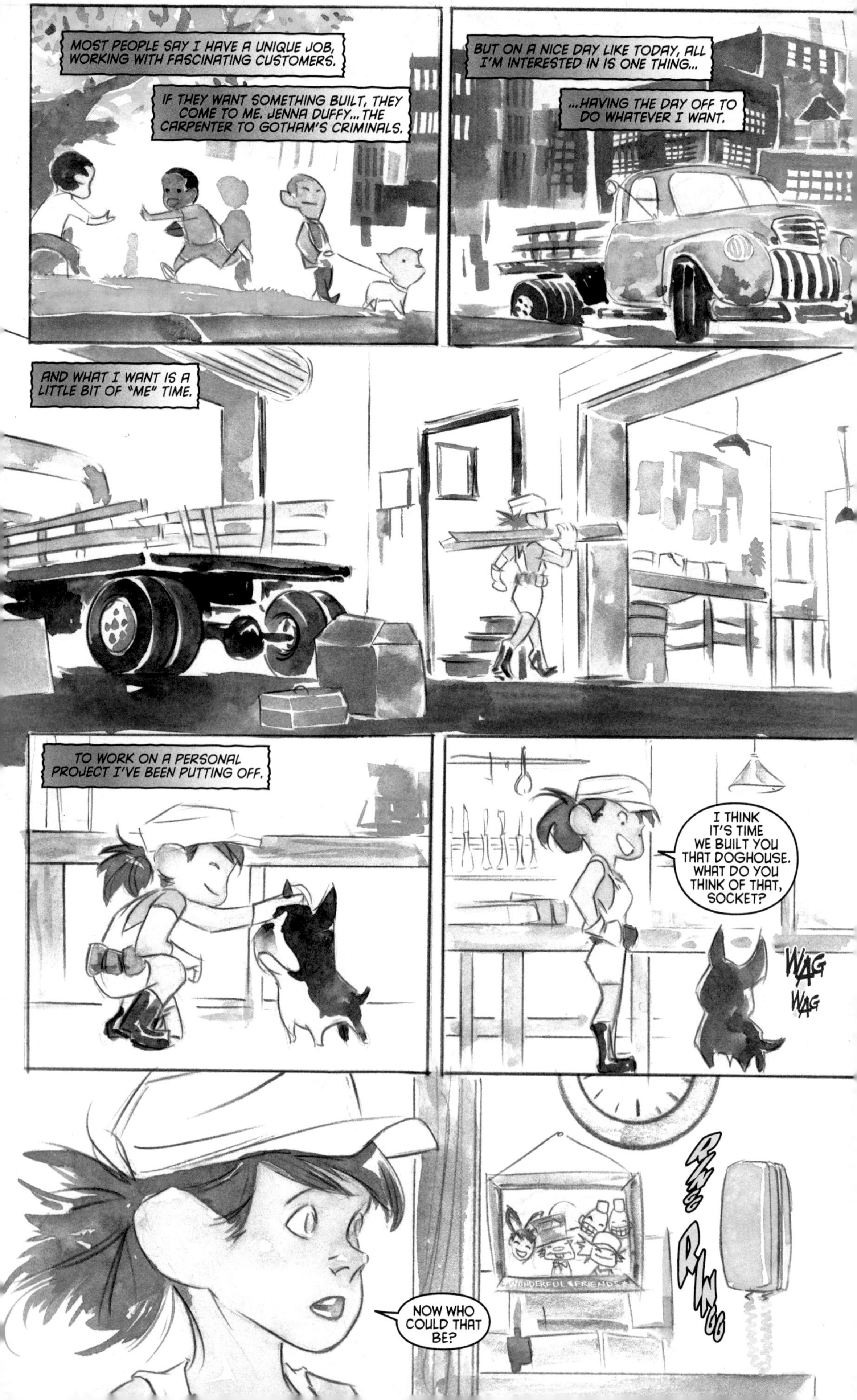

MOST PEOPLE SAY I HAVE A UNIQUE JOB, WORKING WITH FASCINATING CUSTOMERS.
IF THEY WANT SOMETHING BUILT, THEY COME TO ME. JENNA DUFFY... THE CARPENTER TO GOTHAM'S CRIMINALS.
BUT ON A NICE DAY LIKE TODAY, ALL I'M INTERESTED IN IS ONE THING...
...HAVING THE DAY OFF TO DO WHATEVER I WANT.
AND WHAT I WANT IS A LITTLE BIT OF "ME" TIME.
TO WORK ON A PERSONAL PROJECT I'VE BEEN PUTTING OFF.
I THINK IT'S TIME WE BUILT YOU THAT DOGHOUSE. WHAT DO YOU THINK OF THAT, SOCKET?
WAG WAG
NOW WHO COULD THAT BE?
WONDERFUL FRIENDS
RINGG RINGG

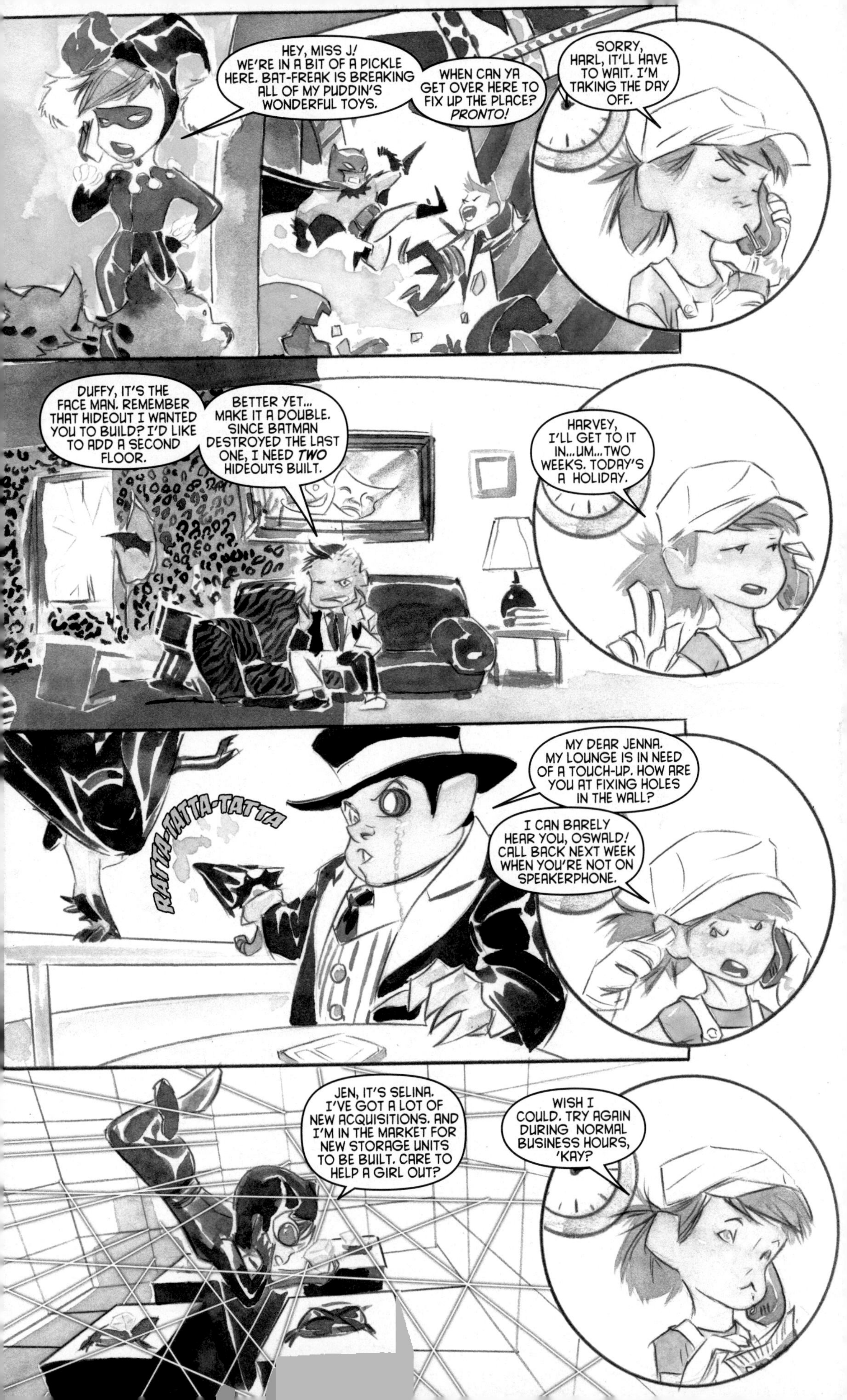
HEY, MISS J! WE'RE IN A BIT OF A PICKLE HERE. BAT-FREAK IS BREAKING ALL OF MY PUDDIN'S WONDERFUL TOYS.
WHEN CAN YA GET OVER HERE TO FIX UP THE PLACE? *PRONTO!*
SORRY, HARL, IT'LL HAVE TO WAIT. I'M TAKING THE DAY OFF.
DUFFY, IT'S THE FACE MAN. REMEMBER THAT HIDEOUT I WANTED YOU TO BUILD? I'D LIKE TO ADD A SECOND FLOOR.
BETTER YET... MAKE IT A DOUBLE. SINCE BATMAN DESTROYED THE LAST ONE, I NEED *TWO* HIDEOUTS BUILT.
HARVEY, I'LL GET TO IT IN...UM...TWO WEEKS. TODAY'S A HOLIDAY.
RATTA-TATTA-TATTA
MY DEAR JENNA. MY LOUNGE IS IN NEED OF A TOUCH-UP. HOW ARE YOU AT FIXING HOLES IN THE WALL?
I CAN BARELY HEAR YOU, OSWALD! CALL BACK NEXT WEEK WHEN YOU'RE NOT ON SPEAKERPHONE.
JEN, IT'S SELINA. I'VE GOT A LOT OF NEW ACQUISITIONS. AND I'M IN THE MARKET FOR NEW STORAGE UNITS TO BE BUILT. CARE TO HELP A GIRL OUT?
WISH I COULD. TRY AGAIN DURING NORMAL BUSINESS HOURS, 'KAY?

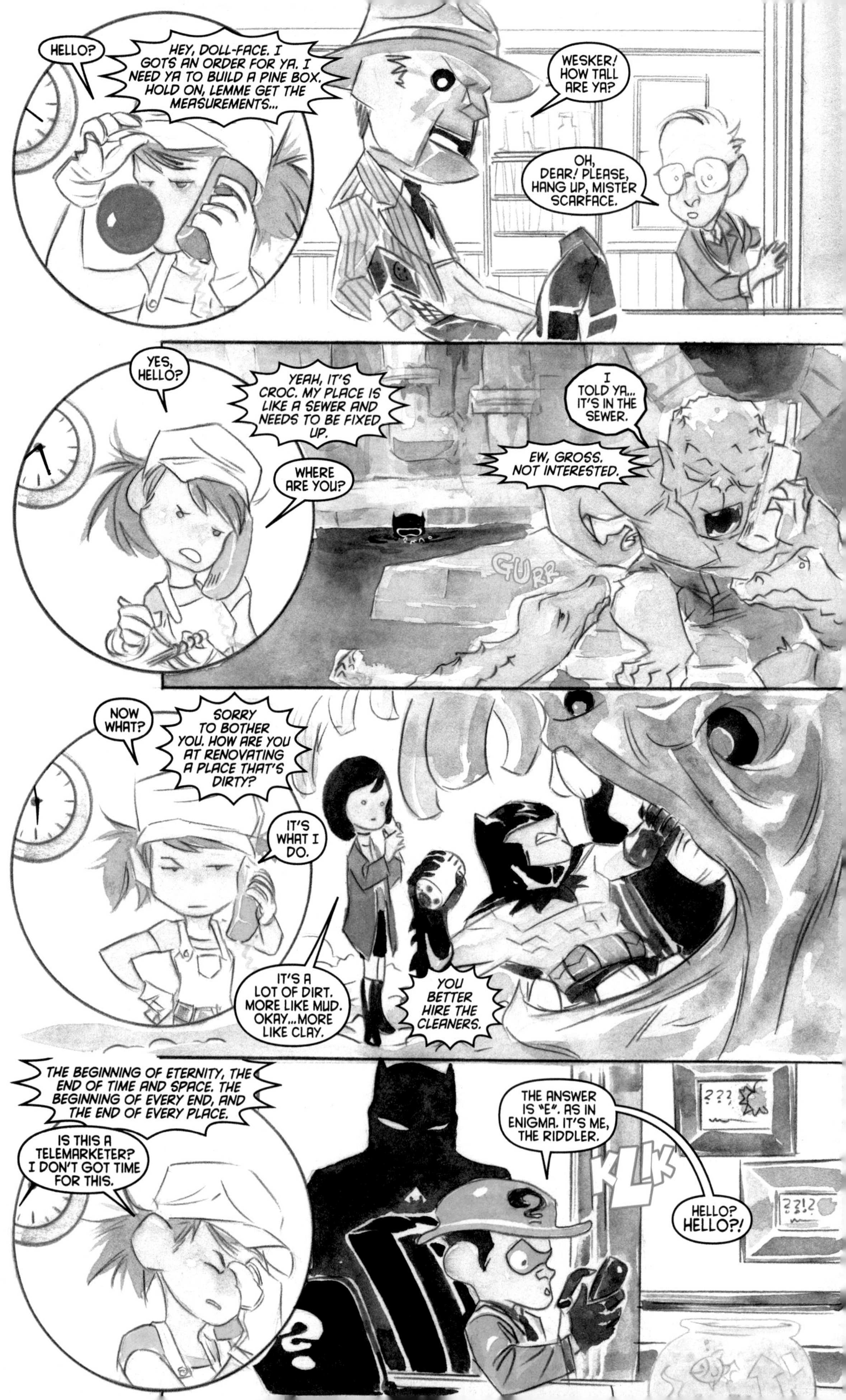
HELLO?
HEY, DOLL-FACE. I GOTS AN ORDER FOR YA. I NEED YA TO BUILD A PINE BOX. HOLD ON, LEMME GET THE MEASUREMENTS...
WESKER! HOW TALL ARE YA?
OH, DEAR! PLEASE, HANG UP, MISTER SCARFACE.
YES, HELLO?
YEAH, IT'S CROC. MY PLACE IS LIKE A SEWER AND NEEDS TO BE FIXED UP.
WHERE ARE YOU?
I TOLD YA... IT'S IN THE SEWER.
EW, GROSS. NOT INTERESTED.
GURR
NOW WHAT?
SORRY TO BOTHER YOU. HOW ARE YOU AT RENOVATING A PLACE THAT'S DIRTY?
IT'S WHAT I DO.
IT'S A LOT OF DIRT. MORE LIKE MUD. OKAY...MORE LIKE CLAY.
YOU BETTER HIRE THE CLEANERS.
THE BEGINNING OF ETERNITY, THE END OF TIME AND SPACE. THE BEGINNING OF EVERY END, AND THE END OF EVERY PLACE.
IS THIS A TELEMARKETER? I DON'T GOT TIME FOR THIS.
THE ANSWER IS "E". AS IN ENIGMA. IT'S ME, THE RIDDLER.
KLIK
HELLO? HELLO?!

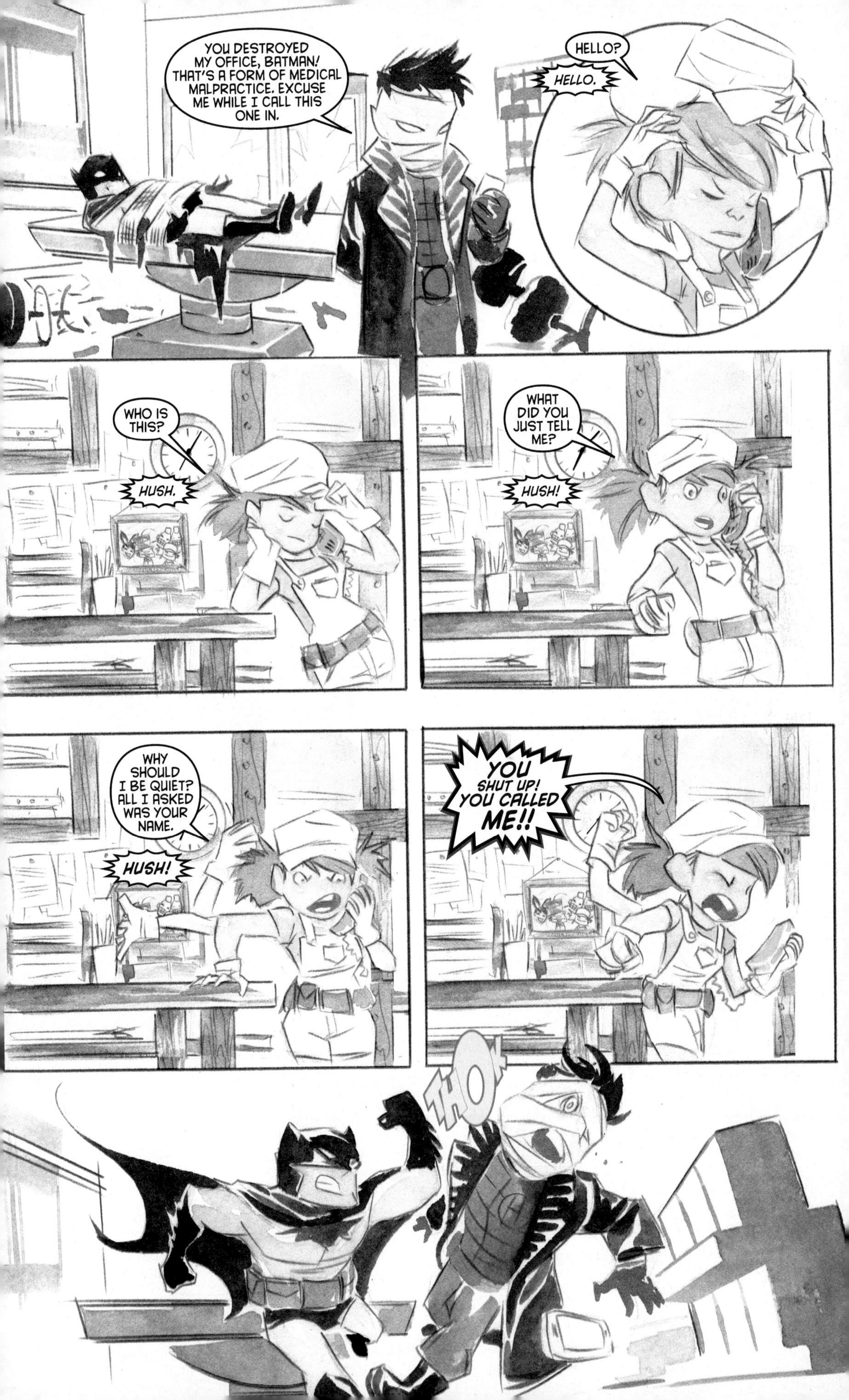

YOU DESTROYED MY OFFICE, BATMAN! THAT'S A FORM OF MEDICAL MALPRACTICE. EXCUSE ME WHILE I CALL THIS ONE IN.
HELLO?
HELLO.
WHO IS THIS?
HUSH.
WHAT DID YOU JUST TELL ME?
HUSH!
WHY SHOULD I BE QUIET? ALL I ASKED WAS YOUR NAME.
HUSH!
YOU SHUT UP! YOU CALLED ME!!
THOK

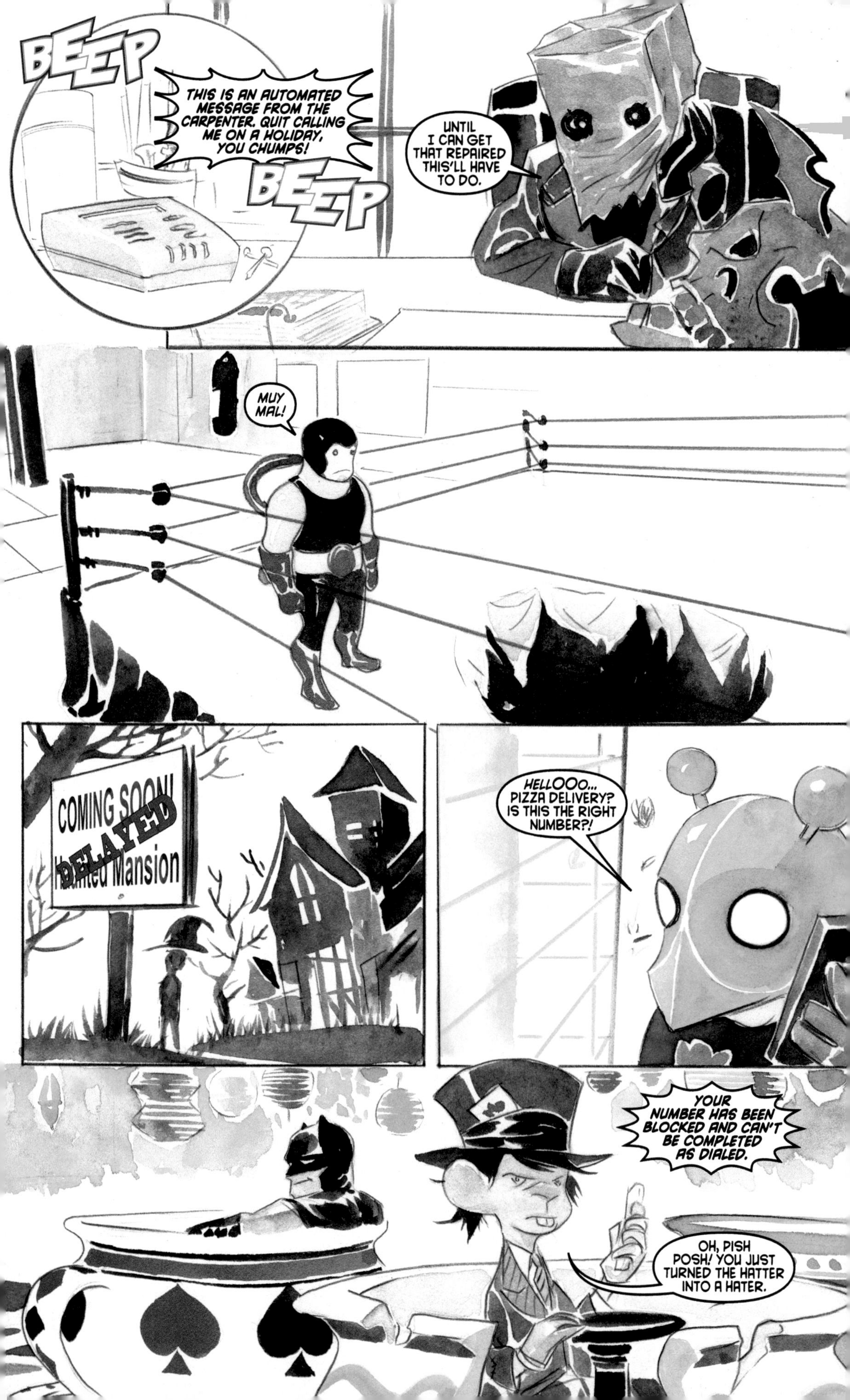
BEEP
THIS IS AN AUTOMATED MESSAGE FROM THE CARPENTER. QUIT CALLING ME ON A HOLIDAY, YOU CHUMPS!
BEEP
UNTIL I CAN GET THAT REPAIRED THIS'LL HAVE TO DO.
MUY MAL!
COMING SOON!
DELAYED
Haunted Mansion
HELLOOO... PIZZA DELIVERY? IS THIS THE RIGHT NUMBER?!
YOUR NUMBER HAS BEEN BLOCKED AND CAN'T BE COMPLETED AS DIALED.
OH, PISH POSH! YOU JUST TURNED THE HATTER INTO A HATER.

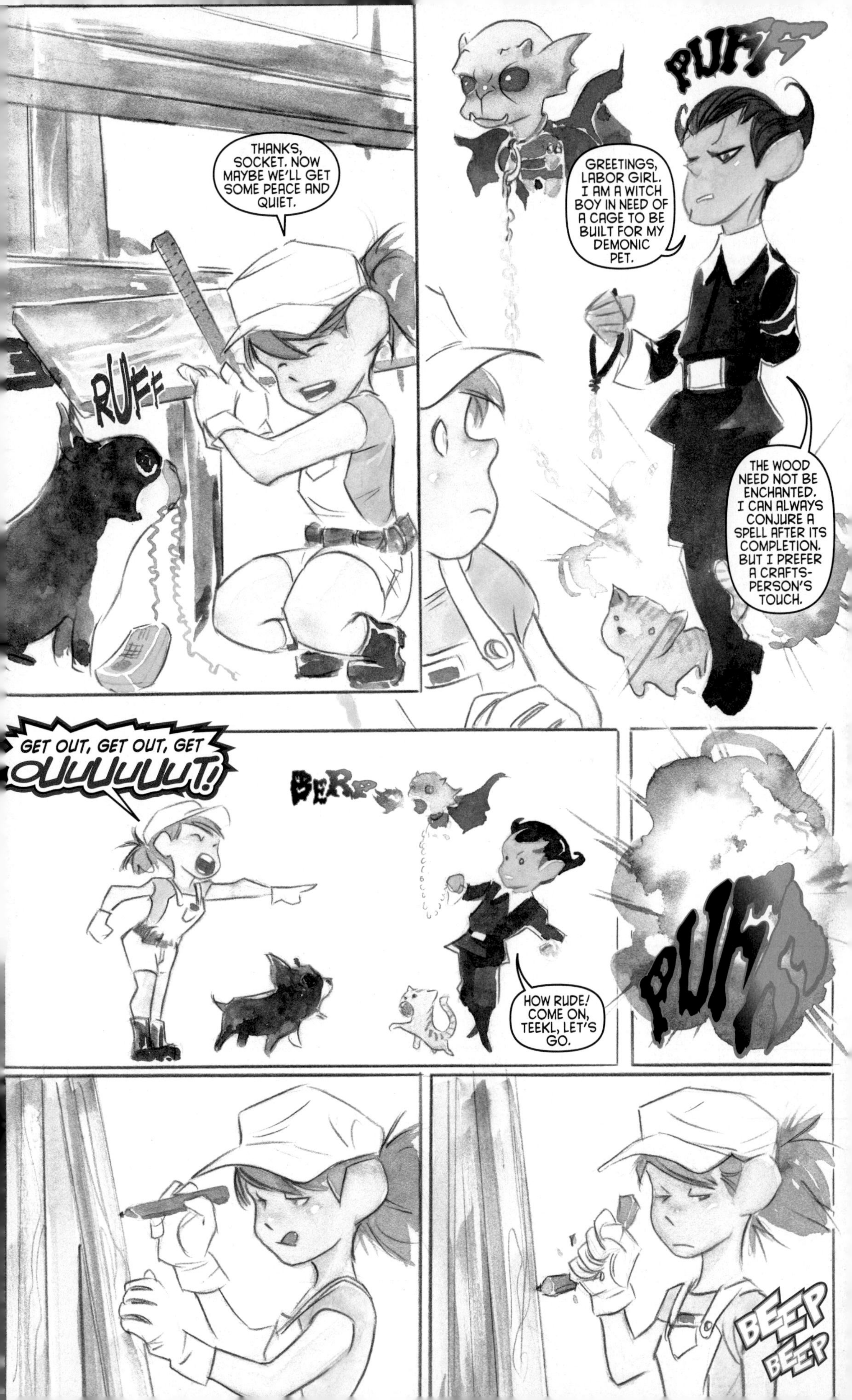
THANKS, SOCKET. NOW MAYBE WE'LL GET SOME PEACE AND QUIET.
RUFF
PUFF
GREETINGS, LABOR GIRL. I AM A WITCH BOY IN NEED OF A CAGE TO BE BUILT FOR MY DEMONIC PET.
THE WOOD NEED NOT BE ENCHANTED. I CAN ALWAYS CONJURE A SPELL AFTER ITS COMPLETION. BUT I PREFER A CRAFTS-PERSON'S TOUCH.
GET OUT, GET OUT, GET OUUUUUUT!
BERP
HOW RUDE! COME ON, TEEKL, LET'S GO.
PUFF
BEEP BEEP

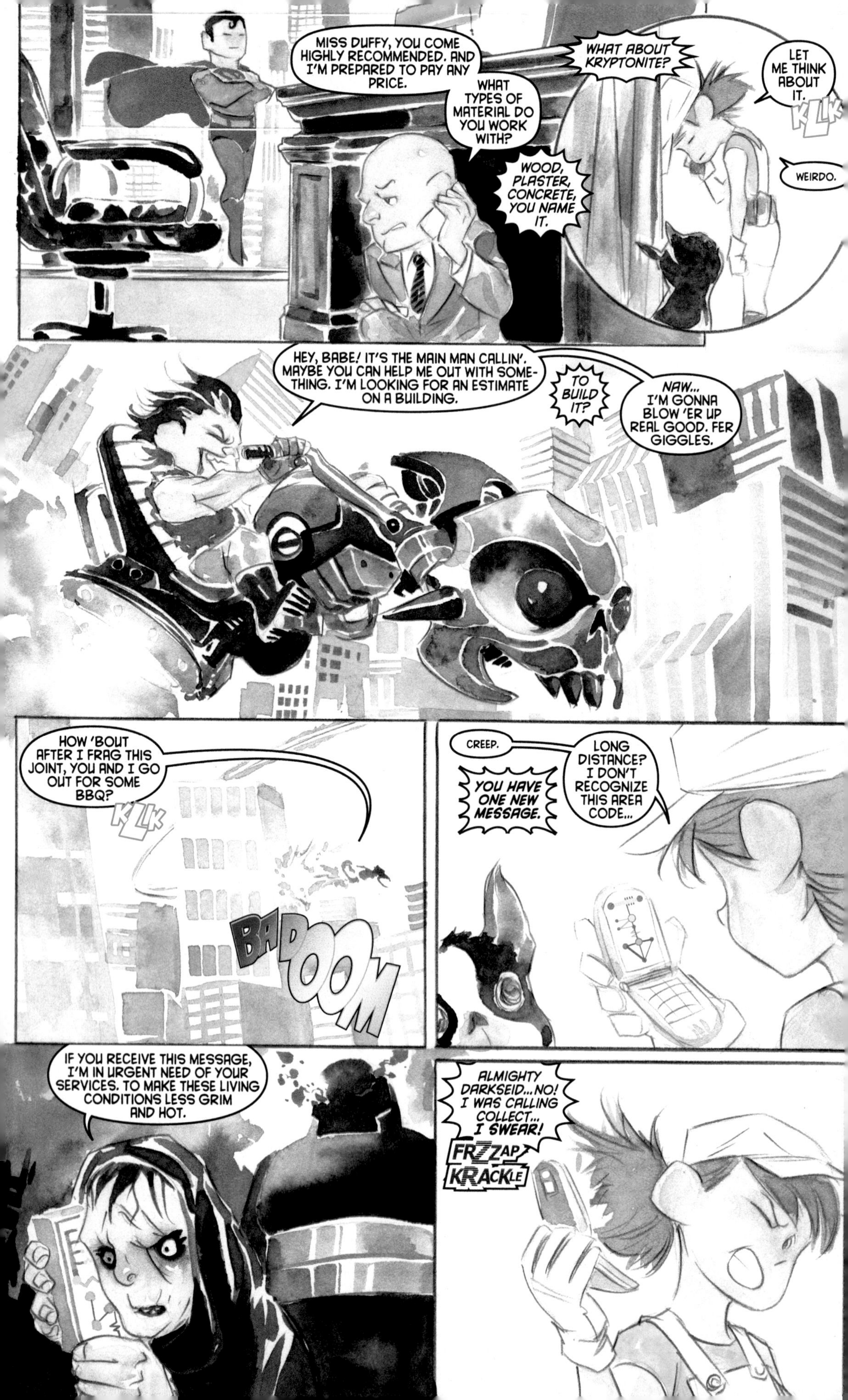
MISS DUFFY, YOU COME HIGHLY RECOMMENDED. AND I'M PREPARED TO PAY ANY PRICE.
WHAT TYPES OF MATERIAL DO YOU WORK WITH?
WOOD, PLASTER, CONCRETE, YOU NAME IT.
WHAT ABOUT KRYPTONITE?
LET ME THINK ABOUT IT.
KLIK
WEIRDO.
HEY, BABE! IT'S THE MAIN MAN CALLIN'. MAYBE YOU CAN HELP ME OUT WITH SOME-THING. I'M LOOKING FOR AN ESTIMATE ON A BUILDING.
TO BUILD IT?
NAW... I'M GONNA BLOW 'ER UP REAL GOOD. FER GIGGLES.
HOW 'BOUT AFTER I FRAG THIS JOINT, YOU AND I GO OUT FOR SOME BBQ?
KLIK
BADOOM
CREEP.
LONG DISTANCE? I DON'T RECOGNIZE THIS AREA CODE...
YOU HAVE ONE NEW MESSAGE.
IF YOU RECEIVE THIS MESSAGE, I'M IN URGENT NEED OF YOUR SERVICES. TO MAKE THESE LIVING CONDITIONS LESS GRIM AND HOT.
ALMIGHTY DARKSEID...NO! I WAS CALLING COLLECT... I SWEAR!
FRZZAP
KRACKLE

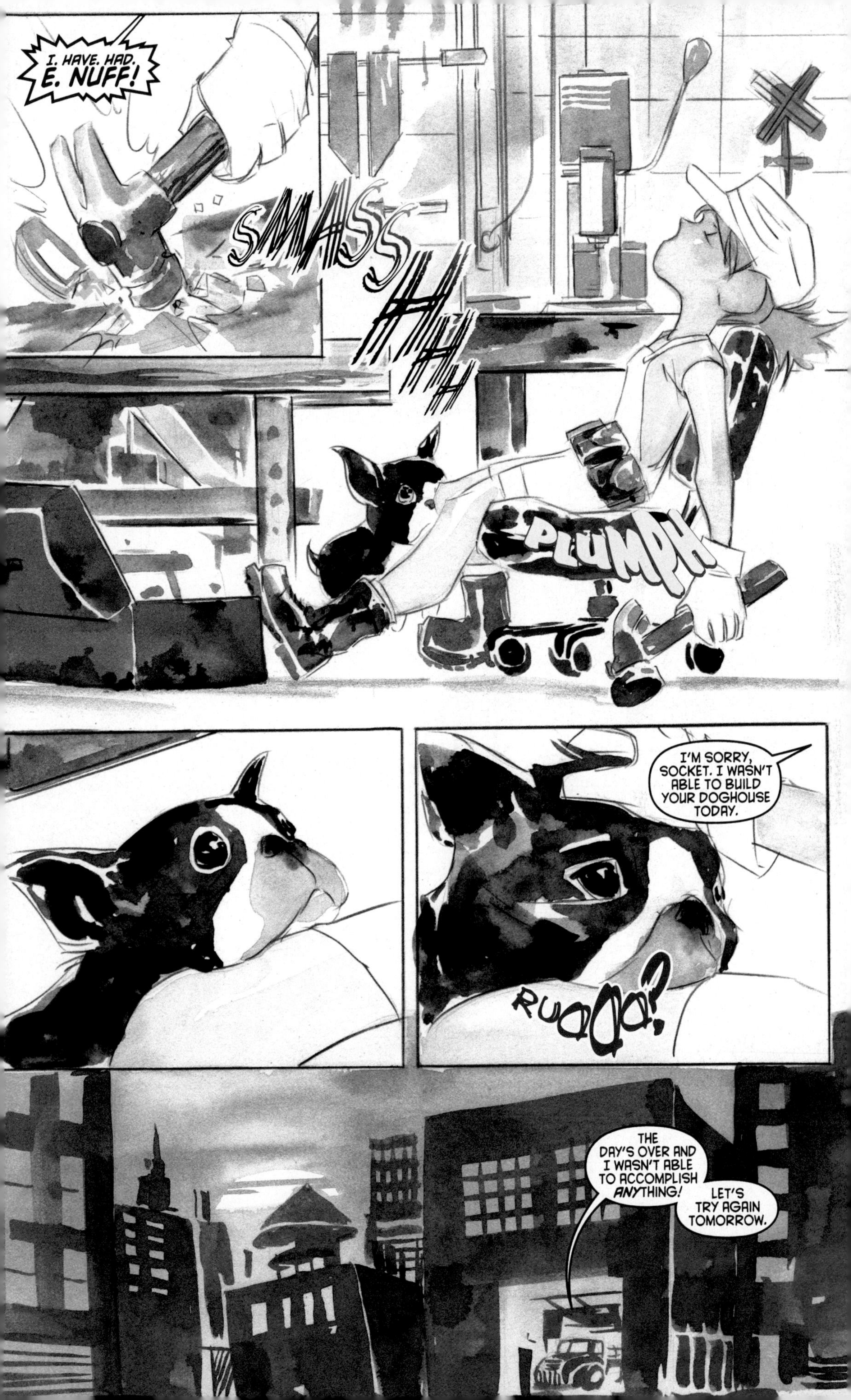
I. HAVE. HAD. E. NUFF!
SMASSHHH
PLUMPH
I'M SORRY, SOCKET. I WASN'T ABLE TO BUILD YOUR DOGHOUSE TODAY.
RUOOO?
THE DAY'S OVER AND I WASN'T ABLE TO ACCOMPLISH *ANY*THING!
LET'S TRY AGAIN TOMORROW.

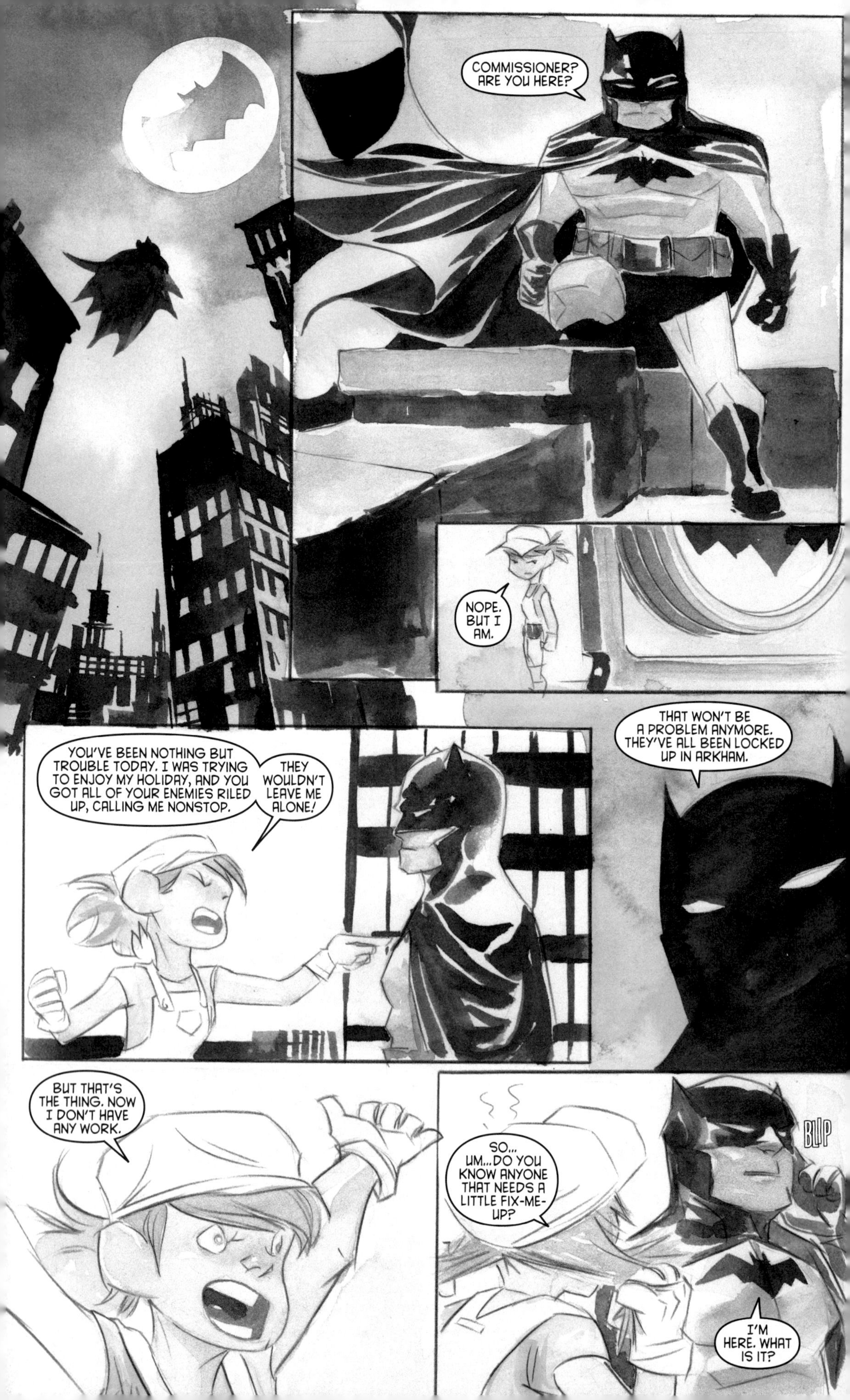
COMMISSIONER? ARE YOU HERE?
NOPE. BUT I AM.
YOU'VE BEEN NOTHING BUT TROUBLE TODAY. I WAS TRYING TO ENJOY MY HOLIDAY, AND YOU GOT ALL OF YOUR ENEMIES RILED UP, CALLING ME NONSTOP.
THEY WOULDN'T LEAVE ME ALONE!
THAT WON'T BE A PROBLEM ANYMORE. THEY'VE ALL BEEN LOCKED UP IN ARKHAM.
BUT THAT'S THE THING. NOW I DON'T HAVE ANY WORK.
SO... UM...DO YOU KNOW ANYONE THAT NEEDS A LITTLE FIX-ME-UP?
BLIP
I'M HERE. WHAT IS IT?

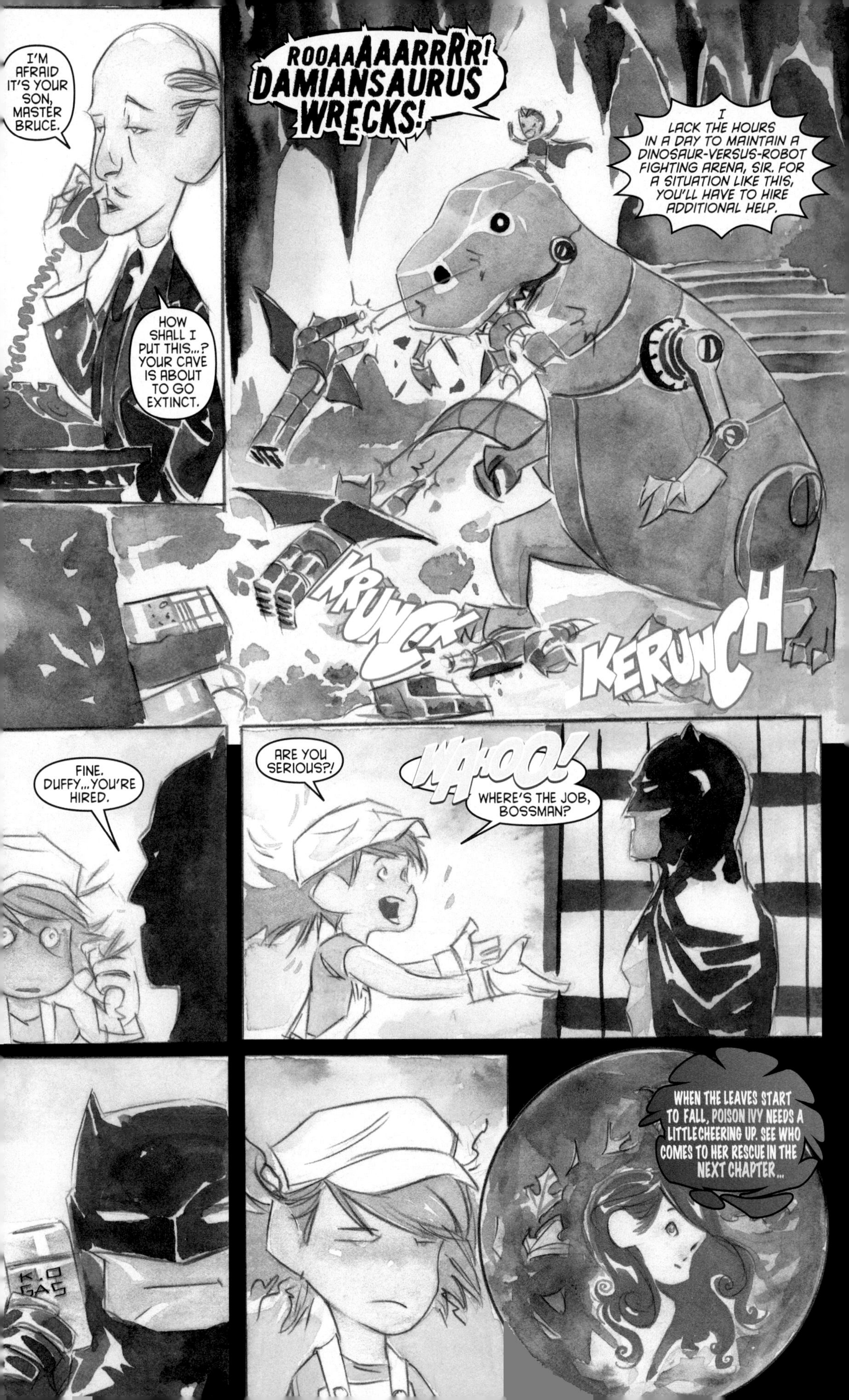

I'M AFRAID IT'S YOUR SON, MASTER BRUCE.
HOW SHALL I PUT THIS...? YOUR CAVE IS ABOUT TO GO EXTINCT.
ROOAAAAAARRRRR! DAMIANSAURUS WRECKS!
I LACK THE HOURS IN A DAY TO MAINTAIN A DINOSAUR-VERSUS-ROBOT FIGHTING ARENA, SIR. FOR A SITUATION LIKE THIS, YOU'LL HAVE TO HIRE ADDITIONAL HELP.
KRUNCH
KERUNCH
FINE. DUFFY... YOU'RE HIRED.
ARE YOU SERIOUS?!
WAHOO!
WHERE'S THE JOB, BOSSMAN?
K.O GAS
WHEN THE LEAVES START TO FALL, POISON IVY NEEDS A LITTLE CHEERING UP. SEE WHO COMES TO HER RESCUE IN THE NEXT CHAPTER...

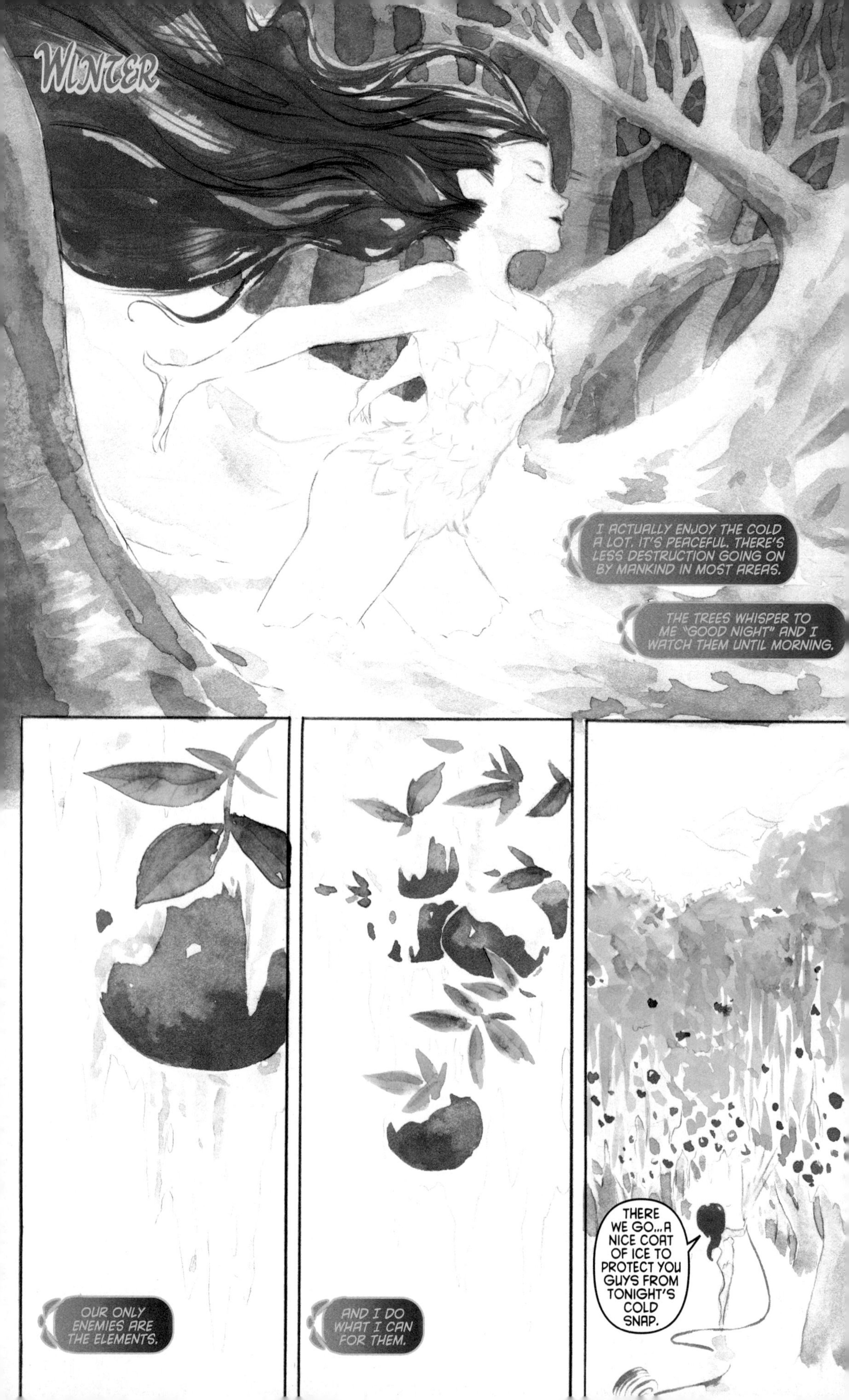
WINTER
I ACTUALLY ENJOY THE COLD A LOT. IT'S PEACEFUL. THERE'S LESS DESTRUCTION GOING ON BY MANKIND IN MOST AREAS.
THE TREES WHISPER TO ME "GOOD NIGHT" AND I WATCH THEM UNTIL MORNING.
OUR ONLY ENEMIES ARE THE ELEMENTS.
AND I DO WHAT I CAN FOR THEM.
THERE WE GO...A NICE COAT OF ICE TO PROTECT YOU GUYS FROM TONIGHT'S COLD SNAP.

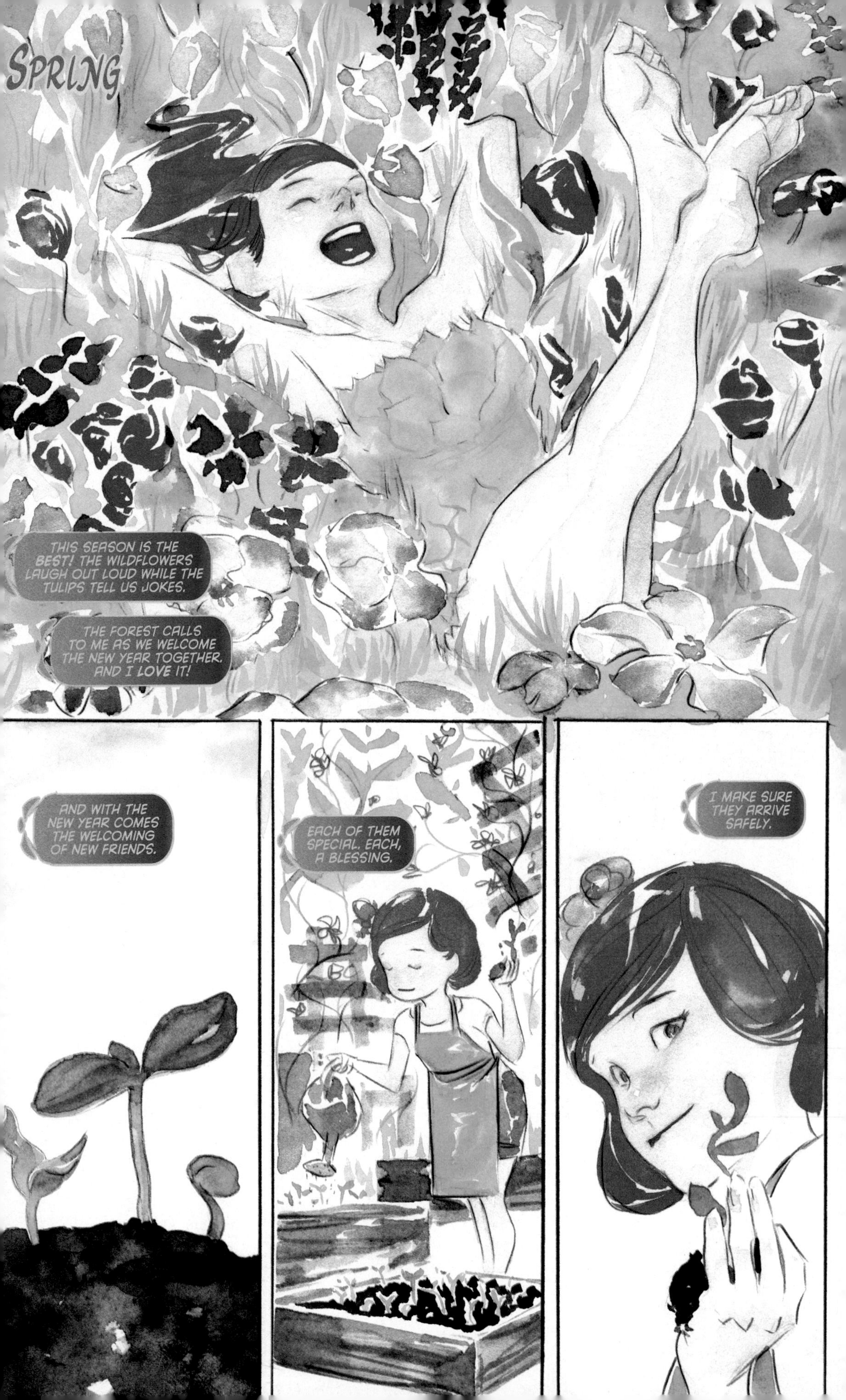

SPRING
THIS SEASON IS THE BEST! THE WILDFLOWERS LAUGH OUT LOUD WHILE THE TULIPS TELL US JOKES.
THE FOREST CALLS TO ME AS WE WELCOME THE NEW YEAR TOGETHER. AND I LOVE IT!
AND WITH THE NEW YEAR COMES THE WELCOMING OF NEW FRIENDS.
EACH OF THEM SPECIAL. EACH, A BLESSING.
I MAKE SURE THEY ARRIVE SAFELY.

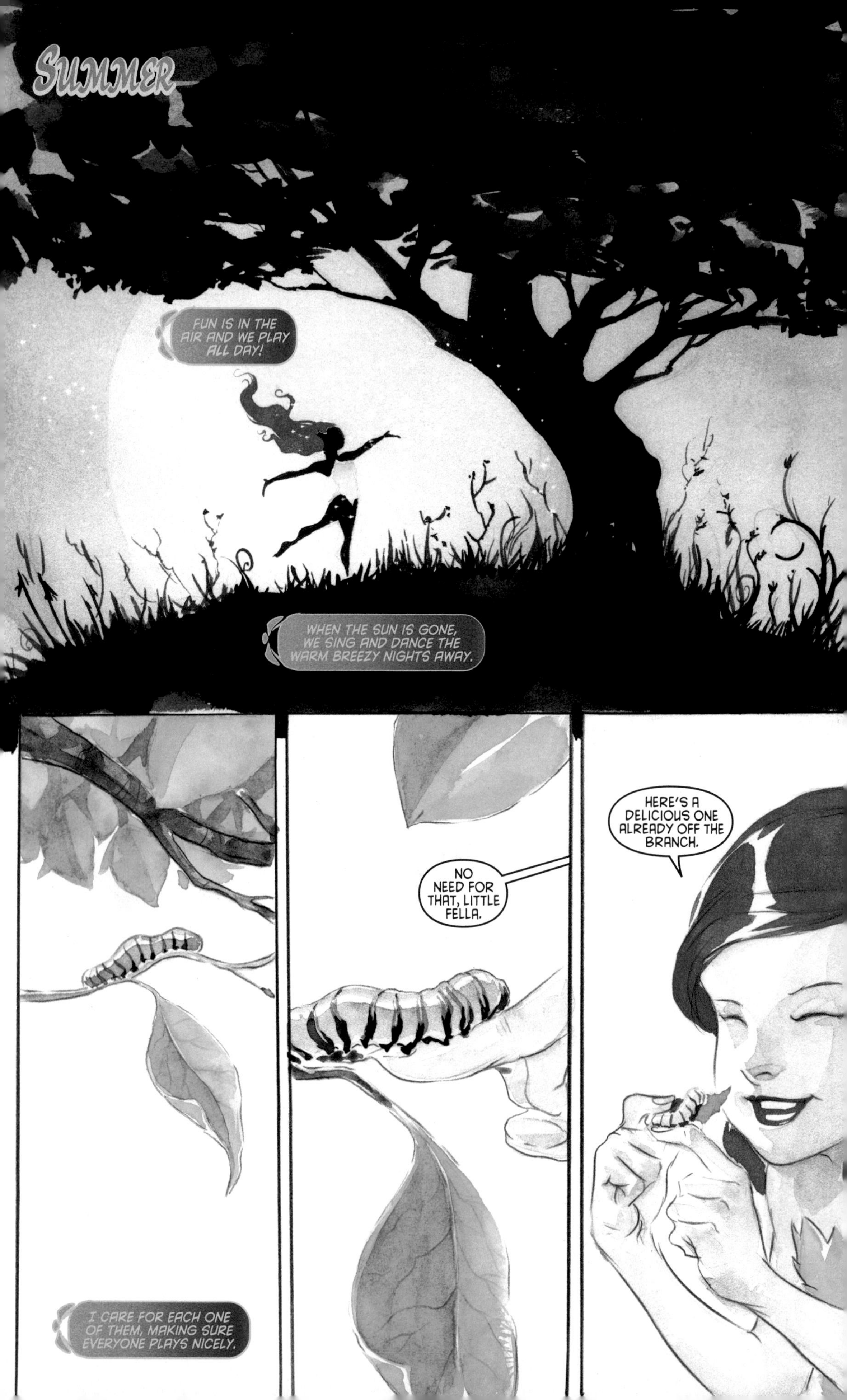
SUMMER
FUN IS IN THE AIR AND WE PLAY ALL DAY!
WHEN THE SUN IS GONE, WE SING AND DANCE THE WARM BREEZY NIGHTS AWAY.
I CARE FOR EACH ONE OF THEM, MAKING SURE EVERYONE PLAYS NICELY.
NO NEED FOR THAT, LITTLE FELLA.
HERE'S A DELICIOUS ONE ALREADY OFF THE BRANCH.

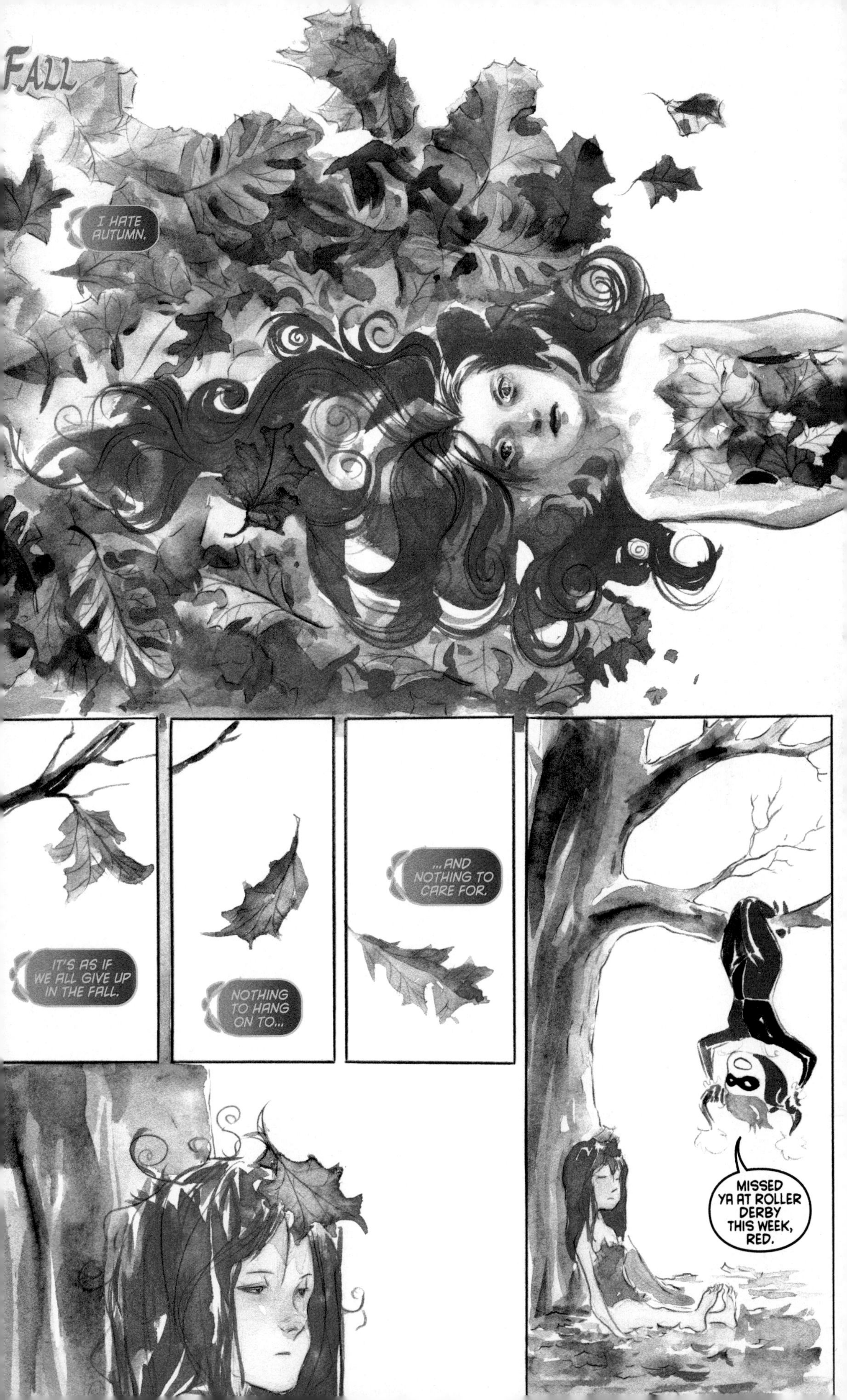
FALL
I HATE AUTUMN.
IT'S AS IF WE ALL GIVE UP IN THE FALL.
NOTHING TO HANG ON TO...
...AND NOTHING TO CARE FOR.
MISSED YA AT ROLLER DERBY THIS WEEK, RED.

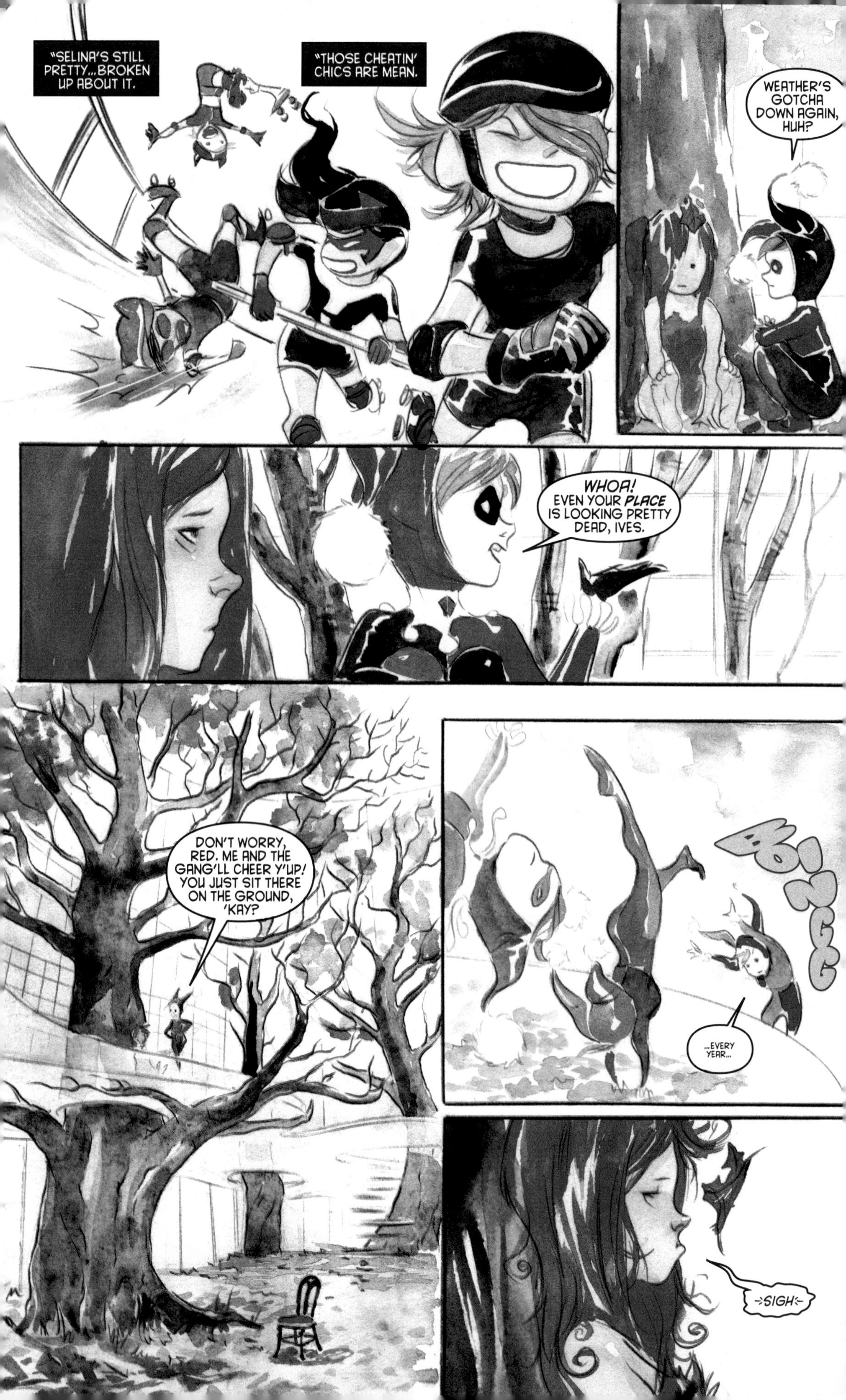
"SELINA'S STILL PRETTY...BROKEN UP ABOUT IT.
"THOSE CHEATIN' CHICS ARE MEAN.
WEATHER'S GOTCHA DOWN AGAIN, HUH?
WHOA! EVEN YOUR PLACE IS LOOKING PRETTY DEAD, IVES.
DON'T WORRY, RED. ME AND THE GANG'LL CHEER Y'UP! YOU JUST SIT THERE ON THE GROUND, 'KAY?
BOINGG
...EVERY YEAR...
SIGH

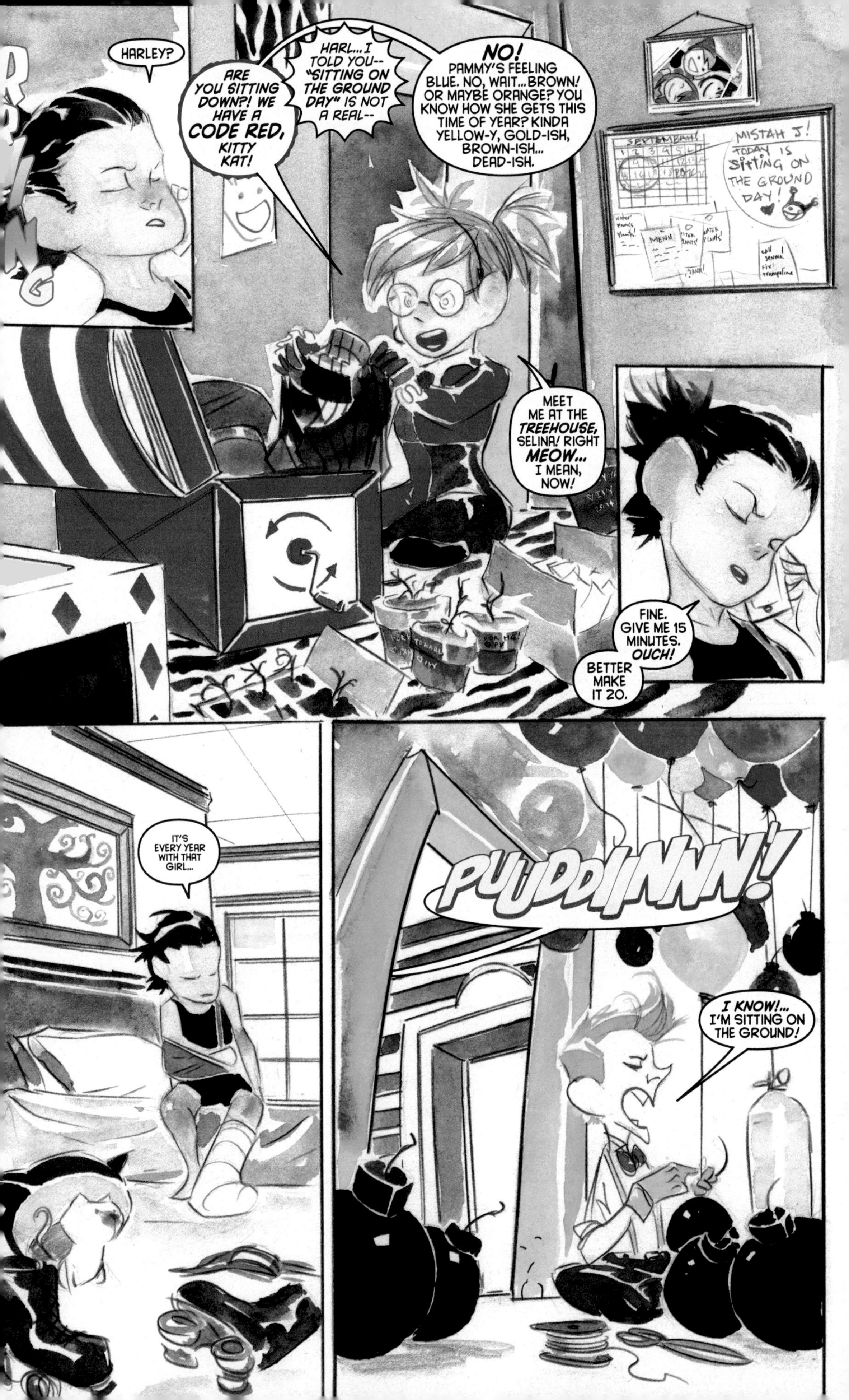
HARLEY?
ARE YOU SITTING DOWN?! WE HAVE A CODE RED, KITTY KAT!
HARL... I TOLD YOU-- "SITTING ON THE GROUND DAY" IS NOT A REAL--
NO! PAMMY'S FEELING BLUE. NO, WAIT... BROWN! OR MAYBE ORANGE? YOU KNOW HOW SHE GETS THIS TIME OF YEAR? KINDA YELLOW-Y, GOLD-ISH, BROWN-ISH... DEAD-ISH.
MISTAH J! TODAY IS Sitting ON THE GROUND DAY!
MEET ME AT THE TREEHOUSE, SELINA! RIGHT MEOW... I MEAN, NOW!
FINE. GIVE ME 15 MINUTES. OUCH!
BETTER MAKE IT 20.
IT'S EVERY YEAR WITH THAT GIRL...
PUUDDIINNN!
I KNOW!... I'M SITTING ON THE GROUND!

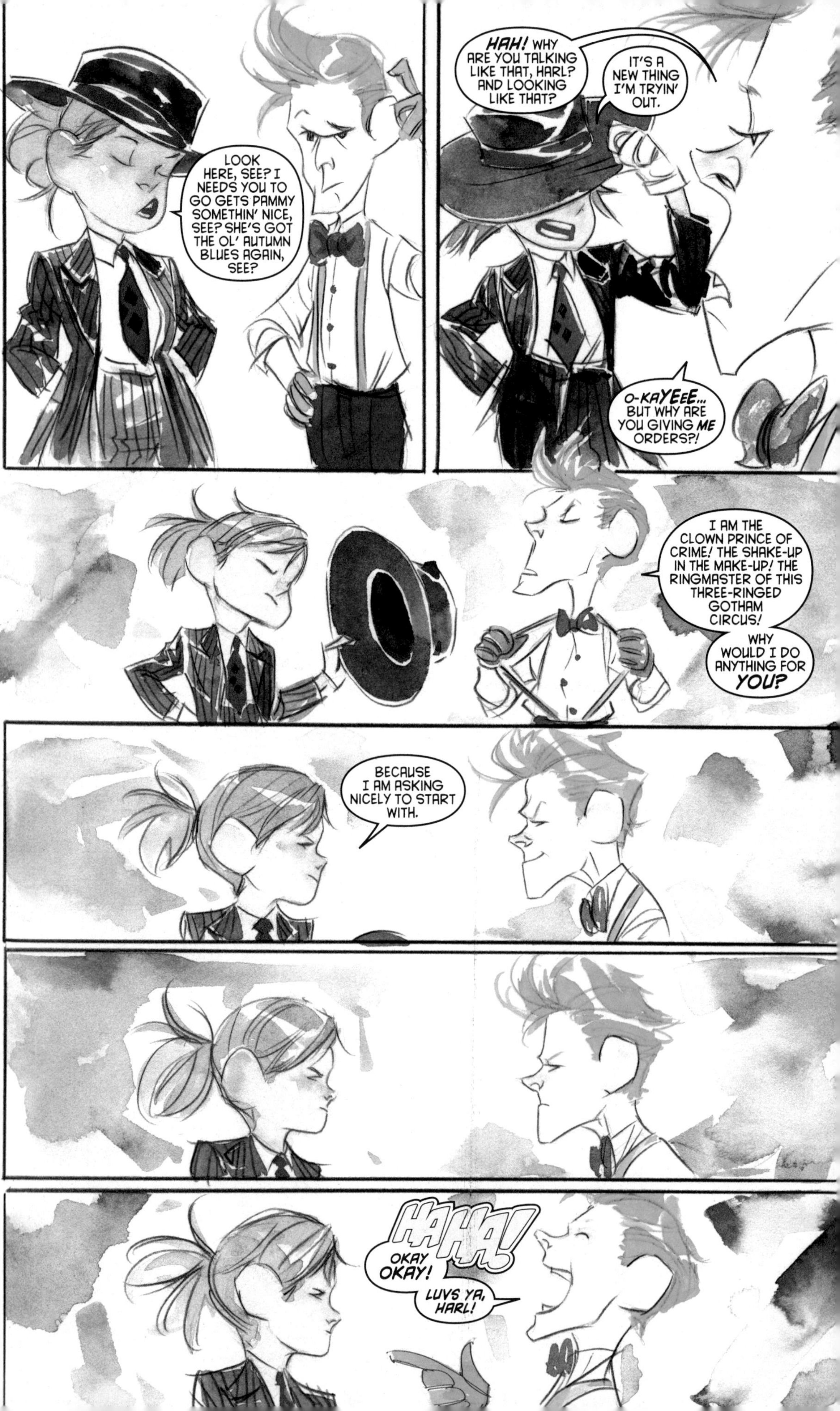
LOOK HERE, SEE? I NEEDS YOU TO GO GETS PAMMY SOMETHIN' NICE, SEE? SHE'S GOT THE OL' AUTUMN BLUES AGAIN, SEE?
HAH! WHY ARE YOU TALKING LIKE THAT, HARL? AND LOOKING LIKE THAT?
IT'S A NEW THING I'M TRYIN' OUT.
O-KAYEEE... BUT WHY ARE YOU GIVING ME ORDERS?!
I AM THE CLOWN PRINCE OF CRIME! THE SHAKE-UP IN THE MAKE-UP! THE RINGMASTER OF THIS THREE-RINGED GOTHAM CIRCUS!
WHY WOULD I DO ANYTHING FOR YOU?
BECAUSE I AM ASKING NICELY TO START WITH.
HAHA!
OKAY OKAY!
LUVS YA, HARL!

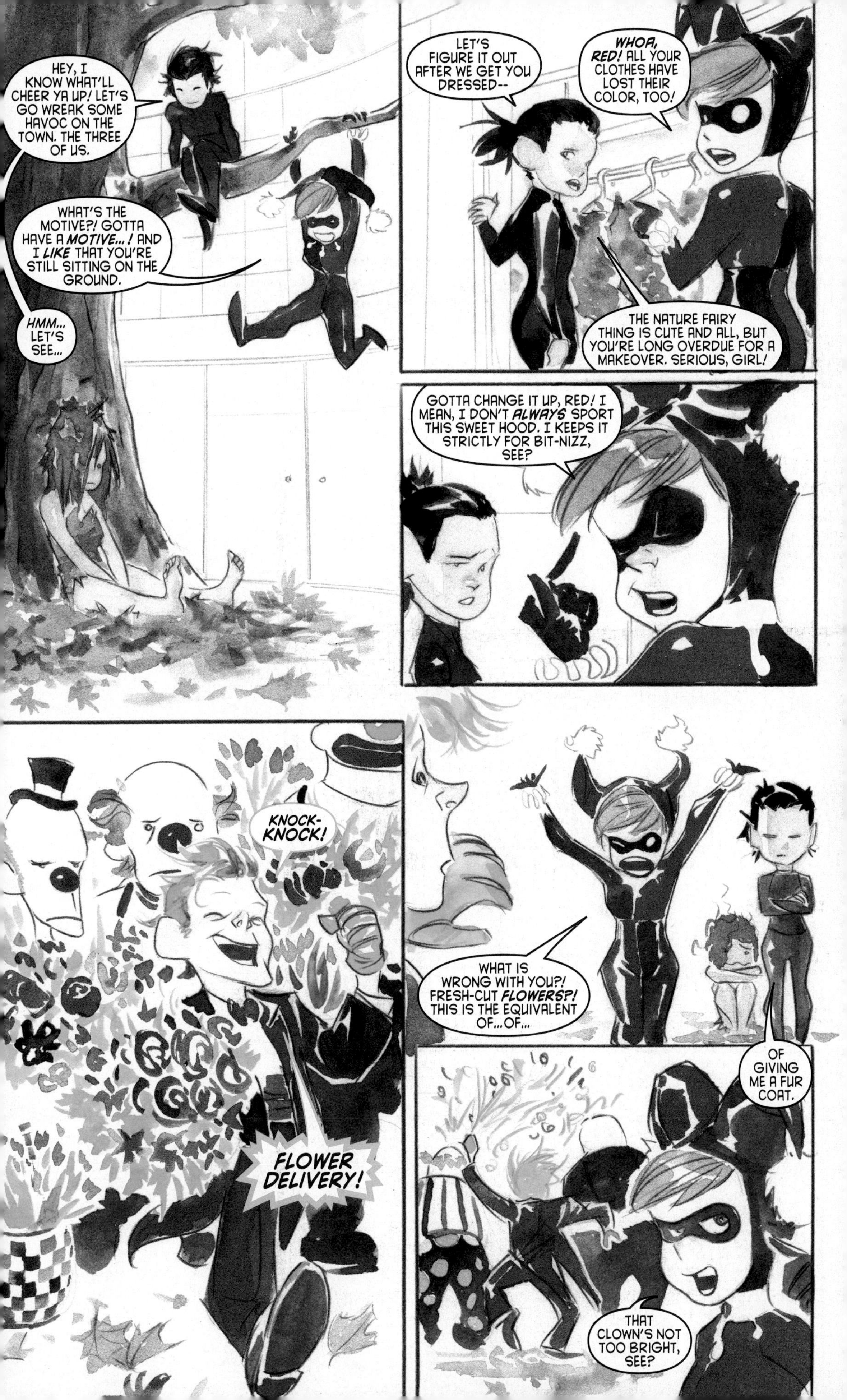
HEY, I KNOW WHAT'LL CHEER YA UP! LET'S GO WREAK SOME HAVOC ON THE TOWN. THE THREE OF US.
WHAT'S THE MOTIVE?! GOTTA HAVE A MOTIVE...! AND I LIKE THAT YOU'RE STILL SITTING ON THE GROUND.
HMM... LET'S SEE...
LET'S FIGURE IT OUT AFTER WE GET YOU DRESSED--
WHOA, RED! ALL YOUR CLOTHES HAVE LOST THEIR COLOR, TOO!
THE NATURE FAIRY THING IS CUTE AND ALL, BUT YOU'RE LONG OVERDUE FOR A MAKEOVER. SERIOUS, GIRL!
GOTTA CHANGE IT UP, RED! I MEAN, I DON'T ALWAYS SPORT THIS SWEET HOOD. I KEEPS IT STRICTLY FOR BIT-NIZZ, SEE?
KNOCK-KNOCK!
FLOWER DELIVERY!
WHAT IS WRONG WITH YOU?! FRESH-CUT FLOWERS?! THIS IS THE EQUIVALENT OF...OF...
OF GIVING ME A FUR COAT.
THAT CLOWN'S NOT TOO BRIGHT, SEE?

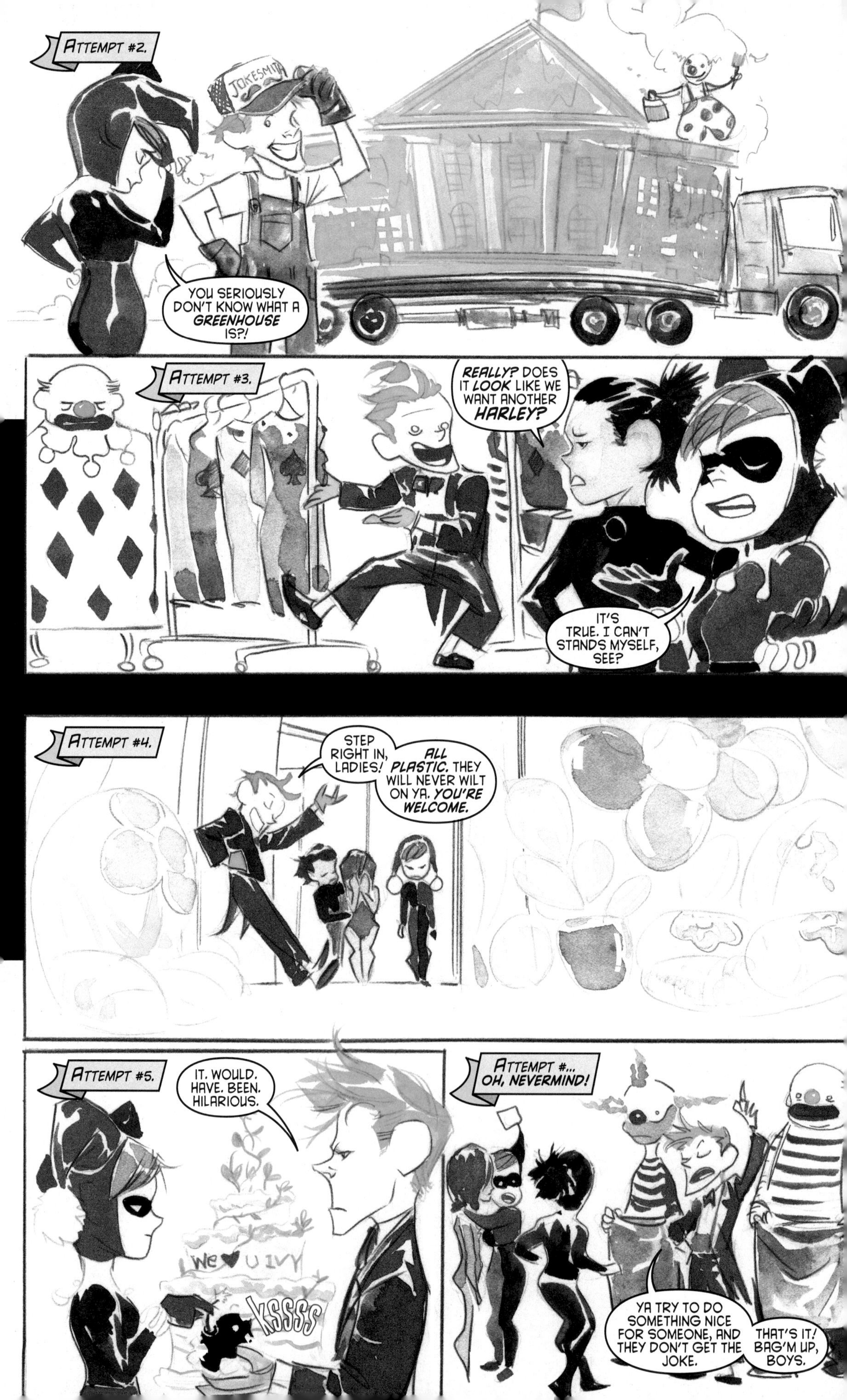
ATTEMPT #2.
JOKESMITH
YOU SERIOUSLY DON'T KNOW WHAT A GREENHOUSE IS?!
ATTEMPT #3.
REALLY? DOES IT LOOK LIKE WE WANT ANOTHER HARLEY?
IT'S TRUE. I CAN'T STANDS MYSELF, SEE?
ATTEMPT #4.
STEP RIGHT IN, LADIES!
ALL PLASTIC. THEY WILL NEVER WILT ON YA. YOU'RE WELCOME.
ATTEMPT #5.
IT. WOULD. HAVE. BEEN. HILARIOUS.
WE ♥ U IVY
KSSSS
ATTEMPT #... OH, NEVERMIND!
YA TRY TO DO SOMETHING NICE FOR SOMEONE, AND THEY DON'T GET THE JOKE.
THAT'S IT! BAG'M UP, BOYS.

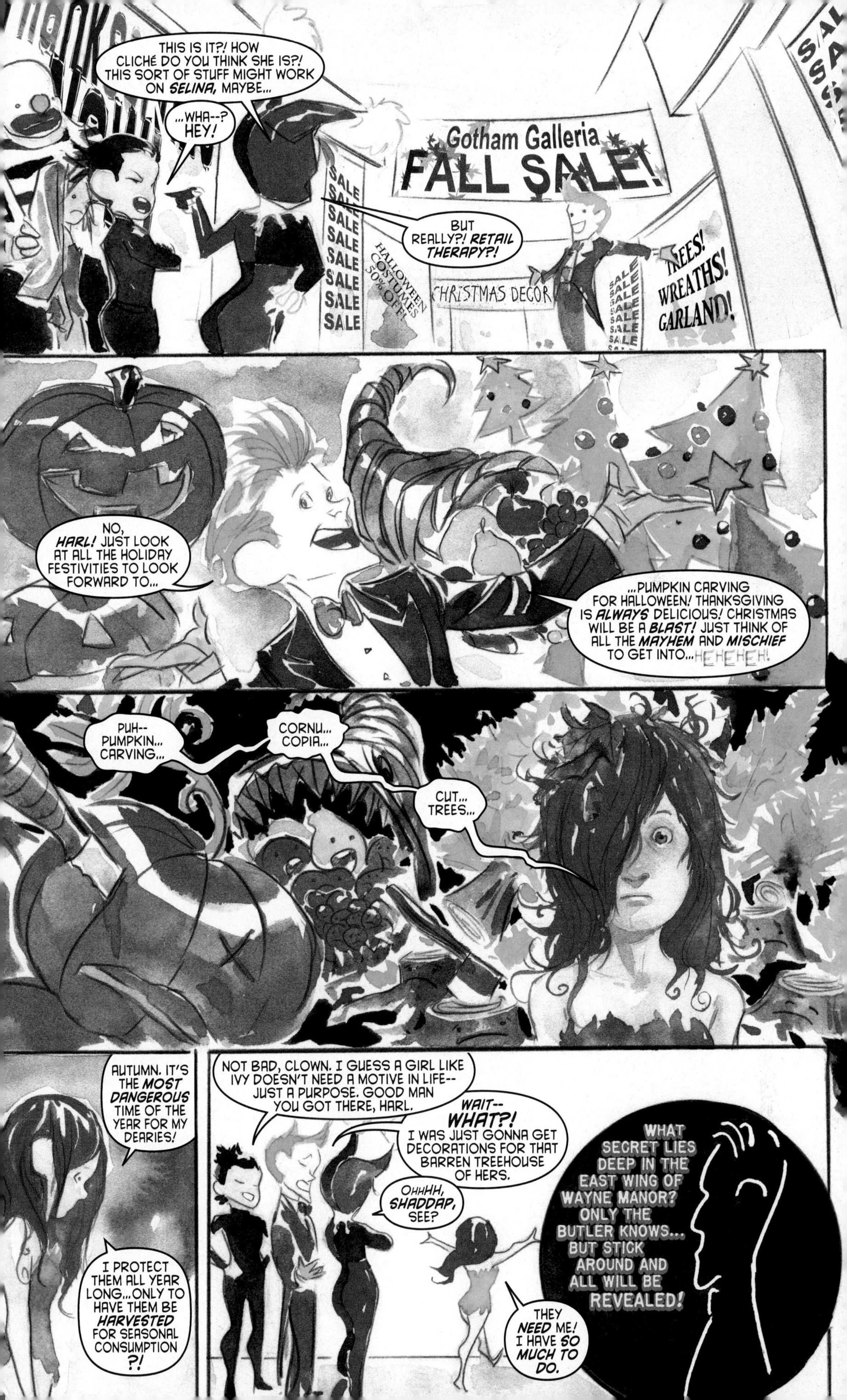
THIS IS IT?! HOW CLICHÉ DO YOU THINK SHE IS?! THIS SORT OF STUFF MIGHT WORK ON SELINA, MAYBE...
...WHA--? HEY!
BUT REALLY?! RETAIL THERAPY?!
Gotham Galleria FALL SALE!
SALE SALE SALE SALE SALE SALE SALE SALE SALE
HALLOWEEN COSTUMES 50% OFF!
CHRISTMAS DECOR
TREES! WREATHS! GARLAND!
NO, HARL! JUST LOOK AT ALL THE HOLIDAY FESTIVITIES TO LOOK FORWARD TO...
...PUMPKIN CARVING FOR HALLOWEEN! THANKSGIVING IS ALWAYS DELICIOUS! CHRISTMAS WILL BE A BLAST! JUST THINK OF ALL THE MAYHEM AND MISCHIEF TO GET INTO...HEHEHEH!
PUH-- PUMPKIN... CARVING...
CORNU... COPIA...
CUT... TREES...
AUTUMN. IT'S THE MOST DANGEROUS TIME OF THE YEAR FOR MY DEARIES!
I PROTECT THEM ALL YEAR LONG...ONLY TO HAVE THEM BE HARVESTED FOR SEASONAL CONSUMPTION?!
NOT BAD, CLOWN. I GUESS A GIRL LIKE IVY DOESN'T NEED A MOTIVE IN LIFE-- JUST A PURPOSE. GOOD MAN YOU GOT THERE, HARL.
WAIT-- WHAT?! I WAS JUST GONNA GET DECORATIONS FOR THAT BARREN TREEHOUSE OF HERS.
OHHHH, SHADDAP, SEE?
THEY NEED ME! I HAVE SO MUCH TO DO.
WHAT SECRET LIES DEEP IN THE EAST WING OF WAYNE MANOR? ONLY THE BUTLER KNOWS... BUT STICK AROUND AND ALL WILL BE REVEALED!

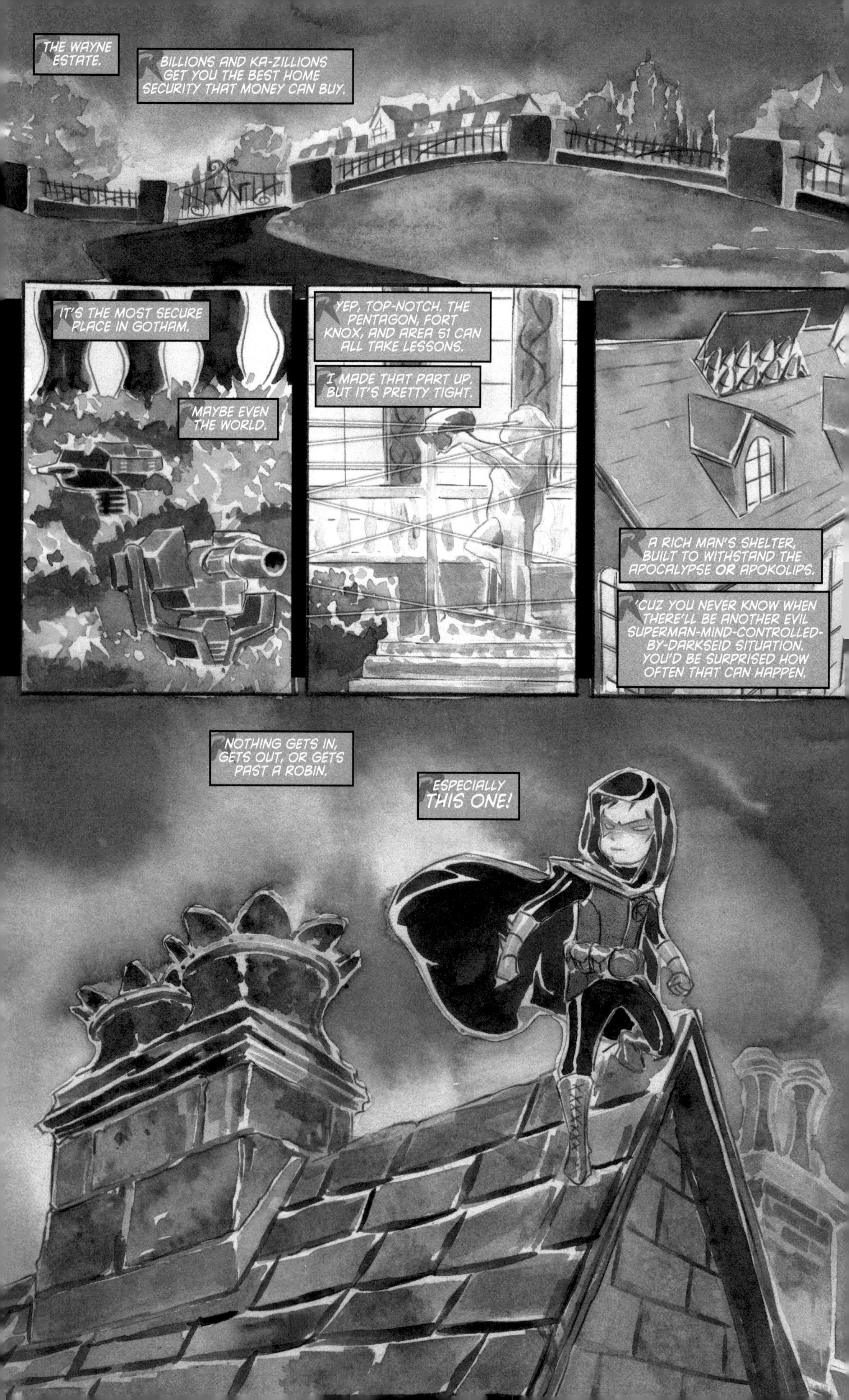
THE WAYNE ESTATE.
BILLIONS AND KA-ZILLIONS GET YOU THE BEST HOME SECURITY THAT MONEY CAN BUY.
IT'S THE MOST SECURE PLACE IN GOTHAM.
MAYBE EVEN THE WORLD.
YEP, TOP-NOTCH. THE PENTAGON, FORT KNOX, AND AREA 51 CAN ALL TAKE LESSONS.
I MADE THAT PART UP. BUT IT'S PRETTY TIGHT.
A RICH MAN'S SHELTER, BUILT TO WITHSTAND THE APOCALYPSE OR APOKOLIPS.
'CUZ YOU NEVER KNOW WHEN THERE'LL BE ANOTHER EVIL SUPERMAN-MIND-CONTROLLED-BY-DARKSEID SITUATION. YOU'D BE SURPRISED HOW OFTEN THAT CAN HAPPEN.
NOTHING GETS IN, GETS OUT, OR GETS PAST A ROBIN.
ESPECIALLY THIS ONE!

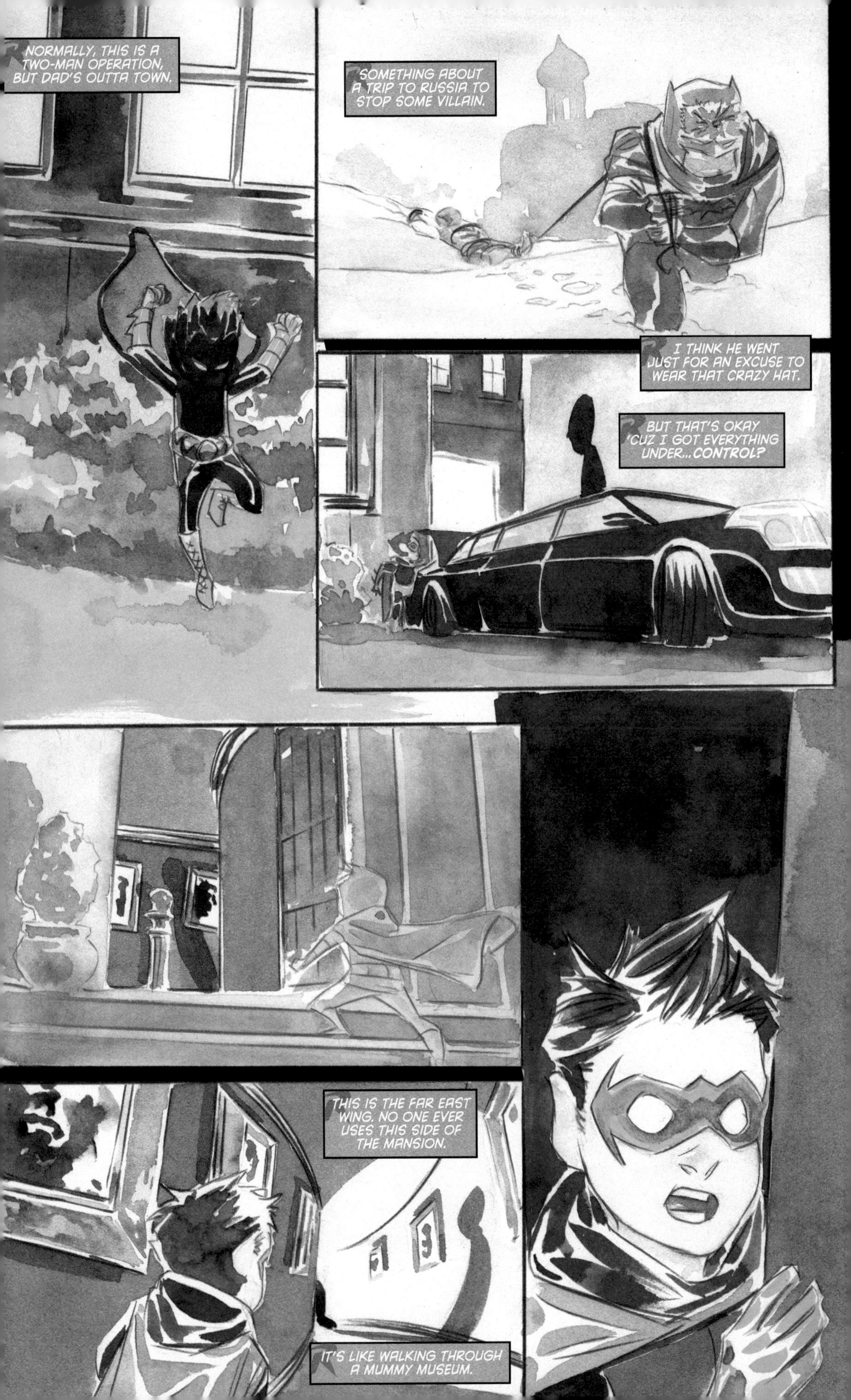
NORMALLY, THIS IS A TWO-MAN OPERATION, BUT DAD'S OUTTA TOWN.
SOMETHING ABOUT A TRIP TO RUSSIA TO STOP SOME VILLAIN.
I THINK HE WENT JUST FOR AN EXCUSE TO WEAR THAT CRAZY HAT.
BUT THAT'S OKAY 'CUZ I GOT EVERYTHING UNDER...CONTROL?
THIS IS THE FAR EAST WING. NO ONE EVER USES THIS SIDE OF THE MANSION.
IT'S LIKE WALKING THROUGH A MUMMY MUSEUM.

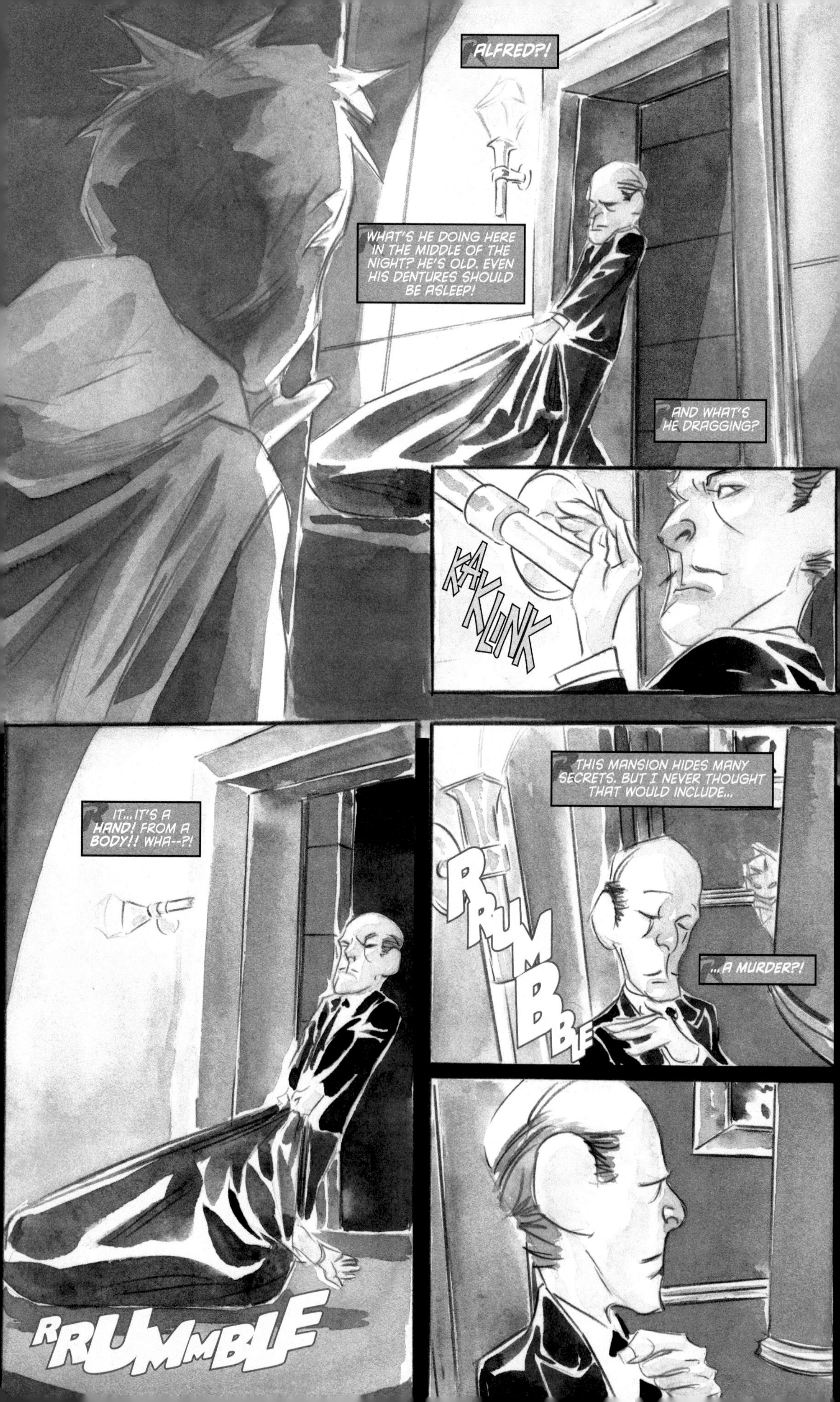
ALFRED?!
WHAT'S HE DOING HERE IN THE MIDDLE OF THE NIGHT? HE'S OLD. EVEN HIS DENTURES SHOULD BE ASLEEP!
AND WHAT'S HE DRAGGING?
KA-KLINK
IT...IT'S A HAND! FROM A BODY!! WHA--?!
RRUMMBLE
THIS MANSION HIDES MANY SECRETS. BUT I NEVER THOUGHT THAT WOULD INCLUDE...
RRUMBBLE
...A MURDER?!

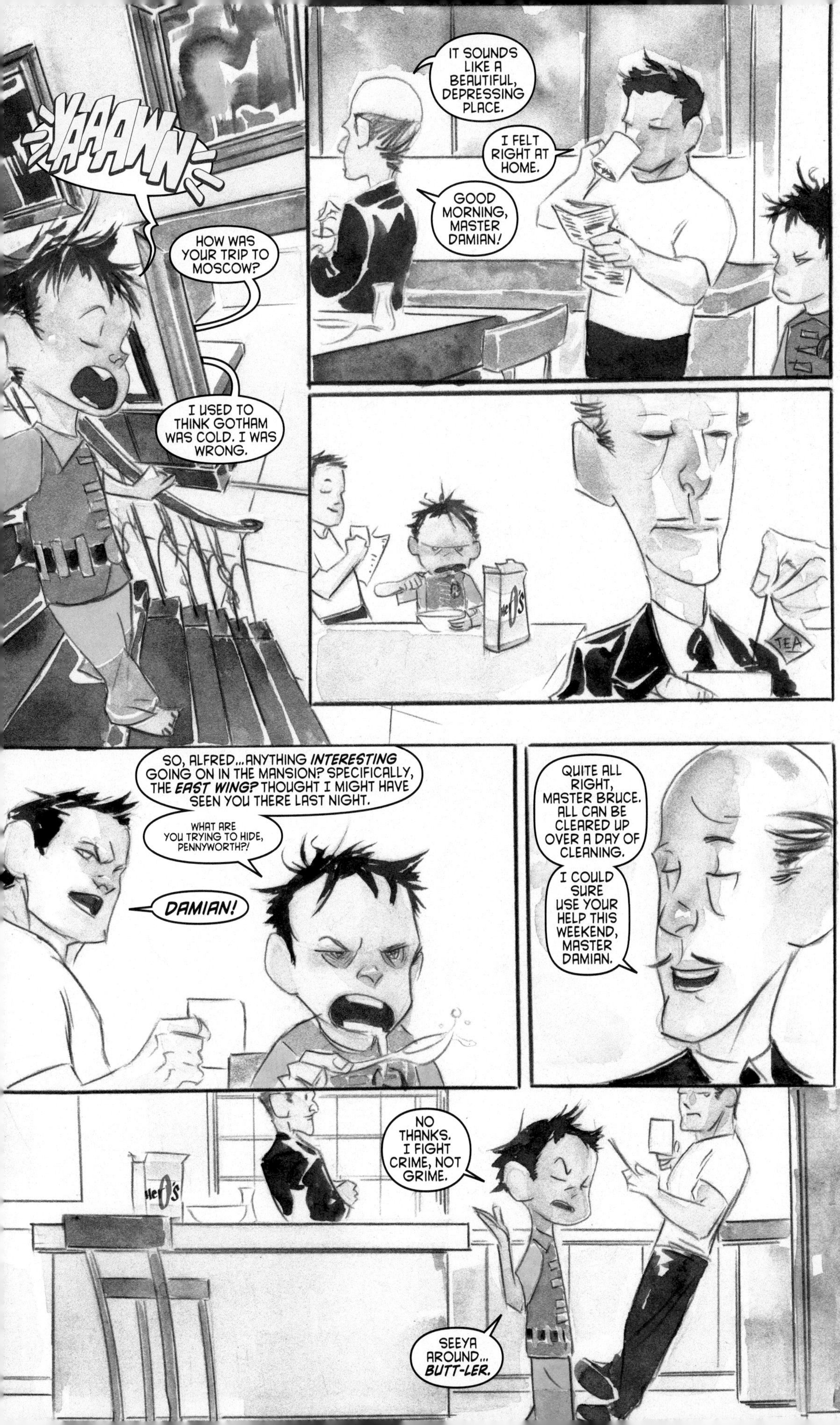
YAAAWN
HOW WAS YOUR TRIP TO MOSCOW?
I USED TO THINK GOTHAM WAS COLD. I WAS WRONG.
IT SOUNDS LIKE A BEAUTIFUL, DEPRESSING PLACE.
I FELT RIGHT AT HOME.
GOOD MORNING, MASTER DAMIAN!
TEA
SO, ALFRED... ANYTHING INTERESTING GOING ON IN THE MANSION? SPECIFICALLY, THE EAST WING? THOUGHT I MIGHT HAVE SEEN YOU THERE LAST NIGHT.
WHAT ARE YOU TRYING TO HIDE, PENNYWORTH?!
DAMIAN!
QUITE ALL RIGHT, MASTER BRUCE. ALL CAN BE CLEARED UP OVER A DAY OF CLEANING.
I COULD SURE USE YOUR HELP THIS WEEKEND, MASTER DAMIAN.
NO THANKS. I FIGHT CRIME, NOT GRIME.
SEEYA AROUND... BUTT-LER.

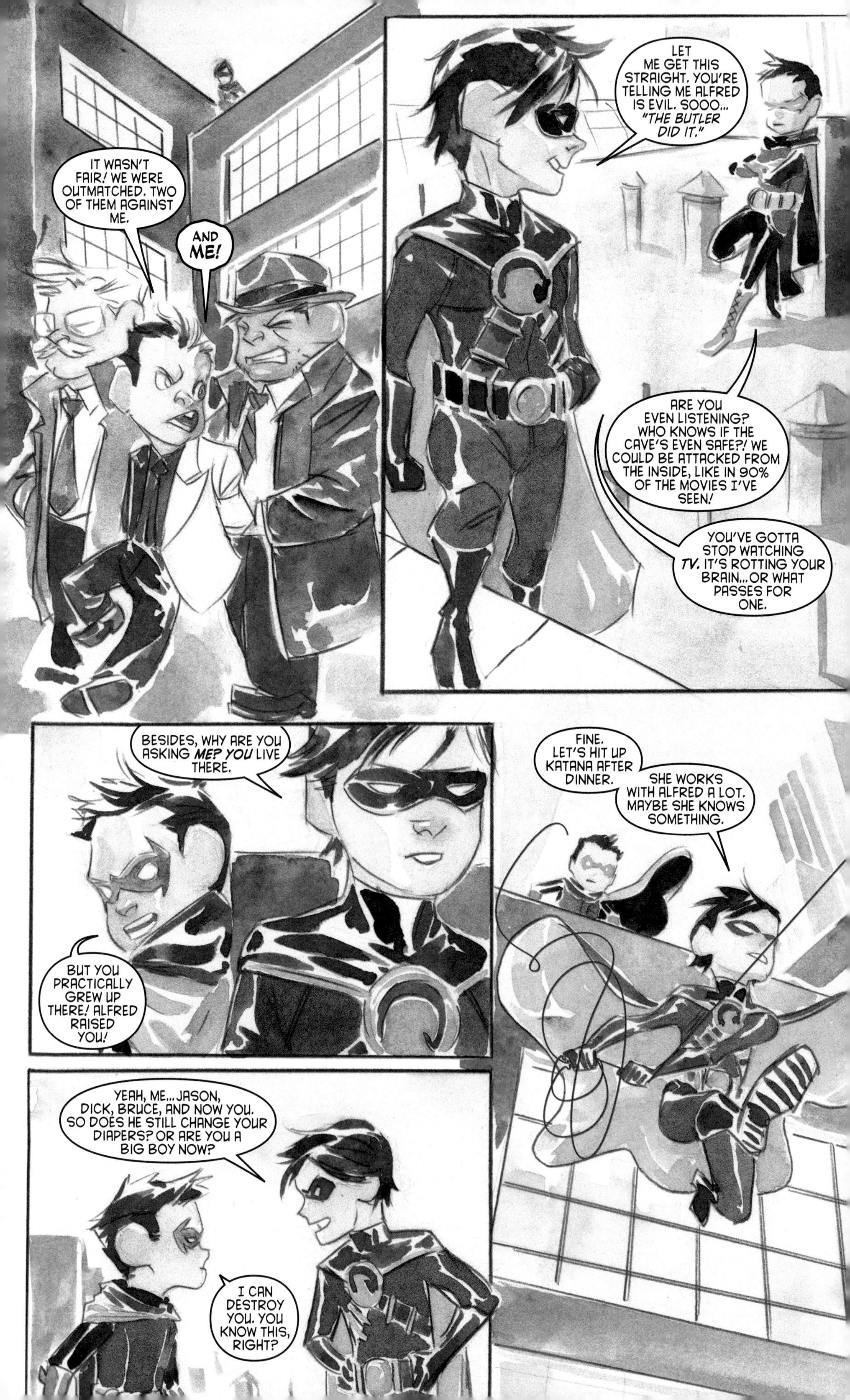
IT WASN'T FAIR! WE WERE OUTMATCHED. TWO OF THEM AGAINST ME.
AND ME!
LET ME GET THIS STRAIGHT. YOU'RE TELLING ME ALFRED IS EVIL. SOOO... "THE BUTLER DID IT."
ARE YOU EVEN LISTENING? WHO KNOWS IF THE CAVE'S EVEN SAFE?! WE COULD BE ATTACKED FROM THE INSIDE, LIKE IN 90% OF THE MOVIES I'VE SEEN!
YOU'VE GOTTA STOP WATCHING TV. IT'S ROTTING YOUR BRAIN...OR WHAT PASSES FOR ONE.
BESIDES, WHY ARE YOU ASKING ME? YOU LIVE THERE.
BUT YOU PRACTICALLY GREW UP THERE! ALFRED RAISED YOU!
YEAH, ME...JASON, DICK, BRUCE, AND NOW YOU. SO DOES HE STILL CHANGE YOUR DIAPERS? OR ARE YOU A BIG BOY NOW?
I CAN DESTROY YOU. YOU KNOW THIS, RIGHT?
FINE. LET'S HIT UP KATANA AFTER DINNER.
SHE WORKS WITH ALFRED A LOT. MAYBE SHE KNOWS SOMETHING.

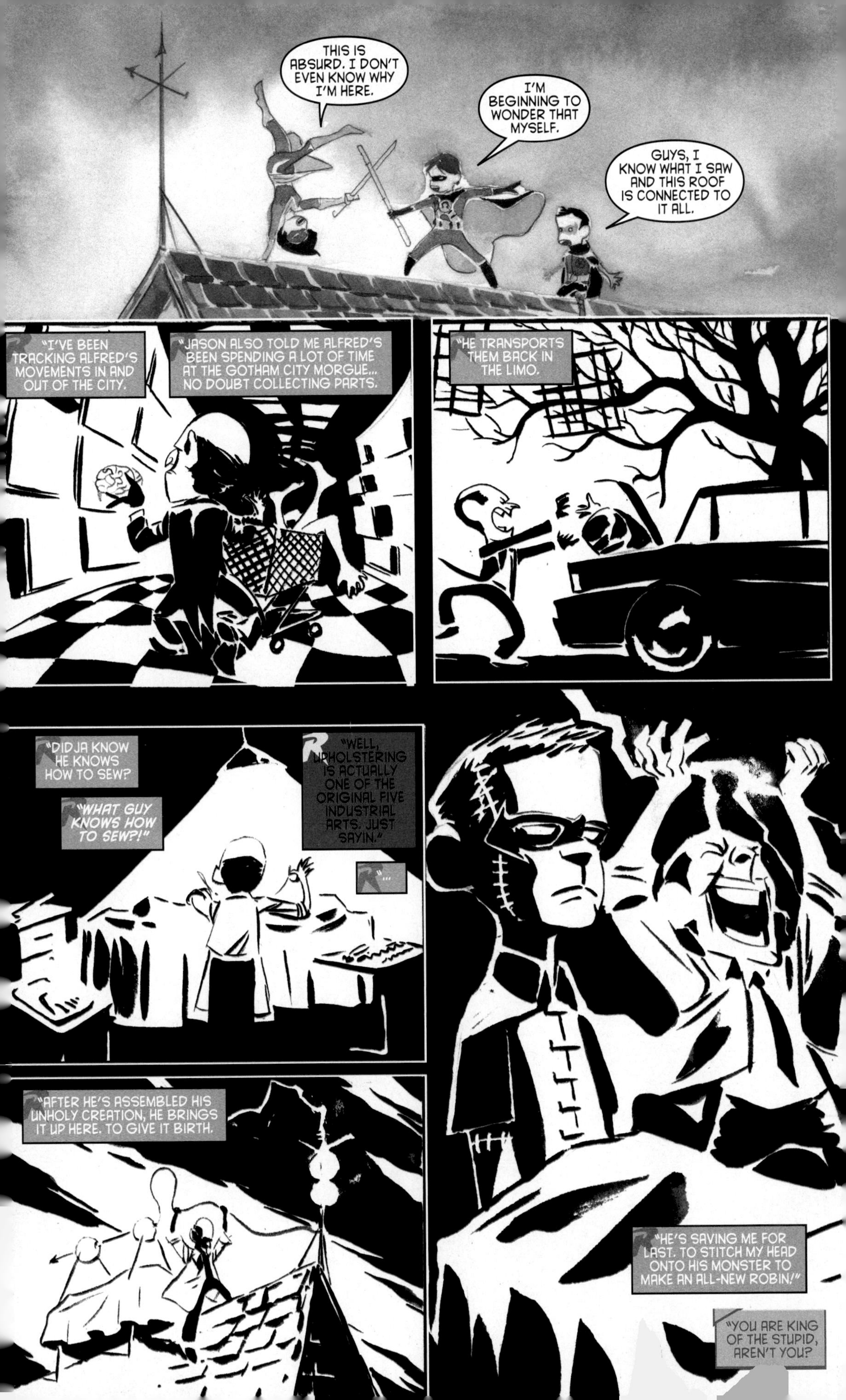
THIS IS ABSURD. I DON'T EVEN KNOW WHY I'M HERE.
I'M BEGINNING TO WONDER THAT MYSELF.
GUYS, I KNOW WHAT I SAW AND THIS ROOF IS CONNECTED TO IT ALL.
"I'VE BEEN TRACKING ALFRED'S MOVEMENTS IN AND OUT OF THE CITY.
"JASON ALSO TOLD ME ALFRED'S BEEN SPENDING A LOT OF TIME AT THE GOTHAM CITY MORGUE... NO DOUBT COLLECTING PARTS.
"HE TRANSPORTS THEM BACK IN THE LIMO.
"DIDJA KNOW HE KNOWS HOW TO SEW?
"WHAT GUY KNOWS HOW TO SEW?!"
"WELL, UPHOLSTERING IS ACTUALLY ONE OF THE ORIGINAL FIVE INDUSTRIAL ARTS. JUST SAYIN."
"...
"AFTER HE'S ASSEMBLED HIS UNHOLY CREATION, HE BRINGS IT UP HERE. TO GIVE IT BIRTH.
"HE'S SAVING ME FOR LAST. TO STITCH MY HEAD ONTO HIS MONSTER TO MAKE AN ALL-NEW ROBIN!"
"YOU ARE KING OF THE STUPID, AREN'T YOU?

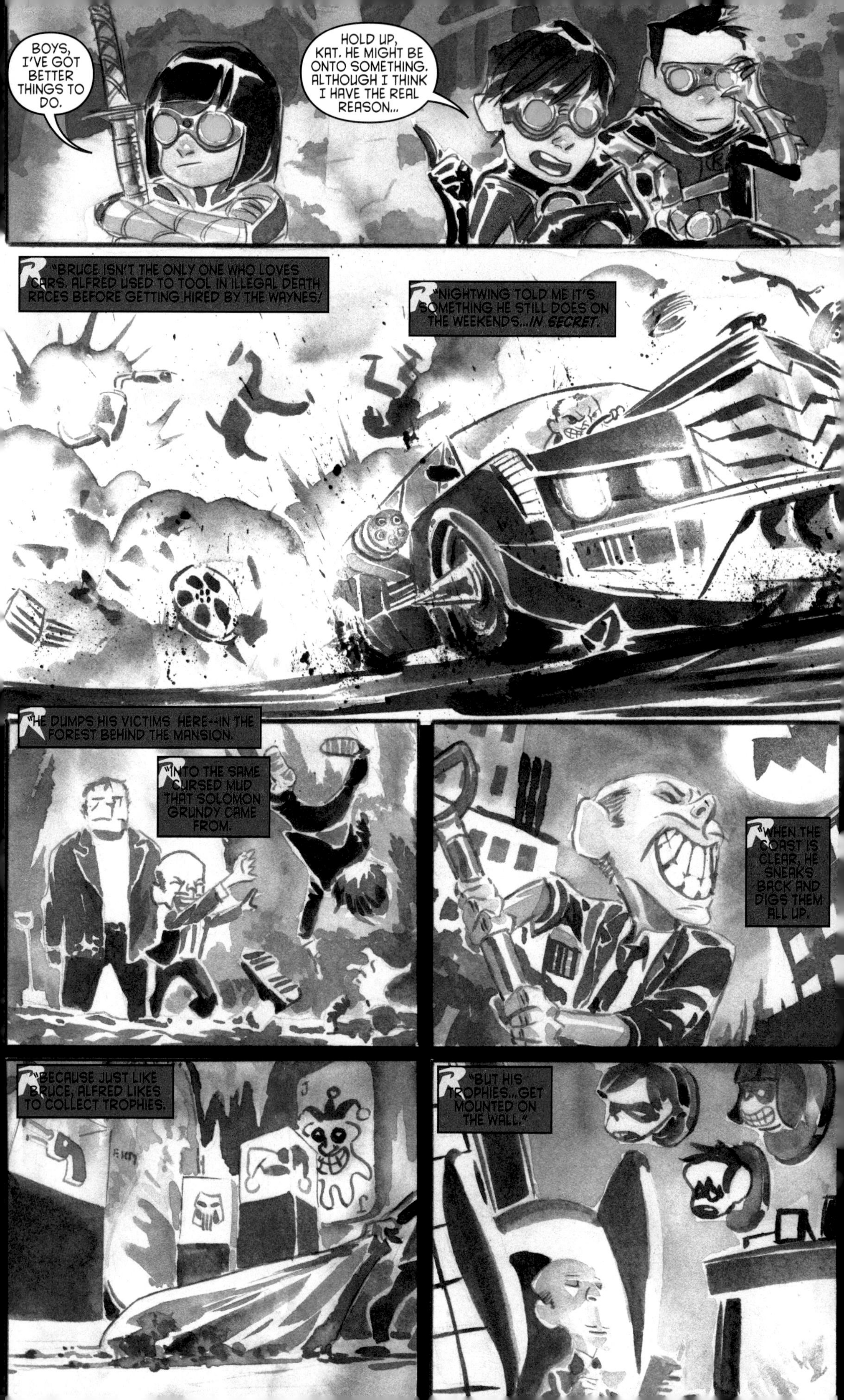
BOYS, I'VE GOT BETTER THINGS TO DO.
HOLD UP, KAT. HE MIGHT BE ONTO SOMETHING. ALTHOUGH I THINK I HAVE THE REAL REASON...
"BRUCE ISN'T THE ONLY ONE WHO LOVES CARS. ALFRED USED TO TOOL IN ILLEGAL DEATH RACES BEFORE GETTING HIRED BY THE WAYNES!
"NIGHTWING TOLD ME IT'S SOMETHING HE STILL DOES ON THE WEEKENDS...IN SECRET.
"HE DUMPS HIS VICTIMS HERE--IN THE FOREST BEHIND THE MANSION.
"INTO THE SAME CURSED MUD THAT SOLOMON GRUNDY CAME FROM.
"WHEN THE COAST IS CLEAR, HE SNEAKS BACK AND DIGS THEM ALL UP.
"BECAUSE JUST LIKE BRUCE, ALFRED LIKES TO COLLECT TROPHIES.
"BUT HIS TROPHIES...GET MOUNTED ON THE WALL."

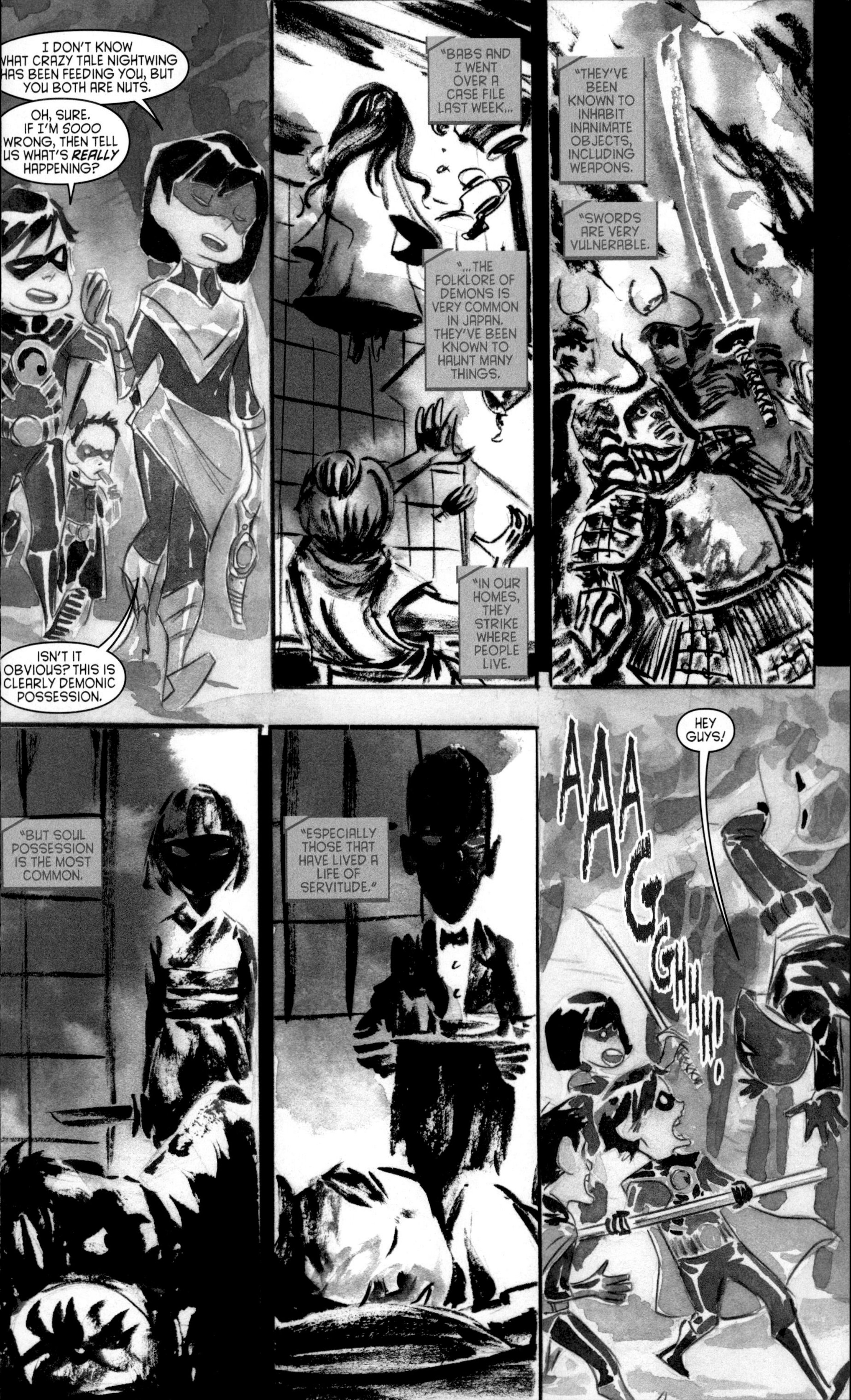
I DON'T KNOW WHAT CRAZY TALE NIGHTWING HAS BEEN FEEDING YOU, BUT YOU BOTH ARE NUTS.
OH, SURE. IF I'M *SOOO* WRONG, THEN TELL US WHAT'S ***REALLY*** HAPPENING?
ISN'T IT OBVIOUS? THIS IS CLEARLY DEMONIC POSSESSION.
"BABS AND I WENT OVER A CASE FILE LAST WEEK...
"...THE FOLKLORE OF DEMONS IS VERY COMMON IN JAPAN. THEY'VE BEEN KNOWN TO HAUNT MANY THINGS.
"IN OUR HOMES, THEY STRIKE WHERE PEOPLE LIVE.
"THEY'VE BEEN KNOWN TO INHABIT INANIMATE OBJECTS, INCLUDING WEAPONS.
"SWORDS ARE VERY VULNERABLE.
"BUT SOUL POSSESSION IS THE MOST COMMON.
"ESPECIALLY THOSE THAT HAVE LIVED A LIFE OF SERVITUDE."
HEY GUYS!
AAAGGHHH!

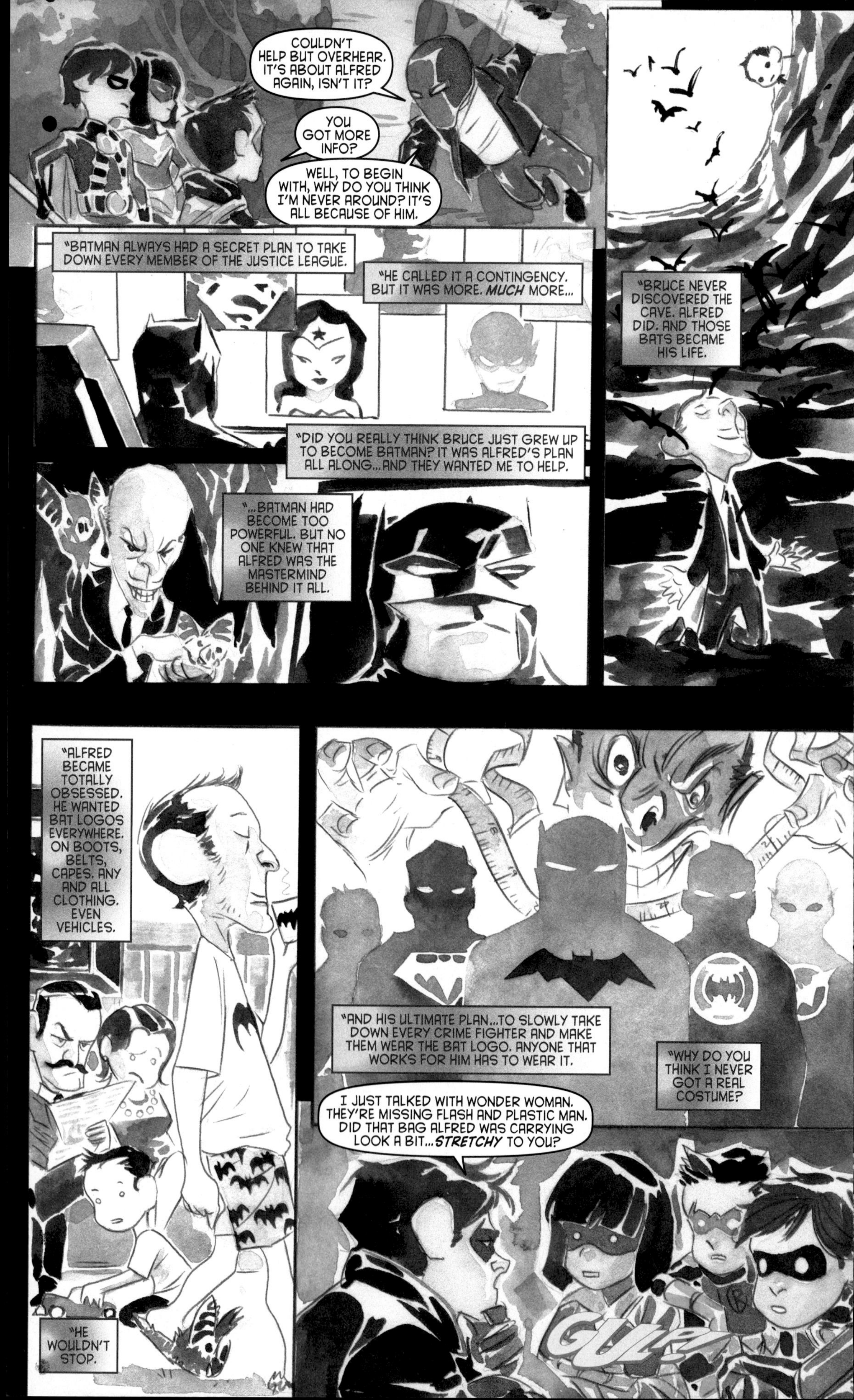
COULDN'T HELP BUT OVERHEAR. IT'S ABOUT ALFRED AGAIN, ISN'T IT?
YOU GOT MORE INFO?
WELL, TO BEGIN WITH, WHY DO YOU THINK I'M NEVER AROUND? IT'S ALL BECAUSE OF HIM.
"BATMAN ALWAYS HAD A SECRET PLAN TO TAKE DOWN EVERY MEMBER OF THE JUSTICE LEAGUE.
"HE CALLED IT A CONTINGENCY. BUT IT WAS MORE. MUCH MORE...
"DID YOU REALLY THINK BRUCE JUST GREW UP TO BECOME BATMAN? IT WAS ALFRED'S PLAN ALL ALONG...AND THEY WANTED ME TO HELP.
"...BATMAN HAD BECOME TOO POWERFUL. BUT NO ONE KNEW THAT ALFRED WAS THE MASTERMIND BEHIND IT ALL.
"BRUCE NEVER DISCOVERED THE CAVE. ALFRED DID. AND THOSE BATS BECAME HIS LIFE.
"ALFRED BECAME TOTALLY OBSESSED. HE WANTED BAT LOGOS EVERYWHERE. ON BOOTS, BELTS, CAPES. ANY AND ALL CLOTHING. EVEN VEHICLES.
"HE WOULDN'T STOP.
"AND HIS ULTIMATE PLAN...TO SLOWLY TAKE DOWN EVERY CRIME FIGHTER AND MAKE THEM WEAR THE BAT LOGO. ANYONE THAT WORKS FOR HIM HAS TO WEAR IT.
"WHY DO YOU THINK I NEVER GOT A REAL COSTUME?
I JUST TALKED WITH WONDER WOMAN. THEY'RE MISSING FLASH AND PLASTIC MAN. DID THAT BAG ALFRED WAS CARRYING LOOK A BIT...STRETCHY TO YOU?
GULP!

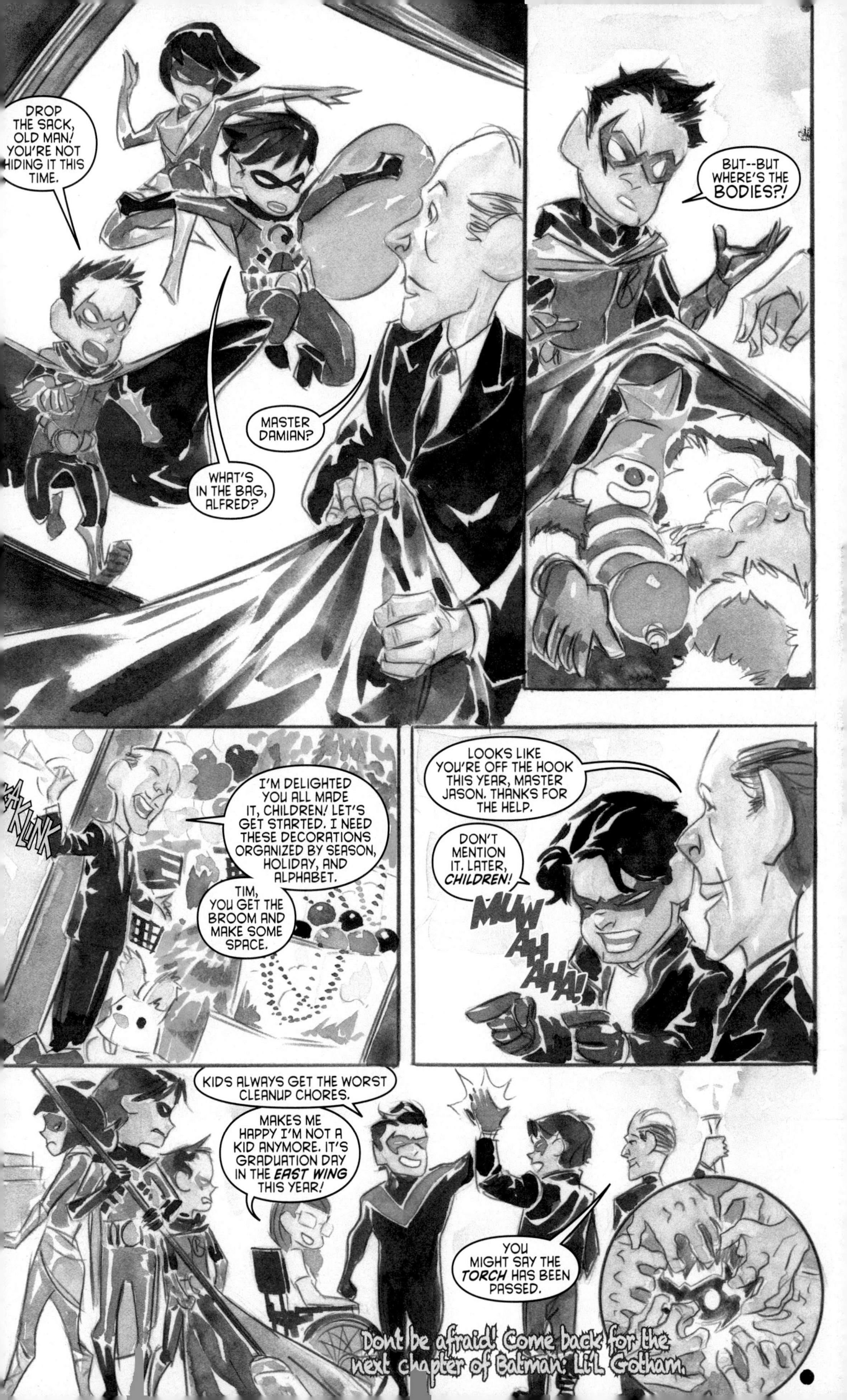
DROP THE SACK, OLD MAN! YOU'RE NOT HIDING IT THIS TIME.
WHAT'S IN THE BAG, ALFRED?
MASTER DAMIAN?
BUT--BUT WHERE'S THE BODIES?!
KLINK
I'M DELIGHTED YOU ALL MADE IT, CHILDREN! LET'S GET STARTED. I NEED THESE DECORATIONS ORGANIZED BY SEASON, HOLIDAY, AND ALPHABET.
TIM, YOU GET THE BROOM AND MAKE SOME SPACE.
LOOKS LIKE YOU'RE OFF THE HOOK THIS YEAR, MASTER JASON. THANKS FOR THE HELP.
DON'T MENTION IT. LATER, *CHILDREN*!
MUWAHAHAHA!
KIDS ALWAYS GET THE WORST CLEANUP CHORES.
MAKES ME HAPPY I'M NOT A KID ANYMORE. IT'S GRADUATION DAY IN THE *EAST WING* THIS YEAR!
YOU MIGHT SAY THE *TORCH* HAS BEEN PASSED.
Dont be afraid! Come back for the next chapter of Batman: Li'L Gotham.

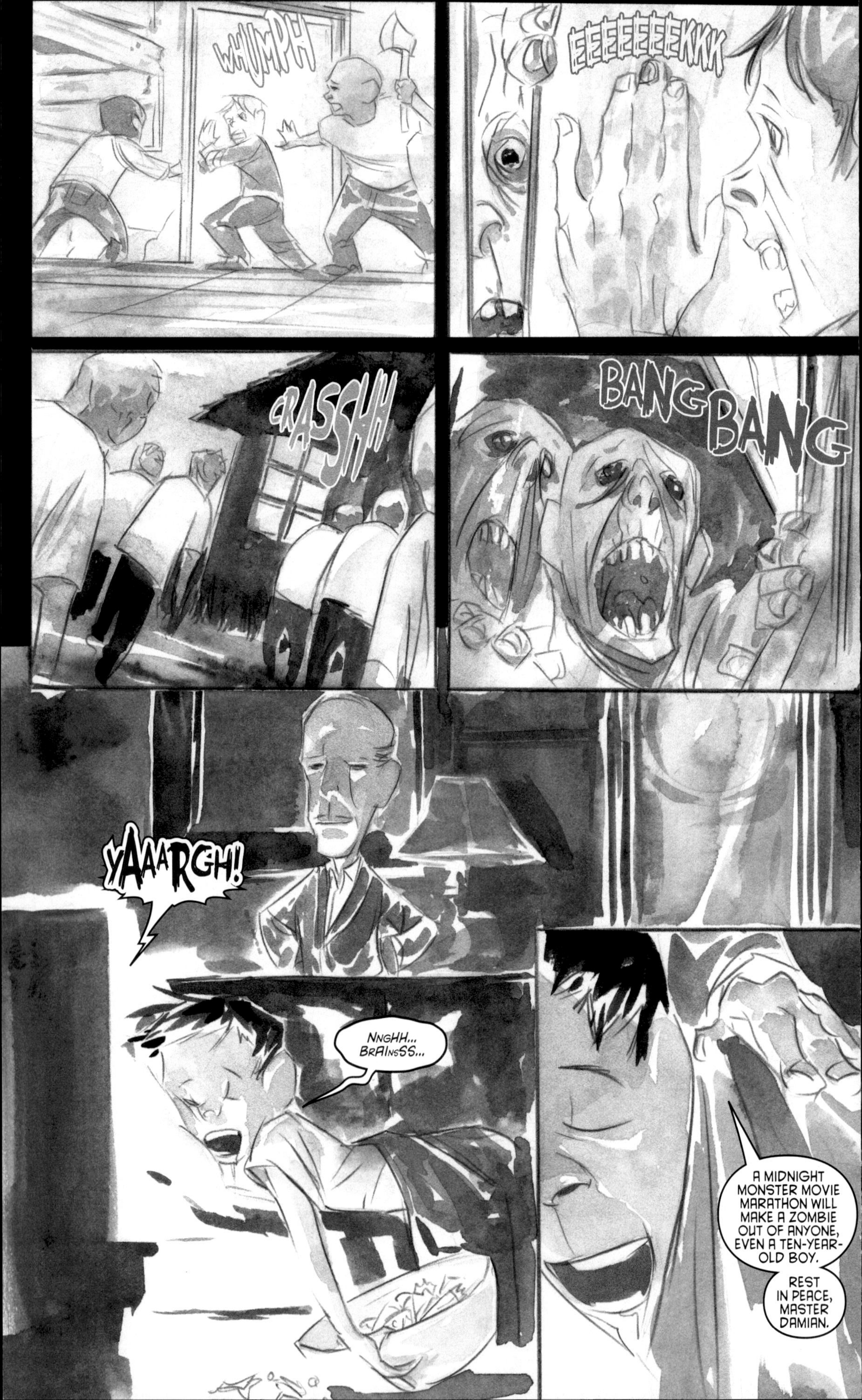
WHUMPH
EEEEEEEKKK
CRASSHH
BANG BANG
YAAARGH!
NNGHH... BRAINSSS...
A MIDNIGHT MONSTER MOVIE MARATHON WILL MAKE A ZOMBIE OUT OF ANYONE, EVEN A TEN-YEAR-OLD BOY.
REST IN PEACE, MASTER DAMIAN.

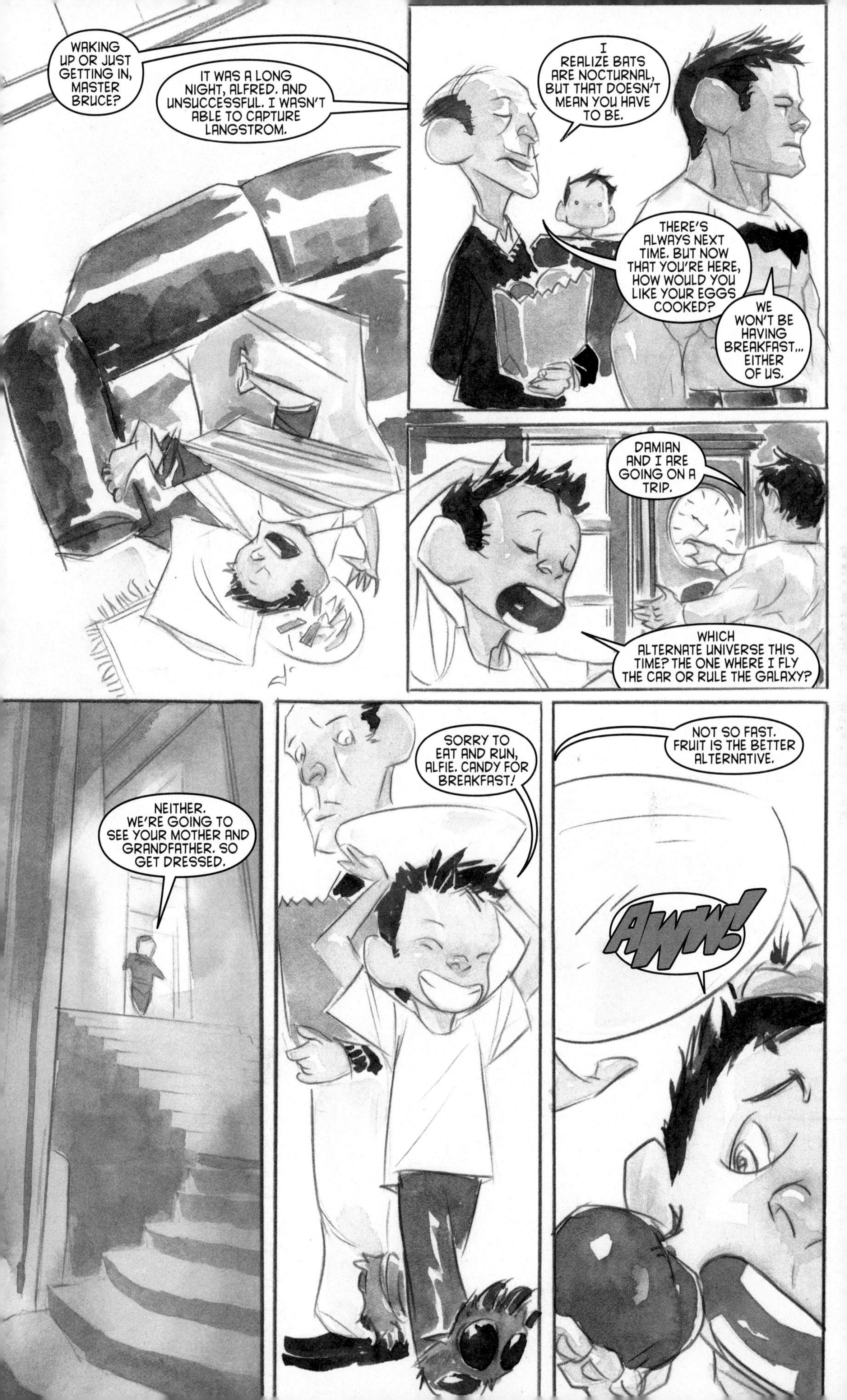
WAKING UP OR JUST GETTING IN, MASTER BRUCE?
IT WAS A LONG NIGHT, ALFRED. AND UNSUCCESSFUL. I WASN'T ABLE TO CAPTURE LANGSTROM.
I REALIZE BATS ARE NOCTURNAL, BUT THAT DOESN'T MEAN YOU HAVE TO BE.
THERE'S ALWAYS NEXT TIME. BUT NOW THAT YOU'RE HERE, HOW WOULD YOU LIKE YOUR EGGS COOKED?
WE WON'T BE HAVING BREAKFAST... EITHER OF US.
DAMIAN AND I ARE GOING ON A TRIP.
WHICH ALTERNATE UNIVERSE THIS TIME? THE ONE WHERE I FLY THE CAR OR RULE THE GALAXY?
NEITHER. WE'RE GOING TO SEE YOUR MOTHER AND GRANDFATHER. SO GET DRESSED.
SORRY TO EAT AND RUN, ALFIE. CANDY FOR BREAKFAST!
NOT SO FAST. FRUIT IS THE BETTER ALTERNATIVE.
AWW!

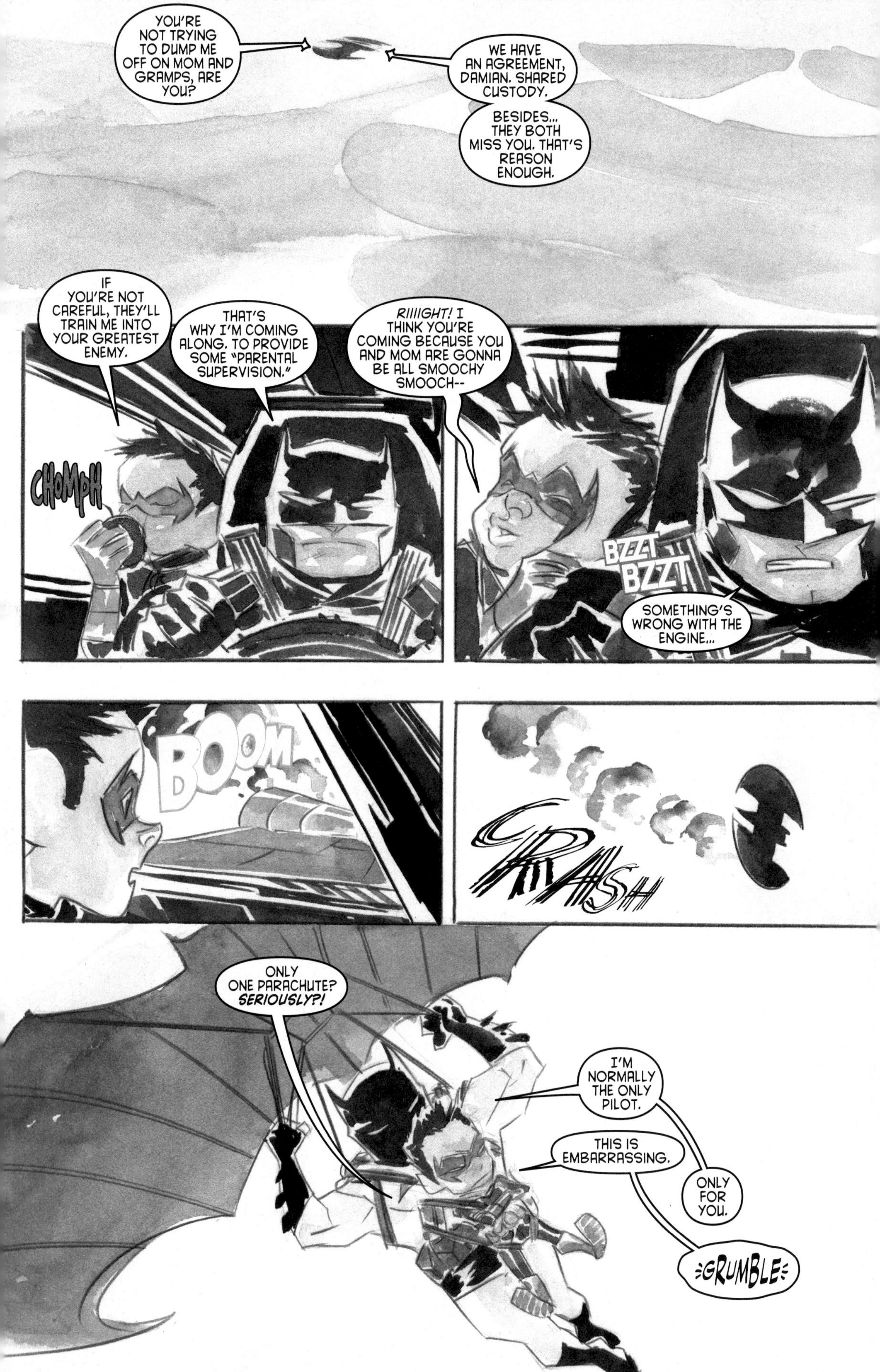
YOU'RE NOT TRYING TO DUMP ME OFF ON MOM AND GRAMPS, ARE YOU?
WE HAVE AN AGREEMENT, DAMIAN. SHARED CUSTODY.
BESIDES... THEY BOTH MISS YOU. THAT'S REASON ENOUGH.
IF YOU'RE NOT CAREFUL, THEY'LL TRAIN ME INTO YOUR GREATEST ENEMY.
CHOMPH
THAT'S WHY I'M COMING ALONG. TO PROVIDE SOME "PARENTAL SUPERVISION."
RIIIIGHT! I THINK YOU'RE COMING BECAUSE YOU AND MOM ARE GONNA BE ALL SMOOCHY SMOOCH--
BZZT BZZT!
SOMETHING'S WRONG WITH THE ENGINE...
BOOM
CRASH
ONLY ONE PARACHUTE? ***SERIOUSLY?!***
I'M NORMALLY THE ONLY PILOT.
THIS IS EMBARRASSING.
ONLY FOR YOU.
GRUMBLE

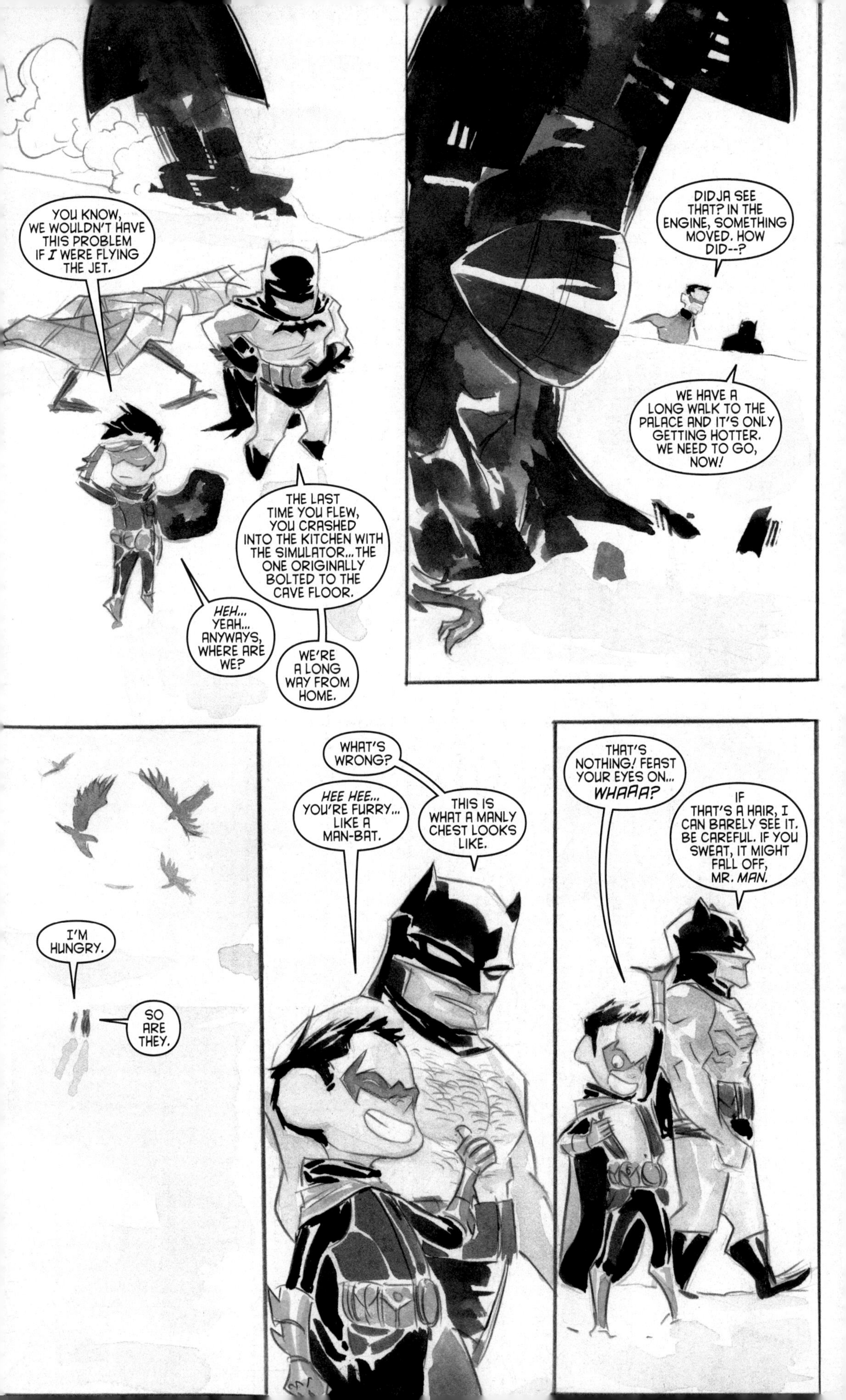
YOU KNOW, WE WOULDN'T HAVE THIS PROBLEM IF I WERE FLYING THE JET.
THE LAST TIME YOU FLEW, YOU CRASHED INTO THE KITCHEN WITH THE SIMULATOR... THE ONE ORIGINALLY BOLTED TO THE CAVE FLOOR.
HEH... YEAH... ANYWAYS, WHERE ARE WE?
WE'RE A LONG WAY FROM HOME.
DIDJA SEE THAT? IN THE ENGINE, SOMETHING MOVED. HOW DID--?
WE HAVE A LONG WALK TO THE PALACE AND IT'S ONLY GETTING HOTTER. WE NEED TO GO, NOW!
I'M HUNGRY.
SO ARE THEY.
WHAT'S WRONG?
HEE HEE... YOU'RE FURRY... LIKE A MAN-BAT.
THIS IS WHAT A MANLY CHEST LOOKS LIKE.
THAT'S NOTHING! FEAST YOUR EYES ON... WHAAA?
IF THAT'S A HAIR, I CAN BARELY SEE IT. BE CAREFUL. IF YOU SWEAT, IT MIGHT FALL OFF, MR. MAN.

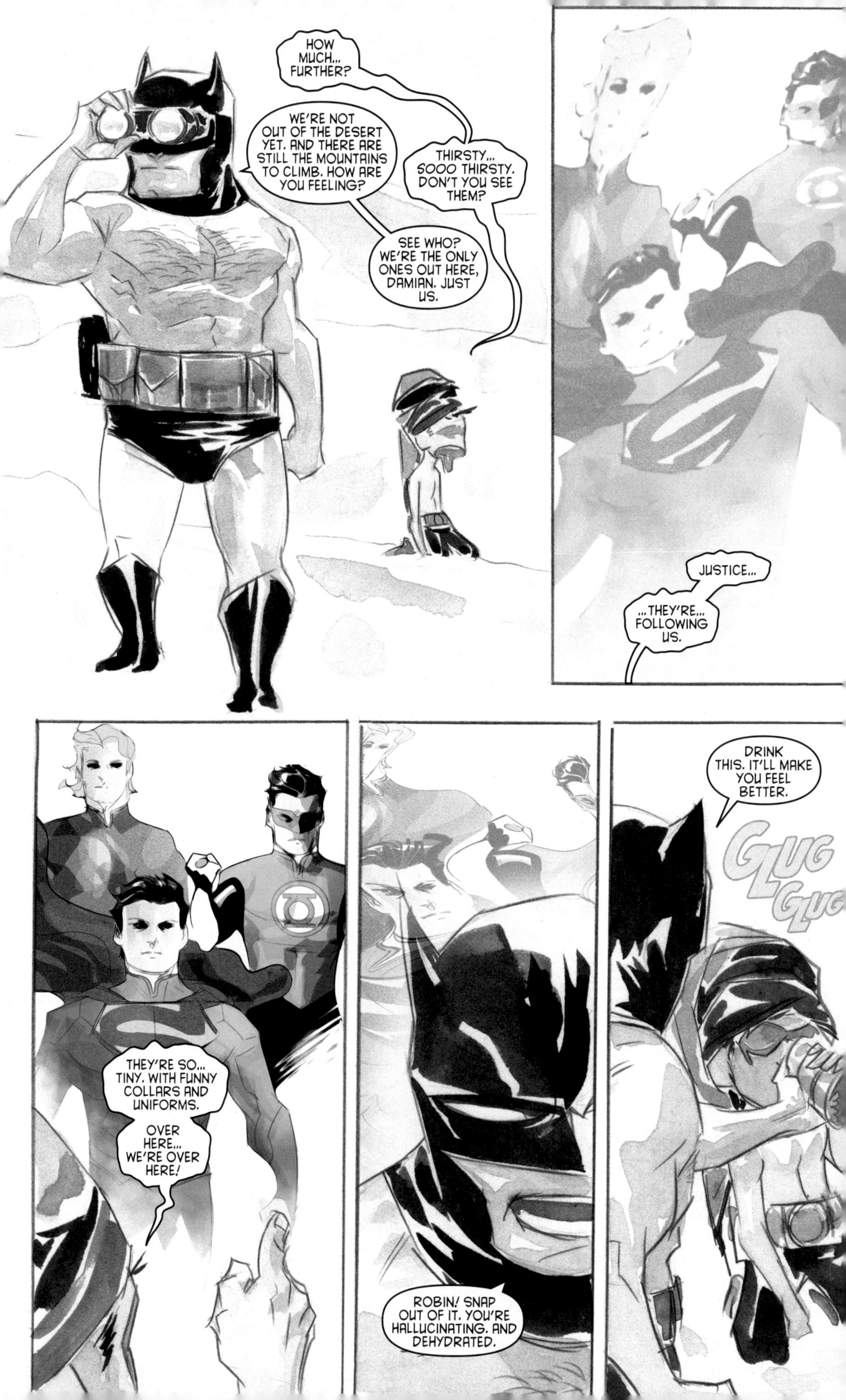
HOW MUCH... FURTHER?
WE'RE NOT OUT OF THE DESERT YET. AND THERE ARE STILL THE MOUNTAINS TO CLIMB. HOW ARE YOU FEELING?
THIRSTY... SOOO THIRSTY. DON'T YOU SEE THEM?
SEE WHO? WE'RE THE ONLY ONES OUT HERE, DAMIAN. JUST US.
JUSTICE...
...THEY'RE... FOLLOWING US.
THEY'RE SO... TINY. WITH FUNNY COLLARS AND UNIFORMS.
OVER HERE... WE'RE OVER HERE!
ROBIN! SNAP OUT OF IT. YOU'RE HALLUCINATING. AND DEHYDRATED.
DRINK THIS. IT'LL MAKE YOU FEEL BETTER.
GLUG GLUG

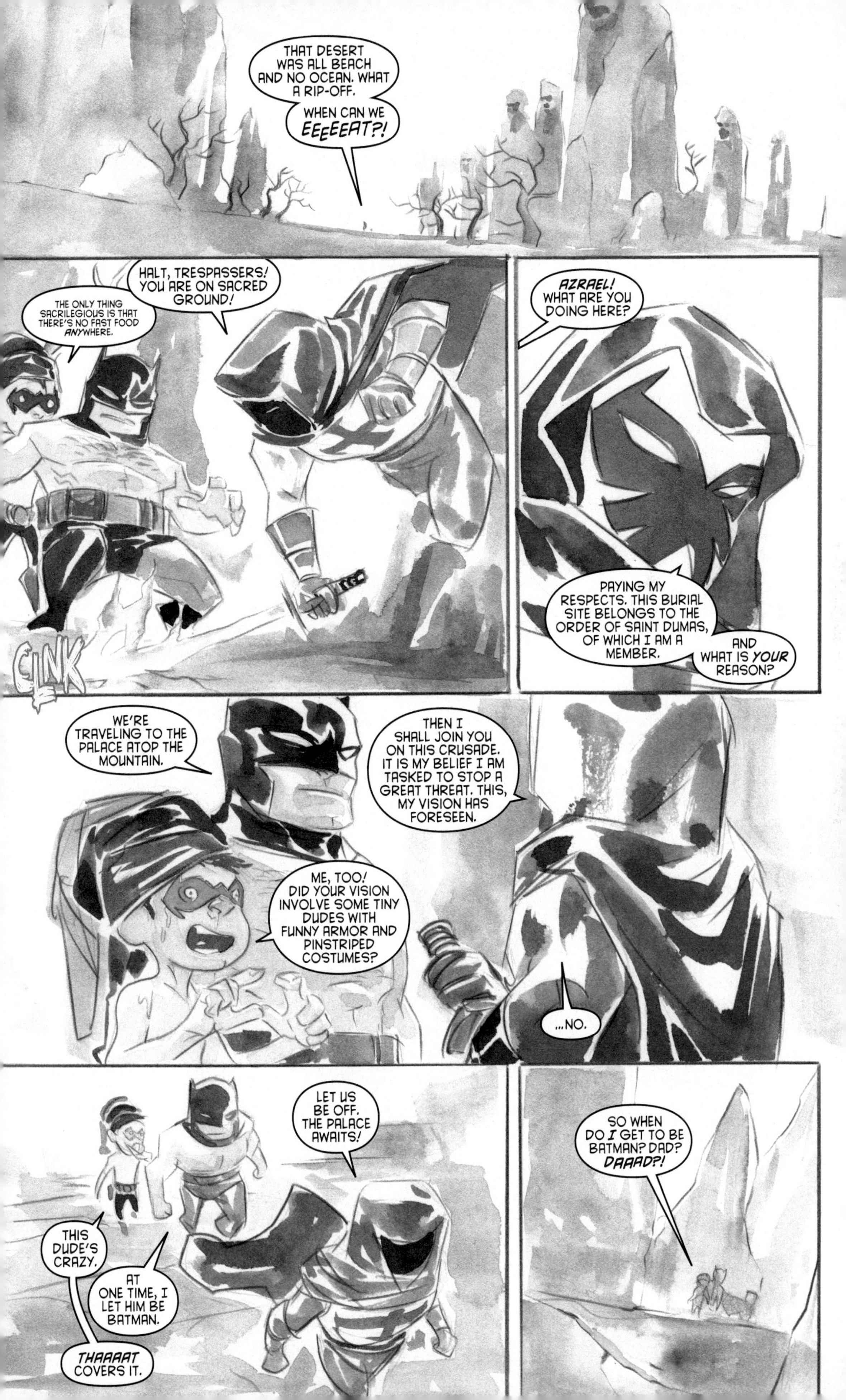
THAT DESERT WAS ALL BEACH AND NO OCEAN. WHAT A RIP-OFF.
WHEN CAN WE EEEEEAT?!
HALT, TRESPASSERS! YOU ARE ON SACRED GROUND!
THE ONLY THING SACRILEGIOUS IS THAT THERE'S NO FAST FOOD ANYWHERE.
CLINK
AZRAEL! WHAT ARE YOU DOING HERE?
PAYING MY RESPECTS. THIS BURIAL SITE BELONGS TO THE ORDER OF SAINT DUMAS, OF WHICH I AM A MEMBER.
AND WHAT IS YOUR REASON?
WE'RE TRAVELING TO THE PALACE ATOP THE MOUNTAIN.
THEN I SHALL JOIN YOU ON THIS CRUSADE. IT IS MY BELIEF I AM TASKED TO STOP A GREAT THREAT. THIS, MY VISION HAS FORESEEN.
ME, TOO! DID YOUR VISION INVOLVE SOME TINY DUDES WITH FUNNY ARMOR AND PINSTRIPED COSTUMES?
...NO.
LET US BE OFF. THE PALACE AWAITS!
THIS DUDE'S CRAZY.
AT ONE TIME, I LET HIM BE BATMAN.
THAAAAT COVERS IT.
SO WHEN DO I GET TO BE BATMAN? DAD? DAAAD?!

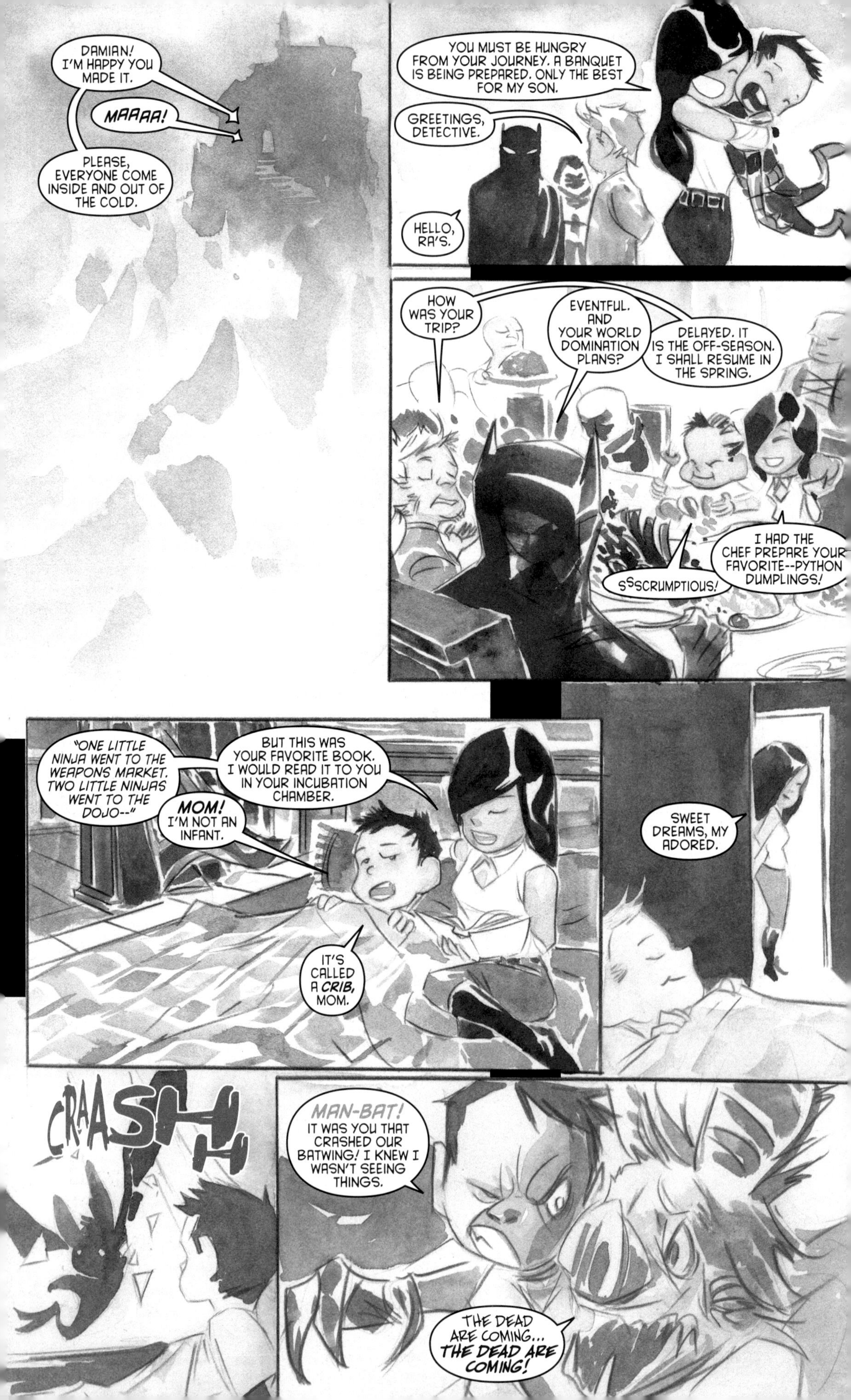
DAMIAN! I'M HAPPY YOU MADE IT.
MAAAAA!
PLEASE, EVERYONE COME INSIDE AND OUT OF THE COLD.
YOU MUST BE HUNGRY FROM YOUR JOURNEY. A BANQUET IS BEING PREPARED. ONLY THE BEST FOR MY SON.
GREETINGS, DETECTIVE.
HELLO, RA'S.
HOW WAS YOUR TRIP?
EVENTFUL. AND YOUR WORLD DOMINATION PLANS?
DELAYED. IT IS THE OFF-SEASON. I SHALL RESUME IN THE SPRING.
I HAD THE CHEF PREPARE YOUR FAVORITE--PYTHON DUMPLINGS!
SSSCRUMPTIOUS!
"ONE LITTLE NINJA WENT TO THE WEAPONS MARKET. TWO LITTLE NINJAS WENT TO THE DOJO--"
BUT THIS WAS YOUR FAVORITE BOOK. I WOULD READ IT TO YOU IN YOUR INCUBATION CHAMBER.
MOM! I'M NOT AN INFANT.
IT'S CALLED A CRIB, MOM.
SWEET DREAMS, MY ADORED.
CRAASH
MAN-BAT! IT WAS YOU THAT CRASHED OUR BATWING! I KNEW I WASN'T SEEING THINGS.
THE DEAD ARE COMING... THE DEAD ARE COMING!

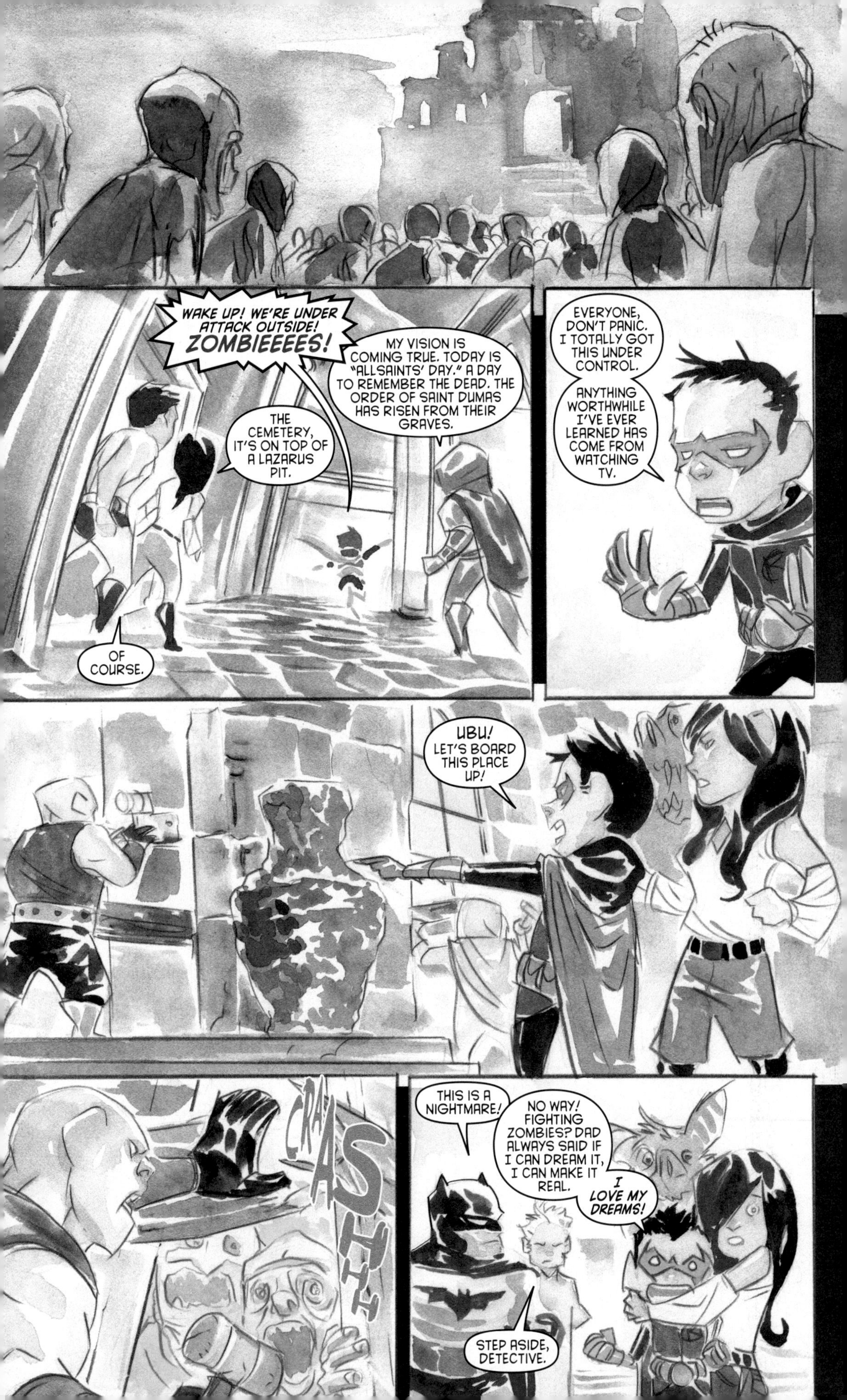
WAKE UP! WE'RE UNDER ATTACK OUTSIDE! ZOMBIEEEES!
THE CEMETERY, IT'S ON TOP OF A LAZARUS PIT.
MY VISION IS COMING TRUE. TODAY IS "ALLSAINTS' DAY." A DAY TO REMEMBER THE DEAD. THE ORDER OF SAINT DUMAS HAS RISEN FROM THEIR GRAVES.
OF COURSE.
EVERYONE, DON'T PANIC. I TOTALLY GOT THIS UNDER CONTROL.
ANYTHING WORTHWHILE I'VE EVER LEARNED HAS COME FROM WATCHING TV.
UBU! LET'S BOARD THIS PLACE UP!
CRASHHHH
THIS IS A NIGHTMARE!
NO WAY! FIGHTING ZOMBIES? DAD ALWAYS SAID IF I CAN DREAM IT, I CAN MAKE IT REAL.
I LOVE MY DREAMS!
STEP ASIDE, DETECTIVE.

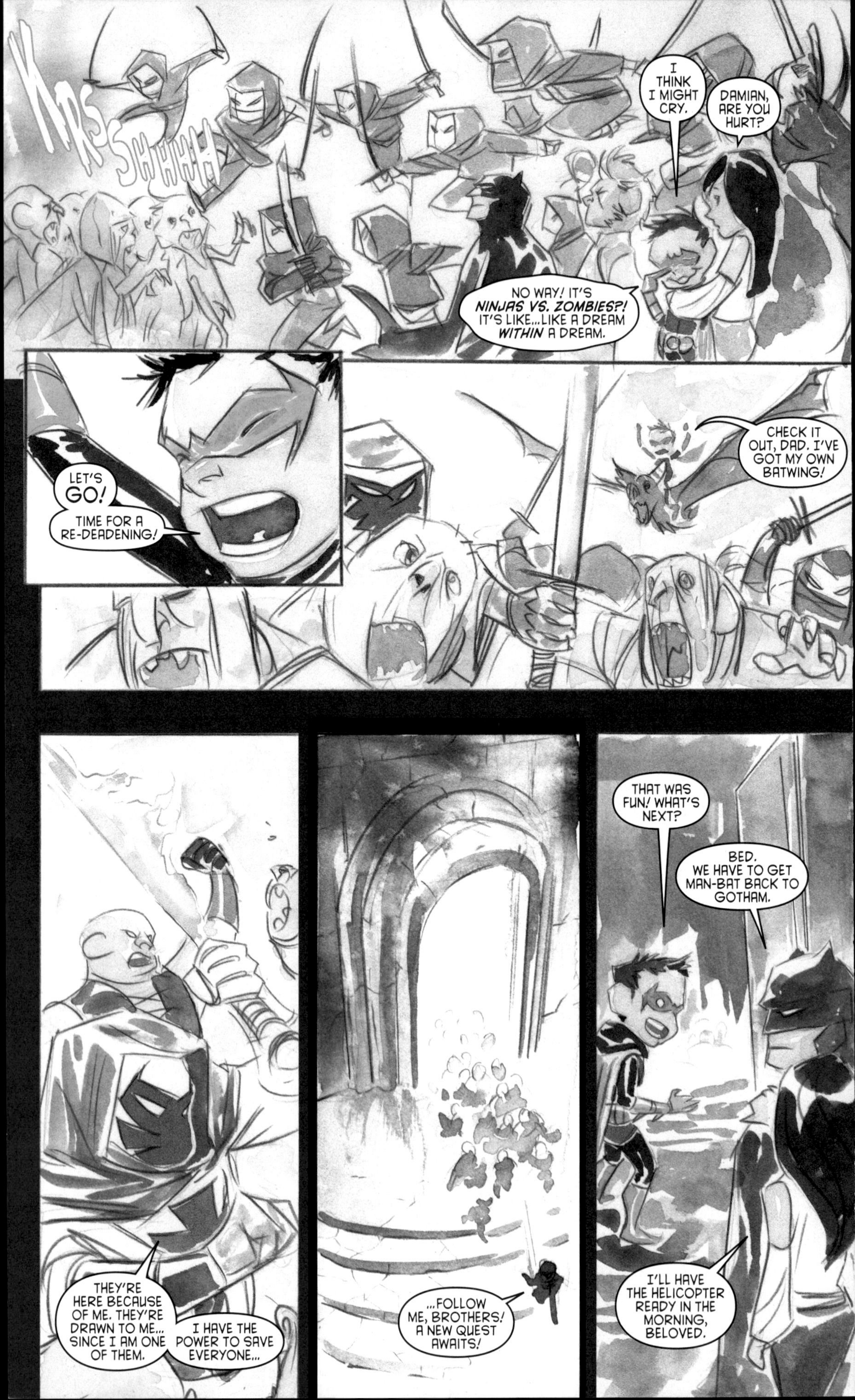
KRRSSHHHH
I THINK I MIGHT CRY.
DAMIAN, ARE YOU HURT?
NO WAY! IT'S *NINJAS VS. ZOMBIES?!* IT'S LIKE...LIKE A DREAM *WITHIN* A DREAM.
LET'S GO!
TIME FOR A RE-DEADENING!
CHECK IT OUT, DAD. I'VE GOT MY OWN BATWING!
THEY'RE HERE BECAUSE OF ME. THEY'RE DRAWN TO ME... SINCE I AM ONE OF THEM.
I HAVE THE POWER TO SAVE EVERYONE...
...FOLLOW ME, BROTHERS! A NEW QUEST AWAITS!
THAT WAS FUN! WHAT'S NEXT?
BED. WE HAVE TO GET MAN-BAT BACK TO GOTHAM.
I'LL HAVE THE HELICOPTER READY IN THE MORNING, BELOVED.

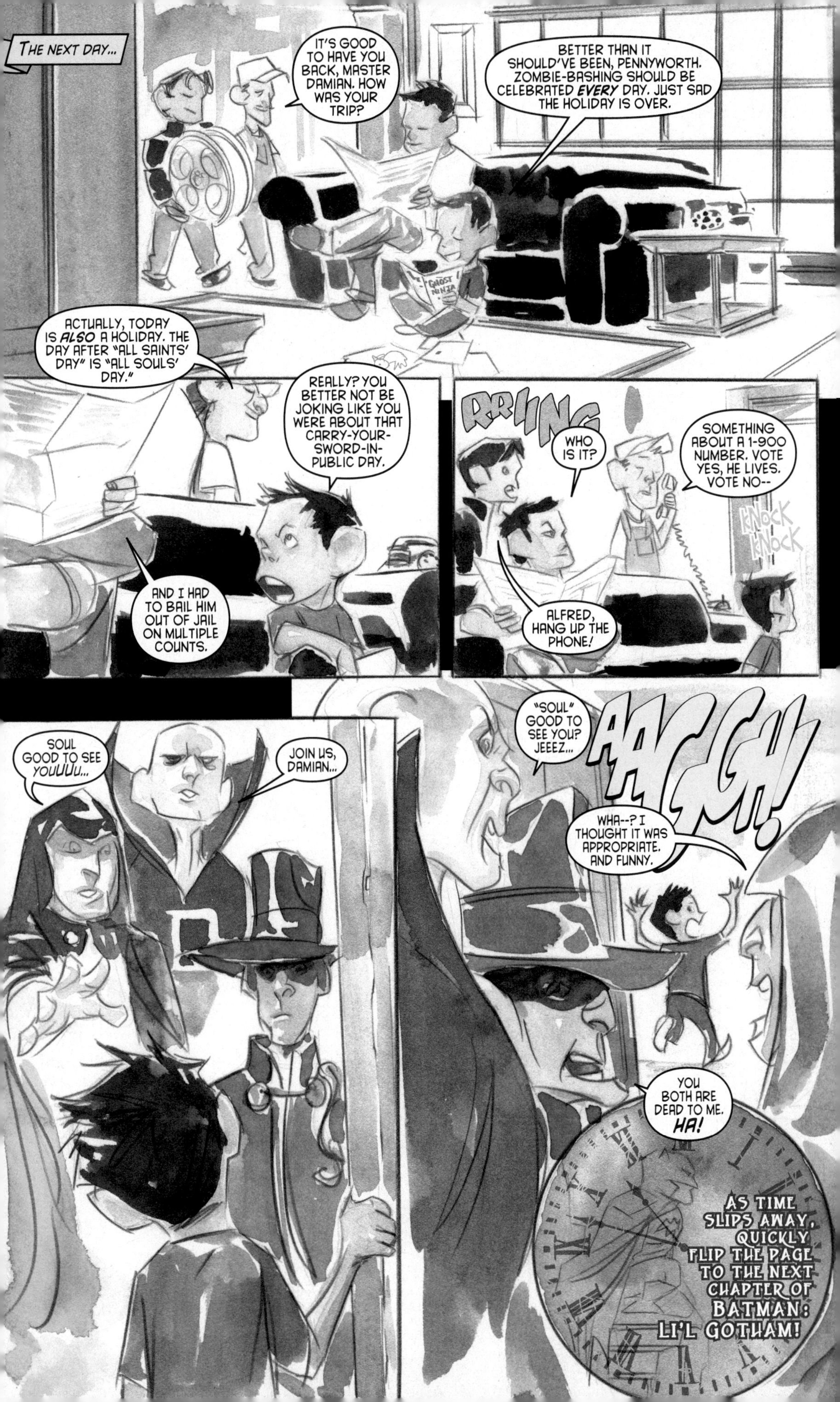
THE NEXT DAY...
IT'S GOOD TO HAVE YOU BACK, MASTER DAMIAN. HOW WAS YOUR TRIP?
BETTER THAN IT SHOULD'VE BEEN, PENNYWORTH. ZOMBIE-BASHING SHOULD BE CELEBRATED EVERY DAY. JUST SAD THE HOLIDAY IS OVER.
GHOST NINJA
ACTUALLY, TODAY IS ALSO A HOLIDAY. THE DAY AFTER "ALL SAINTS' DAY" IS "ALL SOULS' DAY."
REALLY? YOU BETTER NOT BE JOKING LIKE YOU WERE ABOUT THAT CARRY-YOUR-SWORD-IN-PUBLIC DAY.
AND I HAD TO BAIL HIM OUT OF JAIL ON MULTIPLE COUNTS.
RRIING
WHO IS IT?
SOMETHING ABOUT A 1-900 NUMBER. VOTE YES, HE LIVES. VOTE NO--
KNOCK KNOCK
ALFRED, HANG UP THE PHONE!
SOUL GOOD TO SEE YOUUUu...
JOIN US, DAMIAN...
"SOUL" GOOD TO SEE YOU? JEEEZ...
AAAGH!
WHA--? I THOUGHT IT WAS APPROPRIATE. AND FUNNY.
YOU BOTH ARE DEAD TO ME. HA!
AS TIME SLIPS AWAY, QUICKLY FLIP THE PAGE TO THE NEXT CHAPTER OF BATMAN: LI'L GOTHAM!

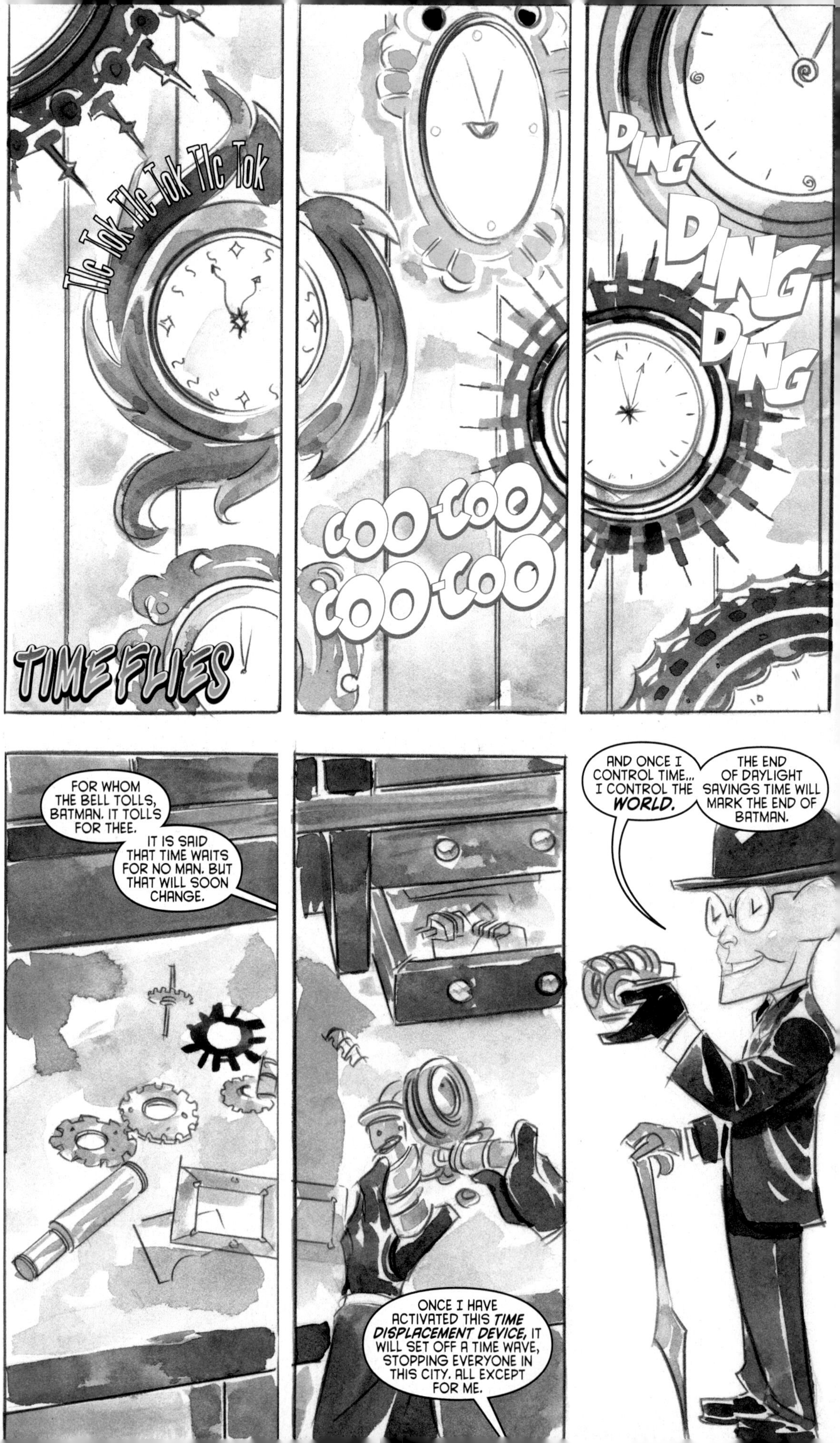
TIC TOK TIC TOK TIC TOK
TIME FLIES
COO-COO
COO-COO
DING
DING
DING
DING
FOR WHOM THE BELL TOLLS, BATMAN. IT TOLLS FOR THEE.
IT IS SAID THAT TIME WAITS FOR NO MAN. BUT THAT WILL SOON CHANGE.
ONCE I HAVE ACTIVATED THIS *TIME DISPLACEMENT DEVICE,* IT WILL SET OFF A TIME WAVE, STOPPING EVERYONE IN THIS CITY. ALL EXCEPT FOR ME.
AND ONCE I CONTROL TIME... I CONTROL THE *WORLD.*
THE END OF DAYLIGHT SAVINGS TIME WILL MARK THE END OF BATMAN.

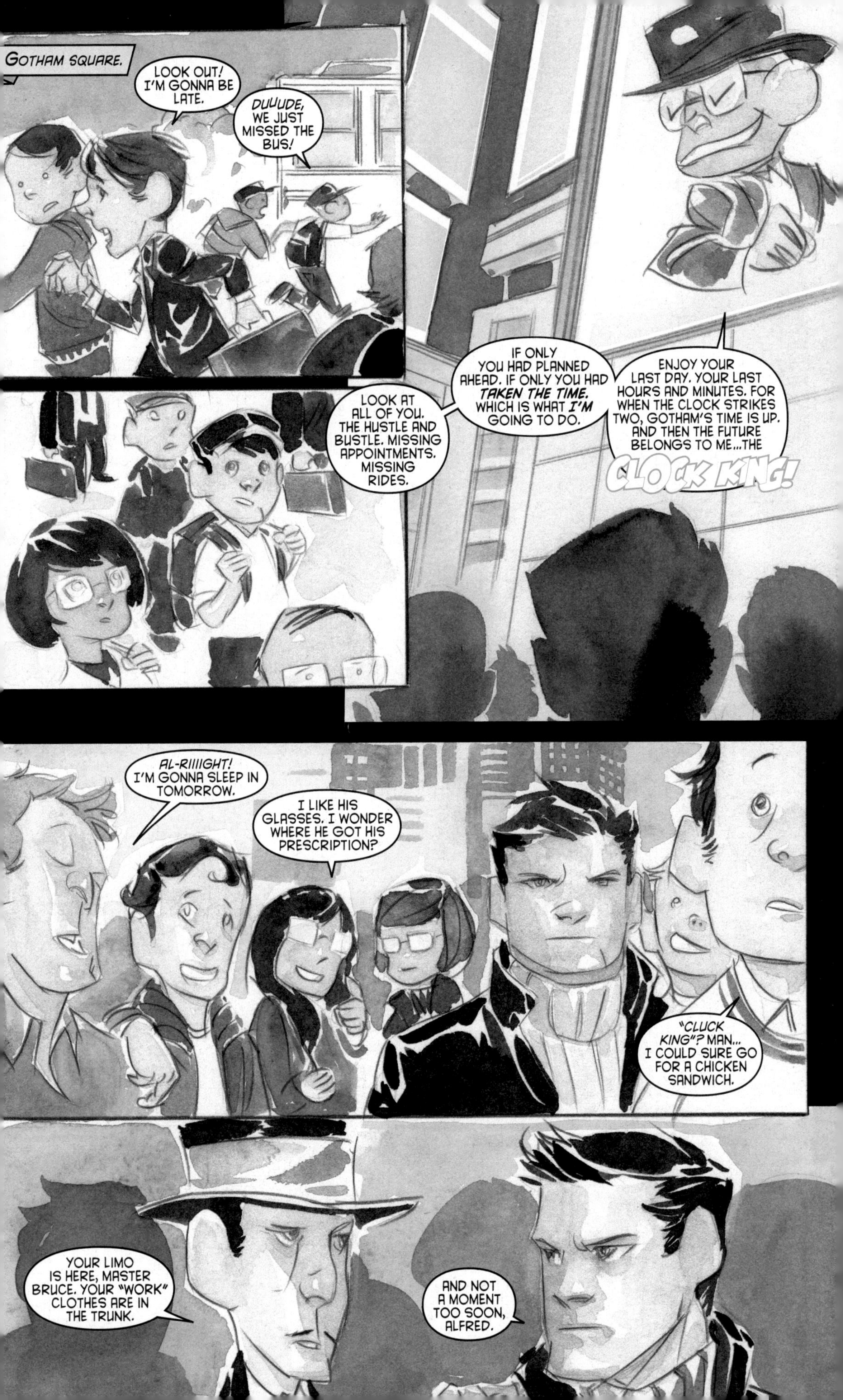
GOTHAM SQUARE.
LOOK OUT! I'M GONNA BE LATE.
DUUUDE, WE JUST MISSED THE BUS!
LOOK AT ALL OF YOU. THE HUSTLE AND BUSTLE. MISSING APPOINTMENTS. MISSING RIDES.
IF ONLY YOU HAD PLANNED AHEAD. IF ONLY YOU HAD TAKEN THE TIME. WHICH IS WHAT I'M GOING TO DO.
ENJOY YOUR LAST DAY. YOUR LAST HOURS AND MINUTES. FOR WHEN THE CLOCK STRIKES TWO, GOTHAM'S TIME IS UP. AND THEN THE FUTURE BELONGS TO ME...THE
CLOCK KING!
AL-RIIIIGHT! I'M GONNA SLEEP IN TOMORROW.
I LIKE HIS GLASSES. I WONDER WHERE HE GOT HIS PRESCRIPTION?
"CLUCK KING"? MAN... I COULD SURE GO FOR A CHICKEN SANDWICH.
YOUR LIMO IS HERE, MASTER BRUCE. YOUR "WORK" CLOTHES ARE IN THE TRUNK.
AND NOT A MOMENT TOO SOON, ALFRED.

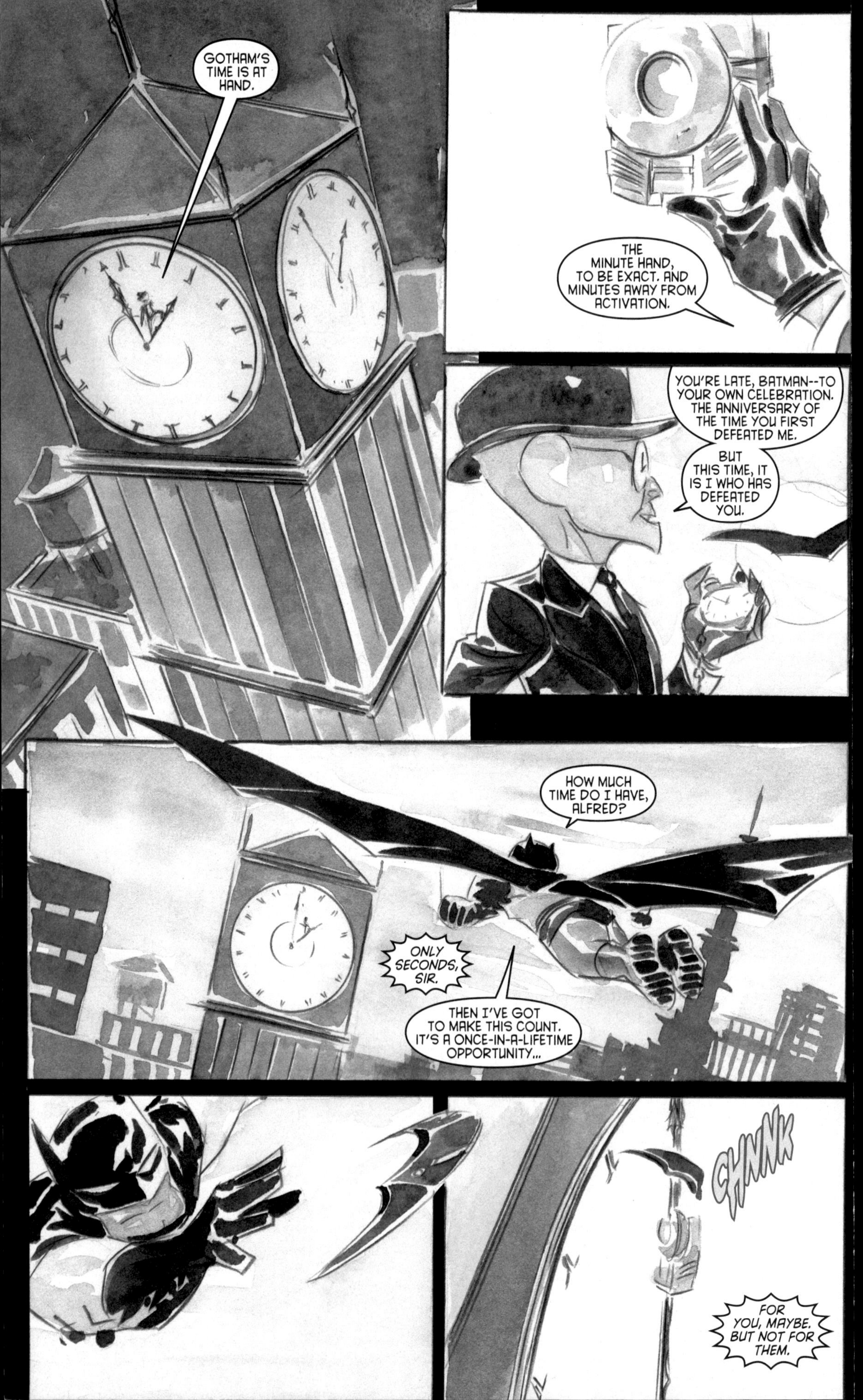
GOTHAM'S TIME IS AT HAND.
THE MINUTE HAND, TO BE EXACT. AND MINUTES AWAY FROM ACTIVATION.
YOU'RE LATE, BATMAN--TO YOUR OWN CELEBRATION. THE ANNIVERSARY OF THE TIME YOU FIRST DEFEATED ME.
BUT THIS TIME, IT IS I WHO HAS DEFEATED YOU.
HOW MUCH TIME DO I HAVE, ALFRED?
ONLY SECONDS, SIR.
THEN I'VE GOT TO MAKE THIS COUNT. IT'S A ONCE-IN-A-LIFETIME OPPORTUNITY...
CHNNK
FOR YOU, MAYBE. BUT NOT FOR THEM.

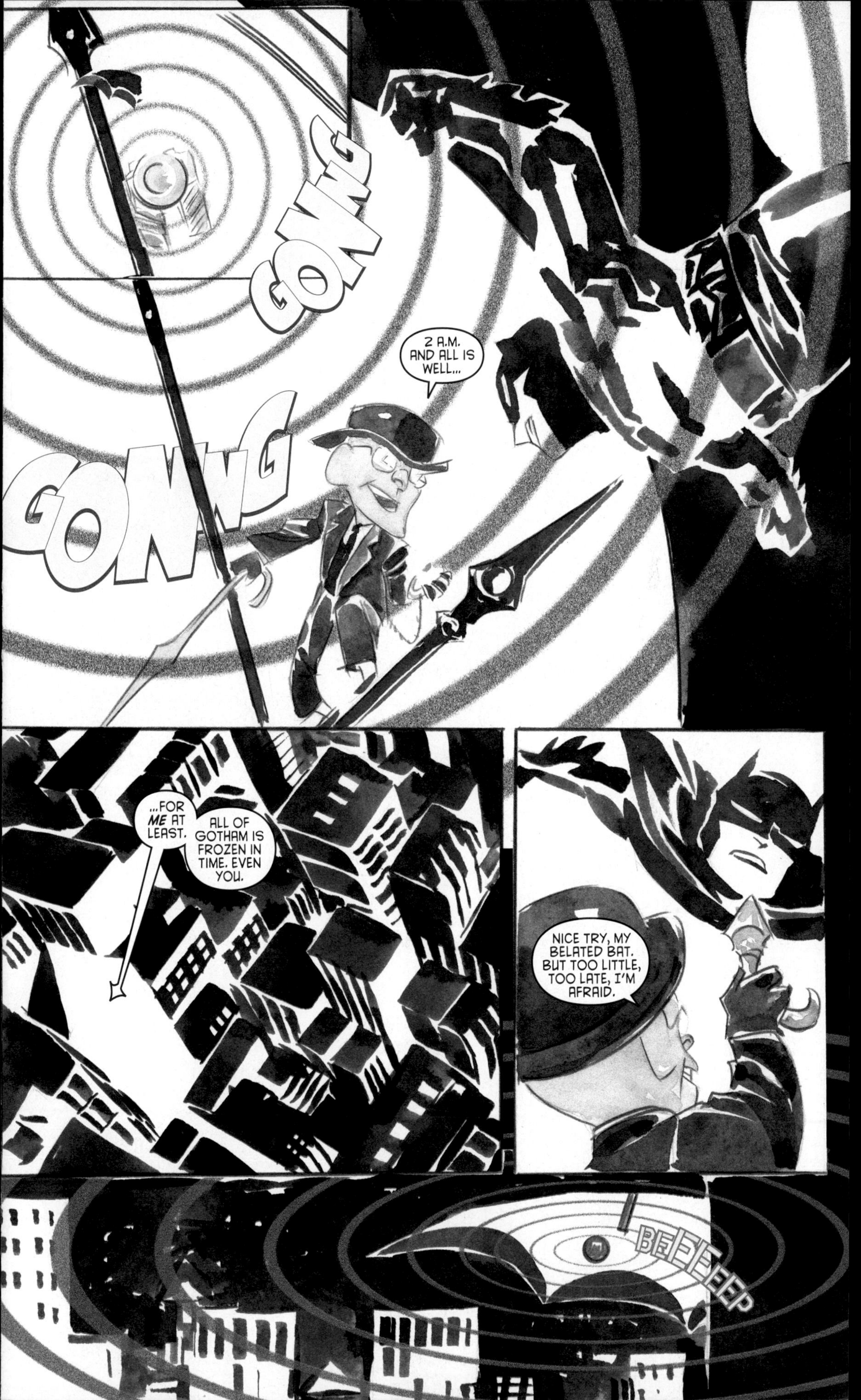
GONNG
GONNG
2 A.M. AND ALL IS WELL...
...FOR *ME* AT LEAST.
ALL OF GOTHAM IS FROZEN IN TIME. EVEN YOU.
NICE TRY, MY BELATED BAT. BUT TOO LITTLE, TOO LATE, I'M AFRAID.
BEEEEEP

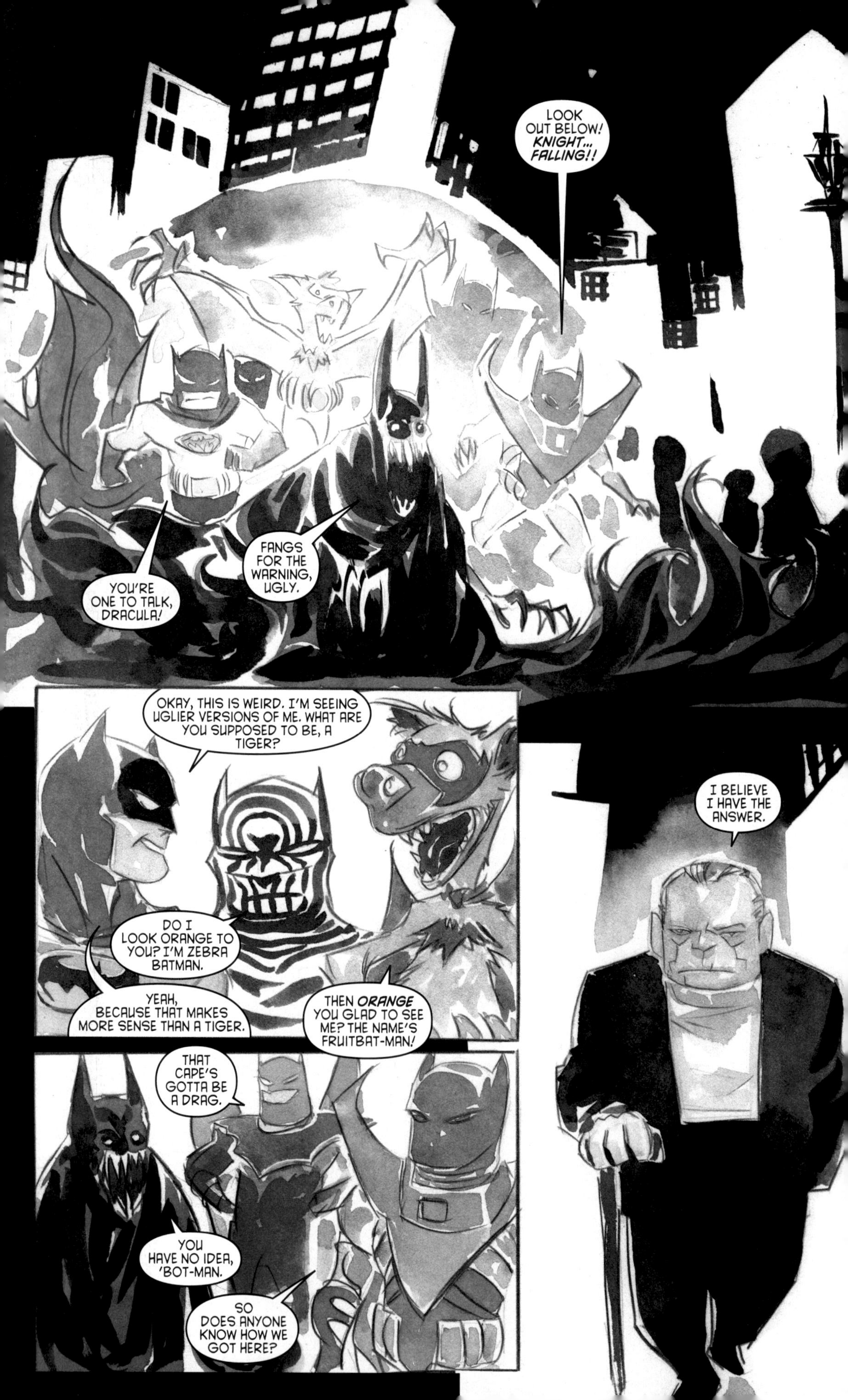
LOOK OUT BELOW! KNIGHT... FALLING!!
FANGS FOR THE WARNING, UGLY.
YOU'RE ONE TO TALK, DRACULA!
OKAY, THIS IS WEIRD. I'M SEEING UGLIER VERSIONS OF ME. WHAT ARE YOU SUPPOSED TO BE, A TIGER?
DO I LOOK ORANGE TO YOU? I'M ZEBRA BATMAN.
YEAH, BECAUSE THAT MAKES MORE SENSE THAN A TIGER.
THEN ORANGE YOU GLAD TO SEE ME? THE NAME'S FRUITBAT-MAN!
THAT CAPE'S GOTTA BE A DRAG.
YOU HAVE NO IDEA, 'BOT-MAN.
SO DOES ANYONE KNOW HOW WE GOT HERE?
I BELIEVE I HAVE THE ANSWER.

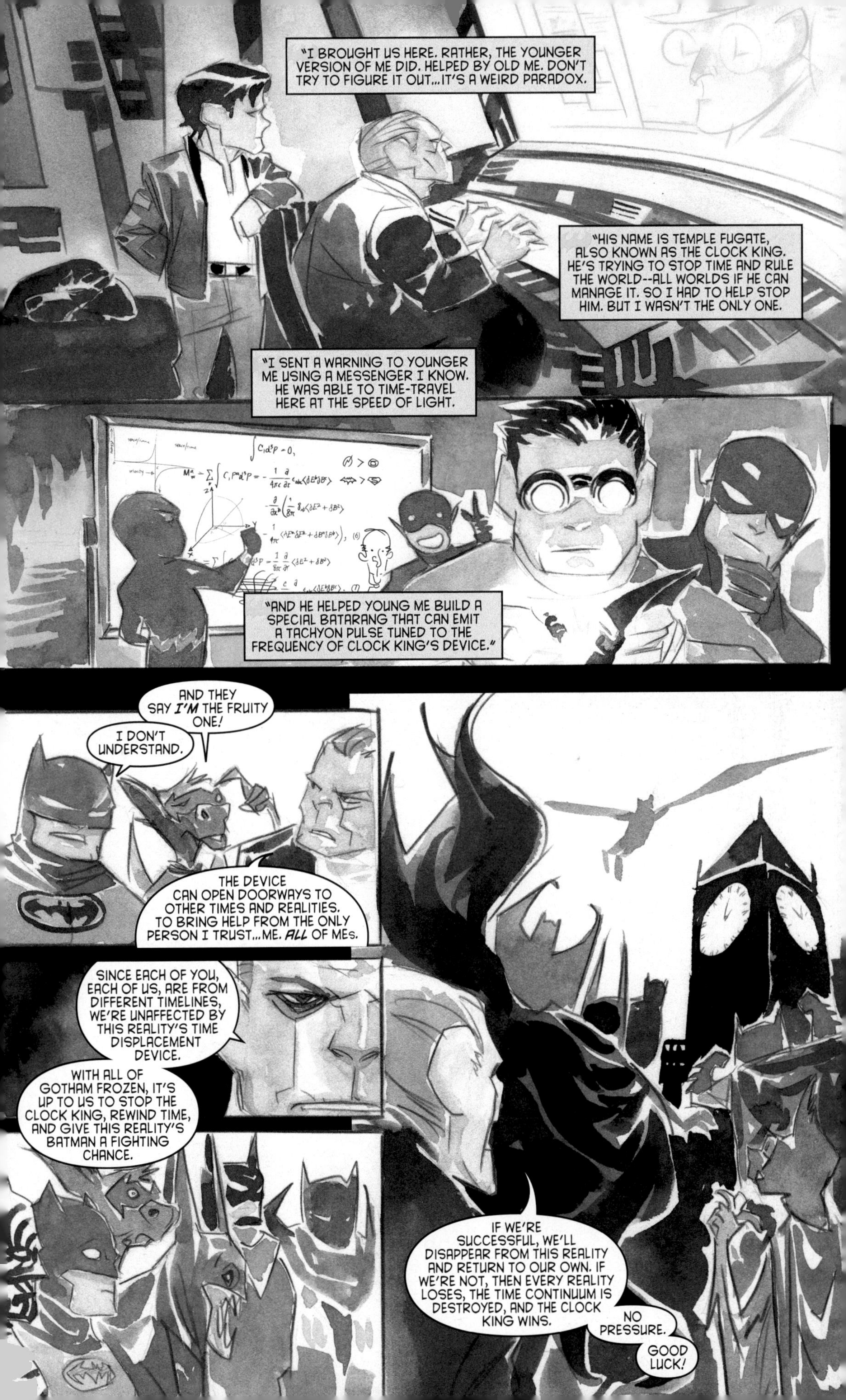
"I BROUGHT US HERE. RATHER, THE YOUNGER VERSION OF ME DID. HELPED BY OLD ME. DON'T TRY TO FIGURE IT OUT... IT'S A WEIRD PARADOX.
"HIS NAME IS TEMPLE FUGATE, ALSO KNOWN AS THE CLOCK KING. HE'S TRYING TO STOP TIME AND RULE THE WORLD--ALL WORLDS IF HE CAN MANAGE IT. SO I HAD TO HELP STOP HIM. BUT I WASN'T THE ONLY ONE.
"I SENT A WARNING TO YOUNGER ME USING A MESSENGER I KNOW. HE WAS ABLE TO TIME-TRAVEL HERE AT THE SPEED OF LIGHT.
"AND HE HELPED YOUNG ME BUILD A SPECIAL BATARANG THAT CAN EMIT A TACHYON PULSE TUNED TO THE FREQUENCY OF CLOCK KING'S DEVICE."
AND THEY SAY *I'M* THE FRUITY ONE!
I DON'T UNDERSTAND.
THE DEVICE CAN OPEN DOORWAYS TO OTHER TIMES AND REALITIES. TO BRING HELP FROM THE ONLY PERSON I TRUST... ME. ***ALL*** OF MEs.
SINCE EACH OF YOU, EACH OF US, ARE FROM DIFFERENT TIMELINES, WE'RE UNAFFECTED BY THIS REALITY'S TIME DISPLACEMENT DEVICE.
WITH ALL OF GOTHAM FROZEN, IT'S UP TO US TO STOP THE CLOCK KING, REWIND TIME, AND GIVE THIS REALITY'S BATMAN A FIGHTING CHANCE.
IF WE'RE SUCCESSFUL, WE'LL DISAPPEAR FROM THIS REALITY AND RETURN TO OUR OWN. IF WE'RE NOT, THEN EVERY REALITY LOSES, THE TIME CONTINUUM IS DESTROYED, AND THE CLOCK KING WINS.
NO PRESSURE.
GOOD LUCK!

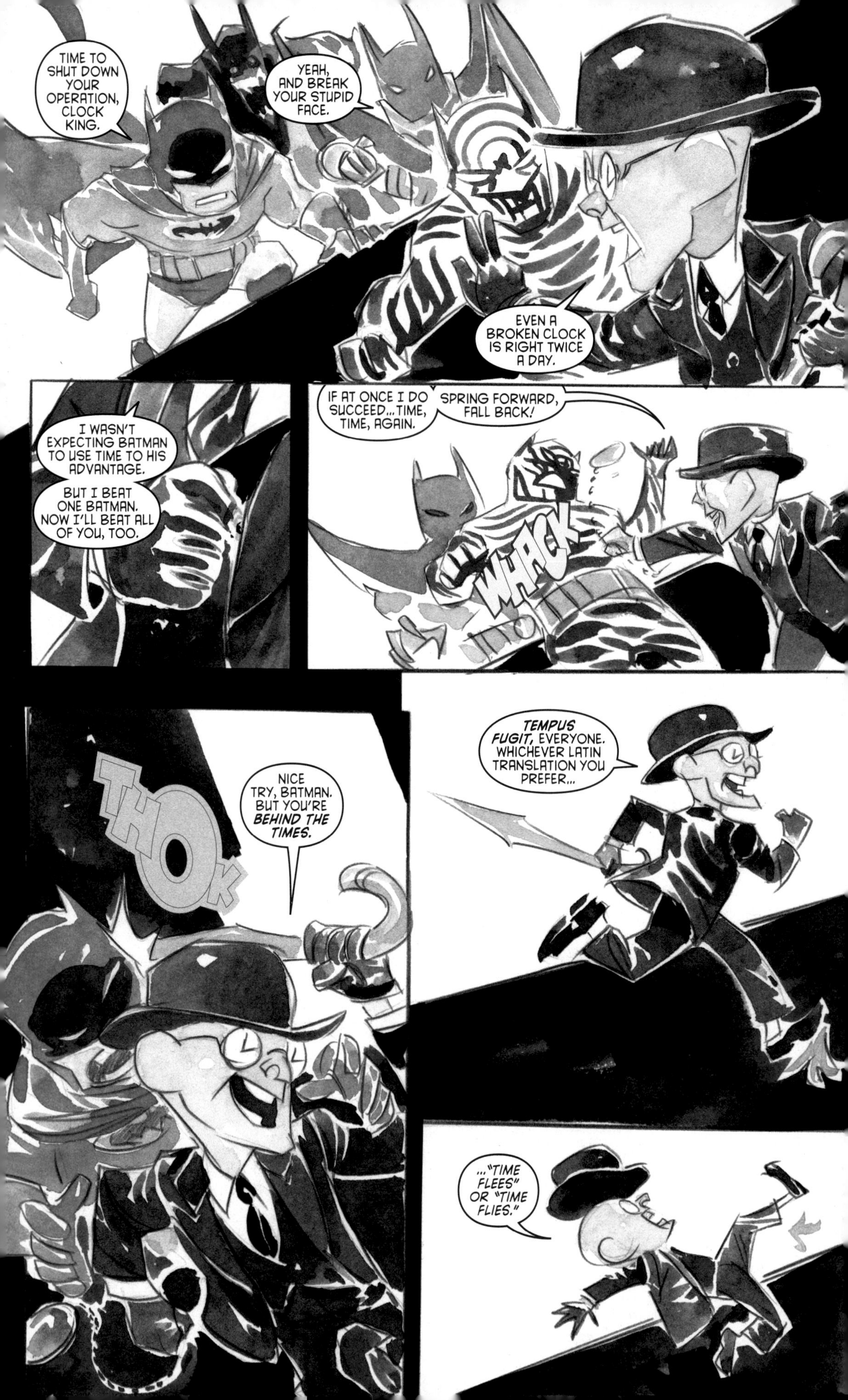
TIME TO SHUT DOWN YOUR OPERATION, CLOCK KING.
YEAH, AND BREAK YOUR STUPID FACE.
EVEN A BROKEN CLOCK IS RIGHT TWICE A DAY.
I WASN'T EXPECTING BATMAN TO USE TIME TO HIS ADVANTAGE.
BUT I BEAT ONE BATMAN. NOW I'LL BEAT ALL OF YOU, TOO.
IF AT ONCE I DO SUCCEED... TIME, TIME, AGAIN.
SPRING FORWARD, FALL BACK!
WHACK
THOK
NICE TRY, BATMAN. BUT YOU'RE *BEHIND THE TIMES.*
TEMPUS FUGIT, EVERYONE. WHICHEVER LATIN TRANSLATION YOU PREFER...
..."*TIME FLEES*" OR "*TIME FLIES.*"

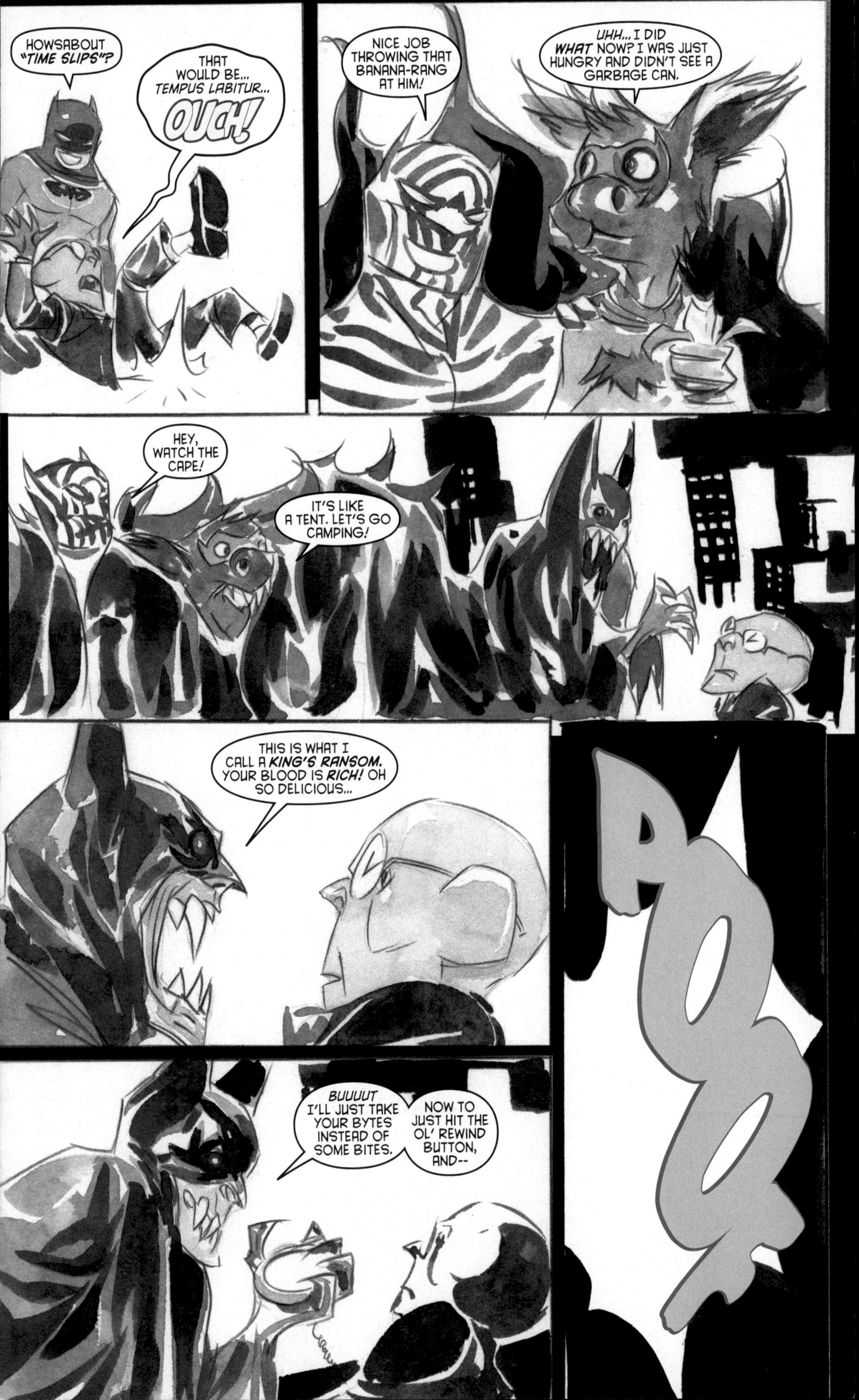
HOWSABOUT "TIME SLIPS"?
THAT WOULD BE... TEMPUS LABITUR...
OUCH!
NICE JOB THROWING THAT BANANA-RANG AT HIM!
UHH... I DID WHAT NOW? I WAS JUST HUNGRY AND DIDN'T SEE A GARBAGE CAN.
HEY, WATCH THE CAPE!
IT'S LIKE A TENT. LET'S GO CAMPING!
THIS IS WHAT I CALL A KING'S RANSOM. YOUR BLOOD IS RICH! OH SO DELICIOUS...
BUUUUT I'LL JUST TAKE YOUR BYTES INSTEAD OF SOME BITES.
NOW TO JUST HIT THE OL' REWIND BUTTON, AND--

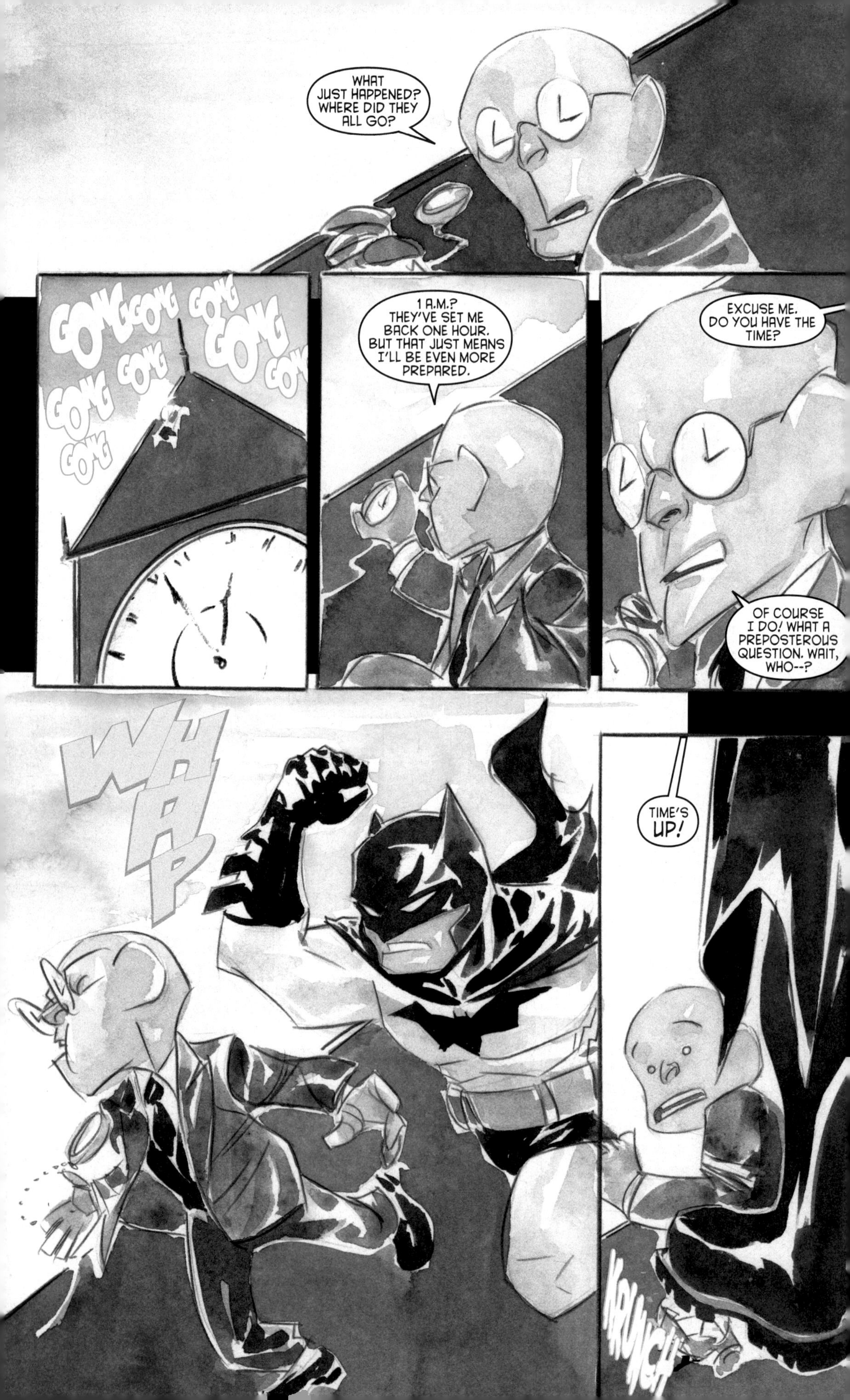

WHAT JUST HAPPENED? WHERE DID THEY ALL GO?
GONG GONG GONG GONG GONG GONG GONG GONG
1 A.M.? THEY'VE SET ME BACK ONE HOUR. BUT THAT JUST MEANS I'LL BE EVEN MORE PREPARED.
EXCUSE ME. DO YOU HAVE THE TIME?
OF COURSE I DO! WHAT A PREPOSTEROUS QUESTION. WAIT, WHO--?
WHAP
TIME'S UP!
KRUNCH

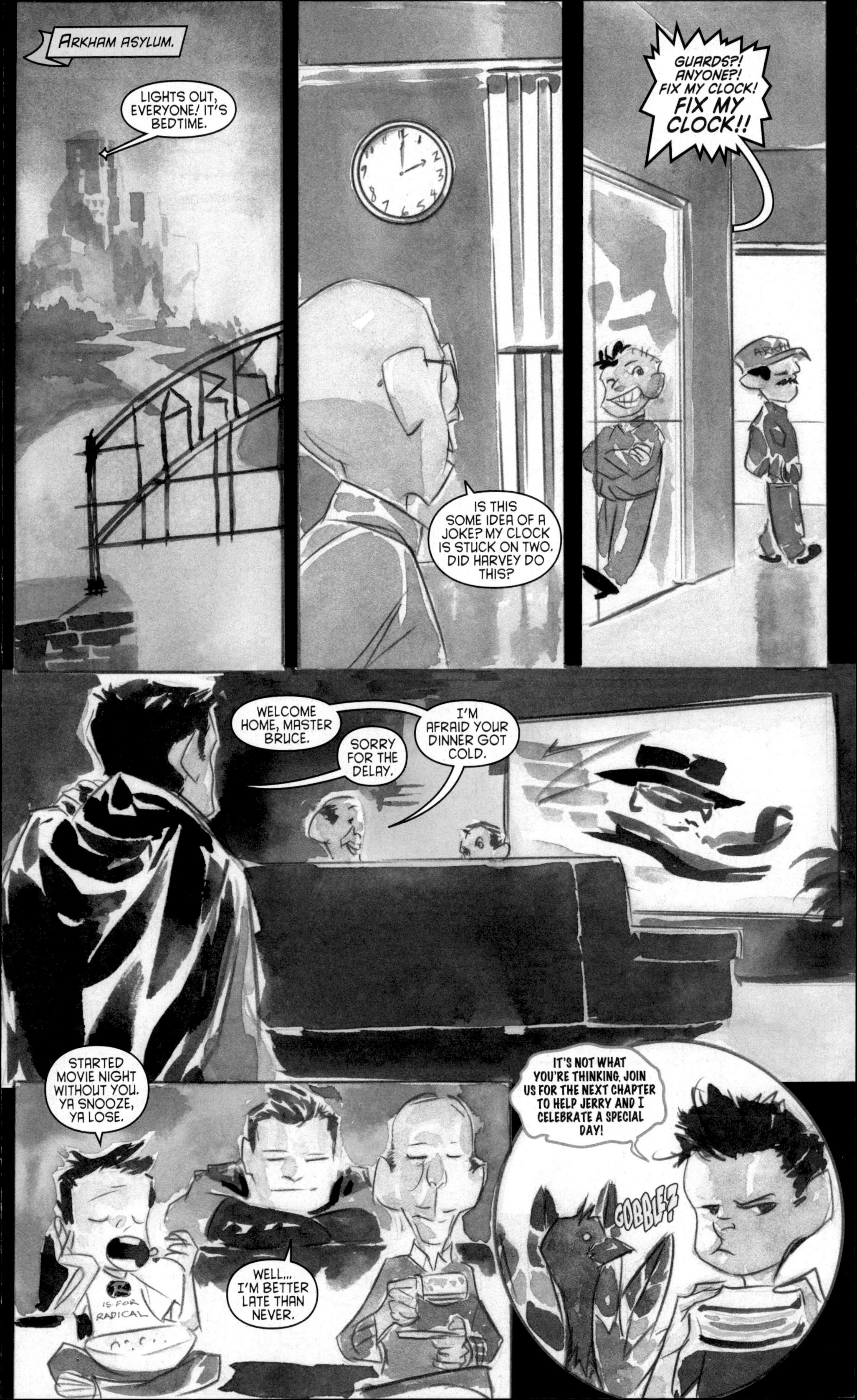
ARKHAM ASYLUM.
LIGHTS OUT, EVERYONE! IT'S BEDTIME.
IS THIS SOME IDEA OF A JOKE? MY CLOCK IS STUCK ON TWO. DID HARVEY DO THIS?
GUARDS?! ANYONE?! FIX MY CLOCK! FIX MY CLOCK!!
WELCOME HOME, MASTER BRUCE.
SORRY FOR THE DELAY.
I'M AFRAID YOUR DINNER GOT COLD.
STARTED MOVIE NIGHT WITHOUT YOU. YA SNOOZE, YA LOSE.
IS FOR RADICAL
WELL... I'M BETTER LATE THAN NEVER.
IT'S NOT WHAT YOU'RE THINKING. JOIN US FOR THE NEXT CHAPTER TO HELP JERRY AND I CELEBRATE A SPECIAL DAY!
GOBBLE?

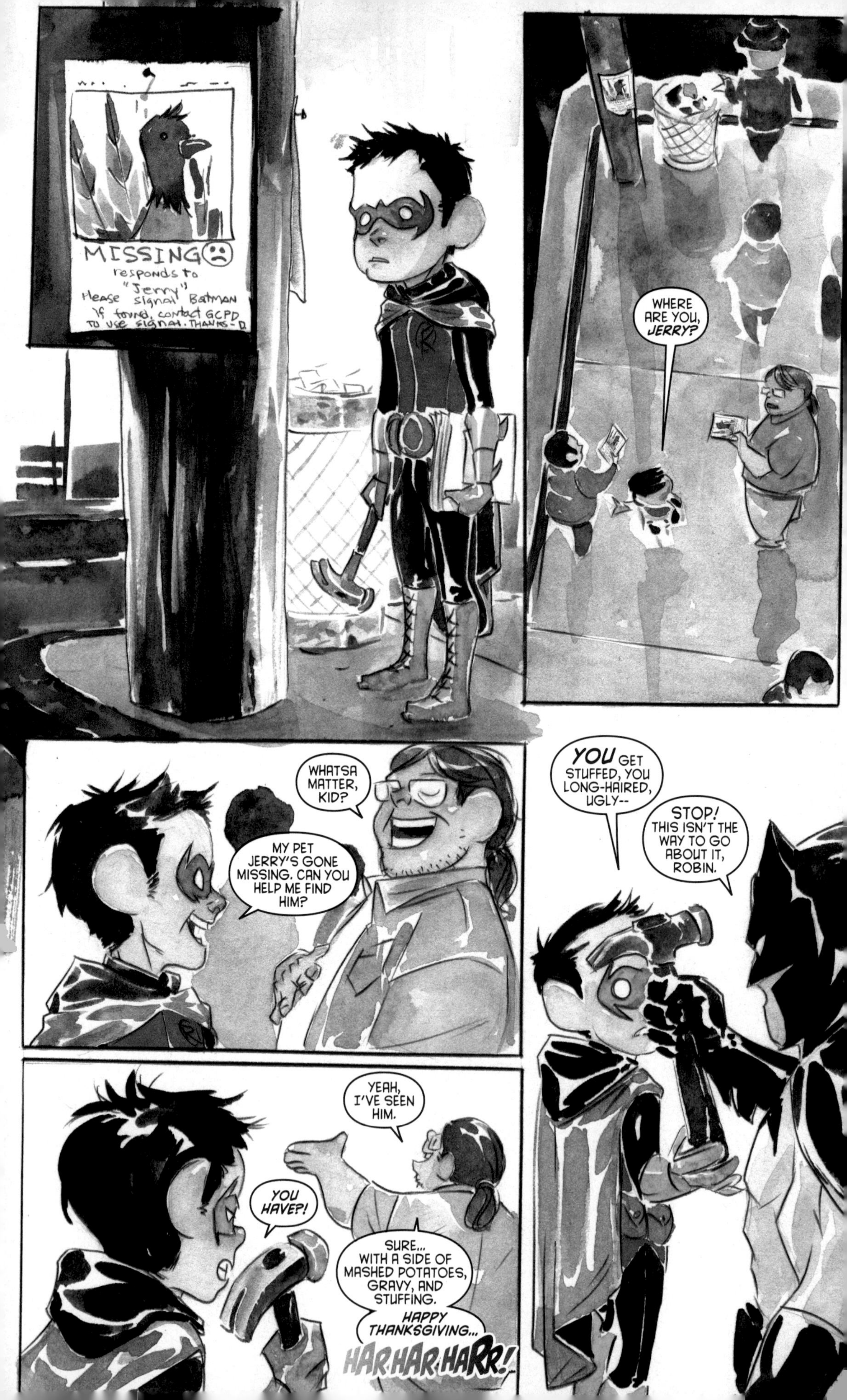
MISSING
responds to "Jerry"
Please signal Batman
If found, contact GCPD to use signal. THANKS - D.
WHERE ARE YOU, JERRY?
WHATSA MATTER, KID?
MY PET JERRY'S GONE MISSING. CAN YOU HELP ME FIND HIM?
YEAH, I'VE SEEN HIM.
YOU HAVE?!
SURE... WITH A SIDE OF MASHED POTATOES, GRAVY, AND STUFFING.
HAPPY THANKSGIVING...
HAR HAR HARR!
YOU GET STUFFED, YOU LONG-HAIRED, UGLY--
STOP! THIS ISN'T THE WAY TO GO ABOUT IT, ROBIN.

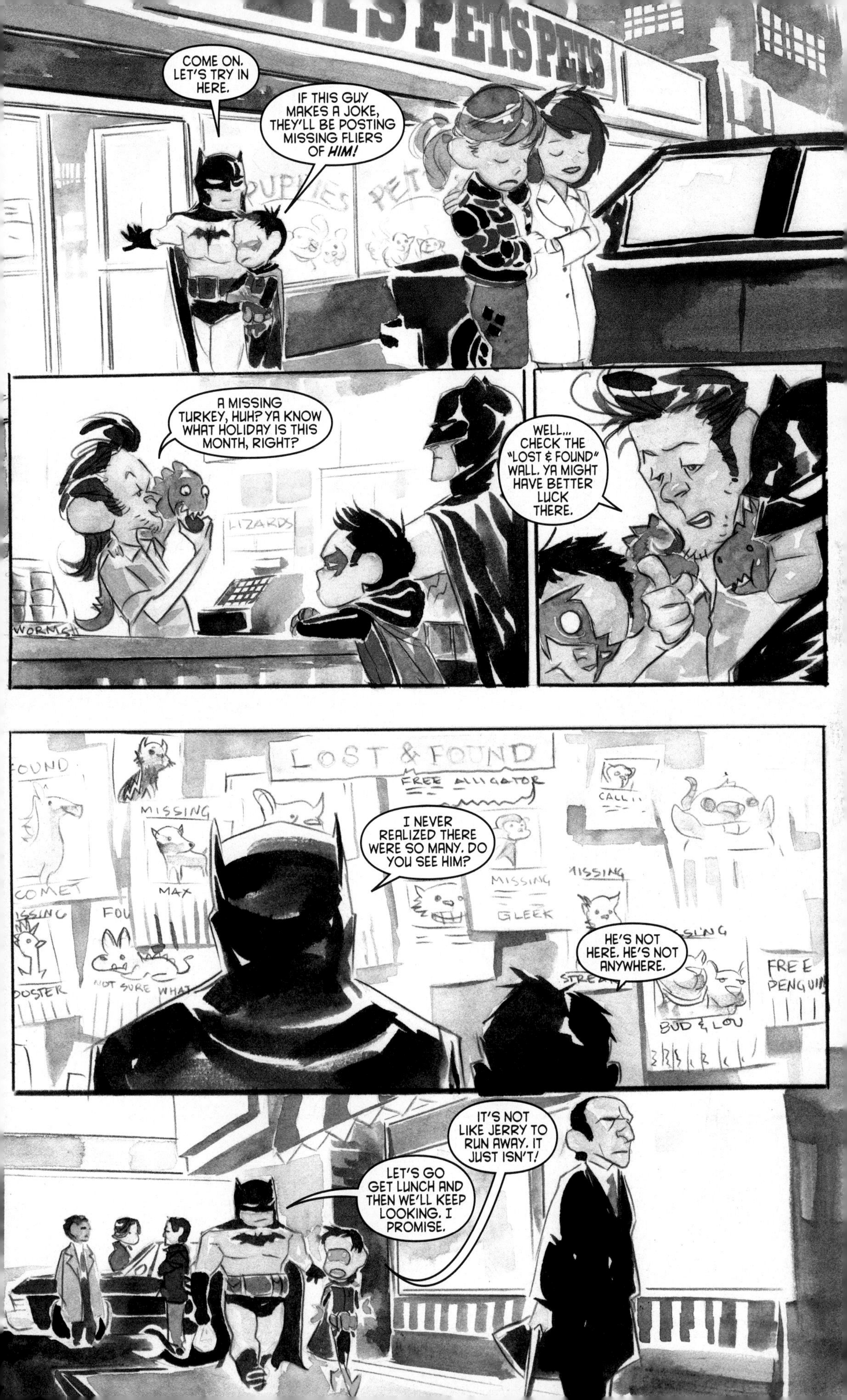
PETS PETS
COME ON. LET'S TRY IN HERE.
IF THIS GUY MAKES A JOKE, THEY'LL BE POSTING MISSING FLIERS OF *HIM!*
PUPPIES
A MISSING TURKEY, HUH? YA KNOW WHAT HOLIDAY IS THIS MONTH, RIGHT?
LIZARDS
WORMS
WELL... CHECK THE "LOST & FOUND" WALL. YA MIGHT HAVE BETTER LUCK THERE.
LOST & FOUND
FREE ALLIGATOR
MISSING
MAX
COMET
GLEEK
NOT SURE WHAT
BUD & LOU
FREE PENGUIN
I NEVER REALIZED THERE WERE SO MANY. DO YOU SEE HIM?
HE'S NOT HERE. HE'S NOT ANYWHERE.
IT'S NOT LIKE JERRY TO RUN AWAY. IT JUST ISN'T!
LET'S GO GET LUNCH AND THEN WE'LL KEEP LOOKING. I PROMISE.

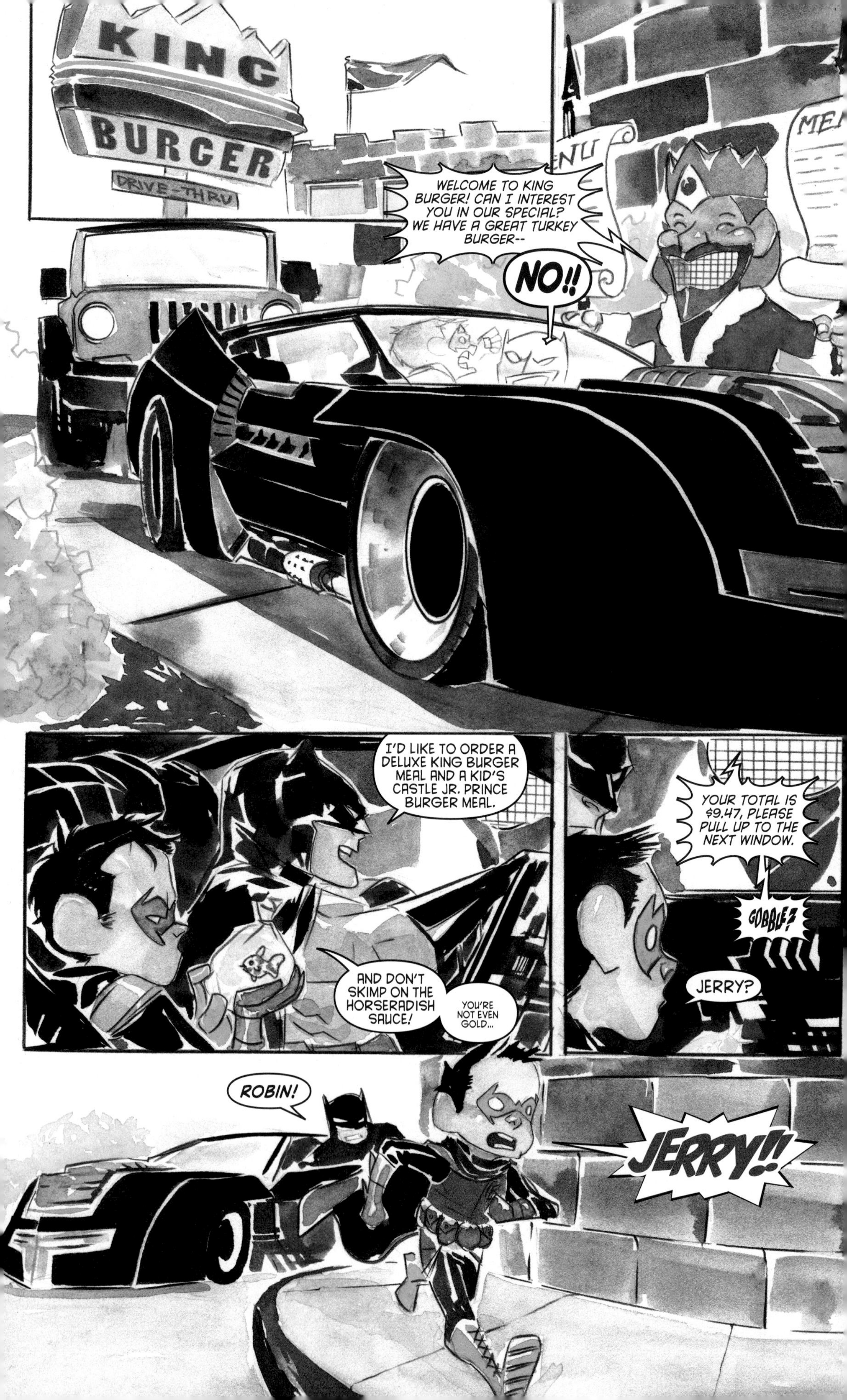
KING
BURGER
DRIVE-THRU
MENU
WELCOME TO KING BURGER! CAN I INTEREST YOU IN OUR SPECIAL? WE HAVE A GREAT TURKEY BURGER--
NO!!
I'D LIKE TO ORDER A DELUXE KING BURGER MEAL AND A KID'S CASTLE JR. PRINCE BURGER MEAL.
AND DON'T SKIMP ON THE HORSERADISH SAUCE!
YOU'RE NOT EVEN GOLD...
YOUR TOTAL IS $9.47, PLEASE PULL UP TO THE NEXT WINDOW.
GOBBLE?
JERRY?
ROBIN!
JERRY!!

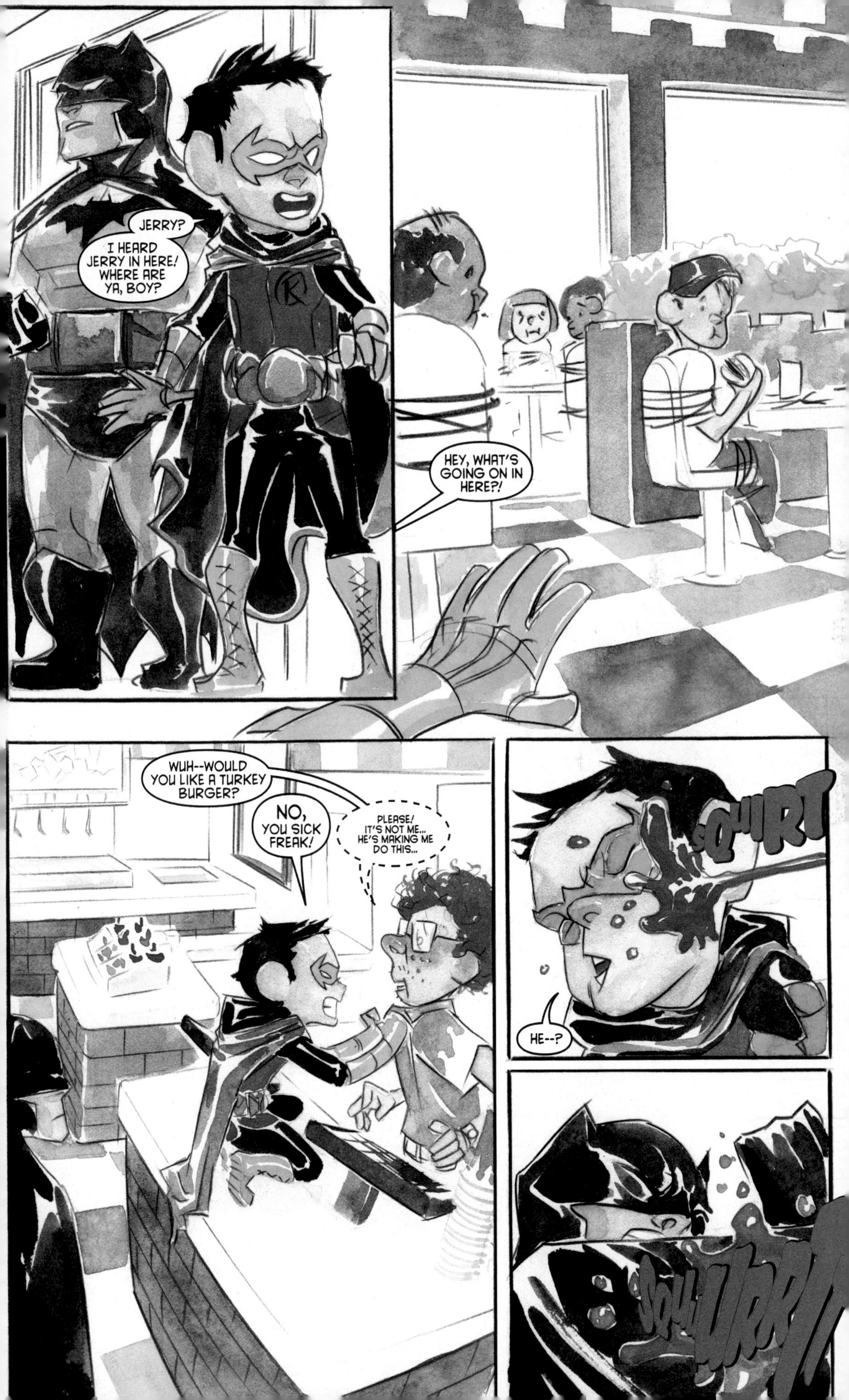
JERRY?
I HEARD JERRY IN HERE! WHERE ARE YA, BOY?
HEY, WHAT'S GOING ON IN HERE?!
WUH--WOULD YOU LIKE A TURKEY BURGER?
NO, YOU SICK FREAK!
PLEASE! IT'S NOT ME... HE'S MAKING ME DO THIS...
SQUIRT
HE--?

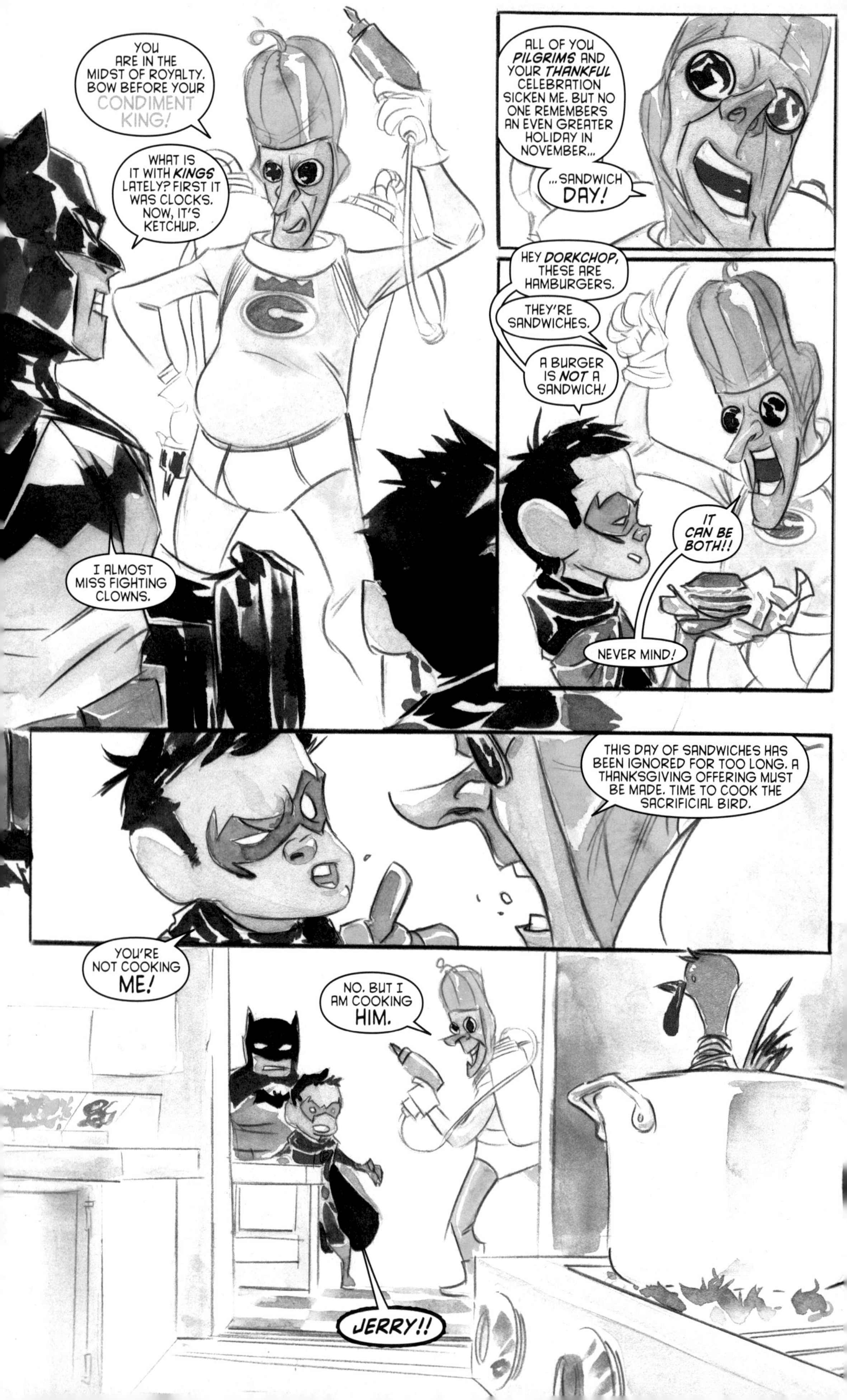
YOU ARE IN THE MIDST OF ROYALTY. BOW BEFORE YOUR CONDIMENT KING!
WHAT IS IT WITH KINGS LATELY? FIRST IT WAS CLOCKS. NOW, IT'S KETCHUP.
I ALMOST MISS FIGHTING CLOWNS.
ALL OF YOU PILGRIMS AND YOUR THANKFUL CELEBRATION SICKEN ME. BUT NO ONE REMEMBERS AN EVEN GREATER HOLIDAY IN NOVEMBER...
...SANDWICH DAY!
HEY DORKCHOP, THESE ARE HAMBURGERS.
THEY'RE SANDWICHES.
A BURGER IS NOT A SANDWICH!
IT CAN BE BOTH!!
NEVER MIND!
THIS DAY OF SANDWICHES HAS BEEN IGNORED FOR TOO LONG. A THANKSGIVING OFFERING MUST BE MADE. TIME TO COOK THE SACRIFICIAL BIRD.
YOU'RE NOT COOKING ME!
NO. BUT I AM COOKING HIM.
JERRY!!

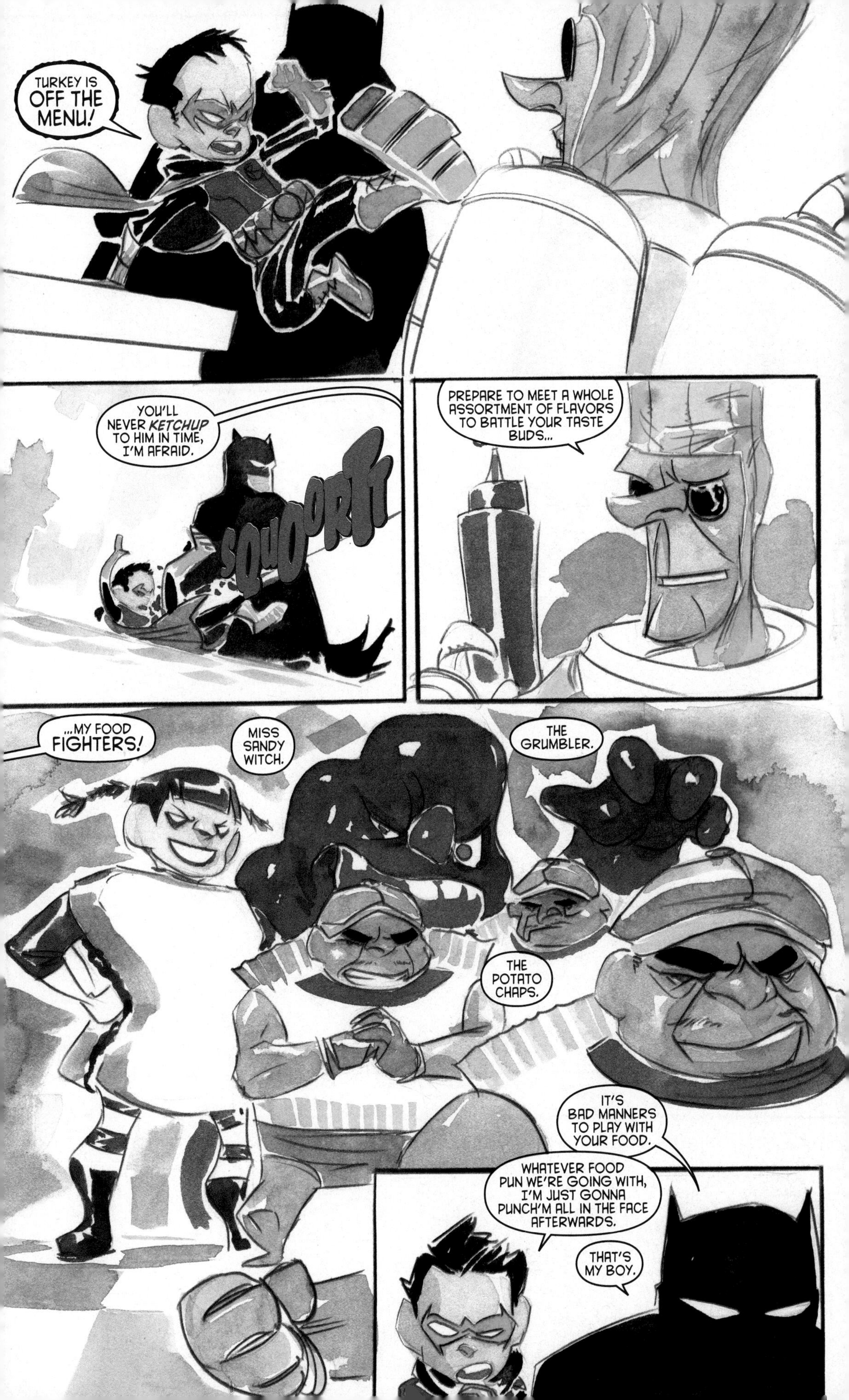
TURKEY IS OFF THE MENU!
YOU'LL NEVER *KETCHUP* TO HIM IN TIME, I'M AFRAID.
SQUOORTT
PREPARE TO MEET A WHOLE ASSORTMENT OF FLAVORS TO BATTLE YOUR TASTE BUDS...
...MY FOOD FIGHTERS!
MISS SANDY WITCH.
THE GRUMBLER.
THE POTATO CHAPS.
IT'S BAD MANNERS TO PLAY WITH YOUR FOOD.
WHATEVER FOOD PUN WE'RE GOING WITH, I'M JUST GONNA PUNCH'M ALL IN THE FACE AFTERWARDS.
THAT'S MY BOY.

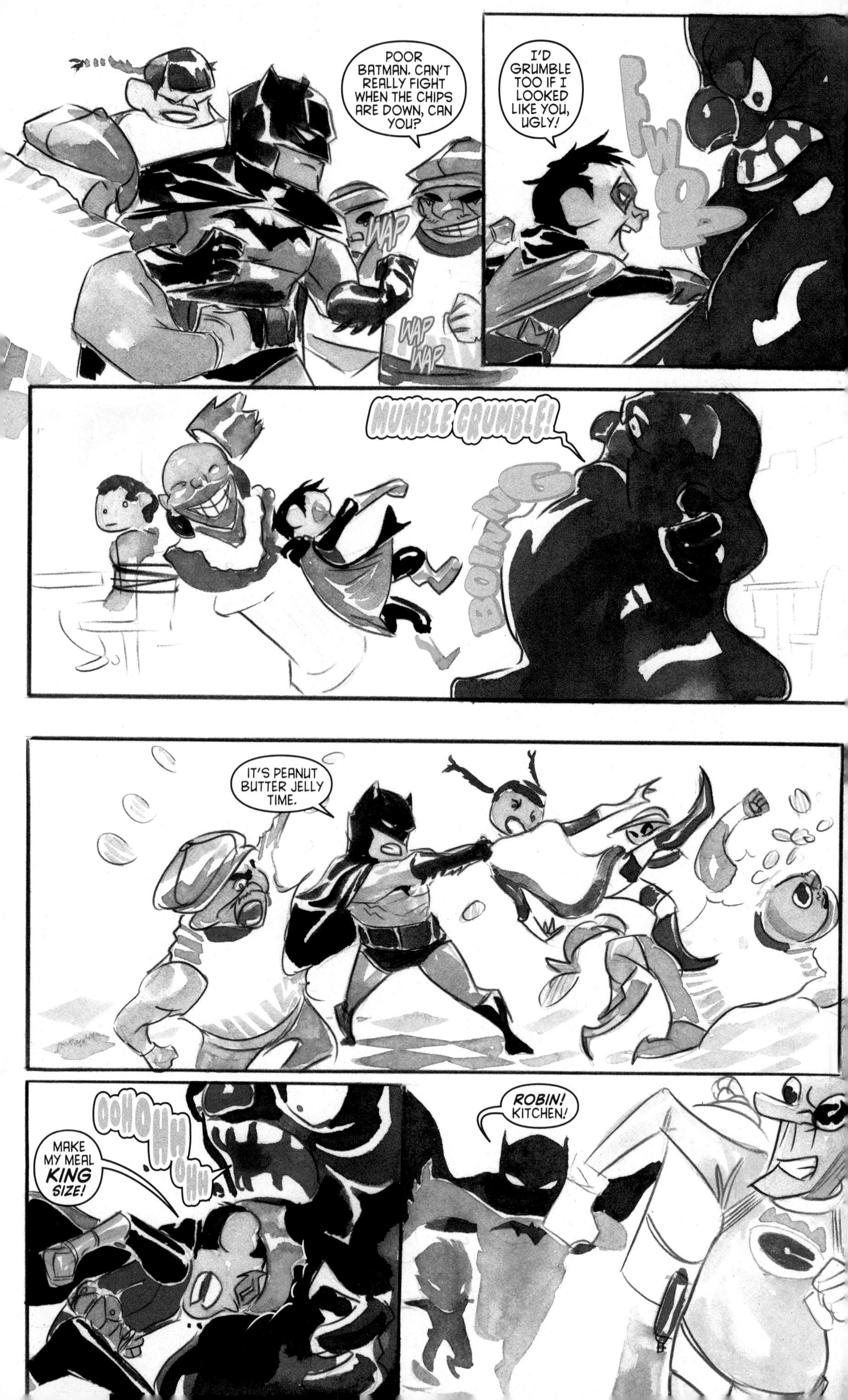

POOR BATMAN. CAN'T REALLY FIGHT WHEN THE CHIPS ARE DOWN, CAN YOU?
WAP
WAP WAP
I'D GRUMBLE TOO IF I LOOKED LIKE YOU, UGLY!
FWOOP
MUMBLE GRUMBLE!
BOING
IT'S PEANUT BUTTER JELLY TIME.
OOHOHHHOHH
MAKE MY MEAL KING SIZE!
ROBIN! KITCHEN!

TAKE A SEAT AND RELISH THIS MOMENT, MY DYNAMIC DUMPLINGS!

FEELING HOT? YOU SHOULD. THAT'S GROUND TRINIDAD MORUGA SCORPION PEPPER IN YOUR EYES.

SKRAH ssss SHH

WHAT A SWEET AROMA! I BELIEVE HIS GOOSE IS ALMOST COOKED.

QUITE THE PICKLE YOU'RE IN.

AND NOW, PREPARE FOR MY SPECIAL MOLTEN BBQ SAUCE. THE SECRET INGREDIENT... IS NITROGEN!

AAAAH!

GOBBLE DOBBLE!

SPLOO

IT BURRRNS!

WHO'S THE TURKEY NOW, NERDLOAF?!

GOBBLE

BROTH'D DOWN BY AN INFERNAL BIRD!

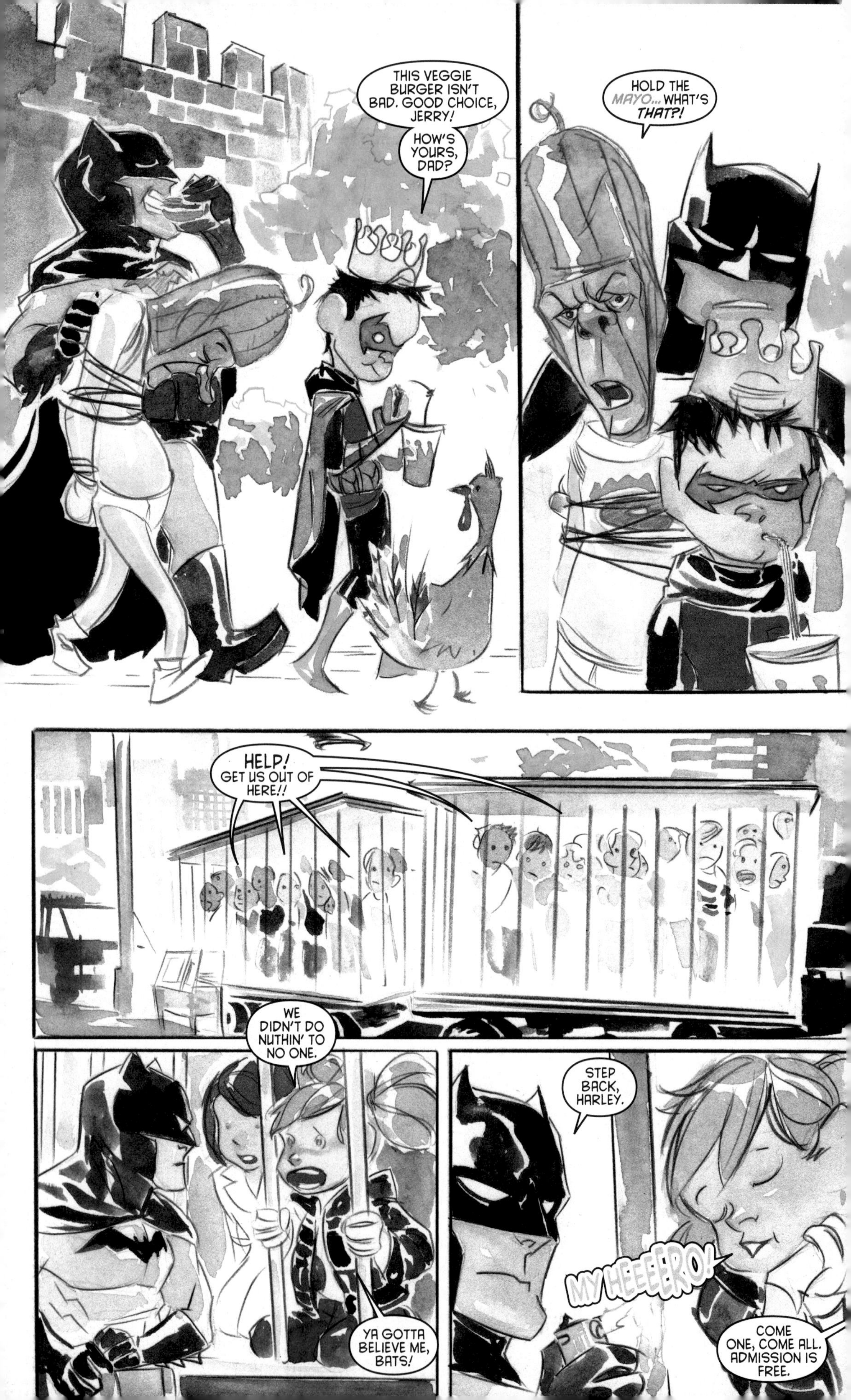
THIS VEGGIE BURGER ISN'T BAD. GOOD CHOICE, JERRY!
HOW'S YOURS, DAD?
HOLD THE MAYO... WHAT'S THAT?!
HELP! GET US OUT OF HERE!!
WE DIDN'T DO NUTHIN' TO NO ONE.
YA GOTTA BELIEVE ME, BATS!
STEP BACK, HARLEY.
MY HEEEERO!
COME ONE, COME ALL. ADMISSION IS FREE.

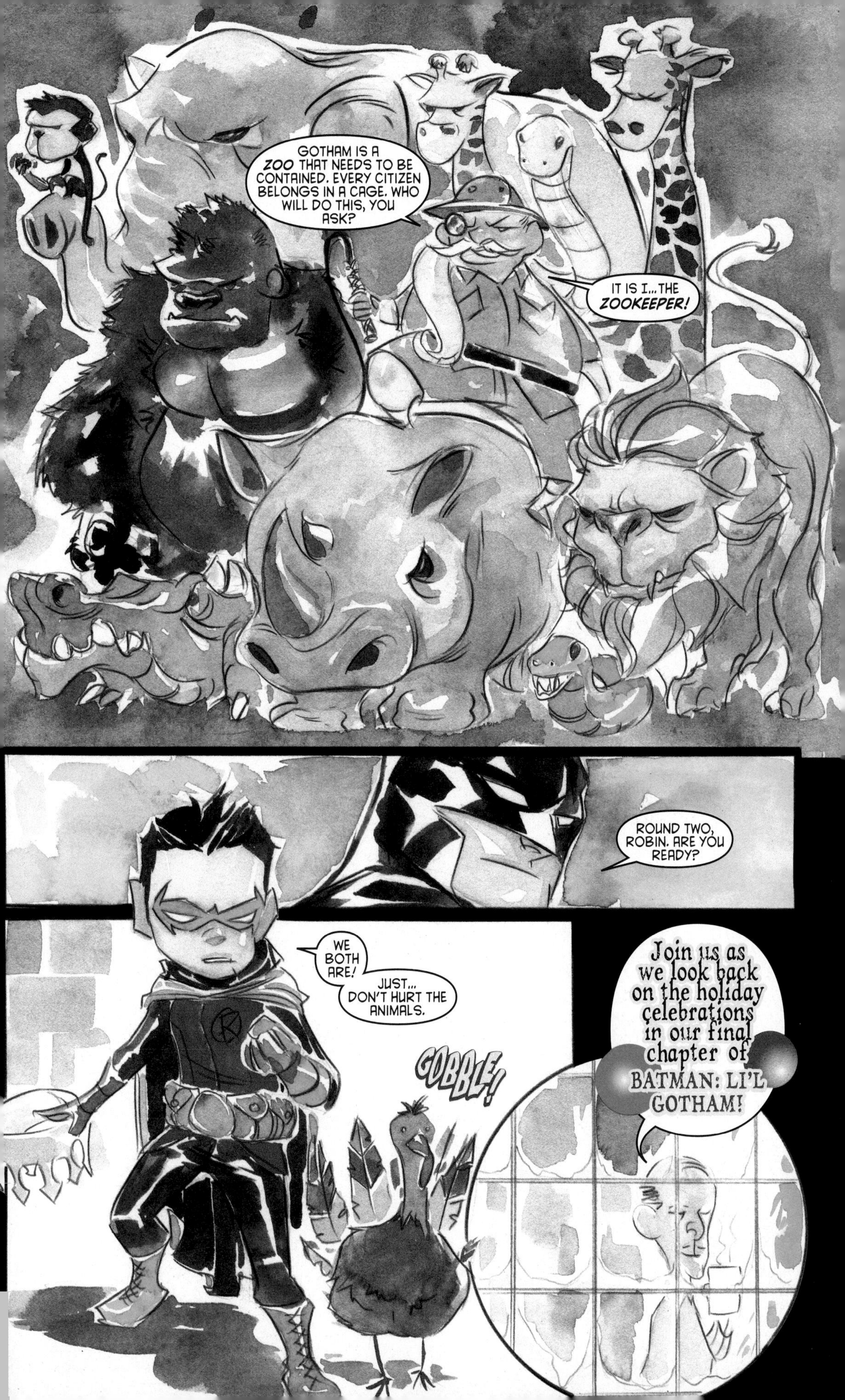
GOTHAM IS A ZOO THAT NEEDS TO BE CONTAINED. EVERY CITIZEN BELONGS IN A CAGE. WHO WILL DO THIS, YOU ASK?
IT IS I... THE ZOOKEEPER!
ROUND TWO, ROBIN. ARE YOU READY?
WE BOTH ARE!
JUST... DON'T HURT THE ANIMALS.
GOBBLE!
Join us as we look back on the holiday celebrations in our final chapter of BATMAN: LI'L GOTHAM!

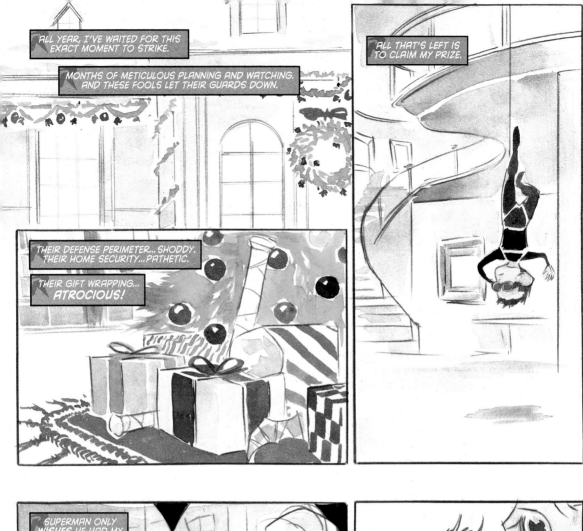

ALL YEAR, I'VE WAITED FOR THIS EXACT MOMENT TO STRIKE.

MONTHS OF METICULOUS PLANNING AND WATCHING. AND THESE FOOLS LET THEIR GUARDS DOWN.

THEIR DEFENSE PERIMETER... SHODDY. THEIR HOME SECURITY... PATHETIC.

THEIR GIFT WRAPPING... ATROCIOUS!

ALL THAT'S LEFT IS TO CLAIM MY PRIZE.

SUPERMAN ONLY WISHES HE HAD MY X-RAY GOGGLES.

ONE MORE ADJUSTMENT AND THEN--

WHUMPP

SNIP

HEY!

THAT'S ASSASSIN-GRADE GRAPPLE ROPE!

IT APPEARS WE HAVE AN INTRUDER. SOMEONE JUST MADE THE NAUGHTY LIST.

BEING UNDER HOUSE ARREST STINKS!

YOU SHOULD'VE CONSIDERED THAT BEFORE YOU TRIED TO HOT-WIRE ALL THE BATMOBILES, MASTER DAMIAN.

AND THE BAT-CYCLE, THE BAT-TANK, BAT-BOAT, BAT-SUB, BAT-BUS, BAT-TROLLEY--

OKAY, OKAY! I SHOULD BE OUT THERE HELPING DAD ROUND UP CRIMINALS.

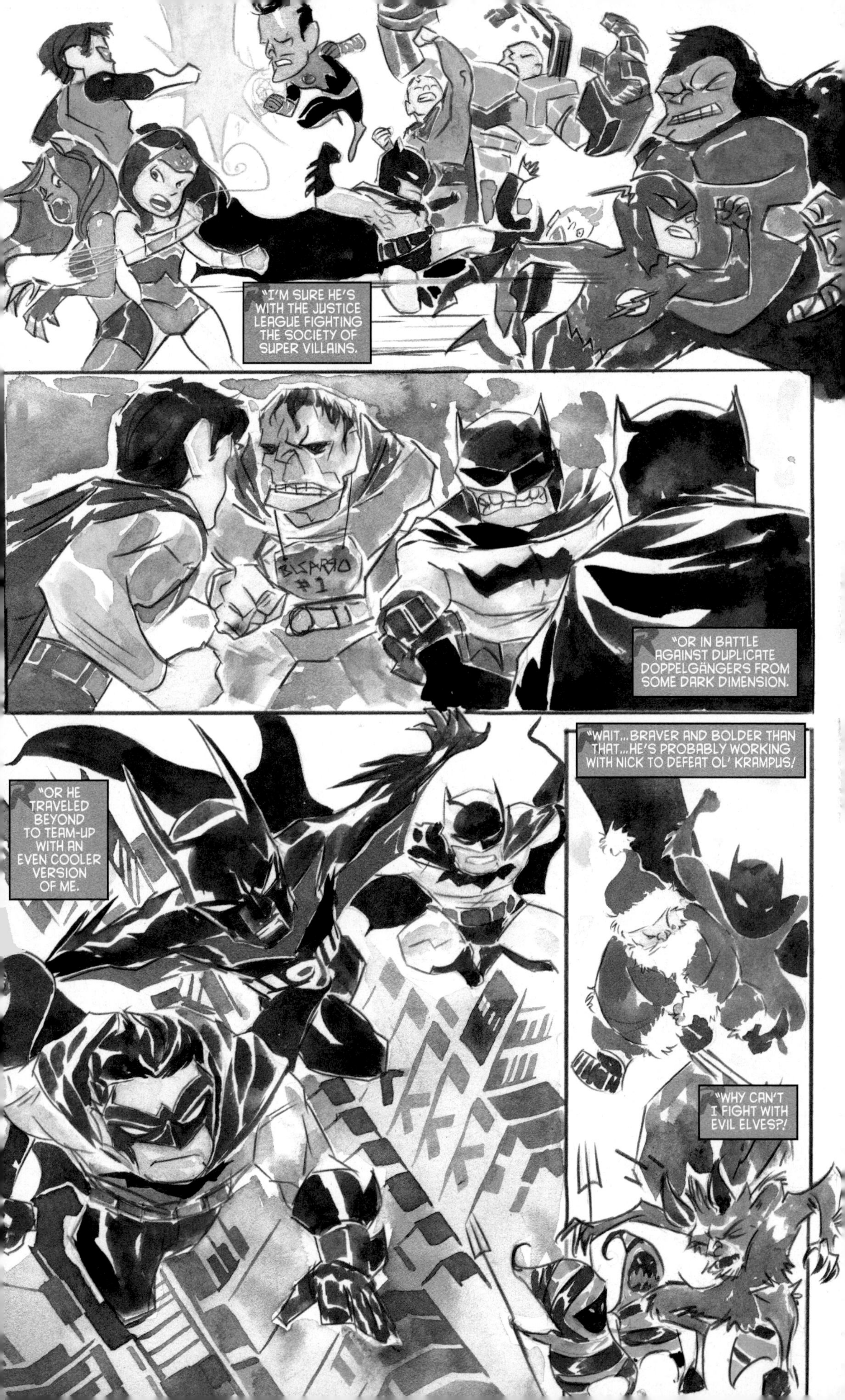
"I'M SURE HE'S WITH THE JUSTICE LEAGUE FIGHTING THE SOCIETY OF SUPER VILLAINS.
BIZARRO #1
"OR IN BATTLE AGAINST DUPLICATE DOPPELGÄNGERS FROM SOME DARK DIMENSION.
"OR HE TRAVELED BEYOND TO TEAM-UP WITH AN EVEN COOLER VERSION OF ME.
"WAIT...BRAVER AND BOLDER THAN THAT...HE'S PROBABLY WORKING WITH NICK TO DEFEAT OL' KRAMPUS!
"WHY CAN'T I FIGHT WITH EVIL ELVES?!

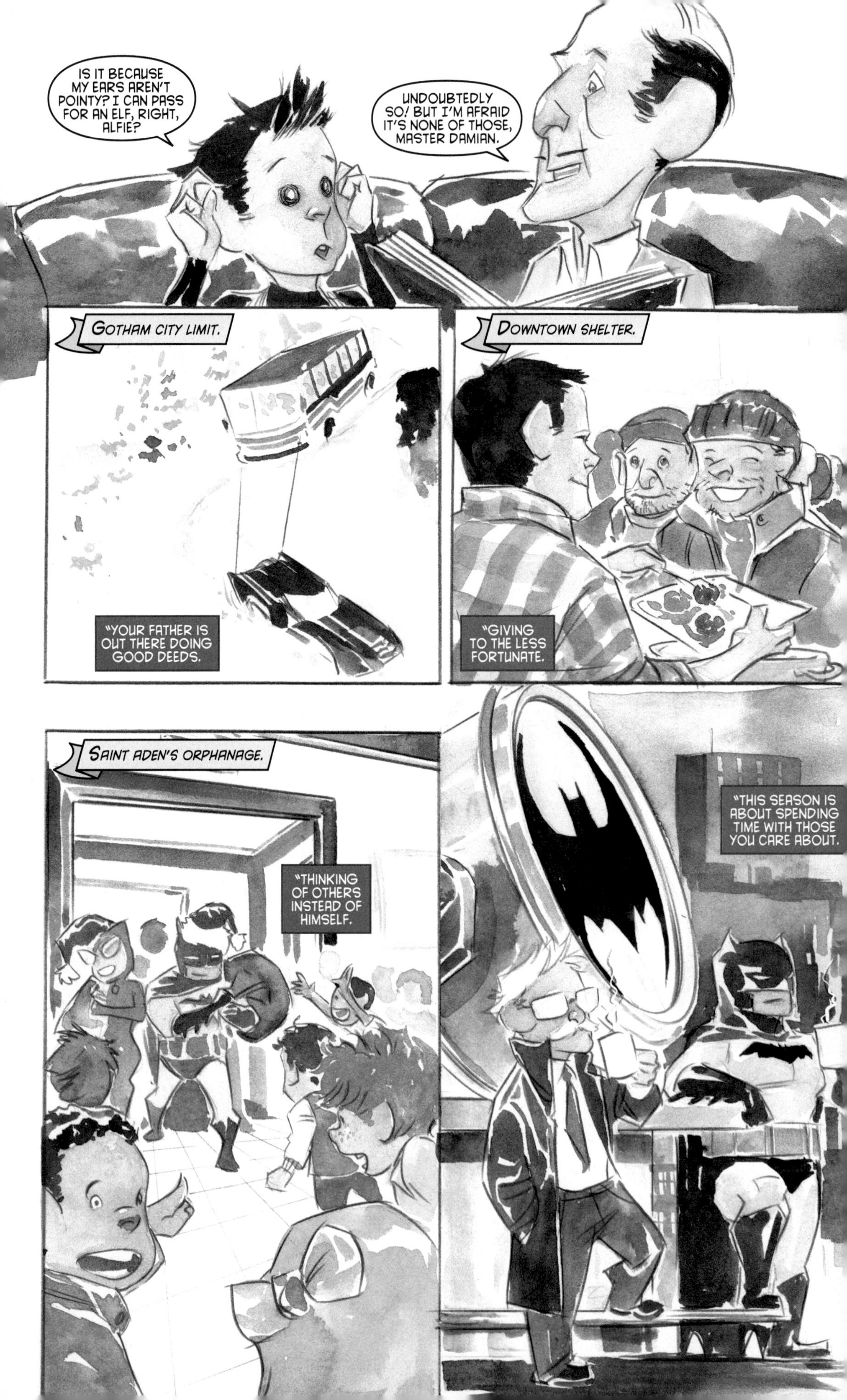
IS IT BECAUSE MY EARS AREN'T POINTY? I CAN PASS FOR AN ELF, RIGHT, ALFIE?
UNDOUBTEDLY SO! BUT I'M AFRAID IT'S NONE OF THOSE, MASTER DAMIAN.
GOTHAM CITY LIMIT.
"YOUR FATHER IS OUT THERE DOING GOOD DEEDS.
DOWNTOWN SHELTER.
"GIVING TO THE LESS FORTUNATE.
SAINT ADEN'S ORPHANAGE.
"THINKING OF OTHERS INSTEAD OF HIMSELF.
"THIS SEASON IS ABOUT SPENDING TIME WITH THOSE YOU CARE ABOUT.

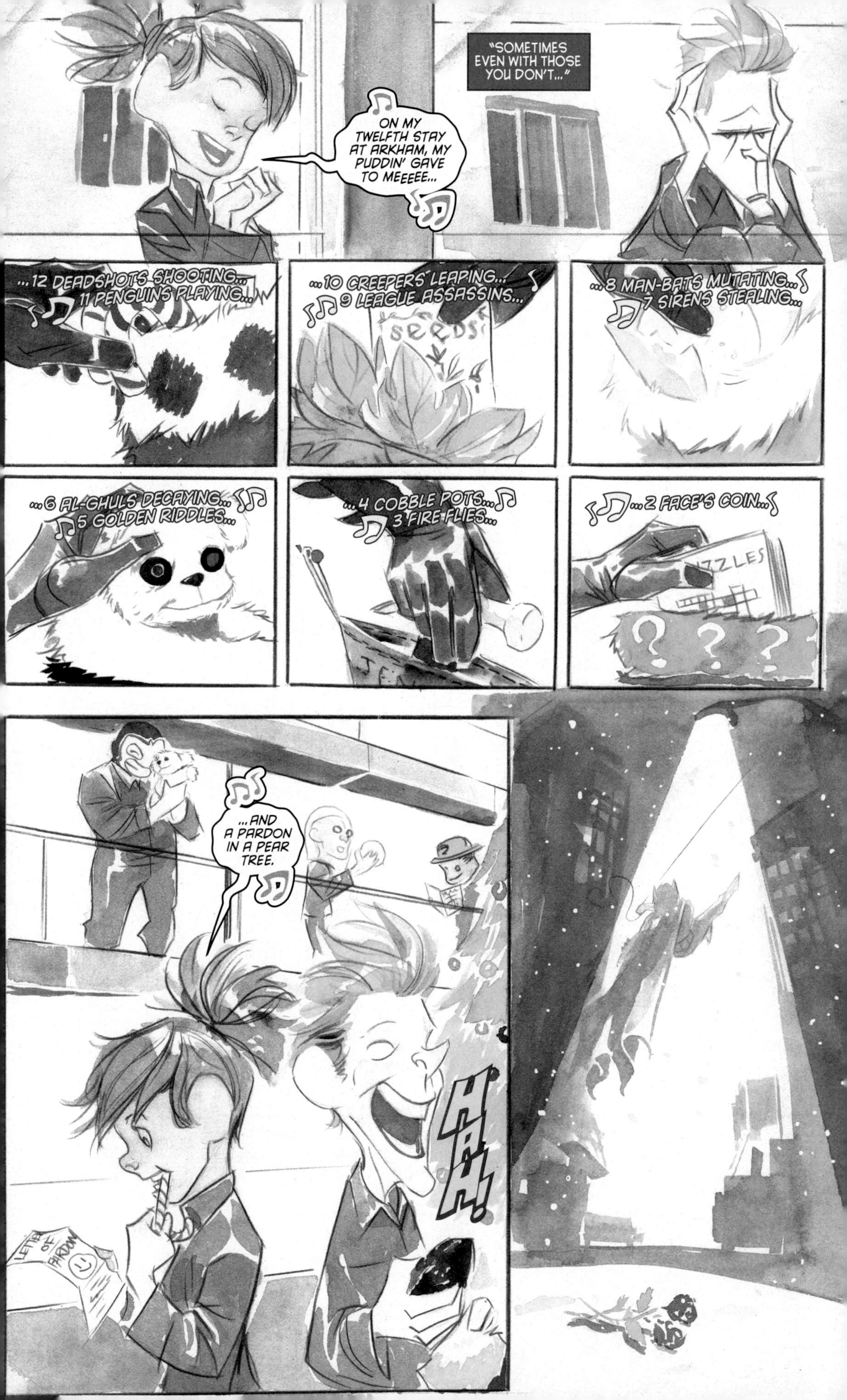
"SOMETIMES EVEN WITH THOSE YOU DON'T..."
ON MY TWELFTH STAY AT ARKHAM, MY PUDDIN' GAVE TO MEEEEE...
...12 DEADSHOTS SHOOTING... 11 PENGUINS PLAYING...
...10 CREEPERS LEAPING... 9 LEAGUE ASSASSINS...
...8 MAN-BATS MUTATING... 7 SIRENS STEALING...
...6 AL-GHULS DECAYING... 5 GOLDEN RIDDLES...
...4 COBBLE POTS... 3 FIRE FLIES...
...2 FACE'S COIN...
...AND A PARDON IN A PEAR TREE.
HAH!
LETTER OF PARDON

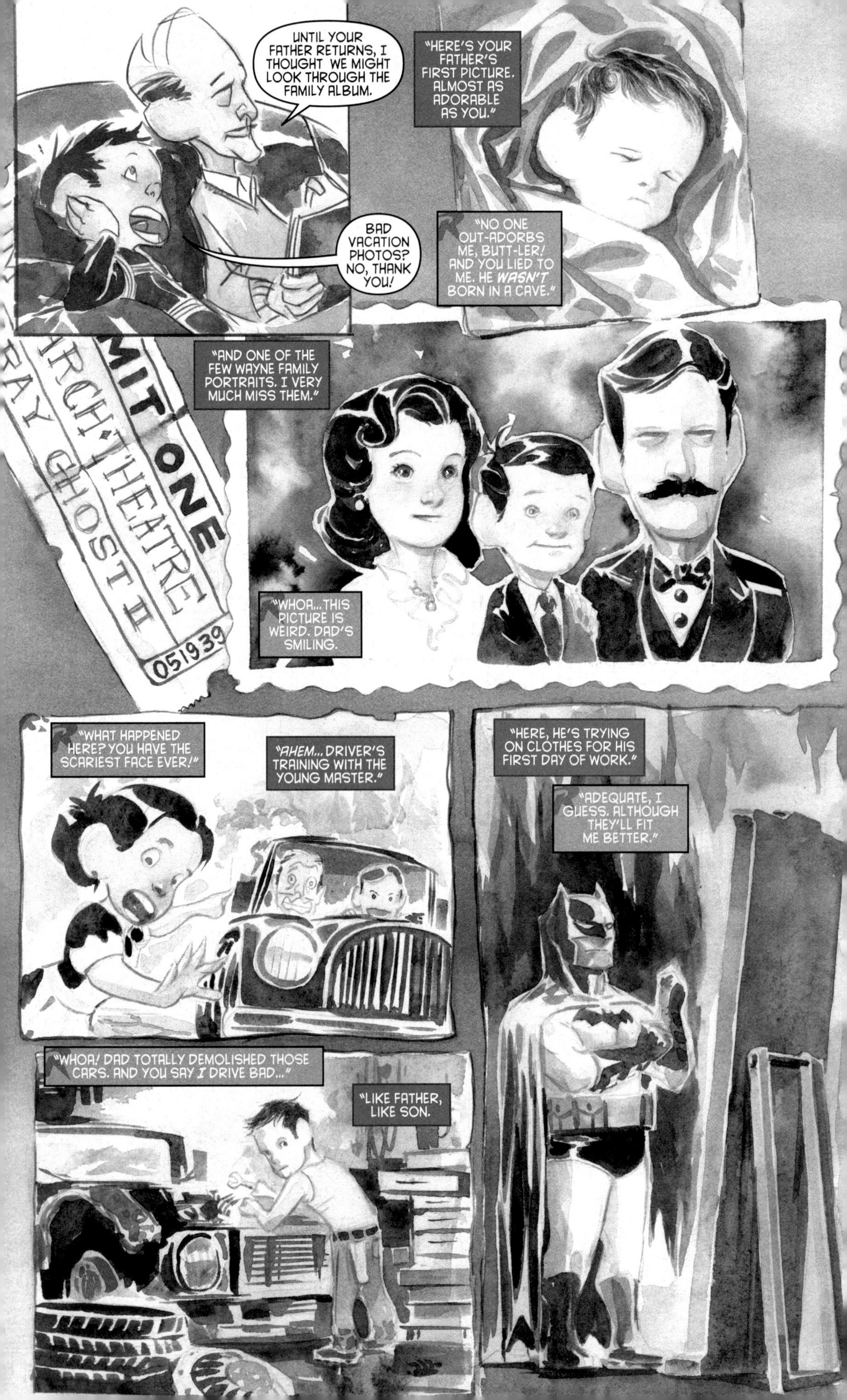

UNTIL YOUR FATHER RETURNS, I THOUGHT WE MIGHT LOOK THROUGH THE FAMILY ALBUM.
BAD VACATION PHOTOS? NO, THANK YOU!
"HERE'S YOUR FATHER'S FIRST PICTURE. ALMOST AS ADORABLE AS YOU."
"NO ONE OUT-ADORBS ME, BUTT-LER! AND YOU LIED TO ME. HE WASN'T BORN IN A CAVE."
"AND ONE OF THE FEW WAYNE FAMILY PORTRAITS. I VERY MUCH MISS THEM."
MIT ONE
ARCH THEATRE
RAY GHOST II
051939
"WHOA... THIS PICTURE IS WEIRD. DAD'S SMILING.
"WHAT HAPPENED HERE? YOU HAVE THE SCARIEST FACE EVER!"
"AHEM... DRIVER'S TRAINING WITH THE YOUNG MASTER."
"WHOA! DAD TOTALLY DEMOLISHED THOSE CARS. AND YOU SAY I DRIVE BAD..."
"LIKE FATHER, LIKE SON.
"HERE, HE'S TRYING ON CLOTHES FOR HIS FIRST DAY OF WORK."
"ADEQUATE, I GUESS. ALTHOUGH THEY'LL FIT ME BETTER."

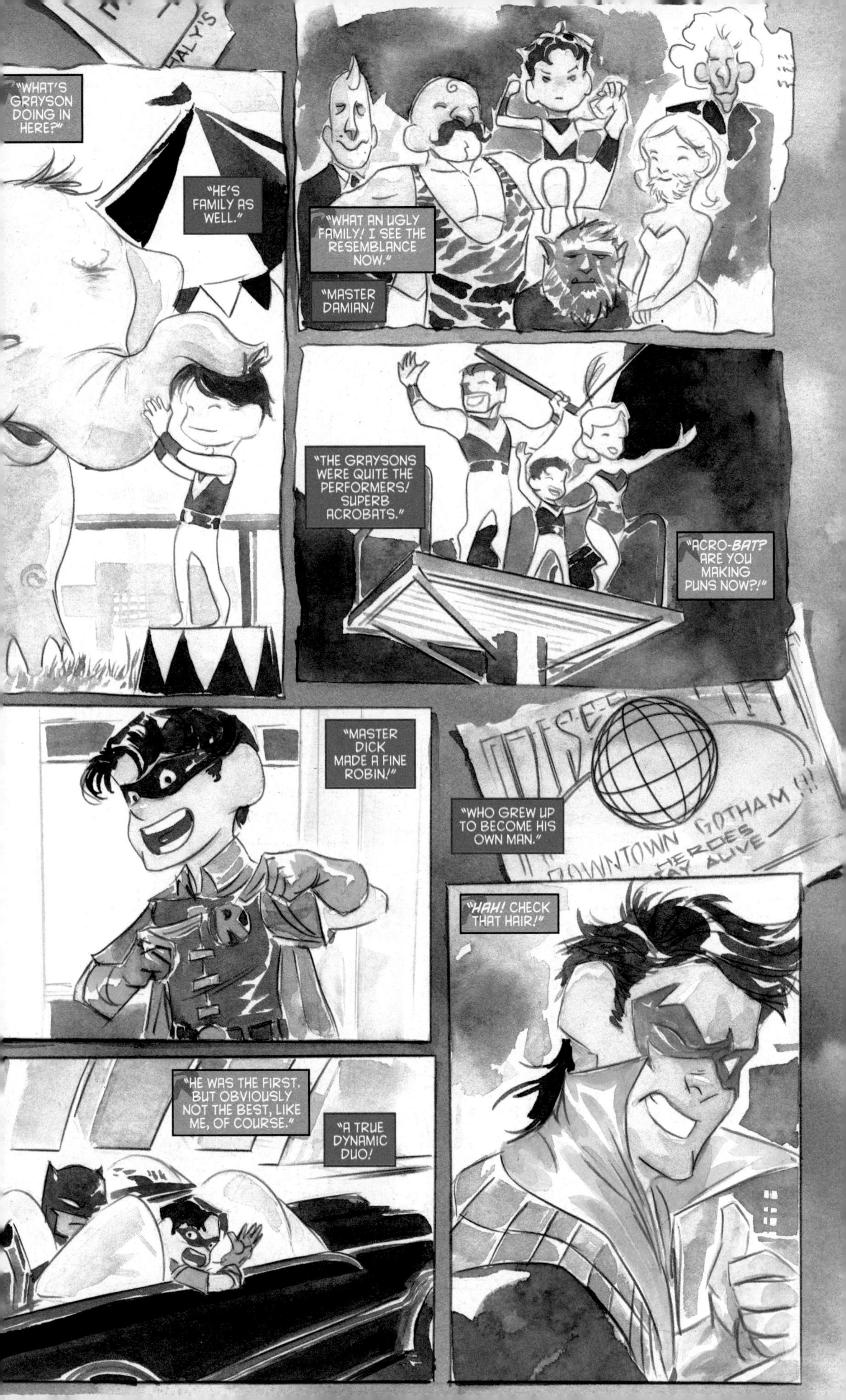
HALY'S
"WHAT'S GRAYSON DOING IN HERE?"
"HE'S FAMILY AS WELL."
"WHAT AN UGLY FAMILY! I SEE THE RESEMBLANCE NOW."
"MASTER DAMIAN!
"THE GRAYSONS WERE QUITE THE PERFORMERS! SUPERB ACROBATS."
"ACRO-*BAT?* ARE YOU MAKING PUNS NOW?!"
"MASTER DICK MADE A FINE ROBIN!"
"HE WAS THE FIRST. BUT OBVIOUSLY NOT THE BEST, LIKE ME, OF COURSE."
"A TRUE DYNAMIC DUO!
DOWNTOWN GOTHAM !!
"WHO GREW UP TO BECOME HIS OWN MAN."
"*HAH!* CHECK THAT HAIR!"

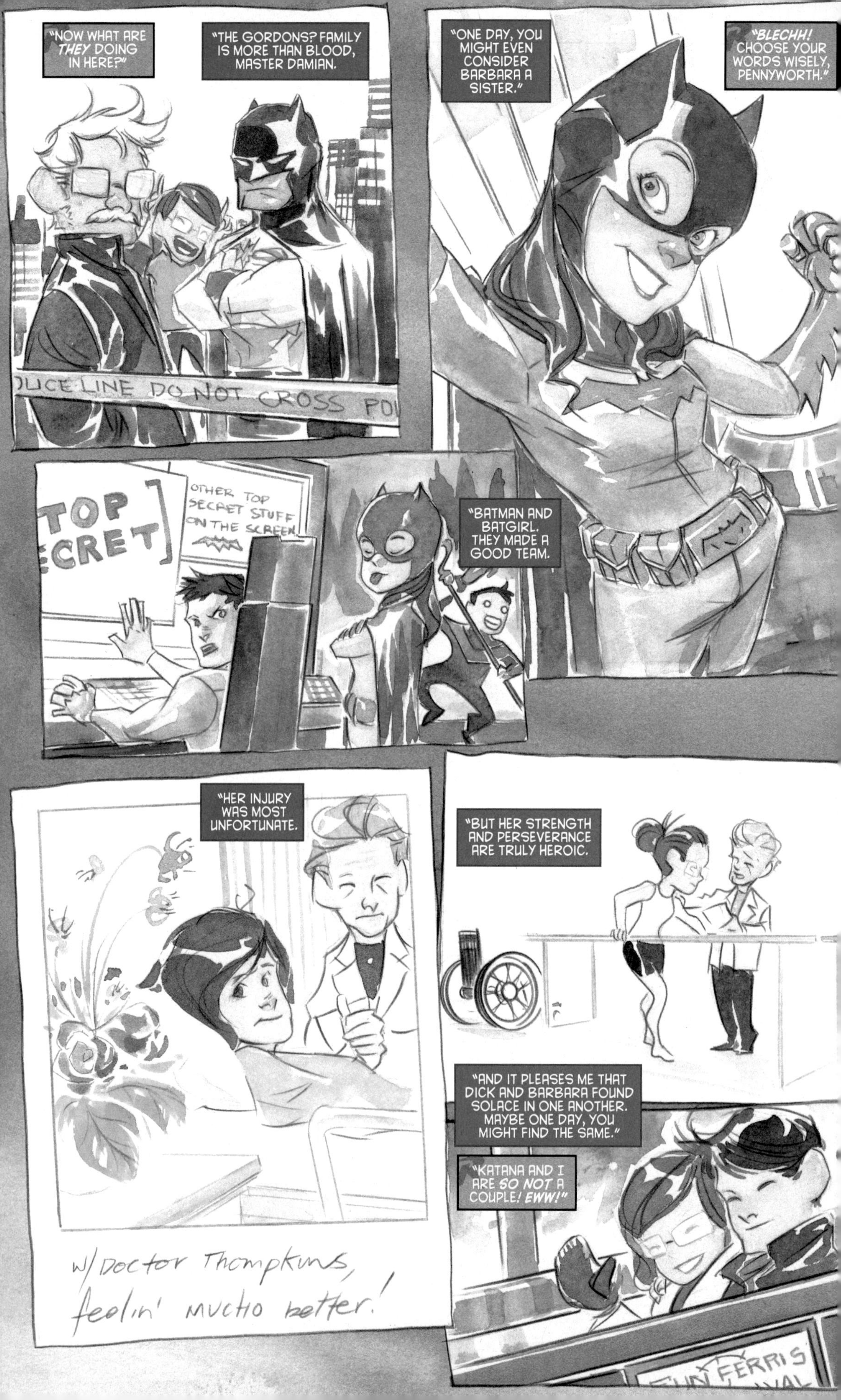

"NOW WHAT ARE THEY DOING IN HERE?"
"THE GORDONS? FAMILY IS MORE THAN BLOOD, MASTER DAMIAN.
OLICE LINE DO NOT CROSS PO
"ONE DAY, YOU MIGHT EVEN CONSIDER BARBARA A SISTER."
"BLECHH! CHOOSE YOUR WORDS WISELY, PENNYWORTH."
TOP SECRET
OTHER TOP SECRET STUFF ON THE SCREEN
"BATMAN AND BATGIRL. THEY MADE A GOOD TEAM.
"HER INJURY WAS MOST UNFORTUNATE.
w/Doctor Thompkins, feelin' mucho better!
"BUT HER STRENGTH AND PERSEVERANCE ARE TRULY HEROIC.
"AND IT PLEASES ME THAT DICK AND BARBARA FOUND SOLACE IN ONE ANOTHER. MAYBE ONE DAY, YOU MIGHT FIND THE SAME."
"KATANA AND I ARE SO NOT A COUPLE! EWW!"
FERRIS

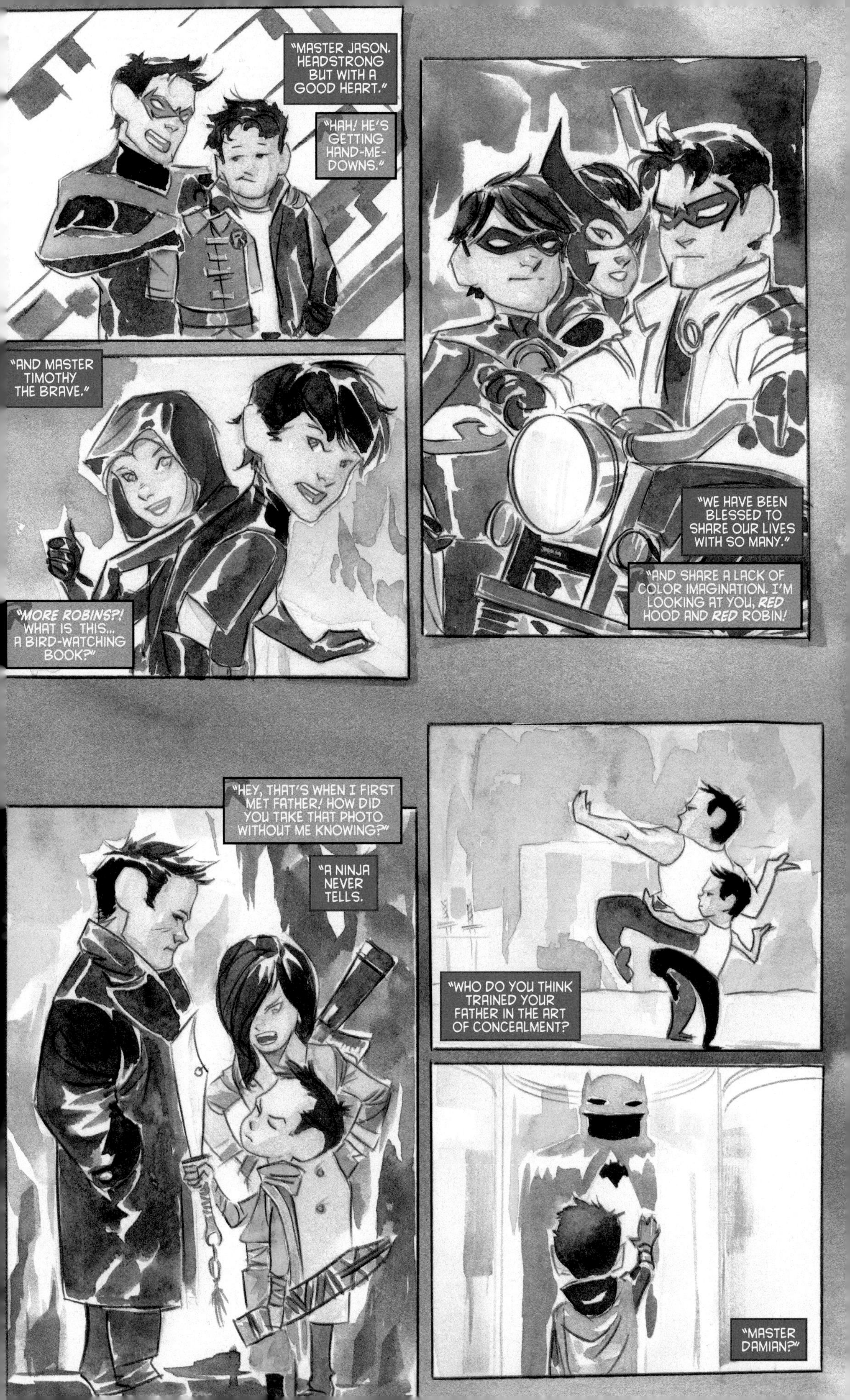
"MASTER JASON. HEADSTRONG BUT WITH A GOOD HEART."
"HAH! HE'S GETTING HAND-ME-DOWNS."
"AND MASTER TIMOTHY THE BRAVE."
"MORE ROBINS?! WHAT IS THIS... A BIRD-WATCHING BOOK?"
"WE HAVE BEEN BLESSED TO SHARE OUR LIVES WITH SO MANY."
"AND SHARE A LACK OF COLOR IMAGINATION. I'M LOOKING AT YOU, RED HOOD AND RED ROBIN!
"HEY, THAT'S WHEN I FIRST MET FATHER! HOW DID YOU TAKE THAT PHOTO WITHOUT ME KNOWING?"
"A NINJA NEVER TELLS.
"WHO DO YOU THINK TRAINED YOUR FATHER IN THE ART OF CONCEALMENT?
"MASTER DAMIAN?"

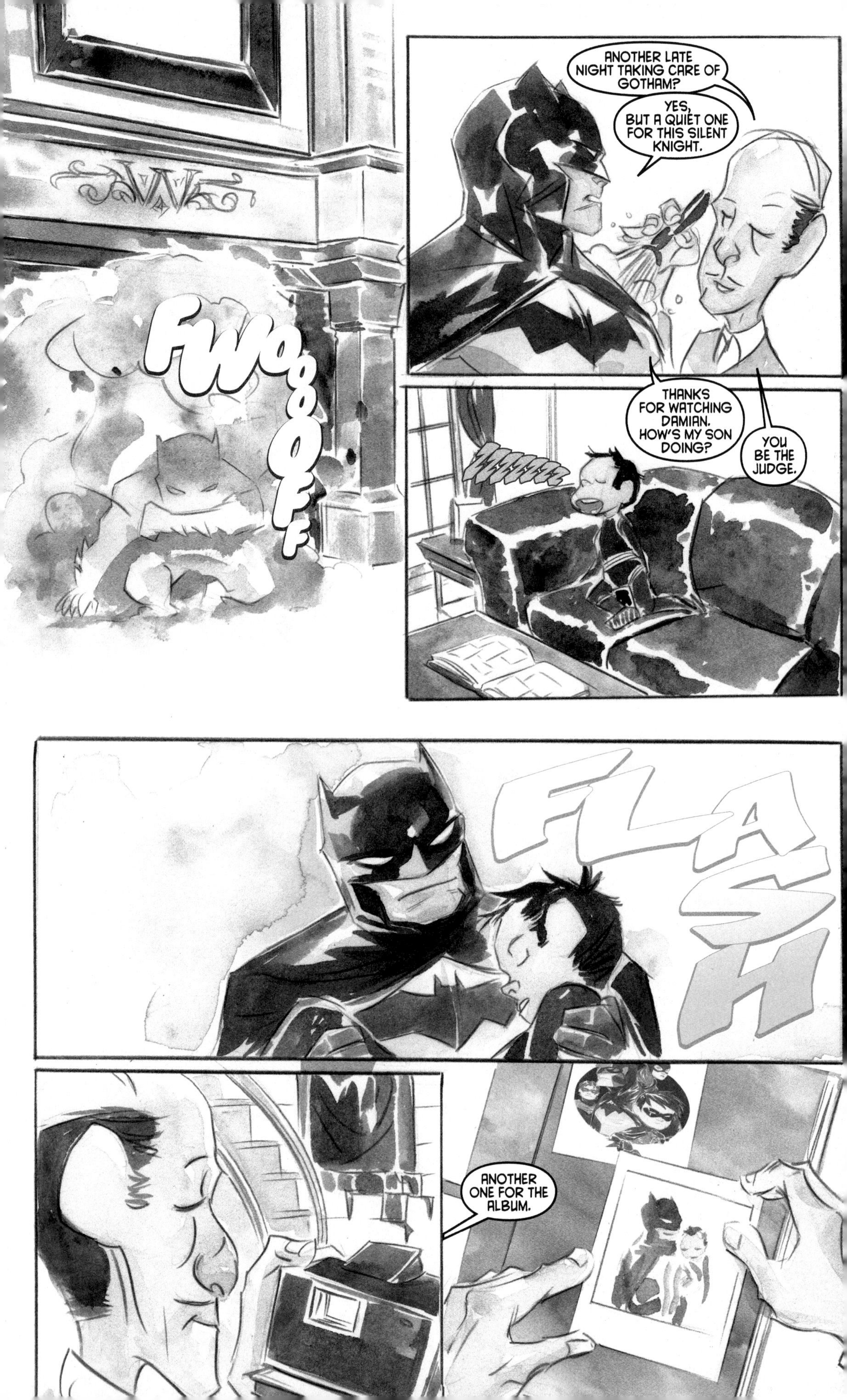
FWOOOOOFF
ANOTHER LATE NIGHT TAKING CARE OF GOTHAM?
YES, BUT A QUIET ONE FOR THIS SILENT KNIGHT.
THANKS FOR WATCHING DAMIAN. HOW'S MY SON DOING?
ZZZZZZZ
YOU BE THE JUDGE.
FLASH
ANOTHER ONE FOR THE ALBUM.

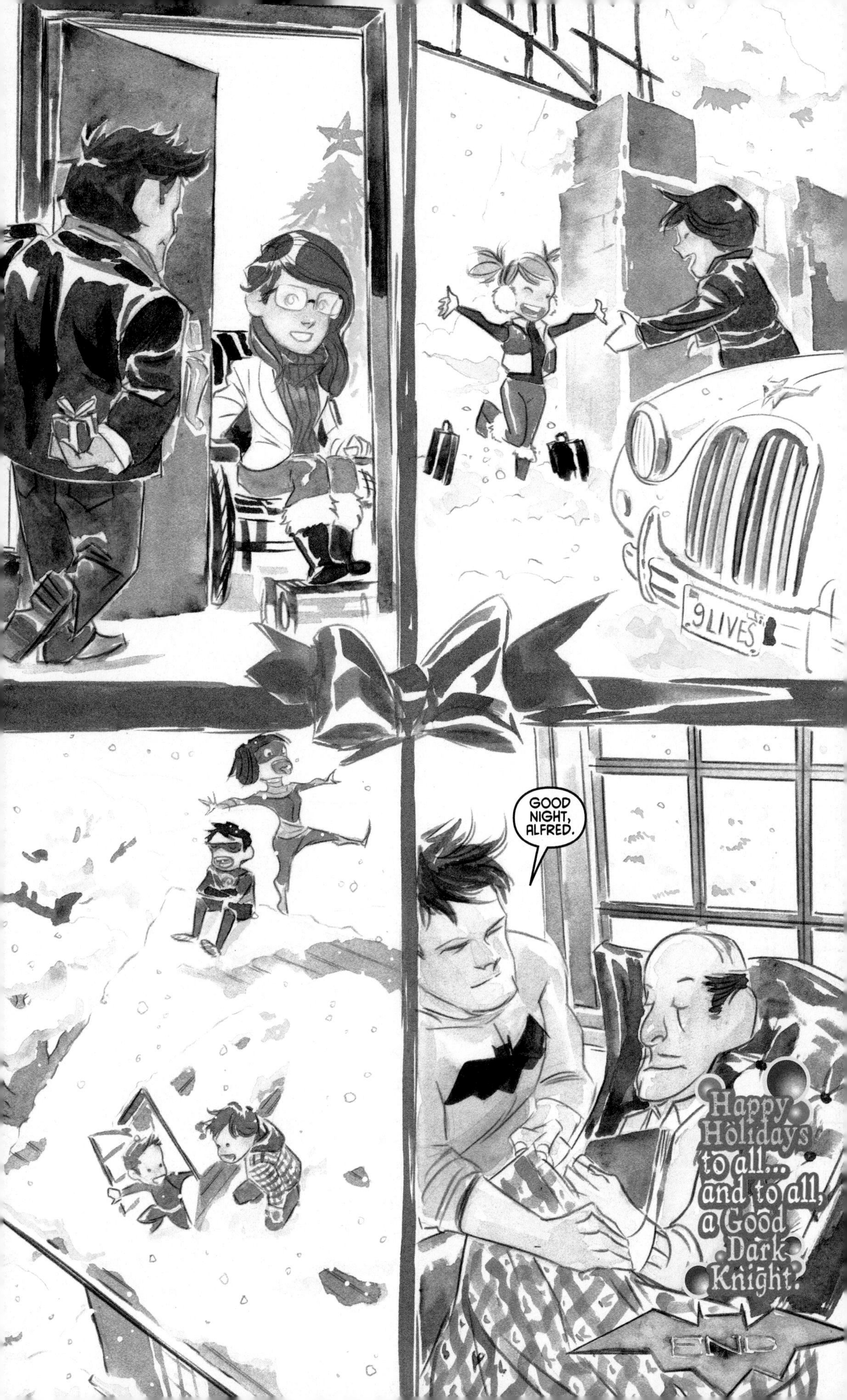
9LIVES
GOOD NIGHT, ALFRED.
Happy Holidays to all... and to all, a Good Dark Knight.
END

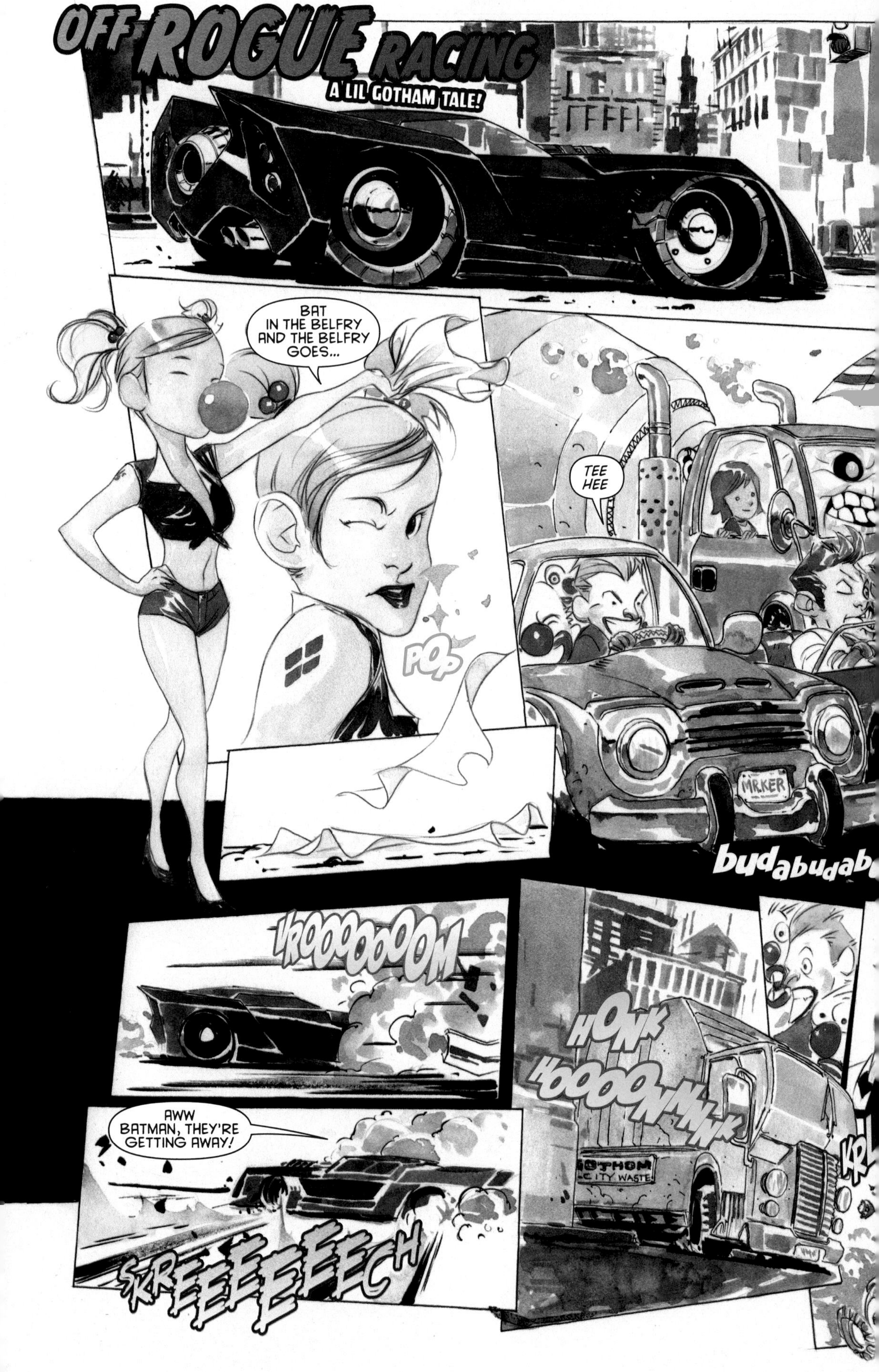

OFF ROGUE RACING
A LIL GOTHAM TALE!
BAT IN THE BELFRY AND THE BELFRY GOES...
POP
TEE HEE
MR.KER
budabudab
VROOOOOOOOM
HONK
HOOOONNNNK
GOTHAM CITY WASTE
AWW BATMAN, THEY'RE GETTING AWAY!
SKREEEEEEEECH

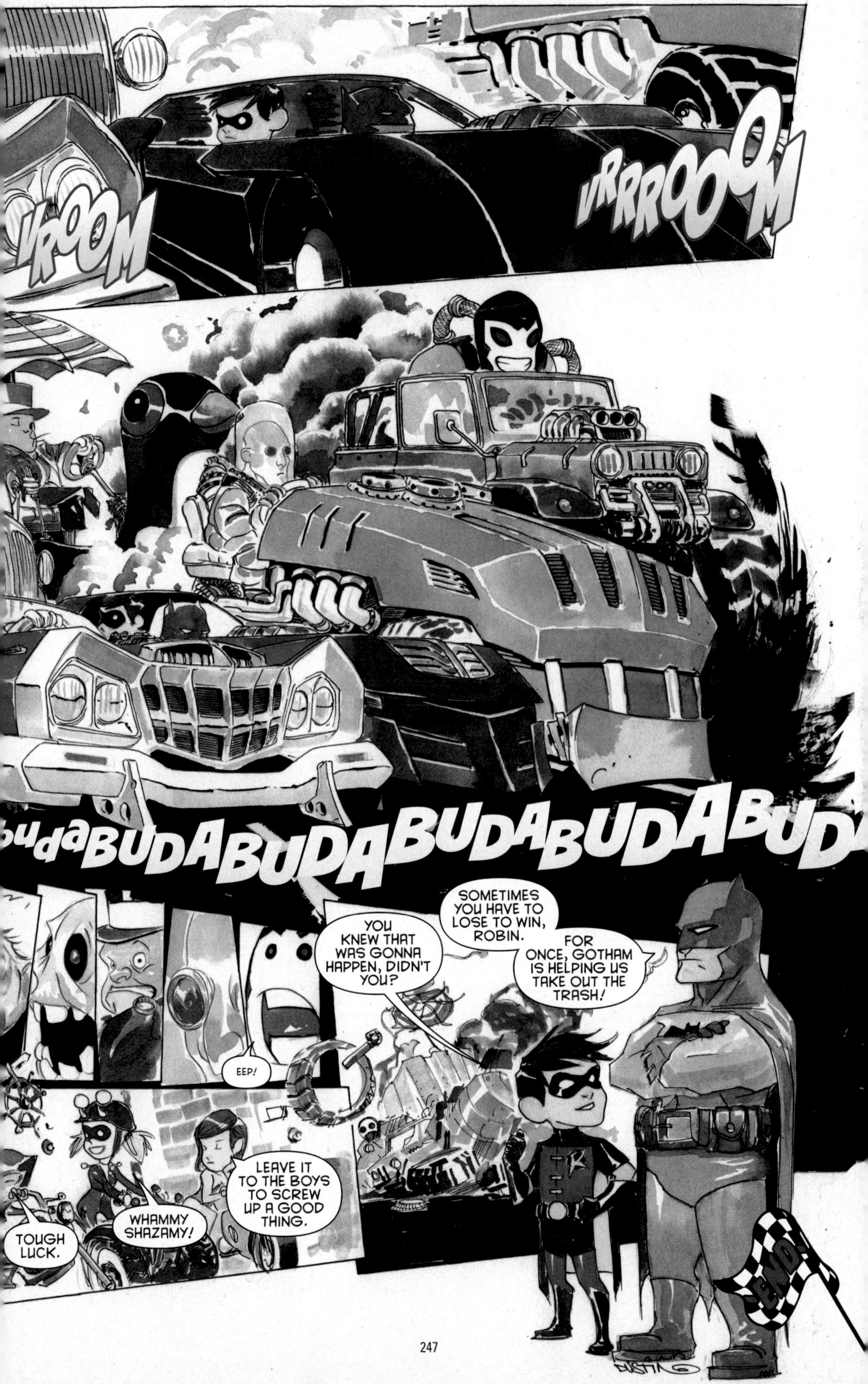
VROOM
VRRROOOOM
budaBUDABUDABUDABUDABUD
EEP!
TOUGH LUCK.
WHAMMY SHAZAMY!
LEAVE IT TO THE BOYS TO SCREW UP A GOOD THING.
YOU KNEW THAT WAS GONNA HAPPEN, DIDN'T YOU?
SOMETIMES YOU HAVE TO LOSE TO WIN, ROBIN.
FOR ONCE, GOTHAM IS HELPING US TAKE OUT THE TRASH!
END

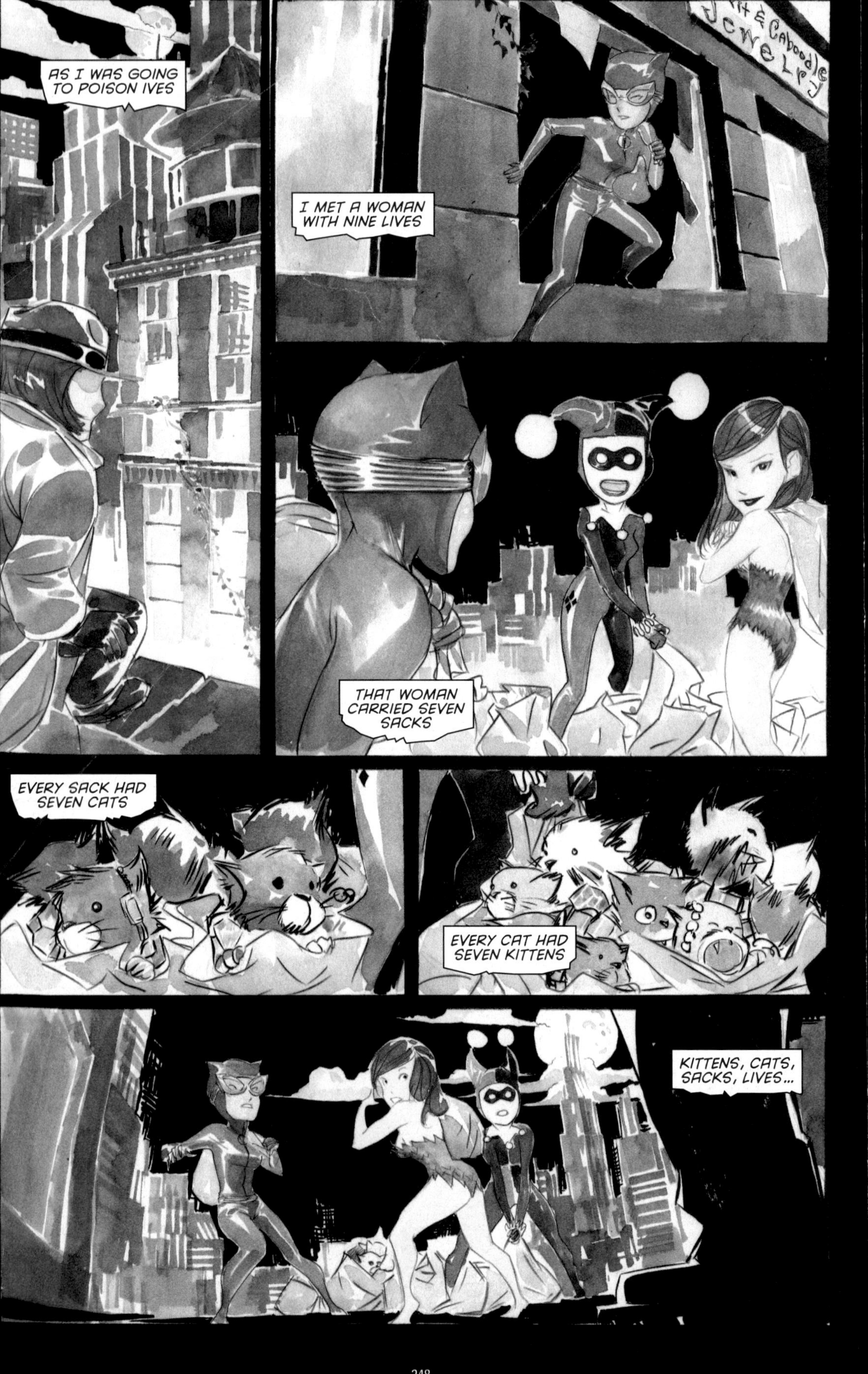
AS I WAS GOING TO POISON IVES
& Caboodle
Jewelry
I MET A WOMAN WITH NINE LIVES
THAT WOMAN CARRIED SEVEN SACKS
EVERY SACK HAD SEVEN CATS
EVERY CAT HAD SEVEN KITTENS
KITTENS, CATS, SACKS, LIVES...

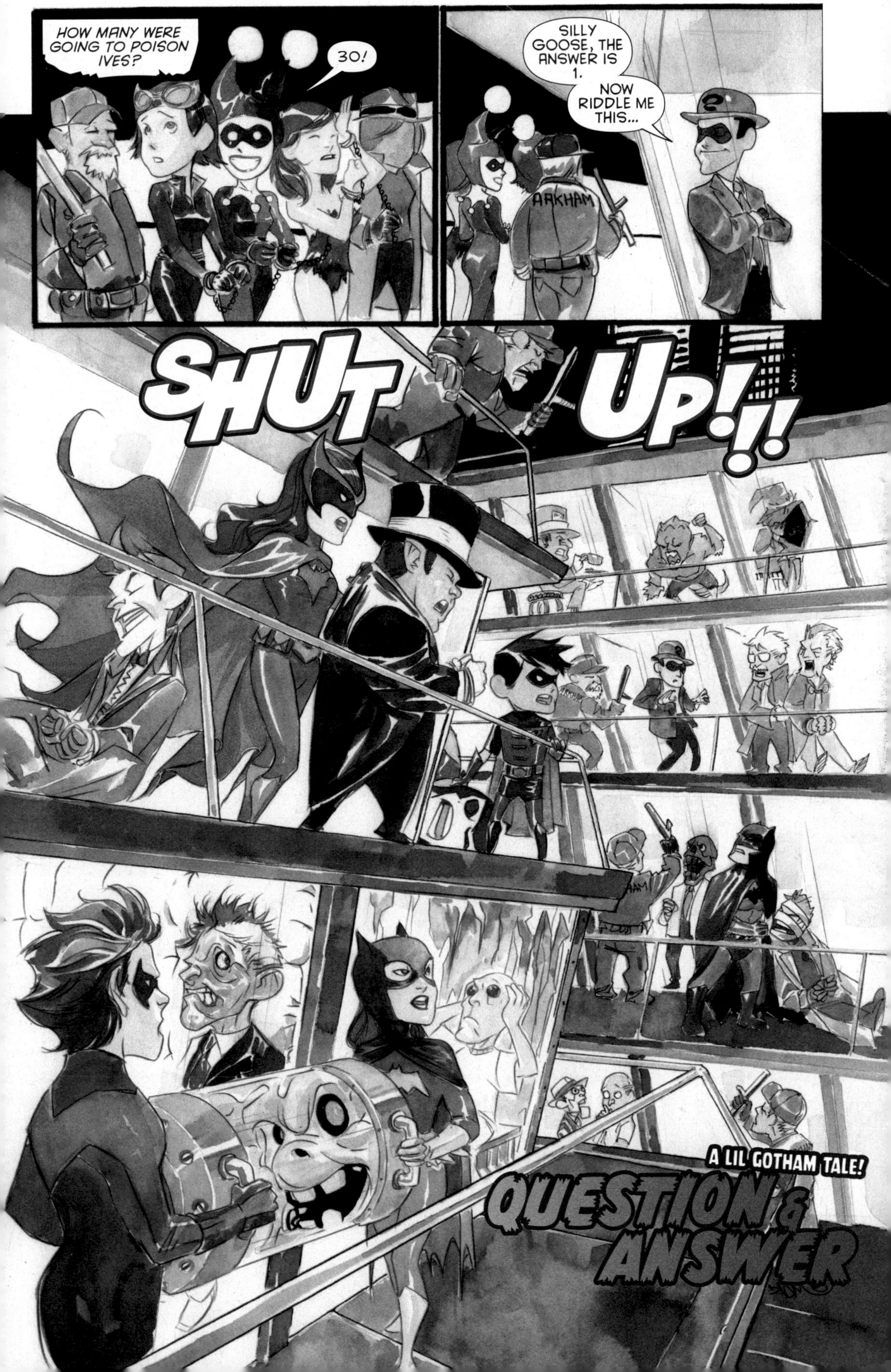
HOW MANY WERE GOING TO POISON IVES?
30!
SILLY GOOSE, THE ANSWER IS 1.
NOW RIDDLE ME THIS...
SHUT UP!!!
ARKHAM
A LIL GOTHAM TALE!
QUESTION & ANSWER

LI'L GOTHAM COVER GALLERY

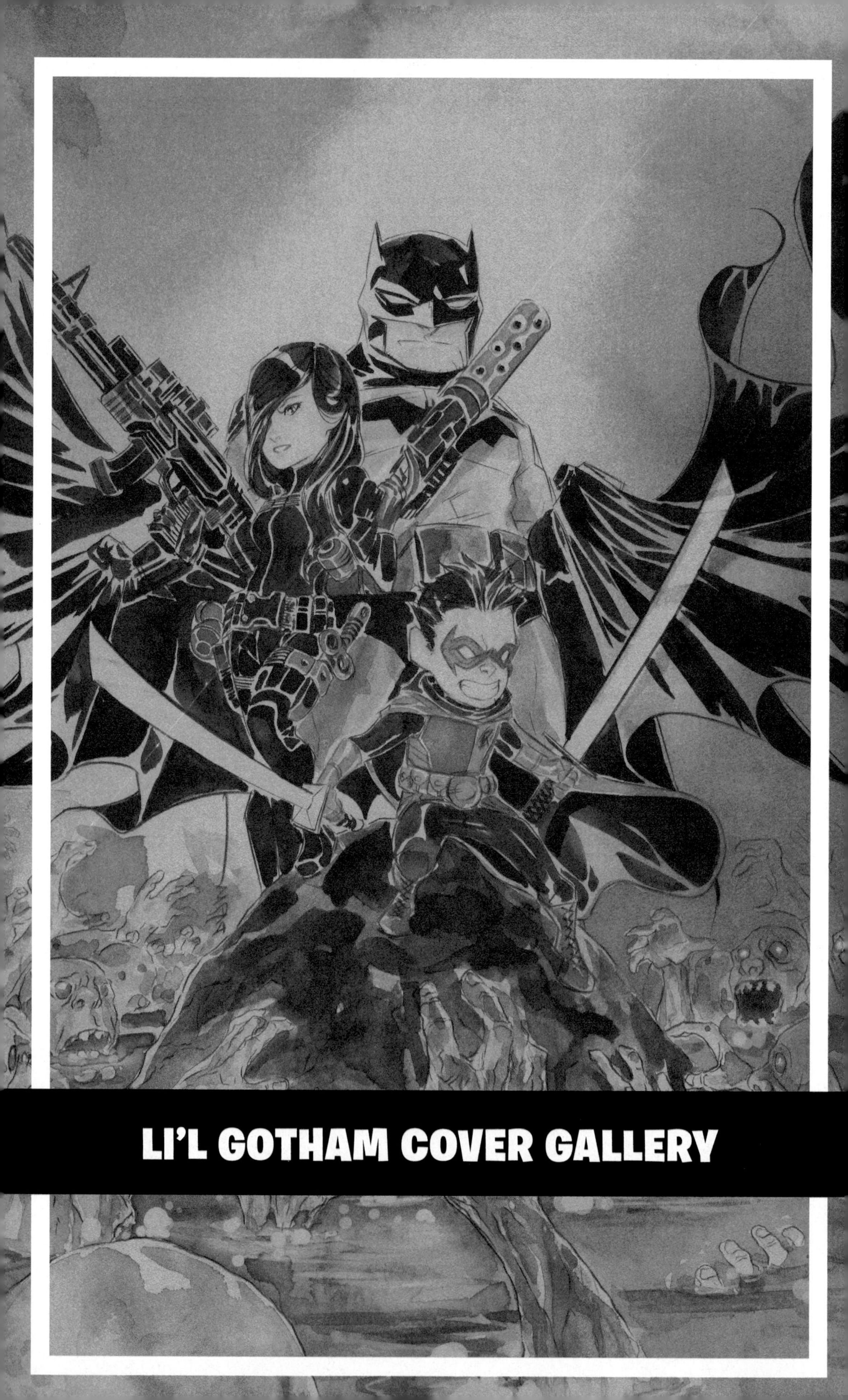

BATMAN: LI'L GOTHAM Digital Chapter #1 cover by Dustin Nguyen

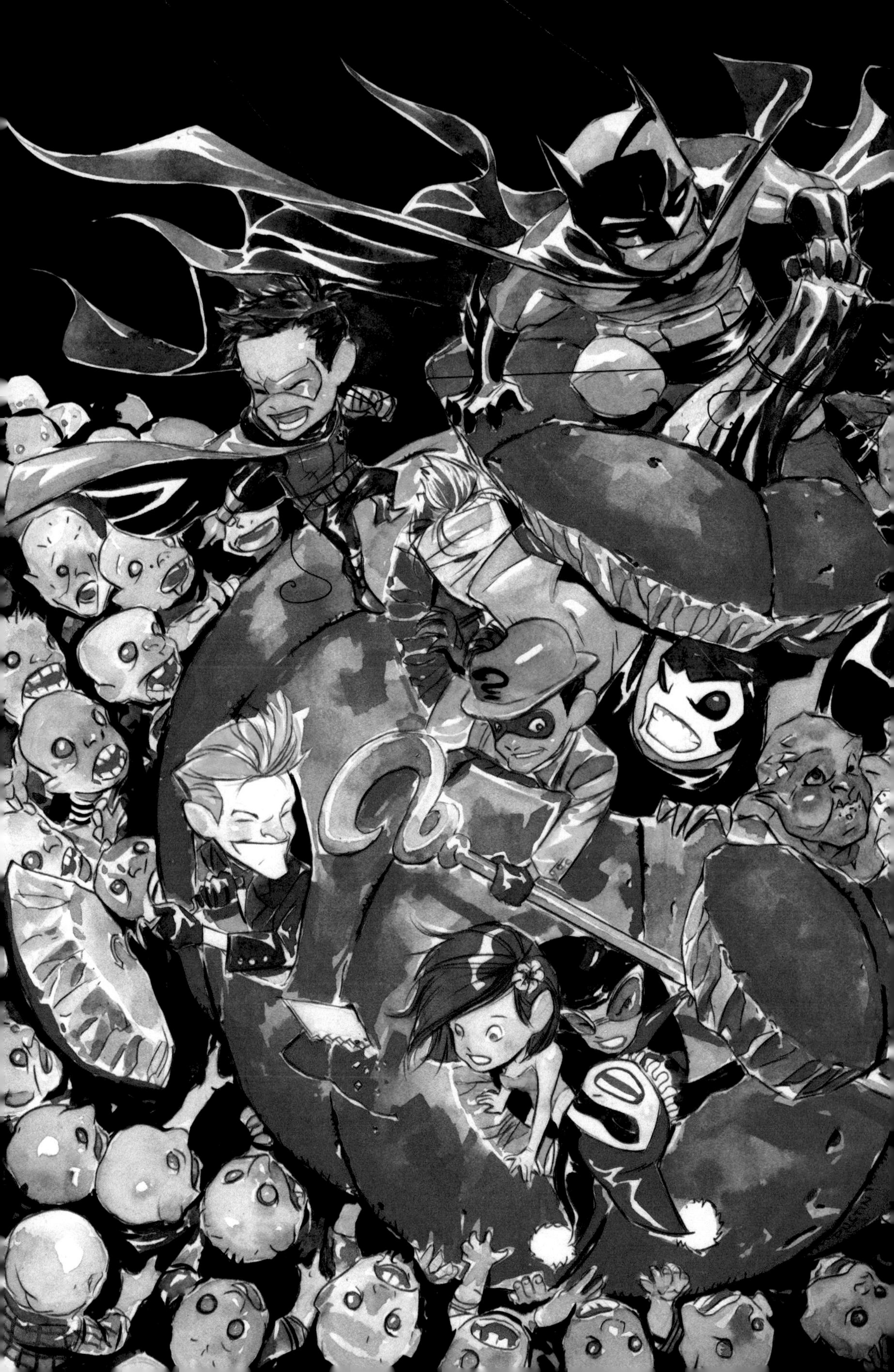

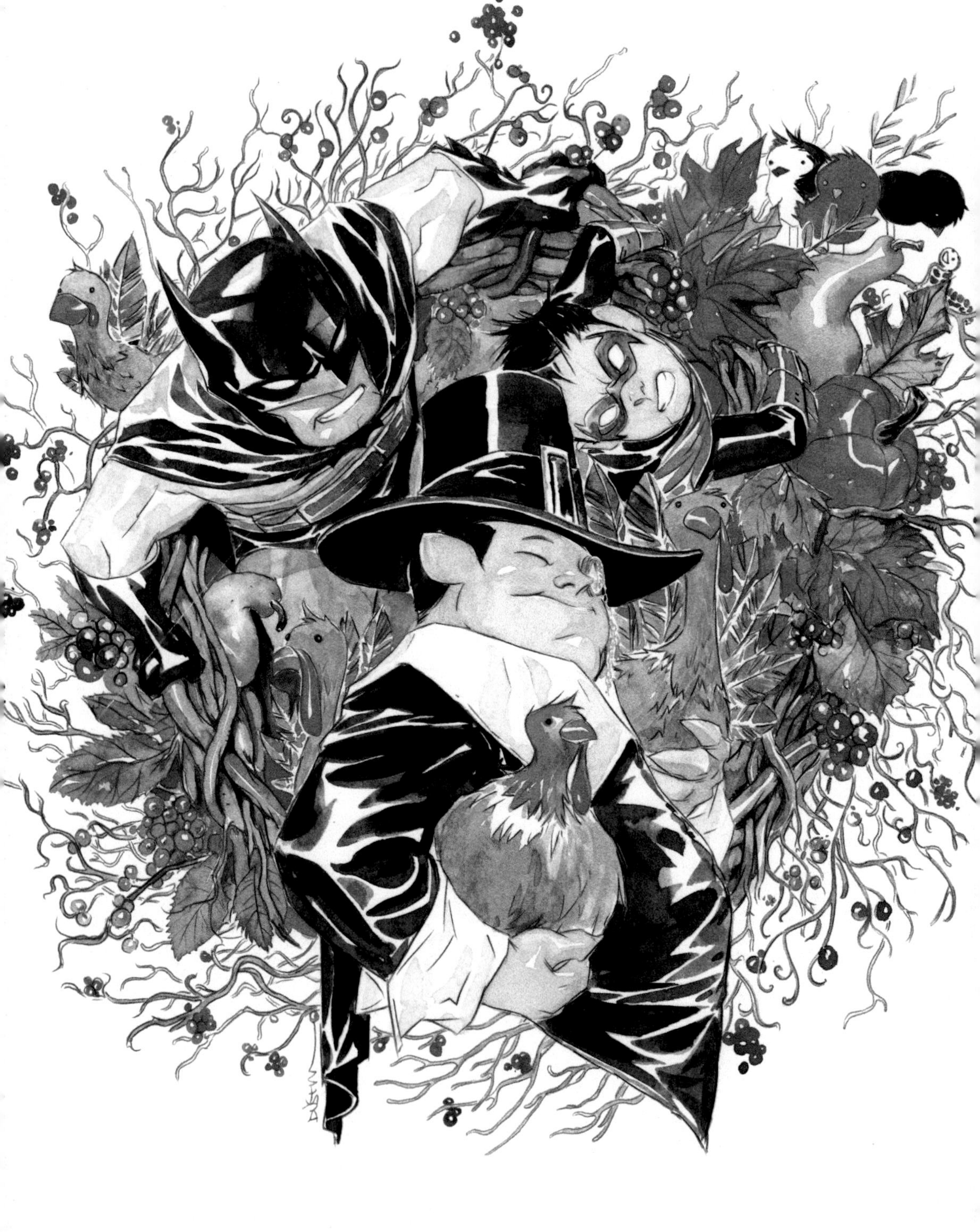

BATMAN: LI'L GOTHAM Digital Chapter #2 cover by Dustin Nguyen

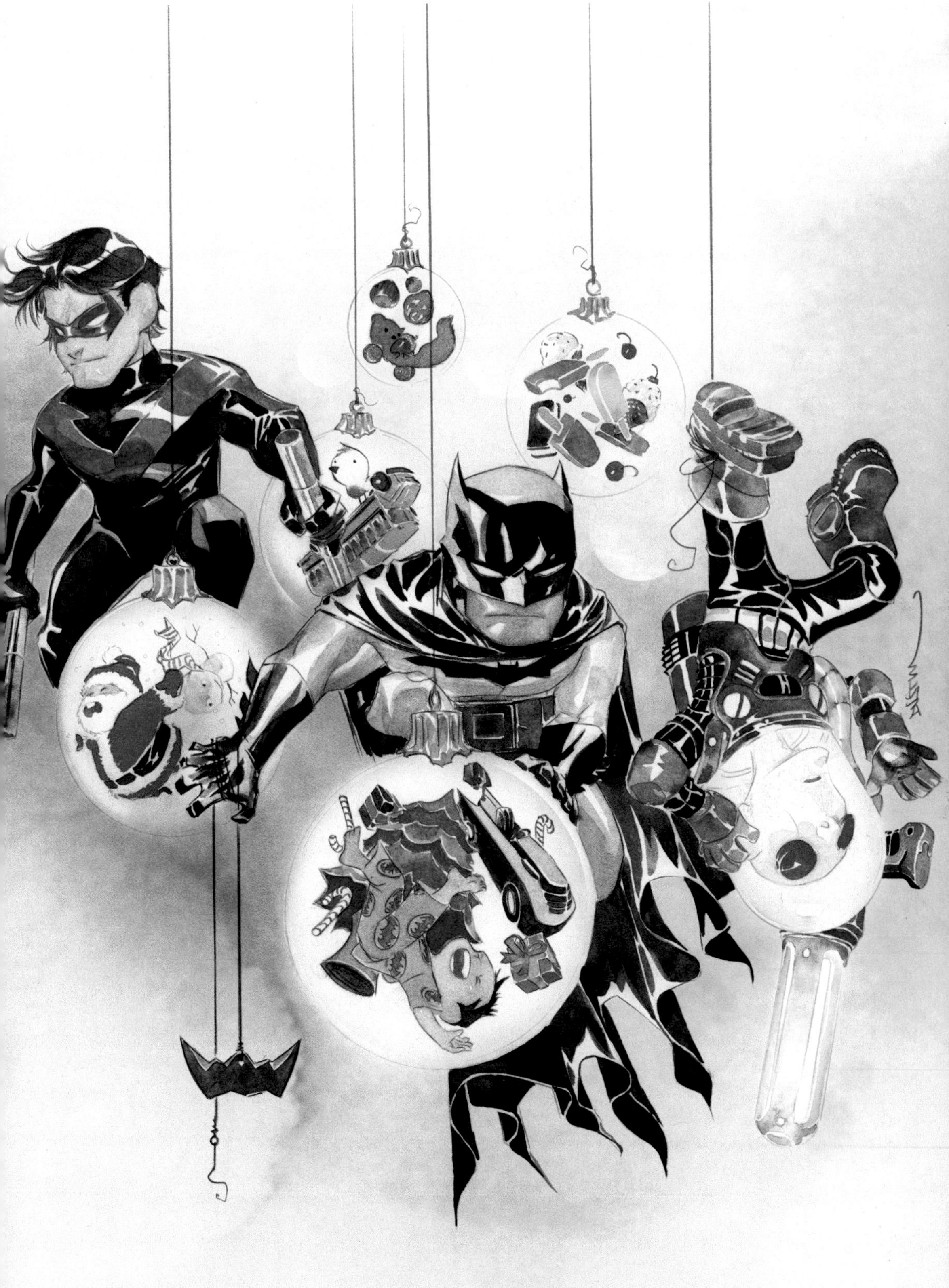

BATMAN: LI'L GOTHAM Digital Chapter #3 cover by Dustin Nguyen

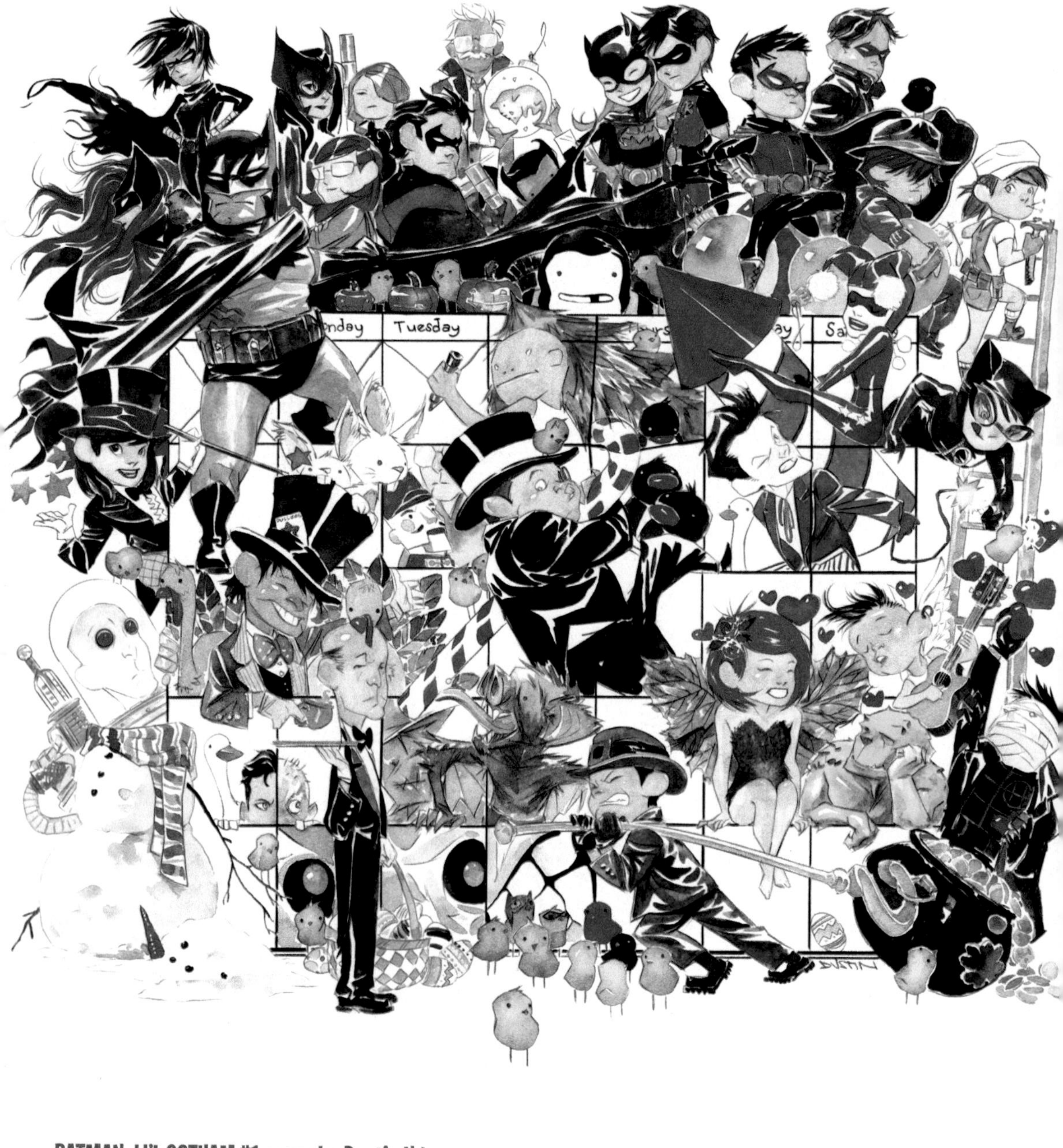

Tuesday
DUSTIN

BATMAN: LI'L GOTHAM #1 cover by Dustin Nguyen

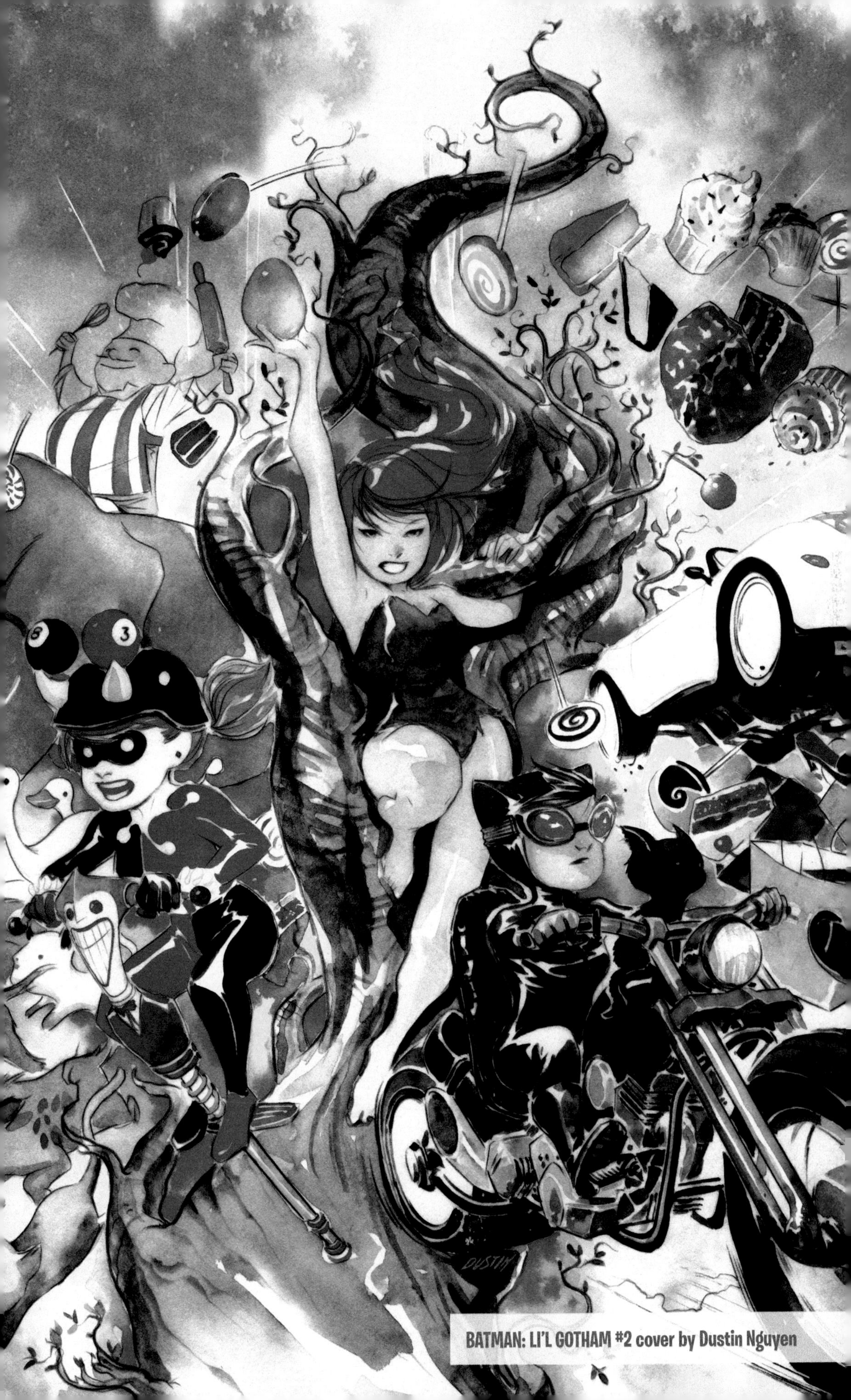

BATMAN: LI'L GOTHAM #2 cover by Dustin Nguyen

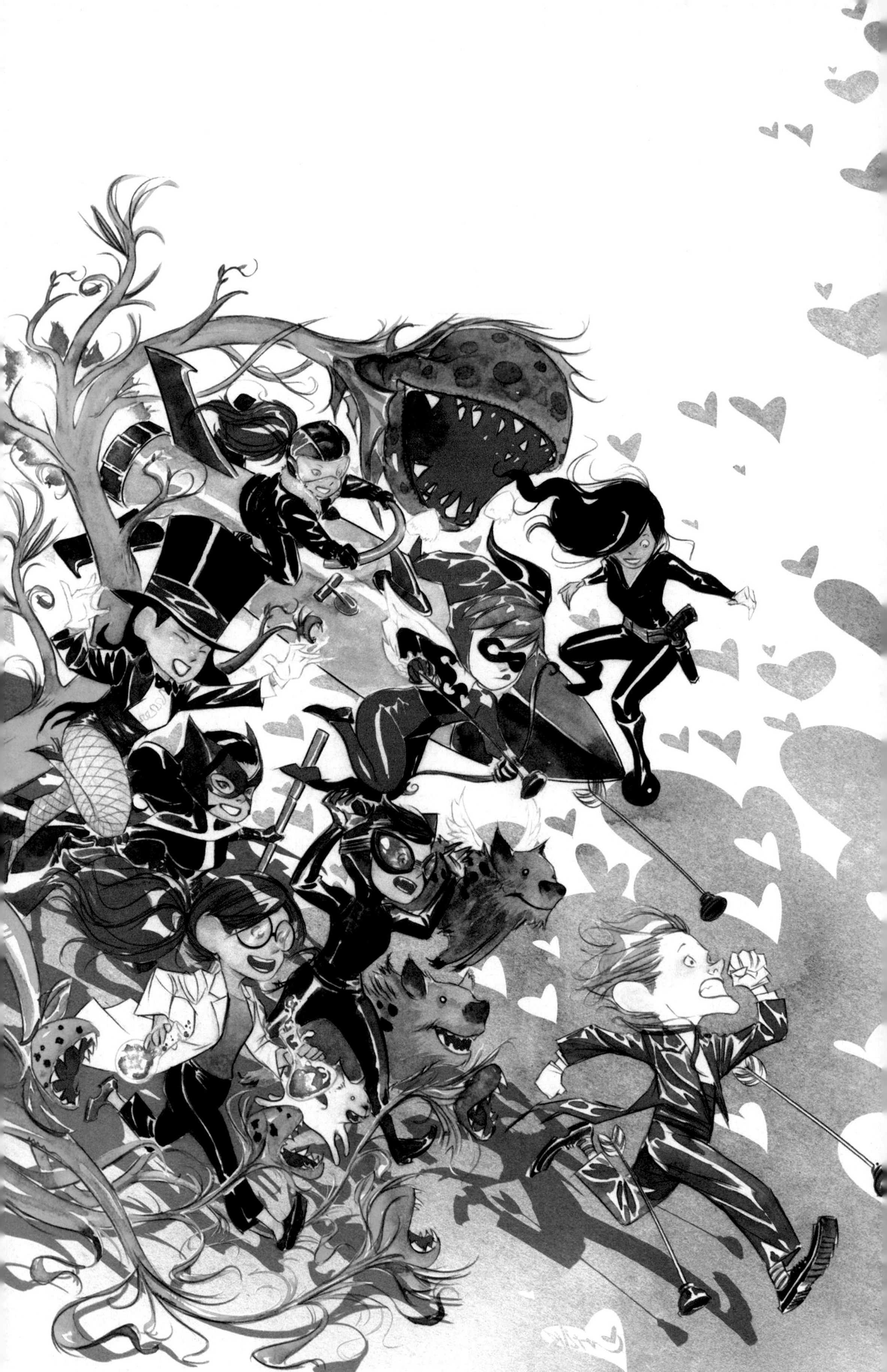

BATMAN: LI'L GOTHAM #3 cover by Dustin Nguyen

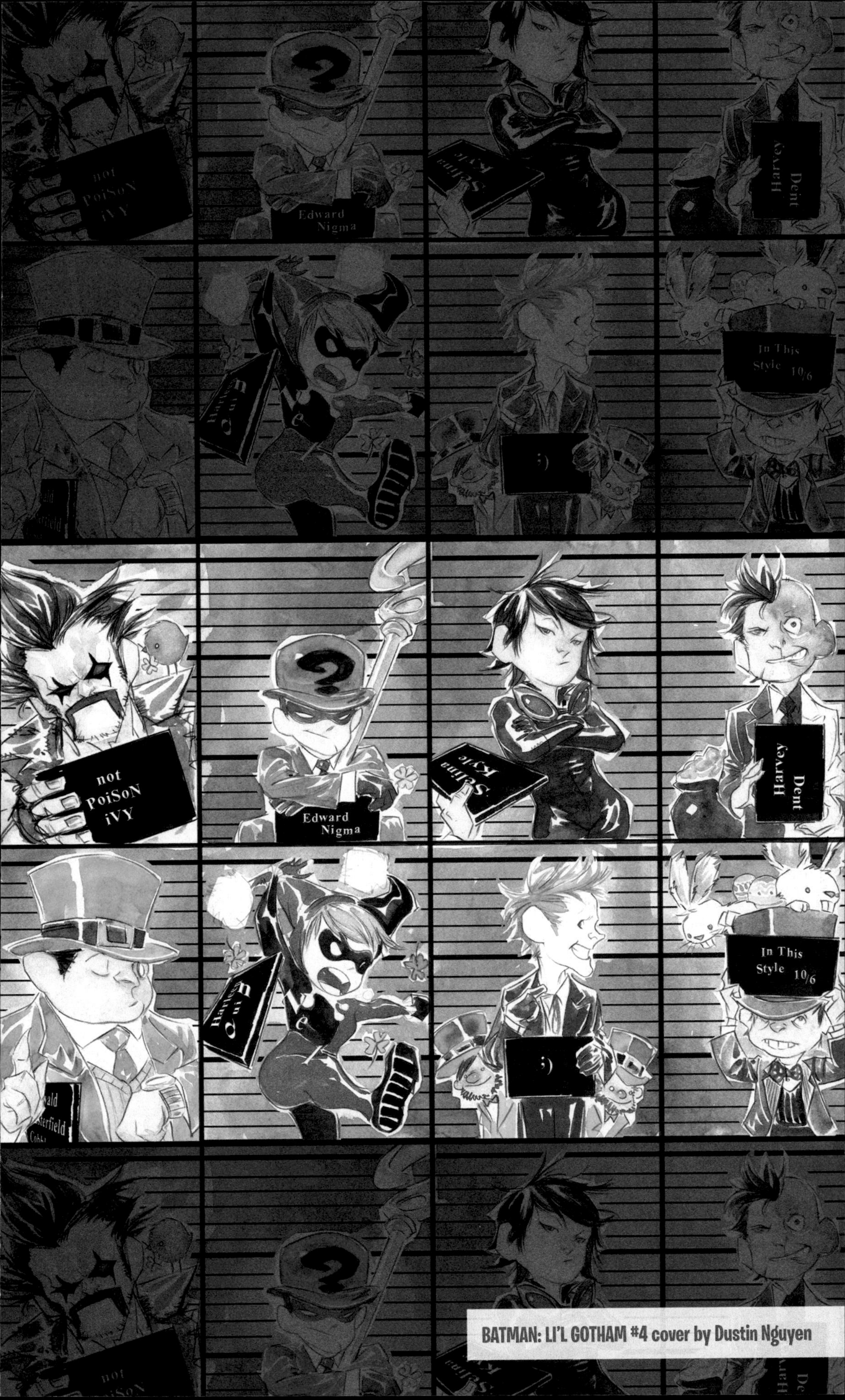
not PoiSoN iVY
Edward Nigma
Selina Kyle
Harvey Dent
In This Style 10/6
;)

BATMAN: LI'L GOTHAM #4 cover by Dustin Nguyen

BATMAN: LI'L GOTHAM #5 cover by Dustin Nguyen

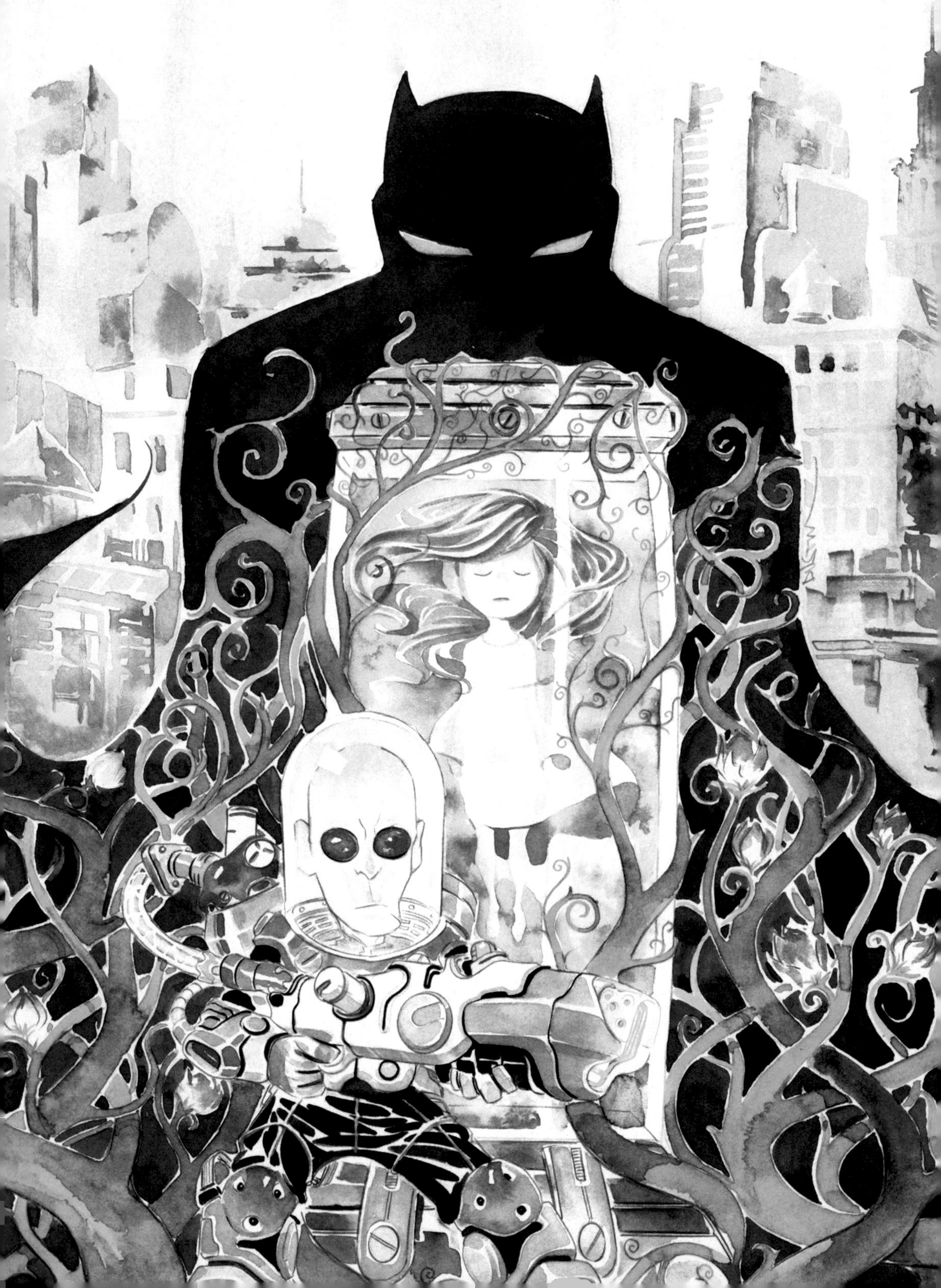

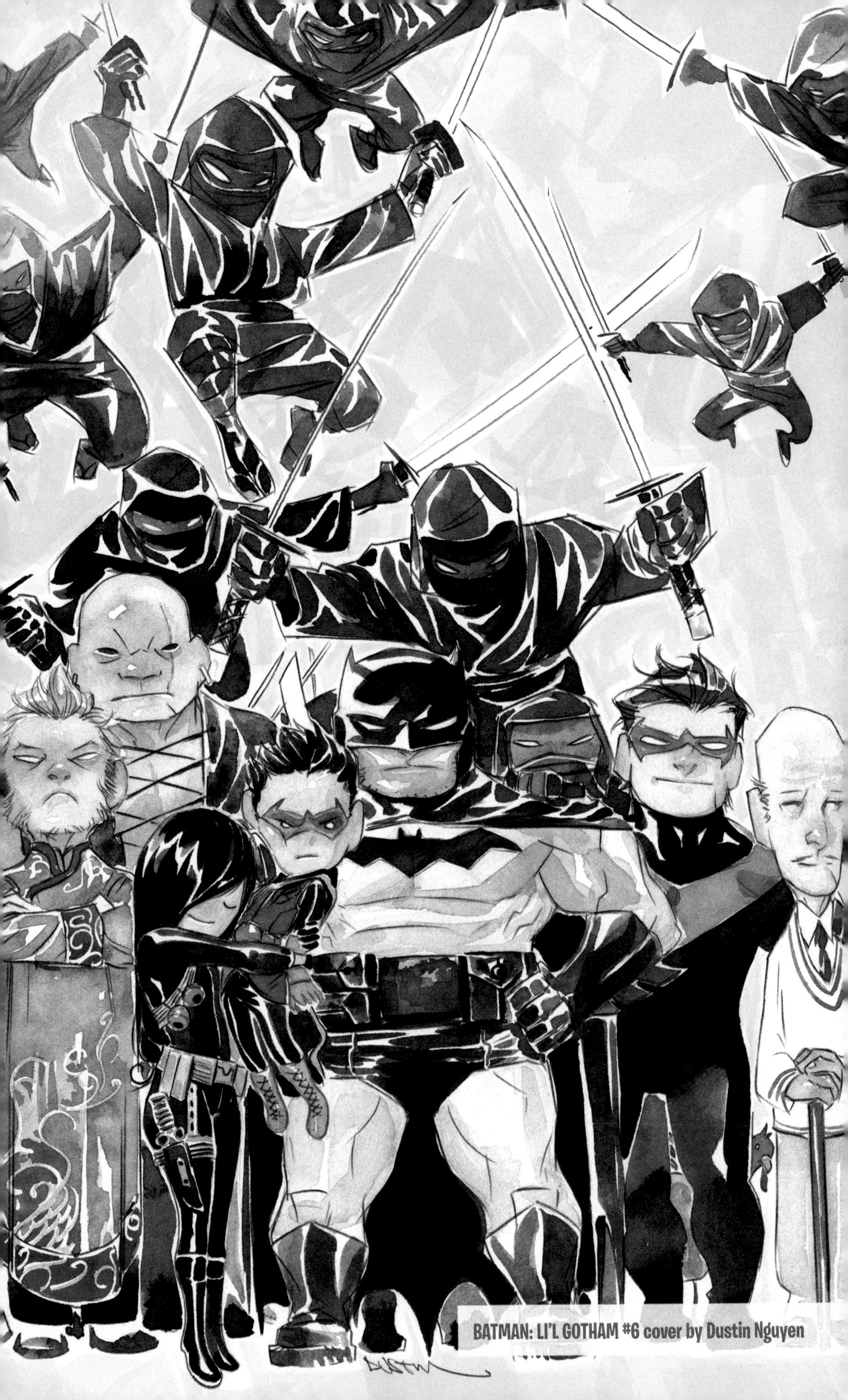

BATMAN: LI'L GOTHAM #6 cover by Dustin Nguyen

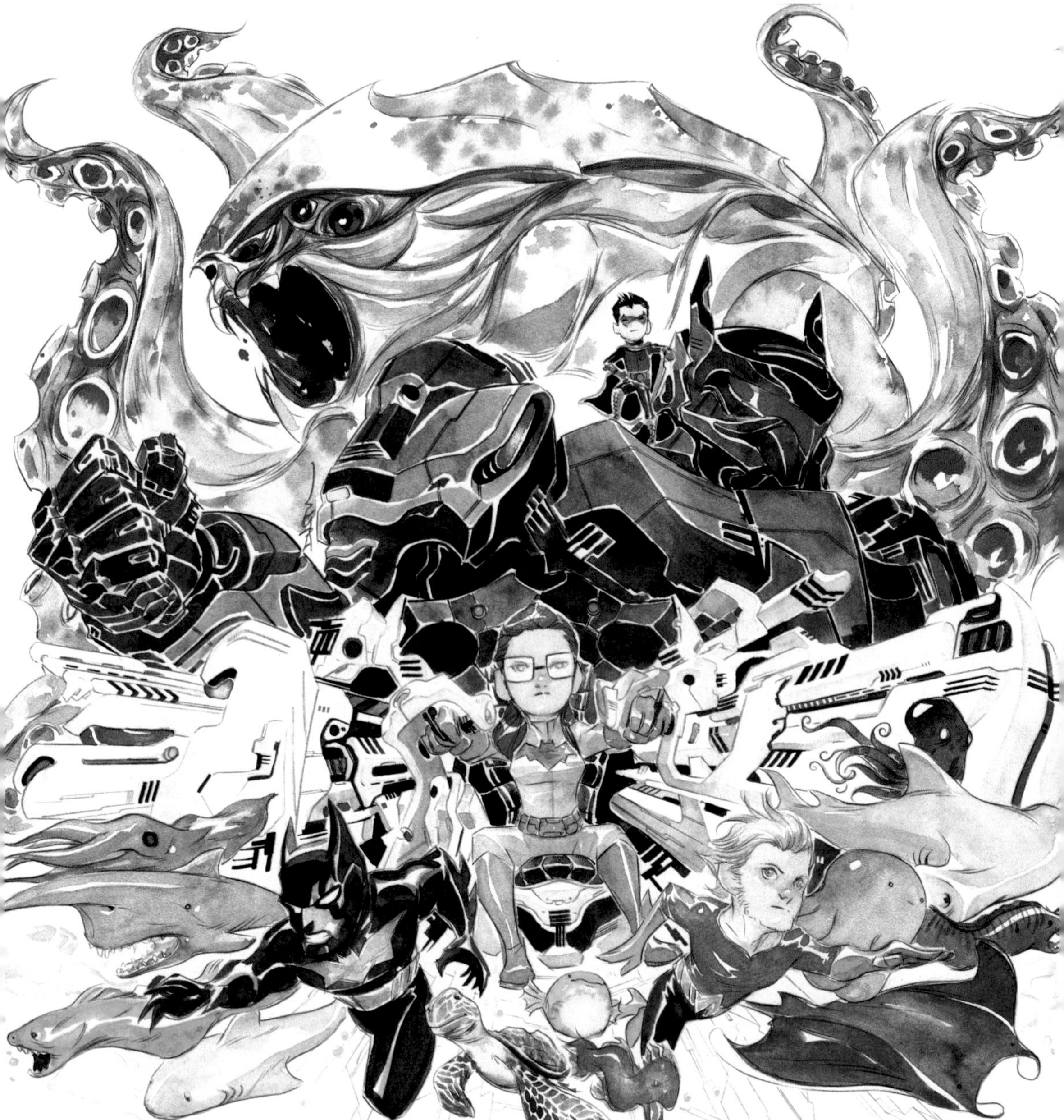

BATMAN: LI'L GOTHAM #7 cover by Dustin Nguyen

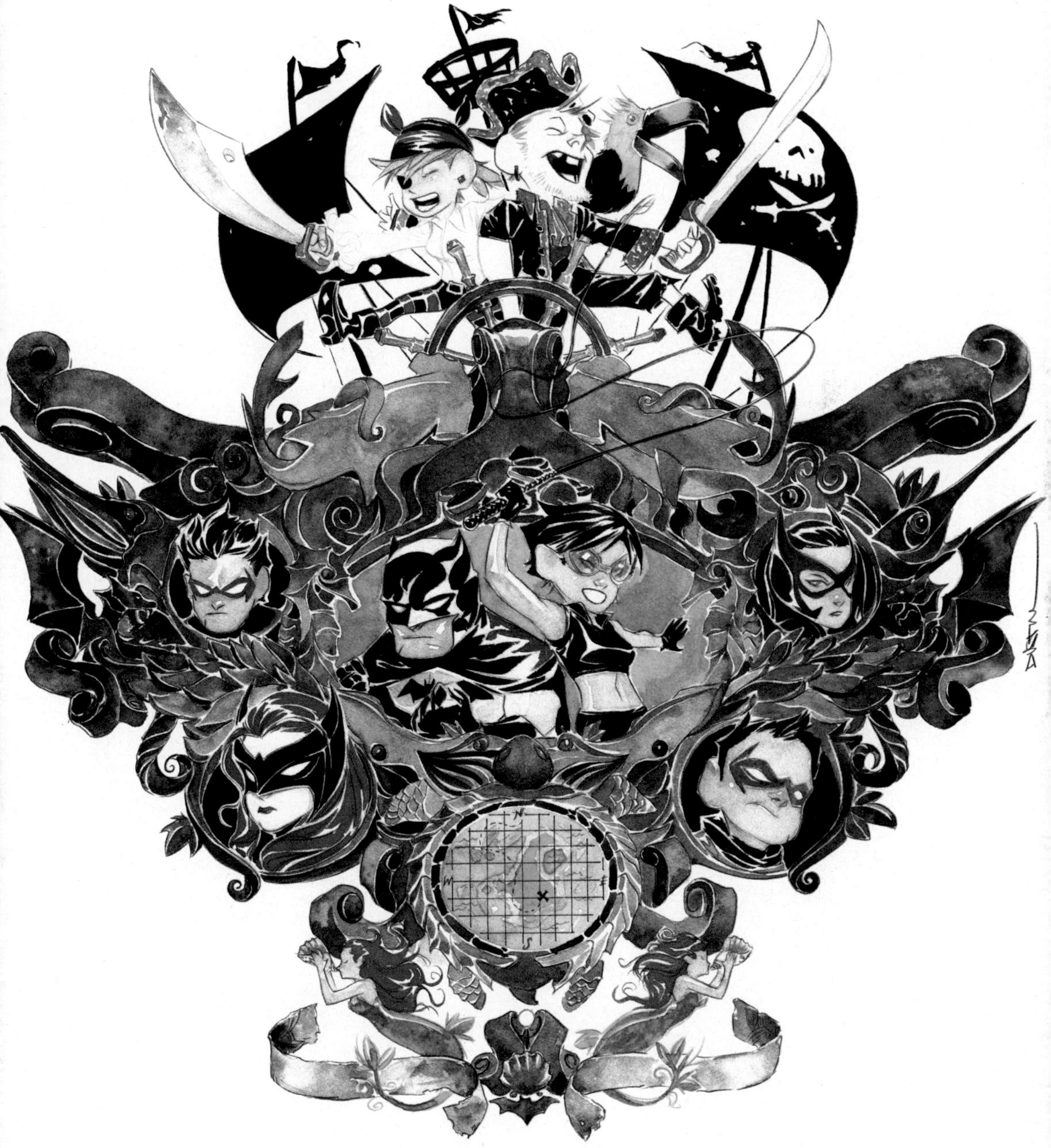

BATMAN: LI'L GOTHAM #8 cover by Dustin Nguyen

BATMAN: LI'L GOTHAM #9 cover by Dustin Nguyen

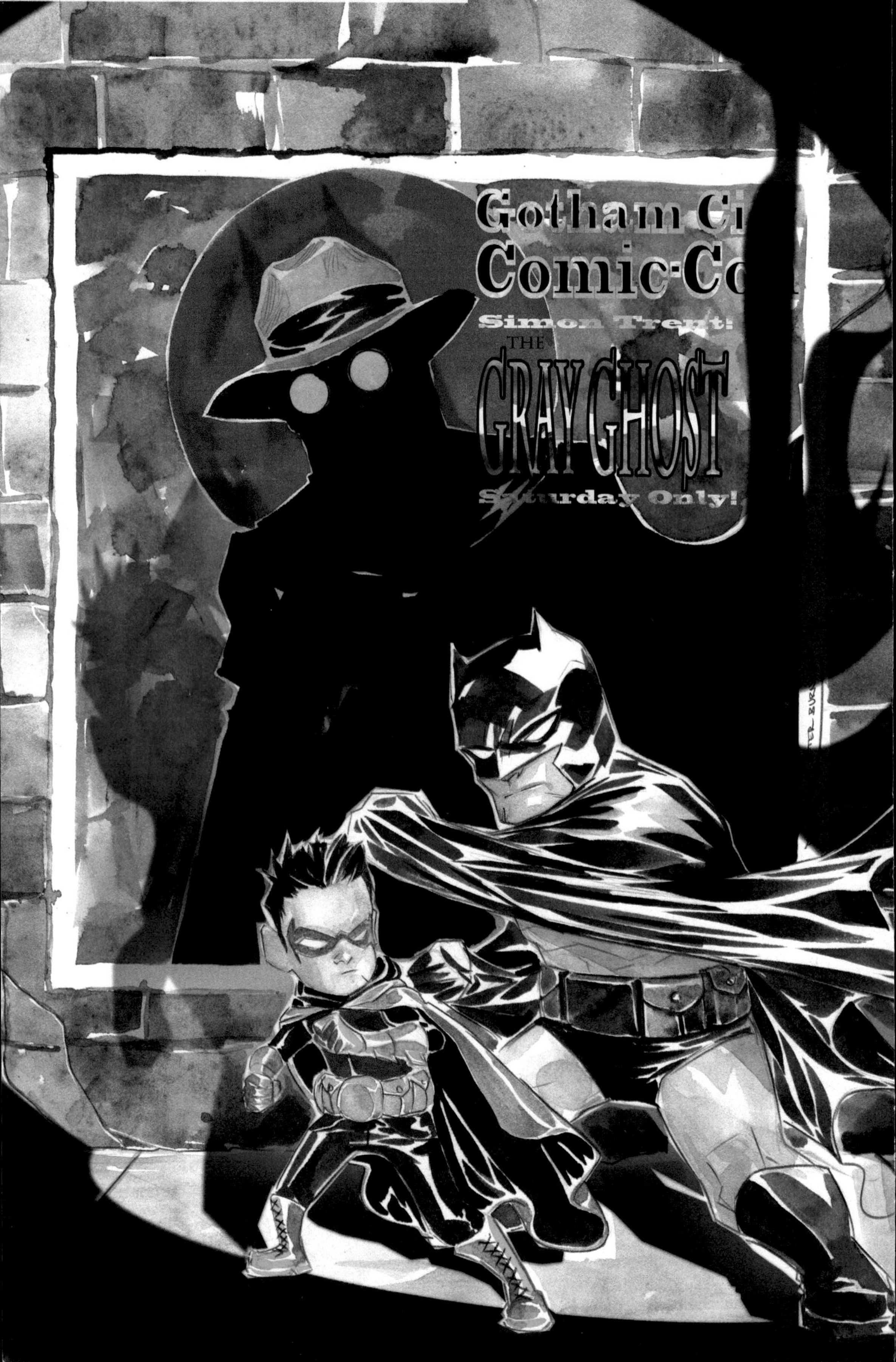
Simon Trent:
THE
GRAY GHOST

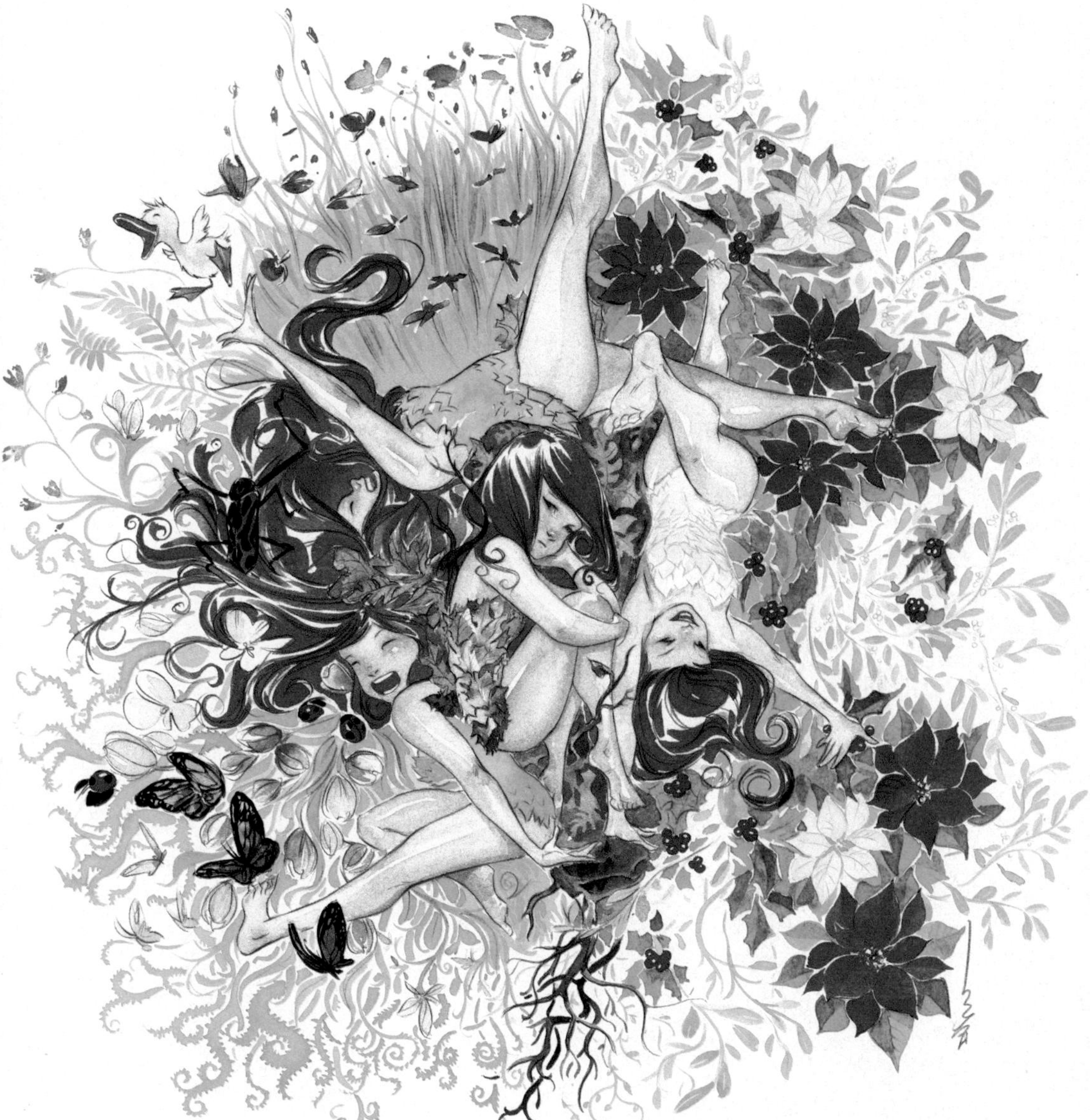

BATMAN: LI'L GOTHAM #10 cover by Dustin Nguyen

BATMAN: LI'L GOTHAM #11 cover by Dustin Nguyen

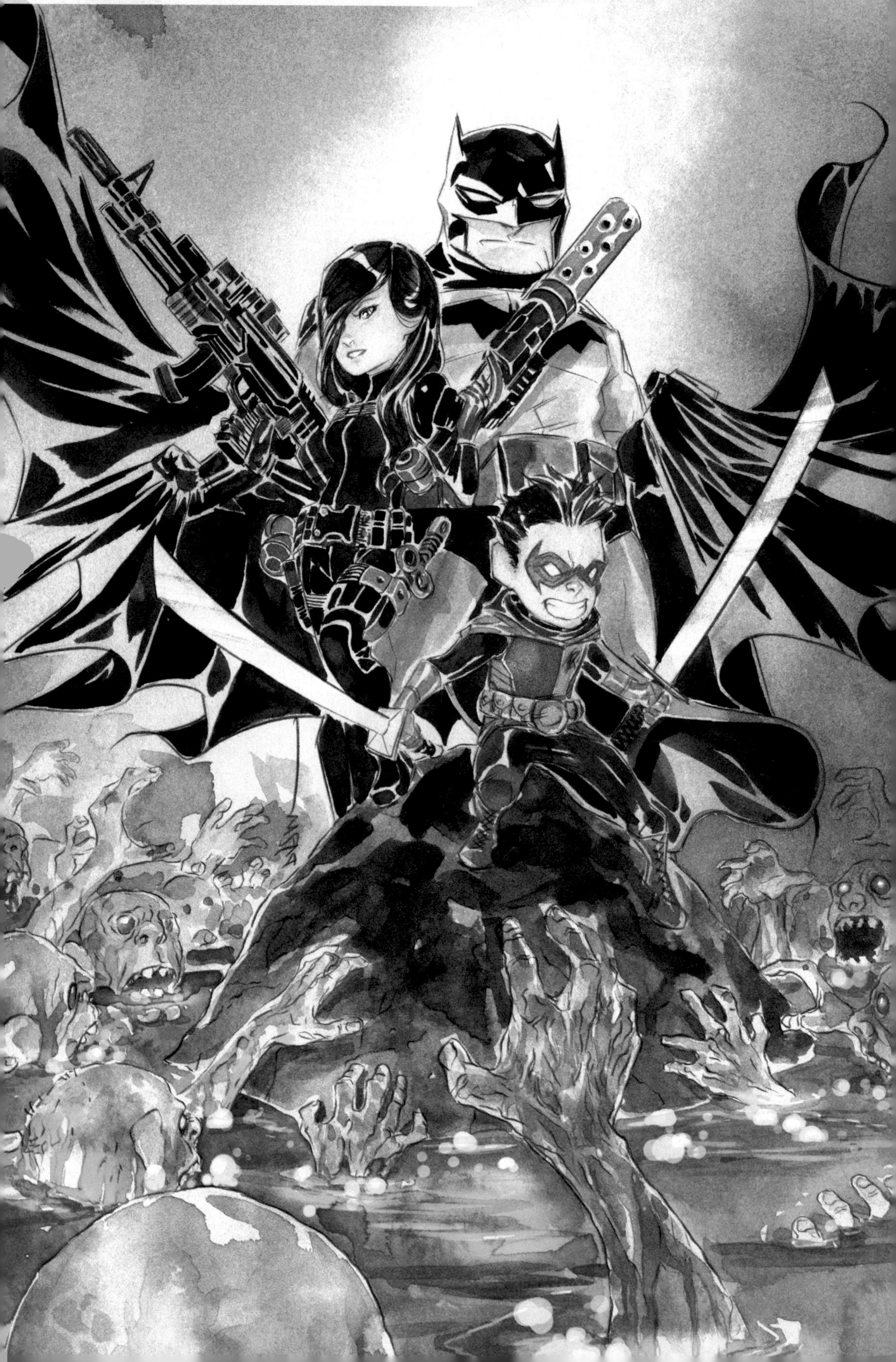

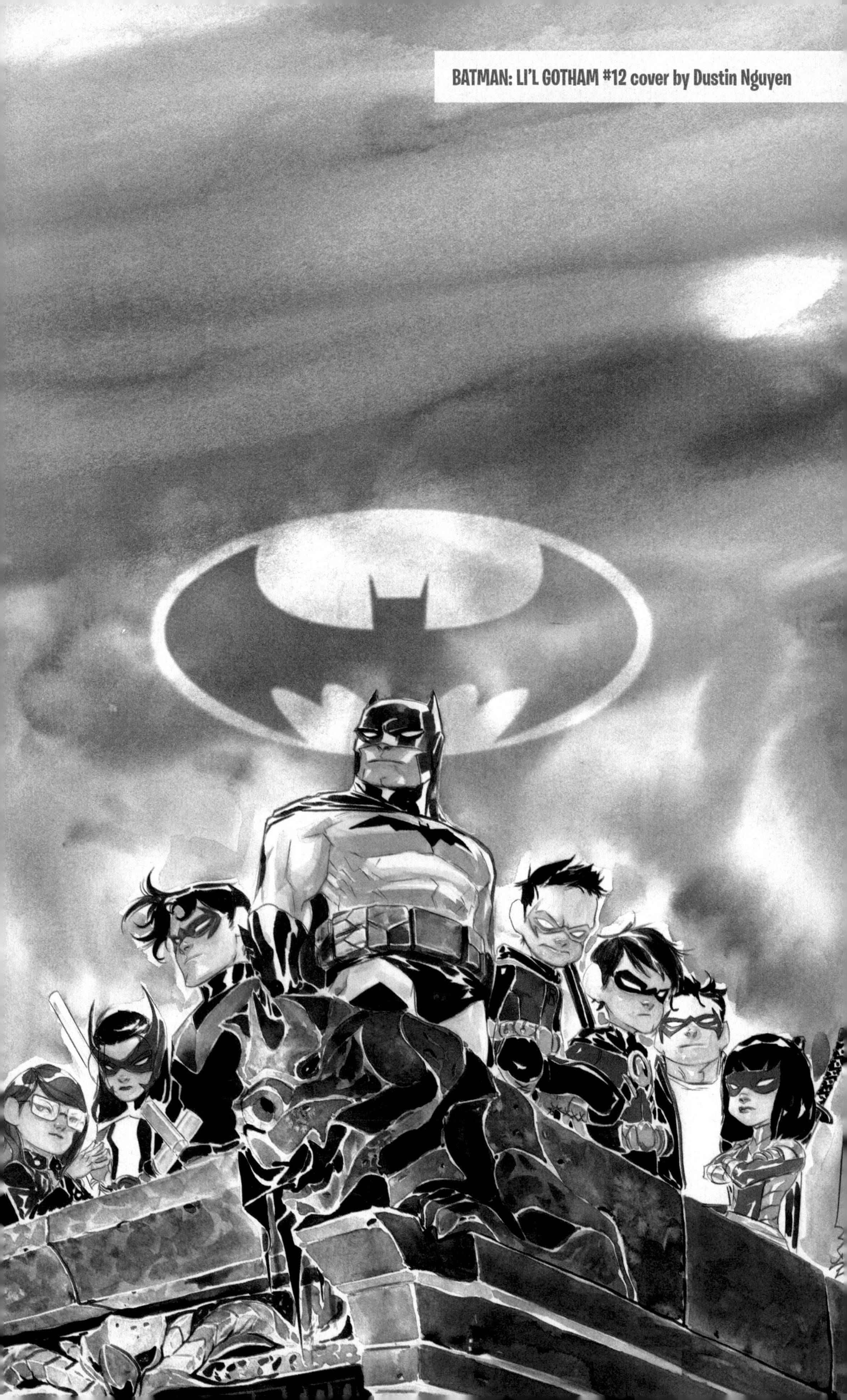

BATMAN: LI'L GOTHAM #12 cover by Dustin Nguyen

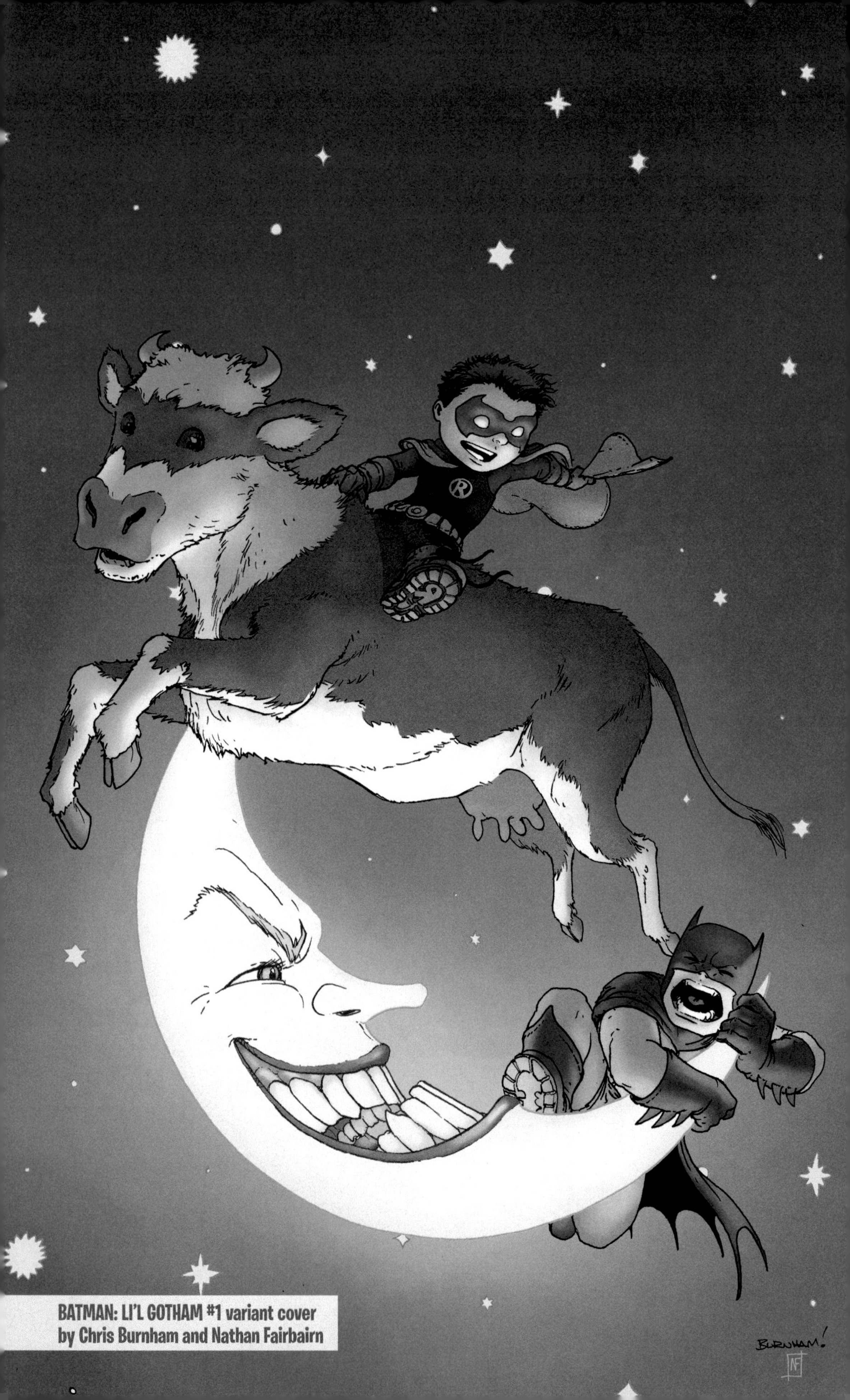
BURNHAM!

BATMAN: LI'L GOTHAM #1 variant cover
by Chris Burnham and Nathan Fairbairn

Li'l Gotham Sketchbook by Dustin Nguyen

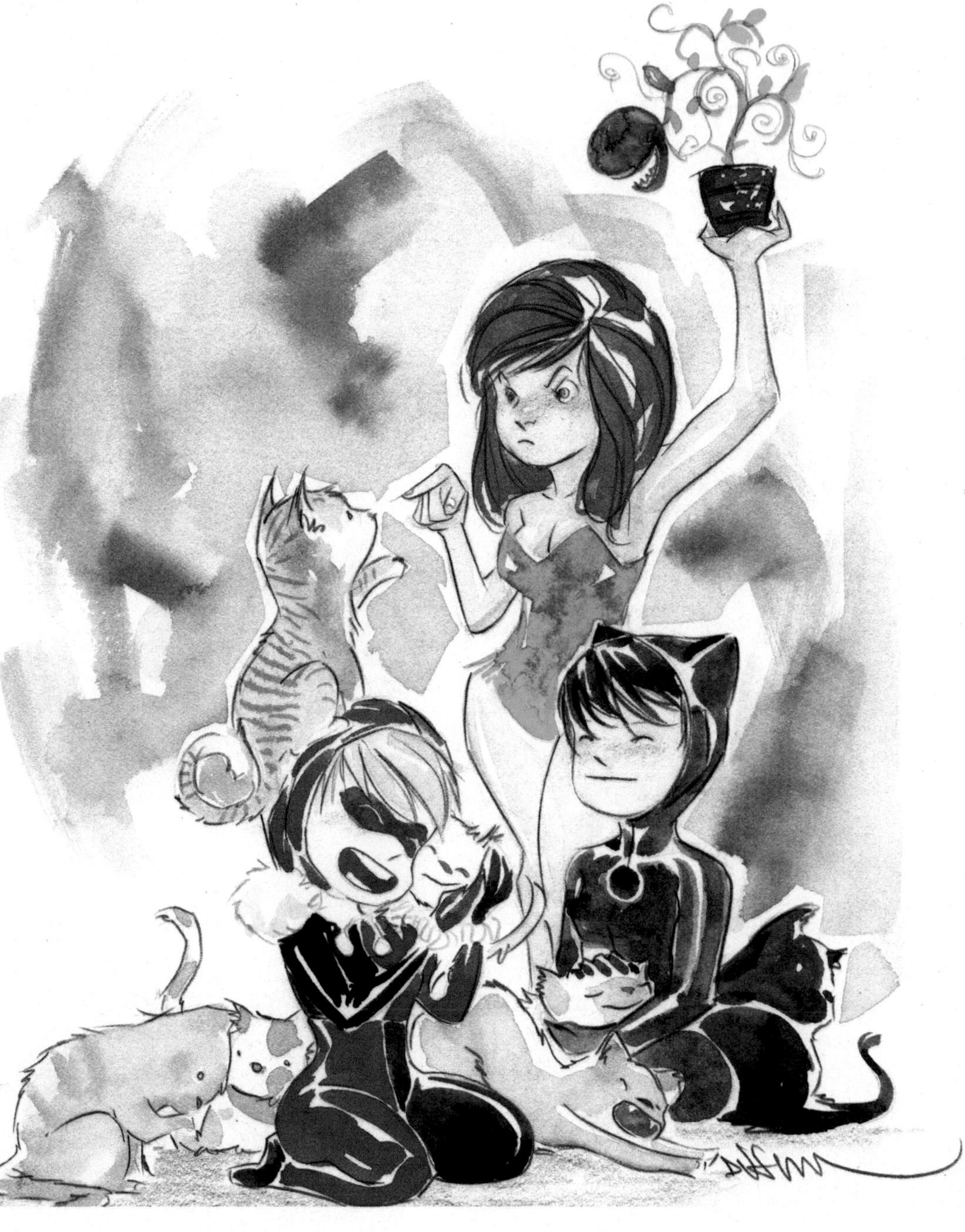

Li'l Gotham cover skecthes

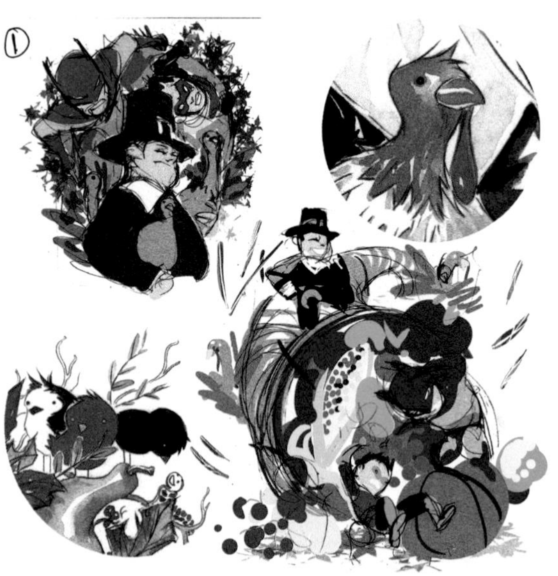

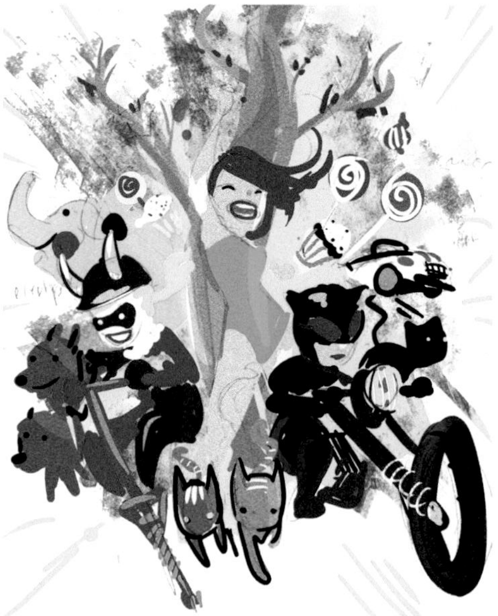

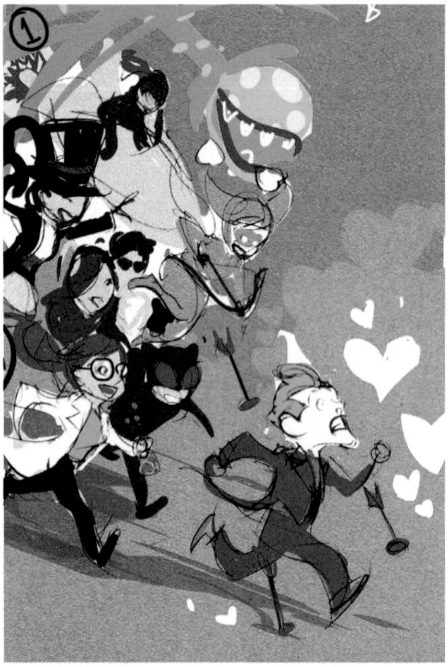

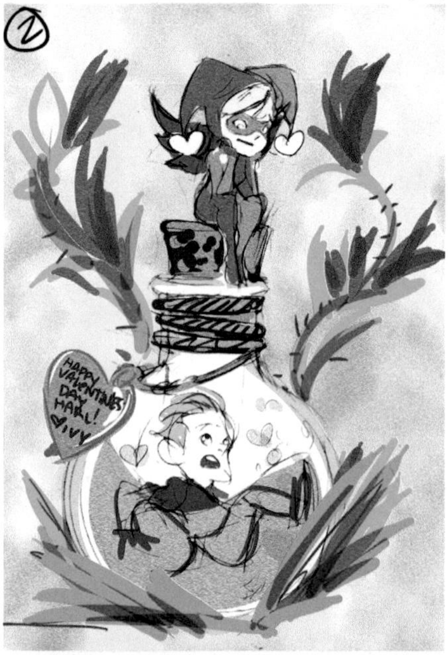
HAPPY VALENTINE'S DAY HARL! -IVY

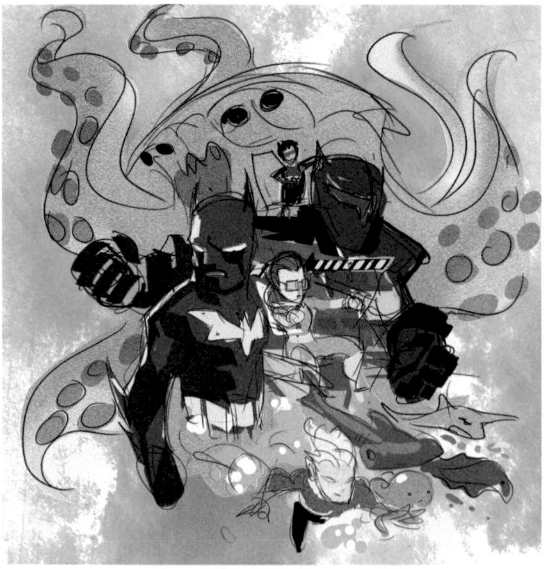

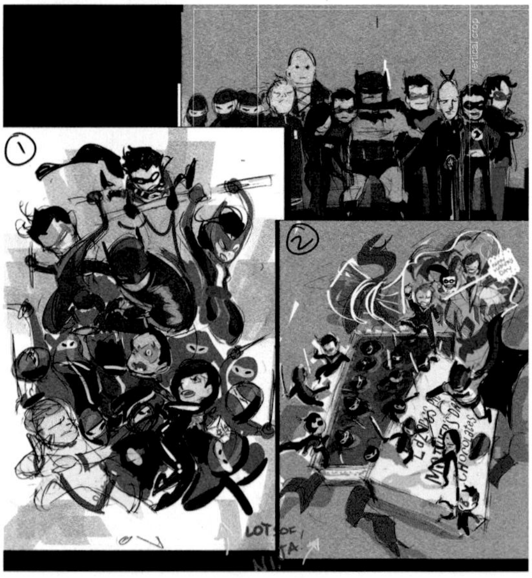

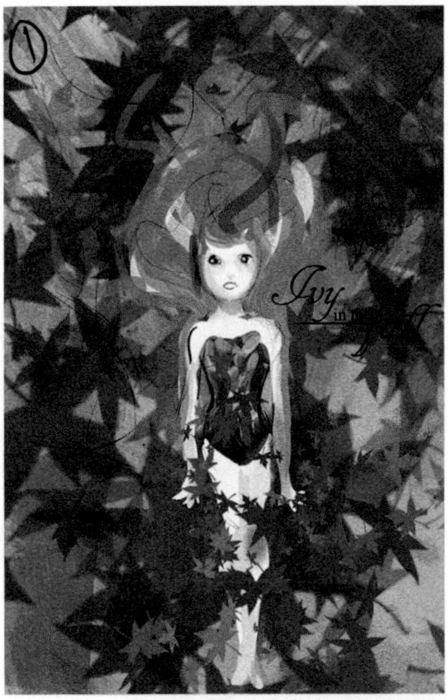
1
Ivy

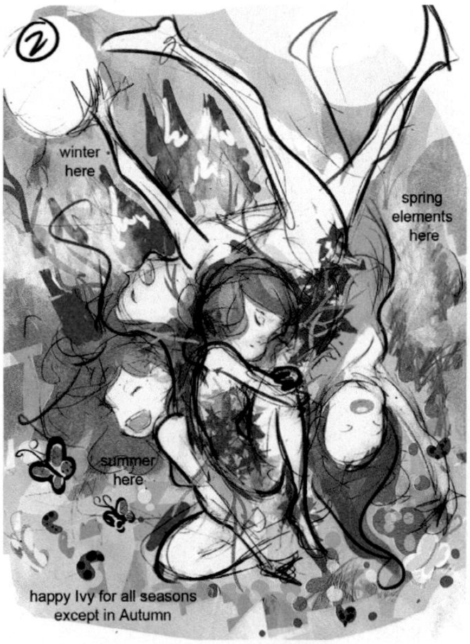
2
winter here
spring elements here
summer here
happy Ivy for all seasons except in Autumn

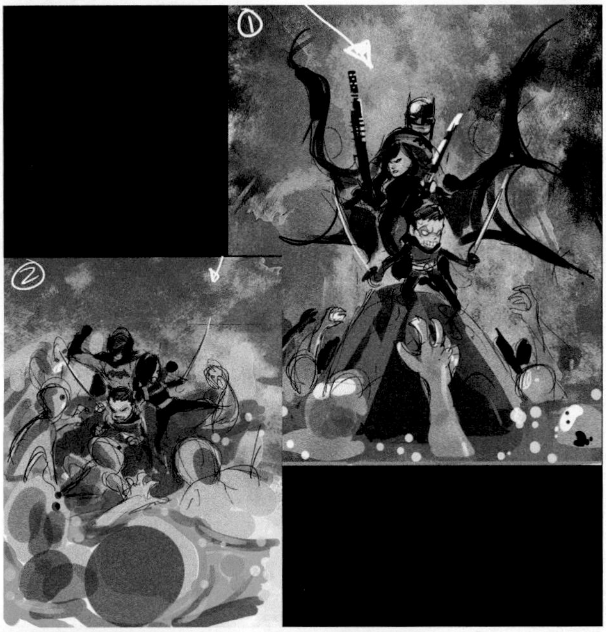
1
2

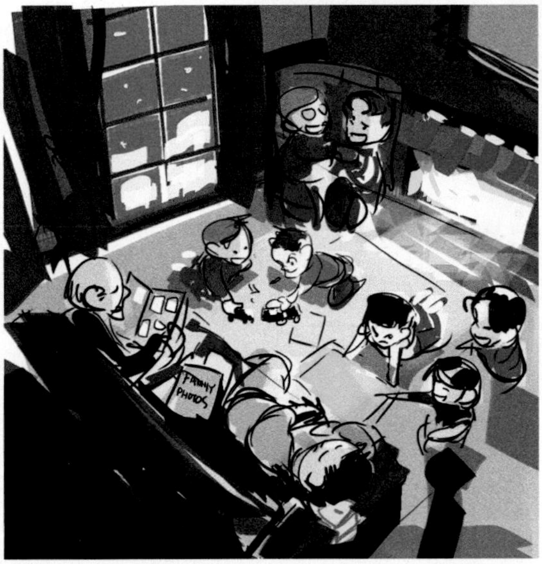
FAMILY PHOTOS

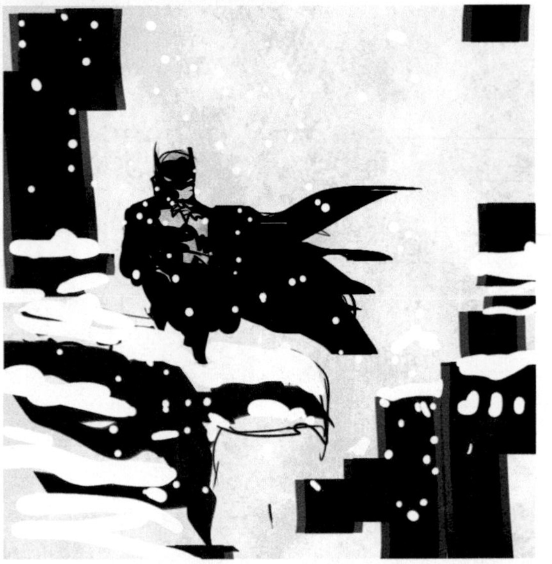

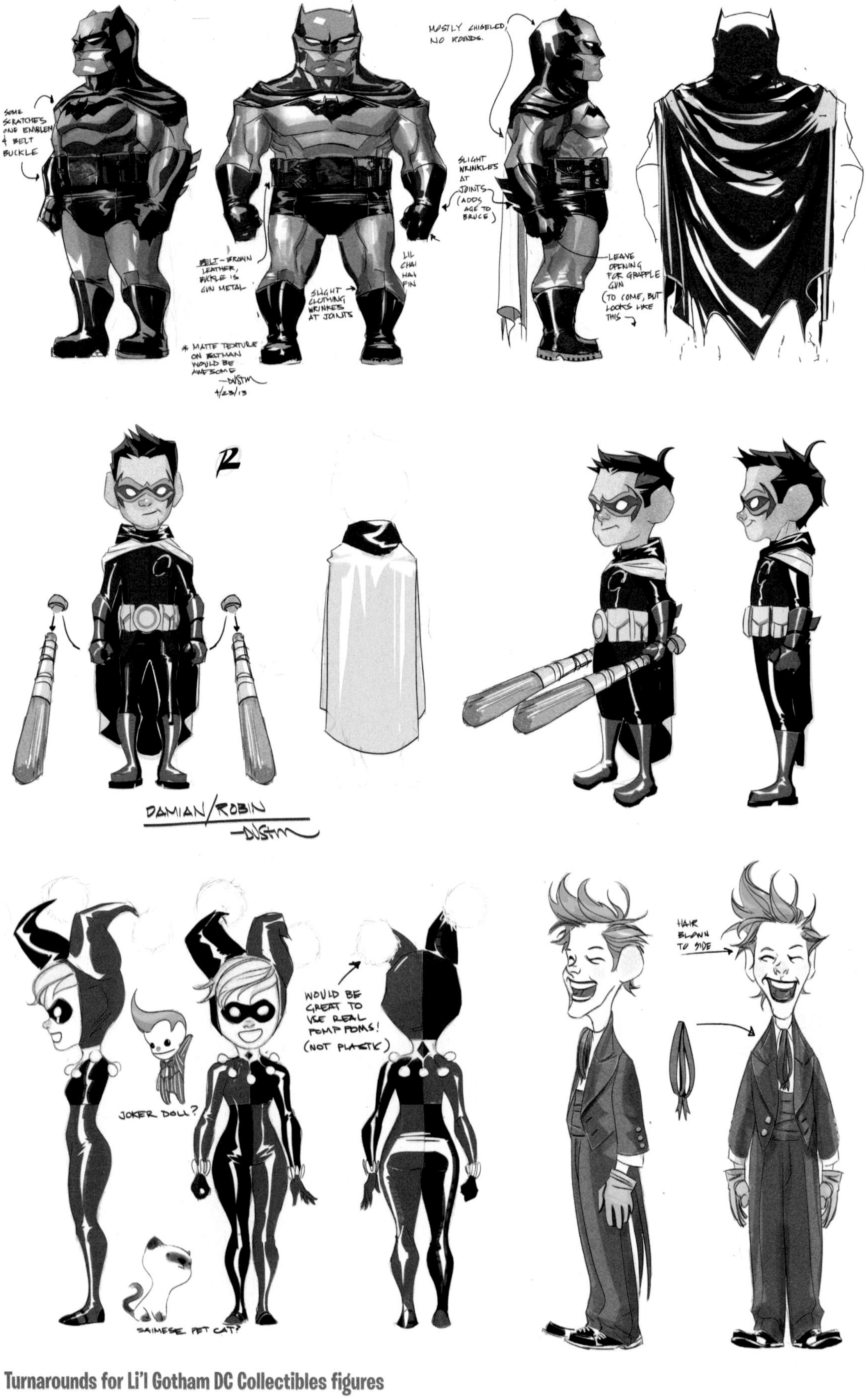
SOME SCRATCHES ONE EMBLEM & BELT BUCKLE
BELT - BROWN LEATHER, BUCKLE IS GUN METAL
SLIGHT CLOTHING WRINKES AT JOINTS
* MATTE TEXTURE ON BATMAN WOULD BE AWESOME
—DUSTIN
4/23/13
MOSTLY CHISELED, NO ROUNDS.
SLIGHT WRINKLES AT JOINTS (ADDS AGE TO BRUCE)
LEAVE OPENING FOR GRAPPLE GUN (TO COME, BUT LOOKS LIKE THIS
DAMIAN/ROBIN
—DUSTIN
JOKER DOLL?
WOULD BE GREAT TO USE REAL POMP POMS! (NOT PLASTIC)
SAIMESE PET CAT?
HAIR BLOWN TO SIDE

Turnarounds for Li'l Gotham DC Collectibles figures

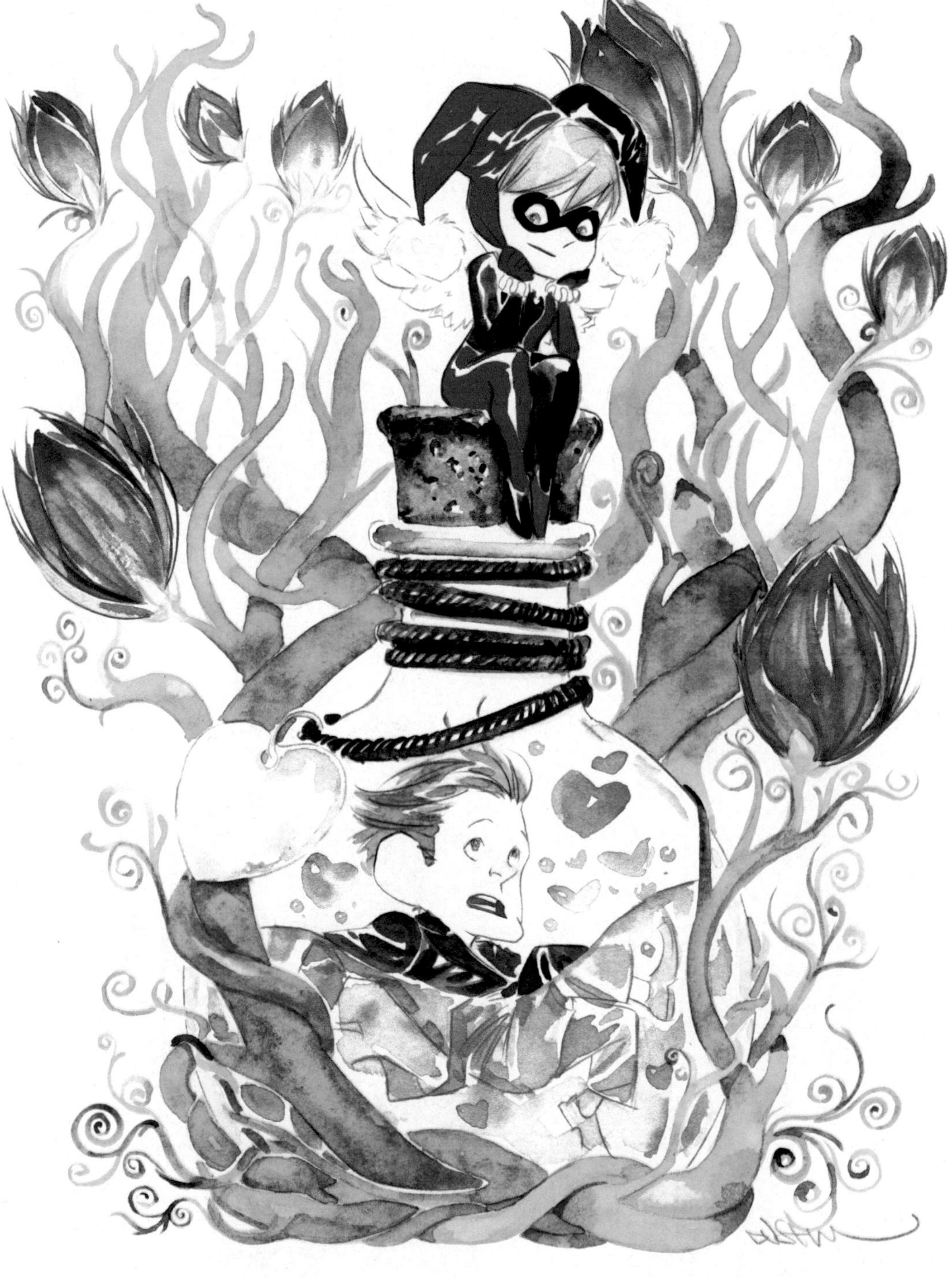

LI'L GOTHAM #3 alternate cover idea

Li'l Gotham character studies

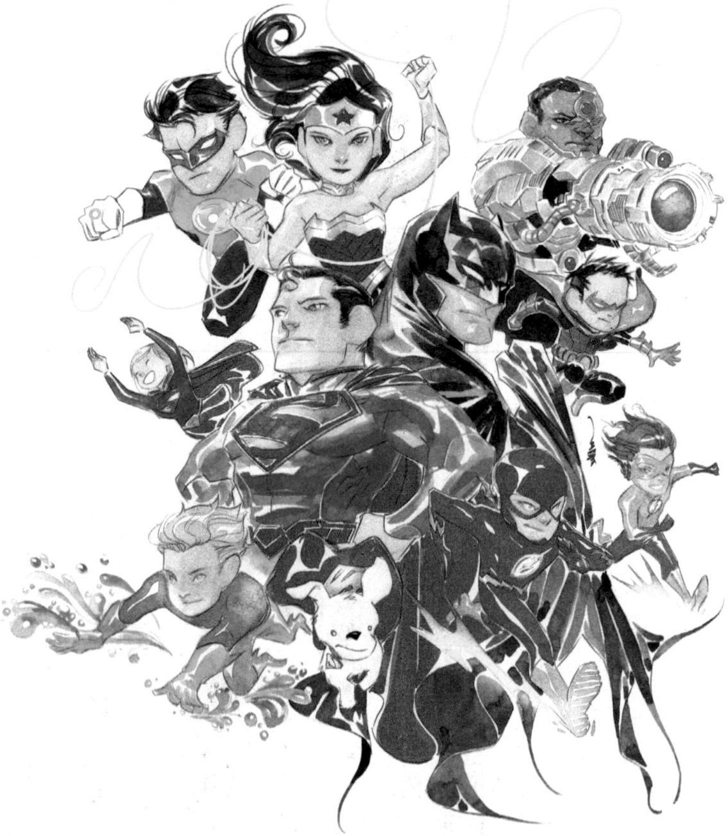

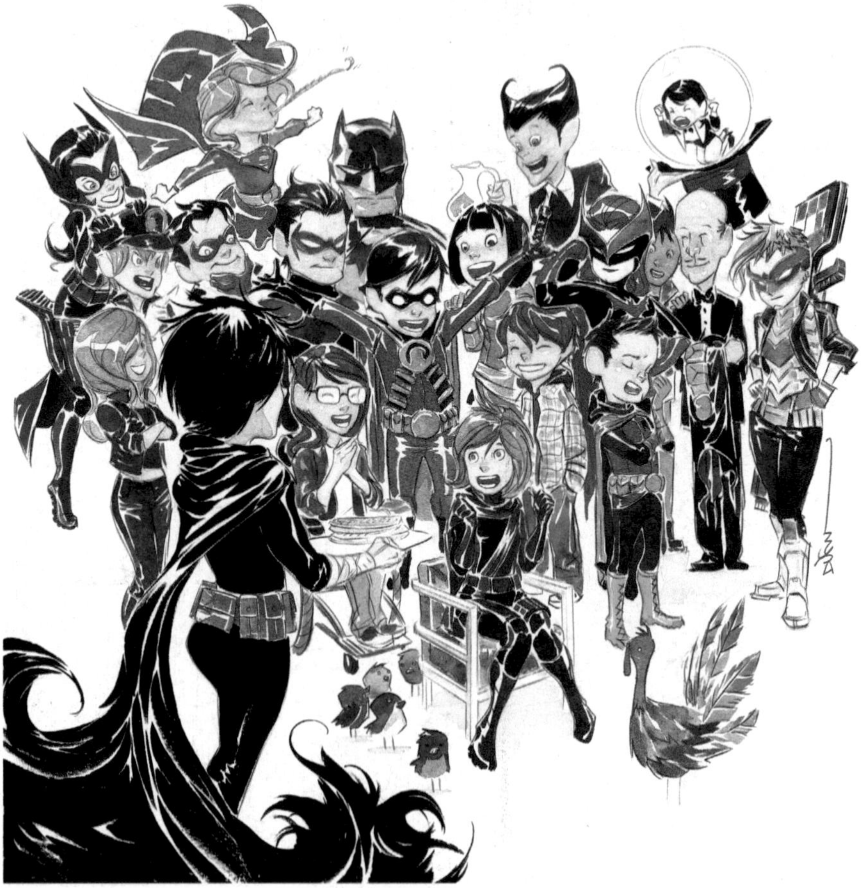